will appeal to all Americans of every political camp and will generate lively discussion." —*Library Journal*

"A heartfelt tale . . . this sprawling domestic history works, revealing not only the likely character of these figures, but also the social undercurrent of political upheaval." —*Kirkus Reviews*

"Engaging . . . [The] women behind the Founding Fathers . . . are brought to life." —*OK!* Magazine

And for the Acclaimed Mystery Series Featuring Free Man of Color Benjamin January

DEAD WATER

A *Deadly Pleasures* Best Mystery/Crime Novel of 2004

"Hambly's brilliantly crafted eighth historical brings the antebellum South so alive you could swear the author traveled back in time to observe her setting firsthand. . . . This riveting novel of suspense is sure to win Hambly many new fans."
—*Publishers Weekly* (starred review)

DAYS OF THE DEAD

"Sumptuous." —*New York Times Book Review*

"Hambly's gifts for vividly evoking long-gone sights, smells and sounds are in full throttle." —*Seattle Times*

High Praise for the Novels of Barbara Hambly

THE EMANCIPATOR'S WIFE
Short-listed for the Michael Shaara Award for Excellence in Civil War Fiction

"Hambly fleshes out the historical record to put before us a compassionate and evenhanded portrait of the 16th First Lady. . . . And she manages to capture . . . the elusive bond between 'Molly' and Mr. Lincoln that endured the snowballing hardships of their lives."
—*Washington Post Book World*

"Just as Lincoln is seduced in the book, Barbara Hambly seduces the reader with a brilliantly crafted opening account of Mary's 1875 insanity trial."
—*Seattle Times*

"Hambly gives history life and breath." —*Mystery News*

"Hambly injects compassion and empathy into the story of a complicated woman living in a difficult time. . . . Compelling." —*Rocky Mountain News*

"A skilled historical novelist limns an absolutely convincing portrait of Mary Todd Lincoln."
—*Kirkus Reviews*

"From its perfect title to its beautiful, poignant last scenes, this is a wonderful portrait of one of the most important, complex and misunderstood figures in American history—a brilliant novel of the Civil War!" —Max Byrd, author of *Shooting the Sun*

"Hambly's novel faithfully describes the factual enslavement and emancipation of a nation. Its fiction details the same cycle of rebirth for one woman."
—*Wichita Falls (TX) Times Record News*

"Hambly gets inside Mary Lincoln's head. Though a fictional account, the book makes you realize that presidents are just men, their wives are just women, and both have their own demons."
—*Sunday Oklahoman*

"Hambly has painted a compelling fictional portrait of one of the most maligned and misunderstood First Ladies in American history." —*Booklist*

"The character Hambly has created is vivacious, impulsive, highly intelligent and 'intoxicated by politics.'" —*Salt Lake City Deseret News*

"Hambly has a knack for bringing historical figures to life in all their flawed humanity. This touching portrait of Mary Todd . . . paints a full, nuanced picture of a talented, tormented woman." —*Publishers Weekly*

PATRIOT HEARTS

"Superior historical fiction, firm in its grasp of history, not showy in its period details. It brings these women out of shadows and endows them with flesh and blood." —*Booklist*

"Look no further for a title to recommend as a reading group choice for the upcoming election years. This

GRAVEYARD DUST

"Seductive . . . Sweeps from lavish balls on elegant river plantations to voodoo rites in Congo Square and savage brawls in men's waterfront dives . . . January proves the ideal guide through these treacherous social strata." —*New York Times Book Review*

FEVER SEASON

A *New York Times* Notable Book of the Year

"A notable writer of mystery fiction . . . This one grips the reader from start to finish."
—*Washington Times*

"From the highborn Creoles in their river mansions to the uncivilized Americans brawling on the levee, Hambly speaks all their languages, knows all their secrets, and brings them all to life."
—*New York Times Book Review*

A FREE MAN OF COLOR

"Magically rich and poignant . . . In scene after scene researched in impressive depth and presented in the cool, clear colors of photography, Hambly creates an exotic but recognizable environment for January's search for justice." —*Chicago Tribune*

"A darned good murder mystery." —*USA Today*

the

EMANCIPATOR'S
WIFE

A Novel of Mary Todd Lincoln

Barbara Hambly

BANTAM BOOKS

THE EMANCIPATOR'S WIFE
A Bantam Book

PUBLISHING HISTORY
Bantam hardcover edition published February 2005
Bantam trade paperback edition published January 2006
Bantam mass market edition / April 2008

Published by Bantam Dell
A Division of Random House, Inc.
New York, New York

All rights reserved
Copyright © 2005 by Barbara Hambly
Cover portrait: *Yulia Teliakovskaya* by Gavril Yakovlev, 1848, reproduced by
permission of The State Hermitage Museum, St. Petersburg, Russia/Corbis
Cover design by Marietta Anastassatos

Library of Congress Catalog Card Number: 2004048797

ISBN: 978-0-553-58565-0

Printed in the United States of America
Published simultaneously in Canada

www.bantamdell.com

OPM 10 9 8 7 6 5 4 3 2 1

FOR KATE

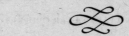

Special Thanks

Are due (in no particular order) to

Kathy Tabb at the Mary Todd Lincoln House in Lexington, KY; James Patton and Barbara Guinan at Lincoln's New Salem; Ed Russo at the Sangamon Valley Collection; Tom Schwartz at the Old Capitol Building in Springfield, IL; John Eden, proprietor of the Long Nine Museum in Athens (pronounced AY-thens), IL; Mr. Wayne Temple for our long phone conversation on the circumstances of the Lincoln marriage; the staff of the library at the Old Capitol Building; the staff of the Library of Congress.

Extra-special thanks to

Roger and David at the Mischler House Bed and Breakfast in Springfield; to Managing Editor Kathleen Baldonado for her usual wonderful job of shepherding my manuscript through the production process; to my long-suffering mother for re-typing the manuscript when the hard drive crashed; and, as usual, to Kate, for the genesis of the whole project.

A NOTE ON NOMENCLATURE

CONFEDERATES AND REBELS

Because it was Lincoln's contention that the Confederate States of America had no legal existence—that his reason for assembling an army was to put down a rebellion, not to invade another nation—I have, in all sections written from the viewpoint of Mary Todd Lincoln, referred to the Confederacy and Confederates as "rebels."

That is her opinion, not mine, and I extend my apology to those whom it offends.

When writing a historical novel, a writer takes as much as possible the voices of those whose lives the book is trying to re-create. It would be as inappropriate to ascribe recognition of the Confederacy to Mrs. Lincoln as it would be to have General Sheridan refer to the Sioux Nation as "Native Americans" instead of "Indians."

All stories are true, and some actually happened.

—ANONYMOUS,
twentieth century

It is very hard to deal with someone who is sane
on all subjects but one.

—ROBERT TODD LINCOLN,
writing about his mother

PROLOGUE

ENCOUNTERING MARY TODD LINCOLN WAS THE NICEST thing that happened to John Wilamet on his first day in the Promised Land. This fact did not speak well for his other experiences in that first twenty-four hours of freedom.

For three weeks he'd been working his way north from his master's plantation in Halifax County, Virginia. As a boy he'd been as far as Richmond twice—once, terrifyingly, when Mr. Henry Wilamet, who owned Blue Hill Plantation, had decided to sell him, but he had changed his mind when he couldn't get the price he wanted. Runaways who'd passed through Blue Hill on their way north to Washington City after the fighting started had told John the route. Such knowledge was a whispered undercurrent among the unfree: which back-roads were safest, what the scrawled marks were on back-fences and sheds that meant, *They'll give you food here.* John could have made the journey quicker, but he had his mother with him, two younger sisters, and a tiny brother.

He was fifteen.

It was October, and the corn had long since been harvested. Mounted patrols seemed to be everywhere, north and south of the river, making it far too perilous to thieve from the houses and the barns they passed. Because Southern troops were camped around the railway junction at Manassas John and his family swung wide and crossed the river in a stolen rowboat near Leesburg, then moved cautiously down the Maryland side: John had been warned that most Marylanders were slaveholders who would as soon secede as not. Just because they'd crossed into Union-held territory did not mean they were safe.

"I'm hungry," whimpered Isaac, who was five. "We gonna have food when we get to Promise Land?"

"We sure will, baby," their mother assured him, a danger-ous sparkle in her eyes. John caught his sister Cassy's wary sidelong glance. Their mother's touchwood temper and bizarre whims had already cost them several days' travel time. Aside from the fact that John had no desire to deal with her ranting herself to exhaustion about what the Promised Land was supposed to be like, you could hear her for miles when she got going. Trying to hush her only made matters worse.

"We'll have food, and shoes, and a cabin all to our own," she added, her voice rising, and Lucy, who was eight, asked, "How we know which one's ours?"

"Don't you back-talk your mama! John'll find him some work, cuttin' wood or drivin' a wagon"—John had never driven a wagon in his life and had no idea where his mother had gotten the idea that he could—"and we'll all have chicken an' biscuits, an' quilts on the beds. You girls'll have pretty new dresses. . . ."

Hooves ahead. The woods here were thin, already blazing with the golds and maroons of autumn. The hard blue of uniforms stood out vivid as jewels. John put a hand on his mother's arm to steer her to the cover of the nearest thicket, but she pulled from him, strode toward the soldiers shouting, "What we got to hide? We here in the Promise Land of Freedom!"

No we not, Mama, we in Maryland. . . .

One of the soldiers reached for his rifle at the sight of movement, but holstered it again the next moment. John panted, trying to keep up with his mother—she could go damn fast when she had a head of steam in her—while Cassy drew Lucy and Isaac to the side of the road, ready to vanish like bunnies if they had to.

"This here the road to Washington, sir?" demanded his mother, looking up at the officer. His mother—Phoebe was her name—was a beautiful woman, and even ragged and di-

sheveled had a fey loveliness that drew the men's eyes. John
was used to seeing that.

Used, too, to the way most drew back after a closer look.

One of the men spit tobacco over the side of his horse and
mumbled, "Damn contrabands. How many does this make
today?"

The officer pointed back along the road. "Left-hand
fork," he said, in a curious yapping voice: *fork* sounded almost like *fahk*. "When you cross Rock Creek, follow the
road till you come to the fort: Ask anyone you meet for Fort
Barker. You contrabands? Runaways?"

"No, sir," began John quickly, with a story he'd used before about searching for a lost master, but his mother shook
off the hand he'd put on her arm and shrilled,

"Yes, sir! We have run away, run away to freedom!" She
swept her arms wide about her, like a raven-haired goddess
of the woods.

John flinched—he had no idea what instructions Northern
soldiers might have received about runaway slaves—but the
officer only shook his head with an air of annoyance. John
drew his mother as gently—and as firmly—as he dared along
the road in the direction the man had pointed, and said,
"Thank you, sir."

The rider in the back ranks spit again. "Damn contrabands." The riders went on.

"Why you pullin' me away?" The sharpness of the slap
that accompanied the words was less worrisome to John than
that hard crazy glitter in Phoebe's eyes. Looking for an argument. Hungering for someone to shout at, the way Mr.
Henry's brother Clive would hunger for liquor. "You
shouldn't be treatin' your mother like that, when you coming into the Promised Land."

They smelled Washington City miles before they reached
it. Richmond had smelled like that, when they'd circled past
it cautiously in the night, and the camps around Manassas railway junction: the reek of thousands of latrine trenches, of
countless corrals of horses, cattle, Army mules.

Washington City was a thousand times worse. As they crossed the Rock Creek bridge the first of the Army camps lay jumbled and dirty to the right of the road, row after row after row after *row* of little round white tents like dirty mushrooms straggling down the brushy hillside. Men in blue uniforms slopped around in mud up to their booted ankles, amid goods-boxes and ambulance-wagons and iron pots slung over campfires. Smoke gritted in the throat. Beyond the camps—and they seemed endless—John saw houses and trees, and farther off a big domed building three-quarters built against the hazy noon sky.

"So this the Promise Land, hunh?" muttered Cassy, though she was careful not to let her mother hear. She was twelve, thin and fine-boned like John, and like John (he reflected gloomily) too smart for her own good. "Don't look so promisin' to me." On the other side of the road, in weedy fields among thin stands of bright-leaved yellow poplar, lay other camps, smaller and dirtier and less organized than those of the soldiers. Through the open sides of some tents John glimpsed makeshift barrooms, planks laid over barrels and card-games going at crude tables. In other places slatternly women loitered, or lines of laundry hung to dry.

Camp Barker, when they reached it at last, turned out to be like these lesser, unofficial establishments, a vast, messy agglomeration of shanties and rude tents—some no more than blankets stretched over ropes—clustered around the packed earth embankments that in their turn surrounded half a dozen wood buildings. The snubby brown snouts of cannon protruded over the earthen walls and the weedy, trash-littered ground stank of garbage and piss.

There seemed to be no order anywhere. Men crouched over smoldering fires among the ragged willows, arguing in the desultory fashion of those who have little else to do. In a rough board shelter a young woman was suckling a baby.

"This here Camp Barker?" asked John, and she nodded.

"They done give out the food this mornin' already, though," she added. Her dress was ragged, the faded calico stained by tobacco leaves, like every garment John had ever owned. He guessed she'd been a field hand, like his mother. "It was just soup, and they was so many, most people didn't even get none of that." She wasn't much older than he, but her eyes were like a tired crone's. Beaten, like those of someone who has come a long hard journey for nothing.

"So what do we do?" John forced cheer into his voice against a dread he could not name. "Where do we go?"

The girl shrugged. "You here."

"And what you all sittin' around here for?" His mother shoved past him, jabbed a knotted finger at the young woman. "You folks all lazy or somethin'? This here Washington City! This here the Promise Land! Land of milk and honey! You free, and you just sittin' here on your lazy ass?"

The young woman stared at Phoebe in shock, as well she might, reflected John, catching his mother by the arm. "Mama..."

She jerked free of his grip. "Don't you *Mama* me! And don't you grab on to me like I was a child!" Her voice pitched high as she rounded on the woman with the baby. "It stink around here! This here the Promise Land, and all you can do is sit out here makin' it stink! We come a thousand miles through the night and through the storm, an' for what? To see a bunch of shiftless folks settin' in the woods..."

People were gathering and John and Cassy tried to pull their mother away. "You turn my own children against me! You gonna call the pate-rollers on us? You gonna send us back?" Phoebe's voice rose to a scream as she fought them. She seemed to get these spells of quick fury more frequently when she was hungry, or worried, or tired. God knew they were all three. Sometimes it seemed to John that his entire life wrapped around his mother's moods like a vine on a stake.

Two or three other runaways came over to them, but backed off when his mother lunged at them, bending to snatch up handfuls of mud, her black Medusa hair tumbling around her shoulders. "Where we get food around here,

hunh? This here the Promise Land, they gotta give us food!"
Isaac, clinging to Lucy's hand, began to cry.

John and Cassy walked their mother to the outskirts of the
camp. In back of the fort near the stink of the sheep-pens,
they settled her under a sycamore tree. John talked her quiet,
then left her with Cassy and walked down the main road into
town. "There got to be some way we can get food," he rea-
soned. "Cuttin' kindling or cleaning some white folks' yard,
somethin' they'll just give me a little food for." He felt light-
headed with hunger and too tired to go far, but he knew
once their mother got an idea in her head, she'd harp and
harp at him until he did what she demanded. It was easier to
just do it at once.

He didn't think they could get sent back to Halifax
County, anyway, and the soldiers hadn't seemed in any tearing hurry to turn them over to Maryland slaveholders.

But after he passed through the muddy Army camps along
the road, and came into Washington City itself, he discovered that he wasn't the first contraband to come looking for
food or a little work to get food, not by a good long way.

"We fixed here just fine," said a man curtly—a slave, John
thought, or a servant, anyway—who was cleaning gardening
tools in the shed of the first yard he asked at.

"There anyplace you know where I could do work for
some food?"

The man grunted. The big yellow house, set among shady
oak-trees, was a nice one, like the houses in Richmond,
though the street in front of it was like a hog-wallow. "I get
four–five niggers a day askin' for food, or work if they honest. Ain't the Army take care of you?"

John shook his head, reflecting that it didn't sound like the
Army was taking care of those "four–five niggers" a day
either.

"Well, we can't take care of you, neither," the man
snapped. He jerked his head back toward the house again.
"With all the Army in town food costs somethin' scandalous.

My missus say we can't be handin' out no food to them that comes beggin'.'"

"I ain't beggin' for food." John prickled with anger, but kept his voice even. "I'm askin' for work."

"An' I'm tellin' you we don't got food nor work. An' I'm wore out with people like you comin' up all the time when the Army's supposed to be takin' care of you. Now get along."

In the alley again John stood still for a moment, his heart beating so hard he could feel it in his ears. He knew his mother's ideas of the Promised Land of Freedom might be exaggerated—a lot of her ideas were—but it had never occurred to him that when they got there, there might not be enough milk and honey to go around.

Or that those who had it wouldn't want to share.

By sunset he'd been turned away from dozens of big white houses along those astonishingly wide streets and any number of the humbler two-room cottages of the free colored in the alleys. Sometimes roughly, sometimes politely, or with sympathy and pity, and admonitions to "let the Army take care of you"—presumably with the small amount of soup the woman at the camp had spoken of. Two or three housewives gave him food—heel-ends of bread and table-scraps—but it wasn't enough to satisfy one person, let alone five. The autumn afternoon had turned chilly, with a nip to the wind. Harsh cookfire smoke mingled with the ever-present stench of the Army camps that lay everywhere over the city, and as he trudged the wide sloppy street back to where he hoped the fort and Camp Barker lay, he felt a stab of longing for the simplicity of life on the run.

After weeks in the variegated stillness of the woods, he found the constant rumbling passage of wagons and ambulances confusing, almost painful. Raised on a rural plantation where he saw no one but the same hundred and fifty people he'd known all his life, he felt as if time had somehow speeded up. There were people everywhere, strangers walking and riding and driving buggies and carriages that he had to watch out for, stray dogs snapping at him, walls and fences

like a dizzying dirty labyrinth. Too much movement, too
many new things coming at him too fast. The stink of the
town was awful, the noise a disorienting clamor in his ears.

He'd been hungry and frightened, all those nights and
weeks up from Halifax County. But he was hungry here
and—though he didn't like to admit it to himself—frightened too, in a different fashion that he couldn't describe. In
the woods at least there was peace.

He was concentrating so hard on remembering all the
turns and streets he'd taken that he didn't even notice the little group of young white men until they crossed the street to
surround him.

They were dressed roughly, wool trousers and coarse calico shirts powdered all over with dust. They wore thick boots
and slouch hats and two of them carried whips, the long
blacksnake kind that teamsters used. When two of them
pointed at him he hastily sprang off the footpath into the
ditch—they were in a street of rough little houses not too far
from the camps on the edge of town, small unpaved streets
darting with half-naked white children who screamed in a
language John had never heard.

But the stockiest of the young men moved to block his
way: "What you doin' hereabouts, then, boy-o?" He shoved
John hard on the shoulder, so that he staggered and almost fell.

"I'm lookin' for work, sir." John lowered his eyes, his
heart pounding. He'd had to do with few enough white men
in his short life and they always scared him, for they had
power and a cruel need to prove their power to anyone
around them.

"You a runaway, then, boy-o?" The white youth wasn't
much older than John, nor were any of his friends, but he
was squat and stocky, with hair the color of a fox and tawny
eyes that seemed yellow against the mask of dust. His body
stank of sweat and his breath of liquor.

"No, sir. My ol' Miss, she died, an'—"

Without change of expression the young man slashed him

across the face with the rolled-up whip. "Don't you be lyin' to me, boy."

John staggered back, and one of the others must have come around behind him and tripped him. His memories weren't clear after that. A boot cracked into his ribs and another into the soft meat below them, and he curled himself together, clenched his thighs to protect his balls and wrapped his arms around his head. He heard someone shout something about going back to where he came from. Weeks later he remembered seeing a Union soldier stroll over across the street to them with his rifle, but he never did remember the actual blow that knocked him cold.

"ARE YOU ALL RIGHT, YOUNG MAN?" A SMALL, GENTLE HAND brushed his forehead. A white lady's voice, with the honeyed inflection of the South.

Even before he opened his eyes the midday light went through his skull like an ax.

He mumbled, "I'm fine, ma'am," out of the sheer habit of never admitting to a white that there was a problem—you never knew what they'd choose to do about it. But when he opened his eyes the pain in his skull cleft him down to his belly, and he rolled over fast, feeling bile flood up his throat, drowning him.

He tried to roll away; the movement only made it worse. Vomit exploded from his lips like the seeds from a squished tomato. The woman was sitting on the ground beside him with her black skirts spread around her and she got a lapful— *How the hell can I throw up so much when I ain't eaten anything?*

Then he was heaving helplessly, conscious of nothing except those small hands holding him steady, agony in his ribs with every spasm, and the smell of vomit that seemed to fill the world.

He sank back to the rough blanket spread on the ground, whispering frantically, "I'm sorry, ma'am, I'm so sorry—I didn't mean it. . . ." Mr. Henry at Blue Hill had beaten a servant for passing wind while waiting at table. John knew perfectly well that white ladies—particularly Southern ladies—did not appreciate niggers vomiting on their skirts.

"Good heavens, don't be silly," she said briskly. Beneath the overwhelming halitus of the vomit he smelled the musk-rose sachet in her clothing as she leaned around him with a wet kerchief, and wiped his mouth and chin.

He opened his eyes, and met her worried gaze, the most beautiful shade of green-touched blue he'd ever seen, like the heart of a flower.

And genuinely concerned that he was all right.

He looked away at once—Mr. Henry would box a pick-aninny's ears for being "uppity," i.e., looking a white in the face—but this woman only went on briskly, "If anyone owes me an apology it's the louts who did this to you. Lizabet . . . thank you."

She held out a tin cup of water to him and in taking it he immediately upset it all over her tightly corseted bosom. She rocked back but caught the cup deftly—"Oh, dear, you *did* take a bad hit, didn't you?"—and put a steadying hand on his shoulder. "Do you want to lie down again?"

"No, ma'am. Thank you, ma'am." He glanced shyly up again at her face, her tone of matter-of-fact friendliness sponging away his fear and his shame. He saw a square, motherly face with a short nose and a determined chin, older than her girlish voice would lead you to think—his mother's age at least and probably more. The flesh around those beautiful eyes was discolored with sleeplessness, netted with fine lines of grief and pain, and he saw she wore the black of deepest mourning.

"I'm all right now, ma'am."

A woman leaned down behind her with another cup of water.

"Thank you, Lizabet. Shall we try this again?" And she gave John an encouraging smile as he took the second cup.

They were under the shelter of an Army marquee. John could see the sloped weedy wall of the fort nearby, yellowing

in the autumn heat. It was nearly midday. It had been growing dark when he had been jumped. Lizabet, who had handed
down the second cup, was a tall creamy-dark mulatto woman.
In Virginia, John would have guessed her to be a housekeeper
or uppermost lady's maid, but she was too elegantly dressed in
clothes that obviously weren't her dumpling-shaped friend's
cast-offs. In a lovely low alto Lizabet said, "He was brought in
last night, beaten up by some Irish teamsters, and at least one
soldier." She handed her white friend a damp towel to wipe
her skirts.

John didn't remember the soldier, but he touched gingerly the pounding nexus of pain on the left side of his forehead and felt a bandage there. His face felt puffy as a
blown-up bladder; his ribs and belly ached from blows.

"Even before the fighting brought refugees into town, the
Irish seemed to think every black man a personal threat to
their livelihood," Lizabet added in a voice like cold bitter
coffee.

The white woman turned back to John, shocked. "Is
what Mrs. Keckley says true?"

"Yes, ma'am," said John, sitting up—cautiously—and sipping the water. "But I wasn't askin' for a job drivin' no team,
I swear. Just cuttin' wood or somethin' so's I could get a little food." His hands shook so badly he spilled the water he
held, and his left eye was swollen almost shut. His clothes
stank of the ditch where he'd been knocked down. "I didn't
start nuthin'."

The marquee around them seemed to be jammed with
people, with more pressing in around its open sides. Three
or four women at the other end of the big shelter dipped
flour and cornmeal and cups of beans from sacks on a rough
table before them. They, like the elegant Lizabet Keckley,
were people of color, mostly lighter-skinned than the runaways—the contrabands, the soldiers had called them—who
shoved each other to get near them, holding out dishes and
gourds and empty sacks to receive the food.

"Well, I should hope not," said the white lady briskly. "If

you *had* started something with a gang of Irish teamsters and an armed soldier I should be obliged to question your sanity. It's a complete disgrace, Lizabet. Something must be done about it! I'm sure this boy . . . What's your name, son?"

"John," he said. "John Wilamet."

"And I am Mrs. Lincoln," she told him, holding out a small gloved hand to shake. "I'm sure John here could do as good a job driving horses as any of those Irish louts." She scrubbed at her fouled skirt with the matter-of-fact touch that made John guess that she'd nursed the sick before—and in spite of the stylish cut of her mourning dress, that she'd washed clothes, too. "Do you have family here, John?"

"Yes, ma'am—Mrs. Lincoln." At least the name was easy to remember, for it was the same one as the Union President whose election Mr. Henry had gotten so worked up about last year. John wondered if she was any relation, though he couldn't imagine how she could be. She was very much a Southern lady. She would have been much more at home among the friends of Mr. Henry's wife Miss Daphne, he thought, than in this Northern place looking after him. "My mama, and the girls an' Isaac. They'll be worried about me. I left 'em yesterday afternoon, under a tree out by the sheep-pens. . . ."

"You rest for a few minutes more, then, dear, and let me know when you're feeling well enough to get up. I'll see you back there. I'm sure your dear mother—oh!" Her head snapped sharply around at the sound of rising voices from the food-tables.

A man—a contraband—was thrusting his gourd back at one of the serving women, shaking it about angrily, demanding more. At the sight of this, Mrs. Lincoln's eyes flared with abrupt fury. "Oh, this is ridiculous! I've told them about keeping order here!"

She got to her feet with surprising speed for a lady of her girth and swept in the direction of the tables, hoops and drapes and ribbons all flouncing like a peony in a tempest. "I *told* that Mrs. Durham that it was no good handing things out piecemeal like this, not that anyone ever listens to *me*. . . ."

John sat up, watching in a kind of horrified fascination, as his stout little friend thrust her way into the middle of the altercation between contraband and server. The nearly instantaneous change in her, from worried kindliness to hot rage, was so total as to be shocking.

Another woman of color, neatly clothed in blue-and-white calico, had already come over to speak to the angry contraband, but Mrs. Lincoln pushed between them. "Stop that at once! You should be grateful you're getting anything at all, rather than demanding more!" When the woman in blue—presumably Mrs. Durham—spoke quietly to her, Mrs. Lincoln whirled upon her.

"Let *you* handle it? I've let you handle the whole of this distribution, and to what end? Nothing organized properly, people shoving in any old how . . ." She positively spit the words, her small black-gloved hands balled into fists. "If you'd done as I suggested and worked through the Army, I daresay in time I could have gotten men in my husband's Cabinet to improve the allotment. I know men in Congress, and I daresay I'm not without *some* influence, in spite of what people like you seem to think. But instead we have only this piddling tent, and people thrusting in as if they owned the whole concern. . . ."

"The only one who's acting as if she owned the whole concern," retorted Mrs. Durham, her voice arctic, "is *you*, Mrs. Lincoln."

"How *dare* you!" Mrs. Lincoln's face went from blotchy red to a furious pallor. "*Mrs.* Durham—if that *is* your name, and I daresay I've often wondered why there isn't a *Mr.* Durham anywhere in sight. . . ."

By this time John was on his feet and almost to her side, heedless of the pain jabbing his ribs. He acted without thinking, recognizing with deadly accuracy in her voice, in her stance, in the narrow blazing focus of her eyes, the echo of his own mother's flash-fire rages. Mrs. Keckley was right beside him, reaching out to touch Mrs. Lincoln's swagged black sleeve before the outraged Mrs. Durham could collect her breath to respond.

"Mrs. Lincoln," Lizabet said, and John put in,

"Mrs. Lincoln, 'scuse me, ma'am, but I feel well enough if you'd take me on back to my family now."

Her blind momentum broken, Mrs. Lincoln stopped, gasping, seemingly dazed by the onslaught of her own emotions. Mrs. Keckley flashed John a grateful look and put in gently, "Come, Mrs. Lincoln, we must help this young man."

For a moment it was touch and go whether she'd respond—whether she'd even heard them—for she was trembling with anger. But she blinked, and looked again at John's ashy face, and the hot wrath in her eyes changed to concern.

"Of course," she said, her voice uncertain. "Of course, poor boy . . ."

As if it were the most natural thing in the world—as if she were one of his own aunties back at Blue Hill instead of a white lady in an expensive dress—she took his arm and put it around her shoulder to take some of his weight. Exhausted, discouraged, and hungry—and sick with the sense of having once more failed to meet his mother's expectations—John could have wept at her kindness.

As they made their way through the crowded tents and makeshift shelters of the contraband camp, Mrs. Lincoln alternated between watchful concern for John and leftover fulminations concerning Mrs. Durham: "The *impudence* of the woman! Who does she think she is?"

Lizabet nodded and made gentle noises that neither agreed nor disagreed, from which John deduced that Mrs. Keckley was also used to this abrupt transformation from lady to Gorgon and back. And whatever the right and the wrong of the matter was, Mrs. Keckley clearly valued her volatile friend too much to sever the relationship.

"Obviously she regards herself as cleverer than a mere *smatterer* like myself, who has *only* been around men organizing major military and political campaigns. I—" Mrs.

Lincoln broke off, pressed her hand to the bridge of her nose. When she took it away her eyes had lost their glitter, and seemed to see him again. "Are you quite sure you can walk, John? You look dreadful."

John felt dreadful, struggling to stay on his feet. But what he felt mostly was deep gratitude for her care and friendship at what was probably the nadir of his short life, coupled with awed fascination. Later, looking back on the incident, he was never sure what shook him up more: that this snub-nosed, haunted-eyed Southern belle, who could show such kindness one moment and such termagant fury the next, was in fact the wife of the notorious President Lincoln—

—or that she was quite clearly as crazy as his mother.

JOHN SAW MRS. LINCOLN MANY TIMES DURING THAT BITTER cold winter of 1862.

She often came to the contraband camp with Elizabeth Keckley—who, Cassy told him a few days after their first encounter, was her dressmaker and one of the most prominent free colored residents of Washington City. Mrs. Keckley had helped found the Freedmen's Relief Association, and had enlisted her friend and employer to help her distribute food and blankets, to find homes for the runaways who continued to flood into Washington City, and jobs they could work at to earn their keep.

John quickly became a sort of page for Mrs. Lincoln when she came. He ran her errands, or helped her unload the bundles of blankets and clothing that she would collect from the wives of Senators, Cabinet members, and officers. Long experience in dealing with his own mother had given John the knack of letting her quick, spit-cat angers slide off his back; had taught him how to talk her out of her rages when it seemed that she did not know or care what words came out of her mouth.

"I really don't know what gets into me," she said, upon one occasion when she returned to the camp a few days after an outburst directed at the commander of Fort Barker that had finished with her departing in tears. "I hear myself saying these *terrible* things, see myself... it's almost like watching someone else." She made a quick gesture as if pushing the memory away. "*So* mortifying..."

Mrs. Keckley put a hand on her shoulder as if to say that she understood. But in fact John guessed that the quiet-voiced, supremely reasonable seamstress didn't understand, any more than he understood why his mother would rant and shriek at total strangers—or, worse, at people who could do her harm if annoyed. They were standing beside Mrs. Lincoln's carriage, a handsome open barouche, in which Mrs. Lincoln had brought clothing collected for the camp children: John guessed that without the necessity of deliver-ing these, she wouldn't have come at all.

"But the Commander really was at fault," Mrs. Lincoln declared, rallying. "He had *no* call to speak to me as he did and *certainly* no call to question my judgment about shelter for the contrabands. He just wants to save himself trouble. If he could find a way not to provide shelter for his *own* soldiers here he'd prefer that, too. *Or* food... 'Surely the men could just go into town for their suppers.'" She aped the Commander's pinched Maine accent with such devastating accuracy that both John and Mrs. Keckley dissolved into laughter.

Later in the winter, when John's little brother, Isaac, fell ill with fever, Mrs. Lincoln helped care for him in the rude shack on M Street that the family occupied. She brought him meat and milk unobtainable in the camp, and when Isaac died, she wept so bitterly that Cassy had to lead her outside, for her stricken wailings only fanned their mother's howling grief.

Later, Lizabet Keckley told John this was because Mrs. Lincoln had only recently lost her own son—and indeed, John noticed, when he next saw Mrs. Lincoln at a troop re-view with the tall, gawky President, that her husband, too, wore the black of deepest grief.

In the spring the armies began to move. Mrs. Lincoln

found John a job with an Army surgeon in General Ord's corps. By that time his family was living with a free colored family named Gordon, in a tiny cottage not far from the unfinished Capitol Building: the Gordons had taken in five other contrabands already and the house was bursting at the seams.

At sixteen, John was small and wiry, but working for Dr. Brainert was less physically taxing than picking tobacco leaves for seventeen hours a day. He and the sturdy, red-faced surgeon got along well.

John still had blinding headaches, especially in cold weather, and the cut he'd taken from the rifle-butt had healed to a curved scar that pulled one eyebrow to a peak and turned his thin, clerkish face oddly ferocious.

He was in Richmond two years later, when President Lincoln came by steamboat to view the captured Southern capital.

Never, in after years, did John forget the host of men, women, children, former slaves—wearing the ragged garments that were all their masters could afford to give them in these days of privation and defeat—pressing up around the President's horse as he rode with his Generals through the rubble of bricks, the soot-black broken walls. Women held up their babies for Lincoln to touch, as if he were a god in one of the books John had begun so voraciously to read. Men struggled through the crush to grasp his boots in the stirrups.

Everything seemed vividly clear to John that day, for he'd recently gotten his first pair of spectacles from the Army, and was still dazzled at being able to distinguish leaves on trees, the letters in his books, the faces of people at a distance with such magical, crystalline brightness. He had glimpsed Mr. Lincoln often at Headquarters—a gangly, almost comical figure, cracking his knuckles as he slouched in a camp-chair with his feet on the table, telling funny stories in that high husky scratchy voice. But today that tall man looked grave and a little shaken, as if shocked by light streaming in from the opened doors of the future, light that only he could see. He had made all these people free, John thought, watching the tall black figure over the heads of the crowd. Had given them not only the rights, but the terrible burdens of the free. That responsibility would rest on his bony shoulders forever.

Ten days later he was dead.

In Richmond John had hoped to renew his acquaintance with Mrs. Lincoln, for he'd heard she was coming with the President. But she quarreled publicly and hysterically with the wives of General Grant and General Ord, and went back to Washington, prostrate with dudgeon and migraine. When she returned a few days later to tour the captured city John was at one of the Army hospitals, puzzling over the case of a Massachusetts soldier who'd been brought in after the fighting at Petersburg, unwounded but paralyzed and unable to speak.

Thus he had had only a glimpse of Mary Todd Lincoln one evening as he passed the steamboat *River Queen* at its dock: saw her stubby black form beside the stooped, bean-pole outline of her husband, silhouetted against the lucid sky. He saw her reach out her hand for his, apologizing maybe for the scene she'd made the week before. He watched Lincoln take off his tall hat and bend—a long way down—to kiss her.

Like Lizabet Keckley, thought John, Mr. Lincoln—he'd learned right off never to call him "Abe" or "Old Abe," names he apparently hated—valued his volatile bride too much to hold her outburst against her. In their touch, in their kiss, it was clear to the young man that they were old friends and partners, who'd come a long, hard road together. And because he was very fond of Mary Lincoln himself, John felt glad that she had at least that faithful lover, those faithful friends.

That far-off image, almost like a picture in a book, was the last John saw of her, until ten years later when he was locking her into a cell.

CHAPTER ONE

Chicago May 19, 1875

SHE WAS SURROUNDED BY ENEMIES.

For the dozenth time Mary Lincoln glanced sharply behind her, heart hammering in her throat with both panic and rage.

Nothing. Bowler-hatted businessmen in natty suits bought newspapers from scruffy boys, barefoot in the spring heat. Tight-corseted women, the ruffled swags that trailed from their bustles sweeping the dirty sidewalk, paused by the windows of shops to admire and chat. Immigrant vendors in grubby corduroy yelled their wares from pushcarts—apples, kerchiefs, mousetraps, toys. A cab darted by along Clark Street, hooves clattering, iron tires banging, as it dodged around trolleys, carriages, drays of barreled beer.

Downtown Chicago on a spring morning. Heat swimming up from the sidewalk bricks; the stink of horse-droppings.

She knew she was being followed. For weeks now she'd been certain of it.

Who? she wondered. *Why?*

And quickened her step. The fear that had shadowed her all her fifty-seven years breathed again at her shoulder. Her feet were swollen in her tight black kid shoes and the snip of breeze that whispered from Lake Michigan died away, leaving her sweating beneath the thick black veils. Why didn't people get out of her way? She dodged past a dawdling woman by a shop window. *Can't they see I'm a widow? I'm entitled to consideration on that score, aren't I? Even if they don't know whose widow I am.*

Thinking about him, even after all these years, made her throat constrict with the grief that had never eased.

She had to get home.

She gazed longingly after another cab that rattled by—they all drove like lunatics in this town! There was money in her purse, and even more hidden in secret pockets of her petticoats, in case of emergencies. But cabs were so expensive. She'd spent enough that morning as it was. Nine pairs of lace curtains at Gossage's, so beautiful! *But I really will have to save after this.*

So no cabs.

And the crowds on the trolleys filled her with nameless but familiar dread.

Why were people following her?

Why that elusive half-familiar glimpse of bulk and movement that she'd seen again and again during the past eight weeks?

Newspapermen? Those vile vampires who'd dogged her every step, twisted her every word . . . called her Confederate spy and worse?

Or was someone plotting to kill her as they'd killed her husband?

Or was it all something she imagined?

She pushed that troubling suspicion away.

Movement in the corner of her vision—were things starting to appear and disappear again? *Not another migraine,* she thought in weary despair. *I had one only yesterday, or was it the day before?* Was the blazing shimmer that came and went only the reflection of the noon sun on the windows of the high buildings? Or the herald of yet another bout of nausea, blindness, pain?

Anxiety swamped the worry about being followed in a greater wave of panic. *I have to get home!* In her room she'd be safe. She could take her medicine before those kinked burning lines started to creep across her vision, before sick disorientation overtook her. The room would be hot and unbearably stuffy—mentally she calculated the cost of even the most modest chamber in the Grand Pacific Hotel against what her husband had left her, against the pension she had finally pried out of those tight-fisted ungrateful liars in Congress. But at least there she would be safe.

She could barely remember a time when she had not felt herself in danger.

A pack of ragamuffin boys flurried past her, like blown leaves among the crowd. Their treble laughter brought back the laughter of her own sons and the stab of grief was as piercing as if they had each died yesterday. Eddie scarcely more than a baby, crying with fever as he clung to her hand. Sweet-faced, sweet-natured Willie, gentle and always so worried about her, bringing her flowers from the weedy lots behind the Capitol. And Tad, flighty and willful, growing daily more like his father...

She squeezed her mind shut against Mr. Lincoln's image. She'd never thought of him as anything but Mr. Lincoln—or Father, when they were alone. His shadow rose behind the shadows of her sons: the looming gawky height, as if his body had been put together from a bundle of slats, the deft lightness of his touch. His hands had been huge, nearly twice the length of hers when they'd press them palm to palm and laugh....

After his death she'd given away everything he'd possessed, lest the sight of even his reading-glasses in a drawer surprise her with heart-crushing pain. In the ten years since then she'd visited hundreds of mediums, speakers with and summoners of the dead, begging for only a glimpse of him. Desperate to hear his voice again, to hear him call her "Mother," and see his smile.

Father, she thought, *how could you have left me in this awful place alone?*

The Grand Pacific Hotel loomed before her, story after story of stone and glaring glass. Only ten years, she thought wonderingly, since Washington's muddy unpaved streets, since the tumult of soldiers tramping by in the sticky night. Ten years since she'd heard the thunder of enemy guns beyond the river. Chicago with its macadam-paved streets, with its trolley cars and bustles and advertising posters and its thousands and thousands of immigrants, seemed like another world, as if she had somehow missed her way coming back from Europe in '71 and fetched up in some bewildering alien land.

Her anxiety lessened somewhat as she climbed the Grand Pacific's marble steps and crossed the lobby's acres of red plush carpet like a determined black bug scuttling for the baseboard. Almost home. Almost safe.

The Grand Pacific was expensive, with its French chef and its conservatory garden. But Abraham Lincoln's widow couldn't be seen to live in common lodgings. That much she owed his memory. And boarding-houses had always been abominations to her.

Mr. Turner, the manager, was understanding and kind. When she'd wake in terror in the night, he'd provide a reliable chambermaid to stay in her room with her at only a very modest charge. He was reassuring and helpful, if occasionally maddeningly stupid, during those spells when voices seemed to be speaking to her out of the walls and floor, when during her migraines she could see the spirit of an Indian warrior pulling the bones out of her face; when she'd wake in panic and terror, thinking she smelled smoke—when she'd see the city in flames, the wall of fire approaching. . . .

Mary shook her head at herself as she climbed the stairs. The Grand Pacific was equipped with modern elevators but she'd never trusted such things. The reminder of her spells of confusion made her headache worse. Maybe it was all only her imagination. Though she only cloudily recalled what she did and said in her spells, it did seem to her they mostly came on her in the afternoons. All she had to do, really, was be a little careful about staying inside.

She pushed the thought out of her mind. Her heart was thudding and her feet, her back, her head were in agony. Her medicine would make her feel better.

And sometimes during her spells—especially at night—one or another of her sons would come to her, beautiful shining figures, smiling and holding out their hands in comfort.

Only Robert was left, of the four beautiful boys she had borne.

Mary paused on the stairs to get her breath, to rest the searing ache in her back. She supposed her shoes were not really made for walking long distances in, but she would *not* be like those absurd suffragist women who went around in Bloomer costumes and ugly boots. Her friend Myra had often expounded on "rational" dress. *That really would give Robert a seizure,* she thought, and smiled a little despite her discomfort at the recollection of her chronically disapproving eldest son. *He thinks I'm eccentric enough without that.*

Poor Robert. As she resumed her climb she wondered whether he suffered from an overdeveloped sense of his own importance, or merely a complete lack of imagination. *Probably both,* she thought. *Such a stuffy man, even before he married that horrid girl . . .*

Yet her heart ached with love for him, and for her granddaughter . . . Mr. Lincoln's granddaughter. Beautiful little Mamie. The terrible dream she'd had in Florida two months ago, the dream of Robert lying ill, dying just as Tad and Eddie and Willie had died, had brought her flying back here, desperate to save him, to push that terrible shadow away if she could. Desperate that he not leave her, as all the others had left her . . .

Mary paid a quick, grateful visit to the ladies' lavatory on the way down the hall. Hot weather always brought back the burning itches that had tormented her since Tad's birth, over two decades ago. Then at last, with a sense of having safely negotiated an unknown battlefield yet again, she unlocked her own room.

It was small, and, as she'd feared, already appallingly stuffy. Since Tad's death she'd found daylight almost too harsh to stand, but even the single gas jet burning in the heavily curtained room added to the already intolerable summer heat. She'd insisted on the least expensive room available in the hotel—really, her money disappeared so quickly!—but for that reason it was already too crowded for comfort. In addition to the eleven trunks she'd brought back from Florida with her—such a beautiful place, and the doctors there most sympathetic and helpful—she'd done a good deal of shopping in these past weeks. Mostly to pass the time, to get herself out—really, what else was there for a woman to do?—but there was no telling when she might get a house of her own, a home of her own, again.

Her plump hands shook as she put aside the packages from yesterday's shopping expedition (an album of poetry and twelve yards of exquisite jade-green satin, and shoes to match) and opened the cupboard, barely to be reached behind the trunks. She was definitely getting a migraine, and she could scarcely see the bottles as she took them out. Not that it mattered which was which. *They're all the same, really. And Dr. Somers in Florida said they're all beneficial.* Godfrey's Cordial, Ma-Sol-Pa Herbal Indian Balm, Dr. Foote's Sanitary Medical Tonic, Nervine, Hunt's Female Revivifier. . . .

She poured them all in a tumbler and drained it, savoring the musky intensity, the burning comforting warmth that rose through her. She'd begin to feel better in a few moments. . . .

A knock sounded on the door.

The delivery boy from Gossage's. That was quick. But it wasn't the delivery boy who stood in the hall when she opened the door. For a flashing, confusing moment, between the uncertain light of the curtained chamber and her own slightly blurred eyesight, Mary thought it was her husband.

Mr. Lincoln . . .

Was it, impossibly, him? As the others had appeared to her, had he finally come?

She blinked, then said uncertainly, "Mr. Swett?"

"Mrs. Lincoln." Leonard Swett took off his hat. It was the high silk hat of a professional that had deceived her migraine-dazzled eyes by adding to his six-foot height. Swett's face was lean, and he wore the same kind of beard that Mr. Lincoln had during the last few years of his life, a jawline Quaker beard without a mustache. Memories flared through her mind, of Swett and his wife, Laura—before Laura's incapacitating illness—coming to dinner at that little cottage on Eighth Street in Springfield. Of Swett laughing with Mr. Lincoln over this lawsuit or that, like boys who've trounced each other behind the schoolhouse, then dusted themselves off and shaken hands.

What was Mr. Swett doing here at her room? Why hadn't he sent up a card? *Had* he sent up a card, and she just didn't remember? No, of course not, she'd just gotten here herself....

"I do apologize." Mary spread her lace-mitted hands across the sable crape of her skirts and wondered how quickly she could get rid of him. She was exhausted, her head was throbbing, and, having taken her medicine, she wanted only to lie down.

Why hadn't he sent up a card and asked her to meet him in the lobby? A gentleman *never* came up to a lady's room.

But it was a basic tenet of Southern womanhood that a lady always gives a gentleman the benefit of the doubt. So instead of asking tartly if he'd been born in a barn, Mary explained, "I've just come in, and have not had time to change. What might I do for you?" She saw now that the boy from Gossage's *was* there, waiting in the hallway gloom, with two men in uniforms she did not recognize. Big men. A problem about the curtains? Probably the fault of that stupid clerk ...

"I regret exceedingly that it is I who must perform this office, Mrs. Lincoln." Swett drew a folded sheet of paper from his coat. He held it out to her in his neatly gloved hand. "This is a writ of arrest from the State of Illinois. You are being charged with lunacy."

If he'd slapped her face she could not have been more surprised. In that first instant she wasn't even taken aback, merely confused, wondering if this were a dream. One of those weird visions, like the Indian spirit who tortured her during her migraines, or the voices that spoke to her out of the walls. Goodness knew she felt unreal enough, as if she'd put her foot down what she'd thought was a step in a familiar staircase, only to find no footing there.

But in Swett's pale eyes she saw that expression with which she was so familiar from a lifetime around lawyers and politicians. That gauging look, waiting for a reaction as a hunter waits for a turkey to step out from behind a bush.

"Lunacy?" Mary thrust her hands behind her. Time and time again she'd heard Mr. Lincoln say to clients, *Whatever you do, don't take any paper they try to hand you.*

Swett was still talking.

". . . courtroom today—this afternoon, in fact—" He took out his watch, as if to emphasize to her how valuable everybody's time was. "—to defend yourself at a hearing..."

"What hearing?" She blinked at him, feeling nonplussed in the most literal sense of the word: at a point from which one cannot go on. He couldn't really be charging her with lunacy. She had to be mistaken about that. She was Abraham Lincoln's wife! "How can it be this afternoon? I need a lawyer...."

"A lawyer has already been arranged for you, Mrs. Lincoln."

"By whom?" Her voice sounded astoundingly calm in her own ears. She remembered all those times back in Springfield, when people would come to Lincoln's office asking for help. You could get a lawyer in a day, but seldom in an hour.

Robert, she thought. *Robert will know how to get me a lawyer. He's a lawyer himself. He'll probably defend me; that way I won't have to spend any money.* Her mind was working slowly, clogged with a dreamlike confusion. It was hard not to simply stare at the pattern of Mr. Swett's silver silk waistcoat. She must keep her mind focused.

Then Swett's next words hit her like a spear in the chest. "By your son Robert, Mrs. Lincoln. Now please." He held out the writ to her and she fell back another step, still refusing to touch it. Refusing to believe.

"Robert knows?" Her mouth felt like someone else's

mouth as she said the words. *Robert knows,* her mind repeated, like a litany that was crucially important for reasons she couldn't recall. *Robert knows. How could Robert know, unless...?*

A portion of Swett's vulpine face disappeared behind a fragment of migraine fire. His beard waggled, temporarily with nothing above it. "Now, Mrs. Lincoln, please. Surely you yourself must admit that much of your behavior is not that of a sane woman."

"I 'must admit' nothing of the kind!" Her mind snapped clear and fury bloomed in her, the blind rage that had all her life lain just beneath the surface, taking her breath away. In a staggering vision of lucid clarity she saw that all her fears had always been true, all her suspicions, all her wariness of betrayal.... She heard her own voice rise to a scream of hatred for them all. "How *dare* you speak to me this way? It's Robert who put you up to this, isn't it? It's Robert who thinks I'm insane, isn't it? He always has! Because I won't put up with that cold little sourpuss he married! Because I want to travel and see the world! Because he wants my money—"

"Mrs. Lincoln, please!"

"Because I see more of the world of the spirits than he does, and he believes that only *his* view of our world can be right!"

"Mrs. Lincoln," said Swett patiently, "all of this can be discussed at the courthouse. That's what a hearing is for. Your son has consulted doctors, and the doctors believe you to be insane."

"What *doctors*?" Her voice twisted at the word. "They don't know me, they haven't even spoken to me!"

"Mrs. Lincoln, look at this room—" He gestured around at the tight-drawn curtains, the trunks piled high against the walls, the packages stacked on the floor, on the table, on the bed all around the small area where she slept, when she slept.

"You come into a lady's room unannounced and pronounce upon her sanity because you did not give her the opportunity to make it presentable for callers? Because you did not give her the option of replying that she was not at home? For shame, sir! Did no one ever teach you that a *gentleman* sends up his card to ask if his arrival is entirely convenient?"

"None of this is to the point." Swett's voice had hardened. Mary, backing from him like a mouse from a cat, saw him suddenly as an alien creature, alien to her as Lincoln had sometimes appeared alien on those few occasions when she'd seen him with other lawyers, wearing his calculating lawyer-face. Hastily she pushed that memory of his cold craftiness from her. Of course he hadn't been like them ever in any way! He'd been a saint. . . .

"The judge and the jury are waiting for us at the court-house. Your lawyer, too, and the doctors who have heard an account of your case." He took out his watch again, and glanced at it significantly, as if, thought Mary, there weren't four other clocks in the room, one of them purchased only last week. . . .

"An account that *you* saw fit to give!" She hurled the words at him like knives. "God knows what lies you've told them! Or did you even have to tell them lies? Just bribe them, the way you have all your life bribed juries to rob the poor!"

He didn't so much as flicker an eyelid at the barb. "You can come with me, or these officers"—he gestured to the stone-faced men in the hall behind him—"will bring you, whether you will or no. There are two carriages downstairs. Unless you yield to me I will either have to seize you forcibly myself, or these men will have to take you and bring you in handcuffs. Now please, Mrs. Lincoln, put on your bonnet and come with me, as you usually would. I'm sure you don't want there to be a scene in the lobby—"

"You are a scoundrel and a coward, and if my husband were alive he would deal with you! Go home and take care of your own wife—about whom God knows I've heard enough tales!—and leave *me* alone!"

She was trembling, and clutched at the corner of the clut-tered dresser for support. *This has to be a dream,* she thought, *a nightmare.* And, *Robert knows. Robert is having them do this thing.* She felt the same nauseating fury that she had when the stylish Washington hostesses would whisper behind her back—or Washington newspapers would print, for all the world to read—that she was a Confederate spy. That she slipped into Lincoln's office late at night to steal Army plans to send to her brothers in Lee's forces across the river. That she should be locked up.

She was surrounded by her enemies, as she had been all her life.

Through blinding tears she screamed, "Let me at least change my dress!" for she was revoltingly conscious of the muck splattered on the hem of her skirt and the stale smell of sweat in her bodice and chemise.

But Swett's hand was on her elbow, and Swett—glancing pointedly at his watch again—was escorting her out the door. She yanked free of him, barely able to see, her hands fumbling with the veils on her bonnet. Mr. Lincoln, she wondered in rising panic, where was Mr. Lincoln? When the big prairie lightning-storms frightened her, in that little cottage in Springfield, he'd come striding home from his office through the pounding summer rain to be with her. . . .

He's dead, she remembered, the memory like yesterday, like a dagger in her guts.

He's dead.

For a minute she smelled his blood on the shoulder of her dress.

The iron elevator doors clattered open. She wanted to explain to Swett how dangerous elevators were, but caught herself: *They'll use that to call me insane.* She held her breath in terror as the car rattled down.

Every word, every action, every glance will give them ammunition, as it did in Washington when they all said I was a spy.

They passed through the lobby, Mary holding herself bolt upright, though her head felt ready to explode. She pulled away, walked ahead of Swett as though he were a servant, hiding her terror under scorn. It was early afternoon: ladies in walking-dresses of summer silk clustered like flowers around the doorway to the conservatory. She felt their glances like knives in her back.

Enemies.

As Swett had promised, there were two carriages at the curb, though it wasn't more than a street or two to the Cook County Courthouse. Single-horse broughams, such as doctors drove—she could guess which was Swett's by the spanking-new paint, the glossy youth of the well-mannered horse. What did the novels all say? *The poor thing was taken away in a closed carriage....*

This can't be happening to me....

She was a Todd of Lexington, whose grandfathers had fought and defeated British and Indians.

This can't be happening to me....

The terrible, agonizing realization of how alone she was.

Swett held out a gloved hand to help her in, for the step was high. It was as if even the inanimate wood and steel mocked the shortness of stature that had all her life been a bitter unchangeable fact.

Mary pulled her hand away. "I ride with you from compulsion," she said coldly, keeping her voice steady with an effort, "but I beg you not to touch me."

Swett climbed in. The carriage moved off with a jolt.

CHAPTER TWO

Lexington, Kentucky July 1825

A CHILD CRIED IN THE DARK OF A SILENT HOUSE.

The breathing of the four other children in the bed was a presence more felt than heard, but Mary knew they were asleep. Twelve-year-old Elizabeth, dark and slim and efficient, had whispered reassuringly to the others as Mammy Sally put them to bed, "Now the doctors are here Ma will be all right." Six-year-old Mary wasn't so sure of it.

On other nights in summer the house smelled of lamp-oil and the straw matting on the floors, of the wet scent of the chestnut-trees behind it and now and then smoke from the kitchen. Now the sticky darkness stank of medicines and blood.

Just before Mammy Sally put the children to bed—Elizabeth, fragile eight-year-old Frances, Mary, and tiny, fretful Ann, with little Levi in the trundle-bed—their Granny Parker had come to the house, something she rarely did after the sun had set. Their father had come down out of their mother's bedroom with a branch of candles in hand, and had embraced his mother-in-law with desperate intensity.

Dr. Warfield had arrived shortly after that, and Dr. Dudley; Mary had heard their voices downstairs as Mammy was tucking the children in. As soon as the old black nurse's candle disappeared down the stairs, Levi had crept up into the bed with the girls, like a frightened puppy seeking the comfort of its litter-mates. When the footsteps of the men vibrated on the stairs, and the door of their mother's room opened and shut, Elizabeth had done her whispered best to comfort them all.

Now Mary stared at where she knew the open door had to be in the darkness, gaping into the still-deeper dark of the hall. Their new brother—George, Elizabeth said his name was—still wailed untended, which meant that Mammy had to be in the sickroom, too.

In time she could stand the uncertainty no longer. She feared the dark—Mammy was full of tales about African demons and the Platt-Eye Devil that lurked under beds—but she feared even more this state of not knowing. Carefully, Mary slipped from Elizabeth's comforting arm and slithered to the floor, a little white ghost in her nightdress, her auburn-bronze braids hanging down her back. Silently she tiptoed to the door, and sat beside it in the pitch-dark hall, listening to her infant brother cry, to the occasional half-heard mumblings behind the closed sickroom door.

Once she heard her mother groan, and smelled fresh blood above the stale odors of sickness. Elizabeth had told her that bleeding would bleed out the sickness, but the smell made Mary's heart quake. Then after a long time the scrape of a chair on the floor, and her father's voice, saying her mother's name . . .

A thump, indistinct and dreadful, like something unknown and unspeakable groping its way toward her in the dark. Mary pressed her hands to her mouth and in her heart whispered the litany with which she'd tried on other nights to keep the Platt-Eye Devil at bay: *Hide me, oh my Savior, hide . . .*

But whatever it was that the future held, it was rushing toward her and there was no way she could hide.

The door down the hallway opened. Candlelight, and the redoubled smells of sickness and blood. One of the doctors emerged with the candlestick in his hand, and Granny Parker, bony and upright in her black dress. Then Mary's father and another doctor, carrying between them a woman's body in a white shift, her long dark braids trailing down to the floor. The shift was spattered with blood and there were bandages on both arms. When Mary's father stumbled a little, the woman's head lolled and Mary saw for the last time her mother's face, pale with the ravages of sickness and death.

MARY'S EYES SNAPPED OPEN, THE TERROR OF THAT HOT DARK hall jolting back hard into the sticky-hot terror of the carriage as it stopped.

Leonard Swett said, "Here we are, Mrs. Lincoln."

Mary had passed the massive gray stone walls of the Cook County Courthouse almost daily since coming back to Chicago in March, and still felt disoriented at the sight. Like everything on the street—in the whole of downtown—it was unfamiliar to her, and the shock of seeing it made her clench her small hands tight until her nails pinched the palms through the silk-fine black kid of her gloves. *I mustn't let them see. I mustn't let anyone see me break down.*

She was a Todd of Lexington, whose grandfathers had fought and defeated British and Indians.

I won't give them that satisfaction.

The tension of her clenched jaw-muscles fired blinding snakes of light through her vision. Her head swam—in addition to the migraine, she was definitely having one of her "spells"—*Why does it have to be now? I must focus my mind, do something.... They said I have a lawyer....*

But terror of the blaze that had destroyed the city seemed to be branded into her brain, tangling thoughts of the present with images of the past. Her mother... the Fire... and Tad had died only weeks before the Fire. Choking out his life, imploring her with sunken eyes, so like her husband's.

He'd left her to face the Fire alone. As they all had left her.

She pulled her hand away again from Mr. Swett's proffered help, hoping she wouldn't stagger on her swollen feet as she stepped down that too-long drop to the curb.

Preceded him in silence from the blinding heat of the sidewalk into the dense gloom of the Courthouse's side door. She had to use the toilet again and didn't dare ask for it, couldn't endure reducing herself before these haughty, scornful men.

The courtroom was full of people.

She heard their voices as Mr. Swett and his guards led her along the corridor, and her heart sank.

She should have realized there'd be an audience to her shame. Of course word would get to the papers. It always did. And of course people would show up, to gape, to listen, to have all the gossip to carry home to their families or their cronies at the saloon. Gossip about the Confederate spy. About Mr. Lincoln's crazy widow who never could keep her temper. *Vampires, ghouls, all of them . . .*

Every chair in the room was full. An usher was already bringing in more from other courtrooms, for those who waited, standing, around the doors.

Mary's whole body turned hot, then icily cold. She wanted to scream at them, to curse them. How dared they treat her this way? She was Abraham Lincoln's wife. . . .

"Mrs. Lincoln . . ." Mr. Isaac Arnold came down the aisle between the wooden chairs, a stringy grim-faced man with an untidy gray goatee. Her heart leaped at the sight of him. He was her friend, Mr. Lincoln's old legal colleague from his circuit-riding days.

"Mr. Arnold, what is the meaning of—?"

And she broke off as she saw the man behind him. A neat-featured man, young and tall and becoming burly, his pouting rosebud mouth nearly hidden under an immense light-brown mustache and his eyes, blue-green like hers—like so many of the Todds'—filled with a calm neutrality in which wariness flickered ever so slightly, his own version of the hated lawyer-face.

Of course it had to be, she thought with despair that held no surprise. *Of course he would be the one to betray me, to drive the knife into my heart.*

A square, firm hand immaculately gloved in gray kid took hers, propelled her toward the front of the room while Mr. Arnold hastened to join Swett by the doors. Robert Todd

Lincoln said nothing to her, and she was not going to give the entire population of Chicago the satisfaction of screaming at her son in front of them.

How dare you?

How could you?

Robert would have an explanation. He always did.

At the back of the courtroom Mr. Arnold was in conference with Swett, and with a man whom Mary had recognized vaguely as Mr. Ayer, Swett's partner. *So he's on their side,* she thought bitterly, *and not my lawyer at all. Who have they got for me, then?*

For a ludicrous moment she wondered if Robert would be defending her after all.

To save money, naturally. *Her* money, of which he was sole heir.

Robert, she thought, *I am sorry....*

Robert sat down next to her, at the small table that, in the United States, constituted the "dock." Though she would not look at him, Mary could smell the pomade with which he combed his hair. She looked around the courtroom, narrowing her eyes a little, trying desperately to discern faces through the flashing scrim of migraine.

There were faces she knew—faces and forms, for as age blurred her sight she had relied more and more on shape, color, and movement as much as on features. Surely that was Mr. Turner of the Grand Pacific! He couldn't possibly think she was insane! He'd said himself, those nights she'd gone to him after nightmares, that several women of his acquaintance needed a hotel maid to stay in their room through the dark hours.... When things she heard or saw in her strange spells of confusion frightened her, he'd said he understood, had agreed that it was all perfectly normal....

And that was Mary Gavin, the stout maid who'd usually stay with her on those terrifying nights when, all too often, she'd hear voices speaking out of the walls and the floor. When dreams of fire would be so real to her that she had to fight not to run out into the streets again, panting with terror. And Mrs. Harrington, the housekeeper of the Grand Pacific, with her gray hair piled in a pompadour eked out as usual with false switches....

The shock of seeing them turned Mary cold. Her fury snatched at all her trusty weapons of sarcasm and mockery, all the secrets about them that she had gleaned: *For a girl whose brother is a simpleton you have little room to talk.... Why should the jury believe Irish trash? I never met an Irish servant who didn't lie like Satan.... Why don't you tell them about your father's bankruptcy instead of about me?*

But then they will say I'm crazy, she thought, forcing her rage back. *If I stand up and say Mrs. Harrington skims money to invest in railroad schemes, I've seen Mr. Turner corner the housemaids in the linen-room, it won't help me. It will just give Robert a chance to twist my words, to point out to them how little self-control I have. I have to think....*

There was one of those moments of quiet that sometimes fall on buzzing rooms, and she heard Mr. Arnold say quite clearly, "...doubt the propriety of my being on this case at all."

"May I remind you," said Swett icily, "of the necessity to have this case over with swiftly? Before there is further embarrassment for all? Back out, and you will put into her head that she can get some mischievous lawyer to make us trouble and defend her. Do your duty."

But it was only when she saw Mr. Arnold coming back down the aisle toward the dock that Mary understood that this friend of her husband—this man to whom she had recently given a complete set of Shakespeare, in gratitude for his support of her during her grief—was in fact going to be her defender.

Do your duty, Swett had ordered him....

Arnold sat on the other side of Robert, so that to speak to him, Mary would have to speak across her son.

The bailiff was saying, "All rise for Judge Wallace...the Court of Cook County is now in session...."

Some of the pounding in Mary's head had now diminished, buried under the warm featherbedding of medicine. Even the itching, the burning pain in her privates didn't seem so bad. But it was hard to concentrate; her mind kept slipping to other thoughts, old memories and dreams, then pulling back in shock so intense that it was easy to slide away again.

I am not insane!

She felt as if, for some inexplicable reason, everyone had started saying she was a black woman, when she could look at her hands, look at her face in the mirror, and see herself as white as she had been yesterday, as white as they....

"I was first called to attend to Mrs. Lincoln in November of 1873 at the home of her son, Mr. Robert Todd Lincoln," declared Dr. Willis Danforth, a stubby and businesslike little man whom Mary chiefly remembered for nodding offhandedly throughout her account of her physical symptoms ("Nervousness is only to be expected of the female system," he'd said, and hadn't taken a single note), and the unquestionable garishness of his watch-fobs.

"She was at the time suffering from a derangement of the nervous system, and a fever in her head."

I was suffering every day from blinding headaches, you self-important dolt, as I've suffered all my life!

"She said that the spirit of a dead Indian was at work inside her head, drawing wires from her eyes—especially the left one—and from the bones of her cheeks. She said that she saw him quite clearly...."

I did! He was there! He's there now, waiting for me with his pincers....

Of course the spirits of the dead are present, are all around us. If the benevolent ones help us and aid us, is it not just as reasonable to suppose that there are spirits of malice who torment us?

"These symptoms were undoubtedly rooted in a physical cause, and under my care they decreased gradually and I ceased to see her. In March of last year, however, I was called back to attend upon Mrs. Lincoln, who was again suffering from a debility of the nervous system, with hallucinations.

She claimed that her deceased husband had told her that she would die on the sixth of September, and this time I could discern no physical cause for her symptoms beyond an abnormal nervous state."

Mary flinched, recalling as if through clouds of gauze the desperate obsession that had possessed her all through that grilling summer. Mr. Lincoln *had* told her, she thought. Had whispered it in her ear, when the candles' light lengthened in her darkened parlor. She would die when she reached the age that he had been when he died. *I will see you on the sixth of September,* he'd said, and her heart had leaped with joy.

She had been alone, and frantically lonely that summer. Her mind had turned and turned again to that date, with a nervous terror and readiness that would not let her sit still. . . .

She'd been afraid—not of death, but of dying. How could she not be, when she remembered with such clarity the horror of his face, like old ivory in the candlelight of that crowded little bedroom, the immense black-red bruise around his right eye where the bullet lodged? When she woke up in the night hearing at the edge of her consciousness the ragged, painful gasps of his failing breath? When she remembered poor Tad, trying to breathe, remembered how Willie had cried and twisted with the fever that ate him like a monster on those stormy icy nights . . .

And then nothing had happened. The sixth of September came and went. She didn't know why. For weeks she had stayed in her room at the Grand Pacific, with the curtains drawn, nursing her headaches and her anxiety—her disappointment—with Godfrey's Cordial and Nervine.

"At Mr. Robert Lincoln's request I called upon his mother again on the eighth of May 1875, ten days ago, at her room in the Grand Pacific Hotel," Danforth droned on. "She spoke of her stay in Florida, of the scenery and the pleasant time she had had there, of the manners and customs of the Southern people. She appeared at the time to be in excellent health, and her former hallucinations appeared to have passed away. She said that her reason for returning from Florida was that she was not well."

"And no mention was made of her fears for her son's health?" asked the lawyer Ayer. "Nor of the telegrams she had sent begging him to 'hold on' until she could reach his side?"

"No, none. I was somewhat startled when she told me that an attempt had been made to poison her on her journey back. She said she was very thirsty, and at a way-station not far from Jacksonville she took a cup of coffee in which she discovered poison. She said she drank it, and took a second cup, that the overdose might cause her to vomit...."

Mary felt her whole face and body grow hot at the bald relation of her story. She remembered vomiting at that station, after two cups of coffee, and remembered wondering if the coffee had been poisoned. But for the life of her could not remember why she'd spoken of it to Danforth, of all people. During his visit she'd felt on the edge of one of her spells, she recalled, and her recollection was hazy, like watching someone else. Like so many things she said, that she wished later with all her heart she hadn't said....

"I could see no traces of her having taken poison, and on general topics her conversation was rational."

"But you are of the opinion that Mrs. Lincoln is insane?"

"Yes," said Dr. Danforth. "I am of the opinion that Mrs. Lincoln is insane."

"Your witness," said Mr. Ayer, bowing to Arnold as he walked back to his seat.

"No questions," said Mr. Arnold.

Mary was so breathless with shock and outrage—*No questions after that?*—that she could not speak, could not take it in, could think of nothing to do or say.

"On April first of this year I encountered Mrs. Lincoln in the third-floor hallway of the hotel at ten o'clock in the evening," said Mr. Turner, the manager of the Grand Pacific Hotel. "She was very carelessly dressed, with a shawl over her head...."

Of course I was carelessly dressed. I was probably on my way to the toilet down the hall! Mary made the trip sometimes seven or eight times a night, to her aching humiliation. All her life she had been one of those people who needed the toilet frequently, especially at night. One could use a chamber pot in the room only so many times. Then those awful, agonizing minutes of listening and surreptitious watching for the corridor to be vacant, the hasty sneaking down the hall. . . .

One of her greatest grievances in the stinginess of Congress in the matter of her husband's pension—one of her deepest resentments at Robert and that fat oily moneybag Judge Davis, who'd probated her husband's estate—had been that their combined machinations had prevented her from having enough money to own her own house and dispense with such humiliating nighttime expeditions.

But that, too, was something she could not say to anyone. The newspapers had mocked her so viciously at the time— "So much for womanly gentleness and obedience," one had commented—that she dreaded even to think about bringing the matter up again.

". . . insisted that the whole South Side of Chicago was in flames. She asked me to accompany her back to her room, and complained that a man was communicating with her through the wall of her room."

Mary stared at him, shocked. She dreamed often of voices speaking to her through the walls and the floor, but could remember nothing of actually telling Turner this. *He's making it up,* she thought. *He has to be making it up. . . .*

"She said that she had a note from a Mr. Shoemaker in room 137, asking her to visit him. Although there is no room 137 in the hotel, she insisted that we seek him: we went to rooms 127, 107, and 27. Then she asked me if she could be allowed to stay in some other lady's room, as she feared that the hotel was going to burn down. . . ."

It's a lie! Mary screamed within her mind, baffled and aghast. *I never said such things.*

Dreamed them, yes, sometimes . . . Shoemaker was the

name of that sad-eyed graying gentleman who had been at the Spiritualist gatherings in St. Catherine's, in Canada, the summer before last. She remembered him quite well, for he, like her, had lost his wife and all but one of his children. He, like her, had been seeking, desperately, for years, to hear them speak, to know they remembered him beyond the grave....

"So great was Mrs. Lincoln's conviction that the city was on fire that she ordered me to dispatch her trunks to the shipping-office in Milwaukee to be safe."

The Fire, thought Mary, shivering as fear rolled over her again in a blinding wave. The memory of running through the night streets, blind with smoke. Of shrieking voices, and the crash of shop windows breaking. Of men staggering from empty houses with bedsheets bulging with silver and jewelry. Of a man hurling a glass of liquor at a girl whose hair was on fire. Of a corpse in the gutter with his head smashed in, staring up at her with accusing eyes.

"Your witness," said Mr. Ayer.

"No questions."

Another surge of sick terror washed through Mary, as she stared disbelievingly at Arnold. He didn't even look at her. Nor did Robert, staring resolutely ahead of him, his hands folded and his mouth set. *They're not going to ask any questions,* Mary realized. *Robert hired Arnold the way he hired Swett and Ayer—to make it look like a trial. Arnold thinks I'm as mad as the others do.*

She felt as if the chair—slightly too tall for her short legs, as all chairs were—swayed under her with the force of this shock. She couldn't imagine what she could do in this situation. For a moment the hilarious irony of it struck her. *All my life I've been surrounded by lawyers—all Mr. Lincoln's friends were lawyers.... Why can't I get a lawyer when I need one?*

A man she'd never seen before was on the stand. She hadn't caught his name, but he was relating how the symptoms described to him by Robert two days previously in Robert's office were definitely the symptoms of madness.

Her extravagant spending not only bordered on mania, it was a *symptom* of mania....

Then go arrest John D. Rockefeller for lunacy! Or John Jacob Astor! Put Potter Palmer the millionaire on trial, with his purchase of all those paintings and statues!

Her uncontrollable rages, long attested in the public press, her uncontrollable grief... tragic, yes...

Tragic? You have the brains blown out of the one you most love on earth, his shattered head falling bloody to your shoulder, and see what it does to your nerves, sir!

Other doctors followed one another to the stand. The symptoms Robert had described to them undoubtedly pointed to madness. The crazed alternation between parsimony and extravagance, the attempt—which all in the court would clearly remember—to sell off the used and soiled gowns she'd worn as First Lady, and the scandal that had followed in the newspapers. Her monomania about trying to contact the spirits of her husband and sons. *(And Robert's embarrassment—let's not forget that!)* "The false sensuous impressions of the mediums force too much blood to the brain, predisposing Spiritualists to lunacy. And it is well known that the female system is by its very nature more prone to nervous debility than the male, being far more intimately connected with the organs of generation...."

The heat in the courtroom was like an oven. Even the men on the jury—stern-faced respectable-looking men in heavy frock-coats and tight cravats—were sweating, and under her layers of black mourning crape and whalebone corsetry, Mary's body was consumed with itches and pain.

"...unnatural fear of fire gives great cause for concern, for the insane will frequently leap from windows in a delusional attempt to escape..."

"No questions."

Unnatural fear? Were none of you driven out of your homes by the Fire? Didn't any of you have to flee to the lakeside, to be crushed and shoved by those screaming crowds as they waded out into the black stinking water?

Am I the only one who remembers that?

"Mrs. Lincoln's closet is piled full of packages, which she has never opened, but are just as they came from the store. . . ."

"Mrs. Lincoln goes out shopping once a day and sometimes twice, and her closet and her room are filled with packages which she never opens. Yes, on the nights when she has me sleep in her room she says that she hears voices coming through the walls, and she's scared to go to sleep. When she goes to the washroom she says people watch her through a tiny little window there. . . . No, sir, there's no window in that washroom. . . ."

". . . called me to Mrs. Lincoln's room, and she asked me to take her down and show her the tallest man in the dining-room. . . ."

"On the twelfth of March of this year"—this was Mr. Edward Isham, Robert's law partner—"I received a frantic telegram from Mrs. Lincoln, who was then in Florida. The telegram stated her belief that her son was ill and dying, and that she would start for Chicago at once. Of course Mr. Lincoln was nothing of the kind, and though the telegraphers and superintendent at the Western Union office in Jacksonville attempted to dissuade Mrs. Lincoln, she and her nurse boarded a train to return to this city."

Face crimson with shame, Mary stole a glance at Robert. That obsession, like the desperate belief that she would die last year, seemed so strange to her now. Yet she remembered the intensity of her conviction, the frantic fear that Robert—the only one she had left—would leave her. Someone had warned her in a dream. . . .

I only did it from fear that you would leave me, too!

That you would leave me the way everyone has left me. . . .

Last of all, Robert Todd Lincoln took the stand.

"For a long time I have suspected that my mother is not sane. She has shown signs of hysteria and nervous disability for as long as I can remember. . . ."

He looked very pale but extremely composed, and spoke

absolutely without the hesitations, the nervous interpolations of "um" and "you see" that so many of the other witnesses had used. It was the professional fluency of a lawyer, of a man supremely used to public speaking—of a man who has planned out in advance his every word and his every pause. Mary remembered Abraham Lincoln speaking before juries, every word honed and ready and without the slightest impression of being prepared in advance—speaking the way everyone wished they could speak in an argument.

"On one occasion she spent $600 on lace curtains; on another, $450 on three watches which she gave to me, for which I had no use. She spent $700 on jewelry last month, $200 on soaps and perfumes, though she has no home in which to hang curtains, trunks full of dresses which she never wears, and she has not worn jewelry since my father's death, ten years ago."

And while we're on the subject of money, thought Mary, *why don't you mention the nearly $10,000 in real estate that I've given you? The $6,000 in bonds from Tad's inheritance from his father? The $5,000 for your law library? Why don't you mention the interest-free loans I've made to you for your real-estate speculations?*

Surely I can buy curtains for a house that I don't yet own?

Not that it's any of your business, or anyone's, what I spend my money on....

Her eyes burned with tears. Robert's image blurred and only his voice remained, the voice of the chilly, reasonable boy who had seemed so apart from his younger brothers, who had spoken to her even as a child with such formality.

The boy who had begged to be allowed to go into the Army, because so many others at Harvard had gone. Because people looked at him, and whispered: *Lincoln started this war and yet he keeps his son back where it's safe.*

How could I let him go into the Army to die?

The boy whose whole life she had shaped, with that single lie that she would give anything not to have told.

The heat in the courtroom was so intense she felt she would die. Her head pounded, and rising through the pain the anxiety and depression that always followed on one of her dreamy spells; the frantic desire to hide in darkness, to be alone, to quaff one more spoonful of medicine to take the edge off her pain and her grief.

"Certainly I was in excellent health on the twenty-fifth of March and remain so. I met my mother's train and urged her to stay with me at my home on Wabash Avenue, at least while my wife was away, for admittedly my wife and my mother do not get along."

As if anyone could get along with that sneaking, cold-blooded hussy!

"She refused and took a room instead at the Grand Pacific Hotel, much against my wishes. Mr. Turner was so good as to give me the room next to hers, where I remained until early in April. I observed many times my mother wandering about the halls in a very disordered state...."

I was on my way to the toilet, you ignorant blockhead! Doesn't that precious wife of yours ever piss?

"On the night of the first of April I stopped her when she would have gone down into the lobby in such a state, and she screamed at me, 'You are going to murder me.'"

"Oh, that is a lie!" gasped Mary, though in fact she had only the dimmest recollections of wandering in the halls. So often she dreamed of such searchings—such fears...

"I told her that if she continued such proceedings that I would leave the hotel; and so at length I did. However, since I knew that my mother habitually went about with at least $10,000 in bonds concealed in a purse sewn into her petticoats—"

And how did you know I still did that, unless you were paying the hotel servants to spy on me?

"—I hired detectives of the Pinkerton Agency to follow her and make sure that she came to no harm."

I knew it! Through the hammering of the heat, through the blinding pain and the sick waves of anxiety and shock, betrayal was only beginning now to penetrate to her inner thoughts. *I knew I was being followed, being watched!*

You spy on me and then you call me crazy for believing that I am being spied on!

She looked around her, wondering if any of the men on the jury—those cold-featured respectable men who hadn't the imagination to realize that there were worlds of spirit beyond what could be bought and sold, those grim-hearted brokers and bankers who thought that a woman was insane if she believed that love endured beyond death—understood what had just been said. They were too far off for her to read their faces clearly, but one or two of them were nodding wisely, approving of this evidence of Robert's care for her.

Or his care for her $10,000 in bonds, which would be subtracted from his inheritance if she were to be robbed.

"Any implication that I might be seeking to obtain control of my mother's affairs is unreasonable, because I already manage her affairs. In fact, I telegraphed her the money that enabled her return from Florida."

Another lie! She shook her head angrily.

"I have no doubt my mother is insane. She has long been a source of great anxiety to me. She has no home and no reason to make these purchases."

Always money, she thought. Robert's mind always returned to money. His, hers, what Mr. Lincoln had left to them—which Robert had held on to as long as he possibly could, Robert and Robert's obese and crafty mentor Judge Davis. Was that because his first memories must be of those earliest days of her marriage to Mr. Lincoln, when they lived in a single rented room in the Globe Tavern in Springfield and she was in constant fear of further destitution, in constant shame when she saw her former friends rattle by in carriages?

Money, and the fact that she would not do as he wanted her to.

"Your witness, Mr. Arnold."

Mary turned in fury to her attorney—now separated from

her only by Robert's vacated chair—but Arnold wasn't looking at her. He was looking at Robert, meeting his eyes across the small space of the front of the courtroom that separated them.

"No questions," he said.

CHAPTER THREE

THE JURY DELIBERATED FOR BARELY TEN MINUTES. WHEN
Robert stepped down from the stand and returned to his seat
beside her he held out his hands to her; Mary turned her face
from him. His face was pale and streaked with tears—Robert
had always, she reflected, been able to talk himself into feeling whatever emotion was most appropriate for the situation.

*Of course a man who's been forced to hold his mother up to the
scorn and ridicule of the entire city of Chicago—the entire nation,
thanks to the press—would shed tears on the witness stand. How
else could he make himself the victim, instead of me?*

She could imagine—as Robert undoubtedly could, too—
what the newspapers would say of a son who *didn't* shed
tears on the witness stand as he asked the Court to lock his
mother up.

"To think that my son would do this to me," she said.

The courtroom was like a slow oven. Beneath layers of
wool crape and black veiling Mary felt her flesh sticky, and
burning as if dipped in acid. As the gentle effect of the medicine subsided the pain in her head mounted, confusing her.
She couldn't bear the thought of asking Arnold—*traitor,
Judas, hypocrite!*—if she might seek out the toilets.... Would
they have a Pinkerton agent follow her there?

Just get back to my room, she thought desperately. *Just get
away, out of the light, into the comforting dimness....* The frantic
anxiety she had felt in the street that morning returned, the
aching need for medicine, the terror of more pain to come.
Back to my room...

And she startled in shock. *What if I can't go back?
What if they find me insane?*

Until this moment it had never truly occurred to her that

this hideous ordeal, this hotbox redolent of the stinks of sweaty wool suiting and cheap pomade, was anything more than a single awful afternoon....

What if they lock me up? Put me in a cell like a prisoner, chained to the walls like the people in pictures I've seen? Hide me and forget me, like Mr. Rochester's wife in Jane Eyre?

Her eyes shot to Robert—who was talking to Swett and Ayer and casting venomous glances at the reporters—and into her mind flashed a memory, the memory of those awful months after her son Willie's death. Willie had died in February: Mary had remained in bed herself for weeks, and as much as six months later the grief had still returned in blinding waves of incapacitating weeping. She remembered how after trying vainly to comfort her, her husband had led her gently to the window of the summer cottage where they were staying.

Mother, do you see that large white building on the hill yonder? She could still hear that high, husky voice, that could carry like a trumpet when he spoke to a crowd, soft now like a troubled lullaby. Could still conjure back the light firmness of that enormous hand on the small of her back. The new lunatic asylum was only partially visible from the windows of the Soldiers' Home—the stone cottage to which the President's family retired during the sticky horrors of Washington summers—but Mary knew what it was.

She could hear beneath the gentleness of Lincoln's voice how frightened he was, how helpless in the face of a grief whose blackness he understood himself, far too well. *You must try to control your grief, or it will drive you mad and we may have to send you there.*

He never would have. She knew that as clearly as she knew her name.

Not to an asylum. Like those hideous reports she had read of patients being doused with icy water or chained behind bars like animals, or like that dreadful story by Mr. Poe...

And I'm not mad....

At first she thought nothing of the scraping of chairs, the

sudden rise of voices. *It has to be the reporters getting excited about something.*

But when she saw Robert hastily return to his seat, and Arnold gathering his papers, she swung around and saw the jury filing back into their box.

But they only just left!

The horrible suspicion seized her that one of her spells had come on her again. Time telescoped during those episodes. Hours could pass in the daydream of what felt like moments. But a glance at the courtroom clock, at the hot gold angle of light high on the wall, showed her that no, in fact only ten minutes had gone by.

"Gentlemen, have you reached a verdict?" The judge didn't look at her. Mary found herself trembling all over, struggling not to scream, not to start flinging things at Robert—books, pens, Arnold's useless and untouched papers....

"We have, Your Honor. This jury finds that Mrs. Lincoln is insane—"

No.

"—and though she is neither suicidal nor homicidal—"

No!

"—she is a fit person to be confined to an asylum."

Reporters came crowding up. Swett, Arnold, Robert, and the two Pinkerton men—*Where were you when my husband was killed?* she wanted to scream at them—formed up around her, thrust their way through them to the back of the room. Mary stumbled in that circle of male shoulders, dark frock-coats smelling of tobacco and Macassar oil, the faces around her a blur.

Robert was speaking to her. Introducing her to a grave-faced man with a splendid chestnut beard, who had testified so learnedly about the vicious effects of Spiritualism and "theomania." *I believe Mrs. Lincoln to be insane from the account given to me by Mr. Robert Lincoln in his office....*

"...Dr. Richard Patterson," Robert was saying. "Dr. Patterson operates a private sanitarium in Batavia."

"You mean a madhouse." Mary's voice sounded flat in

her own ears, and queerly alien, as if someone else were speaking.

Robert's eyes shifted, but Dr. Patterson said, "Bellevue Place is a pleasant house where people can rest and get better, Mrs. Lincoln. We think you'll be very comfortable there."

She opened her mouth to snap, *And it doesn't matter what I think?*

And then realized, *No, it doesn't.*

You're a madwoman. You must go where they send you, and do what you're told.

Forever.

Trembling, she said, "You set this up between you, didn't you? You had a prison all ready for me before we ever walked into this courtroom."

While her heart whispered to her, *It was my doing, my punishment. My shame. No more than my deserving...*

Reporters were craning to listen. Calmly, as if she had said nothing, Robert said, "Mr. Arnold and I will escort you to Bellevue Place tomorrow, Mother. I've taken a room next to yours at the Grand Pacific for tonight. But first, Mother, I must insist that you turn over to me the bonds that you have been carrying with you—"

"The ones you bribed chambermaids to tell you about? Or did you peek through the keyholes at me yourself? That's what you wanted all along, wasn't it? To get hold of my money?"

Robert raised his voice just slightly, though he didn't even glance at the purposefully loitering members of the press. "You're talking foolishly, Mother. You know I've always had the management of your affairs. And you also know that it's dangerous to carry them on your person as you do. Of course I will write you a proper receipt...."

"Surely," put in Swett in his silky voice, "you would wish to spare yourself the humiliation of having the sheriff take the bonds from you by force, Mrs. Lincoln?"

She rounded on him. "Robert will never have anything of mine!"

"Then perhaps you would prefer to hand them over to Mr. Arnold?"

"I will not hand them to anyone! And I'm sure," she added, "that since—as all the world *now* knows, thanks to *your* paid testimony, sir—I carry the bonds in my underclothing, even my son wouldn't wish me to be indelicate in the presence of all the people in the courtroom. Now I'm hot, and tired, and I wish to go back to my room—or do you propose to chain me now in a cage, and feed me through the bars?"

"Of course you will be allowed to go back to your room, Mother," said Robert unhappily.

"Once you promise to give Mr. Arnold the bonds when we arrive there," added Swett.

"He can have what he likes." Mary's voice cracked and she forced it steady, forced herself not to give them even the smallest satisfaction. Hating them, and hating Robert most of all. "Take from me what he likes. Only let me go back."

Leaving the courthouse was like those dreams she'd had as a girl, of attending her classes at Ward's Academy and discovering in the midst of recitation that she was still in her nightgown. . . .

They used to let people tour madhouses and stare at the lunatics, she thought, dizzily sinking into the upholstery of Swett's closed brougham, sweating in pain at every jolt of the pavement. *Do they still?* Evening was beginning to come on, though the bustle of pedestrians and vehicles on Clark Street was worse, if anything, than it had been in the heat of the afternoon. A breath of breeze from the lake brought a little freshness, but not one jot of relief. *We think you'll be comfortable there. . . .*

No. Not that.

She closed her eyes and wondered how much it would hurt to die.

With stony dignity she stepped out of her group of escorts—Swett, Arnold, the two faithful Pinkertons, and a very uncomfortable-looking Mary Gavin, whom they'd

gathered up on their way through the Grand Pacific lobby—
and into the ladies' toilets down the hall from her room.
Blessed relief—blessed, blessed silence, stillness, privacy away
from staring eyes and whispering men...

They were all waiting in the hall for her when she came
out. She almost laughed at their clumsy unease.

"The bonds," Swett reminded her as she unlocked the
door of her room. He reached to take the key from her but
she closed it tight in her palm.

"You shall have nothing from me, sir. My husband left me
those bonds...."

"I'm sure Mr. Lincoln would not have left them to you
had he known you were going to walk around Chicago with
ten thousand dollars' worth pinned in your petticoats!"

Her head splitting, her stomach queasy with the aftermath
of migraine and medicine, her whole body trembling with
exhaustion, Mary shouted at them, raged at them, backed
into a corner of the dark suffocating room with its crowded
packages and high-piled trunks. But they did not leave,
would not leave. They stayed, argued, insisted, and refused
to listen when she begged them to leave, begged them to let
her alone, to let her rest. At last, sick and dizzy and shaking,
Mary retreated to a corner among the trunks and pulled up
her heavy overskirt, so that Arnold could tear the bonds out
of the pocket sewn to her petticoat.

Then they left, all except Mary Gavin, who settled in her
usual chair, as she did all those nights when Mary could not
sleep and paid the stolid Irishwoman to spend the night in
her room with her.

The bonds were gone.

Her money was gone.

She was helpless. She was exactly where she had all her
life feared she would one day be: penniless. And alone.

This is what it is, she thought, frantic, exhausted, fighting
with all her strength not to collapse in tears, *to be a madwoman.*

It is to be a child again, without a penny, with no place to live but what they give you and no place to go but what they permit.

I am not insane!

She lay for a long time on the bed, her hands pressed to her mouth, her face turned to the wall, burningly conscious of the woman on the other side of the cluttered room.

Always watched. Never alone.

The sharp curve of her stays gouged her ribs as she drew in a breath, let it out.

She thought, with aching longing, of the medicines in the cabinet, of their promise of sweet sleep and oblivion.

But if she slept, she thought, she'd only wake in the morning with Robert and that hateful Dr. Patterson at the door, waiting to take her to the madhouse.

If she slept, she'd lose whatever time she had to act before Robert arrived to spend the night in the next room.

She took another breath, and sat up. "I'm going down the hall," she announced.

Mary Gavin hastily screwed the top back onto the little flask she'd withdrawn from her reticule, tucked it away out of sight.

"You don't have to come with me," added Mary, getting to her feet. "I won't be long." She knew the maid never liked to get out of her chair once she'd settled in with her little nips of gin. Through the curtained window, light still lingered in the airshaft. It was seven o'clock. Here downtown, most shops remained open until eight, and those within the hotel itself until ten.

Her heart beat fast as she opened the door, praying the maid didn't see—black against the black of her mourning dress, in the dense dimness of the room's single gas jet—that she had her reticule with her, her reticule that had in it, now, all the money she had in the world.

She prayed it would be enough.

The Pinkerton men got to their feet and one of them hastily stashed the *Police Gazette* in his pocket. Coldly, Mary informed them, "I am going down to Squair's Pharmacy in the lobby, to get some medicine for my neuralgia. I shall be back in a few minutes."

The two men glanced at one another uncertainly and she walked off down the corridor, head high. One of them put on his bowler hat and followed her; Mary stopped, turned back and leveled a freezing glare at him, a glare that only the students of a select Female Academy such as Madame Mentelle's of Lexington, Kentucky, could muster.

Cowed, the man hesitated, fell back, and though he followed her—lumbering rapidly down the stairs as she steeled herself to take the elevator—he kept his distance.

And that, Mary knew, would be enough.

"I WOULD LIKE TWO OUNCES EACH OF LAUDANUM AND CAMphor, sir." Her voice sounded reasonable, if rather flat and distant—it was astonishing, she thought, how difficult it was to sound normal when one was trying to sound normal. What was "normal-sounding," anyway? The doctors in the courtroom that afternoon had seemed to be very sure of it. She thought Mr. Squair's clerk looked at her oddly—had she sounded too normal?—and she added, "I suffer from neuralgia of the shoulder, and bathe it in laudanum and camphor for relief."

"Of course, Mrs. Lincoln. Just a moment, please."

The clerk, a young man with a mustache that made him look like a terrier, disappeared through a white-painted door into the room behind the counter. Mary stared at her reflection in the mirrors that caught the last daylight from the lobby, the gas jets that were just beginning to be lit throughout the Grand Pacific Hotel. For two months now she'd been in and out of Mr. Squair's pharmacy, which opened out of the lobby. It was more expensive than Dole's Pharmacy three blocks down Clark Street, but when her migraines were upon her she was willing to pay almost anything, just to be able to purchase medicine and go quietly to her room. In the mirrors she could see the Pinkerton agent—the fatter of the two, like an immense squash in his cheap mustard-colored suit—in the lobby, looking around him unhappily.

Let him look, she thought. *He can't stop me. If he tries to come in here I shall complain. . . .*

To whom?

She was a madwoman. She was going to be sent to an asylum in the morning. She had only tonight left to her.

Had she dreamed that hideous trial, the way she dreamed and re-dreamed about the Fire? About her mother's death? About that last night in the theater . . .

It would not be the first time that she'd acted on some too-vivid dream.

No. The Pinkerton man was proof of that.

"I'm sorry, Mrs. Lincoln." The clerk re-emerged from the white door. "We—er—the medicine will take a half hour to make up. If you can—please come back in thirty minutes."

"Thirty minutes?" Mary's temper snapped. "That's outrageous! I can't possibly wait thirty minutes! I'm in pain. . . . Thirty minutes for something you only have to pour out of a bottle? Is Mr. Squair here?"

"No, ma'am. He just—he's having his supper—he went home to have his supper. . . ."

The clerk was trying to sound normal, too.

Mary caught at her temper, breathing hard. Waiting infuriated her, but lashing out at Mr. Squair would only cost her time and draw attention to her. Much as she would have liked to get this officious young lout fired, she knew time was what she did not have. Robert might arrive any minute. If he came before she could procure the laudanum, he would never let her go. . . .

He would never let her go anywhere again.

She drew a deep breath and said—still trying to sound normal—"When I come back, young man, I shall have some words to say to Mr. Squair about your incompetence and rudeness to a good paying customer! I have never been so ill-treated in my life!"

There were two entrances to Squair's, which formed a

corner between the main lobby and the hotel's side entrance onto Quincy Street. Mary stormed out the secondary door before the Pinkerton in the squash-colored suit could react—*really, it was no wonder that murdering beast was able to shoot my husband, with blockheads of that stamp for his defense!*—and through the hotel's side door.

There was the usual line of cabs drawn up along the curb on Clark Street and it was no time to count pennies. Mary climbed into one and said, "Rogers and Smith drugstore, please." It was only about a block, but this wasn't the first time she'd taken a cab that short distance. The cabmen didn't like it, but there was no time to waste.

"Shall I wait for you, ma'am?" The driver's voice had the flat vowels of Kentucky. One of the legs propped on the cab's dash was wooden, gone just below the knee. Mary wondered which side he had fought on.

"Of course you shall wait; I'm not in any condition to walk back to the hotel." With traffic as heavy as it was this time of the evening she would have done better to walk, but she was exhausted and in her tight shoes her swollen feet felt as if someone were trying to cut them off at the ankles. The clerk at Rogers and Smith was even stupider and more incompetent than the one at Mr. Squair's. He was gone so long in the back room that Mary left before he even came out, consumed with the fear that the Pinkerton agent would come in, would stop her, would drag her back to the hotel and her guards.

Of course, she thought, *I can always tell him the truth, that Squair's stupid young man wasn't able to fill the order. That my shoulder was hurting so badly I had to seek relief elsewhere. They can't quarrel with that. Even Robert can't quarrel with that....*

"Dole's Pharmacy," she told the cab driver, and the cab lurched away into the thick mill of carriages and drays in the street.

It was dark now, the white glare of the gaslights making the faces of passersby seem harsh, and alien beyond belief. Staring out the cab window, Mary shuddered at that wall of humanity—going where? Doing what? Tomorrow it would be in all the newspapers: "Wife of Lincoln Found Insane." That morning she had cursed at them for not knowing who she was—such unfeeling anonymity seemed a blessing to her now.

And by tomorrow afternoon, she thought, it would be "Emancipator's Widow Dead."

She pressed her hands to her lips, and closed her eyes. They said suicides went straight to Hell. But in the dark parlors where spirits knocked and whispered in the shadows, she had heard the souls themselves give the lie to those joyless preachers and their mistaken ideas of faith. *I will not go,* she thought. *Robert wants my money, well, he may have it: it's all going to him in my will in any case. Rather than be a prisoner for the rest of my life—rather than be stared at, pointed at, hear them whisper "That is Abraham Lincoln's widow, and now she's gone mad, poor thing," I will simply depart. It can't be so terribly difficult. Everyone says that one just slips away.*

And it is no more than I deserve....

And for an instant she was twenty-four again, with the heavy strength of a man's body lying on top of hers. Feeling the rough power of those enormous hands caressing her, seeing firelight reflected in the desperate darkness of deep-set gray eyes.

At Dole's they refused her outright. Time was passing—Robert might arrive at the hotel at any minute—so she did not argue. Would an account of her lunacy have come out in the newspapers already? Why else would they look at her that way, would refuse to sell her laudanum when they'd done so before? She didn't argue. She returned to her cab and ordered him back to the hotel, praying that Mr. Squair wouldn't give her any more trouble.

He didn't, though the cab driver as usual demanded far more than a ride of three blocks was worth: "You'll take fifty cents and like it," snapped Mary, feeling as if her skull were about to split. "In my day gentlemen did not haggle with ladies over the cost of services. Your mother would be ashamed of you." She turned and swept up the steps of the hotel before he could reply, trembling with anxiety and rage.

The bottle Mr. Squair gave her was labeled LAUDANUM—POISON and she drank it on the second-floor landing. She hadn't eaten since lunch and her head throbbed, her feet stabbed with pain as if every small bone in them had been broken. As always she felt, as she climbed the stairs, that she'd safely negotiated some terrible countryside filled with dangers, that she was approaching the place where she was safe, where she could rest....

From the top of the stair she could see the remaining Pinkerton man by the door of her room, talking with Mary Gavin. *Gossiping about me,* she thought. *Whispering how I did or said this, that, or the other. They're all the same.*

Mary Gavin's testimony on the stand stung her, how she'd blithely babbled to everyone in Chicago about Mary's nightmares, and the things she'd confided to her in the dim spells of confusion....

Haven't you ever heard about keeping confidences? Mary wondered bitterly as she forced herself to walk, head high, along that endless hallway. *Or is it customary among you slum-Irish to chat to the neighbors about your friends' secrets and troubles, and how much they spent at the department stores?* She'd given the woman presents, too, and money—which she'd doubtless spent on gin....

"That mentally deficient clerk at Squair's was taking so long to fill my order that I was forced to go down the street to Rogers and Smith," said Mary as the Pinkerton man opened his mouth to admonish her. "Your partner will bear me out, sir, if you suppose that I'm a liar...or insane," she added, with a vicious glance at Mary Gavin. "Provided he didn't stop at a saloon on his way."

She thrust past Mary Gavin, adding over her shoulder, "Please close the door. And please ask those two *gentlemen* in the corridor to keep their voices low. I am, as you may suppose, very tired, and would like to lie down. Since you must be in here, please see to it that I'm not disturbed."

She took off her bonnet, and lay down fully clothed on her bed, wondering how long it would take the poison to work. Everyone was always telling her how dangerous laudanum was, as if she hadn't been taking it without the slightest ill effect for years. But at the moment it didn't seem to be doing much, not even taking away her headache. The room was hateful to her, with Mary Gavin's gin-bottle and newspapers crumpled on the chair, and the empty purse that Mr. Arnold had torn out of her petticoats only a few hours ago lying flat on the table.

How dared he? The shame and humiliation flooded back at having pulled up her skirts in front of all those men—at having been forced to go through what she had been through that day. *How dared Robert subject me to that....*

Shame tore at her, the frantic shame that had followed her all her life, and the burning torment of guilt. The old feeling overwhelmed her, of wishing she could go back in time and scrub out events and scenes; make them be gone, have never happened. *A single lie ...*

How could God be said to forgive, when events followed you through life that way, stacking up more events like tokens in some hellish game?

She sat up, and fished from the cupboard as many bottles as she could reach—Nervine and Catawba Indian Balsam—and poured a dollop of each into her glass, as she had that afternoon. After drinking it she lay down again. The familiar sweet warmth steadied her, lessening her anxiety. With luck when Robert got here they'd tell him she was resting. She pictured his shock and grief when they told him she was dead, when they found the empty bottle—LAUDANUM—POISON—in her handbag, when he realized what he'd driven her to.

Though of course he'd find some way of keeping it out of the newspapers.

Or maybe he wouldn't. Maybe he'd tell the reporters all about it, as proof that she was insane. Only insane people committed suicide, after all.

No, she thought, as sleep stole on her—final sleep, she thought, endless sleep. *One doesn't have to be insane to want to die.*

One only has to be lonely for long enough.

"Oh, my darling," she whispered to that tall shadow that she could half-see, where the dim pink-amber of the lamp-light did not reach. "Oh, my beloved, forgive me."

Though as she slipped over into darkness she could not have said whether she wanted forgiveness for taking her own life, or for keeping him waiting so long.

Chapter Four

IT WAS A FRIDAY AFTERNOON IN APRIL, MUGGY AND HOT. Though the curtains of that large oval parlor on the White House's second floor were closed, still the sharp yellow light pierced the chinks. Sitting in the dimness, Mary tried to summon enough energy to go over and close them more firmly.

But it did not seem worth the effort of getting to her feet, crossing the room.

The darkness comforted her. In the darkness, in the quiet, she could feel that Willie hovered near her. She could almost see the child's sweet spirit tiptoeing out of the shadows, flowers in his hands. He had been her boy, her treasure, the most intelligent of her sons and the most loving. Even when the boys were small, it was Tad who'd go crashing outside at a run to play, Willie who'd stop his headlong rush after him to ask, "Is there anything you need, Mama?"

Is there anything you need?

I need you, my darling! I need your cheer to make me laugh, your smile to make me know I'm alive! When she thought of herself in old age, it was Willie she had pictured at her side. Dear God, the sight of his face, wax-white and so thin, on the satin pillows of his coffin!

"Mother?"

It was her husband. He stood in the doorway of the secret hall that he'd had put in between his offices and the family rooms. For four years he'd had to go through the public hallway on the Executive Mansion's second floor to get from one place to the other, the hallway so crowded with people bringing petitions or seeking favors or asking for jobs for themselves or their family members that it sometimes took him an hour and a half to walk a few dozen feet. He still had a boyish glee about using the inner door, as if it were a secret passage designed to thwart the grown-ups....

His head came within a few inches of the lintel. In the light that came through from his secretary's office beyond, flecks of gray showed in that coarse Indian-black unruly hair that had begun its stealthy retreat back up his forehead. She saw, too, how thin he'd become, not that he'd ever been stout before. But the dark suit that had fit him two years ago hung baggy over his shoulders, and his eyes had a bruised look in hollows under the heavy brow.

"I'm sorry I am late," he said. "Will you come driving with me after all?" He spoke diffidently and a little stiffly, and did not move from the door, as if he feared yet another half-sobbed demand to be left alone.

He was indeed late, and Mary felt a flash of anger at him, for she had looked forward all day to the ride, and now he had spoiled it with his endless meetings. "I thought you had forgotten," she said, "and had gone with Mr. Stanton?" She hated the nervous, masterful Secretary of War who was so often Lincoln's companion on his drives. Couldn't he see the man was dangerous?

"Or perhaps you'd rather go with Julia Grant?" She remembered how her husband had laughed at some witticism of his chief General's bosomy wife, and the attentions he'd paid the woman when they'd gone down to Richmond last week. They were going to the theater with the Grants tonight, too, and she didn't know how she'd manage to sit in the same box with Julia all night, not to mention that coarse drunkard brute of a husband of hers....

The minute the words were out of her mouth she regretted them. Tears flooded her eyes. Her temper had gotten worse since Willie's death and she knew it. As whose wouldn't, she thought defensively, in the face of her husband's growing silences, his absence for eighteen hours out of twenty-four. He had used to share things with her, talk over his plans and his hopes, the cases he had in the courts. He used to ask her advice about his speeches: Would "supremacy of law" offend the Southern moderates she'd grown up with, or should he soften it to "primacy"? Now he talked of nothing but commonplaces, left her out of the circles of power, pushed her aside. . . .

She looked back at the doorway, expecting it to be empty. But he still stood there, though by the deepened lines of his face she could see she'd hurt him. *Good,* she thought. *Maybe next time he'll take to heart what I say.*

Maybe he'll leave me alone. . . .

"I'd like your company best, Mother," he said. "As I always have."

Her mouth opened to rage at him—*A pretty poor way you've had of showing it lately!*

But something in the weariness of his eyes stopped her, the silence like a man who takes a whipping without a sound. For a moment she saw, not a tired man of fifty-six with gray in his beard, but a gawky, gaunt, and painfully shy Kentucky barbarian in a suit that didn't fit, standing in the doorway of her sister Elizabeth's house under Elizabeth's withering gaze. . . .

She smiled at that far-off young man, and said instead, "Pretty poor company I've been, too," and watched the tension melt out of his eyes. She got up and took his hand. "I'd like to go driving with you, Mr. Lincoln. Thank you."

Outside the air was cooler than she'd feared it would be, the first stirrings of breeze wafting across the Potomac to rustle the dogwoods. The dappled sun on her face felt like a blessing, dissolving her disappointed anger. It dissolved even some of the terrible grief over Willie's death that seemed to have turned her heart to stone. The small escort of cavalry that followed the carriage kept their distance. "A lot of use they'll be if a rebel assassin shoots at you from the trees," she said, glancing over her shoulder.

"The only way they could prevent a rebel assassin from shooting from the trees is to surround us like a wall," Lincoln pointed out, in a tone of academic observation, as if he had not been receiving death-threats and letters filled with unbelievable hatred for nearly five years. "And even then they couldn't stop a man from flying overhead in a balloon and dropping a brick on my head."

"*Will* you be serious?"

"No," said Lincoln, and smiled—that sweet lightening of his whole ugly face that the photographers never caught. "I have been serious all morning and I am mighty weary of it." He curled his enormous hand around her small, plump fingers. "Besides, what point would there be in murdering me now? The war is over, all but the shouting—of which I'm afraid there'll be plenty, once Congress hears that there are to be no war trials or hangings or firing-squads for men who were only following their consciences. I want a carriage-ride with the woman I love, not a military parade."

Mary blushed, and tightened her hand over his. How could he still love her? A few days ago she had apologized for the scene she'd made on their trip to Richmond—an apology she wasn't sure she'd have offered if she'd known it would lead to the invitation to spend this evening in a theater-box with General and Mrs. Grant—and things had been easy between them, easier than they'd been in months. It was good, she thought, to have her husband back, at least for an hour or two. . . .

"By the way," he said, "the Grants have been forced to beg off from the theater this evening. Robert's given his excuse as well. . . ."

Mary's lips tightened at this newest evidence of their oldest son's estrangement from his father.

"But we could ask Senator Harris's daughter Clara and her fiancé. . . . Or we could cry off ourselves, which I've half a mind to do. We've both seen the play before, after all."

"Oh, no!" said Mary quickly, the prospect of an evening at the theater *without* Julia Grant and her cigar-stinking husband beckoning like a circus-treat in her childhood. "We've already announced to the newspapers that we would be there; it would be a shame to disappoint them. And it would do me good to get out." She sighed, and settled back on the cushions, looking out over the open barouche's sides at the lush sweetness of the woods north of the last houses of the town, the silver sparkle of far-off water among the trees.

As the carriage rattled along the dusty roads in the slanted evening light they talked of small things: how Jip the dog kept trying to convince one of the kitchen cats to play with him, and the scheme their just-turned-twelve-years-old Tad had evolved to trap the last holdouts of the rebel army in North Carolina. The fighting was over, and Mary reveled in Robert's safe return—not that he'd ever been in real danger, as a member of Grant's staff, but one never knew. It was good beyond computation to see how the years melted away from her husband's face, to see the mischief and the old delight sparkle in his somber gray eyes.

Good to have him to herself, as she had used to do in their old home in Springfield, before office-seekers and Generals and Cabinet members and, as he would put it, "every man and his little black dog" had a claim on his time and attention and energy. For five years now, all she had wanted was to have him to herself.

Good to hear him laugh when she mimicked Julia Grant, conjuring up a scene of the woman measuring the White House for her own furniture. Good to laugh almost to tears at his own imitation of the barely literate brother-in-law of some Ohio Representative's cousin who'd come requesting to be made military governor of New Orleans on account of his services to the Republican Party back home in Cincinnati. . . .

As they came back into town again, and the walls of the White House made a pale blur in the gathering gloom, Lincoln said, "Mother, it has been such a joy only to be ourselves again. We must both be more cheerful in the future; between the war and the loss of our darling Willie, we have both been very miserable."

Mary nodded. "I know. And I have been as guilty of it as you. With the war over now it will be easier."

"I hope so. I find myself looking forward to the end of my term as much as any of the poor slaves looked forward to Freedom. Where shall we go, when I finally get my own emancipation papers? I know you've always said you wanted to travel."

"Oh, yes! Paris first, and then Rome . . . Oh, and we must visit Venice. . . ." She checked herself in her visions of the Opéra and the shops along Rue de la Paix, and asked, "Where would you like to go?" And was surprised at herself, because she realized—even after twenty-three years of marriage—that she didn't know.

"I'd like to go to Jerusalem," he replied, and she thought, *Of course.* For a skeptic who stayed as far away as he could from anything resembling a Church, he knew the Bible, as if it were some marvelous storybook. Of course he would want to see David's city, and the remains of Solomon's Temple. . . .

"And after that," he said, "I think I would like to go to California."

"California?" The name had an almost mythical ring to it, a place at the farthest end of creation.

"To see the goldfields," he explained. "When the men are done in the Army, many of them will go there to find jobs in the mines. And after that," he smiled, "I think the place I look forward most to seeing is Springfield again, and the inside of my old law office. To having things be as they used to be . . . Except with Emancipation, you can bet there'll be more litigation over it than if I'd put a tax on air."

She laughed over that, and in her dream Mary clutched at the happiness she felt; clutched at the white clouds of the dogwood against the graying evening sky, and the sweetness of the air on her face. She knew what was coming next and she tried to run from it, tried to put it aside, like a book whose ending she didn't wish to read. *Let it end here,* she begged. *This is all I want to remember. . . .*

But of course she found herself in the carriage again, later that night, the fog so thick she could see nothing beyond the carriage windows. Senator Harris's daughter Clara was a pretty young thing and her fiancé, Major Rathbone, was overwhelmingly jolly, like some character out of Dickens. But Mary didn't care. In the dark of the carriage she held her husband's hand.

We must both try to be more cheerful, she thought, knowing what he had said was true. She had put off her mourning for Willie that night, and wore a gown of stiff gray silk that rustled like silver as Lincoln helped her down from the carriage, led her up the theater steps and through the dress circle to their box above the stage. The play had already begun, but the conductor of the orchestra spotted them, and broke into "Hail to the Chief." Lincoln—whose main objection to a cavalry guard was that it embarrassed him to be treated like an emperor—nodded gravely and gestured his thanks to the conductor, and to the actors smiling up at them from the stage; Mary basked in the music, as if in that afternoon's sun.

Maybe it embarrassed him to be treated like an emperor, she thought, half-smiling at him. But she felt such pride in him that she knew she must be visibly glowing. Those evenings when he'd come to her sister's house returned to her, that shy tall awkward-looking man whose arms were too long for his sleeves. *That bumpkin,* Elizabeth had called him. *You can't possibly be seriously thinking of marrying that hayseed?*

I showed you, Mary thought, remembering Elizabeth's nearly successful efforts to discourage the match. *I showed you all. . . .*

The Republican Queen, the newspapers had called her.

She hoped Elizabeth had read them, back in Springfield. Hoped everyone had read them who'd looked out their carriage-windows at her walking in the snow, that first poverty-stricken winter of their marriage. One reason she'd wanted to come tonight was her delight in reading about her own smallest movements in the papers the next day, like admiring herself in the mirror back in the days when she'd been the belle of Lexington.

Down on stage, the actor Harry Hawks ad-libbed, "This reminds me of a story, as Mr. Lincoln would say," and the audience roared with laughter and applause. Just as if, thought Mary, half-angry and half-smug, they hadn't been calling her husband nigger-lover, fool, despot, coward, a thousand hateful things during the years of war....

As if every day hadn't brought mail telling him to say his prayers and threatening his life.

But all that was forgotten now. The theater was packed, and a mood of infectious jollity and goodwill rose out of parterre and stage with the usual hot chow-chow of theater smells: pomade and perfume and the stink of the gaslights. The play was delightfully preposterous, with the haughty English grande dame Mrs. Mountchessington conniving to try to wed her unprepossessing daughter Augusta to the homespun backwoodsman she mistakenly believed was a wealthy Yankee.

As sister Elizabeth might have done, thought Mary gleefully, if she'd ever believed that tall skinny lawyer Mr. Lincoln had had two nickels to rub together....

She slipped her hand into Lincoln's, leaned her head on his shoulder: "What will Miss Harris think of my hanging on to you so?"

There was a smile in his voice. "She won't think anything of it."

Maybe he was remembering sister Elizabeth, too.

On stage, Mrs. Mountchessington reeled in horror as she learned the ghastly truth: Asa Trenchard was not rich! Outraged, she sent daughter Augusta from the room, and after a few well-chosen admonitions to the bemused backwoodsman, flounced off herself.

"Don't know the manner of good society, eh?" Trenchard retorted. "Wal, I guess I know enough to turn *you* inside out—you sockdologizing old mantrap!"

Lincoln was just starting to lean down, to make some wiseacre remark in Mary's ear—she never afterwards knew what it was. The crack of a gunshot was hideously loud in the enclosed space of the dark box, and his arm jerked convulsively, wrenching from her hand. Mary caught him as he slumped, smelled the gunpowder and the hot smell of blood. . . .

There was a man in the box, springing out of the cloud of powder-smoke, shouting something. Mary screamed when she saw that he held a dagger, her mind stalled, refusing to understand, her husband's weight bearing down on her heavier and heavier, blood glistening darkly in his black hair.

HER SCREAM PLUNGED HER OUT OF SLEEP, DROPPED HER INTO waking—her scream, the smell of his blood, the weight of him on her shoulder and the knowledge that he was gone, he had left her alone. . . .

And seeing the shadows of her cluttered, crowded room in the Grand Pacific, the looming shadow of Mary Gavin starting up from her chair, Mary screamed again, and again, and again.

She was alive.

It hadn't been laudanum or camphor in Mr. Squair's bottle at all—only one more trick.

And she was going to the madhouse in the morning.

CHAPTER FIVE

Lexington 1832

STRANGELY, WHAT KEPT GOING THROUGH MARY'S MIND ON the train ride from Chicago across to Batavia, Illinois, was that this felt exactly like being sent away from home at the age of thirteen for putting spiders in her stepmother's bed.

She had detested her stepmother from the time that fair, thin, decisive woman had first entered her father's house when Mary was eight. Elizabeth, even then on the threshold of young-ladyhood, could smile at "Betsey" and call her "Ma," as she and their father demanded. Frances, a pale, quiet-tempered nine-year-old, was exquisitely and impenetrably polite as she was to everyone. From the first, Mary loathed that fragile, steely woman who looked at her with so pointed an eye and said, "It takes seven generations to make a lady," and from the first it was Mary who led Levi, Ann, and little Georgie in mischief, petty thefts, and finely-calculated never-quite-disobedience. "She's not our Ma and nobody can make me say she is!"

The spider incident had its roots two days before Elizabeth's wedding, in the icy February of 1832.

It was a Wednesday, and Nelson, the Todd family coachman, had driven Betsey and the elder girls of the household downtown, for a final fitting of the girls' new dresses with Madame Deauville, and to pick up the creamer and sugar-boat Betsey had ordered for a wedding-gift. Under ordinary circumstances this would have filled Mary with unalloyed delight: there were few things in the world she enjoyed more than new dresses. It was not quite a mile from the brick house on Short Street to the paved streets and stylish shops of Cheapside downtown, and the girls could walk it easily, but taking the carriage imparted a sense of style and importance to the expedition, and Mary loved to wave to her friends from Mr. Ward's school when they passed them on the streets.

She loved, too, the hurry and importance of downtown. Lexington wasn't a great city, like Philadelphia or New York, but around the Courthouse square, and along Main Street and Broadway, brick buildings reared two and three stories tall, and it was possible to buy almost anything: breeze-soft silks from France that came upriver from New Orleans, fine wines and cigars, pearl necklaces, and canes with ivory handles shaped like parrots or dogs'-heads or (in the case of Mary's older friend Cash Clay) scantily dressed ladies (but Cash was careful not to carry that one in company). Downtown, every sort of person could be seen walking along the wide flagways that bordered the streets, from her father's friends—planters and bankers in well-fitting fiddleback coats of brown or blue and high-crowned beaver hats—to the young belles of the town, Elizabeth's cronies, in their bright dresses that rustled with petticoats and dangled with a thousand extravagancies of ribbon and lace. Backwoods farmers in homespun shirts brushed shoulders with young gentlemen from the University, studious Yankees who never seemed to have any fun, the swaggering sons of the local planters in their ruffled shirts and varnished boots, and slaves doing the marketing or sweeping the sidewalks in front of their masters' shops, drab dark notes in the colorful scene.

Madame Deauville had the dresses finished—exquisite white silk festooned with blond lace for Mary, Frances, and Mary's cousin Eliza Humphreys, twelve years old and Betsey's cousin, who was living at the Todd house because the schools were better in Lexington than in Frankfort. They would do, her father had said, for the "second day" party as well. This would be given for those who couldn't make the twenty-mile drive out to Walnut Hill, where Elizabeth had gone to live with their Aunt Liza Carr: It was from Aunt Liza's house, and not their father's, that she would be wed. It was almost a day's drive by carriage—the "second day" party would in fact take place on the third day of Elizabeth's married life—and even the acquisition of a new frock did not erase the anger in Mary's heart, that she had lost the sister who had been like a mother to her a month earlier than she had to, because of her stepmother Betsey.

Elizabeth—unlike Mary—had never breathed a word one way or the other about her feelings toward the woman who'd come to take over the household and Robert Todd's six motherless children, five years ago. But about the time Betsey's first baby, Margaret, was born, Elizabeth had started going to Aunt Liza's for "visits" of a week at a time. After Betsey produced little Sam, and tensions in the now-crowded house on Short Street grew, these visits had lengthened. From the final one, a few weeks after Christmas, Elizabeth had simply neglected to come back.

She still called Betsey "Ma," and kissed the older woman's thin cheek whenever they met. But Mary knew that Elizabeth had left rather than let her father's new wife run her life.

And this thought was in her heart as she, Frances, and Cousin Eliza waited in the carriage for Betsey to pick up the wedding-gift from Blanchard the silversmith.

Betsey was taking her time in the shop—"I'll bet she's going over every square inch of it, as if she thought Mr. Blanchard would give her silver-painted tin," she whispered to Frances—and across the street Mary saw a group of her school friends from Ward's. "Will you look at that *beautiful* mantle Mary Jane's wearing?" gasped Mary. "Is that velvet?" Without waiting to hear Frances's speculation on the garment, Mary pulled her own mantle around her and sprang from the carriage in a froufrou of petticoats.

"Now, Miss Molly," called Nelson from the box. "Miss Betsey told you girls to stay in the carriage."

Eliza and Frances drew back at once. "Don't be a baby, Eliza, come on!" called Mary, halfway across the street already. "I'll only be a minute!" she added, turning to wave at Nelson. She knew perfectly well the gray-haired coachman could not abandon either the horses or the other girls. Then she darted across the ice-slick pavement, to Mr. Sotheby's tall brick store.

"Mary Jane, how gorgeous!" she cried, swirling into the lamplit gloom on the heels of the group of girls. "Where did you get the velvet? Who made it up? Will you wear it to the second-day party Sunday?"

The girls surrounded her, exclaiming in their turn over Mary's description of her own new dress, which lay snug in its cardboard box on the seat of the carriage: "Is it true her sweetheart Ninian is the son of the governor of Illinois?" asked Mary Jane Warfield, the doctor's daughter, and Meg Wickliffe chimed in, "What luck, to get a dress from Madame Deauville! Papa simply won't hear of my going to anyone but old Miss Barney!"

The other girls giggled and exclaimed—Miss Barney was in fact every bit as stylish and expensive as her French counterpart—and Arabella Richardson turned from Mr. Sotheby's small case of jewelry and purred, "You couldn't have done better than Deauville, Mary. She can cut a dress so that even fat girls look lovely. My aunts absolutely *swear* by her."

Mary felt the heat of rage scorch her face, since this wasn't the first time the sylphlike Arabella had publicly remarked on Mary's plumpness. But before Mary could make a retort about the provenance of Arabella's dress, the blonde girl turned back to the jewel-case and inquired sweetly, "Mr. Sotheby, could I just have a look at that sapphire pendant? Papa's getting me a new blue silk and it would be just the thing to go with it."

Searing with anger one moment, Mary felt her face grow cold. The chatter of her friends around her seemed to fade into nothingness, as her consciousness focused on Arabella, Mr. Sotheby, and the pendant now in Arabella's pink-gloved hands. Mary had coveted that pendant for weeks, since it had first come into the store, trying to figure out some way of talking her father into getting it for her. It was a beautiful piece, sapphire and tourmaline flowers clustering on golden leaves, more beautiful than anything Mary had seen in her life. But it was a woman's jewel, not a schoolgirl's, and Mary was only thirteen. Arabella—whom Mary had airily referred to as "that blockhead who can't even spell 'cat' " in the hearing of half their class at the Reverend Mr. Ward's school—held it up to her throat as Mr. Sotheby angled the lamp to make it sparkle: "What do you think, Molly dear?" she asked archly. "Does it go with my eyes?"

Nearly strangling with fury, Mary replied evenly, "It does make them look less squinty." The other girls laughed.

"You know," crooned Arabella to Meg Wickliffe, with deliberate thoughtfulness as the girls rustled out of the shop like an ambulatory flower garden, "it's so pretty, I'll just bet I can get Papa to buy it for me. My birthday's next week."

Following them out, Mary was almost too upset to breathe. Her father wasn't due back from the Legislature in Frankfort until tonight, and then he'd be taken up with preparations for tomorrow's day-long drive to Walnut Hill, and Mary had begged a new pair of party-gloves only last week from her other source of fashionable necessities, Granny Parker. What's more, she knew that Mr. Richardson would buy anything for his lovely and stuck-up daughter. Though in Mary's class, Bella was fifteen, and ready for her come-out. On impulse Mary doubled back into the shop, heart hammering with fear that Betsey would come out of Blanchard's and cross the street looking for her. She would not—*could* not—permit Arabella of all people to take that pendant away from her.

Anyone but her, thought Mary, as her small feet thumped hollowly on the plank floor. . . .

But in her heart she knew, that what she really meant was, *No one but me.*

In the instant that she turned back she'd thought, *Maybe I can get him to hold it for me until I can coax Granny Parker.* But she knew already that Mr. Sotheby dealt cash-in-hand. The thought that flashed through her mind shocked her, but her

anger at Arabella—and her sense of grievance that Arabella
didn't have to share her things with sisters or a stepmother's
niece—burned stronger in her, and as she walked up to the
counter and looked up into Mr. Sotheby's horsey face she
opened her mouth and said the first words that came to her.

"I didn't want to say so while the others were here,
sir, but Papa wrote me from Frankfort, that if I truly wanted
that pendant—and I *truly* do—to tell you to put it on his
account."

Her stomach gave a jar of dread as she heard herself—*How
could I SAY that?*—but even as the storekeeper's eyebrows
went up in pleasure and surprise she knew she couldn't take
it back. Then excitement flashed through her like fire on a
powder-trail, erasing her first horror at herself. It was hers
now! That beautiful, beautiful thing was *hers*. . . .

And she'd taken it right out from under Arabella's nose.

I'll talk to Papa tonight, she promised herself frantically,
watching with huge eyes as Mr. Sotheby wrapped the pendant up for her (beautiful exquisite gems, coyly hiding in
rustling white paper!). *I'll beg him . . . I'll cry.* (Tears usually
worked). *And I'll keep it hidden until after he's said I can get it,
and then pretend I got it a few days later, and there's no difference,
really.*

*Then I'll wear it to the Washington's Birthday Dance at Giron's
Ballroom and just see that stuck-up Bella's face. . . .*

She suspected, as she crossed the street again—Betsey, as
she'd hoped, was still searching for minute nicks and imper-
fections on the wedding-present—that God probably
wouldn't think much of this line of reasoning. *But I can't back
out now! And what's the difference, if Papa says it's all right . . . ?*

"I thought I told you to stay in the carriage." Betsey
emerged from Blanchard's with the silversmith at her heels
carrying her parcels. She was increasing *again,* Mary noticed
resentfully, and her thin face looked sallow against the old
gold plush of the pelerine around her shoulders.

"I'm sorry, ma'am, but I just needed some air, and I
thought it would be all right."

Betsey clicked her tongue and allowed Nelson to hand her in, then took the parcels from Mr. Blanchard. The old coachman cocked an eye at Mary as he helped her up the carriage's high step, but didn't comment on the fact that that purported breath of air had involved a trip to Sotheby's and had occupied a good twenty-five minutes.

Mary's father returned to Lexington well after dinner that night, for the roads down to the state capital at Frankfort were icy in this season. Through dinner—always a tumultuous meal, with Ann sulking because she wouldn't be allowed to stand up with Elizabeth at the wedding Friday (and wouldn't get a new dress on the strength of it, as Mary and Frances had) and George and Levi plaguing their tutor, the stiff-backed and bespectacled young Mr. Presby of New England—Mary had almost to shout to make herself heard when she talked to Cousin Eliza. And throughout the meal she was listening, listening for her father's knock at the door.

But when he finally came in he was mud-slathered and cold. "Horse threw a shoe, poor fellow," he said, as his children crowded clamoring around him. "Thank you, Pendleton—" He handed the butler his gloves, riding-cloak, and hat. "Has Nelson got the carriage packed for tomorrow?" Six feet tall, powerfully built, dark-haired and blue-eyed, Robert Todd was in Mary's eyes the handsomest man in all of Kentucky and she would have died for him.

The others were all shouting at once to be heard ("Did you bring me something, Papa?" demanded Ann), and Mary saw at once that he was too tired to listen properly to tear-stained cajoleries about jewelry. She ducked into the dining-room while Betsey clapped her hands and ordered the others up to bed, then found her father's slippers and brought them to him in the small parlor where Pendleton had stirred up the fire.

Betsey glanced impatiently up as Mary came in, but said, "Thank you, Mary," as Mary sat on the footstool to place them on his feet.

As the butler knelt to pull off Robert Todd's boots, Betsey

asked, "Are those fools in Washington still talking of letting the National Bank's charter lapse?"

"They're talking of it. Though what they think is going to happen to the country's credit abroad if they do, I can't even begin to guess."

"Aren't they going to shift the country's specie to state banks, at least?" asked Mary. "That's what it said in the *Kentucky Gazette*."

"That's my clever girl." Her father reached out a hand to stroke the bronze-gold curls that fell forward over her shoulder. "State banks and private banks, which means more power for Jackson's friends, when they've got control of the money to do favors."

"But you run the Bank of Kentucky," pointed out Mary, her concerns about the pendant currently hidden in her jewelry-box vanishing in the double joy of talking politics and having her father's attention. "Won't that give *you* power?"

"Really, Mary. Your father's just come in from a day in the saddle, and I'm sure he's too tired to explain the National Bank to a schoolgirl. Why don't you just run along to bed? Goodness knows we all have to be up early enough in the morning." And Betsey put her arm through her husband's, squeezed it possessively. Robert Todd smiled at her, and covered her hand with his.

"Goodnight, Molly." In his fond eyes she saw herself change from a friend and political partner back into a schoolgirl.

As if the golden joy she'd had in his company had been glass, it shattered in her hands. And left her bleeding.

"Goodnight, Papa," she said tonelessly. "Goodnight... ma'am."

She was trembling as she left the parlor, and Betsey closed the door behind her, leaving her in the icy gloom of the candlelit hall. Too hurt, too furious to go up to bed, Mary snatched her shawl from where it hung over the bottom of the bannister and, pulling it tight around her, crossed through the darkened dining-room and out through the butler's tiny pantry, to the blackness of the yard.

It was bitterly cold out there, last week's patches of snow still dotting the ground. Her Granny Parker's tall brick house, catercorner from her father's on the same big lot, was dark already, but rosy light beckoned from the kitchen, and as she crossed the yard Mary heard the slaves' mellow laughter. The door opened as she approached it, Pendleton coming out with a tray of cold supper for his master. Welcoming warmth puffed out around him, the clatter of dishes and the scents of cooking and soap.

"Lord, child, you should be in bed!" Mammy Sally looked up from the hearth, where she was stirring milk-puddings for the little ones—*Betsey's* little ones—in the nursery.

"You got a long trip tomorrow," added Nelson, sitting at the battered table in the middle of the crowded little room, drinking the watered-down remains of the coffee from dinner. "As do we all." He glanced across the table at Saul, Granny Parker's stableman, a good-natured young fellow who'd managed to keep himself out of the subtle power-struggles between the slaves who'd served the first Mrs. Todd and those that Betsey had, five years ago, brought to the household.

"I think he's talkin' to me," sighed Saul. He put his arm around Jane, who sat beside him. Jane was Betsey's slave, the housekeeper who acted as her right hand and, Mary knew, was resented by most of the others because her mistress had taken the place of Granny Parker's daughter. The house that Robert Todd lived in had been given to him by Granny Parker—the continued occupation was not the most comfortable of situations.

Jane—whom Mary had expected to look down on a mere stableman because she was a housekeeper, and far lighter of skin—wrapped her fingers around Saul's, and gently kissed his knuckles.

"What's the matter, child?" Mammy Sally beckoned Mary

to the hearth, under cover of the murmur and activity as Chaney the cook finished scouring out the pans, and Betsey's maid Judy came in for Betsey's herb tea. "You been quiet all afternoon.... Careful—stand back from the smoke. You get one speck of soot on your dress and neither you nor me'll hear the end of it from *someone* in this house." She glanced across the kitchen at Judy and Jane.

"What's always the matter?" Tears burned Mary's eyes as she drew up one of the kitchen stools. "Mammy, she's poisoning Papa's mind against us! She's keeping him away from us! She told me to run away and not talk to him, because he's too tired, but she doesn't think he's too tired for *her.* She calls me a limb of Satan to my face, or says I'm too fat or will never catch a husband. She's got to be saying that to Papa, too! And he goes along with it!"

She brought up one small white short-fingered hand, dashed the tears away from her eyes.

"I haven't seen him for weeks! He's always gone at the Legislature in Frankfort, and right after the party Sunday he's going back again!" Desolation filled her at the thought of losing him, of always losing him. "She doesn't like to hear me talking politics with him. And I *don't* need it explained to me! I know what we're talking about, I read the newspapers! I'm not stupid, like she thinks I am—like she tells Papa and everyone I am."

"No, child, I've never heard her say to anyone you're stupid," corrected Mammy.

"She says to everyone I'm a limb of Satan."

"That's not the same thing." An expression of gentle amusement pulled the corner of the old nurse's mouth. "Takes brains, to be a limb of Satan." With an almost absent-minded motion she continued to stir the thickening custard in its pan.

"Lord, Miss Mary," added Jane, coming to the hearth to tilt steaming water into the teapot, "why you take everythin' so hard? Why can't you be sweet, like Miss Frances?"

Mary pulled in her breath in a ragged sob, but if there was

one thing her Granny Parker—and her elegant Granny Humphreys, Betsey's mother, in Frankfort—had inculcated into her, it was that you didn't put out your tongue at darkies. So she waited until Jane had gone back to tidying up her account-book at the table before she said, in a low mutinous voice, "If Jane's so smart, let *her* tell *me* why I can't be sweet like Frances. Frances is just a mealy-mouthed wall-flower... and I *am* sweet. Or I want to be."

"Miss Frances is what she is." Mammy Sally raised her eyebrows at the scowling girl beside her. "And you are what you are. Wipe your eyes, child." And she took a clean bandanna from her pocket, lest Mary sully the small square of lace and lawn pinned to her pink silk sash.

Mary obeyed, hands trembling. As always, the sudden swing from the sense of power and gladness that she had in her father's presence, to the rage and tears of having him taken from her yet again, left her exhausted and feeling strange, as if some part of her had separated from herself and couldn't quite fit back together. At such times she had a sensation, almost a fear, of losing herself: an uneasy sense that she was about to start doing or saying things that she didn't want to, couldn't help.

Was that, she wondered, for the flashing split-second before she buried the thought, why she'd lied to Mr. Sotheby?

No. I'll make it all right.

Why *couldn't* she be like Frances? Frances would never have told such a lie. Or like gay Meg Wickliffe, or giggling Mary Jane Warfield, or even Arabella Richardson, who might be a conniving blockhead but never seemed to lose control of either her temper or her tears. Why couldn't she be like any of her other friends and cousins in Lexington, who seemed to get on with their lives with little more than minor heartaches and occasional anxieties over what dress to wear?

She didn't know, and the loneliness of this isolation—worse now that Elizabeth had gone—was like a fish-hook, forever embedded in her heart.

Mammy Sally's heavy-jowled face glistened with sweat as she hooked the pot on its chain down closer to the heat, quickened the gentle rhythm of her stirring. Mary knew she should get to bed—Eliza, who shared her room, would be wondering where she was—but lingered. She felt comforted by the soft clanking of dishes, by the murmur of talk in this familiar room, with its sieve hung on the door to keep the witches away.

She wished she could hang a sieve on the door of the house, to keep Betsey out forever.

"Sometimes when I hears them old stories about wicked stepmothers, I wonder how the poor stepmothers feel," said Mammy Sally at last, still so low that the others could not hear. "Can't be easy for Miss Betsey, you know, coming down here from Frankfort where she had her own property and her family was just about kings and queens of that town. Coming away from being free, to marry a man with six children already and your grandmother lookin' over her shoulder . . ." She shook her head. "That'd be enough to give *me* headaches all the time like she gets, and to make me spit poison in all directions."

"How dare you take her side?" The betrayal cut Mary's heart like a knife.

"Child, I'm not taking her side." Mammy Sally turned from her stirring to give Mary a hug, her uncorseted flesh yielding as a feather mattress under the faded calico of her dress. "I'm just sayin' she *has* a side."

"Well, I have a side, too. Why couldn't she stay in Frankfort, and be free and queen of everybody there like you say? Why did she have to come here?"

Mammy Sally smiled, and poured out the cooling milk into the shallow ramekins for Patty the nurse-girl to take up to little Margaret and baby Sam. "Maybe she wonders that now, too. But she got to make the best of things as they are, the way we all do."

The door opened into the frosty night and Saul came back in, breath blowing steam. "Everythin' loaded up ready to leave in the mornin'," he reported, and went to put his arms around Jane's waist. The housekeeper turned, startled, then closed her eyes and with a motion that went straight to Mary's heart leaned her head back against the man's heavy shoulder, as if relaxing into the pillow of a bed.

"Because you know she can't go back," Mammy Sally's quiet voice went on. "Can't none of us ever go back."

Chapter Six

MARY LEFT THE PENDANT HIDDEN IN HER JEWEL-BOX AT home the following morning, when the family set out on the daylong drive to Aunt Liza Carr's. She knew she'd be sharing a room that night not only with Eliza, but with Ann, who kept a ruthless eye on Mary's trinkets to make sure their father never gave Mary more than she herself got. Mary had meant to take her pony and ride beside her father's tall horse—a ploy she used whenever she could, to get time alone with him—but Betsey ruled that ladies didn't spend all day in the saddle the way men did. A few hours was all that was proper for a girl.

So Mary and Eliza were drafted into the chore of looking after little Georgie, who chose that morning to act up, racing wildly around the house, refusing to dress, and shrieking at the top of his lungs.

Betsey's babies, mercifully, were left back at home with Mammy Sally. Only those whom Mary thought of as Robert Todd's "real children"—Frances, herself, Levi, Ann, and George—plus Cousin Eliza, of course—would be with their father to witness the wedding of Elizabeth, who had stood in as a mother to them all.

Even in wintertime, Mary loved the hilly bluegrass country, with its sharp outcrops of granite, its shadowy thickets and dense woods. The dangers from Indians, from cougar and bears, that had given this land the name "The Dark and Bloody Ground" fifty years ago, had given place to plantations of tobacco and hemp, where blood-horses looked mildly over pasture fences, but the shape of the land remained, dramatic and untamed. Though pale sunlight filtered through the leafless boughs of tulip and paw-paw trees, the silence of the woods seemed to hold secrets that tugged at Mary's heart.

The ceremony at Walnut Hill was quiet, and small by Southern standards, meaning fewer than a hundred people: Todds and Parkers and Logans and Russells and all the other connections that made such unbreakable chains all across the South. In addition to Mary and her brothers and sisters, several of her father's brothers and their wives were present, and her exceedingly handsome cousin John Stuart, who had recently gone to practice law in the recently-admitted state of Illinois. The bridegroom himself had come from Illinois to study law at Transylvania University in town, and it was understood that though he would take up residence with Elizabeth at Walnut Hill until he finished his studies, he would (*what else?* thought Mary) be welcome in Robert Todd's house as an overnight guest several times a week.

Her throat ached with renewed desolation as she watched Elizabeth speak her vows in Aunt Liza's parlor. All those years of going to Elizabeth for comfort against Betsey's sharp tongue, all those years of knowing her oldest sister was her refuge, and now Elizabeth was leaving her for good. Even the fantasy that somehow, some way, Betsey would disappear and Elizabeth would come back from Walnut Hill dissolved in the glowing happiness of Elizabeth's words, "I do." Elizabeth would go with Ninian, wherever Ninian decided to go.

No quantity of sapphire pendants would ever assuage that hurt.

The second-day party held at Robert Todd's house in Lexington on the following Sunday was four times as big as the wedding, and wildly more gay. The house, which wasn't even large enough for the family (not to mention the cousins, brothers, and family connections Betsey unhesitatingly invited to take up residence from time to time), was jammed to the doors with well-wishers and friends. Arabella Richardson showed up in the promised new dress of blue silk so elaborate, and so much more beautiful than Mary's new white frock, that Mary darted back upstairs and put on the sapphire pendant, on a blue velvet ribbon around her neck.

The blazing chagrin on Bella's face was everything Mary had hoped it would be.

Robert Smith Todd was a popular man in Lexington, and his friends crowded the parlor. From the chattering circle of her school-friends, their voices drew her like the Pied Piper's magic music toward them around the refreshment table. Fond as she was of Meg Wickliffe and Mary Jane and the others, their conversation was centered wholly around beaux and earbobs...subjects all very fine in their place, but nothing to the headier mental delights of politics. Her father was saying, "...just because Jackson fought the British and can hold his liquor doesn't mean he has honest friends."

"The voters will find their mistake if Jackson does do away with the bank." Mr. Henry Clay took a julep from the tray Pendleton offered, a tall man, thin and hawk-faced and leonine, and also the handsomest man in Kentucky, Mary thought, right after her father. "Think about some of the bankers you know, gentlemen...present company excepted." Clay's warm gray eyes twinkled as he raised his glass toward Robert Todd. "Can you imagine putting the finances of the *country* into their hands?"

Mary edged closer, and the man beside her glanced down at her with an understanding flash of a grin: Mr. Clay's cousin Cash, who'd stayed at the Todds'—naturally, at Betsey's invitation—when he and his body-servant had managed to inadvertently burn down the dormitory of Transylvania University a few years before. Though everyone was crowding close to hear Henry Clay speak, Cash squeezed aside to make room for Mary. He was a big handsome young man with black hair and a devil in his green-eyed smile.

Mary's new brother-in-law Ninian Edwards said, "And every one of them can make as many friends as he needs for votes, just by extending credit...."

"Hell," snorted Cash, "Old Hickory's idea of raising

money is betting everything he owns on a horse-race and hoping for the best—not that I mean to disparage a single one of his horses."

"I daresay some of them have more sense than some of the men Mr. Jackson's been putting into office," remarked Mary impulsively, and that got an even bigger laugh.

"You have a smart little girl there, Todd," approved Old Duke Wickliffe, Meg's father and the wealthiest of the planters near-by Lexington. He spit—with perfect politeness and excellent aim—into the cuspidor half-concealed among the ferns at the end of the refreshment table.

Mary looked up at Mr. Clay, who had served in the government under every President from George Washington on, who had been one of the last to flee the capital in the face of the invading British, who was as close to a fighting hero as Kentucky had. "You *will* run for President against Mr. Jackson again, won't you, sir?" And, with her dimpled, one-sided smile, she added archly, "I still hold you to your promise of an invitation to your inaugural ball."

Henry Clay laughed at the reminder of the old jest between them. Mary had known Mr. Clay for most of her life, admiring him with her father's admiration, and later loving him as a friend when she'd go riding out to the gates of his plantation, Ashland, along the Richmond road outside of town. Only gradually had she understood that he was something more than a kingly, lion-haired family friend with a voice like an avenging god's. She'd heard her father talk of Mr. Clay being elected President of the United States long before she had any clear idea that President of the United States was very different from state Assemblyman or state Senator, both offices her father had held.

"My dear." Clay bowed over her hand. "Since you remind me of my promise, you give me no choice but to run."

The men applauded, and Cash likewise bowed to Mary and said, "Then you have my personal thanks, Miss Mary, for spurring my cousin on to his duty again. . . ."

"Like he needed it," commented Meg's brother Young Duke Wickliffe with a cheeky grin at the tall statesman.

"And I, in turn," said Clay, with becoming gravity, "claim *your* invitation, Miss Mary, to your husband's inaugural ball . . . whoever the lucky gentleman may be."

Cash and the other men laughed again, and Mary fluttered her fan and glanced up at Mr. Clay sidelong, as she'd seen Elizabeth and Meg Wickliffe glance at their beaux. It was another old joke between her and Mr. Clay that if she couldn't grow up and marry him, whoever she *did* marry would have to become President to even things out. Even at thirteen Mary understood how to flirt as well as talk politics, how to look shyly under her lashes, and which angles of her head best became her. This knowledge was almost second nature among the well-born belles of the South. In fact, for a woman to talk politics, she was almost obliged to flirt, to take the edge off what she said so that men wouldn't think her mannish.

Besides, Mary had always enjoyed flirting.

"Elizabeth, you'd best go fetch that good-looking husband of yours away if you're ever to get started on your wedding journey," said Granny Parker, leading Elizabeth into the parlor and fixing Ninian with a beady dark eye. Old Elizabeth Parker had come over the Cumberland Gap in a wagon and had lived in a blockhouse among the canebrakes before Lexington was founded. She had scant regard for husbands, having buried her own decades ago. "I take it you'll still be with Liza when you get back from White Sulphur Springs?"

"Until Ninian's done at the University, yes." Elizabeth's gaze followed her grandmother's, to where Ninian's dramatic raven curls could be seen over the crowd around Mr. Clay and her father. Something in her face, in the way her expression softened, brought back to Mary the way Jane had settled into Saul's shoulder in the kitchen, like the same passage of music, played in a different key.

"Where's she put you these days, Frances?" inquired

Granny Parker of the second sister, who trailed along behind Elizabeth, holding her hand. "In the attic?"

"I think I heard her tell Nelson to move a blanket out to one of the sheds," provided Mary archly, which got another laugh. "That way she can rent out the room."

Frances, who had no sense of the ridiculous, only said, "Oh, no, ma'am, I share the small room at the top of the stairs with Ann." But Betsey, making her way to her husband's side, stopped and stiffened with anger, and her narrowed gaze focused on Mary as if seeing her clearly for the first time in that very crowded day.

Mary turned quickly, and looked around for her father. She had to catch him now, had to make it all right.... *I'll tell him I don't know what came over me*—that was true enough.... *I'll tell him Bella Richardson said she deserved to have the pendant because her father is richer than Papa.... And I ... and I got so angry that I couldn't let that pass....*

She began to tremble as she nerved herself up for the interview.

But the group of men had shifted, Ninian and Cash coming over to the knot of girls around Granny Parker, Ninian to put an arm around Elizabeth and Cash to sidle as close to Mary Jane Warfield as he could without her father seeing them. Mary slipped away as soon as she could, joining the group of girls who accompanied Elizabeth up to Frances's room, to collect the last of Elizabeth's things as the carriage that would take her and Ninian to White Sulphur Springs was brought to the door. The girls hugged Elizabeth as they mounted the rather narrow stairway, blocking the way completely with their wide mountains of petticoats: Frances and Meg were already in tears and Arabella Richardson was pretending to be.

Mary saw Betsey emerge from the parlor and come toward them, and tried to get up the stairs before her, but there were simply too many girls in the way. Her stepmother reached out and caught the sapphire pendant in her hand, jerking so hard Mary thought either the ribbon or her neck would snap.

"Why don't you tell me which is worse, Miss: to hold household in the face of needless expenditure, or to lie to tradesmen in order to get something you want?"

She spoke in a level tone, but quietly, so quietly Mary wasn't sure, afterwards, how many of her friends heard. Mary's stomach gave one sickening heave under her tight-laced corsets and she felt her face grow cold. Then blood flamed to her cheeks and her throat and her chest, and she retorted, "At least I don't spy on people behind their backs!"

With a gesture as smooth and swift as swatting a fly, Betsey dealt her a stinging box on the ear, and every girl on the stairway stopped dumb, staring down at the two of them at its foot. "You can go to your room, Miss," said Betsey, "and stay there. I think I've seen enough of you for the day."

As Mary thrust her way blindly up through what felt like a patchouli-scented forest of petticoats, she heard the voices behind her, whispering questions. . . .

Whispering answers.

She slammed the door of her room like a wordless curse flung at her stepmother, then stood hanging on to the handle, her knees trembling so hard she didn't think she could make it to the bed. Shame washed over her like the waves of a bottomless ocean.

Shame and terror. *She'll tell Papa.* The words hammered the inside of her ribcage until she felt she would die if she did not scream.

Liar. Liar. Mary Todd is a liar.

The whole town would know about it and nobody would ever speak to her again.

Her father . . .

She felt sick, as if she were going to throw up. *I didn't mean it. I only wanted something pretty!*

Thief. Liar and thief.

Please, God, don't have everybody in town be whispering that. Papa will be disgraced, too. He'll never speak to me again.

And then I really will die.

Somehow she made it to the bed, and lay trembling, listening to the hushed whispers of the girls in Frances's room next door. *Thief, liar.* Mary dragged the pillow over her head, heedless of Mammy Sally's careful hours with the curling-irons. She lay that way for a long time, her mind blank to everything except dread and shame.

Betsey would tell everyone. Betsey had practically announced it to all her friends, right there on the stairway. What would Eliza and Frances say? They'd never be able to hold up their heads at Ward's again, unless they joined in the cry against Mary. . . . Mary knew exactly how those alliances worked. Her heart curled up at the thought, like a giblet in a dry oven.

Daylight was fading from the windows when Mammy Sally knocked on the door. Mary snatched the pillow from her head. "Go away!" And, when Mammy knocked again and opened the door, "Don't you say a word to me! I don't want to talk about it!" She was shaking all over. Somehow that was almost worse than her father being disgraced for having a liar and a thief in his family: that every darky in town was going to be whispering her name in kitchens, tack-rooms, garden sheds. *Did you hear what that Mary Todd did . . . ?*

Mammy's eyebrows went up, but she only said, "Turn round, child, let me unlace you. No sense gettin' that pretty dress all creased up layin' on it."

Mary obeyed in silence, too angry—and too humiliated—to further humble herself by crying. When Eliza came up a few hours later Mary pretended to be asleep. When she did sleep, her dreams were of walking down Broadway hearing everyone she knew whispering behind her: *Liar. Liar and thief.*

The next morning Mary stayed in her room. She heard the voices of the family going down to breakfast, but knew better than to even try it herself. All she'd need would be Betsey dragging out the whole story in front of them. She trembled at the thought of the upcoming interview with her father. He would ask her why she'd done it—with the look of hurt in his eyes, as he'd asked her about countless acts of disobedience over the years—and she had nothing, literally nothing, that she could tell him.

She didn't know why she'd done it. Just thinking about saying that made her want to cry.

But she wanted above all things to have it over with, done. *He will never speak to me again,* she thought, and the next moment, *He has to say it's all right. He has to say it or I'll die.*

She strained her ears for the sound of his boots on the stairs, and wondered if she should pray. But she could think of nothing God would even consider granting her.

Boots at the bottom of the stairs. Muffled voices, her father's and Betsey's. She held her breath: *It's going to be now. . . . I'll cry. He'll forgive me if I cry. . . .*

Then, very dimly, the sounds of hooves in the street. A saddle-horse being brought around to the front of the house. The sound of the front door opening . . . "I'll be back on the first," said her father's voice.

The door closed. Betsey's light decisive step retreated to the parlor. A moment later, the sound of hooves rattled down Short Street as her father rode away.

Mary sat up, her mouth literally ajar with shock and, a moment later, outrage. There would be no confrontation. No bargaining, no tears, no forgiveness.

He had left without any of them. Without saying good-by.

"She told him you weren't feeling well," reported Eliza, when she came up an hour later after helping Betsey and Frances wash the good breakfast china—a task never relegated to darkies. "She said you were still asleep."

And SHE *called* ME *a liar!* The hairs on her head prickled with wrath.

Her father was going to be gone for almost two weeks, and Betsey had taken it upon herself to step between them, and prevent them from even having the chance to say good-by.

"What did she say to you yesterday, anyway?" asked Eliza, digging through her own little painted tin box for a ribbon to go in her yellow curls. "Is your ear all right?"

Mary barely remembered Betsey hitting her in front of her friends. All she could think was, *She told him in private. Of course—she doesn't want to hear the darkies in every kitchen in town saying, "That Mary Todd's a liar and a thief," any more than I do. Not because she cares one single thing about me, but because of Papa's reputation at the Legislature and the bank.*

But she'd told him. Betsey wouldn't pass up the chance to drive the wedge more firmly between Robert Todd and his "real children." She had taken him from Mary, and had driven Elizabeth from the house, Elizabeth who had been like a mother to Mary, to make way for her own children. She had struck Mary in front of all her friends, and had lied—*lied* to keep her husband away from his daughter before he rode back to Frankfort.

Mary managed to whisper, "My ear is fine."

Later that day she made it her business to linger in the kitchen, and when Betsey's back was turned abstracted a handful of coffee-beans from the tin caddy that was usually kept locked. These she used to bribe Saul to procure for her a dozen live spiders, an astonishing number considering it was the middle of winter. The result was everything Mary had hoped it would be, Betsey's voice screaming wildly in the darkness a few minutes after bedtime—she was always too stingy to carry a bedroom candle—and Patty, who had her own reasons for disliking her mistress, reporting the next day in the kitchen that she'd found Miss Betsey standing on a chair naked as a jaybird, shrieking and trying to claw the confused arachnids out of her long unbraided hair.

She can't prove I did it, thought Mary, with a kind of burning complacency as she lay listening to the cries and thumps. *She can't prove a thing.*

But Betsey didn't need or want proof. Despite the fact that Mary had sworn Saul to secrecy and dropped down the outhouse the candy-tin in which the spiders had been delivered, Betsey confined Mary to her room for the ten days intervening before her father's return from Frankfort—days of anxiety, loneliness, and alternating waves of defiance and agonizing shame.

Worse still, she refused to let her have any books, not even the Bible. Only sheets to hem.

So there was nothing to do but wait for her father's return.

She wished there were something she could do to punish herself, so that he would forgive her. Wished there was some way she could go back in time and rub out everything that had happened since that Wednesday afternoon in Mr. Sotheby's store. Make it all not have happened, make everything go back to what it had been before.

She knew she mustn't wish for Betsey to die before her father got home—she could just imagine what God would have to say if she prayed for it—but the thought was frequently in her mind.

Sometimes, when she thought of what her father would say to her, she wished she could simply die herself.

Her father came home just before suppertime on the first of March. Mary was so exhausted with shame, with remorse, with anger at herself and Betsey and all the world, that she started sobbing the moment she heard the hooves of his horse in Short Street, and was still weeping after supper, when Betsey came into her room—wordlessly and without knocking—and escorted her down to his study.

"Your mother and I have been talking," said Robert Todd, when Betsey had closed the door and went to stand beside him at his desk.

Mary protested, "She's not my mother!" Then she clapped her hands over her mouth and stood, tears streaming down her face, looking from Betsey's stony countenance to her father's weary one. She saw in his eyes only a kind of tired peevishness. There wasn't even anger, she realized, with a sick shock of disappointment. Only that he didn't want to be troubled with the conflict between his first wife's children and their stepmother.

He just wants everything to be all right, so he can be like his friends and not worry about it.

The knowledge was like opening a beautifully-wrapped present and finding it empty. Like biting into a delicious-looking piece of cake that had been made without sugar or salt.

And I'm the one who's hurting him.

It seemed that there was nothing that she could do or feel that was not wrong.

"Your mother and I have been talking," he said again, and Mary flinched, waiting for the words of anger, of disappointment, of rejection. *Liar. Thief.* She wished she could shrink in on herself and disappear. Then he said, "And we've agreed that you're old enough now to go away to school."

Mary looked up. This was so unexpected that she was caught breathless, as if she'd stepped through her familiar bedroom door and found herself falling down the backyard well. Then the meaning of his words sank in, and her disappointment evaporated, her volatile spirits leaped.

School . . .

Mary had listened in hungry envy when the Reverend John Ward had spoken to his classes about the seminaries for higher education that girls could go to, in Philadelphia and New York. Meg Wickliffe—who at sixteen was almost finished at Ward's—said she might go to Sigoigne's very prestigious Female Academy in Philadelphia, next year or the year following, and Mary's soul had ached with the desire to go, too. To learn more of history than the Reverend and Mrs. Ward could teach. To have access to all the literature of England and France that she'd only just heard about . . . to learn to speak French properly, and maybe Italian, maybe even Latin like the boys.

The sudden shift from shame and dread to the great longing of her heart was so unexpected that for the first few moments while her father was speaking, Mary only felt confused, as if she were dreaming. *Betsey didn't tell him. She can't have told him....*

"...know that we don't have the money to send you to Philadelphia or New York. But Madame Mentelle at Rose Hill teaches a very fine course of studies...."

Madame Mentelle! Mary's thoughts came crashing back to earth. She'd seen the tall, rangy Frenchwoman striding about Lexington's muddy streets in her hopelessly old-fashioned, high-waisted dresses. In the frame of her short-cropped hair her angular face and pale eyes had a decisive expression even more witchlike than Betsey's.

Mary's glance shot to Betsey's face, and she understood. This was Betsey's way of getting her out of the house. Of having Robert Todd that much more to herself.

She, Mary, had handed her the wherewithal to convince him to do it....

And because of the pendant—because of the falsehood she had told—she couldn't even protest.

"You'll like it there," said her father, with encouraging cheer.

How do you know?

She managed to say, "Yes, Papa. Thank you, Papa."

He held out his arms to her, and Betsey moved aside a half step, as if giving permission for Mary to sit on her father's knee. "That's my little girl," he said, rocking her, holding her—taking comfort, she felt, though it was something never said between them, in her nearness and her unquestioning love.

Betsey didn't tell him, Mary thought again, disbelieving. Her heart ached with gratitude—not to Betsey, but to God.

Betsey was getting exactly what she wanted, spiders notwithstanding.

Mary was still her father's little girl, his child for whom he could make everything all right without effort when she wept, and not a liar and a thief.

But the price of that miraculous salvation was exile.

"Mary," said her father's deep voice in her ear, "I want you to apologize to your mother for what you did."

Mary nodded, and at his urging slipped down off his knee. She curtsied to Betsey, whispered, "Ma, I'm so sorry."

Betsey's face was enigmatic. "I accept your apology, Mary. We will say no more of it." A formula? A promise? A simple acknowledgment that certain things were best kept quiet for the good of the family's reputation? Mary's eyes searched her stepmother's face briefly, then fell before the cold gaze. Betsey had kept her secret, and Mary, now, was obliged to keep it, too. The shame of being caught in a lie—of being trapped by her lie—burned in her like the scar of a red-hot knife, sealed in her secret heart. She knew she would never, ever speak of what she had done.

Not even to obtain forgiveness.

"Run along now," said Betsey, "and tell Chaney to give you some supper."

As Mary backed from the little book-crammed study she saw her stepmother take the place she had had moments ago on Robert Todd's knee. "Well," said Betsey, as Mary shut the door, "now maybe we'll have some peace."

CHAPTER SEVEN

Rose Hill was a low, rambling house built in a grove of locust trees, out on the Richmond Pike. From earliest childhood Mary would pass the place when she'd ride her pony to Mr. Clay's graceful stucco house at Ashland, which stood nearby. She'd seen Madame Mentelle in town, too, and had overheard Betsey and her bosom-bow Sophonisba Breckenridge talking about her—"virago" and "bluestocking," and "very well educated I *suppose,* but those *dresses* she wears..." The roll of Sophy's eyes had been worth a thousand words. "I'll bet that poor husband of hers lives under the cat's foot." And the two women had giggled like malicious girls.

Now the tall Frenchwoman stood at the top of the front door's three brick steps: "Dulcie will show you where to put Miss Mary's things," she told Nelson, as the old coachman unstrapped the trunk from the back of the carriage. The slave woman of whom she spoke stepped down to help Nelson carry in Mary's many boxes, and Madame herself glanced sidelong at Mary, her pale eyes unreadable. "Take the books into the library. *La bibliothèque de votre père, c'est renommé ici à la ville.*" Her French was so fast, and so slurred, that Mary had to grope for the words addressed to her, picking the sentence apart.

La bibliothèque... the library... *de vot' père*... your father's library...

"*Merci, Madame,*" she replied carefully, meeting that disconcerting gaze unflinchingly. Understanding that this woman was testing her—probing to see how much work her French would need to achieve the proficiency of a truly accomplished young lady, she went on in that language. "Papa says you are a scholar."

Madame winced, as at the scraping of a nail on tin. "*Une scholaira?* This isn't Latin! I was afraid all you'd learned here was American French. Good God, the Chickasaws speak it better than those imbeciles at Ward's."

Mary's spine stiffened, for she liked the Reverend Ward and his wife. "Maybe the Chickasaws learned it while selling American scalps to the French before the Revolution," she retorted.

Madame's eyebrows shot up at this impertinence. Then, slowly, she smiled, revealing long yellow teeth like a horse's. "From what I hear, your grandfather kept the local market in such commodities fairly scanty."

And as they crossed the threshold into the dim entryway Mary's heart flooded with warmth, that this forbidding woman knew something of her family. That she wasn't just another nameless schoolgirl to be pushed aside, as she was always pushed aside at home unless she raised a fuss or made them laugh. And at the same time it burst upon her like sunlight that French was a language in which one could talk about things that were important and fun, not just about the pen of the gardener's aunt.

"Grandpa Todd held off the Indians at Blue Licks, Madame." She had no idea what the French word for a salt-lick was, so simply gave the vowel a Gallic twist. "My Great-Uncle John was killed in that battle."

"'My Great-Uncle John, *he was* killed in that battle,'" Madame corrected. "This is how it is said in Paris. I too had an uncle killed in battle, fighting for the King of France against the rabble." She paused in the hallway; through a door on her right Mary glimpsed dark bookshelves and busts of bronze and marble and gilt-trimmed porphyry in niches; through another, wide windows and dappled light. Somewhere in the house a woman sang as she worked, a light air, and in French. There was a smell of wood-smoke, and of pine boughs brought in to freshen the winter stuffiness. The quiet felt like the blessing of God, after the constant turmoil and children crying of her father's house—her stepmother's house.

"I understand you are something of a scholar yourself."

"Yes, ma'am."

"And I suppose you've been told all your life not to tax your poor little female brain with such heavy matters as history and mathematics." Madame led the way down a passageway, and across a narrow court tucked in like an open-air hallway between the main block of the house and its western wing. Plum-colored nubbins of new canes punctuated the thorny stems of roses along the brick of the wall. A green film of moss on the bricks underfoot showed where the shadows lay longest. "At least that's what people were always telling me."

"Did they call you a bluestocking, ma'am?" It was the worst thing Betsey and Sophy Breckenridge could say of another woman, and Mary was astonished she remembered the phrase for it in French.

"Bluestocking? To hear them tell it, I was blue all the way up to my chin." Madame walked beside her down the court, which had several doors opening onto it and a little iron gate at the end. "And do you know what? It didn't change how I felt. One cannot change what one feels, child. Any more than one can change what one loves." She paused with her hand on the door-latch. "We're a bit crowded this season. I hope you don't mind a room in the family wing, instead of over on the east side with the other boarders? Dinner is in the main house at five, and perhaps we'll have a little music afterwards—do you play?"

Before Mary could reply Madame opened the door, to reveal a room every bit as constricted—and as innocent of a fireplace—as her own on Short Street. The two small beds it contained seemed to fill it. Mary's own three trunks were piled at the foot of one, with hatboxes and satchels stacked neatly on top. Beside the other, just removing an armful of folded linen from a stylish portmanteau, was Meg Wickliffe, a smile of welcome and delight on her face.

"I shall see you girls at dinner," said Madame. "Don't put

spiders in my bed, and I daresay you and I shall get along fine."

WITH THE POSSIBLE EXCEPTION OF MAMMY SALLY'S KITCHEN, Mary had never known a place where she felt so profoundly at home as she did at Rose Hill. She missed Frances and Eliza—missed Mammy Sally and even months later missed Elizabeth—but she had never known a sense of peace like the peace she knew at the rambling, tree-shaded house on the Richmond Pike.

For all Lexington's brick shops and paved streets, for all its University and bustling little downtown, it was still only a few minutes from the hilly bluegrass meadows, from the dark woods and the fields of tobacco and corn. When Nelson came with the carriage on Friday evenings to bring Mary back to Short Street, they drove for the most part through groves and woodland before the houses of the town rose around them, windows glowing amber in the freezing winter dark, or, later, somnolent in the grass-scented twilight of summer. Mary would wave to friends both black and white as they passed them, and then they'd be on the other edge of town, where the hills started up again and the trees clustered thick.

Mary settled quickly into the sleepy rhythm of those days, the peculiarly Southern blending of countryside and town.

During the week, Meg Wickliffe was like a sister to her. They'd braid each other's hair at night, and laugh over the running feud between Madame Mentelle's parrot Xenophon and Dulcie the maid—Xenophon had learned to imitate the sound of the silver bell Madame used to summon Dulcie, and called the exasperated woman into the parlor a dozen times a day. Xenophon also swore in Italian—"I shall never be able to teach Italian so long as that bird is in the house," remarked Madame.

At sixteen Meg was very much a belle, and would be sent, she said, to Sigoigne's next year, as soon as her French was up to Philadelphia standards. Her beaux would come to Rose

Hill in the evenings and make careful conversation in the drawing-room with Meg and the older girls, under Madame's watchful eye. Meg instructed Mary in the intricacies of curling-irons, chignons, and how to wire one's braids into the latest and most fashionable styles as seen in fashion plates from France; they giggled over the courtships of their friends, designed elegant dresses for one another, and stayed up far too long after bedtime reading *The Monk* to one another by the light of a single shielded candle.

Mary would flirt with Meg's beaux in the parlor, when Madame's back was turned.

When she was home on Saturdays, she would stroll down to Cheapside to shop with Frances and Eliza, with Elizabeth if she was in town, and sometimes with Ann. Mary had learned her lesson and never lied to Mr. Sotheby again, though she found that she didn't feel quite right about the sapphire pendant and seldom wore it. Still, her father bought her other things, earbobs and slippers and gloves, as if deep in his heart he understood that he'd really sent her away to buy peace with his wife. Mary sensed the guilt that lay behind his unwillingness to see her cry, and occasionally used it, if there was something she really, really wanted . . . though whenever she did this, she always felt ashamed.

Sometimes after Nelson brought her back to Rose Hill on Sunday evenings, Mary would sit in her room and take her special things out of the little casket where she kept them: brooches, necklaces, handkerchiefs bordered in lace. Proof that her father loved her.

Hope that he loved her best of all.

Frances, at fourteen, had finished Ward's school and was already a belle, her fair hair dressed up in elaborate side-curls and serpentine plaits adorned with silk flowers from Sotheby's. As far as Mary could see, she did little but shop, and stroll, and chat with her friends, and sew dresses to wear at the dances held in the long salon above M'sieu Giron's confectionary. On those rare occasions when their father was home from the Legislature, he would shake his head and say,

"Now, a girl must be able to amuse her husband, and to raise intelligent sons for the nation," but Mary observed how Robert Todd would puff with pride when planters' sons like Nate Bodley or Young Duke Wickliffe would come calling.

And though there was nothing Mary liked better than to shop and stroll and chat with Frances and Elizabeth—nothing that excited and interested her more than the selection of lace for a pelerine, or of silk for a dancing-dress, or being made a fuss over by Mr. Sotheby or Mr. Fowler when she'd come into their stores—she loved, too, the peaceful stillness of the library of Rose Hill, away from the noise and confusion of too many children in too few rooms. There she could savor in peace the way Shakespeare's words sounded in her mind: *If I profane with my unworthiest hand / this holy shrine, the gentle fine is this / My lips, two blushing pilgrims ready stand / to smooth that rough touch with a tender kiss....*

She had to be careful, of course, not to speak of it too much—no gentleman liked a bluestocking—but she found great pleasure in being able to talk sensibly about Shakespeare if the subject arose.

Spring advanced and the dogwood bloomed. The high tide of summer transformed the hills to lush green, the shade of the thick groves to mysterious blue-black. Like the savor of burgoo against the sweetness of toffee, the social delights of dances and picnics were flavored with politics that were the heartbeat of the South, as men wrangled with the framework of power and law to shape and enable their quest for money and the comforts of life.

Henry Clay was running for President. An ardent Whig like Robert Todd, Ninian took Mary, Frances, and Elizabeth out to hear the candidates speak at a picnic at Trotter's Grove. Elizabeth joined at once with the other matrons, young and old, of Lexington, in directing their slaves to set out the tables and the food—cornbread, Brunswick stew, imported oysters, homemade jams—and Frances, who cared little who became President, gravitated at once to the young gentlemen who'd come to listen, but Mary found herself a place by the speakers' platform. Cheap draperies of red, white, and blue bunting adorned it; the American flag had had a couple of extra stars scootched into its blue field for Maine and Missouri, and looked a bit ragged and out of balance. Ninian, also maneuvering his way through the crowd to stand close, caught her eye and winked.

Mary had followed the campaign closely in the several journals available in Lexington, both Democrat and Whig, and wanted to hear what men from elsewhere in the state were saying about Clay's American System of public works and strong currency. But when she tried to edge closer, Elizabeth gestured to her to come to the food-tables.

"Really, Mary," she whispered, as soon as Mary came close. "You mustn't push yourself in among the men that way."

"I was close to Ninian," protested Mary. And then, when Elizabeth simply pursed her lips and handed her a dish of beans to set out, she added in annoyance, "I'm not going to flirt with him, if that's what's worrying you."

"The things you do say." Elizabeth's expression was that of a woman requesting a servant to remove a dead mouse from the soup tureen. "A gentleman never *seems* to mind anything a lady does, but what he *thinks* of a young lady who has so few qualms about unsexing herself is another matter. In any case," she added, "gentlemen are more comfortable talking politics *without* ladies present ... if you know what I mean."

Mary scowled rebelliously, but when she looked back in the direction of the platform, it was pretty clear to her what Elizabeth meant. She could hear Old Duke Wickliffe's voice rising in anger about the God-damned bill to forbid the importation of slaves to the state, see his son Young Duke lashing the air with his riding-whip. Cash Clay was squaring off with the bull-like young Nate Bodley, gesticulating furiously. By the sound of it, Nate—whose father owned Indian Branch, one of the wealthiest plantations in Fayette County—was already half drunk.

Before nightfall, thought Mary uneasily, somebody would call somebody out, or someone would end up thrashed with a cane behind the line of carriages where black grooms walked the blood-horses to be raced later in the afternoon. And the young ladies of her acquaintance, Frances and Meg, Eliza and Mary Jane and Isabelle, all clustered together, giggling at Arabella Richardson's jokes or crying out admiringly at Meg's new walking-dress of pleated jaconet, as if nothing more serious existed in all the world.

Don't they remember that Isabelle's brother KILLED Meg's brother three years ago, over a letter written to a newspaper? Mary wondered, puzzled and angry. *Don't they care who gets elected, who runs the nation?*

Of course, it didn't do for a girl to thrust herself in among the gentlemen once the talk got heated, for fear of hearing words no young lady should hear. But that didn't mean girls had to act like imbeciles, just get young men to like them.

She realized that the sun-dazzle in her eyes was growing brighter, that sections of leaves were disappearing from the chestnut trees, appearing and disappearing, as things do in dreams. Her stomach curled with dread. In a small voice she said, "I think I'm getting a headache," and Elizabeth's annoyance changed swiftly to her old protective sympathy.

"Maybe if you sit down in the carriage where it's shady it'll go off." She put her arm comfortingly around Mary's shoulders, though Mary knew perfectly well that her headaches never "went off."

She had had them, on and off, for a year or more; it seemed to her that since she'd begun having her monthlies they'd become more frequent, and worse. Sometimes Mammy Sally's remedies of bitter herbs would stave them off. More frequently nothing helped.

"Well, I'm not going back home," Frances hastened to put in. "You just sit still and be quiet, Mary." And as if to emphasize her words she fluttered off in the direction of Arabella and her cronies. Even in her agony, Mary felt a stab of furious resentment, that she could not be joining her as the center of the boys' attention. Wittier and quicker-tongued than the fairy-like Frances, she surreptitiously enjoyed the game of drawing beaux away from her sister.

It was like the knowledge that her father sent her more presents than he sent Frances or Ann.

"I'll get you a wet napkin to put on your eyes." Elizabeth guided Mary gently to the carriage, with clearly no intention of leaving the speaking either. "Ninian, I think I saw Dr. Warfield over near the tables. Do you think he might come and see Mary?"

By the time Ninian came to the carriage, with the gray-haired professor of obstetrics and surgery from the University in tow, old Nelson had fetched a glass of ginger-beer and had put up the hood of the barouche in a vain effort to approximate by shade the darkness that Mary's throbbing head craved. As Mary heard the voices approach, she heard Nelson offer, "I can take Miss Mary on home and be back in an hour, Miss Elizabeth."

"That's probably best," agreed Elizabeth.

And Dr. Warfield—whose daughter Mary Jane had been shyly slipping away all afternoon to speak to Cash Clay among the trees of the groves—asked, "How often does your sister have these nervous headaches, Mrs. Edwards?"

"Sometimes two or three a week. Sometimes she'll go a few weeks without one."

Old Dr. Warfield climbed into the carriage, making it rock like a ship in the storm and bringing Mary's lunch heaving back into her throat. She wanted to scream at him to go away, to leave her alone. . . . Elizabeth and Ninian climbed in also *(rock, sway, lurch!)*, Elizabeth taking her seat beside Mary and the two men opposite. It would have been, of course, completely improper for any man to have been in the carriage alone with her. "May I take your pulse, Miss Mary?"

Elizabeth turned down the cuff of Mary's glove; the medical man's gloved fingers felt warm on her icy wrist.

"Your sister is of a nervous disposition, is she not, Mrs. Edwards?" There wasn't a soul in town who hadn't heard of Mary's alternating charm and tantrums.

"Yes," replied Elizabeth, "very much so."

"And I believe Mr. Edwards told me that this is your little family politician?"

"She has a very lively mind." Much as Elizabeth might disapprove of Mary's unladylike zest for politics and study, she would never admit this to even so prominent an acquaintance as the professor.

Just let me alone! Mary wanted to scream at them, and began to weep as the hammering in her head increased. She opened her eyes a slit: Dr. Warfield looked like a buzzard, with unhealthy skin and a straggling beard. As she watched, half his head and a portion of his right shoulder disappeared into a fiery cloud of migraine light.

"That explains it," said the doctor wisely. "A female's constitution is far more nervous than a boy's would be. The entire system of the female is rooted in the nerves and the generative functions rather than in the higher organs of thought and reason. For this reason mental activity tends to overload and debilitate her, resulting in these headaches, which are much more characteristic of the female system than the male."

"But what can we do about them?" asked Ninian.

Her brother-in-law might be a blockhead about tariffs, thought Mary, but that was the first practical remark she'd heard concerning her headache from any white person that afternoon.

"Personally, I would recommend that she be bled, to lower her constitution. If bleeding does not relieve the pressure on the overactive nervous system we shall try a blister, to draw the heat away from her brain."

There's nothing wrong with my brain! Just take me home and leave me alone in the dark! Get Mammy Sally to make me some of her herbs....

But of course nothing would do for it but that Dr. Warfield and Ninian accompanied Mary and Elizabeth back to the house—and to Betsey, who was sent for and who was less than pleased about being obliged to leave the picnic and her friends to tend to a stepdaughter whom she half-suspected was putting on this show of pain simply to gain attention.

Mary was put to bed, swathed in her green-and-gold-flowered wrapper. Dr. Warfield came in with a china bleeding-bowl and a sharp little knife. He was brusque and rough-handed, his breath smelling of bourbon, and the blade gouged deep. In the stuffy, curtained bedroom the blood stank. Mary wept, wondering if she were going to die as her mother had died, but her headache didn't go away.

"Do you feel better, darling?" asked Elizabeth, and Mary had the good sense to nod. The last thing she wanted was a blister to draw the heat away from her brain.

"I'm afraid that as long as she is kept in school, she will run the risk of continuing to suffer in this fashion," she overheard Dr. Warfield say, outside the bedroom door, as Elizabeth made sure no chink of light came through the curtains and Ninian tucked her in with brotherly affection. "Education, and the mental overstimulation of attending a political speaking, invariably react thus on the female organism."

"Well, I know how much Mary loves school. . . ." Her father's voice. He must have ridden back from the political speaking too. He sounded doubtful, because it was true that the headaches had become much worse in the three months Mary had been at Mentelle's. But before Mary could do much more than think in panic, *Don't take me out of the school . . . !* Betsey's crisp voice cut in.

"We shall speak to Madame Mentelle about modifying Mary's course of study, but I see no reason why she cannot continue to attend. I've heard wonderful things of her there, and of course her French has improved tremendously."

Of course, thought Mary. *She doesn't want me here.*

She desperately hoped her father would come in and see her, maybe sit on the edge of the bed and hold her hand a little. But he didn't.

"We'll keep you informed of Mary's progress, Dr.

Warfield." Tongue click. "Now we really must be getting back—folks will wonder what's become of us...." The voices trailed away down the stairs.

Hooves and the jingle of carriage-harness in the street, dimly perceptible even through the shut curtains, the closed windows.

Mama wouldn't have left me alone, thought Mary, grief welling up in her, almost worse than the pain. *Mama wouldn't have sent me away—or made me share a room with her cousin.* She barely remembered her mother, barely remembered sitting on her lap, enfolded and safe, in the days before Levi came along. But the memory was precious. After Levi's birth—and then Ann's and George's—her mother had had little time to give to her. But what she had had, Elizabeth Parker Todd had given. As always when she felt sick and alone, Mary tried to picture what life would be like now if her mother had not been carried out of her room like that in the dead of night, never to return again.

The anger she felt made her head hurt worse, swamping her grief in pain.

After a little time soft bare feet creaked on the hall floor, and Mammy Sally came in, bearing a cup that smelled sharply and sweetly of hot ginger and sugar. Mary drank it thirstily, and lay back in the darkness while those warm strong hands unbraided her hair, gently brushed out the long, heavy curls. She whispered, "Thank you," and slipped over into sleep.

THAT WAS ALMOST THE LAST OCCASION ON WHICH MARY stayed in that small room. The following Saturday, when Nelson brought her home for dinner, her father announced that he had "closed the deal" on Palmentier's Tavern on Main Street, and would be converting it into a house for the family—he cast a significant eye at Betsey as he spoke, and she simpered in acknowledgment of what the novelist Mrs. Radclyffe would have called the "token of his affection" that currently swelled the front of her white lawn gown. *You didn't even ask us,* thought Mary resentfully, as Eliza gasped, "May I have my own room?" and Betsey heaved a visible sigh of relief.

"Now maybe we'll be able to entertain properly."

Robert Todd said quietly, "Now maybe my family can come and go from our own front door without crossing paths with coffles of Mr. Pullum's slaves."

And young Mr. Presby the tutor said, "Amen."

Mary glanced sharply at her father from beneath her lashes, then across at Elliot Presby, the theology student who hailed from some tiny rock-ribbed village in New England. Bespectacled, skinny, with a face like a saint who's just bitten a sour lemon, young Mr. Presby had little that was good to say about the South or Southerners, and on more than one occasion had reacted to Mary's teasing with sharp anger.

Above all he detested the institution of slavery, and looked upon all slaveholders—including Mary's father—with ill-concealed disapproval. When she was younger Mary had teased him mercilessly, but now she was more and more conscious herself of the brick-walled yard on the corner near her father's house, of the men and women who sat on benches under Pullum's awnings out front, with chains around their ankles....

And of old Nelson's silence when he drove her past the place on the way to and from Rose Hill.

Cash Clay had returned from his year at Yale an abolitionist, afire to end slavery, or at least forbid the importation of more slaves to Kentucky. According to Frances, after Mary had left the political-speaking Nate Bodley had attempted to cane Cash over it.

Of course it isn't the same with our people, thought Mary, watching as Pendleton circulated the table with a platter of boiled ham. The darkies were slaves, yes, in that they were legally her father's property—or more properly Granny Parker's property—but she knew he treated them well. Slavery in Kentucky wasn't at all like slavery in the deeper South. She'd been in and out of the kitchen all her life, listening to Nelson tell his stories, or watching Mammy Sally make her custards for the children, as lovingly as if they were her own.

Her father would never sell Nelson or Mammy Sally or Jane or even grumpy old Chaney. They were part of the family.

And where would they go if they didn't live with us? That was something that had always bothered her about Cash's wild insistence that all slaves be freed immediately, for their own good and that of the owners' souls. *What would they do? Who would take care of them?*

Then she thought, *If we move down to Palmentier's Tavern, it will be harder for Jane and Saul to meet.* It was only a few streets up from Main Street to Granny Parker's big house, of course; but she knew Granny Parker was strict about keeping her people at their duties, as was Betsey.

And she, Mary, had been consulted about the move no more than had been the slaves.

Why should I care? she wondered, as Nelson drove her back to Rose Hill early Monday morning, with the horses' breath and her own a faint mist in the chill. *It isn't as if it were my home anymore.* She had shared a bed with Eliza, because Ann had taken over her old bed. Though they all laughed and giggled as they always did when she came home, she felt like an interloper. Ann and Eliza had to move their things around to admit her, cheerfully as they always did. But she felt, as she always felt, that things went on without her. That if she did not return, she would not be much missed.

Still, the thought of complete strangers sleeping in that bedroom, of another family reading the newspaper by lamplight in the study where she had read on those rare, precious evenings with her father, filled her with desolation. As if she were invisible, and no one cared if she lived or died. She stayed away from the house on the Saturday when the furniture was moved, joining instead with Meg and the Trotter sisters, with Mary Jane and her sisters Julia and Caroline, and her other friends from Ward's, to gather hickory-nuts in the woods along the Richmond Pike.

It was a warm day at summer's end. The leaves of the maples had begun to turn and the air within the woods felt heavy, mysterious with the coming of the year's change. The girls were joined by several of Meg's numerous beaux—Nate Bodley, Jim Rollins, Buck Loveridge, and a few others, sons of the local planters or the gentlemen of the town—and there was a great deal of laughter and chasing around the laurel thickets among the trees, under the benevolent eye of Isabelle's widowed Aunt Catherine. Mary, with her curls bobbing under a new hat of pink straw and a new dress of pink-sprig voile, flirted with Nate and let him hold in his handkerchief the nuts she gathered, a curiously exhilarating experience. In the dappled green light his handsome face looked different, gentler than it did when she'd seen him among the cronies at the political speakings. His brown eyes caressed her when he called her "Miss Mary," and she realized, for the first time in her young life, that something might lie beyond flirting.

That instead of the delight in being the center of attention in a ring of young men held by her saucy wit, she might draw to her a single man, who would love her as Saul loved Jane.

It was a revelation to her, and one that confused her, as she had lately been confused by the stirrings in her body of feelings she didn't understand. She pulled her hands away from Nate and he chased her, laughing, through the sun-dappled woods.

They came out of the undergrowth to see Cash Clay sitting alone in the clearing, his long legs stretched out on the grass, hulling the hickory-nuts the others had gathered, striking them on an outcrop of rock. Nate and Mary stopped, unseen, for at that same moment Mary Jane came into the clearing by herself, her bonnet gone, her fair hair undone and lying over her shoulders. She was looping it up and working a hair-pin into it when she saw Cash; Mary caught Nate by the sleeve and tugged him deeper into the laurel, touching a finger to her lips. Nate nodded, his eyes bright. He knew, as Mary knew, the trouble Cash had in getting a word alone with Mary Jane. Since Cash's return from Yale as a new-fledged abolitionist ("He'll get over it," Nate had sighed. "With Cash it's always some damn thing"), Dr. Warfield had barely been able to tolerate the young man's presence in his house.

By all rules of propriety, of course, Mary Jane should have gone immediately to seek the others, for even the slaves had left to set up the picnic-baskets by the spring. Betsey—and certainly Mary Jane's mother, the formidable Maria Warfield—were quite clear on what a young lady must and must not do. Watching her, Mary thought, *Go to him!* As if she watched a play—like reading *Twelfth Night* and whispering to Viola, *Tell him who you are!*

And slowly, Mary Jane crossed the clearing, her long hair falling unnoticed down over her shoulders again, and stood above Cash, who held out his hand to her, and moved his long legs aside. She hesitated for an endless moment, then settled beside him, her butter-yellow skirts billowing as she sank down, covering his shins in a froth of tucking and lace. Nate's hand closed around Mary's behind the screening laurels, and she was suddenly, profoundly conscious of the warmth of his grip, the soft whisper of his breath on her hair. Like actors in the green-and-golden proscenium of the glade, Cash laid his hands on either side of Mary Jane's face and kissed her; her own hands closed briefly, hungrily, on his arms.

Then quickly she was on her feet, and hurrying away.

CASH AND MARY JANE WERE MARRIED IN FEBRUARY, AT DR. Warfield's house in Lexington near the University. For two days before, there had been whispers, panic, excitement. Another of Mary Jane's suitors had sent a letter to Mary Jane—which her mother had then passed along to Cash for reasons best known to herself—calling Cash a rake, an abolitionist, and a traitor, and Cash had ridden down to Louisville and publicly caned the man. The result, predictably, was a duel, to be fought on the eve of the wedding.

"Cash is really going to *fight*?" demanded Mary, aghast, when she and Elizabeth went to call on Mary Jane on the afternoon before. Elizabeth would be Mary Jane's matron of honor. They'd found the distraught bride with her sister and four other friends, pacing the parlor and fighting not to weep.

"What else can he do?" demanded Bella Richardson, widening her long-lashed violet eyes. "After the things Dr. Declarey called him in that letter . . ."

"And getting himself killed is going to help Mary Jane?" retorted Mary. She remembered how her friend had looked up at Cash in the clearing in that hazy autumn light, the way she'd held his arms, wanting and yet afraid. On the back of the parlor sofa, where the light from the bow-window fell, Mary Jane's bridal gown lay in a cascade of ivory-colored silk and point-lace. Mary felt sick at the thought of not knowing whether in the morning she would put on that dress, or black mourning for what was never to be.

"It's a matter of honor," protested Bella. "I couldn't marry a man who would not fight for his honor."

"That's the stupidest thing I've ever heard," snapped Mary, rounding on her fiercely, and Elizabeth said, *"Hush!"*

Elizabeth put her arms around Mary Jane, almost forced her to sit in one of the parlor chairs. Mary Jane was visibly trembling, her face waxen, but she held herself calm. In her place Mary knew too well that she herself would be in hysterics. Meg Wickliffe knelt beside the chair, gripping Mary Jane's hands. Not speaking the name of the brother who had been shot.

"The matter is in God's hands," said Elizabeth quietly. "Very often in such affairs no one is hurt at all."

Meg turned her face away.

But in the morning Cash appeared at McChord's Presbyterian Church, muddy from his hard ride back from

Louisville but otherwise none the worse for wear. The matter vanished as if it had never been, save for the tears Mary saw in Mary Jane's eyes, and the way she trembled as she stood at the altar with her dark-haired, savage bridegroom. Mary, just turned fourteen and clothed in her own new status as a budding belle, wondered if she were the only person still troubled by the implications of the duel. At the reception in the Warfield parlor afterwards, she watched Mary Jane and her friends laugh and chatter and felt as alien from them as if they were characters in some fantastic book. *Isn't anyone going to ask Mary Jane if she has second thoughts about marrying Cash?* From the group of men around the punch-bowl she heard Cash's booming voice:

"...of course the news had spread of the duel, and the whole state had turned out to watch, it seemed like—Lord, it was like a fair! So I said to Declarey..."

Could you marry a man who would stake his life—and your happiness—on a letter written in anger, that should simply have been put on the fire?

Her eyes traveled the room, picking out the way Elizabeth touched Ninian's sleeve as she murmured something to him; the way Mary Jane's gaze turned, again and again, in mingled love and pain, toward Cash's dark, tousled head among the crowd around the punch-bowl. She saw Nate Bodley in the crowd, and saw how he turned also to scan the big double-parlor...seeking her? She remembered the way he'd taken her own hands in the woods, the whisper of his breath on her hair. She had dreamed last night that she was Mary Jane, sinking down to be kissed in the green and gold of the glade.

Nate had come often to Rose Hill in the evenings, when the older girls would sit in the parlor or, in warm weather, on the pillared porch, exchanging shy commonplaces with the sons of planters, the students at the University. He'd laughed uproariously with the rest at Mary's jokes and witticisms, and had shown a marked disposition to seek the chair beside hers.

I will marry, Mary reflected again. The feelings stirred that day in the woods had changed the words' meaning for her. It had always been, *I will marry someday, when I'm grown. . . .*

But she was grown, or close to it. She'd coaxed a new dress from her father for today, white tarlatan that rustled and whispered with silvery sweetness, the sleeves so wide they were held out with hoops and everything trimmed with green velvet ribbons. More and more young men were riding out to Rose Hill to see her, and she had become adept at the secret language of sidelong glances and gentle laughter, of kisses promised or withheld.

But it came to her that this was more than a pleasant game, a way to collect beaux as tokens of her beauty and to score off her sisters. It was a hunt, to find a husband. To not be an old maid, scorned and pitied by all.

To hear Meg talk, or Bella or Isabelle, any husband was better than having people whisper about you in that sweetly hateful way, and urge their brothers or cousins to dance with you so you wouldn't be a wall-flower.

Even a husband who would leave you a widow on your wedding-day because some other man called him an abolitionist in a private letter that was intended for no one's eyes but yours.

There was Nate of course, whose quest for her seemed to have been sidetracked by a promising discussion of the proposed railroad between Lexington and Frankfort. A golden Hercules, and well-off—stupid as a brick, Mary thought, and not likely to get anywhere in the world except to be a slave-owner and raise tobacco and horses.

When I marry, she decided, *it will have to be to a man who's going somewhere. A man like Father, or Mr. Clay.*

Her old jest with Mr. Clay, about marrying a man who would be President of the United States, returned to her. Naturally there was no way of guaranteeing that, though it would be intensely gratifying to stand at the center of power, to shine as first among all the women of the land. But it occurred to her that marriage to someone who just stayed at home and minded his slaves and his business would be appallingly dull.

And what if I don't want to get married at all? She thought of Betsey, always pregnant, more and more frequently ill, confined to the quiet of her room. *What if by the time I'm nineteen*—the last possible outpost of belle-hood before people started calling you an old maid—*I haven't met anyone I love the way Mary Jane loves Cash, the way Elizabeth loves Ninian or Jane loves Saul! What if I don't meet someone like that at all? What then?*

As soon as Cash and Mary Jane left in the carriage for Crab Orchard Springs for their wedding-trip, Mary took the opportunity to walk home with Elizabeth, Frances, Eliza, and Ann. There would be dancing that night, and while the men lingered over the punch-bowl and their cigars the girls retreated, to change clothes and have a beauty-nap, for the dancing would last most of the night. The other girls' chatter saved Mary from having to talk. She felt troubled and lonely, doubly so because she had never felt completely at home in the tall-fronted brick house on Main Street.

The other girls went rustling up the stairs, but Mary passed through the dining-room and pantry to the big kitchen in the back of the house, where she knew the servants would be gathered, taking advantage of the warmth there on this icy day and also of the fact that the family was out.

But coming into the pantry she saw Nelson and Pendleton standing in the kitchen door, and beyond them, heard the sound of a woman weeping.

"What is it?" Mary slipped between the two men and into the brick-floored room. "What's wrong?"

Nelson turned, and Mary saw that his eyes burned with impotent rage. Past him in the kitchen Jane sat huddled on a stool beside the big brick hearth, her face buried in her hands. Mammy Sally held her, rocked her gently, tears running down her face.

Softly, Nelson said, "Your Granny Parker took Saul to Mr. Pullum, to help your Uncle David out for having backed a

bill for one of his friends. Saul's gone. Taken away with a coffle for Louisville this morning."

"Saul . . ." Mary fell back a step. After the biting air of the
street the kitchen was warm, the smell of vanilla and steaming cider incongruously sweet. Jane leaned her head back
against Mammy Sally's shoulder, still hugging herself, as if
without the binding strength of the older woman's arms her
heart would tear itself out of her ribcage and flee to some
land where things like this didn't happen. Where a man
couldn't be taken away and sold just to raise a little extra cash,
without anyone once asking if he had family or loved ones.

Saul was gone, just like that. Without warning, without
good-by.

Not because of some stupid dispute about honor, thought
Mary, that he would have had the choice to take up or leave
alone. But because it suited her grandmother to help out
Uncle David, and this was the quickest and easiest way.

Marriage, and honor, and sapphire pendants, and not being an old maid—even having a stepmother who sent one
away from home for putting spiders in her bed—suddenly
seemed insults to the silent agony on Jane's face. The petty
luxuries of the free.

Mary gathered up her skirts and went quietly back
through the pantry, and up the stairs.

⚜

CHAPTER EIGHT

AFTER CASH'S WEDDING, MARY UNDERSTOOD THERE WERE two worlds in Lexington. She had always been aware of the division between them, but had slipped back and forth across it with the blithe malleability of a child, to whom the fairies in the garden are as real as the horses in the stable. Besides the storybook tales of King Arthur and his knights, and the heroes of Troy, Mary had grown up on Nelson's narrations of talking foxes and clever rabbits and of little boys and their conjure-wise grannies; of the Platt-Eye Devil who waited for bad children in the dark and of the jay-bird who'd fly to Hell every Friday night to tell Satan of little girls' iniquities.

Everyone always said that slavery in Kentucky "wasn't like it was deeper south," and that, to Mary's mind, had made it all right.

When Granny Parker sold Saul, the division between the worlds sharpened into focus for her: how narrow the gap was, and how abysmally deep.

The world of the whites was itself divided into two: the world of men, of politics, of speculation for new lands opening in the West, of horse-racing and money-making and the casual, noisy, whiskey-smelling friendships of men; and the world of women. Mary wasn't sure which she liked best. She reveled in gossip, in shopping, in flirtations on the porch of Rose Hill and beautiful new dresses—she'd grown adept at coaxing promises from her father, and at holding him to them, if necessary, with tears. She loved afternoon-calls and the intricate ritual of who was at home to whom and who left cards on whom. But she understood that the ultimate power lay with the men.

And the men, who would gallantly offer their arms to

help women cross puddles that they assumed the women didn't have the brains to walk around, guarded their power jealously. To get drunk, to shoot or thrash one another, to whip any darky who needed it or gamble the fortunes on which their families depended, were prerogatives not to be shared with addlepated females or Northerners like Mr. Presby who couldn't comprehend what things were like in the South.

Yet it was also a world of enchantment, of sultry evenings on the porch listening to the cry of the crickets, a world of taffy-pulls and dances in the big ballroom above Giron's Confectionary. A world of writing letters to friends and brushing Meg's hair and frantically trying to sneak time to get back to the literary adventures of the blameless Isabelle and her flight from the loathsome and doomed Duke Manfred . . .

A world of sweet peacefulness where day succeeded quiet day, and season gentle season, in a land where the rules were always clear—if sometimes byzantine and never spoken— and people could be counted on.

On the other side of that narrow abyss lay the world of kitchens, backyards, and dusty alleys in the deep shade of elm-trees, refuges for whoever could get away from their unceasing work for a quick chat with friends who might disappear tomorrow. It was a world of back-fences and the tiny economies of vegetable-plots, fish-hooks, second-run coffee-grounds, and dresses too worn for "the missus" to want anymore.

A world where there was no power, and no redress. Ever.

For weeks after Saul's departure Mary thought of him. She would see him in her mind, chained to the deck of the steamboat going down the Ohio to the Mississippi, and down the Mississippi to New Orleans, and thence to harsh labor and early death in the sugar and cotton lands of the deeper South. In her dreams he would gaze silently at the dark walls of trees gliding past, and Mary would sometimes hear the wailing slave-songs that would drift from behind the brick walls of Pullum's slave-yard.

"I'm goin' away to New Orleans,
  Good-by, my love, good-by,
  I'm goin' away to New Orleans,
  Good-by, my love, good-by,
  Oh, let her go by."

Papa would never sell any of our people, she thought, and most of
the time truly believed it. But in fact, Mammy Sally and
Nelson and Chaney and Pendleton belonged, not to her father, but to Granny Parker. As Saul had done. When that
thought came to her, Mary would close her eyes in panic,
her heart hammering at the fear of losing her friends.

At the idea of her friends losing their homes and each
other, weeping as Jane had wept.

And there was nothing she could do about it, as there had
been nothing she could ever do about her mother's death.

When Cash came back from Crab Orchard Springs with
Mary Jane, Robert Todd gave a reception for the newlyweds
at the new Main Street house. At this party Mary took Cash
aside and asked, *"Are* you an abolitionist, Cash?" She'd heard
the word bandied about a great deal, usually as a deadly insult. Even her father would argue that, though opposed to
slavery in principle as Mr. Clay was, he was not an abolitionist. Cash looked down at her with his arms folded, his piercing eyes grave.

He said, "Yes, I am."

"But you own slaves." He had been left fatherless young,
at sixteen inheriting the plantation of White Hall, where
they grew tobacco and hemp.

"That will only be until I can establish my brothers in
some profession where they can make their own way, and
until I can establish myself in a way that will not do injustice
to Mary Jane." He glanced across the spacious double-parlor
that had once been the common-room of Palmentier's
Tavern. Mary Jane, clothed in the brighter colors and more
modish styles of a young wife, laughed with her friends as if
she had never felt fear in her life. The company overflowed

the double-parlor and filled the family parlor across the hall, and the dining-room beyond that. "Then I will free the people whom my father left to me—and in freeing them, will free myself."

Mary was quiet. She had heard this before, from Elliot Presby—and had gotten into screaming arguments with the tutor on the strength of it. But from Cash it was different. Cash *did* understand the South, as the sanctimonious young New Englander never could.

"People in this country talk about slavery as if it were a matter of choice," Cash went on. "Like the decision whether or not to keep a carriage, or whether to become a Methodist or a Baptist. We have lived with it so long that it seems like that to us, and not what it really is. Not what Mr. Lloyd Garrison has shown us—showed *me,* when I went to hear him speak at Yale—that it is."

Cash's voice had grown grave, without his usual edge of theatrical anger. "And it is a sin, Mary. It is an evil, the most wicked of injustices, perpetrated and carried on simply because it is profitable to *us* to buy and sell black men and make them do work for us. Garrison describes it for what it is, and describes slaveholders—myself still numbered among them—for what they—*we*—really are: oppressors beside whom Herod and the Pharaoh of Egypt were fiddling amateurs. It cannot be allowed to continue."

A few days later Cash rode out to Rose Hill in the evening, at the time when young gentlemen customarily called on the girls. In warm weather, chairs would be brought out onto the lawn beneath the chestnut-trees, for Madame frowned on such visits, but in the bitter cold of early spring she relented, and admitted them to the fire-warmed parlor. There she would take out her violin and play, to the accompaniment of her daughter Marie on the piano. Most of the young gentlemen were terrified of her.

Madame had long ago ceased to frighten Mary. When the school-day was done and the day-students went home,

Madame and her husband seemed more human, like parents to the handful of boarding-students. Evenings in the big parlor were like the family that Mary had always wished she had; they made up, in part, for the desolation she still felt each time she left her father's house.

That evening Cash brought her a note from Mary Jane, a commonplace invitation to tea the following week. When Mary walked him out to the porch, he slipped her a closely folded packet of papers: "Mr. Garrison's newspaper, *The Liberator*," he whispered. "Read it yourself, Mary, and see if you do not agree with us, that slavery is a moral issue, and not merely a question of white man's property and white man's law."

She stowed the papers under her mattress, where she was fairly certain no one would find them. The girls made up their own beds each morning, and changed their own sheets on Tuesday nights, the linen fresh-washed and fresh-pressed by Dulcie and Caro. It did not seem, thought Mary, that you could get away from slaves. Once she'd read *The Liberator*, tucked between the pages of *A Young Lady's History of the United States*, it seemed to her that slaves were everywhere, in every corner of Lexington.

They did all the laundry. They cut all the wood, for kitchen fires, bedroom fires, heating water to wash clothing and dishes. They ironed sheets and napkins in every house she knew of, from the wealthy plantations like the Wickliffes' Glendower and Dr. Warfield's The Meadows to houses like her father's and Granny Parker's. They worked on road-gangs, cutting trees and leveling grades so that wagons could come and go from Louisville on the river, taking hemp and tobacco down to market or hauling up the *batiste de soie* and *gros de Naples*, the feathers and ribbons and buttons of mother-of-pearl that made shopping-expeditions in Cheapside so entrancing. They milked everyone's cows and shoveled out everyone's stables; they spread the manure on everyone's gardens so that roses and carrots and potatoes would grow.

She realized she didn't know anyone—except old Solly, the town drunk and gravedigger—who didn't own a slave.

Yet it was clear to her, reading Mr. Garrison's impassioned writings, that the owning of slaves, the selling of slaves, did more than just make a mockery of the liberty that the United States had claimed as a birthright in separating from England. It was evil in and of itself, in the eternal eyes of God. The men who owned other men were tyrants, the men who sold other men were kidnappers, the men who punished other men for not accepting bondage as their lot were no better than robbers who beat their victims. Garrison's words burned her, left her breathless and deeply troubled.

Because she knew in her heart that they were true. But if she accepted them, she understood that she would have to accept that her father was a tyrant and kidnapper. That Mr. Clay, whom she both admired and loved, was, in Garrison's words, "a patriotic hypocrite, a fustian declaimer of liberty, a highway robber and a murderer."

Then she would look around her at the friends chatting of beaux and dresses—good people, dear and sweet (except maybe Arabella Richardson)—and she wouldn't know what to feel or think.

She would have liked to talk to her father about this, but on those Saturdays and Sundays when she returned to the Main Street house, her father, if he was home at all, was always surrounded by family: always talking to Ninian—who frequently came up with Elizabeth from Walnut Hill if the couple weren't staying outright at the Main Street house for a few weeks—or admonishing Levi and George, or playing with little Margaret, little Sam, or baby David. . . . Or if he were doing none of those things, Betsey was there, and Mary felt robbed and abandoned all over again.

Even a new pair of slippers or the promise of a new dress did not entirely make up for the ache—and confusion—in her heart.

Nor could she bring the matter up to M'sieu Mentelle without opening the subject of where she'd gotten hold of copies of *The Liberator.* No young lady at Rose Hill was permitted to receive correspondence that had not been scrutinized by Madame. The parents of her boarders expected her to be aware of such things. And in any case the rule about speaking only French within the house was strict, and Mary did not feel up to discussing "the popular fury against the advocates of bleeding humanity" in French.

One Saturday evening in the summer of her second year at Mentelle's—1833—Mary found her chance. Supper at the Main Street house was done—a reduced group around her father's table, for Ninian had received his law degree not long ago, and had taken Elizabeth north to his family home in Springfield, Illinois, leaving Mary bereft. Mr. Presby had returned to Boston to visit his family, and the Todds had begun to make plans to retreat to Crab Orchard Springs—or perhaps to Betsey's small country house, Buena Vista, five miles outside town, as soon as Mary was out of school for the summer.

Mary herself felt depressed and strange, as if she were going to have a headache later. She had had a nightmare the night before, about the town being flooded with water that shone ghastly green with poison, and the thunderclouds building over the mountains filled her with uneasy dread.

After supper she'd followed her father out onto the rear porch that overlooked the small formal garden that was Betsey's pride, and beyond it the woodland that bordered the stream at the rear of the property. In buying Palmentier's, Robert Todd had also purchased the three town lots surrounding it—practically the only vacant lots remaining near the center of Lexington—so that this green and pleasant prospect would remain his.

This evening he sat smoking in the gloom, listening to the muted burble of the creek. Betsey had retreated early to bed with a headache—she was, Mary suspected, increasing yet again—and Mary herself shivered at the far-off sounds of thunder.

But she sat on one of the cane-bottomed chairs beside her

father, and said, "Is Mr. Clay going to run for President again, when Mr. Jackson's term is up?"

Her father grinned, and pinched her cheek. "Always the little politician, eh?" He sighed. "Maybe. Jackson's a sick old man. Even if he could, I don't think he'd court accusations of being a dictator by running for a third time when Washington was content with only two."

"Mr. Clay is against slavery, isn't he, Papa?" Mary leaned against her father's arm, taking comfort in his bulk and size, in the scent of tobacco and Macassar oil and horses, the faint sweaty smell of manhood in his coat. "Yet he owns slaves, the way you do."

Her father sighed again. "A man can be against slavery and still not be a crazy abolitionist, Molly," he said. The darkness, broken only by the faint glow of light from the kitchen windows, seemed to bring them closer; Mary treasured the delicious quiet of the moment, the man-to-man matter-of-factness of her father's voice as he spoke to her. Like a woman and a friend, not like a child.

A closeness better than all the sapphire pendants in the world.

"Slavery is evil. I don't think you can argue that. But simply turning all the slaves loose would bring down a greater evil, in terms of poverty, and chaos, and lawlessness. Darkies aren't like you and me, daughter. They don't understand principles—you know how you have to keep instructions to Chaney or Judy very simple, if you're going to get anything like what you're asking for—and in most ways they're like children. Even a smart darky like Jane isn't more than a few generations removed from the jungle, you know. It wouldn't be any kindness to them to turn them loose to fend for themselves, any more than it would be to let loose your sister Frances's pet canary in the woods."

Thunder rumbled above the hills. The metallic drumming of the cicadas in the trees seemed to accentuate the heat and closeness of the dark. Mary shivered, hating the electric feel of the air that pressed so desperately on her skull, as if the lightning itself flickered in her brain. Nelson emerged from a side door, descended the back steps, and crossed through the garden to the coach house, in whose attic he and Pendleton had their rooms while the women slaves slept above the kitchen. "But couldn't they do their same jobs at wages?"

He shook his head. "It doesn't work that way, sweetheart. No planter could make a profit if he had to pay wages, and if the wages were low the darkies would go looking for higher ones, and drive white men out of work. No, Mr. Clay's scheme is best. You don't free the Negro race until you're able to provide a home for them. Either colonize them out in the West beyond the Mississippi—which would certainly spark problems with the Indians or the Spanish—or set up colonies for them in Africa, where the benefits of what they've learned in this country will gradually civilize the heathen tribes around them."

"Wouldn't that be like letting loose a canary in the woods?" asked Mary.

"Of course it would, baby." Her father patted her gently, and glanced longingly at the cigar he'd stamped out the moment Mary had appeared in the dark door to the house. "That's why we have to do this slowly. It's only the abolitionists who want to rush pell-mell into things, to solve the problem *their* way, in *their* time, the minute they think they see a solution. They're not thinking about the consequences, to the country or to the darkies themselves."

Lightning leaped white across the sky, blanching the leaves of the chestnut-trees. Mary screamed—at the same moment the trees bent in the rushing wind, as if reaching for the walls of the house, and thunder ripped the darkness that dropped like a smothering blanket in the lightning's wake. Trembling, she retreated to the house as a second blast of lightning split the night, and torrents of rain began to fall. Her head aching in earnest, she ran up the stairs to the guest-room, flung herself fully clothed on the bed, covered her head with the pillow so she would not hear.

But she did hear. And she saw, through the pillow and her

shut eyelids, the white blasts of lightning that ripsawed the night. She heard, too, the hammering of the rain, until it seemed to her that the house and the whole town would wash away. Once she crept from her bed and looked out the window, to see the spring at the bottom of the garden overflowing, its waters spilling everywhere, glittering in the lightning's blue flare. She remembered her dream, of overspilling water bringing poison, bringing death.

The following day, Sunday, the bells of McChord's Church were tolling. Her father came in while the family was seated at breakfast and said, "That was Jim Rollins outside, coming up from the University. There's a woman down on Water Street, where the Town Branch flooded last night, down sick. They're saying it's cholera."

Betsey clicked her tongue. "Nonsense. They can't tell so quickly."

But Mary glanced over at Eliza, cold terror gripping her. Last summer's newspapers had been filled with reports of the cholera that had killed thousands in New York and New Orleans, like the ravenous plagues of medieval Europe. Frances set down her spoon rather quickly, and said, "I know Mary has a few weeks of school yet, but if some of us could go down to Crab Orchard Springs early this year she could join us as soon as she's done."

And little Margaret, glancing from face to face of her shaken seniors, asked, "What's cholera?"

"It's a sickness, sweetheart." Betsey stroked her eldest daughter's blond curls. "A sickness that only bad people and poor people get."

"Aunt Hannah wasn't bad, or poor," pointed out Mary, "and she died of it last year." Betsey looked daggers at her, but Mary turned to her father, whose sister Aunt Hannah had been. He didn't admonish her for contradicting her stepmother.

Instead he said, "I think I'll just ride over to the University, and see what they're saying at the Medical College. I won't be long—and I think it's probably best if no one goes outside for now."

Just before dinner he was back, with the news that ten other cases of cholera had been reported in the town. Nelson was sent to the market to buy tar and lime: "The disease seems to spread through the night air, according to Dr. Warfield," said Robert Todd, to his wife and children assembled in the family parlor. "Until we can get packed, and get out of town, I think the safest thing we can do is stay indoors, keep the windows shut, spread lime on all the windowsills and thresholds and burn tar to cleanse the air. I think the Mentelles will understand if you leave school a few weeks early this term, Molly," he added, glancing over at Mary. "I understand the air is better in Crab Orchard Springs. If we leave now, we can probably get a cabin there, until the epidemic is over."

But the next morning Mary came down to breakfast to hushed whispers and bad-news voices. "Pendleton is sick," her father told her. "We've got him isolated and I've called Grant Shelby to take a look at him"—Grant Shelby was the local veterinarian, who also handled slaves—"but Mammy Sally says it looks like the cholera, and from what I've seen I agree with her. I'm afraid there's no question of leaving town now—or of leaving this house."

There followed three of the most nightmarish weeks Mary had spent in her life. The summer's heat lay on the city like a soaked blanket. The air was unbreathable from the white streaks of lime on every window- and doorsill, and from the flambeaux of tar that Nelson made up and burned all around the house. In the dark of the shuttered house the smells thickened daily, hourly, in every stuffy, shadowy room. Mary felt the stink of it would never leave her throat. Yet she was forbidden to so much as venture out into the yard, though Betsey crossed back and forth to the coach house a dozen times a day, to help with Pendleton's nursing.

Mary herself felt very little fear that she would catch the disease. She feared it far less than she feared lightning-storms, or the silence that lay over the stricken town. Generally the creak of wagons and carriages, the clop of hooves and clamor of voices from Main Street, reached to every corner of the big house, shutters or no shutters. Now Lexington was silent, and under the summer's heat the only sounds that could be heard through the shutters were the occasional creak of a single wagon passing, or the tolling of a funeral bell. If she had no fear for herself, she was frantic with fear that Frances, or Ann, or Eliza would come down sick, or that, when the quarantine was over, she would hear the news that Mary Jane or Meg or Nate Bodley was dead. Every night when she prayed—as Granny Parker had instructed her from earliest childhood—she added to the rote litany of OurFather-WhoArtinHeaven...the fervent request that her friends be spared.

But she had no sense that God heard her. The last time that she had truly petitioned God was when she was six, that her mother return to comfort her, for she needed her so.

God apparently had not heard.

Nearly as bad as the smells was David's crying, which went on and on, sawing at the terrible silence. That, and the fact that as fruits and vegetables were thought by some to cause the disease, in the height of the season of peaches and mulberries the family lived on beaten biscuits and beef tea. After the first week there was no more newspaper, for so many of the men who printed it were either sick or tending the sick in makeshift hospitals. Betsey, wraith-thin, took to her own bed with exhaustion, and was snappish and impatient, and Robert Todd spent most of his days at her side. Mary kept to the semi-dark of her shuttered bedroom, reading books from her father's library to shut out her fears, or peering through the chinks in the shutters to watch the dead-carts rumble by below. One afternoon the noise of clumping and thumping in the hall brought her to the door, and she saw her father and Nelson bringing trunks down the attic stairs.

"What is it?" she asked. "What's happening?"

"Old Solly the gravedigger's outside," said Nelson. "He's asking for whatever trunks and boxes folks have, since the coffin makers can't make enough coffins for those that're dead."

Shoulder to shoulder in the lamplight, both men were dirty and dusty, shirtsleeved and daubed with the smuts of burned tar: black man and white man, of the same age, in the same household, feeling the same fear—helping others as well as they could. Mary opened doors for them and helped them maneuver the heavy trunks down the stairs, with a sense of seeing the front-parlor world of the whites, the shadow-world of the back alleys and kitchen-yards, merge....

Do men like Papa and Dr. Warfield think they're going somewhere different than Pendleton and Nelson when they die?

Pendleton recovered, though he was weeks in bed and lost a good thirty pounds. By July the funeral-bells had quit tolling, and Robert Todd packed up his family and took them, belatedly, to Crab Orchard Springs. Later Mary heard that five hundred people had died in Lexington, including half the patients at the lunatic asylum that stood beside the University.

COMING BACK THAT FALL TO LEXINGTON, MARY HAD THE same unsettled feeling that she had had at Mary Jane's wedding: a sense that fear and upheaval were all being swept tidily away out of sight. Fate had asked questions about the two dusty men bringing trunks down from the attic, and those questions were put aside unanswered. White men and black men had died, but when the shadow of death withdrew, business at Pullum's Exchange revived more quickly than at any other establishment in town. When Mary would go down to the perfumers and milliners on Cheapside with Frances or Mary Jane, she would see the hickory whipping-post beside the Courthouse, the place where disobedient slaves were chained and flogged, and she would sometimes look at her companions and think, *Don't you see? Don't you understand?*

But how could they, when she didn't really understand herself? All the argument that year was about the National Bank, and Andrew Jackson's iniquities, and the takeover of Indian lands in the West. Perhaps her father and Mr. Clay were right, she thought, and freedom was something to be given to the darkies only with due care, and not handed out rashly. . . .

But the sight of slavery still sickened her.

One night shortly after the family's return, just before Mary was to go back to Mentelle's, she was waked again by the distant rumble of thunder. Her sleep was never sound, and some nights she would lie awake until nearly dawn, listening to the soft breathing of Eliza and Ann, whose room she shared in summer so that the guest room could be kept ready for visitors. Neither of the other girls stirred. For a time Mary lay silent, listening to the slow ticking of the clock in the hall and wondering what time it was and what had wakened her. . . .

Voices, she thought. Voices, and the sound of a door opening in the yard.

Silently, she slipped out of her low trundle-bed. The night was hot, the smooth old wood of the floor cool under her feet as she stole to the bedroom door and out into the hall. The door was a bone of contention between herself and the other two girls, for since childhood Mary had been unable to endure an open door—even of a closet or armoire—in a room where she slept. She opened it now, and slipped into the upstairs hall, knowing that if she opened the bedroom shutters they would awaken, too.

Moving by touch in the dark she unlatched the shutters of the window in the hall. There was no light in the yard below, but by the moon's gleam she could see figures moving at the bottom of the high kitchen stairs. Mammy Sally, Mary thought, identifying the woman's figure though she wasn't wearing the headrag that kept kitchen soot and grease out of the hair of the women servants. And the tall man with short-cropped silver hair could be no one other than Nelson. They faded back into the shadows of the wall, but having seen them, Mary could see them still.

Waiting.

Curious, and wide-awake, Mary eased the shutter back into its place. She knew she ought to go back into the bedroom for a wrapper or a shawl—Betsey had repeated over and over that for a lady to move about in her nightgown was only a half-step above walking about naked—but to do so would risk waking Eliza and Ann. Besides, Mary frequently made surreptitious nocturnal expeditions to the outhouse clothed only in her nightgown—when she'd already used the chamber pot two or three times in the night and didn't want to risk Ann or Eliza deriding her—and didn't think it so horrible. She was covered, after all.

Crickets and cicadas made a strident chorus outside as she crept down the wide staircase, her long braids lying thick down her back. Somewhere a dog barked.

Hoodoo? she wondered. Though Mammy Sally would deny it to every white member of the household, the old slave knew more about nursing than the herbs and willow-bark she'd employed to get Pendleton through the cholera. More than once, on her stealthy trips to the outhouse, Mary had seen the old nurse out at midnight, drilling a hole in the south side of one of the chestnut-trees at the bottom of the yard, to "blow the chills" out of her own body and into the tree. Mary knew, too, that servants from other households would sometimes come to their kitchen, asking for a conjure of peace-plant and honey to sweeten up a harsh mistress, or balls of black wax and pins to send an importunate master away. These they'd deny wanting, if they saw Mary watching.

The dining-room with its graceful table and glass-fronted cabinet of silver service was a cavern of nameless shadow. Mary kept to the wall, feeling her way along, till she reached the pantry door, and slipped through into the kitchen, smelling of grease and ashes, warm as a bake-oven even hours after the big hearth-fire had been banked.

From there she stepped out at last into the blackness of the porch. Shadows stirred in the dark beneath the house's tall brick walls, and Mary saw the harlequin squares of a man's gingham shirt, the brief flash of eyes.

"Lou?" came Mammy's voice, and a whisper replied, "'S'me." A moment later Lou stepped across to the bottom of the kitchen steps. In the moonlight Mary identified him; one of Mrs. Turner's slaves, whom she rented out as a day laborer to the hemp and bagging factory in which Robert Todd was a partner.

Mammy stepped out of the shadows, handed Lou a bundle. Not bulky enough for blankets, Mary guessed; it had to be food or clothes. "There's a hay-barn five miles down the Louisville road," Mammy whispered. "Don't sleep there, they always look there, but there's a cave in the creek-bank just behind it."

"Patrols ride that road mostly early in the night," added Nelson. "Whatever you do, you keep away from them."

"With Mrs. Turner behind me," said Lou, "you got no worry there." In the kitchen Mary had heard talk of Mrs. Turner, things the white folks of Lexington never knew. The chill-eyed Boston woman was hated and feared throughout the slave community. If even half of what Mammy and Nelson and Jane had whispered was true, Mary wasn't surprised Lou would run away.

"When you get to Louisville keep to the edge of town. There's a tavern on the south side called Bridges, the owner don't care who sleeps in his sheds. Look for Mrs. Chough that lives behind the Quaker meetinghouse there, she'll get you across the river. You see this sign on a fence, it means they'll take you in." Kneeling, Mammy sketched something in the dust of the yard, smoothed it over at once. "You see that sign, it means they'll give you food at least. When you been gone three days, I'll let Tina know you got away."

Lou bent quickly to kiss Mammy's sunken cheek. "Tell

Tina I'll send for her, I swear it. . . ." Tina must be the woman he loved, thought Mary, in some other household, some other kitchen in the town. "Tell her I'll find a way somehow."

Nelson said, "She knows you will."

"God bless you." The runaway clasped Nelson's hand, kissed Mammy again. "God bless you both."

The two Todd slaves waited until Lou had disappeared into the dark of the trees. Like a ghost Mary fleeted away before Mammy could reach the top of the steps from the yard. In the dark of the downstairs hall she paused for a moment, overwhelmed with a wild urge to laugh, to cheer, to dance.

She felt she had learned a secret, and the secret was this:

That the people most concerned in the subject of freedom weren't sitting around tamely waiting for the abolitionists and the colonizers to quibble the matter out between them. The people most concerned didn't really care whether Mr. Clay and his friends were thinking "what was best for the darkies," or whether the issue was moral or political, or whether, as Nate Bodley's father claimed, abolitionist pamphlets stirred up slave revolts.

They were doing whatever they had to, to be free.

CHAPTER NINE

For the most part, however, Mary's awareness of the shadow-world that underlay the gracious brick houses of Lexington, the horse-races and picnics and the ubiquitous network of kinship ties that spread from Kentucky to the Virginia tidewater, was simply that: an awareness, like her awareness of the earth underfoot. Cash, and Mr. Clay, and increasing numbers of men in the town might be preoccupied with the subject of that earth—might see everything in terms of mud and worms and stones—but except on those occasions when the veil between the worlds of black and white lifted, Mary's days were shaped and colored by other things.

She turned sixteen. Nate Bodley kissed her in the shadows of the cherry orchard behind Rose Hill; she slapped him, and burst into tears, as a young lady must (Betsey said), but the sensation of being held, of being touched, of being wanted stirred her deeply. She found herself watching for opportunities to engineer such a scene again.

Along with the girls she'd gone to Ward's Academy with—some of whom were now day-students at Rose Hill as well—she and her sisters were part of the vast web of Todd cousinry that stretched back into Virginia and extended its tentacles across the river into Illinois: Porters and Parkers and Stuarts, Logans and Russells and Richardsons and ramifications still more distant. Girls and young men, they had known each other from childhood parties, from picnics in the woods and on the banks of the Town Branch and the Kentucky River, chasing each other through the trees as Nate Bodley had chased her. And as she now looked at Nate, they all looked at one another with changed eyes.

It was a happy time. In addition to Nate—and half a dozen other beaux—Mary had her studies and her beloved books at Rose Hill. She had Frances and Eliza and her friends, friends she'd known all her life. No longer forced to live under Betsey's roof, she came to dearly love the small half-brothers and half-sisters whom she had formerly so resented. Secure in the knowledge that she would be returning to her own pleasant room at Rose Hill on Sunday afternoon, she could hold little David on her lap, play with small Margaret and small Sam, and bask in their uncomplicated love.

There were balls and cotillion parties almost every week, either in the long room above Giron's Confectionary or in the private houses of friends. Summer lemonade or Christmas eggnog, crickets calling in the warm nights or the diamond glow of silent winter stars. Her father and the other men arguing cotton and politics. There were lectures at the Lyceum about nitrous oxide, galvanic batteries, cold-water cures for fever, and the Reverend Zaccheus Waverly's talks on travel in the Holy Land, from which Nate or one of the young law students at Transylvania would beg for the privilege of walking her home.

There were exhibitions of waxworks, and rides under the lilac trees of Ashland, Mary straight and graceful in a rifleman-green riding habit that flowed down over the left side of the neat-stepping little hackney her father had bought for her. There were student plays at Rose Hill, not amateur fit-ups but careful productions with elaborate props and scenery: *Pizarro, Hernani, Macbeth* in which everyone exclaimed over the passion with which Mary played the mad scene to a couple of tall, thin senior students grimly bedight in false beards. There was the true theater too, with troupes visiting from New York or Philadelphia. There were bonnets and coiffures, and the always-delightful challenge of extracting promises for new frocks from her father, and holding him to them with tears; there was *La Belle Assemblée* and the *Royal Ladies Magazine*.

The second Monday of every month was Court Day, when the justices of the peace would assemble in the County Courthouse. But most of the people who crowded the square before the Courthouse had little interest in what went on inside. Peddlers, horse-traders, trappers from the hills would set up their pitches, shouting the virtues of bloodstock or coonskins, milk-cows or Old Sachem Medicinal Bitters. Slave-dealers would be there, too, to buy up debtors' Negroes at the Courthouse door: stony-faced black men tricked out in blue coats and plug hats and women in neat-pressed calico ("Strip off, gal, let the gennleman have a look at yuh...." "See his back? Not hardly a stripe on 'im; he don't need much whippin'....").

On the benches along the iron fence, idlers spit and whit-tled, smoked and swapped tales: Nate Bodley in his ruffled shirt bought a peg of hard cider for ragged old Solly the gravedigger, who had once been so drunk and disorderly that in desperation the town council had sold the old white man to a free Negro woman for thirty cents so he'd have someone to look after him.

Even young Mr. Presby would stop to hear the news and ask what was being said in New York and Philadelphia. The young ladies went in rustling groups with aunts or brothers or fathers to shop for ribbons and silk flowers, but Mary found herself drawn as always to the men who argued about improvements and the National Bank.

"Good gracious, Mary, you don't want gentlemen to think you're a bluestocking!" exclaimed Frances, and Mary flipped her fan at her and lowered her long eyelashes, and said, "Silly!" Mary was always meticulously careful not to "parade" her learning more than was seemly for a girl, and in any case a girl with as many beaux as she had was in no dan-ger of being considered "blue."

But afterwards at the Court Day cotillion, Mary was hard-pressed to keep her mouth shut when Buck Loveridge or Jim Rollins speculated on possibilities of government contracts and the jobs that could be traded for favors, votes, and influ-

ence. Her newspaper reading gave meaning to chance fragments of conversation overheard at dances: "What the hell
we need some Yankee Congressman takin' money from us,
every time we turn around?"

"Because if Congress didn't build a road down to
Louisville with its taxes you'd sit on your tobacco and starve,"
Mary retorted. The men all laughed, but later, as she edged
her way to the lemonade table through a flowerbed of petticoats and gowns, she heard Arabella Richardson purr to
Nate Bodley, "Honestly, Mary's so quick with a comeback, I
just don't know how she does it! Myself, I never could tell a
demi-crat from a demi-john." And Bella smiled meltingly up
into Nate's bedazzled eyes, like a trusting child.

A few evenings after this, Mary treated the other
boarding-students at Mentelle's to a hilarious imitation of
Bella's simpering, during one of those quiet evenings when
the handful of boarders gathered after supper in the library to
study their lessons. From the secretaire in the corner where
she was doing the household books, Madame observed her
without comment. But when the other boarders went to
bed, she crossed to where Mary sat reading at the marble-
topped circular table beneath the chandelier, and said gently,
"It hurt, didn't it?"

"What did?" Mary looked up from *Les Trois Mousquetaires*.
"Little Miss Demi-crat?" And she mimed Arabella's languishing flutter of eyelashes—then had to turn her face aside at the
sudden sting of tears.

Growing from girl to woman hadn't lessened the wild
swings of her moods. At balls and cotillions she still burned
with the wild glow of exultation, simply at the pleasure of
dancing; from this she could pass almost instantly into volcanic anger that left her ill and shaking. She still had those
strange periods in which it seemed to her that she was two
people, that she stood on the edge of saying and doing some
unthinkable word or deed. And try as she would to control
her temper, in her anger she would still say cutting things
that had to be apologized for later, with agonies of anxiety

and tears. She had wept on and off, in secret, for two days, for Quasimodo and Esmeralda when she'd finished *Notre Dame de Paris;* sometimes it only took a caring look or a gentle query if she felt all right, to bring on tears she could neither explain nor control.

But she refused to weep for the "slings and arrows," as she scornfully termed them, aimed at her by the other girls in the town, the ones who said she was a bluestocking, or who raised their eyebrows or rolled their eyes when she'd quote from Shakespeare. She shrugged and replied, "As if I care what that little—" She fished in her French vocabulary for the word for "knothead" "—imbecile thinks."

"You are right not to care, child," said Madame gently. "In five years what will she be? The wife of some planter who fritters his money away on pretty dresses and jeweled earbobs, with nothing to look forward to in this life but the squalling of children and listening to her husband talk of horses and slaves."

Mary's mind returned to the cotillion, and Bella in her gown of shell-pink silk, surrounded by young gentlemen. To herself, likewise the center of a group who vied to get their names on her dance-card. To the sheer sensual thrill of the fiddles, the sweet scents of the night outside. To Nate in his ruffled shirt and coat of black superfine, swinging her out onto the dance-floor with such gay strength. To the joy of being held, and the empty ache when she looked through her little chest of her father's gifts.

"And in five years," she asked softly, "what will I be, Madame?"

Madame's hand rested gently on her shoulder. With her angular face and mannishly short-cropped hair, she looked like the embodiment of all those sniggering warnings: *virago, harridan, bluestocking.*

If you're not careful you'll end up like that....

Mary didn't even know whose voice it was, speaking that warning in her mind. Because in a way she envied Madame. Madame was happy, with her husband and her daughter and her books and her fiddle, doing exactly what she pleased and not caring what others said.

Mary wondered what it would be like, not to be always looking over her shoulder, wondering if Betsey or Elizabeth or Granny Parker were approving of what she did.

"The world is an enormous place, Mary, and there is a great deal in it. Good plays by actors a notch above the strolling players who come to Mr. Usher's theater. Opera, sung by men and women of talent and long training. Buildings that are older than your grandmother and that speak of the ages they have seen."

For a moment the schoolmistress's pale eyes softened, remembering perhaps those gray streets of Paris in the days of the kings, where lush moss grew on stones that had been set into place before the first Pilgrims boarded the *Mayflower.* Then she smiled, and shook her head: "Somehow, child, I cannot see a girl of your intelligence spending the whole of her life within a dozen miles of the Kentucky River."

No, thought Mary. And yet sometimes as Nelson would drive her to her father's house on Main Street on Friday evenings, and back to Rose Hill on Monday mornings, and she'd watch the slaves sweeping down the board sidewalks in front of McCalla's Pharmacy, or old Mrs. Richardson gossiping with Mr. Ritter—M'sieu Giron's cook—in front of the confectionary, she'd wonder how she was ever going to leave this place.

Meg was gone, at Sigoigne's Select Female Academy in Philadelphia. Her letters were full of playhouses and opera and dazzling dresses. Frances and Eliza were fully occupied with the leisurely lives of helping Betsey run the household, making dresses, riding out with their friends to pay "morning-calls." Though Mary loved her studies at Rose Hill, loved the exhilaration of taking first in recitations and of knowing more about history than any other girl, she sometimes wondered what Betsey's reaction would be if she said some Sunday evening, "I don't want to go back."

Would she reply, "You must"?

Rose Hill was her home, and Madame Mentelle like a mother to her, giving her what no one ever had. But as the years flowed stealthily by, and her father and Mr. Clay started talking of who would run for President again—as Mary realized that from being among the younger girls at the school she was now eighteen and the oldest—she began to feel a kind of desperation.

It wasn't that there had been any falling-off of her suitors. A belle to her lace-gloved fingertips, she knew how to make the most of her rosy prettiness, and had the advantage of being sharply intelligent, well-read, and with a name for witty repartee. She was skilled enough on the dance-floor to follow even the most awkward gentleman and make him feel he was actually dancing rather well; she used a variation of the same technique in conversation.

Nate Bodley continued to seek her out at subscription dances and cotillions and balls, and there had been a number of kisses stolen in quiet parlors and secluded woods.

If she had loved any of the regiment of town boys and sons of planters whose names filled her dance-cards, she knew it wouldn't be difficult to find a husband.

But she didn't. And a husband wasn't what she wanted to find.

She didn't know the name for what she wanted to find.

Increasingly, it was dawning upon her that many of the Lexington boys frightened her. It wasn't that she disliked them, although she considered a number of them complete idiots on the subject of paper currency. Some, like Cash and Nate, she was deeply fond of.

But the first time Cash got into a duel after his wedding— with Mary Jane expecting their first child—Mary was shocked, and furiously angry. The whole scene in the parlor, this time of White Hall, was repeated, except without the wedding-dress lying like a mute and gorgeous intimation of tragedy over the back of the sofa. Mary Jane weeping, Frances and Mary and Mary Jane's sisters all gathered around to comfort her—old Mrs. Warfield, too, muttering, "I told you how it would be. . . ." in the background, and Cash, of course, nowhere to be found.

And just as well, thought Mary, stroking her friend's icy hand. She didn't think she could have seen Cash without screaming at him, "How can you do this to Mary Jane?"

Four years had changed her view of what it was for a man to defend his honor. It was no longer a case of the romantic agony of a bride widowed upon her wedding-night, trading bridal white for somber veils of woe. Cash's death would leave Mary Jane a widow and his unborn child an orphan, to be raised by the gloomily triumphant Mrs. Warfield and whatever new husband Mary Jane might eventually find. Their suffering was the price Cash would cheerfully pay, thought Mary, for his precious honor.

Yet no one—not even Mary Jane—seemed to share Mary's awareness. When she spoke her thought to Frances in the carriage on the way out to White Hall, Frances stared at her and said, "For God's sake, Mary, keep your mouth shut! Don't you think Mary Jane is suffering enough?" As if Cash had come down with cholera, and had not chosen to make his wife suffer rather than let some other man call him "nigger-lover" unpunished.

And Mary, sitting mute beside Frances as the team pulled the vehicle up one of the long steep hills by the river, had the queer, sudden sensation of kinship with Mr. Presby. She felt a stranger in an alien land, wanting to shout things in a language that nobody there understood.

That night, at her father's house, after the exhausting afternoon comforting Mary Jane, Mary had dreamed of Cash and the other man both firing into the dirt at their feet. In the dream it was the earth that bled, as if in justification of the Indian name of Kentucky, "The Dark and Bloody Ground." On her way down to breakfast a few hours later Nelson caught her with the news that both Cash and his opponent had shot deliberately wide, and Mr. Presby subjected everyone at the breakfast-table to a scathing sermon on the evils of dueling, a practice never engaged in in the North.

("Except by Alexander Hamilton and Aaron Burr," remarked Mary, shaking out her napkin, which earned her a bespectacled glare from the tutor.)

But every man Mary knew—including her father and both her uncles—carried weapons when he left his front door. In the glass showcases of half the shops, braces of pistols were displayed along with silk scarves and necklets of pearls. Men showed off their knives to one another, which they carried sheathed beneath their superfine swallow-tailed coats, and spoke with pride of the swords concealed within the hollow shafts of their canes. During the election of 1836 feelings ran high, and there were shouting-matches at political-speakings, the hot tempers fueled by Kentucky bourbon. The ladies mostly kept clear of these—as ladies must—but unlike most ladies of her acquaintance, Mary could not pretend she didn't see what she saw: red faces, mouths stretched by shouted oaths, the vicious blaze of violence in men's eyes.

Men spoke admiringly of the "code duello" of the South, but there was little of that punctilious tradition in the brawling that broke out at Court Days. On one occasion Mary saw Cash holding back the crowd while his friend Jim Rollins kicked and lashed a Louisville Democrat who'd sung a song insulting Henry Clay: *"In spite of his running he never arrived. . . ."*

Dust stinging her eyes and the smell of blood in her nostrils, Mary thought, *I can't live like this. I can't.*

She turned her face aside and found herself looking down a quiet street near the Courthouse, in time to see her neighbor Mrs. Turner being helped by her coachman into a carriage. There was a slave boy with them, carrying two small parcels his mistress had bought from the peddlers in front of the Courthouse. At the sound of the ruckus around the fight the boy checked his steps and craned his neck, and without word or admonition Mrs. Turner took the coachman's light whip from beside the dashboard and caught the youth a savage lick across the backs of his legs that dropped him to his knees. The parcels went tumbling into the dust. Mrs. Turner lashed the boy a second time, this time across the face, and stood quiet as a schoolmistress in her walking-dress of lavender-gray while the boy picked up the parcels and staggered to his feet, blood running down his face.

Then she handed the whip back to her coachman, and got into her carriage, the boy handing in her packages and scrambling up behind.

Where will I be in five years?

That year, Frances went to Springfield, Illinois, to visit Elizabeth and Ninian.

"I daresay it won't be long till Elizabeth finds a husband for her," remarked Betsey in a tone of deep satisfaction, when Frances's first letter reached them in Lexington, speaking of her warm welcome to Ninian's big house on the hill, and the cheerful entertainments planned by the best of Springfield society. Like Lexington, Springfield was a new town, rough and raw on the bluffs above the Sangamon River, but growing fast. Like Lexington, it was a hotbed of state and local politics, with money to be earned and money to be grabbed in land-dealing and political patronage.

Like Lexington, too, Springfield seethed with Todd cousins and Todd connections. Half of southern Illinois was populated by Kentuckians who had crossed the river rather than compete, in industry or agriculture, with the slaves the Virginians brought in. Mary's uncle John Todd was a physician in town; another uncle there was a judge. Her handsome cousin John Stuart was a lawyer there, as was her cousin Stephen Logan from the other side of the Parker family: both were active in the Legislature in Vandalia, and there were female cousins as well, Lizzie and Francy and Annie. In her letters Frances sounded very much at home.

"And high time," Betsey added, folding up the letter and glancing along the table at Mary. Margaret, Sammy, David, and Martha had been joined in Mammy Sally's care by beautifully dimpled little Emilie, and Mary suspected her stepmother was increasing yet again. Robert Todd was as usual in Frankfort at the Legislature. "A girl who isn't married by the time she's nineteen just isn't trying." Mary would be nineteen in December. "I don't know what she's waiting for."

"Maybe to fall in love?" Mary dusted sugar over the dish of mulberries and cream that Pendleton had handed her. She didn't look up, but felt her stepmother's glare.

"Girls fall in love every other week—most girls do, that is. I hope your sister isn't too high in the instep for the Springfield boys."

"And in any case," added Mr. Presby disapprovingly, "the whole idea of young females 'falling in love' and marrying willfully whoever takes their fancy is, I believe, responsible for a great deal of heartache and unhappy matches." He spooned a frugal pinch of salt onto the oatmeal he'd requested Betsey have Chaney make for him—everyone else in the household ate cornbread or grits. "The writers of romantic novels have a great deal to answer for."

"Surely you aren't advocating the selection of husbands by professional matchmakers, as they do in China, Mr. Presby?" Mary fluttered her eyelashes. "Or perhaps by the lawyers of the young ladies' families?"

Mr. Presby's upper lip seemed to lengthen with disapproval. Over the years their relations had not improved—once they had nearly come to a screaming-match over molasses. "It is to be hoped that Mrs. Edwards, with a certain amount of experience in the world, will be able to guide Miss Frances's choices and make sure that she marries a gentleman, and a man of means sufficient to support her in the comfort to which she is accustomed. I am sure that otherwise there is no happiness to be expected."

She would miss him, Mary thought, when he returned to New England to take up a parsonage in one of those gray little towns where no one seemed to have any fun.

Already she missed Frances. Ann—now fifteen and finished with whatever the Reverend Ward could teach her—she had never liked, bearing her an obscure grudge from the days when she'd learned that her own name would be short-

ened from Mary Ann to simply Mary . . . as if Ann had willfully stolen half her name. Ann was a tale-bearer, a crybaby,
and had a temper almost as bad as Mary's—without Eliza to
keep the peace between them, they had come to hair-pulling
more than once.

Eliza finished her schooling and had returned to
Frankfort. Mary wrote to her weekly, as she wrote to Frances
and Elizabeth and Meg in Philadelphia, but it wasn't the
same. One by one the friends Mary had made at Ward's
school had married, or were engaged. When she went to the
dances at Giron's, the talk among them was all of servants and
babies, or the latest of them to be engaged. There were new
young belles "coming out"—including Ann—girls four and
five years younger than Mary. Though Mary laughed and
flirted, she felt increasingly alone.

It was her last year at Rose Hill. She was the oldest girl in
all the classes, and helped Madame Mentelle with the younger
ones. She still had the room she'd shared with Meg, at the end
of the narrow courtyard on the family side of the house, but
she now occupied it alone. More than once Madame had said
to her, "You are like a daughter to me." Her own daughters
were married, Marie to the son of Henry Clay ("A drunkard
who'll break his father's heart," predicted Betsey, with gloomy
satisfaction).

"It is a shame and a disgrace that there is no possibility for
a young woman to attend college the way a young man
does," declared Cash, when he encountered Mary at a Court
Day in the spring of 1837. "You're a perfectly intelligent person—God knows more intelligent than half the men of my
acquaintance. You're well read, well informed, politically astute." He frowned, his black brows plunging down over the
slight hook of his nose. "Yet this country can find no better
use for you than to marry you off to a bucolic ignoramus like
Nate Bodley."

He jerked his head in the direction of the planter's son,
standing with half a dozen of his cronies around Bill Pullum.
Pullum had a young slave woman with him, and by the

sound of their voices, and the stony expression of the girl's face, there was bargaining going on. Nate's voice rose over the others: "Yeah, but will she breed, that's what I want to know." He grabbed the front of the girl's yellow calico dress in both hands, pulled it open and down over her arms, to squeeze her breasts.

"Yet what choice does a woman have in this country—or in any country?" went on Cash, not quite rhetorically, but with his usual habit of preaching to Mary about her rights. " 'Female seminaries' . . . 'young ladies' academies' . . . Faugh! Marriage-marts by another name!"

Cash had recently expanded his interest in abolition into what he sometimes termed "the rational treatment of females"—something Mary Jane laughed gently over, because her husband still hadn't the faintest idea what it cost to run a household. "This country will remain in bondage until women as well as men free their slaves, make up their own beds, wash their own clothes, throw away their corsets. . . ."

"Why, Cash," purred Mary, flipping open her fan and widening her eyes at him over its lacy brim, "I never *dreamed* you wore corsets."

Caught off-guard in mid-tirade, Cash burst into laughter, his eyes twinkling: "You, young lady, are a minx," he said. "Now you tell me whether you don't think women should have the same rights to be educated as well as men—to hold property in their own names—even to vote!"

"I'm not sure," said Mary in a judicious tone, "that I'd sleep well at night knowing Arabella Richardson could vote for the President of the United States," and Cash laughed again.

"I don't sleep well knowing Nate Bodley can. You aren't going to marry him, are you, Molly?"

Mary sighed, and turned her eyes away in sick distaste from the sight of Nate and his friends clustered around Bill Pullum and the slave girl in yellow. "He's rich," she said. "And Betsey has been trying to push us together. When he comes to the house on Saturday evenings she always finds some reason to leave us alone in the parlor, and whenever I go to the theater or the Lyceum, it's 'Why don't you send a note to Indian Branch?' I don't..." She hesitated, looking up at the man by her side, the eagle profile, the lively sparkle of his mad green eyes.

There was a man, she thought, who was going somewhere, who was going to make something of himself.

Maybe she wouldn't end up marrying the President, she reflected. But a man who wasn't in politics at all—who only followed what all his friends proclaimed—seemed to her not wholly a man. And though she knew that other men examined female slaves in the same fashion in the open markets, she also knew it wasn't the same.

Then she tossed her head again, making the ribbons dance on her bonnet and her bronze curls bounce. "I can't imagine spending the rest of my life listening to Nate Bodley go on about his racehorses and his slaves.... Not that there's anything the matter with his racehorses, of course."

But when Cash had conducted her back to where her father and Betsey stood on the Courthouse steps, and she asked—hesitantly—about going on with her education, her father frowned in puzzlement, and said, "Do you mean to be a schoolteacher, then?" in a voice of disappointment and disbelief.

As if, thought Mary, she had expressed an interest in becoming a nun. A Presbyterian one, presumably...

Levi and George snickered and nudged one another. George, at thirteen, had already been in half a dozen brawls at Court Days and political-speakings. Levi, four years older and living now in a boarding hotel, was drunk, though it was early in the afternoon.

"I think it's an excellent idea." There was something in Betsey's tone of a woman in a shop slapping down a coin to buy the last packet of pins before a rival's hand can touch it. "The Reverend Ward was telling me only the other day what an exemplary student Mary was when she attended the Academy, and how he would have loved to have her return for further study and to teach the younger children. Although really," she added, with a titter of laughter and a sharp look at Mary under her bonnet-brim, "now that Frances has gotten engaged up in Illinois I bet it won't be long until *you* catch a husband—"

"I didn't say I wanted to be a teacher," Mary interrupted, feeling as if her stepmother had given her a shove toward the door of the house.

"Then what did you say?" Betsey's glance was like steel. "Honestly, Mary, I'm only trying to help you. . . ."

"You're only trying to get me out of the house," retorted Mary hotly, "so there'll be more room for your own children. Don't think I don't know that's why you've been shoving Nate Bodley at me like that purple fright of a hat you made for me—"

"Mary!" exclaimed her father, with a fast look around to make sure none of his friends had heard this outburst. Mary clapped her hands over her mouth, tears of shame flooding her eyes.

"I'm sorry," she gasped in a stifled voice. She turned and, springing down from the Courthouse steps, darted into the crowd.

"Mary, come back!" called out her father, and Betsey added her voice to his:

"Come back here this minute!"

She dodged around a gaggle of skinny cows, caught up her green-striped skirts, fled between a countrywoman hawking lettuces and a trader trying to sell a farmer a donkey, ran from the square down Main Street. . . .

And stopped, shocked, seeing behind the shelter of two drawn-up carriages a little knot of men beating another, savagely, with their canes. Two of the attackers held the victim's arms as a third struck him, over and over. Mary first saw the struggling shapes, almost without meaning: the figure bent under the blows, the glint of the brass cane-head, the white straw hat lying in the mud near the wheels of the Breckenridge carriage, the glint of broken spectacle-glass. A fourth man stood apart, his hands on the shoulders of a young black woman in a yellow dress.

The silence was eerie, broken only by the thwack of the cane, the grunt of the wielder as he raised it above his golden-blond head.

Nate. The man with the cane was Nate Bodley.

And the man he and his friends were beating was Mr. Presby.

They flung the tutor to the ground and Nate said, "Goddamn Yankee abolitionist, you keep out of my business after this, you hear?" He kicked him, then turned, grabbed the slave girl roughly by the arm, and thrust her ahead of him down the street, trailed by his friends. Presby lay in the dirt where he'd fallen, blood gleaming in his hair.

Mary ran to him, fell on her knees beside him, turned him over. Panic filled her, blind terror. . . . He wasn't dead, he moved his hand, *thank God, thank God*. . . .

And all the while she repeated, over and over in her mind, *I must get out of this place. I must get out.*

CHAPTER TEN

"A VERY SAD CASE." DR. RICHARD PATTERSON LAID THE SLIM
bundle of papers on the worktable in John Wilamet's little
cubicle off the sunny parlor of Bellevue House. John drew a
clean folder from the drawer, scanned the top page of the
bundle—a letter in his mentor's careful, tidy handwriting—
for the new client's name, then raised his eyes to Dr.
Patterson's in startled shock.

Dr. Patterson nodded at the unspoken question—*Yes, it
really is who you think it is.* "A most tragic case. And one
which requires special consideration, of course."

"Of course," John murmured, and let his body settle back
in his chair again. His long fingers flicked through the correspondence and doctors' opinions that would make up the basis of the file. A letter from Robert Todd Lincoln dated April
tenth: "*. . . If you would meet with me and Drs. Jewell, Danforth,
Isham, Smith, Davis and Johnson at my Chicago office on the twentieth . . .*" A much longer letter from Dr. Patterson's younger
brother DeWitt, also—like Patterson's son—a physician: "*I
treated Mrs. Lincoln during her husband's tenure of office as
President of the United States, for weakness of the bladder and for
head and back injuries resulting from a carriage accident on the second of July 1863. I do not believe any permanent injury was sustained in the carriage accident, though for the remainder of her
residence in Washington she complained of increased headaches. . . .*"
Several letters from Dr. Danforth, whom John had met now
and then during the past two years, when he came to Bellevue
Place to consult.

He looked up at Patterson again. "Is she violent?" Thinking of that stout little black-clothed figure in the Army tent

by the walls of Fort Barker years earlier, screaming imprecations at the ladies of the Freedmen's Relief Association.

Thinking of his mother.

"Good heavens, no." Patterson sounded vaguely horrified at the idea, although even some of his own carefully selected patients had their moments. Through the open door of his cubbyhole, John could see Miss Judd and Mrs. Goodwin, two of the twenty or so well-to-do white ladies who were the only people Dr. Patterson would admit to Bellevue, both writing letters.

Miss Judd, fragile and ethereal-looking in the shaft of sunlight from the wide windows, looked better than she had a few nights ago, when John had settled down to the tedious task of coaxing her to eat. She'd entered Bellevue at less than seventy pounds and there had been times John had feared she would die simply because her heart would not endure the deprivation that she seemed to so desperately crave. Mrs. Goodwin was thumbing through the notepaper in the box, looking for a sheet that was sufficiently clean not to repel her.

That bore watching.

"No," Patterson repeated, and drew up another of the cane-bottomed chairs that furnished—barely—the stark little room off the parlor. "Nothing of that kind, dear boy. Mr. Lincoln—Mr. *Robert* Lincoln—is of the opinion that his mother's insanity dates to her husband's death. Scarcely surprising, given the terrible circumstances of her widowhood. And a woman's nervous system naturally suffers from the burden of modern civilization more than does that of a man. Greater noise, greater stimulation, the greater stresses engendered by a need for order and punctuality..." He shook his head.

"In my opinion Mrs. Lincoln should have retired to some country retreat following her husband's assassination, and lived quietly, instead of choosing such over-stimulating venues as Chicago and Europe. Mr. Robert Lincoln concurs with me on that. Her mental powers, already dangerously overtaxed, seem to have been further irritated by the death of her youngest son four years ago. Again, she followed this bereavement not with the total rest that is the only possible amelioration of such a condition, but with further travel and stimulation that eventually deteriorated her nervous tissue. Her attachment to Spiritualist séances, and the excitation engendered by their rejection of the divine authority of Scripture, only hastened the inevitable."

In the parlor, Mrs. Goodwin finished her search through the small packet of notepaper at the rosewood desk, sat back, her narrow, rectangular face pursed with pent emotions. Then she leaned forward and began to thumb through again. Her movements were quicker now and she'd begun to rock a little in her chair. Bad signs.

Dr. Patterson went on, "According to Drs. Danforth and Isham, Mrs. Lincoln suffers from a hysterical bladder and frequent urination, as well as from spinal irritation, and theomania. Of course all of this must be confirmed by observation. According to Mr. Lincoln there's no family history of insanity or alcoholism, certainly no syphilis or epilepsy involved. I'm afraid, if indeed her illness is of ten years' standing, that she may be with us for some time."

John held up a finger, caught Patterson's eye and nodded out the door to where Mrs. Goodwin had just sat back a second time, trembling now and looking restlessly around. Patterson smiled a little at John and said, "You go speak to her." John got to his feet, crossed the parlor without appearance of hurry or deliberateness to the woman's side.

"Maybe it's time for a little walk in the garden, ma'am?" he suggested, and she turned on him, her face contorted with anger.

"Why can't this filthy place provide clean paper?" Mrs. Goodwin's gloved fists bunched together on the table's waxed and polished top. Unlike Miss Judd, who wore lace house-mitts of the kind wealthy ladies often did in company—and who was regarding the stout stockbroker's wife with more alarm than was usual in her lackluster blue eyes—Mrs. Goodwin had on kid gloves of the sort usually worn for visiting and outdoors. She took them off only to bathe. "Every single one of those pieces of paper is disgusting!"

"Dr. Patterson does the best he can here, ma'am," said John in his most reasonable voice. "Let's talk about this outside in the garden...." He had observed that Mrs. Goodwin generally calmed down and felt better after a few minutes among Mrs. Patterson's roses with the sun on her face. "When we come back, I'll help you find one that's clean."

Mrs. Goodwin got to her feet—John carefully moved her chair aside without touching her—and, he thought later, would have walked outside with him had not Dr. Patterson, who had been watching from the cubicle door, come over and said, "Now, Mrs. Goodwin, surely you know those notepapers are for everyone. We can't bring in paper specially to suit your tastes."

"They're dirty!" She whirled, her cheeks reddening and her eyes unnaturally bright. "I couldn't write to my children on those disgusting rags! There's a spot—look at it!" She jabbed a gloved forefinger at a nearly invisible speck on the small, clean buff sheets. "Every page is like that! Goodness knows what they'd catch!"

"But no one here is sick," pointed out Patterson in his deep, reasonable voice. "The papers are quite clean, you know...." He touched the top of the stack, at which Mrs. Goodwin drew back as if he'd spit on it. "And we can't make special cases for everyone."

"You can give your patients something that's clean enough to touch without giving them every disease from smallpox to cholera, and passing them along to their families!" And with that she turned and fled up the wide stairs in a storm of blue faille ruffles. Minnie Judd pressed a clenched fist to her mouth and burst into silent tears.

"I suspect hydrotherapy is what she needs," said Patterson to John. "You'd best tell Peter to prepare the tub. She's been progressively excited for the past two days. I've only been waiting for an outburst like this. But you did quite well," he added. "We shall make an alienist of you yet."

"Thank you, sir," said John. He wondered whether, if he had been allowed to take Mrs. Goodwin for a short stroll in the sunlight before bringing her back to the subject of the notepaper, the whole scene could have been avoided. As Dr. Patterson climbed the stairs after his recalcitrant patient, John went to reassure Minnie Judd, who was trembling like a whipped greyhound and weeping without a sound.

JOHN HAD BEGUN CORRESPONDENCE WITH DR. PATTERSON three years earlier, when he'd written to him asking for copies of the proceedings of the Fox River Medical Association, of which Patterson was president. At the time John had been working as a secretary for the resident surgeon of the state asylum in Jacksonville. He read old journals, and the proceedings of medical associations, whenever he could lay hands on them in the offices. The overworked white men who ran the institution spoke approvingly of John's "desire to improve himself," but it never seemed to cross anyone's mind to put him in a position of any responsibility. Those positions—or more probably the salaries that went with them—were the purview of white men.

At times during those years at Jacksonville, John had wondered why he didn't simply become a carpenter, or work in a brewery, or shovel horse-shit in the streets—God knew Chicago's streets could use more full-time shovelers. Lionel Jones—whose family shared the rear cottage of a two-house lot on Maxwell Street with Cassy, Cassy's children, Lucy's children, John's wife, Clarice, and their daughter, and Phoebe—was a laborer at the Armour stockyards and made enough to pay his share of the rent and keep body and soul together, something John was not always able to do. Lionel lived day to day, ate and slept and walked out with his family along the shores of the lake on Sundays, and sometimes fought with his wife, Lulu, and sometimes loved her....

Why, John wondered, did he want more?

Why did anyone want more?

Why this driving curiosity to learn what insanity *was*? To help the insane?

As Cassy put it, "Don't you got enough to do lookin' after one insane lady?" with a sharp nod at their mother.

John had no answer to that. For the first few years after the War's end he had worked for Dr. Brainert, under whom he'd served in the Army; the red-faced Army surgeon had resumed his private practice in Chicago, specializing increasingly in diseases of the nerves. Working as his assistant, John had studied the works of Greisinger, Charcot, and Johann Reil, trying to fathom the shadowy world of lunacy while at the same time trying to cope with his mother's intermittent hysterical rages, her long periods of silent refusal to get out of bed, to wash or dress herself—her increasing tendency to seek release from her inner demons in drunkenness or opium or "hop."

During those first few years in Chicago, immediately after the War, John had felt a good deal of hope. In spite of living in a rattletrap cottage "back of the yards," and being refused service in all but "Negro" stores, he had a sense of being given a chance to prove what he could do.

When Brainert had died, suddenly, of heart-failure—struck down as if smitten by lightning as he stepped from the trolley-car near his house—John had learned how illusory that sense of well-being actually was.

That was in 1869; the first optimistic flush of Reconstruction was over. The sense of rebuilding a new nation, of educating and helping the freedmen to "take their places in American society," had faded before the realization that those freedmen wanted the same jobs that white men held. By the common consensus of everybody but the former slaves themselves—who weren't asked—their "places in American society" seemed to be doing exactly the kind of jobs they'd been doing before the War: that is, anything that was too nasty, too backbreaking, or too time-consuming for anybody but slaves to undertake, and for not much more profit than they'd had as slaves. Less, in most cases, because at least

slaveowners *had* to provide shelter and food, or their neighbors would talk.

After months of finding no work at all, John had secured a
place as assistant to a surgeon attached to a private sanitarium
in Lake Forest, for a third what a white man would be paid.
The sanitarium had closed in '71; that was when he'd gone to
work at Jacksonville, after yet more months of helping Cassy
do white people's laundry, and rolling cigars in the Maxwell
Street room by the light of a single kerosene lamp to make
the rent. When the banks all failed in '73 he'd been let go from
Jacksonville—not that they could spare a single man from that
overcrowded and hellish warehouse for the permanently insane—and with that failure, it seemed to him, even the nasty
and backbreaking employment tended to go to the white
men, who mostly had brothers-in-law or cousins or friends in
city government or the packing-yards or the railroads. At least
they got paychecks.

And he was, for all intents and purposes, back on that
street in Washington being beaten up by the Irish teamsters,
who feared that newly freed slaves would take their jobs.

The recollection of that day was clear in John's mind as he
read over the reports from Mrs. Lincoln's trial, and the eval-
uations of Drs. Jewell, Isham, Danforth, et al. concerning the
sanity of the President's widow. For years John had regarded
Abraham Lincoln with skepticism for backing the colonizers,
the men who'd wanted to free the slaves only if they could be
shipped out of the country where they wouldn't interfere
with the white men. Now, he wondered if the man hadn't
simply guessed what would likely happen if all black men
were given their liberty at once, as the abolitionists had demanded: that in such numbers, most black men would be
unable to find jobs.

John lowered the papers, looked out through the window
of his tiny office—like a dressing-room off Dr. Patterson's
handsome study, with its shelves of books, painted lamp-
globes, and imposing rosewood desk—and thought about the
stout little Southern belle who would come to the contraband

camps with boxes of clothing or blankets, brisk and busy and bossy. The woman who would give such wickedly funny accounts of the reactions of the pro-Southern society matrons of the town to her requests for help. Swinging from energy to tears to hysterical rage with the same unexpected violence, fragile in the same way that his mother was fragile.

But Mr. Robert Lincoln—and Drs. Jewell, Danforth, Isham, etc.—were wrong if they thought her insanity began when her husband's blood had been splattered over her gray silk dress at Ford's Theater that Friday night in 1865.

Whatever was wrong with Mary Lincoln, it started long before that.

Dr. Patterson had Argus—the attendant who doubled as coachman—harness the team and rode down to the train-station late in the afternoon. They returned in the evening, an hour before supper, when the first cooling breezes rustled the trees around Bellevue Place. Mrs. Patterson shut her daughter, Blanche, into her room in the family wing— Blanche was simpleminded and often kept out of the way— and with her son, also named John but referred to throughout Bellevue as Young Dr. Patterson, went out onto the steps.

John Wilamet watched from the window of his cubby-hole as Peter opened the iron lodge gates to admit the vehicle. When it reached the steps, two men—one lean and bearded with a mouth like a bracket, the other burly, mustachioed, and dressed with the finicking care of a dandy— helped a stout black figure out. Dr. Patterson made a sweeping gesture with one arm, taking in the three-story brick house, with its lower wings and comfortable-looking bow windows. Mrs. Patterson came down the steps and held out her hands to the veiled widow; Mrs. Lincoln pulled her hand sharply from the other woman's grip. John saw Mrs. Patterson's back stiffen, and knew Mrs. Lincoln had already made an enemy, before she even crossed the threshold.

Somehow, that didn't surprise him.

A number of the other patients were in the parlor when

Mrs. Lincoln was escorted in. Mrs. Goodwin, of course, was still confined to her hydrotherapy tank, wrapped in wet sheets with a steady stream of water flowing over her to calm her spirits. But Minnie Judd was there, sharing the green-tufted sofa with Mrs. Edouard—up and around for once—and the restless-eyed Lucretia Bennett. By herself at the table sat Mrs. Johnston, to whom most of the other ladies gave a wide berth. Mrs. Munger quietly brooded in a corner. Mrs. Patterson made introductions, not mentioning that "Mrs. Lincoln" was in fact the wife of the man whose idealized image, decorated with an incongruous halo, was appearing coast-to-coast on china souvenir plates and allegorical paintings of apotheosis in Heaven.

Behind them, in his study, Dr. Patterson was saying to Mrs. Lincoln's two escorts, "I know your mother will be comfortable and happy here." So one of them—it had to be the younger man, in the natty gray suit, with the watchful, suspicious eyes—was Robert, Abraham Lincoln's oldest—and only surviving—son.

"Here at Bellevue we offer the modern management of mental disease through moral treatment, not restraint. Rest, proper diet, baths, fresh air, occupation, diversion, change of scene, an orderly life, and no more medicine than is necessary are all that are required, we believe, to restore the failing reason to health, if in fact it can be restored. And I believe we have had a good deal of success in that field."

"As to that," said Robert Lincoln in a light voice that reminded John at once of his father's, "I'm not sure how much success anyone could have with my mother. The important thing is that she is placed somewhere safely, where she can do no harm to herself. Beyond that . . ."

If in fact it can be restored, thought John, quietly leaving the cubicle and following Young Doc, Mrs. Patterson, and Mrs. Lincoln into the hall that led to the family wing. *Aye, there's the rub.* At Jacksonville, where he'd sometimes doubled as an attendant, he'd seen those upon whose restoration to reason family, doctors, state had given up: the maniacs pounding on walls, writhing in the metal-barred cribs to which they were confined, shrieking or weeping as they were held down for "water cures" considerably more rough-and-ready than Mrs. Goodwin's hydrotherapy. He'd watched the delusional confined to "tranquilizing chairs"; the melancholy wasting silently away unnoticed, except when force-fed through tubes; the syphilitic screaming in pain and the filthy avoided by everyone.

Many of them hadn't seemed worse than some of the ladies here—only poorer, long ago abandoned by families who could deal with them no longer, and picked up on the streets by police or strangers who turned them over to the courts.

Could some of them be cured, he wondered, if treated with *rest, proper diet, baths, fresh air* and all the rest of it instead of the Utica crib or the metal collar? How could you reach them if they barely heard you? What could you do?

"Now, I'm sure you'll find this room very comfortable." Mrs. Patterson's voice drifted around the corner from the hall that ran down the center of the wing where she, Dr. Patterson, Blanche, and Young Doc had their private rooms. John had guessed, a few days ago, when one of the small patient rooms on that wing—and its next-door "attendant's room"—had been aired and made up, that someone of some importance, a "special case," was being brought in. "You'll be free, of course, to walk around the grounds and in the garden—I'm quite proud of my garden—and of course you'll have the use of the carriage for riding anytime you care to. Our grounds are quite extensive. We encourage our ladies to walk in the fresh air."

Argus had brought in Mrs. Lincoln's trunks already, five of them, and half a dozen carpetbags. They crowded the bright, bare little room with its single iron-framed bed, its white curtains that did not hide the window-bars, its small barred judas-hole in the door. Mrs. Lincoln put back her black veils and regarded Mrs. Patterson with those large, tourmaline-blue eyes John remembered: eyes red with weeping now, and settled into unhealthy-looking pouches of pale flesh. In Washington, struggling to regroup from the death of her beloved son, Mrs. Lincoln had struck John as brittle, changeable, volatile.

Now she looked beaten. In her small, silvery voice she said, "I don't suppose anyone in this place has bothered to tell you that I'm not a well woman? I suffer from headaches—not that my son will admit that they're anything but a *figment of my imagination,* as he wishes they were—and from pain in my back."

"Of course Dr. Danforth has been over all that with us—"

"Dr. Danforth," retorted Mrs. Lincoln witheringly, "would undoubtedly prescribe poison for me—if he thought he could get away with it. And my son would thank him for it, always supposing he didn't request it to begin with."

"Now, Mrs. Lincoln," smiled Mrs. Patterson, "you know you don't mean that. You're just tired. Of course you'll have medicine here, all the medicine you need. This is John Wilamet. . . ." She gestured toward him as he stood in the doorway. "John helps my husband, and he will bring you whatever you ask for."

John supposed there were worse things than being treated like an attendant by Mrs. Patterson. At least Dr. Patterson consulted with him over treatment of patients, and taught him what he had learned in over twenty years of dealing with those troubled in their minds. And it certainly beat rolling cigars until your fingers bled, or ironing shirts that white folks' servants brought to be washed.

But such an attitude didn't bode well for his chances of becoming a doctor of minds himself.

Mrs. Lincoln regarded him bleakly. He couldn't tell whether she recognized him or not.

"Supper will be at six," said Mrs. Patterson. "You'll want to wash up, of course, and change your dress. You shall take your meals with the family, rather than with the other patients. . . ." She smiled in what she'd probably been told was a kindly way. John wasn't sure her square, expressionless face was capable of much else. "Someone will knock on your door."

She rustled off down the hall, like a solid rectangle of corsetry. John knew what was expected of him. His hand on the door, he asked, "Can I bring you anything, Mrs. Lincoln, or do anything for you?" He had to check on Mrs. Goodwin before supper, and look in on Mrs. Wheeler, who frequently became disoriented at this time of the evening. But he could not, he thought, simply leave this woman here without a word. There was something in the way she looked around the small room in the graying light that reminded him of a child, sent to a strange place alone.

She snapped, "No." And then, as he began to withdraw, her square, heavy face softened infinitesimally, and she added, "Thank you, Mr. Wilamet."

John closed the door, and bolted it from the outside.

CHAPTER ELEVEN

ON FRIDAY AFTERNOONS, DR. PATTERSON WAS DRIVEN IN the carriage to the railway station to take the Chicago and Northwestern to the city. John had learned to lie low and stay quiet until the superintendent's return. Though neither Young Dr. Patterson nor Mrs. Patterson had ever spoken a word of disapproval about taking a man of color to train as an assistant—and though neither was ever anything but polite— neither treated him in any way different from Gunther, Peter, and Zeus, the men who made the rounds of the rooms with the door-keys every night and were ready at call to restrain unruly or hysterical patients, or from Amanda, Katie, Gretchen, and Louise, who were in charge of making up beds and walking with the patients in the gardens. John had once overheard Mrs. Patterson say to her husband, "I don't see what the point is, since there are no Negro doctors anyway," and had been unable to hear what Patterson replied. Her tone had carried the self-evident inflection of one who says, *You know they don't enter sheep in the Kentucky Derby.*

John knew that there were, in fact, black doctors, most of them trained overseas. But there weren't many of them, and those there were made an extremely poor living, as few blacks had the money to call a doctor when they were sick.

And no blacks that he knew had the money to seek out help for the terrifying agonies of the mind.

So on the Fridays and Saturdays while Dr. Patterson was gone, John slipped into the invisibility he had perfected most of his life. He mixed medicines for the patients—camphor, laudanum, morphine, saline draughts, chloral hydrate, belladonna, ergot, cannabis indica...despite Dr. Patterson's assurances about "no more medicine than is necessary."

Croton oil for those who stubbornly refused to move their bowels and tartar emetic for those whose frenzies or obsessions were best controlled by keeping them semi-nauseated most of the time. He helped Gunther and Gretchen with the hydrotherapy patients, making sure the water in which they lay was tepid—Dr. Patterson at least didn't believe in such "stimulating" treatment as "the bath surprise," unexpectedly pouring ice water down a patient's sleeve in the hopes of snapping their mind back to sanity, a favorite at Dr. Marryat's sanitarium in Lake Forest. He helped Young Doc in leeching those patients like Mrs. Wheeler who had exhibited signs of over-excitement and mania, and took his turn at observing those who were confined.

He prepared a blister for the back of Mrs. Johnston's neck—as a counter-irritant to the irritations of her brain—and more tartar emetic to puke Miss Canfield out of her lethargy. Young Doc gave an electrical treatment to Mrs. Hill, who was also slipping into a lethargy, but unlike Patterson he did not permit John to observe.

At least, John reflected, Patterson's refusal to deal with the chronically violent precluded such techniques as refrigeration—or maybe it was only that the wealthy gentlemen who installed their female relatives here didn't wish to see them going about with their heads shaved.

In any case, John didn't see Mrs. Lincoln again until late Friday afternoon, twenty-four hours after her arrival.

Bellevue Place, before Dr. Patterson had purchased it, had been a school. Although most of its sixteen-acre grounds were occupied by graveled paths, green lawns, and little copses of trees, there was a formal garden to one side of the main house. This Mrs. Patterson had had put into shape again, so that the twenty or so ladies under Dr. Patterson's care—he admitted neither epileptics nor syphilitics, no "furiously insane" nor of "filthy habits" (except of course Mrs. Johnston)—could have at least a chance of regaining the balance of their minds by fresh air and quiet. After the hellhole stench and noise of the state asylum at Jacksonville, John wholeheartedly agreed with this treatment. He loved the garden, though he did not walk there or sit there except in attendance on one of the patients.

It would not do for these wealthy ladies to think that the silence and repose being paid for by their families were being shared—and gratis at that—with a black man.

So on Friday afternoon he stepped out the side door as he usually did, and stood near it where the corner of the wall shielded him. Feeling the sun on his face, listening to the silence and birdsong and drinking in the scents of warm mulch, of grass, of sweet alyssum and June roses. Thinking of those, like Mrs. Wheeler, or Mrs. Edouard who had spent most of the night screaming and who now lay in opiated sleep, so lost in their lightless inner labyrinths that they were cut off from this beauty, this peace.

The door creaked behind him and he straightened, turned back to the house with the air of one hurrying from one duty to the next, as a stout crape-clad figure stepped out. "Excuse me," she said, "I was looking for—" Mary Lincoln stopped on the threshold, gazing out at the brilliant green, the neat hedged squares, and the exuberant colors—Ispahan and La Noblesse, Painted Damask and Ville de Bruxelles. Her face, puckered a little with annoyance, relaxed into her slightly crooked smile.

"How beautiful," she sighed, and looked up at him, shading her eyes with her hand though she wore the black bonnet of a widow. "We had a rose garden, when we lived in Washington.... Will you walk with me, John? Mr. Wilamet, I should say now. It's good to see you after all these years." She seemed relaxed and cheerful—as well she should be, thought John, considering the amount of laudanum she'd had that morning for back pains, headache, and what Mrs. Patterson had described as "agitation." Her voice had the slight dreaminess with which he was well familiar. "I had no idea that being clapped up as a madwoman could be so pleasant."

"I wish I could say I was delighted to see you, ma'am."
John smiled and offered her his arm. "And I would be, under
other circumstances, I hope you know."

"What a dilemma for the writers of etiquette books." Mrs.
Lincoln laid a small plump hand on his elbow, and with her
other hand opened her fan. Her black straw bonnet—worn
without a veil—was in the latest style, John observed. He
knew she'd been assigned Amanda as a permanent attendant
and wondered how that quiet, matter-of-fact quadroon
woman had dealt with the contents of those five trunks and
numerous hatboxes and carpetbags in the confines of the small
room. He'd already heard from Peter that another eleven
trunks were expected later in the week.

"I'm sure my husband would have come up with a dozen
formulae for introductions and greetings when one meets an
old friend in a madhouse, or in jail, or in the gutter outside a
tavern: 'Why, whatever are you doing here?' seems somehow inadequate to the task. Is there any possibility of getting
a decent novel to read here rather than the collection of mor-
alizing tracts they have in the library? Or will I be put in a
straitjacket only for asking?" Her voice was careless, with an
echo in it of a Southern belle's ineradicable flirtatiousness,
but John heard the tension hidden beneath. *She doesn't know
the rules,* he thought. *She is in a new place, and, in spite of the
laudanum, watchful.*

She may, too, have heard some of the commotion last
night when Mrs. Edouard started beating the walls and
screaming.

"You won't be put in a straitjacket," he replied. "Dr.
Patterson practices what they call moral treatment, rather
than chaining up lunatics the way they used to...." *The way
they still do,* he reflected, *in every institution but those wealthy
enough to hire the staff needed for adequate attention to their patients.* "In a way it's almost like letting the mind heal itself, the
way the body heals itself, provided there is no infecting agent
poisoning the system. There are lectures every Sunday night,

and concerts—and of course you may call for the carriage to go riding anytime you wish."

Beyond the garden, he could see Mrs. Johnston walking with young Miss Canfield and ignoring the nurse Louise, who walked in attendance behind, as if she weren't there. Maybe to Mrs. Johnston she wasn't. At the far end of the aisle of roses, Mrs. Hill sat alone on a bench, rocking back and forth and presumably communing with the voices that spoke to her out of the air. With a kind of wry bitterness John reflected on the filthy brick wards of Jacksonville, on the never-ending smells, on the notorious "swing" that the few overworked doctors there told themselves and each other was actually calming and therapeutic . . . and had the added benefit of being a threat that all but the most frantic lunatic understood.

"There seem to be lectures night and morning here." Mrs. Lincoln's light, silvery voice was dry. "I got a good one from Dr. Patterson before breakfast concerning my 'will to insanity,' as he called it. And another about my dear son's concern for me. Is that part of moral treatment, as well?"

"It's part of Dr. Patterson's system to instruct and convince patients in changing their ways."

"And to censor what they read, the way they do in Russia?"

And in Virginia, reflected John, *if you happened to be black there sixteen years ago.* "I admit the library isn't the most modern in the Western Hemisphere," he answered. "If you asked for a book I think it would depend on what it was, whether Mrs. Patterson would procure it for you or not. They're cautious about anything that would affect the balance of the mind. . . ."

"The balance of my mind is perfectly fine!" She rounded on him, her cheeks flushing red. She almost shouted the words.

John was silent.

"I'm not a child." Her voice was trembling. "Or a lunatic." Turning her back on him, she burst into tears and strode away down the path. John started after her. Swinging back, she shouted, "Let me alone!" and quickened her steps, almost running—running in any direction that presented itself, because within the wall that surrounded Bellevue Place, all directions were ultimately the same.

Chapter Twelve

On Wednesday afternoons John walked into town and took the train to Chicago. An hour and a quarter through flat warm prairies, green with summer's advance, combed by wind and broken by the emerald tufts of wood-lots. Then a quarter-hour through thickening lines of brown brick workingmen's cottages—white workingmen—that eroded into a ring of shacks and shanties, boardinghouses and clapboard saloons, the streets dirtier and more crowded and the steel rails doubling and trebling and quadrupling and the stench of the packing-yards growing until it was impossible to believe that the stink could still be invisible: John always felt that somewhere it stood in a glowing green wall of filth, he was only looking in the wrong direction....

And that was Chicago.

He knew most of the people who rode on Wednesday afternoons in the third-class "Negro" car. These were men who worked as gardeners or stablemen during the week in Batavia or Geneva, and women who were maids in Wheaton. There wasn't much work for blacks in Chicago, let alone out in the white peaceful towns of the prairie countryside. Those few who had it, tended to leave their families in the city where they had friends to help them if anything went wrong. Amanda, the attendant at Bellevue, had two children in town whom she left with her parents, and would visit every other Tuesday when she had the night off. The Germans and Poles and Hungarians who crossed through the rattletrap car for their own less-than-palatial third-class accommodations—men who'd flocked west in search of jobs that simply weren't to be had in New York—regarded the black enclave with occasional curiosity, occasional suspicion, when they regarded them at all. Mostly the blacks were invisible, as long as they stayed quiet, which they did. Nobody wanted any trouble. The week was hard enough as it was.

All the car windows were open—those that weren't jammed permanently shut—and still the air was hot. Sweat ran down the sides of John's thin face, itched in his close-cropped hair under his mouse-brown derby and stuck his shirt to his back. The thick lenses of his spectacles slipped down heavy on his nose. As the train slowed down flies came in, the flies that seemed to hang over Chicago in the summer like a roaring, glittering cloud.

Once they got into the city itself the noise of the other trains, coming and going all around them as the tracks converged, drowned any attempt at conversation. John gritted his teeth, bracing against the din as he always did, as if it were a physical pain. Once he was out of the train he hurried through the echoing immensity of the half-built station to the platform where the southbound local would depart, chugging its slow way through the crowded neighborhoods south of downtown. The shriek of train-whistles, the yelling of the porters, the clamor of the engines, even after all these years, still made his chest feel as if it would burst.

Since the War's end he had lived in cities. In Richmond, briefly and terrifyingly, knowing that his blue uniform and his black skin made him a potential target whenever he stepped outside the Army Headquarters; then this nightmare metropolis where everyone seemed to be rushing, scrambling, fighting at all times amid the unending stink of factory-smoke, horse-dung, and the all-drowning stench of decaying meat. The moments he could snatch in the garden at Bellevue were the more precious, in contrast to this. No wonder women sometimes got well there, away from these hideous streets.

No wonder Dr. Patterson was of the often-expressed opinion that "the Negro race is constitutionally unable to adapt itself to the pace and demands of civilized life." Most representatives of "the Negro race" that John knew had come, like himself, from the quiet of country plantations.

Chicago was enough to drive anyone, black or white, insane.

From the Twelfth Street station he turned west again, picking his careful way across and through the mazes of tracks. This whole neighborhood between the Galena yards and those of the Illinois Central—which included the river levee and the lower end of Satan's Mile—lay under a permanent pall of sooty smoke, rasping in his lungs. Dead cats and dead dogs lay by the rails, some cut nearly in half. Now and then the trains would claim a child, or a drunk. This close to the river the stink of the packing-houses, of the soap and turpentine plants, was enough to knock you down. Constant, unending, the squeals of the dying pigs, the lowing of cattle terrified and in agony made an aural curtain as palpable as that green, rotting wall of smell.

The houses here, cramped two on a lot along the unpaved streets, sweltered in the clammy heat. The Great Fire of four years ago hadn't reached this far and this part of Satan's Mile was much as it had been for a dozen years: clapboard cottages of two and three stories that had started life as sheds; stables and shacks that still housed goats and pigs; muck-filled alleys and rough frame houses whose very kitchens and hallways were sub-sub-sub-let to make the exorbitant rents. Elsewhere in the city it had been as bad or worse, but the vile "patches"—neighborhoods so rough they were a law unto themselves, like Hell's Half-Acre or Hairtrigger Row—had been supplanted by endless dreary zones of clapboard cottages.

The inhabitants of those ramshackle dwellings still grouped according to nationalities, as they had before the Fire—why live among people you couldn't talk to, even supposing they wouldn't beat you up on sight? But there was a sort of neutrality accorded to the main thoroughfares. John walked quickly as everyone walked in Chicago, tired and hot with his coat slung over his shoulder and his little carpetbag of laundry in his other hand. He mentally counted his way through the neighborhoods: Judd Street, Russians; O'Brien Street, Hungarians; Kramer Street, *now we're down to the Italians*—skinny children with glossy black curls chasing one another through the alleys behind saloons where the kerosene lamps had begun to throw their orange glow over shirtsleeved men in derbies and the thick blue pall of cigar-smoke . . .

Griffe Moissant's on Maxwell Street—red-peeling paint, shutters thrown wide to the reeking heat—marked the last two blocks before the dump where refuse from a nearby packing-house was thrown. In heavy rains the runoff was the color of coffee, the texture of phlegm, and smelled like nothing of the human earth. The neighbors here were mostly like John, born slaves and either runaways during the War or freed in its wake. Many of the men had fought, in the 22nd C.I. or the 107th or the 2nd Light Artillery. Many more of them had been told, when news of Lee's surrender reached their home plantations, that the government would prefer it if they'd stay put on the same land they'd worked for their former masters, and work it for a wage.

"Funny thing about that," had said Lionel Jones, when John and his family had first moved in with Lionel, whose brother had still been alive then and married to Cassy. "Once Marse Barton finished takin' out the rent for the cabin, an' the bill for food from the plantation store, an' new shoes for wintertime, an' hire of his hoes an' his plows an' his mules, *we* owed *him* money. . . . But he was nice enough to let us stay on an' work for free."

"What a good man," John had replied drily, and Lionel gave him a wink and a savage, broken-toothed grin.

Most had stayed in the South. Seeing some of those who lived along Maxwell Street—none of whom could read and few of whom had any training or experience at anything except agricultural work, much less the connections with police and city politics that were so vital to borrowing money and establishing businesses—John understood why. The devil you knew, in the quiet world of familiar faces and familiar countryside, be it ever so stricken by poverty, was infinitely less terrifying than the grinding, bewildering, many-visaged unknown demons that waited grinning at the end of the tracks.

There were times, when the hammering of the train-engines and the stink of the smoke and the rotting meat seemed about to crush him like a spider between two stones, when he wondered if he shouldn't have gone back to Virginia himself.

John passed Griffe's, and then Cuff's Grocery, where another gaggle of drinkers sat on the porch sipping the stale dregs that Cuff bought from the downtown saloons for a few cents a barrel. As he did so John felt his stomach begin to tighten with dread. It was nearly dark and above the smells of privies and stockyards he could scent the drift of side-meat and beans, cornbread and red-eye from the open doors of those weathered shacks. Could hear old Aunt Machie singing through her open door as he passed her house, singing at the top of her lungs as always, sweet and beautiful as an angel:

"Shoo, shoo turkey, throw your feather way yonder,
  Shoo, shoo turkey, throw your feather way yonder. . . ."

He was almost home. That cold quivering behind his breastbone tightened up like a fist around his heart, wondering what the hell he'd find.

Every week—every Wednesday night when he came home to spend his half-holiday with Clarice and Cassy and the rest of his family—it was a toss-up whether he'd have rest and joy, or an agony of chaos and awfulness.

As he walked past the Bonfreres' house in the front of the lot, he found himself listening for his mother's screaming voice.

Nothing.

But no sound of the children either, and they always made

a noise as they went about their chores. Cassy and Nando Jones had had three: Selina, Abe, and Miranda, before Nando's death from pneumonia in '71—'71 had been a bad year all around. John's little sister Lucy had grown up wild all her short life, refusing to work with Cassy as a laundress and taking up with a gambling man when first they'd come to Chicago. She'd died birthing her second child, Josephine—Cassy had taken in Josie and Josie's sister, Geraldine. You didn't turn family out-of-doors. Then there were the brothers and sisters John's mother, Phoebe, had borne in Washington during the War, and in Chicago afterwards, those who had survived: Rowena, Sharon, Ora, Ritchie.

With the children of Lionel and his wife, Lulu—George, Tom, Ish, and baby Dellie—that made enough and more than enough to support, and most of them too young to be of much help. A year and a half ago, against every resolution not to do anything of the kind, John had fallen in love with a girl named Clarice, and now their child, Cora, was just learning to walk. Clarice helped Cassy with her laundry business, her sweetness and tact increasing the number of their clients in times when nearly everyone else was losing them to hard times, tight money, the closing of factories and shops.

But it was backbreaking work, and it took every minute of daylight for the four grown women while nine-year-old Selina looked after the babies and marshaled the younger children to the household chores. When times were good John could hear Selina's sharp, sweet voice calling out commands, encouragement, teasing, sometimes getting Tom and Abe to sing part-songs with her as she swept and they hauled wood for the boilers set up in the narrow yard, just the way Cassy had done, he remembered, with Blue Hill Plantation's "hogmeat gang" all those years ago.

But there was only silence now and the silence went to the pit of John's stomach as he came into the yard. Clarice and Lulu were gathering in washing from the lines that strung back and forth, taking up the whole of the yard between the Bonfreres' house and his own. In the cobalt dark of the porch the open door shone with red-gold kerosene light. Clarice saw him, laid the shirts and sheets carefully back over the line and ran to him, caught him in her arms—"God, I'm so glad to see you!" and their lips met, hard. Hers tasted of sweat, with the slightest whisper of honey. He could have stood there kissing her in the dark all night among the wavering lines of sheets. "Your Mama's gone off."

Shit. "Where?"

She shook her head. She was a few inches short of John's own five-foot, eight-inch height, and like John and Cassy built slim; darker than they, nearly full-blooded African, like Lionel and Lulu, but delicate-featured, a coal-black gazelle. She had her hair wrapped up for work and he wanted nothing more than to tear off her headscarf and gather those great, soft, scrunchy handfuls of her hair in his hands, and to hell with Phoebe....

"The kids have gone out after her." Meaning Selina, Rowena, Abe, and Tom.

"And Cassy didn't?"

"Cassy maybe got other things to do." His sister appeared at the top of the porch steps, her sleeves pushed up and her arms folded, slim as a strap. He could only see her silhouette, but knew what her expression was from the sound of her voice. "I got ten sets of sheets that need to be delivered tonight if we're going to eat next week, and I'm just starting into the ironing now, brother. Mama was in and out all morning, saying how she had a headache, and a backache, and a bellyache, and how she was just going to stay in bed and get herself better, and then just before the sun started going down she lit out of here, said she was gonna go buy medicine."

Shit. John was perfectly familiar with his mother's "medicine-buying" expeditions. "I'll go look for her."

"Get yourself something to eat first."

"Save me some." Though with the youngest nine children home and the three grown women—and Lionel coming in God knew when from Griffe's—whatever would be left by the time John located his mother wouldn't be much. "I'll be back when I can, baby," he whispered to Clarice, cupping the side of her face for one more kiss, the anger and weariness of going through all this yet again tight in his chest.

Then he set out on his search.

If Phoebe were a simple drunk, he reflected, taking a quick look through the door at Griffe's—where as he suspected Lionel was having a couple with his friends from the stockyard—the matter would be an easy one. Even the drunks in the neighborhood knew enough not to stray across Kramer Street, and that was a piece of wisdom just about impervious to liquor.

But for Phoebe, liquor was only an adjunct to whatever dark things inhabited her skull. When her voices started talking to her, there was no telling where they would lure her, or what would appear to her to be a good idea at the time.

So he worked his way south and east, making for the dives and flophouses and tawdry saloons of the levee. This was the way his mother had gone last time she'd wandered away, when she'd been picked up, with a blacked eye and a bloodied lip, naked in an alley behind the Eagle of the Republic saloon on Grove Street and telling the cops at the Twenty-second Precinct House about the revelation God had given her—John winced at the memory. For weeks at a time she'd be more or less the woman who had raised him, who had fled with her children from Blue Hill, with her wry sense of humor and her bitter, sardonically funny observations, telling amazing tales to the children of princesses and warriors and the serial adventures of the Hebrew Children in the wilderness that had nothing to do with any Bible story John had ever read. . . .

And then she'd be gone. Even when she was there, she was gone. Abusive, angry, shouting, or simply silent, staring at the wall. For the past four years he'd been keeping a log of her moods, and knew she was getting worse, much worse.

He didn't know what to do about that.

He hunted for her until nearly midnight, through steamy dark streets illumined only by the smoky glare of the bar-room doors. A one-legged white beggar in the shabby re-mains of a blue Union uniform claimed he'd seen her, on the plank sidewalk outside Dapper Dan's on Judd Street. The man, though drunk himself, was good enough to go into the saloon to ask after her and thus prevent John from getting his head broken by the men inside. Dapper Dan's was one of those places where the "regulars" were all white. Through the door John saw him pause long enough to pull off his wooden leg, untie his real leg from among his rags, park prosthesis and crutches in a locker, and ask the other plug-uglies in the place about her—he came back out, said she'd been seen and thrown out.

From there John asked for her at the shabby dives along the levee, where merchant sailors were incapacitated with chloral hydrate and relieved of their pay, their shoes, and fre-quently their lives; at the catacombs that doled out needled beer and murder. He went to the lakefront bagnios where the clap was probably the mildest and most benign thing that would happen to you. . . . His sister Lucy, John knew, had died in one of the places along here.

One of the waterfront gangs shoved him up against a wall, drunk and looking for sport: "Christ, you mean that nigger bitch who went on about the river of flamin' locusts pourin' down out of the moon?" marveled the bulldog Irishman who led them.

"She's my mother," said John, keeping his voice steady with an effort. The man who pinned him against the wall had on brass knuckles and there were blackjacks, sticks, and chains dimly visible in the gang's shadowy hands. John knew if you showed fear you were dog's meat.

"Let 'im go, boys. He got trouble enough."

The men passed on, bawling with laughter.

In time John found her, where the tracks of the Illinois Central ran into the lakefront yards. It was a nightmare world of darkness and lights, like a shooting-gallery of trains switching back and forth, engines clattering, bells hammering, all night long without cease. The night was still hot and the occasional chuff of breeze off the lake like smelly glue, mosquitoes roared and swarmed around the railroad lanterns that hung before the doors of dark little dens where crooked games, camphor-laced wood-alcohol, and whores too far gone to work even the levee beckoned to those with nowhere else to go. John heard Phoebe's voice singing, cracked and beautiful and silvery, the skipping, almost child-like march the Union soldiers had sung, with words that always raised the hair on his nape:

"Mine eyes have seen the glory of the coming of the Lord. . . ."

John always wondered what that woman had actually seen, the one who had written that song. What the glory of the coming of the Lord had looked like, in the deep of the night.

Phoebe was staggering along the tracks in the middle of what looked like a river of ties and steel. Her black hair hung down her back to her hips and her pink dress lay torn and ragged over her shoulders and she sang full-out as if she were in a choir.

"I have seen Him in the watchfires of a hundred circling
*   camps,*
They have builded Him an altar in the evening dews and
*   damps,·*
I can read His righteous sentence by the dim and flaring
*   lamps—*
His day is marching on."

The groaning shriek of pistons and wheels drowned her voice and a train clanked by between them, medium fast. Steam blasted John in the face. He stopped on the tracks, aware that if another engine bore down on him the noise was so great all around that he wouldn't hear it; he kept looking over his shoulders, left and right. There was an engine there, lamp burning, but unmoving as of yet—at least he could perceive no movement, in the shifting shadows and dark. Two cars went by, tramps dimly perceived in their open doors, and the lights beyond framed Phoebe's body and caught like dark fire in the ends of her hair. She was walking toward another moving engine, her arms outspread as if welcoming a lover.

> "I have read a fiery gospel writ in lines of burnished steel,
>   As ye deal with my contemners, so with you my grace shall
>   deal,
>   Let the hero born of woman crush the serpent with his heel,
>   While God comes marching on. . . ."

With one panicky look over each shoulder—and yes, there was another train coming, though not fast—John darted over the tracks. His eye was caught by the rats swarming between the ties, by the dark slumped form of a drunk asleep or dead on the ground with a bottle glistening under his hand.

"Get your hand off me!" ordered Phoebe, when John caught her, pulled her from the track. "I don't got to go with you! I don't got to go anywhere with you!" Her breath smelled of oil of turpentine, a favorite tipple at the rough joints along the tracks.

"It's me, Mama, it's John."

"No it ain't. John wouldn't come look for me. John too good to go out lookin' for his own mama. John thinks he's too good to speak to her, when he see her on the street."

"Ain't you got no place to take her?" One of the trainmen emerged from the dark at the edge of the switch-yard. "State asylum or someplace? She sure crazy."

The way the man looked at her—the familiar way he helped her over the last couple of ties and over the filth-swimming ditch into Water Street—John suspected the man had had her, in the shadows of one of the alleyways. Maybe six or eight of his friends as well. He always suspected that was how she'd ended up bearing Sharon, Ritchie, and her last baby, who had died.

John said shortly, "State asylum don't take colored."

"Oh." The man nodded vaguely. "Damn shame."

Yes, thought John, escorting his mother back through the now-quiet streets. *It certainly is a damn shame.*

About halfway home Phoebe abruptly decided that he was who he said he was after all, and commenced on a rambling account of why she'd had to go looking for medicine for her back and her belly and to shut up the ants running through her brain. John murmured, "Yes, Mama," and "No, Mama," as she spoke of the things she'd done.

At home he found Clarice had saved out some supper for him, but Phoebe announced, "I'm hungry," and took the pot from her. When John tried to get a share she shouted at him so loudly that, mindful of Lionel and Lulu and the older kids asleep in the next room—or out on the porch, draped in makeshift tents of sheeting against the mosquitoes—he let her have it. As she gorged down all that remained of the beans and rice, Clarice took him quietly aside and showed him what she'd found under the house beneath the corner of the room where his mother's bed was: twelve patent medicine bottles, all of them new and all empty.

"How much pain is she in, to need that much medicine?" asked his wife worriedly. John sniffed the necks of one bottle and then another, and glanced back through the door at his mother in the single candle's quavering light. All her favorites, Godfrey's Cordial and Nervine and Pritchard's Female Elixir. Two definitely had the bitter smell of laudanum and two more the pong of alcohol beneath the mingling sweetness of herbal tonic. "You think if you ask your Dr. Patterson about her, to have a look at her...?"

"That's all I'd need," sighed John. "To tell the man I work for that my mother's crazy? That anytime she might take it into her head to come out to Batavia and look for me?" All the way out to the levee, and all the way back, the anger had been building in him, anger and grief and shame that he'd hold her craziness against her. Shame even that he'd hold her drunkenness against her, for it clearly was no fault of hers.

He knew those ants had been running through her brain long before she'd started trying to shut them up with alcohol.

Clarice asked softly, "What are we going to do?" She too raised her head, looked back through the doorway at the packing-box in which Cora slept. At Cassy curled in a tight ball on her mattress with Miranda and Ritchie. Though Cassy kept a hand on her money-box and slept with it under her pillow at night, still Phoebe had managed to raid it two or three times in the past few years, spending the rent-money inexplicably on toys for all the children, or games of keno. "You know this can't go on."

"I know."

By the time they got Phoebe to bed—after an endless argument during which she refused to lower her voice—it was nearly dawn. John could do no more than lie on the mattress with Clarice in his arms, trembling with anger and frustration, listening to the clanging of the switch-yards in the dark.

CHAPTER THIRTEEN

SLANTING SUNLIGHT DAPPLED THROUGH THE DOGWOOD TREES along Pennsylvania Avenue; the horse of one of the Union Light Guard shied at a passing dog and snorted, tossing its head. Mary glanced over her shoulder at the sudden clatter of hooves, then back at Lincoln in the carriage beside her: "A lot of use they'll be if a rebel assassin shoots at you from the trees."

Lincoln leaned back against the leather of the carriage-seat: "The only way they could prevent a rebel assassin from shooting from the trees is to surround us like a wall. And even then they couldn't stop a man from flying overhead in a balloon and dropping a brick on my head." And he looked up, shading his eyes as if to search for such a craft.

"*Will* you be serious?"

"No." Lincoln smiled, and put his arm around Mary's shoulders. "I have been serious all morning and I am mighty weary of it."

Deep in her dream, feeling as if she were trapped in quicksand, Mary thought, *No . . . Let me out. Let me wake up.*

I know what's coming and I don't want to see it. Not again.

But she couldn't wake—couldn't put from her the happiness of each relived second in his company, even if she knew that each one was a knife in her heart.

". . . I want a carriage-ride with the woman I love, not a military parade. . . ."

Sometimes—tonight was one of those times—Mary caught fragments of other events in her dreams: hurrying downstairs to the carriage in her silver-gray dress, her tippet of black and ermine wrapped around her shoulders. Hearing Lincoln in the hall behind her knock at Robert's door. "We are going to the theater, Bob; don't you want to go?"

She didn't hear Robert's reply, but in the carriage, on the way to Fifteenth Street to pick up young Major Rathbone and Miss Harris, Lincoln shook his head and said, "I can't blame him, the poor boy hasn't slept in a bed in two weeks. I told him to do just what he felt most like."

And then they were in the theater. Mary was conscious of the damp cold of Lincoln's coat-sleeve as he escorted her up the dark little stair, of the scent of Major Rathbone's hair-pomade and of Miss Harris's lavender sachet. Her heart was crying *No! Let me out!* but she tightened her grip on the sinewy arm, still strong enough, after all these years, to pick up an ax by the last inch of its handle and hold it out straight before him. . . .

Strong enough to swoop her up in his arms as easily as he'd swoop Tad.

The Pinkerton guard John Parker, burly and disheveled and smelling faintly of liquor, rising hastily from the wooden chair beside the door of the box to salute; Lincoln stopping for a moment to say something to him as Major Rathbone opened the door and bowed Mary and Miss Harris through. The box itself, dark and a trifle stuffy, with its drapery of red, white, and blue, and the glow of the stage lights beyond it outlining the rocking chair the management always brought in for Lincoln. The band breaking into "Hail to the Chief," and Lincoln moving the draperies aside a little to bow to the audience.

Laughter and cheering gusted up from below, warming Mary with a glowing satisfaction—a sense of deep vindication—that she felt even through her rising panic, her desperate struggle to get out of the dream before the end. Six months previously every newspaper in the country had been calling him "that giraffe from Illinois" and claiming that re-electing him would damage "the cause of human liberty and the dignity and honor of the nation." "There was never a truer epithet applied to a certain individual than that of 'Gorilla.'"

He had suffered—not from those slurs, but from the

grinding toll of the War itself. She could see it in his face, in the shadowy glow of the gas-lights. The deep lines, the sadness in his eyes, made her want to weep. The cheers from the audience were a balm, to her and, she thought, to him. At least there was the lightness in his movement that he'd had during their carriage-ride, the relaxation, as he sat beside her, that she hadn't seen in him in months. Major Rathbone and Miss Harris settled in the other two seats, hand in hand, heads together: the young soldier's mother had married Miss Harris's father, an irascible and sharp-tongued Senator from New York, and now it looked like the children of their separate first unions would themselves unite. Mary's hand stole into Lincoln's, and down onstage the sprightly Florence tried to tell a joke to Lord Dundreary, with predictably sparse results.

Florence: "Why does a dog wag its tail?"

Lord Dundreary: "Good heavens, I have no idea."

Florence: "Because the tail can't wag the dog."

"There's Charlie Taft," murmured Lincoln, looking down into the audience below them, and Mary hid a smile; in any crowd, Lincoln was always looking for people he knew. And the other Mary, the Mary who lay locked in the dream of these minutes, felt the minutes passing as if she heard the ticking of a clock. . . .

Ten more minutes to go. Nine. As if she walked with him down the road to a ferry, dreading the sight of every tree, every path-side stone that told her it was getting closer, and there was nothing she could do to stop the approach of the crossing-over point, when he was with her one moment, and the next. . . .

Maybe if I scream I can wake myself. . . .

"Don't know the manner of good society, eh?" sniffed the bumpkin Asa Trenchard, down on the stage. "Wal, I guess I know enough to turn you inside out—you sockdologizing old mantrap!"

Lincoln leaned down, to make some wiseacre remark in Mary's ear; she felt the brush of his beard against her temple.

NOOOO...!!!

The gunshot was like the cracking boom of thunder, like the lightning that had always so terrified her. Lincoln's arm jerked convulsively in her grip, and Mary caught him as he slumped sideways in the rocking chair. Gunpowder stink filled her nostrils, gunpowder and the horrible hot smell of blood.

Someone was shouting, rushing forward through the smoke. Major Rathbone tried to seize him, struggling in the reflected glow from the stage, and a knife flashed in the gaslight gleam. Miss Harris fell back against the box rail, screaming, and on Mary's shoulder Lincoln's weight grew heavier and heavier as he sagged against her. She saw the blood in his hair and began to scream too, screaming as all that she had feared for four years came rushing to catch her, to sweep her into the darkness that lay on the other side of that dividing-line of her life....

THERE MUST BE SOMETHING I COULD HAVE DONE.

Mary looked back on the dream—like looking back into a room, through a window from the outside—as she sat beneath the elm-trees of Bellevue's parklike grounds the following morning. Beside her on the bench sat Mrs. Olivia Hill, black-clothed like herself, a widow like herself, who had come up to her last Friday, after she'd run away from John Wilamet in the rose garden: "Is there anything I can do, my dear?" she had asked.

There wasn't, of course, and both of them knew there wasn't. But it was good at least to know that someone in this place actually cared. Like John...Imagine meeting John here, after all those years! Olivia had sought her out again after breakfast this morning, and offered to walk with her, the gray-clad form of Amanda trailing inconspicuously behind. "They don't like to see us in conversation, you know," whispered Mrs. Hill, and widened her enormous blue eyes at

Mary. "Especially not those of us who were put here for our beliefs."

Mary turned her head sharply, met that gentle gaze. There was something in Mrs. Hill's voice that told her exactly what "beliefs" her family had considered marked her as insane, and she lowered her voice before she asked, "Do you think it might be possible to speak to our loved ones here?"

Olivia glanced back at Amanda, then at Mary again.

"Have you ever tried it?" Mary persisted. "Since you've been here, I mean?"

Olivia's thin, intent face grew troubled in its frame of black veiling. "The problem is the daylight," she explained, and Mary nodded. Every medium she'd ever spoken to had emphasized that the yellow vibrations of sunlight were absolutely inimical to the materialization of ectoplasm. "You notice how careful the good doctor is, to keep us separated once it grows dark."

Mary looked up at the trees overhead: elms like the clouds of a prairie thunderstorm, even in the brightness of morning casting a dense blue shade. "Surely," she urged, "we can at least try. Is there anyone else here, who might form a circle with us? Who might lend their strength, to summoning the spirits across the Veil?"

"Oh, yes. Lucretia Bennett was put in here for exactly that reason—because, her husband says, she believes that their sons speak to her from the Land Beyond. And that, of course, must be madness." She smiled her sweet, sardonic smile. "And little Miss Judd as well, though I'm afraid, poor child, she does have a terribly nervous constitution.... She says she knew you when she was a little girl."

Mary smiled at the recollection of that fairy-like child she'd known in Chicago, in the chaotic days of 1860 before the Republican Convention. "She did. Her father was one of my husband's great supporters.... The President of the Illinois Central Railroad, you know. My husband did a great deal of work for them, in his lawyer days. *And* had to sue them to get paid, I might add."

"Oh, well, one can understand how the *poor* Illinois Central Railroad would be so *poverty-stricken* that they wouldn't have the money to pay their lawyer. . . ."

And both women laughed. Bellevue Place, Mary thought, looking out past her companion to the thick green lawns, the winding graveled carriage-drive that circled the grounds, did not seem so very different from the Spiritualist camps she'd attended in the green country of upstate New York. There was that same relaxed air of not having anywhere else to be, of having all arrangements for room and meals taken care of in advance. . . .

The difference, of course, being that in those places one was treated like an adult capable of making decisions despite one's grief, and not like a willful and deluded child.

And even when she was a child, Mary didn't recall this horrible sense of being always watched, always spied upon, tattled on for the slightest deviation from what Dr. Patterson considered "normal" behavior.

It was worse than living with her sister Ann.

"I've never had success in materializing the spirits since I've been here," went on Olivia, with a sigh of regret. "It's what one can expect, of course, in this atmosphere of con-centrated skepticism—I should think the look on Mrs. Patterson's face would send any spirit fleeing. But if nothing else, we can transmit to our loved ones the assurance that *we* are thinking of *them,* even if they cannot come to us."

"But they know that anyway," Mary pointed out.

"Of course," agreed Olivia, with a beatific smile. "But is it not good to receive a letter full of love and cheerful thoughts, even from one to whom you are prevented from writing?"

No, thought Mary crossly. *Mr. Lincoln hears me speak to him every day, hears me tell him how much I love him, need him. . . . My sons hear my words of love daily, hourly. One holds séances in order to hear from THEM. In order to see their dear faces again, to hear their words, touch their beloved hands. It isn't that I don't think they hear, there in the Summer Land. But I miss them so!*

"When those medical lackeys my husband hired came

with their statements about conversing with the dead being proof of madness, I told them, if belief in the survival of the soul in Heaven is madness, then I claim the sisterhood of madness with Christ and all his saints." Scorn flicked in Mrs. Hill's voice and she squared her slim shoulders. "If it is madness to believe that love survives death, and that my precious boys in Heaven still love and comfort the mother they loved on earth, then how I pity your bleak and loveless sanity!"

Mary assumed there was some kind of grapevine telegraph in operation, as soldiers exchanged from rebel prison camps during the War had assured her existed in Andersonville and Libby Prison under the very noses of the guards. She was certainly aware that every darky in Lexington had known news and information long before a single white was aware of it, apparently by telepathy. In any case, the following morning directly after breakfast, she and Olivia Hill made their way to the densest copse of elm-trees, that stood farthest from the house at a corner of the grounds, and found Minnie Judd and the white-haired Mrs. Bennett waiting for them there.

"It's *good* of you to come with us here," said Lucretia Bennett in her oddly-inflected voice. "*Good* of you to *help* us in trying to reach out to our *loved* ones on the Other Side."

"I don't hold much hope." Olivia took Mary's other hand and drew her down onto the bench in the secluded shade. "We have twice attempted to hold gatherings here—mostly at this early hour, when the sunlight is not so harsh. Perhaps there were not enough of us to invoke the energies needed to build a bridge of thoughts for the souls to pass from the Summer Land to this world. We can only trust, and pray."

In the dense shade the four women recited, very softly, the Lord's Prayer, and just as softly, sweet voices harmonizing, sang "Shall We Gather at the River." Despite her misgivings about the daylight, Mary felt herself relaxing with the familiar words, the peaceful sense that these circles always brought her. Others over the years had included more prayers, and many had incorporated more music, drawing the Seekers together into calm and ready thought.

But always was that awareness that they understood her loss. Who young Minnie might have lost, Mary did not know—a friend, perhaps? She was too young to have given a sweetheart to the War. But Mrs. Bennett's black dress told her at least that this woman, like Olivia Hill, had walked the road she had walked. And all of them, she knew, had this in common: that they had found life without their loved ones literally beyond bearing.

In her mind Mary painted the darkness of those shuttered, curtained parlors, the enclosed sense of comfort and safety. The flicker of candles that always recalled the dim parlors of her girlhood, before the pallid glare of gaslight chased shadows away.

Please come, beloved, she whispered in her heart. *Please speak to me through these kindly women. Rest your hands on my shoulders, let me know that even here you're with me. That you've forgiven me . . .* The dreams of the night before last, and of last Wednesday night—was it only a week ago?—were the clearest she had seen him in many months. Even the knowledge that they would end with his head slumping down to her shoulder, blood gleaming blackly in his hair, wasn't enough to make her thrust them aside, even if she could have. They were all she had.

Give me something to live on, something to hold! I miss you so.

"Now, ladies." Dr. Patterson's deep voice broke the sweet silence that succeeded the song. Mary's eyes snapped open and Olivia and Mrs. Bennett dropped her hands at once, like guilty schoolgirls. The superintendent strode across the grass toward them, with his wife and Amanda striding purposefully behind. "You know this kind of excitement isn't at all good for you. Mrs. Hill, I'm surprised at you."

Mary replied, since Olivia seemed unable to answer. "Are we not then even permitted to pray? I should think *you,* of all people, would approve."

The doctor smiled, that impenetrable and eternal smile that she was coming to hate. "Of course you may pray, my dear Mrs. Lincoln. But prayer is for Sunday in chapel, or qui-

etly and privately in your room, as St. Paul recommends, and
in a spirit of Christian resignation. Mrs. Bennett, Mrs. Hill, I
have a little treatment I'd like to try on you now before
lunch, to see if we can make you feel better. . . ."

"He always does that," whispered Minnie Judd, in her soft
thread of a voice as the doctor and his wife led the two other
women away. "He doesn't like to see us gathered together.
Not even in daytime."

"And you put up with it?" Mary's voice snapped with
scorn for this thin girl in the dazzlingly fashionable dove-gray
gown, scorn that reflected the surge of rage burning through
her. Minnie regarded her with surprise in her cornflower-
blue eyes.

"We must put up with it, ma'am. What choice do we
have?"

What choice indeed? thought Mary, shaking with anger as
Minnie, too, walked away under the trees toward the big
stone house, her demi-train rustling on the grass. *When you
have been judged a madwoman, you have no choice. You must take
what they give you, and rejoice that it is no worse.*

And all the peace beneath those lush trees, all the pleasant
treatment and hollow professions of understanding, could
never make up for that indignity.

THAT NIGHT MARY TOOK SUPPER WITH THE PATTERSON FAM-
ily. Mrs. Patterson smiled her wooden smile and tried to
make gracious small-talk, but the fourth time she broke off to
berate her daughter for not "behaving like a lady" when the
poor young woman was clearly doing her best not to upset
her food in company, Mary was hard put not to slap the doctor's wife.

Dr. Patterson had just returned from his bi-weekly visit to
Chicago, and though he spoke kindly to his daughter he said
nothing in her defense. Mostly, he chatted with his son about
the affairs of his practice in Chicago. All her girlhood Mary
had been ingrained with the idea that Yankees had no

manners, and though she'd found that in many cases this was
an exaggeration, she'd never been able to get used to this particularly Yankee combination of sanctimoniousness and pre-
occupation with work to the exclusion of one's company.
Even after all these years, even in this situation, it annoyed her.

After supper Dr. Patterson mixed Mary a glass of medicine to take before she went to bed, for her back had begun
to ache again, and her head, and she found herself both depressed and unable to rest. But when Amanda had helped her
change into her nightgown and wrapper, and had locked the
door for the night, Mary sat up for a time in the chair beside
her bed, her eyes closed in the silence.

She whispered the Lord's Prayer, as the women had done
that morning in the shade, and sang softly under her breath,
"Shall we gather at the river / the beautiful, the beautiful river. . . ."

Prayer and song were an incantation, like Mammy Sally's
hoodoo rhymes. Hoping against hope that even without the
circle of loving hands and hearts, the spirits would come.
The gas hissed softly, its flame turned down low behind a
painted globe of glass—never since childhood had Mary
been able to sleep in a completely dark room. Through the
pink mosquito-bar tacked over the window a whisper of
breeze stirred the dense, hot air. The big house was silent
around her. Even the woman who had screamed last night—
screamed so loudly that she could be heard here on the family side of the house—made no sound.

How many nights she had sat thus in her great bedroom
in that cold dreadful mansion on Pennsylvania Avenue, that
fraudulent white-painted sepulchre of her dreams. . . . Had sat
late, so late that even the incessant noise of soldiers marching
in the street, of bugle calls from the camps on the near-by
Mall, had ceased. Her husband was absent, as he was so often
absent, having slipped down the service stairs and out of the
house through the basement, to walk alone through the
chilly fog to the War Department to wait for dispatches.
Sometimes he'd even sleep there on the sofa in the telegraphers' room. Or coming back, he would go to his office, his

stockinged footfalls passing her door, to read petitions or pleas or the papers related to a thousand and one details of the War that only he could decide upon, until he fell, exhausted, asleep at his desk.

In that silence—Mary remembered it so clearly now, called it back to her, *willed* it back—it had seemed to her that the gaslight had burned blue, just as candles did in the romances she read, and she had seen those beautiful, glowing forms pass through the closed door of her bedroom and come to her, holding out their hands.

Willie. . . ! She had seen him so clearly. His face—a round Todd face, just beginning to lengthen as he passed his eleventh birthday—wore that expression of thoughtful calm that had nothing in it of solemnity. A Todd face and his father's gray eyes. Sometimes he wore the gaudy little uniform the militia Zouaves had given him, along with an honorary commission of Colonel; sometimes the dark wool suit in which he'd been buried. He did not seem ghostly at all, only wrought of a pale light, and he led a smaller child by the hand, little Eddie in the long toddler's dress of tucked linen that Mary had sewed for him.

Her dearest boys! She had clasped them to her heart, though now she could not remember whether their flesh had felt solid in her arms. *Yet it wasn't a dream!* she told herself. It happened, just as Nettie Colburn, and Lord Colchester, and the other mediums of the spirits had assured her it would!

She breathed deep, the swoony warmth from Dr. Patterson's medicine enfolding her. If Dr. Patterson had not interrupted them, would not a few more minutes have sufficed for the Circle they'd formed? Even in daylight, even in the midst of this terrible place? Would not the spirits have found some way of communicating with those they loved? In her mind she formed the scene, Mr. Lincoln shyly smiling as he walked toward her through the deep shadows of the elms, with Eddie on one hip and Willie clinging to his hand, and Tad—young thin tall Tad like a half-grown Thoroughbred colt—striding alongside.

Could she not at least have felt on her shoulders the pressure of strong hands, as occasionally happened in the darkness of those séance rooms, when the medium would tell her that he sensed the presence of a tall and bearded man?

She sat awake—or mostly awake—in the gloom for what felt like hours, before lying down on top of the covers, and crying herself to sleep.

CHAPTER FOURTEEN

Springfield 1837

IN JUNE OF 1837 MARY PACKED HER MANY TRUNKS AND HAT-boxes, and in company with her father and Judy, made the jolting coach journey down to Louisville, to take one of the Ohio River steamers to Cairo.

Her father hired a stateroom for her, barely big enough to swing a mouse in, let alone a cat. He himself took a curtained bunk in the men's cabin, and spent a good portion of each day in the gentlemen's parlor, smoking long nine cigars, playing vingt-et-un and talking politics with the highly assorted crowd of slave-traders, land-speculators, cotton- and sugar-brokers, merchants, and lawyers who journeyed up and down the Ohio from Cairo all the way up to Pittsburgh. "I don't believe you talk politics with them at all," teased Mary, when her father took her for a walk around the upper deck in the evening cool after supper. "I believe you just use that as an excuse to gossip, the way you always accuse us poor women of doing." And she twinkled a smile at him from beneath her bonnet-brim.

"And isn't that just what you do?" he countered with a grin.

And Mary laughed, for she didn't want to complain of the company in the ladies' parlor. But in fact she found it excruciatingly dull, consisting as it did of a New England woman whose husband was engaged in "something to do with land" in Mississippi, a merchant's wife whose whole soul was occupied in the cost and difficulties of running her husband's business (and his life as well, in Mary's opinion), and the wife and daughter of an Ohio state Assemblyman who weren't entirely clear whether the husband/father of the family was a Democrat or a Whig.

The talk was all of servants, and of the expense of running a household, and the best way to get wine-stains out of damask. Why was it, Mary wondered, that married people became so *dull*? When Mary said she was from Kentucky the Yankee woman had asked disapprovingly if her father owned slaves, and had proceeded to lecture her—in Mr. Presby's best style—on the evils of slavery without bothering to ask first what her own views on the subject were.

"You'll like Springfield," prophesied her father, leaning his elbows on the upper-deck rail. "With your taste for politics you'll feel right at home there." On the stern-deck below them hogs squealed in their pens among high-piled sacks of corn, bushels of oats, barrels of whiskey and apples. Now and then above the incessant pound and splash of the two great paddles, Mary could hear the voices of the slaves who'd come onboard at Louisville, chained to the walls along the narrow walkways on either side of the engine-room. Sometimes singing, sometimes calling out in whatever gambling-games it was they played to pass the time and take their minds off where they were going. Sometimes, from the starboard where the women were chained, she would hear a child cry.

"It's going to be the state capital now, isn't it?" Elizabeth had mentioned that in her latest letter, in the midst of a host of Ninian's concerns, as if it were important only because it raised the value of Ninian's town lots.

"If Ninian and the Long Nine have anything to say about it, it will."

"The Long Nine?" Mary raised her brows. "So my brother-in-law has become a cigar? It's a guarantee of popularity, I suppose...."

Her father laughed. "That's the name someone gave the representatives of the Sangamon County delegation at the Legislature. There are nine of them—the biggest county delegation in the state—and every man of 'em's over six feet tall, the tallest six feet four. Springfield's already the center of trade and farming in the state, and the biggest town. Vandalia's a mere village by comparison."

He shifted his broad-brimmed straw hat on his head, and looked out, as if he could see, beyond the wall of forest along the riverbank, the small settlements marked by pluming smoke, the tiny farms. "Illinois is one of the fastest-growing states of the Union, daughter. The key to our nation's future lies in the West. You'll meet the best of the coming men there."

"Are you trying to marry me off, Pa?" Mary regarded him coquettishly.

He pinched her chin. "I just want my girl to be happy."

She turned her eyes away to the green monotony on either side of the river, the forest that seemed to stretch on forever, trying to unthink the thought that had sliced across her mind: *You want to be happy knowing you've done your duty by "your girl."*

Happy with Betsey. And Betsey's children.

With the problem of those she supplanted all happily gone away at last, and no man to say you didn't do your duty.

She had so looked forward to this journey—to seeing Elizabeth and Frances again, and Elizabeth's new baby— Julia, named for the first tiny daughter, who had died. She still felt wild, dancing excitement at the sound of the churning paddlewheels, a bursting exhilaration at these new lands, this new *world*. But the suspicion that this was only a farther-away version of Mentelle's snagged in her mind. It caught on her thoughts like a burr in a petticoat, filling her with unthinkable shame.

At Cairo they transferred to another steamboat, this one going upriver on the Mississippi, which even in those high reaches was a broad yellow-brown stream whose banks were a tangle of snags and bars that the pilot had to negotiate with care. Sometimes they'd pass a flatboat, wide rafts a hundred feet long and laden with pumpkins and corn and hogs, riding the current all the way down to New Orleans. The paddles would churn the water and the men working the sweeps would shake their fists, sun-browned men who looked like they'd been braided out of strips of rawhide, with their faded hair and faded shirts and heavy Conestoga boots. Mary made the acquaintance of a French lady from New Orleans and her even-more-French aunt from Paris, and had a good time speaking to them in their native language of the cities she longed more than anything to see. She had a sense, riding the river, of profound delight, of moving out of the lush hollows of Kentucky and into a wider world.

They debarked at St. Louis, and then truly the world did change.

All of her life Mary had lived in Lexington, traveling no farther than Frankfort to visit Betsey's haughty, thin-nosed old mother. Her world had been a rolling verdant world of dense forests and granite outcrops, of patches of laurel, paw-paw, tulip trees. When the stagecoach climbed from the river-valley where St. Louis lay, the full harsh sweep of the prairie wind struck them, and she saw for the first time the prairie emptiness: green, flat, endless, unbroken to the horizon, baking with that indescribable scent of curing grasses under the morning sun.

Clinging to the strap in the swaying coach, Mary gazed at the stage-ruts sweeping away into the unimaginable distance and thought, *I'm going in the wrong direction! I should be going south, to New Orleans, or east to New York and Europe. Where am I going, and why?*

AT LEAST THERE WERE TREES IN SPRINGFIELD. FOR TWO DAYS on the stage, jolting through that vast untenanted world of tall grass and meadowlarks, Mary had had terrible visions—her sister's letters to the contrary—of yet another desolate constellation of board shacks, weathering slowly to grayness in the hot wind and unending glare of the sun.

But Springfield stood on the bluffs above the Sangamon River, and the fertile country along the bottomlands was set-tled up with scattered farms and cattle grazing contentedly in the waist-deep prairie grass. It was late in the day when the stage pulled into the yard of the Globe Tavern, an unpromising quadrangle of whitewashed buildings whose long porch sheltered an assortment of the local bumpkins and a pair of sleepy dogs. A bell clanged from the cupola on the roof, to announce the arrival. Dust and smoke hung in the air, as did the smell of livestock.

"What do you want to bet that's Ninian's carriage?" Robert Todd helped his daughter from the big high-wheeled coach and nodded toward the lower-slung and more elegant vehicle that stood waiting. "I wrote him the night we arrived in St. Louis, that we'd be on the next stage. The team certainly looks like Ninian's taste in horseflesh," he added, with an admiring glance at the glossily-groomed bays. "Have a seat and I'll go find him. He'll be inside."

He handed Mary into the carriage and signed to the stagecoach guard to pile their luggage beside it, then crossed the yard and climbed the plank steps to vanish into the inner darkness of the porch. The slave girl Judy, exhausted and intimidated by the journey, retreated to a bench near the woodpile. Mary put up her parasol against the slanting light of the afternoon sun and looked eagerly around her, taking in what she could see of the town that Elizabeth—and now, apparently, Frances—had chosen for their home.

The tavern yard certainly didn't look promising, and the street visible beyond—rutted and unpaved under a miasma of yellow dust—even less so. In addition to the carriage in which Mary sat, the yard contained half a dozen infinitely more plebeian vehicles, mostly farm-wagons, and a decrepit buggy, as well as a number of saddle horses hitched to the porch railing. Dogs snored in the shade. Chickens scratched. An occasional hog wandered in from the so-called street.

Whereas in Lexington there would have been a variety of people in evidence—wealthy planters, students of law and medicine from the University, slaves on errands for their masters, and young ladies in silks and fine muslins shopping in the Cheapside stores—here there seemed to be nothing but farmers and teamsters. In the shadows of the tavern porch a gang of rough-looking idlers drank, spit tobacco, and

laughed uproariously over some tale being spun for them by
a tall skinny idler sitting on a barrel with his long legs
sprawled out before him. Presumably, reflected Mary, sitting
up quite straight in her new pink ruffled dress, there was a
better class of citizen farther into town.

Movement in the tavern doorway. Mary turned, hoping it
was her father and Ninian. But instead a blocky, broad-
shouldered man in the tattered remains of a black long-tailed
coat, bewhiskered and filthy, staggered across to the carriage,
jabbed a grimy finger up at her, and declared, "And another
thing, Missy: if slavery was to be expanded into the Western
territories, how long would it be before the white slave-lords
of the South would demand white slaves as well as black?
How long before the wealthy factory-lords would take the
indifference of the government for license to enserf the luck-
less laborers who are already de facto slaves, by further robbing them of what little liberty they still enjoy? Eh?" He
glared up at Mary, red-faced with anger. "You answer me
that, Miss!"

Mary looked away, cheeks burning. The man reeked of
cheap liquor and clearly was incapable of taking—or even
recognizing—a hint that his conversation was not wanted.
Judy, who'd gotten to her feet, was looking around in an
agony of uncertainty, not about to go up and tell a white man
to go away. In Lexington, of course, it simply wouldn't have
happened. Too many people knew Mary—any shopkeeper
or clerk in town would have headed off the drunkard from a
girl they'd waited on since her earliest childhood.

But since the alternative was to take refuge in a public
tavern—presumably among this man's equally inebriated
comrades—and since Mary wasn't sure she could make a dismount from the rather high carriage without providing
every idler on the porch with a glimpse of petticoats, pan-
talettes, and ankles—she remained where she was. Her
frozen silence seemed to enrage her interrogator still further.

"A government system which condones the domination
of any man by any other man has automatically doomed to

destruction all those it pretends to protect!" bellowed the whiskered man. "Of course the government will permit the extension of slavery into the newly formed territories and of course the result will be—"

"Professor Kittridge, come on up here on the porch and let me buy you a beer." The storyteller unfolded himself from off his barrel and ambled over to the carriage. Mary had an impression of enormous stringy height, of coarse black hair sticking out in all directions and high, sharp cheekbones. The stranger's features all seemed too big for his face—nose, brow, mouth—and his eyes were deep-set and gray as winter rain. He was dressed like the men on the flatboats in what seemed to be the uniform of the country, a faded calico shirt and linsey-woolsey trousers tucked into Conestoga boots, and there was a small straight knife-scar on his right temple. His voice was a husky tenor, high without being reedy, and underlaid, Mary thought, by a soft Kentucky flatness about the vowels.

"Lay not your hand upon me, servant of the servants of Mammon!" Professor Kittridge swung around and lashed at the storyteller with a punch that would have stopped an ox in its tracks. "Pettifogger! Serpent! *Diabolos!*"

The storyteller met this barrage of invective by putting his hand on his attacker's forehead and holding him off at the length of his gorilla-like arm, Kittridge's frenzied punches slashing inches short of his ribs. At the same time he backed off, so that Kittridge's own momentum propelled him by degrees to the porch. As he did so, the storyteller glanced up over Kittridge's head to Mary, checking to make sure she wasn't harmed or alarmed. His gray eyes met hers, and when he saw that far from fainting with affront she was struggling not to laugh aloud, they sparkled with a deep answering delight.

Barely had the Professor and the servant of the servants of Mammon vanished into the darkness of the porch when Robert Todd, Ninian Edwards, and a skinny little man carrying a coachman's whip appeared from around the corner, quickening their pace as they crossed the yard. "Miss Mary, I beg your pardon," called out Ninian. "I thought I'd have time to pick up sugar and coffee from Irwin's. Can you ever forgive me?" His eyes twinkled as he, the coachman, and his father-in-law loaded the trunks onto the back of the carriage and strapped them into place. Judy, looking infinitely relieved to have the world return to situations with which she was familiar, hurriedly crossed to join them.

"Shall I horsewhip Jerry here for leaving the carriage?" Ninian indicated the coachman with a grin, and the black man grinned back.

"I should think it massively unjust to punish the servant for a sin he shares with the master." Mary put on her most pious expression, and all three men laughed. "Just don't you dare let it happen again."

Ninian and her father sprang into the carriage, Judy climbing up to the coachman's box. Jerry unhitched the team and swung himself up beside her. "You are just, as well as beautiful, Miss Mary," said the coachman gravely, and clicked to the horses. Ninian leaned forward to point something out to her father about his team. As the carriage turned, Mary saw the tall storyteller emerge from the porch again, a couple of saddlebags over one bony shoulder, making for the saddle-horses tethered on the other side of the yard. He stopped a stride beyond the porch steps, seeing her with the men of her family.

Mary met his eyes, raised her hand in a little gesture: *I'm well. Thank you.* And he lifted his enormous hand to her in return.

The wheels of the carriage threw dust on him as it pulled out of the yard.

CHAPTER FIFTEEN

MARY WAS THREE MONTHS IN SPRINGFIELD. IT WAS HEAVEN, to be with Elizabeth again, mothered and fussed over as she had been when she was a child. Heaven to share the second-floor front room of Ninian's handsome brick house with Frances, instead of with the whining tattletale Ann. Frances slept promptly and soundly, and didn't make a fuss when Mary sat up reading: didn't moan and mumble, "What, again?" on those nights when Mary had to use the chamber pot half a dozen times. It was heaven not to spend all day, every day in a battle of wills with Betsey; heaven not to have a gaggle of little half-brothers and -sisters playing in the library when she wanted to read.

That made up for a lot.

And Springfield was lively. Ninian's house—the "House on the Hill," though personally Mary wouldn't have called that *hill* more than a bump—was the center of all the best society there, the young lawyers and politicians who were starting to flood into town, now that it would be state capital. As a member of the influential Long Nine, and the son of the former governor, Ninian had connections with all the spider-threads of influence and favors and promises of government jobs in the county.

For the first time in her life she could discuss politics freely, without Betsey throwing up her hands and making remarks about schoolgirls and bluestockings, and Mary reveled in this like a cat in catnip.

She had plenty of chances to talk politics. With the State Legislature coming to Springfield, single gentlemen were ten to a lady, and a girl had to be really trying, not to have her dance-card filled days before a ball.

That, too, made up for a lot.

But it didn't make up for the prairie thunderstorms, whose violence Frances hadn't lied about. When the forks and sheets of lightning drove down out of the blackness, when thunder ripped the sky as if the whole of the universe were tearing to pieces, Mary could do nothing but hide herself in bed, weeping with a fear she didn't understand and sometimes screaming inconsolably as if Death itself stood just outside the bedroom door.

And it didn't make up for the fact that Ninian's modest collection of books was one of the finest libraries in Sangamon County: Its few volumes of edifying fiction Mary either had already read or made short work of in the first week. The only bookstore in town, C. Birchall and Company, refused to stock novels on the grounds that they were immoral, and thus she spent her three months in Springfield engaged in a constant quest for something—*anything*—to read.

Professional theatricals were immoral, too. No amount of picnics and buggy-rides in company with admiring young gentlemen could make up for that.

If Lexington was provincial, Springfield was rustic.

Much as she enjoyed that summer, she could not rid herself of the feeling that she should have gone in the other direction when she got on the steamboat at Cairo.

Though Springfield was officially now the state capital of Illinois—with a cleared field for the new State House and ox-teams hauling stones through the unpaved streets to prove it—the Legislature still met in Vandalia, a sleepy village sixty miles to the south. Teamsters, laborers, and ruffians associated with the building jostled along the few board sidewalks that dignified the downtown, and clogged the barrooms of the shabby and unprepossessing taverns that dotted the outskirts of town.

On Mary's second evening in Springfield, when Ninian gave a party for the regiment of Todd and Stuart cousins—and their most privileged friends—Mary couldn't help missing the students and professors who had added a note of sophistication and learning to Lexington parties. The talk was either gossip concerning all the Todd, Logan, and Stuart cousins, or of state politics, of government contracts, and of who had influence with the state's Congressmen and Senators in Washington—fascinating topics enough, but not to the exclusion of everything else.

"Of course it's not much," grinned her cousin John Stuart, as they stood together on the porch in the semi-darkness, with the dim glow of the oil-lamps within shining on the bower of polished honeysuckle leaves. "It's rough and raw compared to Kentucky—and I'll say it myself, though I love this place. But that's why we're all here. To be in on a good thing from the beginning."

From within, Elizabeth's voice lifted, calling for a game of Speculation. There was warm laughter, and the scraping of chairs. "Can I help you, Eppy?" asked Frances's voice—Eppy had been introduced to Mary as "our cook," and though legally Illinois was free soil, it was quite clear to Mary that Elizabeth regarded the handsome young black woman in the same light that she'd regarded Mammy Sally, as a well-loved slave.

Springfield was, Mary reflected, in some ways very like home.

"Sure, you can walk three blocks and be out on the prairie . . . now." Cousin John tucked a thumb into his waistcoat pocket, and turned his head, a strong, blunt profile against the dark masses of the trees. The air felt dense, and even this far from the river the occasional mosquito whined. Mary felt the preliminary ache behind her eyes that whispered of a thunderstorm somewhere, over those endless grasslands.

"But you mark my words, Mary, in five years, Springfield is where everything will be happening in this section— maybe in this country. The prairies are the best farmland there is. Land that people are trading around now as if it were shoelaces is going to settle up. Town lots that people give me to pay bills with will be worth what they are in

Boston or Philadelphia. The State of Illinois will swing a lot of power in the country. You could do worse than to settle here and make it your home."

"Are you trying to hitch me up with someone already, Cousin John?" Mary forced aside fears of the coming storm and gave him a sidelong look.

John Stuart merely laughed. "I don't think you'll need any help from me, Cousin Molly."

He might even be right, thought Mary, as she let the big man take her arm and lead her back into the parlor, though she'd heard far too many land-speculators and schemers in her father's parlor in Lexington to be dazzled by encomiums about "this section's going to go far...." She'd heard much the same about the proposal to run a railway line from Frankfort to Lexington, which had ended up in disastrous failure when it was discovered that the grade was too steep and that the weight of the trains very quickly destroyed the granite ties between the tracks.

The section may indeed have been destined for greatness, but the thought of living in a town with no bookstores and no circulating library filled her with dismay.

And if her destiny in life was to marry the President of the United States, Mary reflected, with a wry nod to her early passion for Mr. Clay, it was pretty clear she wasn't going to meet him here.

It was enough, on the occasion of that first party, to sort out relatives she'd only met upon occasion years ago, if at all: the courtly cousin John Stuart and his wife; Uncle John Todd—a doctor—and his schoolgirl daughters, tall Lizzie and chubby Francy; Ninian's brother Benjamin and *his* wife Helen; the Leverings, who lived nearby on the Hill; quiet, saturnine Dr. Wallace, who was Frances's leading beau. Then there was Senator Herndon—another of Ninian's Long Nine—and his chinless and pompous cousin Billy, and a short, dandified little lawyer with the manners of a dancing-master and the voice of Jove speaking from Olympus, Mr. Stephen Douglas.

"I thought your partner was going to make one of us this evening, Stuart," remarked Dr. Wallace, when the rather extended family party settled down in the parlor for a game of Speculation.

John Stuart shook his head and grinned again. "He's ridden over to New Salem, courting."

"What, still?" laughed Ninian. "Is he never going to bring himself to the scratch?" And Elizabeth rapped his elbow with her fan and scolded, "Shame!"

"Your sister's been trying for months to get Mr. Lincoln married off," said Mercy Levering, a fair and rather reserved girl of Mary's age to whom Mary had taken on sight. "Mr. Lincoln is Mr. Stuart's law partner. . . ."

"It would challenge any matchmaker in the world," teased Frances. "Which is why Elizabeth is so keen on it. . . ."

"I am not," replied Elizabeth, with the matronly dignity she'd already begun to assume back in Lexington, and went on handing out the little mother-of-pearl fish tokens for the game.

"Is he that ugly?" asked Mary, and Mercy put her hand over her mouth so as not to be seen giggling.

"He is ugly as Original Sin," replied Frances grandly. "*And* he eats with his knife."

"Frances . . . ," reproved Elizabeth, who would have taken the lead in the gossip if she didn't have her position to uphold.

"Well then, dearest," said Mary judiciously, "I can only say that your encouragement of the match is terribly irresponsible, both for the sake of the poor woman *and* whatever children they'll bear. . . ."

"That is unjust." Elizabeth was struggling not to burst out laughing. "He isn't *that* ugly."

"But you must admit he *does* eat with his knife," pointed out Frances, amid gales of chuckles around the table.

"He's a backwoodsman," protested Ninian. "It's taken Cousin John a year to teach him not to sit on the floor."

"Stuart met him in the militia during the Black Hawk War," provided Uncle Dr. John, "and taught him to read. . . ."

"I didn't *teach* him," laughed Cousin John, turning to Mary as Elizabeth went back primly to handing out counters. "I just encouraged him to read law. He was a captain under me, elected by his men, a gang of toughs from the rough side of New Salem. . . ."

"As if New Salem had a polite side," added Frances, rolling her eyes.

"I remember one day Lincoln was marching them across a field someplace in the north of the state, beating the bushes for Black Hawk and his braves, and they come up on a fence. It's clear across their line of march and there's a gap of about three feet in the fence; I could see the look on Lincoln's face when he realized he didn't remember the command to form a column—to get in a single line to pass through the gap. He looked aghast for about half a minute as the fence gets closer and closer, then he yells out: 'Company to fall out for two minutes and reassemble on the other side of that fence!' I almost fell off my horse laughing."

"Mr. Lincoln is engaged to a Miss Owens from Kentucky," supplied Elizabeth, seating herself at the head of the parlor table in a demure rustle of taffeta petticoats. "I'm hoping—we're all hoping, for he is really the best-natured soul on the planet—that she'll succeed in teaching him a few social niceties."

Frances shuffled the cards. "He'll always be ugly."

"Well, there *is* that."

Mary's father returned to Kentucky the following day— or more probably, she reflected wryly, he returned to Frankfort, or Louisville, or some other town where there was business that would keep him from the too-crowded house in Lexington, and the sharp-voiced demands of his wife. The bitterness that flavored her old grief at being left behind Mary hid, as she tried always to hide it, beneath flirtation and jests and fun.

And it was fun. Frances had already formed around herself

and Elizabeth a coterie of the young men and girls of Springfield—with more young men coming in all the time—and there was no more talk of being an old maid at nineteen. On the afternoon of Robert Todd's departure, Mr. Douglas appeared in a buggy to take Mary riding out on the prairies, and as if Elizabeth had hoisted a flag from the topmost gable of the House on the Hill, every eligible bachelor in Springfield put in an appearance that first week.

Mary was usually accompanied by Frances, and by Mercy Levering, with whom she quickly became fast friends. Lively, dark-haired Julia Jayne often joined them, the daughter of yet another town doctor. The four of them went together to the orgy of militia reviews and barbecues that surrounded the great Daniel Webster's visit to Springfield, and the ceremonies and speeches that accompanied the laying of the State House cornerstone on the Fourth of July.

Mr. Douglas was a dandified little dynamo, barely an inch taller and only a few years older than Mary and already registrar of the land-office of Springfield, a position of considerable power. Of all the men in Springfield, Mary felt that he was the only one who had potential to go beyond the small politics of state and county. When he would take her to picnics and cotillions, his talk was of the close maneuverings of money and land, and the promise of new inventions that would open the frontier country to men of enterprise and resource.

"Douglas is a Democrat," said Ninian, over supper one night. "And a demagogue, with his eye always on the main chance. I don't trust him."

"Just because he votes for Van Buren doesn't mean he's going to break my heart." Mary smiled a little as she said it, because charming as he was, she found something about Douglas's Yankee single-mindedness slightly repellant.

"Doesn't it?" Ninian glanced sharply at her from beneath those level black brows. "Could you really love a man whose politics were that different from yours, Molly? You take politics seriously, as all intelligent people should. Could you really live with a man for whose intellectual mainspring you had contempt?"

Mary delicately buttered one of the beaten biscuits that were Eppy's pride before replying. At home she would have dodged the question, since most of Betsey's questions had some ulterior motive, but in Ninian's eyes—and Elizabeth's peaceful silence—she read only interest in what she actually thought. At length she said, "I hope I'll never be put to the test of falling in love with a man whose ideas differ radically from mine."

"That would hardly be possible, would it?" asked Frances. Mary and Frances had spent the day—a Saturday, hot with the breathless humidity of high summer—picnicking with Dr. Wallace, Mr. Douglas, and Mercy Levering, in the woods that fringed Sutton's Prairie to the east of town. That huge expanse of empty grassland, rising imperceptibly to a too-close horizon, filled Mary with a kind of panic, and she had been glad for the company of her sister and her friends.

Having watched the matter-of-fact understanding, the peaceful teamwork, of Frances and William Wallace—having seen her sister's obvious happiness with the soft-voiced young doctor—Mary wasn't sure what to answer. *Could* she wholeheartedly love someone whose mind was alien to hers? She had certainly not loved Nate Bodley.

She felt a lump of envy in her chest, and the lump of loneliness that never quite ever went away. She said, "Would you love Dr. Wallace, if his ideas differed from what you believed was right?"

"Of course." The prompt self-evidentness in her sister's voice told Mary that Frances had never given the matter a thought and hadn't the slightest idea of why Mary hesitated.

"Which I suppose is why," smiled Elizabeth, "everyone says that women should stay out of politics. In how many households do you think there's really room for *two* politicians?"

By her tone of voice that ended the matter, but Mary persisted. "Next you'll be saying that women shouldn't have an education."

"Of course not, dear," said Elizabeth. "I know how you love your books. Just don't let your education interfere with your happiness."

Mary opened her mouth, and shut it again, overwhelmed with the familiar sense of speaking to people from some unknown land.

In any case the point was a moot one, because much as Mary enjoyed flirting with Stephen Douglas—and he, clearly, with her—she felt in his presence no such stirring of the senses as she'd experienced with Nate Bodley, let alone the delicious and instantaneous raptures occasioned by the heroes of *Belinda* and *Glenarvon*. What she did experience—with more and more frequency as the summer drew on—was an odd sense of desperation.

"Elizabeth is less insistent about it than Betsey," sighed Mary a few nights after that conversation, as she and Mercy sat on the porch of Ninian's house watching their escorts for the evening drive off in a rented buggy. Merce had been asked to a lecture on Phrenology at the Mechanics' Institute hall by Josh Speed, a partner in Speed and Bell's Dry Goods—a twinkly-eyed Kentuckian who had the gift of getting along with nearly everyone in town—and Mary had been escorted along by Mr. Shields, a bantam Irish lawyer who quite plainly considered himself God's gift to the female sex. "But she wants to marry me off, too."

Mary felt a twinge of anger as she said the words—at Elizabeth, at Betsey, at her father. At the world that was so constituted that an unmarried girl would, when she died, spend Eternity leading apes around Hell.

"They just want you to be happy," pointed out Mercy, breaking off a spray of the sweet-smelling honeysuckle to twine around her fingers. She spoke a bit diffidently, for in spite of their friendship Mary had lost her temper at her once or twice over trifles, and though they'd made up with tears and apologies, Mercy now tended to pick her words carefully.

"Can't they see I'm happy as I am? Why does a woman need to marry some *man* to be happy?"

Mercy replied, her voice peaceful in the thickening twilight, "I suppose because we can't stay forever in our fathers' houses." Sitting straight-backed on the rush-bottomed porch chair, she seemed to give off an aura of quiet from her rustling lavender muslin skirts, her smooth fair hair. "Because if we're not part of some household—father's, brother's, brother-in-law's, husband's—we won't be comfortable, and will have to make our livings at some horrid task like sewing or ironing or teaching school. And because without a husband or children of her own, I don't think any woman can truly be happy."

Mary was silent, thinking of her mother, thin and worn with childbearing. Of Betsey, always pregnant, always angry, more and more often ill and confined to her room . . . With a flash of insight Mary realized her stepmother felt the same anger she did, at the husband and father who found it so easy to be away for weeks at a time with the Legislature.

"Elizabeth sees Mr. Speed, or Mr. Shields, and sees they'll be rich, and have nice homes, and that as Mrs. Shields you'll never want for nice dresses or a carriage."

"As if that mattered!" retorted Mary. "I should rather marry a poor man whom I loved, a man who is going someplace—even a Yankee—than an old rich one with all his fortune secure. I've told Elizabeth that."

"And I think Elizabeth doesn't see why you can't love a wealthy man as easily as a poor one," responded Mercy. "Or why you can't love Mr. Douglas, who is certainly going someplace. He's used his position as registrar to buy up some of the choicest property in the state, Mr. Speed tells me, up near Chicago. . . ."

"Chicago?" exclaimed Mary, startled. "You mean that village where the lumber boats come in?"

"Mr. Speed said Chicago will be a major city one day, and that Mr. Douglas will end as a very rich man."

Mary sniffed, amused. "If I paid ten cents for one town lot in every village someone told me was going to be a major city one day, I'd be bankrupt tomorrow. And Ninian doesn't trust Mr. Douglas." She hesitated, turning her fan over in her hands. "To tell you the truth I don't either, after the way he went on about Mr. Sampson's Ghost."

Sampson's Ghost was the pseudonym used by a writer of letters to the *Sangamo Journal* during a local campaign for probate justice that had been closely followed by every inhabitant of the House on the Hill. The Democratic candidate, a General Adams, lived on land deeded to him by the deceased Mr. Sampson; the letter-writing Ghost offered proof that not only had Adams forged the deed to Mr. Sampson's land, he had earlier forged a judgment to gain title to the land of a man named Anderson, robbing Anderson's widow and son. The letters were entertaining, written with a wry satiric humor that had most of the town laughing. Stephen Douglas had bristled when Mary had laughed at them, however, and had defended Adams hotly.

"A fool can write whatever he likes to the papers, and get another fool to print it." Douglas, Mary had learned already, had little use for the editor of the *Journal,* the bespectacled and cheerful Simeon Francis. Then he had added—fatally, if he'd ever had any intention of winning Mary's hand—"What does a pretty girl like you need to go reading that farrago for, anyway?"

"I think," said Mary slowly now, looking back from her vantage-point on the porch with Mercy in the scented dusk, "that Ninian is right about Mr. Douglas. He probably wouldn't appreciate two politicians in one household. Certainly not if the other one wasn't a Democrat."

A mosquito whined in her ear, and she swept at it with her fan. It was time to go inside. She gave Mercy a hug and a kiss, and the girls exchanged promises to meet the next day to go downtown to look at ribbons at Birchall's Store.

Within the house the hall was dark, though lamps burned in the dining-room where Frances helped Eppy to set the table. Mary ascended the dark stair to her room, Mercy's placid words lingering uncomfortably in her heart.

We can't stay forever in our fathers' houses....

What if Father dies? She hastily pushed the thought from her mind, turning from it as she'd physically have averted her face.

But the image of him standing in the upstairs hall with Nelson rose out of the shadow, both men covered with dust, the stink of lime and gunpowder hanging heavy in the stuffy heat of the enclosed house and the glowing green ghost of cholera flitting from window to window, just waiting to slip inside.

One day he will die. What then?

Live with Betsey? Mary shuddered.

With Levi? Or George?

Father will be fine!

But panic whispered to her, nevertheless. *What then? What then? What then?*

A letter lay on her dressing-table, its green sealing-wafers cracked across. Of course it was Ninian's right—and Elizabeth's, as her guardians this summer—to read letters that came to her under their roof. But the sight of the opened correspondence filled Mary with the sudden desire to go storming downstairs and inform her sister that she would not stand to be treated like a child.

But until I marry, she thought furiously, *I am only a child in her household....* Elizabeth certainly read Frances's letters. As Merce's sister-in-law read Merce's.

And there was nowhere but Betsey's house to go back to.

Her hands trembled as she carried the letter to the window, where the last twilight gave enough of a faint blue flush for her to read.

It was from the Reverend John Ward, her old Lexington schoolmaster.

My dear Miss Todd,

I hope this letter finds you in full health and happiness. Often in the years since you left my tutelage I have spoken of you as the best and most promising pupil I have ever had the pleasure and privilege to educate; and frequently my good wife and I have wondered whether, in fact, you might find your calling in the education of the young.

Owing to my wife's illness this summer, she has been unable to assist me as she formerly did, making it necessary for us to seek help in the education of the younger students here at Ward's. Yours was the first name that rose to both of our minds. Your deep love of learning, combined with your affection for small children, impressed us both deeply. I have already spoken to your father and your stepmother concerning the propriety of your returning here to board and to teach. . . .

Mary's hand tightened hard on the paper and she thought, *Oh, I'll just bet Betsey leaped to tell Papa how proper it is, as long as it keeps me out of the house. . . .*

But as she sat in the window, looking out into the last of the twilight, she thought again, *We can't stay forever in our fathers' houses.*

A schoolmistress.

The thought made her smile. She remembered Madame Mentelle. Maybe an eccentric and happy schoolmistress, who did as she pleased and could stay up all night reading if she wished, and whose letters no one would read without her permission.

One who did not have to live in this desolate and book-less hog-wallow in the midst of the empty prairies, waiting in terror for the next storm.

Still she leaned in the window, her forehead against the glass that was no cooler than the stifling air. A man walked by in the street, a tall skinny silhouette, whistling an old backwoods tune. Darkness settled thick.

After a long time Mary got up, shook her petticoats straight, and went downstairs, to ask Ninian if, when he journeyed to Lexington next month to investigate railroad stocks, she could return with him.

It was time to go home.

CHAPTER SIXTEEN

Bellevue Place May 1875

"Mrs. Lincoln."

A soft tap at the door of her room. John's voice—it was hard for her to think of him as Mr. Wilamet, though he was so grown-up now, with his thin, serious face and his spectacles. They changed so, boys. . . .

Mary pressed her hands to her face, unwilling to think about the boys who would change no more.

"Mrs. Lincoln?"

She didn't even look at the curtained judas on the door, the curtain that could be nudged aside by anyone in the corridor.

"What is it?"

"Your son is here to see you."

Mary's voice rang hard as flint in her own ears. "I have no son."

John Wilamet said nothing in reply to that. But he didn't go away. Mary had learned the distinctive creak of the floorboards in the quiet downstairs hall of the family wing, even through the muffling of the Turkey carpets. When she couldn't sleep—as often she couldn't, this past week that she'd been here—it seemed to her sometimes that the comings and goings of Mrs. Patterson and Young Doc shook the house, forcing her to demand paregoric or chloral hydrate to help her drift off. How anyone could be so inconsiderate . . .

She repeated, raising her voice, "I have no son!"

Still Mr. Wilamet remained. Mary watched the curtain on the door, waiting for it to move, as it did when Gretchen or Mrs. Patterson would peep in on her—believing they were so clever and subtle! But it didn't stir.

She got impatiently to her feet and went to the door,

yanked the curtain aside to face the young man through the wooden bars. "Didn't you hear me?"

"I heard you, ma'am." John still retained the gentle burr of the South that Mary had not heard about her in years. "But the man who's here seems to think he has a mother."

Mary put a hand to her head; a tear leaked from her eye. She wasn't even sure why she wept—Robert never had any patience with tears. But it had become such a habit with her to weep that she did it almost without thinking. "Get me some paregoric, then, if you will," she said fretfully. "I have such a headache. If I'm to see him I must be at my best."

"Of course," agreed John. "But if I may say so, ma'am—he'll be watching for that."

"Watching for what?"

"Watching for you to be a little sleepy, the way paregoric makes you. Maybe a little less sharp. More forgetful."

Mary opened her mouth to snap that paregoric never had that effect on her, but closed it. It *did* make her a little drowsy and more than a little forgetful—so much so that she'd sometimes sit for many hours gazing into the dimness of her hotel-room, and come out of a dream to discover she'd drunk half the bottle without being aware of it. But she'd hoped that no one had noticed.

The thought that Robert would be watching for weakness had never occurred to her. But of course he was a lawyer. He'd watch, as lawyers all watched. And use everything she did and said.

"Just a little, then—water it down. I won't give him that satisfaction. And send Amanda in here to me, so I can change my dress."

"Good for you, ma'am," grinned John. "Don't give him a thing."

As she dressed, Mary's anger rose, sharpened by the sense of restless unhappiness that had so frequently attacked her over the years. In her mind she saw Robert in the courtroom again, tears in his eyes as he announced to the entire world that his own mother was a lunatic.

But when, at last, she entered the parlor and saw him sitting there, physically so like her father, tall and barrel-chested, with wariness in his Todd-blue eyes, her rage overflowed into tears again and she could only sob, "How could you?"

He was on his feet at once, to conduct her to a chair. She jerked her arm away. "Mother, you know you are not well," he said, in his even, rather light-toned voice. "You know you haven't been well—"

"I haven't been well for twenty-three years!" Mary lashed at him. "You try living with headaches, neuralgia, back pains, and internal complaints for that long and see what it does to *you*! But I am not insane!"

"No one is saying you are *completely* insane, Mother. . . ."

"You are. A week ago, in a public courtroom, you said exactly that!"

"I didn't come here to argue with you." Robert took her hands, his tone indicated that he didn't want to discuss the matter further—Mary was familiar with that from a lifetime of dealing with her own father. "I came to see how you are feeling. You look more rested than you did, more at peace. How has your week been passed here?"

Mary started to snap back at him that it had been passed in much the fashion anyone would expect, for a woman locked up unjustly by her own family, but she hesitated, his words penetrating past her fury.

How *had* she passed the week here?

And she realized, with a sense of panicked shock that shook her to her core, that she did not exactly know.

It was a realization that took her breath away. It was not that she had been unconscious: she remembered small incidents quite clearly, like the attempt at a séance in the garden with Mrs. Hill, and the carriage-rides—twice? three times?—with Mrs. Patterson and Blanche. But they all came back to her as if part of a cloudy and pleasant dream, without anxiety or pain. She recalled telling Mrs. Bennett—that haunted-eyed old woman with the extraordinary delusion that parts of her body had been taken away and replaced by parts of someone else's—that she had not been so happy or comfortable in her life.

Except when she slept.

She wasn't even sure if her conversation with Mrs. Bennett had been real, or on what day it had taken place.

Was that madness?

"Mother?" Robert was still holding her hands.

"I'm so sorry, dear," said Mary automatically, and made herself smile. She added, because Robert was looking at her as if she'd begun talking about her tormenting Indian spirit again, "Things go along so quietly here I was just trying to remember what I *have* done all week." And she laughed, the light sweet conversational laughter of an accomplished belle.

But her heart had begun to pound and her thoughts to race, and she thought, *I must keep his suspicions at bay.*

And then, *I can ask Mr. Wilamet. He will know about such things, and he won't betray me.*

"I'm delighted to hear it, Mother," Robert was saying, in the pleased tone of one who has put everything into its proper drawer. "That's precisely why I wanted you to come to Bellevue Place—so that you could rest."

No, thought Mary, looking into her son's face and seeing only a stranger's. *You wanted me to come to Bellevue Place so you wouldn't be worried that I'd embarrass you in public. You wanted me to come here so that I wouldn't have to live with YOU. So that you wouldn't have to think about me again, except maybe to say to yourself, "Poor Mama."*

And in her secret heart of hearts, a voice whispered: *You wanted me to come to Bellevue because of what I did to you, all those years ago.*

Because of the lie I told.

The lie that had made, and destroyed, his life and hers.

Lexington 1837

MARY RETURNED TO LEXINGTON IN THE COLD AUTUMN RAIN of 1837, jolting up the hill in the stagecoach with Ninian and almost in tears with the pleasure of those craggy familiar hills, the dripping tangled trees. She spent a week at her father's house—which was still hard for her to think of as "home"— sharing the upstairs front bedroom with Ann. Then Nelson loaded her trunks and hatboxes into the carriage and took them over to Ward's school, where she would occupy a room of her own five nights a week for what turned out to be the next twenty-five months.

Ward's school being ten minutes' brisk walk down Main Street and up Market Street, it was seldom that Nelson would bring the carriage, as he had to Mentelle's. Instead Mary would walk—shaded by a ruffled parasol or muffled in a stylish coat of her favorite hunter green—to the big brick house on Main Street every Friday afternoon, and back after Sunday dinner. Under these circumstances she could be pleasant and friendly with Betsey, and have the patience to teach Margaret and Martha—Mattie, they all called her— their sewing-stitches while her stepmother looked after golden-haired little Emilie.

It was good to be back in the South, back in the world whose rules she instinctively knew.

Yet that world had changed, and the subtleness of the changes made the alteration more, not less, disturbing.

There were still the dances in the long room above Giron's Confectionary, and laughter and French gallantries from the little Frenchman who was so delighted to be able to hold conversation in his native tongue. There were plays at Usher's Theater—heaven after three months in the wilds of Springfield!—and danceables at the Meadows and in the big double-parlor at Ashland. There were picnics at race-meetings in the spring, and young men jostling discreetly to sit beside her while the horses galloped down the long green turf, glistening like polished bronze and copper in the sun. There was the wonderful gossip that only Southerners could understand, of vast tangled family trees and acquaintance that went back generations.

But many of the shops in Lexington were closed up now, owing to the collapse of the banks in the wake of President Jackson's economic woes. Girls Mary had known no longer came to the dances, or they came in dresses that bore the mark of discreet refurbishment from last season, and people like Bella Richardson were extra-sweet to them and whispered, "Poor things..." when she thought they didn't hear. Many of Mary's former beaux no longer raced their own horses, and wore a look of grimness, as if they'd grown suddenly old.

Mary Jane Warfield Clay had a son, and was expecting another child soon. Though Mary delighted in little Elisha's soft curls and bright, knowing blue eyes, she found Mary Jane almost wholly preoccupied with servants, high prices, and the household budget. Meg and Mary Wickliffe were likewise both married, and talked exactly like the Yankee women who'd ridden with her on the steamboat down the Ohio, of teething babies and the shocking cost of lamp-oil. When Mary stood at the dances among the single girls, she was disconcerted to realize that some of them were in the upper year or two at Ward's—as she herself had been, when first she'd put up her hair and entered the fascinating world of a belle.

They seemed so *young.* Mary laughed about it with Isabelle Trotter and Julia Warfield, before one of Mr. Clay's sons came over and swept her into a cotillion on his arm. Then for a time she could dimple and laugh and be once again the belle of the ball. But that night, listening to Ann's soft breathing beside her in the dark of the upstairs front bedroom, Mary stared at the ceiling with panic racing in her heart.

Nate Bodley came to call on her, the second or third afternoon after her return from Springfield. "What is it?" he asked, when she stood up and stepped away from his attempt to clasp both her hands, and they both glanced at Betsey, who smiled pointedly and said,

"Well, I'll leave you two young people to get re-acquainted." She rustled out into the hall, leaving them alone together in the double-parlor. Mary heard her sharp voice call out to Chaney about laying another plate for dinner.

"I've missed you, Mary." Nate stepped closer, smiling his old devilish smile, and still Mary didn't answer. In her mind she saw the brass head of his cane flying up and down, smelled the mud of the gutter, and the bitter tang of Mr. Presby's blood. "What is it, sweetheart? Now, don't you freeze up on me...."

At that she glanced up at him, her eyes bright with anger. "Do you honestly need to ask that, sir, since Mr. Presby lived here under our roof?" The young tutor had returned to his family's New England home at the same time Mary had gone to Springfield. He had not returned.

Nate's face flushed. Mary wondered whether it was because of guilt over the caning, or because the caning involved the pretty quadroon slave girl he had bought. She wondered too whether that girl was still in Nate's father's household. "That was politics," he protested. "You gotta understand, Mary, there's things a man can't put up with another man layin' on him."

A well-bred young lady would have simply said, *Then we can only agree to differ, Mr. Bodley*—with or without shyly downcast eyes—and left it at that. If she really wanted to sever the connection, there were a thousand social ways to avoid Nate without fuss. Mary felt her *own* cheeks flame.

"It was not politics, sir," she replied in a steady voice. "A righteous man accused you of evil and you had no argument in your favor but violence. That doesn't sound like politics to me."

"What it doesn't sound like to me is any of your business, begging your pardon, Miss Todd, or any woman's business...."

"It is every right-thinking person's business—"

"It is not!" Nate cut her off, jabbing his finger at her, his eyes blazing with the gunpowder violence that had so frightened her that spring day half a year ago. "I see you've become an abolitionist in the North, talking to people who haven't got the slightest idea what it's like here—"

"I didn't need to travel to the North to see what's right under my eyes here, Mr. Bodley!"

"But it's no man's right to tell me what I can and can't do with my own property in my own house!"

"And not the right of the woman you'd make your wife, either, whether or not you have a concubine under your roof?" Mary lashed back.

Nate's mouth flew open with shock at hearing her say the word; for an instant he was silenced. Then he laughed harshly. "God help the man that makes *you* his wife, Mary Todd!" Turning on his heel, he strode from the room. Mary heard Betsey call out, "Mr. Bodley..." as the front door slammed.

Mary stood by the hearth, trembling, tears of anger blurring her vision and her head starting to pound as her stepmother came into the parlor. "Mary, honestly, how can you quarrel with Mr. Bodley so soon after your return? You really must strive to get the better of your temper, my dear, or you stand in grave danger of ending an old maid."

"Oh, leave me alone!" Mary turned in a whirl of turkey-red skirts. "What woman wouldn't be better off an old maid, than living with a yellow rival beneath her husband's roof?"

"Mary!" gasped Betsey. "You didn't say such a thing to Mr. Bodley?"

"It's true!"

The older woman's lips pursed impatiently. "A good many things are true in this world, Miss, but that doesn't mean that a lady ever speaks of them. If you don't curb your temper, men will say—"

Mary screamed, "Leave me alone! I don't care what men say!" And pushing past her, she blundered into the wide hall and up the stairs. Her vision was beginning to dissolve into jagged lines of flaming wire. She wanted to curse, to beat on the walls, to shriek at them for a parcel of fools. Later, lying in her room on the big four-poster bed, she felt sick and depleted. Frightened, too, and half-nauseated with guilt. Nate would tell everyone he knew—all the young men in Lexington—that Mary had become a termagant and an abolitionist since she'd been in the North.

And Betsey...!

She remembered screaming at Betsey—who would be certain to tell her father when he came home, not to mention all her gossipy friends....

The floorboards outside the bedroom door creaked. There was a gentle knock, familiar from a lifetime of tantrums and headaches and darkened rooms, and Mary whispered, "Come in. Please come in," without turning her face from her pillow.

She heard Mammy Sally enter, and cross at once to the windows, pulling the curtains against the light that Mary had been too angry and too sick to block out. The day was hot for September, and Mary heard the dim voices of children in the street—Sam and David and Margaret and Mattie and little Emilie all shrieking at one another like baby birds. She peered dolefully up from beneath the tangle of her disordered hair as the elderly nurse looked down at her for a moment, then sighed and shook her head, and sat on the bed at her side.

"Your head ache, child?"

Mary nodded. Even with the curtains shut the light in the room seemed blinding.

The strong hand stroked back the tumbled chestnut curls. "Nelson told me you took up for that poor yeller gal Serena, that Mr. Bodley bought last spring, and thrashed Mr. Presby over. That was good of you, child, but it wasn't any business of yours. Not to lose a beau over. And not to get yourself into trouble with Miss Betsey, so soon after you come home."

"He wasn't my beau," said Mary softly. "Not from the

minute I saw it happen." She sighed, and dropped her head back down to her arm, wondering that her skull didn't split. Mammy Sally reached to the bedside table, where she'd set a cup of her herbal tea. Mary managed to sit up, took it with trembling hands and sipped the sharp-tasting, nasty brew. In the day's heat the steam only made her head feel worse. "And Betsey would marry me off to the Sultan of Turkey, if she thought it would get me out of the house."

She turned over, tangled in her petticoats and stiff with corset-bones, and Mammy Sally, instead of saying—as Betsey certainly would—that she would crumple her dress and rip a sleeve-seam by lying on the bed fully clothed, merely helped straighten the heavy volutes of fabric around her, and brought up the other pillow for her head.

"Why can't I keep my temper, Mammy?" Mary whispered. "Betsey talks like she thinks I *like* to shout and scream and feel sick the way I do. I can't help it—I don't mean to get angry like this. I know what I'm supposed to do and say, and I just . . . I just *can't*."

"I know you can't, child," the older woman said softly, reaching out a gentle, work-roughened hand to wipe the tears away. "All you can do is watch yourself, and do what you can so you'll have less to fix later. And maybe the Sultan of Turkey likes a wife with a little temper to her, to keep him from getting bored."

And in spite of her pain, and the sickness rising in her stomach, Mary laughed, and hugged the old woman.

It was truly good to be home.

NATE BODLEY BECAME ENGAGED TO ARABELLA RICHARDSON the following week. For the next year, in between teaching French and listening to the smaller girls at Ward's read their lessons in the chill of early dawn, Mary periodically suffered the spectacle of the radiant Bella shopping for her trousseau, or comparing notes about it with the other unmarried girls of the town.

Mary had not been the only girl whom Nate had squired to picnics, Court Days, and danceables, and Nate had been far from Mary's only beau. Still, when young gentlemen who were slaveholders or the sons of planters asked Mary to dance, or came to sit beside her beneath the trees of Trotter's Grove, there was a note in their voices, a difference in the way they disposed their legs and arms and bodies, that told her—and every other girl in town as clearly as an announcement taken out in the newspaper—that they no longer considered her marriage material.

She was a good friend from childhood, and would of course go on being a good friend. She was Robert Todd's daughter, cousin or second cousin or kin to most of them, and there was no question of cutting her: people were entitled to be abolitionists if they wanted to, they supposed. It was a free country, wasn't it?

But none of them danced more than one dance with her, and only after the younger girls' dance-cards were full.

And because—of course—nobody would speak of the scene between her and Nate, she never had the opportunity to explain to anyone whether she was actually an abolitionist or not.

Gentlemen who believed, with her father, that the slaves should be one day freed—when they'd been sufficiently educated and prepared for freedom, or when they could be relocated to some other country suitable for them—continued to court her. The older students at Transylvania University were joined by some of the younger professors. If Mary had to suffer the spectacle of Bella Richardson hanging possessively on Nate Bodley's arm, at least—for a time—she could contemplate it from within a circle of her own admirers.

For two years she was happy at Ward's, happier than she had been at any time since she'd left Madame Mentelle's in 1837. She loved her pupils, who ranged in ages from seven to eleven—girls and boys both, for the Reverend believed that if the two sexes mingled in the backyards, nursery wings, and parties of the town, there was no reason they shouldn't do so in the classroom. She loved, too, having her own room, having access to all the books she wanted—being able to travel, in thought at least, to those places where she longed to visit: Venice, Constantinople, Paris, Scotland. When Elizabeth wrote the following summer inviting her back to Springfield, Mary passed it by in favor of a visit with the family to Crab Orchard Springs, as they had done in her girlhood.

There were good times even with her family, helping to look after the littler children when baby Alex was born, in '39, almost two years after her return. She would sit in the kitchen as she used to, watching the stir and bustle of the big house. Elizabeth's Eppy had taught her some cookery in Springfield—Chaney began to instruct her in more.

Yet during those two years Mary found herself lying awake more and more, either in her small pretty room in Mr. Ward's house or at her father's house—with her father gone to the Legislature in Frankfort yet again—wondering if this was what she wanted. If this was all there was. All there was going to be. Sometimes she'd take out her casket of jewels, as she'd done at Mentelle's, and turn over the earbobs, the gold chains, the sapphire pendant in her fingers, as if the sight of them were reassurance that though she didn't live in her family's house, still she was loved.

Sometimes this worked.

Sometimes it didn't.

She was perfectly aware of it, when people first started treating her as a spinster.

That was at Christmas of 1838, shortly after she turned twenty-one. Nellie Clay—who had been one of her senior pupils at Ward's when first Mary returned from Springfield—got married then, in a huge party held at Ashland, Nellie being a twice-removed cousin of Mr. Henry Clay's. Mary had coaxed a new dress of pink and green silk from her father for the occasion, and her curls, threaded with dark-green velvet ribbon, shone like copper in the light of the candles in the octagonal central hall as the bride descended the stair. And it gave her a sense of pride, almost as if

Nellie were a daughter she had raised, when Nellie ran to hug her after the ceremony—girls wed young in Kentucky, and Nellie was seventeen.

Yet at the reception afterwards, hearing the babble of voices and seeing so many familiar faces—Mr. Clay a bit grayer than he'd been at Elizabeth and Ninian's second-day party, Nate already getting thick under the chin—Mary felt a sudden stricken, shaken fear, as if the ground beneath her feet had been rocked by an earthquake.

All the belles, in their rustling skirts of ivory or rose or pale-blue silk, were now decidedly younger than she, some by nearly five years. The young men crowded around them, offering cups of punch and slices of cake; eyelids were fluttered, blushes half-concealed behind blond lace fans. The young matrons—Mary Jane Clay, and Margaret Preston, who had been Meg Wickliffe when she'd shared a room with Mary at Rose Hill—were gathered in the rear parlor, watching with the satisfied air of soldiers whose battle has already been won as the fiddles struck up a dance-tune. Madame Mentelle glanced around from conversation with Mr. Clay and M'sieu Giron, and beckoned Mary to join them, but halfway there Mary was intercepted by Nate Bodley.

"Will you dance with me, Mary?" he asked. "For old times' sake?"

Nellie, in the arms of her bridegroom—a planter from Louisville—was smiling dewily at her, gratified, Mary realized with a flare of alarm, that anyone was dancing with her teacher at all.

It was then she realized she was becoming someone that other people had to look after socially.

She danced with Nate, but she talked to him as if she were talking with a stranger, asking after his horses, his plantation, his wife—all the polite small-talk that rose so easily to her lips. He replied in kind, perfectly happily, as if he'd never taken her in his arms in the orchards behind Rose Hill, or chased her through the green-and-golden woods. She wondered if he still had the quadroon girl in his household, or if he'd sold her off.

It was something a lady wasn't supposed to ask, or even think about.

In May Elizabeth wrote to her again, announcing Frances's wedding to Dr. Wallace and asking if Mary would like to come back to Springfield when the Legislature finally opened there in the fall.

Mary wrote back, saying that she would be delighted to come.

Even then she knew that, books or no books, theater or no theater, thunderstorms or no thunderstorms, she would never live in Lexington again.

CHAPTER SEVENTEEN

Springfield 1839

SPRINGFIELD HAD GROWN IN TWO YEARS. THE STATE HOUSE was nearly finished, though the earth around it was the same hog-wallow of mud, torn-up rubble, and trampled gravel—scummed now with ice—that it had been, and the Legislature would be meeting in shop-fronts all over town because none of the building's rooms were finished inside. The State Supreme Court had been given quarters in a commercial building across the street. But the town swarmed with lawyers, clerks, minor officials eager to get government jobs or government patronage. Ninian's house was always full of men, eager to do favors or to buy small gifts—flowers for his wife and sisters-in-law, a stick-pin or a pair of gloves—to curry his good opinion. Political wives were now bringing their daughters to husband-hunt in the man-heavy town.

Springfield's atmosphere had changed, from bucolic sleepiness to the aggressive sparkle of power. It went to Mary's head like drink.

Mr. Douglas called on Mary's first afternoon in Elizabeth's house, to bespeak a waltz at the upcoming cotillion to be held for the legislators at the new American House Hotel. He wore a well-tailored tobacco-colored coat and a yellow silk waistcoat, and looked like a man who was going places in the world.

"He's still a Democrat," remarked Ninian, and Mary laughed.

Elizabeth had spoken of holding a ball to celebrate Mary's return, but since her arrival was so soon before the American House cotillion, they settled on a festive supper for all their friends before going *en masse* to the more general fête.

"Somehow it doesn't surprise me," remarked Dr. Wallace, helping Frances and Mary into the carriage after supper, "that Mary would manage to get the entire Legislature to welcome her to town."

In the long, lamp-lit common room of the American House, Mary, clothed in a ruffled gown of fawn and rose silk—her father's parting gift—was again the center of a court of gentlemen, laughing behind her fan and teasing them as they vied to bring her up-to-date on all that had happened in the town in the two years since her departure. Since she'd had Ninian send her both the *Sangamo Journal* and the *Illinois Republican,* there was little she didn't already know about the wild mudslinging that had gone on between the *Journal*'s claque of "Young Whigs" and the *Republican*'s "Young Democrats" over every conceivable subject from the State Bank to the digging of local canals. Legislators and would-be government employees from Chicago to Cairo clustered around her, and nobody even asked what her opinions on slavery were or how old she was.

She danced two waltzes with Mr. Douglas, who was her height to an inch, so that their steps matched beautifully. He was a wonderful dancer, light on his feet and firm in his lead—"Of course that's how he'd dance," she giggled to Frances later, over a cup of punch. "That's what his politics are like, too—leading you right along and making you like it."

"I don't know, Mary," teased Frances. "If you really want to marry the President of the United States, maybe you'd better think about changing your politics." But she laughed when she said it, knowing—as all of them knew—that Mary took her politics far more seriously than she took Mr. Douglas.

Senator Herndon's chinless cousin Billy—who after a number of opening shots at various careers was currently a clerk at Speed and Bell's Dry Goods—asked her to dance too, declaring that she moved as gracefully as a serpent; Mary rolled her eyes, and replied, "That's rather severe irony, sir, especially to a newcomer. Now I think I've torn a flounce, and need to go repair it." As she retreated upstairs with Merce and Julia she added, "Remind me to wear a torn flounce next time, in case he ever asks me again." All three of them were still laughing over this—and over Billy's newly-grown whiskers, which resembled nothing so much, in their patchy fairness, as socks hanging on a clothesline—when they returned to the dancing a few minutes later.

Merce's new sweetheart, a patrician New Yorker named Jamie Conkling, came up and claimed Merce with a bow—"If you'll excuse me, Miss Todd, I think I need Miss Levering to keep me from dying of loneliness out on the floor. . . ." Across the room, Dr. Wallace caught Mary's eye and started to approach, but beside her a quiet, very light voice asked, "Miss Todd?"

She turned, looked up—and up and up—and saw to her enormous surprise the tall stringy storyteller who'd rescued her from Professor Kittridge in the Globe Tavern yard over two years before.

He wore a suit now of very ill-fitting dark wool, and a black string tie, and his black hair was firmly pomaded to his narrow, rather bird-like head. In his eyes was the look of an unarmed man about to go into single combat with a Gorgon.

"If you please . . . Miss Todd . . . That is, if you don't mind . . ."

Beside him Josh Speed gave him a nudge closer to her, and whispered, "Just ask her, Lincoln."

Lincoln swallowed hard. He had an Adam's apple like a lime on a string. Mary realized this had to be Cousin John Stuart's partner. Frances certainly hadn't lied about his looks.

He blurted out, "Miss Todd, I'd sure like to dance with you in the worst way."

Speed shook his head and groaned.

Fighting to keep from laughing, Mary held out her hand and answered, "I'd be delighted, Mr. Lincoln."

He did, in fact, dance with her in the worst possible way. But while Mary would have been merciless about someone like Billy Herndon—who had done himself no good with his "serpent" remark—she felt oddly protective of this gangly backwoodsman, and did her best to keep her new slippers out from under the Conestoga boots that she guessed were Lincoln's only footwear.

The fact that the dance was a schottische didn't help the situation any. Halfway through Lincoln stopped abruptly, abashed, with all the other couples swirling around them. "I guess I better let you go 'fore I kill you, Miss Todd. I thank you...."

"Mr. Lincoln." She looked up into his eyes, clear gray under the overhang of his brow, and smiled. "How dare you slight a lady's courage, sir? I'm made of hardier stuff than that. *Lay on, Macduff....*"

His whole gargoyle face transformed with delight at the quote. "*And curs't be he that first cries 'Hold, enough.'* But let's sort of get ourselves out of the main channel here, and practice a little in the shallows."

In a corner of the common room away from the main ring of dancers Mary took him carefully through the steps: hop-hop, slide-slide, hop-skip-slide....

"Like tryin' to learn to march in the Army," Lincoln said, gravely studying the toes of Mary's pink Morocco-leather slippers, which she made just visible with the tiniest lifting of the hem of her skirt. "Only then it was just right and left, and once I'd tied a string around my right wrist I could remember it most of the time. I guess folks would just laugh at us if I was to ask you to lead."

"You did all right leading old Professor Kittridge across the yard the way you did. *What* did he call you? For two years now I've been dying to ask...."

Lincoln laughed, and scratched the back of his head, a habitual gesture that made rapid inroads on the pomaded neatness of his hair. His smile transformed his face, dissolving its gravity into comic mobility, and lightening it like sunlight on stones. "*The servant of the servants of Mammon.* Bad enough, he says, that humanity has enslaved itself to the Devil of

Property. But lawyers who haggle over other men's property for pay are the lowest of the low. Lookin' at it that way, I reckon he's got a point." He gingerly held out his hands to her. "Can we slow down to half-speed, till I get the blame thing figured out?"

"Of course." Mary took his hands—the biggest hands she'd ever seen, straining at the seams of his much-mended kid gloves. "Everyone else in the room is so busy minding their own feet, they'll never notice."

It robbed the dance utterly of the reason that one did a schottische—the exhilaration of its flying speed—but it did give Mary enough time to get her toes clear of his boots. Now and then, when she glanced up, she could see his lips move as he counted the steps.

"Did he ever marry his lady from New Salem?" asked Mary, after Lincoln had bowed awkward thanks, fetched her a cup of punch (at Speed's whispered reminder), and beaten a hasty retreat to join the men in the hall. The musicians—a German, a free black farmer, and Ninian's quadroon coachman Jerry—were likewise refreshing themselves before the next dance: Mary, her sisters, Merce and Julia clustered at the rear of the room, all except Elizabeth flushed and rumpled.

Elizabeth heaved a long-suffering sigh. "No. After all our urging..."

"Well, you could hardly blame him," retorted Frances. "Apparently Miss Owens didn't trouble to watch her figure and got enormously fat."

"*I* heard *she* was the one who called it off," put in Julia Jayne, tossing her dark curls. "One *can* have enough of a man who falls into brown studies and can't be troubled to converse with a woman for hours on end. Not to mention leaving the poor thing to fend for herself when a group of their friends went riding and had to cross a stream on horseback...."

"Lincoln's trouble," observed Josh Speed, who had joined them, "—other than not having a lick of sense about women—is that he's risen out of the world he was born into, and so cannot marry the kind of woman he grew up with. Yet he's still enough of a backwoodsman that he's never learned how to talk to ladies of this new world that he hopes to make his."

"I'd say," remarked Frances, looking over at the unruly black head rising above the jostling group in the hall, "that he's never going to learn to talk to ladies at the rate he's going. He must be thirty if he's a day."

There were shouts of laughter from among the men: "... *so about the third time the top of the hogshead fell down inside the barrel, the cooper figured he'd put his son inside the barrel, to hold the top up while he fixed on the hoops....*"

Mary remembered Court Days at Lexington, and the backwoodsmen who'd come in from their rough cabins in the canebrakes. Most held a few acres of corn which they chiefly made into whiskey, their herds of cattle and pigs which they let rove wild in the woods. Illiterate, coarse, woodcrafty as the Indians they had supplanted, they lived from hand to mouth and from day to day, their women barefoot in faded calico with trains of tow-headed silent children.

What became of those children? Mary wondered, comparing them with her well-mannered little pupils at Ward's, with Betsey's little ones at home. What became of the ones who yearned for something beyond the woods, who looked about them at men dying of pneumonia or accidents or sheer hardship at thirty-five or forty, when their strength gave out? The ones who thought—as she had thought—*There must be something else?*

She glanced across at Speed, and she saw the deep, amused affection in the young storekeeper's eyes as he watched his lanky friend: a servant of the servants of Mammon, in his shabby suit and rough boots and mended gloves, an ungainly interloper in the world of gentility and power. "Mr. Lincoln's come a long way," she said softly, and Speed's gaze shifted to her.

"That he has."

"And he'll have to go a long piece farther," sniffed

Frances, "before he's likely to come across a woman willing to put up with him."

ABRAHAM LINCOLN WAS LIKE NO MAN MARY HAD EVER MET. Frances still made fun of him, but when they encountered one another at dances that winter, he would awkwardly maneuver to speak to Mary, to dance with her if he could. She was used to having beaux jockeying for her attention and trying to cut one another out for dances, but Stephen Douglas, and the elderly widower Edwin Webb, Josh Speed, cocky little Jimmy Shields, handsome Lyman Trumbull—for whom Mary had a passing *tendre*—and the suave John Gillespie were men who knew how to play the game, with women and with one another.

Lincoln was different. He was agonizingly shy, laboring under the double burden of his very odd looks and his excruciating awareness of social backwardness. Mary guessed, from the hesitant way he spoke to her, the way he would hang back when Douglas or Shields deftly claimed her attention from under his nose, that he'd had harsh rebuffs from women before, and had no idea how to make a neat riposte. Mostly he just retreated to the world of men, a world in which he was a quite different man.

Across the room at Ninian's or the Leverings' she would watch him with Ninian, with Jamie Conkling or Ed Baker—a brisk little cock-sparrow Englishman and another of her Coterie, as their circle of friends came to be called—or others who knew him through Legislature and the courts. The shyness fell off him there like an ill-made coat, and he'd joke, and listen to other men's stories, and speak with a sharp and quiet acuteness that vanished utterly the moment one of the Springfield belles addressed him.

Elizabeth referred to him as a "cracker from the canebrakes'" but he had, despite deficiencies in table manners, an inherent dignity that went far beyond which fork to use, and a genuine kindly consideration for others. Moreover, Mary knew perfectly well that a man couldn't become a lawyer, much less a member of the State Legislature, without being able to read and write. "No, it's perfectly true," Josh Speed told her, one freezing January afternoon when Mary came into Speed and Bell's to buy ribbons. "Most of what Lincoln knows he taught himself. I don't think he's had more than a year of schooling in his life. He really did grow up in a log cabin, in the Indiana woods. His father used to hire him out to the neighbors to cut wood and husk corn, and keep the money he made—which is legal," he added, as Mary opened her mouth in indignant protest. "Up until a boy's twenty-one. It's just most fathers don't do that kind of thing anymore."

"So that's what they mean when they speak of a 'gentleman of the old school,'" sniffed Mary, and Speed laughed, and came around the end of the counter to hold out his hands to the iron heating-stove.

"Well, Lincoln left Indiana the minute he could, and I haven't seen him in any tearing hurry to get back. He told me once his pa used to thrash him for reading. When he was living in New Salem, about a day's ride from here up the Sangamon River, he used to walk ten or twelve miles to borrow books, if he heard of people who had them."

Speed and Bell, Mary knew, generally had a small stock of books, whatever could be brought in from the East. These were mostly almanacs and volumes of sermons, though once they did get in a volume of Shakespeare's sonnets, which Mary bought. The store was built of sawn lumber and whitewashed inside and out. It smelled of wood and soap, and now the heavy scent of smoke and burnt coffee. Barrels and bins ranged the center of the room near the stove, where men would sit through the winter evenings talking politics and spitting tobacco. Shelves occupied every foot of wall with bright bolts of calico and sheeting, pots of white-and-blue enamel, caddies of tea and coffee and dishes to whose edges packing-straw still clung. They didn't stock the variety of

fancy goods and ribbons that Birchell and Irwin did, but Mary
liked Josh Speed.

"Is he in?" she asked impulsively, because she knew
Lincoln lived upstairs with Speed, in the big loft. Speed
shook his head.

"He'll be at your cousin's law offices if he isn't in the
Legislature—Stuart left him in charge of the whole practice
when he went to take his seat in Congress. Lincoln's a devil
for work: between riding the circuit courts all summer, and
now working to organize the Whig Party the way the
Democrats are organized, my guess is once the snow melts I
won't see much of him."

"That must be what happens," remarked Mary lightly,
"when you're allowed to keep some of the money you
make."

Speed laughed, then glanced at the empty wooden chairs
around the stove with a reminiscent grin. "He'll be here
tonight—the whole bunch of them, Baker and Conkling and
Douglas..." He shook his head, with a kind of wonder and
delight in his eyes. "I've never heard arguing the way it is
when Lincoln and Douglas get after each other over the State
Bank or divorce or Indian lands or anything that's on their
minds. It's amazing, like watching two gods throwing
lightning-bolts at each other. One night Douglas wasn't here
and Lincoln did an imitation of him, and argued with himself.
That's the closest I've come in my life to dying laughing."

Mary chuckled at just the thought of it—by this time
she'd seen Lincoln do imitations of people. But as Joshua escorted her across the muddy plank sidewalk to Ninian's carriage she felt a pang of bitterest jealousy, that this world of
politics and power and informal alliances around the stove
was something she would not be permitted to join. For a
moment she was a child again, seeing the shoulders of her father's guests close in a rank against her.

Hearing Betsey say, *Really, Mary....*

And being relegated to conversation about earbobs and
beaux.

The next time she saw Lincoln, at a Washington's Birthday ball given by the Leverings, Mary caught his eye and edged from the group of her admirers to stand with him in the corner by the stairway. "Mr. Speed tells me you're an admirer of Robert Burns, sir," she said, glancing up at the tall man who towered over her. "I have a book of his poems, if you'd ever care to borrow it. Mr. Speed says come spring you'll be riding all over the state to the circuit courts—that has to be unbelievably dreary."

The lined gargoyle face lit up first with surprise, then with pleasure, and the uncertainty he always had around women vanished from his eyes. "Why, thank you, Miss Todd. You're right, it's tiresome and lonely, riding the circuit courts, and Burns would be the best companion I could ask for, aside from Mr. Shakespeare. It's kind of you to think of me, Miss Todd."

Any other man of her acquaintance would have spoken the words as a formula: It's-kind-of-you-to-think-of-me-Miss-Todd, with a bow and a knowing smile. But the way Lincoln said them, Mary knew that it was not only kind, but almost unheard-of in the lawyer's experience.

"I promise I won't let it come to harm."

"Good heavens, I never thought you would!" She smiled. "I can tell you're a man who knows how to take care of books. God knows I've spent enough of my time here in Springfield trying to find things to read to have sympathy for someone cast ashore in places like Petersburg and Postville!"

He laughed at that, his nose wrinkling up and his big horselike teeth flashing. "And in some of those places I feel cast ashore, like Mr. Crusoe—and wasn't it just lucky for him that ship of his didn't sink under him at the outset, and leave him without any of those guns and axes and ropes and the rest of his plunder."

"Which I think was just a *little* providential on Mr. Defoe's part," remarked Mary consideringly. "On the other hand, if he hadn't provided him with all that 'plunder,' as you say, poor Mr. Crusoe would probably have starved in the first week, and Mr. Defoe couldn't have made much of a story out of that."

Lincoln laughed again, and scratched his head, augmenting the crazy ruin of his hair. Seeing the way his whole frame relaxed, Mary understood that this sad-eyed man truly loved to laugh. "Though I will say, you'd be surprised what you can do with just an ax. Still, there should have been an almanac someplace on that boat, and if you're real desperate you can get some good reading out of an almanac."

After that Mary would lend Lincoln books, which he consumed like a child devouring candy. He usually returned them on Sunday afternoons, when Elizabeth held open house for the Coterie at the House on the Hill. Frances would act as co-hostess for these gatherings, for she and Dr. Wallace were still living in a rented room at the Globe Tavern. Mary—who was becoming quite a notable cook under Eppy's tutelage—would assist with the refreshments, but for the most part she was free to mingle with her guests, and many of those freezing winter afternoons ended with her and Lincoln lingering in the darkening parlor, long after the others had departed.

They talked of the books she lent him, and Mary was surprised at the scope of his reading, and the depth and acuteness of his mind. Her other suitors—Douglas and Shields, Trumbull and Webb—were educated men, familiar as a matter of course with Shakespeare and Homer. Lincoln, uneducated, had discovered the stories for himself, and had read them as Mary read Gothic novels, with an almost sensuous pleasure. On one occasion he recited to her "John Anderson, My Jo," which he had memorized as he casually and easily memorized entire speeches and scenes from Shakespeare, and she thought she heard a catch in his voice on the ending line, *"We'll sleep together at its foot, John Anderson, my jo."*

"I got to memorizing poetry for when I travel," he said. "It's three days' ride down to Carthage, and four days to someplace like Belleville, and most days you don't meet a soul on the roads. Back when I didn't have a horse I'd walk, sometimes two and three days, if I'd delivered a load of goods by raft and had to get back home."

On other evenings they spoke of the issues in the Legislative committees he was on, or of the suits he had before the courts. "Yes, the state needs a strong central bank, but if it has one, who's going to run it?" pointed out Mary, one lamp-lit evening when they sat, half-forgotten by the other guests, in the dim rear parlor. "What if you get a scoundrel in charge, like Biddle in the National Bank, who spent his time buying influence and manipulating credit to favor his own supporters? Wouldn't that discredit the bank and cause more ruin than it amends?"

"Oh, I would love to see some politician go to the polls sayin' he's gonna tell the banks what to do," sighed Lincoln, with a comical shake of his head. "He'd be the first man in the country's history to not only get *no* votes, but to have 'em taken away from him, so he'd be a vote-debtor and have liens against him for the next six times he runs. . . . But this whole mess the state's in now, with no money for canals or railroads or anythin' else we need, is because there's nuthin' sayin' what money is and what it ain't, which is all banks really do, when you think of it. . . ."

When she spoke of her father's slaves, he asked if she were an abolitionist: "I hate slavery—one trip to New Orleans was enough to do that for me—but the way the abolitionists are goin' about their business will surely tear this country apart. When I see the violence that's come about in the last few years, that printer Lovejoy murdered over in Alton, and the mob in St. Louis that burned that poor Negro sailor to death—when I hear that some state governments have put bounties on the heads of abolitionist publishers—all I see is that *both* sides are turnin' their backs on reason, turnin' into a mob."

"It's easy enough for us to say," replied Mary softly, "because we're white. For us it *is* a matter of reason. People like the slaves of that horrible Mrs. Turner who lived back in Lexington, who would beat them literally to death over things like a broken teapot, don't really care about what the Founding Fathers intended. They just want to be able to leave a place where they're being mistreated, and not have their husbands and wives taken away from them to pay for someone's gambling debts."

If he spoke easily and earnestly of how the state could raise money for internal improvements through the sale of federal lands, or at what point Macbeth could have turned aside from his disastrous course, he did not speak of his family, or the Kentucky canebrakes where he'd been born. The stories he told were of people he'd met on the road, or folks he'd known in New Salem or Cairo or points between. And Mary remembered what Josh Speed had said of Lincoln's father on that winter afternoon in the store, and of Lincoln himself on the night of the Legislature's cotillion: that he was an exile from the world he'd grown up in, who had found no place yet in the world for which his starved mind yearned.

And Lincoln was ambitious. That was one of the first things Mary learned about him, and one of the most surprising: that behind his diffidence in polite company, his razor-sharp wit and his deep, gentle love for animals and children, he had his eyes on political power and studied how to achieve it the way he had once, he told her, studied to become a surveyor.

"Which you don't expect, when you speak to him in company," said Mary to Speed, on a rainy day in early March. She'd heard the rumor that there was a new shipment of Irish lace—the first of the spring—and because Elizabeth was out paying calls with the carriage, she had convinced Merce to walk downtown through the slushy muck of the streets, hopping from plank to plank of building material dropped off the construction drays and carrying a bundle of shingles they'd found to bridge the gaps. Speed was astonished to see her—the weather had been foul all morning and promised worse—but, as she'd calculated, Mary had first pick of the lace, and put money down on the two best pieces for herself, plus gifts for Elizabeth, Frances, Merce (who was thumbing through the books), and Julia.

"He appears so humble—like Duncan, *he hath borne his faculties so meek*—but I notice he doesn't put a foot wrong when he's negotiating with delegates from the other districts for Legislative votes, and at Court Days I don't think there's a man he doesn't speak to." Mary dimpled, and shook her head. "Yet he likes to present himself as a bumpkin who couldn't tell a wooden nutmeg from a barleycorn."

"Only when it suits him." Speed leaned on the counter and scratched the ears of the fat marmalade tomcat who shared the building with Lincoln and himself. "People like to hear that, when he makes a speech—Lincoln's figured that out. It lets him slip his point across when their minds aren't closed to argument by highfalutin' words. I think his ambition springs from a different root than, for instance, our little Stephen's—though they're both poor boys who want to end up richer than their fathers were. But Lincoln's ambition goes beyond that. He wants power so that he can do the job right, while other men want it only so they can collect the job's pay."

He glanced at the windows, gray with dreary afternoon light. The brown puddles in the street lay still as glass, but the sky lowered sullenly above the wet board buildings of the town. Work had resumed on the State House the week before and the downtown streets were rivers of half-frozen slush. "You two had best get home, if you're going to do it without getting wet. Would you like to wait here where it's warm, and I'll see if I can find someone to take word to Ninian's house to get the carriage here?" And after one look at the ocean of goo beyond the plank sidewalk's edge, he added, "I'd take you home myself but the canoe's got a hole in it."

"We'll manage," laughed Mary. "We got here, didn't we?" But when she and Mercy reached the edge of the sidewalk Mary saw, to her alarm, that most of the dropped planks and shingles that they'd used for stepping-stones had already sunk in the mud.

A few wagons creaked past, hauling roof-slates to the State House before the rain should start again.

Mercy looked around her anxiously as they retreated toward the shop's door again where Joshua waited. "I promised my sister-in-law I'd be home. Jamie's coming to dinner...."

"And Mr. Gillespie's coming to our house," said Mary consideringly. "And goodness knows if Elizabeth's back yet with the carriage...Oh!" she called out, hurrying back to the edge of the sidewalk and waving her handkerchief at the driver of a passing dray. "Oh, Mr. Hart!" For she recognized the man as a laborer whom Ninian had hired on several occasions to fix fences and mend the stable.

"Mary!" cried Merce, shocked. "What are you...?"

The little Irishman drew rein and touched his soaked hat-brim, and Mary gave him her most flirtatious smile. "Mr. Hart, could I possibly, *possibly* trouble you to drive past my brother-in-law's house on your way back to the freight depot? It isn't so very much out of your way...."

"Miss Todd...!" said Speed, half-shocked and half-laughing, and Merce gasped, "Mary, don't you *dare*! Everyone will talk!"

"Oh, pooh. We need to get home."

"*We* nothing! That dray is..." She visibly bit back the word *filthy*, out of consideration for Mr. Hart, and finished with, "My sister-in-law will *kill* me!"

"Well," laughed Mary, "I think I'm a match for my sister. I can't make poor Mr. Speed go hunting someone to take a message for me, Mr. Speed, I really couldn't.... And I think we can trust Mr. Hart, can't we, Mr. Hart?" She turned to the carter appealingly, with a helpless flutter of her lashes, and the unshaven, stocky little man laughed good-naturedly and held out a dirty-gloved hand.

"I'm not too proud if you're not, Miss Todd."

Speed rolled his eyes. "Your sister will skin me for letting

you do this. Here," he added, pulling off his apron, "you'd
better put this over the seat...."

"Are you sayin' the seats of me vehicle aren't all they
should be?" Hart bristled with mock indignation, as if the
plank on which he sat wasn't wet with rain and slick with spattered mud, and all four burst into laughter. As they jolted
through the streets—Merce having remained, like a stranded
mariner, on the boardwalk outside Speed's store—Mary saw
Douglas and Lincoln emerging from Birchall's store, Douglas
natty in a new broadcloth coat and Lincoln looking like he'd
dressed in a high wind in some scarecrow's hand-me-downs.
Mary lifted her hand like a queen and waved as Betsey had admonished her for years: move the wrist, never the elbow.

Douglas looked shocked, and as if he asked himself if he
really wanted as a Senatorial—or Presidential—wife a woman
who'd ride unchaperoned on a construction dray through the
middle of town.

Lincoln removed his dilapidated hat and executed a profound bow.

CHAPTER EIGHTEEN

IT WAS THROUGH LETTERS THAT THEIR LOVE FIRST GREW.

Even with Mary—who had reason to believe that she was the woman he talked to most easily—Lincoln was often silent as a clam, as if at some time in the past he'd been told that he mustn't speak to women as he spoke to men and had no idea how one *did* speak to women. He was not, Mary noticed, a good speaker extempore, even on politics, and needed to prepare his notes carefully. Had they not shared an interest in both politics and poetry, she thought he'd never have been able to put two words together with her at all.

Writing freed his thoughts.

In his letters she had the feeling of seeing the man, and not what his awkward body or his barren upbringing had made of him.

And Mary, as quick with witty repartee as she could be with defensive sarcasm, found that she, too, could write of deeper thoughts than she could express aloud... certainly than she could express to Elizabeth and Ninian. Not only was Lincoln different from any man she had ever met—*she* was different, with him.

Through the winter of 1839 they met each other socially, at the House on the Hill or the homes of friends: the Leverings, or the Englishman Edward Baker, the acerbic Dr. Anson Henry or Simeon Francis, who published the *Sangamo Journal*. The *Journal's* little one-room board building, or Simeon's big house on Sixth Street near-by, were de facto club-houses for the Young Whigs of the capital, of whom Lincoln was acknowledged chief. Mary became very fond of the sturdy editor and his forthright wife, Bessie, and read the

Journal regularly. Any trace of romantic possibility between herself and Stephen Douglas was swept away when in the wake of a particularly nasty round of political mudslinging Douglas lost his temper and tried to cane Simeon in the street.

Lincoln was one of those who pulled the two men apart. Mary, who had just stepped from Diller's drugstore when it happened, flattened back against the wall, her gloved hand pressed to her mouth, almost in tears with the wave of unreasoning terror that washed over her at the sight.

"What is it?" asked Lincoln, crossing the street to her when Douglas had jerked himself free of other men's restraining hands, and stormed on his way. "Are you all right, Miss Todd?"

"Yes." Mary's voice was a toneless whisper, but she was shaking as if she, not Simeon—not Elliot Presby—had been attacked. Lincoln just stood there, looking down at her as if he hadn't the slightest idea of what to do in the face of feminine emotion. Mary fumbled in her reticule for a handkerchief and guessed, wryly, that if Lincoln had a bandanna in his pocket it probably wasn't clean. "No. It's just...a friend of mine was caned in the street, back home, and...and hurt very badly. And one of my cousins...shot his best friend, over an article printed in the newspaper...." She fought to keep her face from crumpling into weeping again.

Nothing really happened! she reminded herself desperately.

Why did she feel the panic terror, smell again the mingling of gutter-mud and blood?

She tried to draw a deep breath.

Douglas of course would have had a clean handkerchief and dabbed away her tears with it.

Douglas with his cane flashing through the air...

But it was Lincoln who'd seen her pressed against the wall, her face white with shock, while everyone else went about their business.

"Would you like me to take you home, Miss Todd?" he

asked gently, and she nodded, and laid her hand on his offered arm.

THE MUDSLINGING, OF COURSE, HAD BEEN PART AND PARCEL
of the campaign to elect General William Henry Harrison
President come November.

As soon as the roads were clear in spring, Lincoln was on
them, making speeches in support of General Harrison and
debating political issues with every Democrat in every corner of the state. He wrote to Mary from Jacksonville, from
Alton and Belleville: brief notes, mostly concerning the political debates, in which he knew she was interested. (Catch
Stephen Douglas telling me what his rivals said about him, she
thought.) Though the tall, gawky man was almost as reticent
about stating his thoughts on paper as he was on Ninian's
porch, his feelings came through in those simple, lucid para-
graphs, his deep sense of politics as service, as the duty that
must be taken up as the price of power. Mary, who like her
father and Ninian and nearly everyone she knew, had only
thought of government in terms of privileges, perquisites, favors, and contracts, felt surprised and a little ashamed: it was
as if she had mistaken a woodland pond for the Atlantic
Ocean.

She had, she realized, operated under the assumption that
men who'd lived most of their lives in the backwoods, if not
invariably stupid, were certainly simple.

There was nothing simple at all about Abraham Lincoln.

When the Legislative session closed for the summer, Mary
accepted the invitation of her two uncles—the Honorable
North Todd and Judge David Todd—to spend the summer
in Columbia, Missouri. She packed her trunk and Ninian escorted her on the two-day stage-ride to St. Louis, then by
steamboat up the Missouri to Rocheport. Ninian had his
own reasons for going to Rocheport, for there was going to
be a gathering of Missouri Whigs there in a few weeks.

Mary had always held a little grudge in her heart against

her uncle David, because it was to pay his debts that, long ago, Granny Parker had sold poor Saul. But the feeling dissolved when the big, jovial man sprang down from the buggy where he'd been waiting for her at the landing, and gathered her into his arms. "What, you haven't got our girl married off yet?" demanded Uncle David of Ninian, and pinched Mary's cheek. "What's that wife of yours been doing?"

"Fending off suitors with a broadsword and shield," returned Ninian with a grin, and shook Uncle David's hand. "And she needs to, sir, with the way this girl draws 'em."

Mary gave him her sidelong smile, said, "I'm quite capable of fending off my own suitors, thank you, sir," and flipped open her fan. A drift of breeze came off the river, but the air felt thick and hot, damper than the dry prairie winds of Springfield.

And Uncle David laughed and shook his head.

It was curious, after even a few months in Springfield, to be back in a slave state again. And though Mary was as strongly opposed to slavery as ever, she could not deny that she loved the gentler pace of the lands where scrabbling competition was tempered by a more easygoing outlook on life. Uncle David's house in Columbia—most of a day's buggy-ride from Rocheport—though roughly built by even Springfield standards, ran with quiet efficiency. Mary reveled in being brought coffee in bed by the housemaids, and in knowing that if the ribbons on her pink muslin needed pressing before a party, they'd be pressed without arguments from the maids about how much other work they had to do.

And there were parties. It was twenty miles back down to Rocheport, but when the Whig Convention opened with a grand ball on the night of June 16th, Mary and her cousin Annie were there, strictly chaperoned by Annie's mother, plump Aunt Bet. The town was crammed with delegates and only the fact that cousins on the other side of the family had a house in Rocheport guaranteed the David Todd party anyplace to stay—every boardinghouse and hotel was jammed. Mary was secretly disappointed that Lincoln wasn't among the Illinois delegates—he'd written her he had a court case on the seventeenth—but on Sunday morning, after the closing of the convention, when Mary was just wondering whether Rachel the cook's wonderful pancakes were worth pulling herself out of bed for, she heard the far-off sound of knocking downstairs.

The creak of footfalls—one of the housemaids running, Abigail or Kessie. Cousin Annie was already awake and brushing her hair—Mary didn't understand how she did it, after both girls had danced until nearly four in the morning at a party given for the delegates who'd come up to Columbia after the convention closed. "Oh, my goodness, if that's that Mr. Teller from Hannibal, who kept asking me to dance last night...," moaned Annie, with a comical grimace, and listened.

Mary listened too, and heard, unmistakably, that light, husky voice saying, "I am terribly sorry to disturb you, Miss, but is this where I might leave a note for Miss Mary Todd?"

She jolted upright in bed, coppery braids tumbling. "Get Abigail and tell her not to let him leave." It didn't occur to her until later to ask herself why it was *his* voice that elicited such a reaction. Had it been James Shields, or Lyman Trumbull, or any of her other suitors, she'd simply have rolled over and thanked God for servants to tell them to go away. "Where are my stays?"

"I do beg your pardon for not sending a note," apologized Lincoln, when Mary—in an unbelievably brief half-hour—appeared, corseted, dressed, washed, and not a curl out of place, in the parlor. "I didn't know how long it would take to get the judgment, but I figured if I could get to Rocheport in time to have a talk with some of the delegates before they left town, it'd be a good idea to try."

"So faithful in love, and so dauntless in war / There never was knight like the young Lochinvar?" And then, a little shyly, she added, "You must have ridden all night."

Lincoln scratched his long nose. "Pretty near," he admitted. "I've got to be in Shelbyville Saturday to speak. If we can't *dance but one measure, drink one cup of wine,* I thought maybe I might at least walk you to church, Miss Todd? If it's all right with your uncle, that is."

They lagged behind the rest of the family party all the way to the Presbyterian church, comparing notes about the delegates and their positions, and lingered under the trees until the lifted notes of the first hymn dragged them unwillingly indoors. Then they had to run the gauntlet of eyes. In Missouri there was no slipping unobtrusively through the door and onto the nearest bench and pretending they'd been there all along. Lincoln started to do this and Mary tugged him sharply by the sleeve; it was only on a second glance that it apparently dawned on him that those rear benches were entirely the province of the slaves.

The laundresses, gardeners, kitchen girls all grinned good-naturedly and slid over to make room for them, since Miss Molly was already known all over town as the young cousin staying with Judge Todd and they were used to seeing young couples sneak in late, but Mary pulled him down the aisle to the Todd family pew.

As they walked back to the house afterwards for Sunday dinner—still far in the rear of the rest of the family—Lincoln mused, "I spent most of yesterday evening catching up on the platform for the election, and I never saw so many men dodgin' and skirtin' an issue in my life. It was like watching folks tryin' to dance under a leaky roof in a rainstorm. You'd think to listen to 'em nobody'd ever heard the word *slavery* in their lives."

Mary rolled her eyes in sympathy. "I thought Kentucky was bad," she sighed. "*Nobody* here will talk about it, not even if they're *not* trying to avoid offending delegates. Like at home," she added. "Betsey—my stepmother—always impressed on us that we call darkies 'servants,' or 'our people.' Even her mother did—Granny Humphreys—and she was against slavery like my father. But if you can sell someone, they're not a *servant.*"

Lincoln shook his head. He'd sat beside her in her uncle's

pew—the first time Mary had ever heard of him entering a church—listening respectfully to the sermon ("Render unto Caesar those things that are Caesar's") but mostly, she'd thought, he watched the faces of the congregation around them. As he always watched, wherever he was.

"They can't go on pretendin' forever that slavery doesn't exist," he replied quietly. "Not with the abolitionists callin' every slaveholder a murderer, an' the slaveholders claiming the abolitionists are incitin' rebellion, and working men in the North gettin' into the act by killin' Negroes in the streets. Here we're choosing a man to run the country for the next four years, we're putting on the line for the world to see what we, the Whigs, believe in an' don't believe in, and all most Whigs want to say about General Harrison is that he's a plain honest man who drinks hard cider an' lives in a log cabin, unlike that frippery fop Van Buren. What kind of election is *that*? It's like we're in a runaway buggy headin' straight for a brick wall. Sooner or later, we're gonna have to do *somethin'* about that wall."

"I cannot tell you," said Mary quietly, when they sat alone on the porch again after dinner, "how good it is to talk to someone...." She hesitated. What was it about Lincoln that she found so restful? Why did she feel that, alone among all the people of the world, she could speak her mind to him, be her true self?

Of course, she never discussed slavery with any of Uncle David's family—it wouldn't have been polite. Nor with any of the young gentlemen of the town who, in the weeks before the Whig Convention, had given such promise of a summer rich with dances, flirtations, compliments, and proposals of marriage. And as she'd found in Lexington, once slavery as a topic became forbidden ground, there was very little of politics that *could* be discussed. The unspoken darkness permeated every thread and corner of life.

But most of those young gentlemen—clerks and land speculators, young farmers or the sons of the small cotton-planters and dealers who made up the town—who'd come calling as potential beaux hadn't even offered to discuss politics. Not with a lady. It was unheard-of. With them, Mary had been all that a lady should be: flirtatious and clever, laughing at their jokes and twinkling at their wit (such as it was), lively and breathless and filled with energy....

And only half herself.

Impulsively she said now, in the quiet shade of the porch, "How good it is to talk to you, Mr. Lincoln. I've missed you."

He studied her for a moment, as if weighing up how much to say about himself. Then he said, "And I you, Miss Todd."

She held out her hand to him, plump white fingers emerging from a mitt of lace. Uncle David's house was of squared logs, added to and clapboarded over, and its wide porch boasted only a bench to sit on, to take the hot feathers of breeze that floated from the hills beyond the town. "You can make that Molly," she said softly, "if you want."

He hesitated, then his big hand closed gently around hers. She remembered Speed telling her how Lincoln's father had handed him an ax at the age of eight and put him to work; he had the hands and arms of a laborer. "It's a pretty name," he said. "Molly." He smiled uncertainly, like a man stepping over the threshold of an unknown room in the dark, then bent his head suddenly and pressed his lips to her fingers.

At the touch of them, and the sight of the dark rumpled head bending over her hand, Mary felt a kind of a calm shock, as if she understood something she had only known intellectually before, like the first time she'd dreamed in French. And she thought, *I love him.*

And it was in her eyes, as he raised his head and met her gaze. Her heart felt clear, and peaceful, and as if all things had suddenly simplified in her life: *I love you.*

His big hands caught her arms, crushed her to him, as if she weighed nothing. His mouth was hot on her lips and his breath burned her cheek. Then the next second he thrust her away, or thrust himself away from her. For a moment he sat half turned from her, his breath fast and thick as if he'd been running, then he stood up abruptly and had made one long stride toward the porch steps before Mary sprang up and caught his sleeve.

He turned, and looked down into her face. "Miss Todd," he whispered, "I am sorry. . . ."

"It's all right." She could feel the shivering tension in his arm. Could see, for one instant, the naked desire in his gray eyes, before he looked aside. As if he feared, she thought, that if he didn't hold himself in check with a rein of iron he would back her to the wall and devour her.

And it was hard to remember any reason on earth not to let him.

She said again, "It's all right, Mr. Lincoln. And you may still make that Molly, if you'd like."

He drew a shaky breath, held it for a moment, and let it out; his shoulders relaxed a little as he looked back at her. The expression in his eyes was of a man who expects to have his face slapped hard.

On a similar occasion back in Springfield, Stephen Douglas had made a gallant remark about how a woman ought to forgive a poor man's gesture prompted only by her beauty, and had begged debonair forgiveness on his knees. And James Shields had protested—rather smugly—that he did not know how it had come about that he'd been over-whelmed enough to steal a kiss. . . .

But Mary knew that love was something Lincoln—the perpetual jester—did not joke about. And he wasn't going to say he didn't know how it had come about when he knew very well.

He said again, more collectedly, "I am sorry . . . Miss Molly."

"You understand that every girl has to *say* she is sorry, too." Her twinkling eyes belied her words, and under his deep tan his cheekbones colored. The corner of his big mouth moved in a smile.

"I can step down off the porch if you'd like to slap me," he offered, in the grave voice he used for jests, and suited the action to the word, bringing his face down almost on level with hers.

Mary reached out with her folded fan and touched him—like the breath of a butterfly—on his cheek. "There," she said. "Don't let it happen again."

They both knew it would.

Lincoln was on the road the rest of the summer and fall. His letters came to her from Carlinville, from Belleville, from Shawneetown. He mostly spoke of rallies and speeches, of the discreet horse-trading that went on among the delegates: *I promise to throw contracts your way if your friends vote for me.* Mary had told him that her Aunt Bet read her letters, as Elizabeth read them back in Springfield—he'd been horrified at this and even more shocked when Mary had told him that this was customarily done in all polite households—so he was circumspect in what he wrote, both about his own feelings and about the careful jockeyings among the politicians on the issue of slavery.

But under his wry observations and astute commentary, she sensed his pleasure in having someone with whom he could share his thoughts. "Man does not live by politics alone," he wrote her from Waterloo, after ten days of travel and political meetings in southern Illinois, "and sometimes I wish I could only sit beside a stream in the woods as I used to, watching to see what leaves would float past." The decision on the part of the Whig leaders to evade the issue of slavery completely, for fear of offending Southern, slaveowning Whigs like the Todds, annoyed him: "The sole argument of this election seems to be that General Harrison doesn't use gold dessert-spoons like President Van Buren does. By this argument I too would be qualified for the Presidency, and I don't see anyone rushing out to vote for me."

Because even sleepy little Columbia—which made Springfield look like New Orleans in comparison—was galvanized by the election, there was plenty for Mary to write to him about, and between her accounts of rallies and excursions and parades, she wrote of her affection for him, and her hopes to see him in Springfield in the fall. "Julia writes me that in October there will be a grand circus and menagerie coming to Springfield, which will display a gigantic elephant, the *first ever* seen in the State, as well as a giraffe and exhibitions of horsemanship and trapeze artistry," she wrote. "I do hope that, even amid the final stages of General Harrison's campaign, we can take the time to behold such a *spectacle.*"

Of course, knowing that she loved Lincoln did not keep her from flirting with half a dozen of the Columbia beaux. She made herself the life and soul of the entertainments surrounding the Presidential campaign, kept her mouth properly shut about both Shakespeare and politics, and in the three months she was in Missouri received two proposals of marriage, one from a young cotton-planter and another from a delegate from one of the southern counties. She walked out with a number of gentlemen and received posies and danced whenever she could, and this almost—but not quite—made up for the fact that there wasn't a book in the town besides a couple of Bibles and what she'd brought in her own trunks, and there was nothing resembling a theater closer than St. Louis, a hundred miles away.

During a political campaign, one didn't really need plays.

With the dances and parties attendant on the campaign there were always refreshments—pies and taffy, picnics of burgoo and barbeque—and, a little to Mary's alarm, she found her sleeves getting tight and her corset-laces harder to pull close. "Oh, it's nothing, everyone gets a little plump in the summer," consoled Annie—no sylph herself—and the two girls talked Uncle David into an expedition down to St. Louis on the steamboat for new dress-goods. Mary laughed about this, and made jokes with Annie and her other girl-friends in the town as they cut and fitted lettuce-green sprig muslin and pink dimity, but her recollection of Betsey's remarks about fat girls never finding husbands gnawed at her mind.

Yet the food was so good! Sweet and comforting, and doubly so because Elizabeth wasn't always looking over her shoulder, making remarks about the need to catch a beau.

Nevertheless, when Mary was packing her trunk to return to Springfield, it was with a pang of horrified shock that she realized how many of the dresses she'd brought with her at the beginning of summer she hadn't worn in some weeks—and how many of her favorites had had the seams let out two, or in one case three, times. Even as she ate a last breakfast of Aunt Bet's justifiably famous blueberry-maple pancakes before Quincy the coachman brought the buggy up to drive her and Uncle David to Rocheport, she quailed at the thought of facing Elizabeth. Quailed, too, at the recollection of Josh Speed's humorous account of Lincoln's reaction when he discovered that the Miss Owens he'd been tepidly engaged to a couple of years ago had grown enormously stout in his six-month absence.

I'm not enormously *stout,* Mary told herself, as she got into the buggy. Her heart began to pound with guilty apprehension, though it would be a good four days' travel before she'd have to face her family and friends. *And that'll soon disappear, once I get back to Springfield. If I just don't eat much on the steamboat....*

But almost the first thing Elizabeth said to her, when Mary came downstairs the morning after her arrival in Springfield four days later, was, "Good God, Molly, you've put on flesh! I would scarcely have recognized you, now that I see you in the light." The stage had been late coming into town, and Mary, her head aching from its swaying, had been glad only to come home and go upstairs after a swift embrace to Ninian, Elizabeth, little Julie, and Eppy in the kitchen.

She flushed now to the roots of her hair. "Well, and I'm *delighted* to see you too, Elizabeth! Thank you for making me feel *so much* at home already."

It was Elizabeth's turn to color up. She said, "I'm sorry. You're right, it wasn't my place to say anything...."

"I should say not!"

"But if your own sister can't give you a hint, who can? I can see we're going to have some work cut out for us, letting out your winter dresses." She spoke in a mollifying tone, but Mary, stung to tears, was in no mood to forgive and forget.

"Well, thank you *very much*," she retorted. "Please don't hesitate to use the tape-measure so you can have the most *accurate* information when you tell your friends about it."

"I'm sure no one in town," replied Elizabeth icily, "is going to need *my* word that you've gotten stout, once they see you. I only say this for your own good, dear, for you are twenty-one now and as you know, gentlemen as a rule don't ask fat girls to marry them."

"Well, I wouldn't know about *that*! As it happens, I got *four* perfectly decent proposals of marriage in Columbia— not that I had the *slightest* interest in any of them! And Mr. Lincoln finds me attractive enough to come to an understanding with me."

"*Mr. Lincoln?*" Elizabeth stared at her, appalled. "Molly . . ."

"What's wrong with Mr. Lincoln?"

"He is a bumpkin," stated Elizabeth, with cold finality. "A backwoodsman, and a penniless bankrupt to boot. Why don't you accept a proposal of marriage from Mr. Hart the carter while you're at it?"

"And why don't *you* admit—while you're at it—that you have no use for a man unless he's wealthy and high-born! That you'd as soon have married some crippled old dotard, if he'd had a big house and land and wealth—"

"*Molly!*"

"—and have whistled Ninian down the wind if it weren't that he was the son of the governor!" All Mary's pent-up resentments about having her letters read, about being called fat, about her father's long absences, frothed to the surface. "*You* have no more notion of love than does that snippy old harpy our father married! Only love of money . . ."

Elizabeth—who had never had any trouble holding her own in the noisy Todd household—reddened with anger, but as usual her voice remained cuttingly level. "If you marry that backwoods pumpkin-roller with his load of debts you'll find out soon enough what money means!"

"Money means nothing beside love!" Mary screamed at her. She felt as if she were burning up inside. "I'd rather by far marry a poor man who's going somewhere than a rich incompetent who couldn't even get on the electoral ballot of his own party in his own state!" (Ninian hadn't.)

"Honestly!" Elizabeth threw up her hands. "There's no talking to you when you get like this! I'd hoped that a little time away would cure your temper...."

"There is nothing wrong with my temper!!!" Mary shrieked. "It's you who don't want to admit that you're—"

Movement caught Mary's eye and she turned—they both turned—to see Eppy frozen in the parlor doorway.

And behind her, his eyes bulging out of his head with horror, was Mr. Lincoln.

CHAPTER NINETEEN

LINCOLN AND MARY WENT TO THE CIRCUS TOGETHER A FEW
days later, and tried to pretend everything was still all right.
Mary tried hard—and succeeded well—in being her usual
bright, flirtatious self, but the excursion was not a success.

Lincoln marveled over the elephant—Sultan, his name
was—and asked the dour Scotsman in charge of him all kinds
of questions about what elephants ate and how they worked.
"I never did see anything like it," he remarked, in one of his
rare relaxed moments that day. "Though my ma told me of
them—my stepmother," he corrected. "I'll have to write her
of this. She'd tell me tales of wonderful things, things I'd
never seen, growin' up in the woods; the only person back
then who treated me like a human being."

But for the most part Mary felt, all that day, that Lincoln
was studying her uneasily. He had little to say to either
Elizabeth or Ninian and she wondered exactly how much
Lincoln had heard of what she and Elizabeth had said to one
another, and how much of a shock it was to him, to see how
her bust and waist and hips had expanded since their last
meeting in June. Wondered if he were re-thinking, in that
new light, all the local gossip that Mary Todd "had a temper." Certainly Elizabeth never went beyond glacially exquisite politeness to him, and when they returned to the house
that evening, he was not asked to stay to dinner.

Mary had another screaming-match with Elizabeth and
cried herself to sleep.

Lincoln left town soon after that, and was gone almost a
month.

His journeys up and down the state all summer in the cause
of the Whig Party and William Henry Harrison showed on

his face and his form, during the few October days before his
latest departure. While Mary had grown plumper from the
thrill and jollity of campaigning, Lincoln had grown more
lean. Even in repose, he looked tired. The skin over his high
cheekbones was tanned dark from riding long distances between the prairie towns, and lines were settled around his
eyes. His notes to her were short, and when he did see her, he
was very quiet. Mary tried to convince herself that this was
only the result of days and weeks spent exerting himself to
charm and convince voters.

She failed. And as usual when she felt fear, it transformed
itself to anger. When Lincoln left for Pontiac to take cases at
the DeWitt County Circuit Court—because of his campaign
journeys he hadn't worked all summer—Mary returned, almost defiantly, to the round of rallies and speeches, balls and
barbeques, attendant on the final throes of the election, cul-
minating in a glorious, dazzling, torchlit procession on
Election Night.

Tippecanoe and Tyler, too!

But she wished Lincoln were in town at her side.

After making speeches, trading favors, promising votes,
talking to delegates, crisscrossing the state on horseback for
six solid, weary months—to the total neglect of the work
that might buy him new clothes or would pay his board bill
at Butler's, where he and Speed both ate—Mary wasn't even
sure whether Lincoln himself cast a vote.

She flirted with Douglas, danced with Gillespie and
Trumbull, walked out with Jimmy Shields and sweetly tried
to discourage—but not discourage too much—the attentions
of the avid and elderly Mr. Webb, all the while trying to eat
as little as possible. But she found her temper was shorter on
short rations and her headaches, which had plagued her on
and off through the summer, grew worse. She longed for
Mammy Sally's mouth-wringing tisanes, for the gentle care
of Uncle David's old cook Rachel . . . for something other
than Elizabeth's tart remarks about "overcoming her ten-

dency" to headaches, as she admonished her to "overcome" her temper.

On the ninth of November, the Sangamon County Circuit Court would begin its session. On the twenty-third, the Legislature would begin meeting, in the Springfield Methodist Church, since the State House was still not done. Mary was determined that when Lincoln returned to town, she'd demonstrate to him that she wasn't a girl to wait sighingly for a man's attention. He'd see how popular she was— plump or not, spirited or not, twenty-one or not—with every other bachelor in that man-filled town, and she wrote to her father in Lexington for the money for three new dresses to make sure the point was carried across.

And on the seventh of November, Ninian's Uncle Cyrus arrived in town, with his daughter Matilda.

Mary liked Matilda Edwards immediately. She and Elizabeth waited impatiently in the parlor, on the evening that Ninian had Jerry harness up the carriage and rode to meet the stage at the American House Hotel—a total of three blocks, but there would be luggage and the streets were unpaved and soupy after the first of the autumn rains. Cyrus came in with Ninian, big-shouldered and tall like all the Edwards men, elegantly dressed, even for travel. He was a prominent politician and man of business, and one of the wealthiest citizens of Alton, which lay just upriver from St. Louis. He bowed over Elizabeth's hand, smiled at Mary: "Here's my girl Tilda," he told her. "I know you'll be great friends."

Matilda Edwards was sixteen years old, tall for her age and blonde and ethereally slender. She was exquisitely dressed in dark-blue delaine and what appeared to be at least ten petticoats beneath her rustling skirts, and had the gentlest, most natural smile Mary had ever seen. "Oh, dear, I hope you'll be able to put up with me," she murmured guiltily to Mary, as Mary led her up to show her the bedroom they would share. "I sleep like a cat—up and down and moving all around. . . ."

"It's all right, I get up about a dozen times a night. . . ."

"Oh, dear, neither of us will get any sleep...."

"Do you read in bed?"

"Shhh! Papa would *slay* me if he knew.... Oh, you have a copy of *Belinda*...!"

The two girls stayed awake, whispering and giggling, until nearly dawn.

Every man in Springfield fell instantly and violently in love with Matilda Edwards on sight.

Including Abraham Lincoln.

And no girl could be really angry with her because she was so sweet.

"Oh, Papa will be *so* pleased," Tilda sighed, after the first small party at the House on the Hill—to which Mr. Lincoln was not invited—at which Cyrus renewed his political connections with the wealthier inhabitants of Springfield and his daughter was introduced to the Coterie. It was nearly two in the morning; she and Mary were brushing out each other's hair and getting into their nightgowns, while the rain pattered gently on the leaves outside. "He wants me to meet other gentlemen. That's why he brought me here."

"*Other* gentlemen?" Mary cocked her head at the significance of the modifier. Any other girl would have driven her wildly jealous, the way the young men had clustered around her—including several of Mary's own beaux.

Tilda turned her enormous blue eyes upon Mary. "You won't tell?"

Mary shook her head.

"There's a... a gentleman." Self-possessed and matter-of-fact as she had been all evening, the girl blushed. "Back home. Mr. Strong." She could barely bring out his name above a whisper, as if the syllable was a precious thing. "Papa thinks I must look about me a little—he says I am too young. A girl must have beaux, you know," she assured Mary anxiously, as if she thought that after flirting with a dozen men herself Mary would somehow object. "But... I could *never* truly look at another man, you know."

Mary gave her a smile that beamed with understanding. "I

know." And made a resolve to encourage her young cousin in exactly that course of action, no matter how long she should stay beneath Ninian's roof.

The fact that at no time did she worry about losing Lincoln to Tilda did not, however, make it any easier to watch him follow the girl with his eyes, and stand talking with her for fifteen minutes at a time at the American House ball that marked the opening of the Legislative session. In response, Mary flirted and danced with every other suitor she could attract. Back in Lexington, she had learned that if a girl wanted to gain and hold a man's attention, all she had to do was lavish her smiles upon another man. Stephen Douglas danced as divinely as ever; Jimmy Shields was most assiduous in bringing her cups of punch (with superhuman resolve, she eschewed the cake).

And Lincoln, hovering at the edge of the cluster of young clerks and delegates around that slim, blonde vision in pink silk, barely seemed to notice Mary was in the room.

As far as Mary could see—and she kept as much of an eye on the group around Matilda as she could while engaged in holding as many other men as possible on her own string—Lincoln never worked up the courage to so much as approach the girl as a suitor. That could have had something to do with whatever he might have overheard Elizabeth snap at Mary about him during their quarrel.

And it could have been because Josh Speed had also fallen—apparently quite seriously—in love with Matilda, too.

Mary's temper shortened as the evening progressed, until she finally lashed out at Julia Jayne over some casual jest about Mary's new dress. She left the assembly-room in tears. Jamie Conkling—who had become great friends with her, since their mutually beloved Mercy had returned to her parents in Baltimore—escorted her home.

After that Mary saw little of Lincoln. As a practicing attorney and a member of the State House of Representatives he was, she knew, frenziedly busy. With his party in the minority in both Houses and the whole state's finances in disarray he was fighting an uphill battle to salvage the internal improvement measures that the Whigs had put through. With banks and businesses closing right and left, nobody was about to release funds to build roads, no matter how badly they were needed.

Sometimes he would call after supper in the evenings, or walk with her on those few Sundays before rain—and then snow—closed in on the prairies. Once, he took her sledding.

But he was always withdrawn, as if struggling with his own thoughts. On the sledding excursion he spent a good deal of the time talking with Matilda, who had accompanied them in company with Josh Speed.

Even before Tilda had appeared on the scene—even before Lincoln had walked into Elizabeth's parlor to discover that the prettily plump, high-spirited girl he'd danced with and written to was now a fat, shrieking termagant—there had been times when Mary had wanted to hit him over the head with a book. He was abstracted, absentminded, and perpetually late through becoming absorbed in whatever case he was working on or story he was telling to the loafers who hung around Diller's drugstore. He would drift away into thought and pay no attention to what Mary or anyone else was saying to him. On some occasions, when she was late coming down to the parlor, she'd find him so engrossed in one of Ninian's books that he'd been unaware of her entering the room.

And if there was something on his mind—and she would take oath, as the winter days advanced toward Christmas, that there was—he was as tight as an oyster about saying what it was.

Raised in a vociferous family where everyone spoke their mind and if you didn't ask for what you wanted you certainly wouldn't get it, Mary found this silence maddening.

Yet when, after Lincoln had walked her home one snowy night from a Missionary Society lecture on the South Sea Islands, she asked him what the matter was, he turned the question aside with a story he'd heard about what the native ladies of those islands actually did with the dresses the missionaries sent them: "And I don't know whether the moral of that story has to do with innocence, modesty, or only just the weather there." Mary had to laugh, in spite of her annoyance, and stepped up on the porch, two steps up so that their faces would be on level when he kissed her, gently, on the cheek. Her hands tightened over his, big and awkward in his mended gloves, and his fingers returned the pressure.

But he turned away hastily as Ninian came out onto the porch, and as she rustled into the hall to shed her jacket and muff, she heard her brother-in-law say, "A word with you, if I may, Lincoln."

Mary froze. She was starting to turn back toward the door when Elizabeth appeared from the parlor: "How was the lecture, dear?" And, when Mary took an impulsive step toward the door, Elizabeth purposefully crossed the room to head her off. "Come into the parlor, dear, and get warm. You must be frozen."

"What's Ninian talking to Mr. Lincoln about?" She could hear Ninian's voice on the porch, but he'd closed the door. An understandable thing to do—the night was freezing—but anger and panic stirred in her heart at this exclusion.

"Good heavens, dear, I don't know." Elizabeth's usually soft laugh was tinny. "Politics, I suppose...."

"Ninian sees Mr. Lincoln every day at the State House."

Elizabeth put a hand on Mary's elbow to guide her into the parlor, and when Mary balked, her hand tightened. "Darling..."

Mary tried to yank her elbow away and Elizabeth's grip closed like a claw.

"*Darling,*" she repeated, and closed the door of the parlor behind them. There was an edge to her voice, and a wariness in her eyes, bracing for another storm. "Ninian and I have your best interests at heart, you know that. Mr. Lincoln is a very fine man, a very honorable man. But you cannot deny that he is a very cold man, a man who has no particular liking for women...."

"He is not!" cried Mary, who had the best of reasons to know the volcanic physical desires masked by the lawyer's wary reserve. "Just because he doesn't say a lot of pretty words—"

"And you cannot deny," cut in Elizabeth inexorably, "that he is a man ten thousand dollars in debt due to poor business practices. You keep saying that wealth doesn't matter, but you have never been poor."

"And I suppose *you* have?"

Elizabeth's lips tightened. "Your happiness is my duty, Mary. I assure you, you would not be happy with Mr. Lincoln, even if he should ask for your hand. . . . Which I doubt he will do, the way he's been dangling after Tilda."

"That isn't true!" Mary flashed back. "We have an understanding. . . ."

Elizabeth rolled her eyes.

"Tilda isn't the slightest interested in him. . . ."

"Good God, I should hope not!" cried Elizabeth, clearly startled that Mary would even consider an idea so grotesque. "Her father left her here to make a decent match, not to ally herself with a bankrupt clod-crusher, never mind how clever he is. He has no family, Mary, and no—"

"If you tell me again how he has no money I shall scream!" Mary screamed at her. She pulled free of Elizabeth's grip and slammed through the parlor door and into the hall just as Ninian came in from outside, his sharp nose red with cold. Mary jerked open the front door and stumbled onto the porch.

"Mr. Lincoln!" she called out into the coal-sack blackness of the snowy night. The glow of the parlor lamps touched the drifting flakes, a foot or two beyond the edge of the porch, but there was no sign of any tall figure in the blackness.

Sick dread in her heart and tears flowing from her eyes, Mary thrust past Elizabeth and Ninian, and ran up the stairs to her room.

"Darling . . ." Matilda turned from the mirror where she

was brushing her hair as Mary slammed into the big front bedroom. "I'm worried about Mr. Speed." Speed was the beau who had escorted Matilda to the lecture. "He's become so serious about me—about himself and me—and this evening he said he couldn't endure to remain in Springfield, if he and I could not be together. I'm afraid that—"

"Oh, leave me alone!" cried Mary, and flung herself down on the bed in a huge storm of crushing petticoats, and buried her face in the pillows. She was crying.

Matilda, being Matilda, took her at her word and left her alone. For nearly forty minutes she brushed and braided her own lovely flaxen hair while Mary sobbed. Only after Mary's grief began to subside did she wrap every shawl in the un-heated room around her for warmth, and cross to the bed and silently take Mary in her arms. Mary held on to her and wept afresh. After a long time, her head aching, she finally consented to be helped to undress.

She dreamed she was trying to catch up with Mr. Lincoln on an overgrown woodland path; running and stumbling through the sun-splashed green shadows, calling out to him again and again. But her legs were too short, and she was fat and out of breath, and her head ached too terribly. She saw him ahead of her, the flecks of sunlight mottling his coarse Indian-black hair and the faded blue of the homespun shirt he wore, and his long legs carried him away from her, out of sight.

NEW YEAR'S EVE CAME, AND WITH IT A GIANT COTILLION AT the American House. Though Lincoln spent most of the evening talking with the men, he was standing beside Mary when midnight tolled, and like every other young couple with an understanding, they kissed. His hands closed tight over hers, though his lips scarcely brushed her cheek. Not much else was possible, with Elizabeth and Ninian only feet away. But as always, Mary felt the hunger in him, the powerful physical desire of an active man coupled with the desperation of an unwanted child. She wanted to drag his mouth down to hers, to let his embrace overwhelm her as it had on her uncle's porch in Columbia, to revel in it as she had then. That physical desire, unspoken of by either, held taut between them, as much a part of their understanding as any amount of Shakespeare and Whig politics.

Her eyes closed, Mary didn't even see who Matilda kissed as midnight struck.

But when Lincoln went back immediately to the men, gathered around the long tables that had been set up to the left of the great common-room fireplace, Mary decided he needed a lesson, and proceeded to flirt, turn and turnabout, with every man of the dozen gallants who preferred dances with the ladies to speculation about who President Harrison would appoint to government jobs. With the Legislature and the courts both in session, even the presence of the Vandalia political matron Mrs. Browning and her daughters didn't lessen the ratio of men to women much. Clerks, delegates, and lawyers jockeyed and nudged for a chance to dance with the flaxen Matilda, black-haired Julia, and plump, lively, fascinating Mary Todd.

Josh Speed danced with them all, but as she circled the room with him in a gay polka, Mary saw Speed's dark eyes follow Matilda's graceful white form. "Mr. Speed," said Mary worriedly, her small hand resting on his arm as they lilted through the figures.

The dark gaze returned to her. She saw the marks of sleeplessness in the lined lids, the crease between nostril and mouth, and remembered Matilda's words in their bedroom after the South Sea Islands lecture, and later gossip of Elizabeth's.

"Tilda . . . is very fond of you. I know she wouldn't want to think that you would . . . would do anything rash or foolish because of her."

"You mean, like selling up my half of the store and leaving town?" Speed's smile, usually light as sunshine, seemed tired, with the wryness of a beaten man. "Word gets around fast.

No." He shook his head. "Miss Edwards isn't why I decided to sell up, if I sell up ... and I still haven't completely made up my mind to do it. Though since Pa's death they do need me now at home." He managed a chuckle. "God knows what'll become of Lincoln if I do."

It was something that had gone through Mary's mind, too. Not that Lincoln couldn't have found someplace—even in the overcrowded boardinghouses of the new state capital—to live. But she knew he depended on Speed's friendship far more than most people suspected. For a man as gregarious as Lincoln was, very few people pierced the iron wall of isolation he kept around his heart.

Then Speed sighed, and shook his head. "But it's time for a change, Molly ... Miss Todd. Time to ... I don't know. Fish or cut line on a lot of things. What better time than the New Year?"

So when Lincoln knocked at the door of the House on the Hill late on New Year's afternoon, when the curtains of cinder-colored twilight were winding themselves thick beyond the windows, Mary thought only that he brought news concerning Speed's decision—or perhaps sought solace for the separation he knew would come.

New Year's dinner at the House on the Hill was always a special occasion. They had spent the morning, like everyone else in town, in obligatory calls, leaving their cards at every house. Elizabeth was justly proud of her hospitality, and Eppy had worked like the Israelites in Egypt to prepare cakes, pies, gingerbread, and an enormous savory ham for the Leverings, for Ninian's brother Ben and sister-in-law Helen, for Dr. Wallace and Frances, Uncle John Todd and his daughters, plus the thin, red-haired, and irascible Cousin Stephen Logan. After dinner there had been open house, for all the wealthy and fashionable of Springfield: Senator Herndon and the chinless, slightly inebriated, and now-married Billy; Dr. Merriman and Lincoln's friend Dr. Henry, and their wives; Dr. Jayne and his wife with Julia and her brother William;

Stephen Douglas and Jimmy Shields and a whole train of other bachelors come to pay court to Mary and Matilda....

Elizabeth and Eppy had spent the afternoon and evening darting back and forth to the kitchen for claret cups, platters of gingerbread, and cups of coffee, resolutely refusing all offers of help from the girls.

The last suitors had been gone for an hour. Matilda—who had been extremely quiet all day—had gone upstairs. When the clock struck six, Mary guessed that there would be no more callers, and with a grateful sigh took off her gloves—which were still too tight for her, much to her annoyance—and stood to see what help she could give in the kitchen.

Then there was a knock on the door. After a long time—Lina, the housemaid, was back in the kitchen helping Eppy clear up—Mary heard the girl's swift feet running to the hall to answer.

"Is Miss Todd here?" asked the familiar voice.

And Mary thought, *Thank God, Elizabeth's in the kitchen....*

And there he stood, the top tousle of his unruly hair seeming to reach for the wooden archway that separated front parlor from rear.

She melted into a smile. "Mr. Lincoln! Do sit...."

He held up his hand to silence her. In the firelight—only a single lamp had been lit in the other parlor—she saw his face was haggard, his eyes filled with the last extremities of wretchedness.

"Miss Todd," he said.

And Mary felt the tears rush to her eyes at the formality of his address. Had it been another man who had gone back to calling her by her surname after the more intimate "Miss Molly," she would have twitted archly on the defection, fluttered her eyelids, and made her dimples peep....

Her heart was sick within her. She could say nothing.

Lincoln took a deep breath and went on, as if he were speaking from memorized notes, as he did in court and on the political platform.

"Miss Todd, I had meant to communicate with you by letter, setting forth all the reasons why our understanding—if understanding it is—cannot any longer endure. But a better man than I am put that letter on the fire, and convinced me that I was honor-bound to speak to you in person. . . ."

Mary began to tremble uncontrollably. Her vision of him blurred with tears but she heard the miserable desperation in his voice as he said, "Molly . . ."

"I didn't mean to flirt!" she sobbed frantically. "Oh, the deceiver is deceived! I never meant . . ."

"Molly, it hasn't got anything to do with you flirting!" The formal tone broke from his voice as he abandoned his rehearsed lines. "Good Lord, I know you flirt with everything in britches! That's just how you are!"

"I've played fast and loose with you, and now you turn from me. . . ." Shudders wracked her whole body. She collapsed back on the sofa, hands pressing to her face, praying, desperate her tears would change his mind, as they so often changed her father's. "I never, never meant to—"

"No!" She heard him cross the room to her, felt his arms, so astonishingly strong, gather her to him. Felt the warmth of his body through the wet cold of the coat he still wore. "Molly, it's just it would never work out between us! I'm . . . I'm saddled with debts. . . ." He stumbled, groping for words. "Poverty is the only thing I'd have to offer any woman. . . ."

And I can't keep my temper, thought Mary, pressing against him, her hands locked around his lapels, *and I let myself get fat. . . . No wonder he wants to run away!* Terror of losing him—of losing the one man she could talk to easily, the one man who understood her—ripped at her like the shock of a wound, and she sobbed, "I love you! And you said that you loved me, too!" *Don't leave me. . . .*

"Molly . . . !"

He lifted her onto his lap, cradled her to him like a child. The physical power that had shocked her, drawn her on the porch in Columbia, now comforted her and she clung to him, her face against his chest, sobbing that it was all her fault and wanting to hold him and never let him go. *There has to be something I can say, some way I can undo the damage....* "You promised me," she sobbed again and again, as she had sobbed to her father, to coax dresses out of him. "You said you loved me! I trusted you, I believed you—was your love a lie, then?"

"No!" He wiped her eyelids, and kissed her cheek, and turning in his arms she pulled his mouth to hers, frantic for reassurance of love. He tried to pull away and she wept harder, refusing to let him go. The next moment he was holding her close, kissing her, not with the passionate hunger of before, but with great gentleness, as if he understood how deep ran her need to be loved.

Footsteps in the hall.

Mary stumbled to her feet, Lincoln rising above her. "I must go," he said tonelessly, and Mary nodded, clutching one final time at his hand. He strode from the house just as Elizabeth came into the front hall. Mary fled past her, up the darkness of the stairs. *Let her make of that what she pleases. If she thinks I'm weeping because he said good-by, so much the better.*

She knew that above all else, she didn't want to see Elizabeth's satisfied face.

Matilda was sitting in bed, reading by the light of a branch of candles, her fair hair shining in the amber light. She looked up and saw Mary's face. "Dearest..."

Mary shook her head violently, and went to stand by the window, though the cold seeped through the panes and made that whole side of the room as icy as outdoors. She pressed her forehead to the glass, hoping that the pounding pain starting behind her eyes would subside. Hoping that she'd catch a glimpse of that tall form striding away into the night. But there was only darkness outside.

"It has been a day, hasn't it?" came Matilda's voice softly behind her. "I'm so sorry, dearest. And I'm afraid I hurt Mr. Speed terribly this morning...."

"Mr. Speed?" Mary turned back from the window, re-membering how Speed had seemed to see no one but Matilda, all through the ball last night.

Speed, she recalled then, had been one of the few members of the Coterie who had not passed through the parlor that day.

"He came by just after breakfast, while you were still upstairs," said Matilda softly, shutting her book. "He asked me to marry him, so tenderly—it quite broke my heart to tell him that I could not."

Mary whispered, "Poor Speed." And turned to look out once more into the darkness.

So Lincoln had heard that Matilda had turned down Speed—and that he was now free to court her without fear of hurting his friend.

And had rushed immediately to end whatever existed between Mary and himself.

Mary closed her eyes and knew she hated all men.

"Not a very good start for the year 1841, is it?" Matilda's voice was sad.

"No," said Mary, softly. "Not a very good start."

CHAPTER TWENTY

WITHIN A WEEK, JOSHUA SPEED SOLD OUT HIS SHARE IN Bell's dry-goods store and made arrangements to return to his family in Kentucky. If Tilda shed any tears at the prospect of his departure, she didn't do so in Mary's presence.

When Lincoln neither called on Mary nor sent her a note by the second week of January, she made an excuse and had Jerry drive her down to the offices of the *Sangamo Journal*.

Any lady who was a proper lady would, of course, have sent in her card to Simeon Francis and waited in the carriage. But by the standards of Lexington society, no true lady would have gone seeking word of Lincoln in the first place—certainly no self-respecting belle would have *dreamed* of letting herself be seen wearing the willow for any man—and Mary had always been a believer in the sheep-and-lamb principle.

She could just imagine what Betsey, or Betsey's re-doubtable mother, would have to say about the single big room of the print-shop, with its bare wooden floor reeking of ink and spit tobacco. Though the *Sangamo Journal* was the leading Whig newspaper of the state, Simeon Francis still couldn't afford to hire a clerk or turn down job-printing work to make ends meet. When Mary entered, the stocky editor was setting type for calling cards for the wealthy Mrs. Iles, working as close to the iron heating-stove as he could in the bitter cold.

"Miss Todd!"

"I realize it's not terribly ladylike of me to come here, sir," said Mary, with a wan twinkle. "But it wouldn't have been ladylike of me to make you come out to the street and freeze to death, and..." She hesitated, holding out her hands to the stove, wondering what Springfield gossip had spread so far about herself and Lincoln.

She finished, "... and there were reasons that I couldn't write you, to come to the house."

"I take it—" Simeon wrapped an inky rag around his fist to pick up the tin coffee-pot and pour her a cup "—this concerns Lincoln?" Mary flushed, and looked down into the black depths of the liquid he handed her, unable for a moment to reply. "Since I understand your sister and Ninian aren't exactly in favor of your engagement?"

"Did Mr. Lincoln tell you this?"

She glanced up as she spoke, saw the compassion in his blue eyes, and wondered what Lincoln had told him. Wondered for the thousandth time what Ninian had said to Lincoln, back on that snowy night in November.

She sipped the coffee. It was utterly poisonous.

"I've heard nothing from him, sir," she said, in what she hoped was a matter-of-fact voice. "I was concerned he'd been taken sick. I haven't wanted to ... to ask Ninian."

"No." Simeon sighed and propped his small square spectacles up onto the bridge of his nose. "No, I understand."

"*Is* he ill?"

Dear God, she thought, suddenly aghast, *don't let Mr. Francis say he's been fancy-free and happy as a lark and going about his business....*

"Not in body, no, I don't think so," replied the editor slowly. He drew up a wooden chair for her, of the several that stood around the stove, silent reminders of the male political camaraderie from which Mary was forever excluded. "As far as I know he's been hauling himself down to the Methodist Church to vote in the Assembly most days. I'm glad he has, to tell you the truth, for it gets him out of his room. He and Speed are both rooming at Bill Butler's these days, while Speed gets his affairs together. When Lincoln's not actually in the Assembly he's up there alone. Pacing, sometimes, Speed tells me. Sometimes just sitting staring out at the sleet."

Mary was silent, shocked. Lincoln had told her he was subject to fits of sadness—hypochondria, he called them deprecatingly. But he had jested about them, as a man might jest about breaking out in a rash when he ate strawberries.

To her mind, unbidden, rose the desperation in his voice as he'd cried, "Molly..." The passion of his kisses and the shocked horror in his eyes as he'd seen her for the first time in the full spate of her fury against Elizabeth. *I've driven him away,* she thought, and tried to push the thought from her mind. *He loves me, but...*

Or have I killed his love for me?

Yet how could he have kissed me with such frenzy, if he didn't love me?

Had he kissed Matilda that way? Had he dreamed of doing so? Was he only waiting for his best friend to leave town so he could have his chance to try?

She felt her eyes fill with tears, not knowing whether they were of sorrow or blind, screaming rage at the man she loved. She fought them back: *I must not, must not, have a tantrum, or a fit of crying, for Mr. Francis to tell him about....*

Are they all talking about me like that?

The recollection of every spurt of rage, every sharp-tongued retort, speared through her mind like a rainstorm of daggers: remorse, panic, shame. Then murderous anger at everyone for talking of her when it wasn't their business, for laughing at her behind her back.

Very carefully, she said, "May I... would you take him a note, sir?" She fought the impulse to run out to the carriage, to tell Jerry to take her to Butler's boardinghouse. To rush into that dark and lonely—and probably icily cold—room and tell the tall, silent man there how much she loved him, how much she needed him....

To beg his forgiveness, to make him say that he loved her, too.

To hear him say that he wasn't really in love with Matilda, that he wasn't really in torment of mind because Matilda was really the one he wanted to wed.

But of course it was ridiculous. No young woman *ever* called on a bachelor in his room.

Ever.

No matter how much she needed to hear his voice.

Tears began to flow down her cheeks, hot against her chilled skin. If she'd ever doubted she loved him, she knew now that she did.

Simeon said gently, "Of course, Miss Todd." He moved toward the end of the table closest to the stove. Mary guessed that the ink at the far end would be frozen.

She brought her hand from her muff, held it up to stay him: "Thank you, Mr. Francis. I'll... I'll send one over later, if you'd be so kind."

Back in her room Mary prayed, *Dear God, don't let him be really in love with Matilda.* But she felt as always that she was speaking the words into an empty room. She had always been able to move her father by her desperate tears of contrition, and to move Lincoln.

She'd never managed to move God.

Sitting at the little vanity—profoundly thankful, cold as it was, Matilda was out paying calls with Elizabeth—Mary tried to compose a note to Lincoln. But again and again her mind turned to the thought of that tall skinny storyteller sitting alone in his room—the new room that he now occupied alone—with a blanket around his shoulders, staring out at the driving sleet.

An exile from the world he sought to leave behind, and an unaccepted sojourner in the world of ideas, power, and the responsibility for not only his own actions but the well-being of others.

And she could find nothing to say to him except, *I love you. Don't leave me.*

The following day she still hadn't found the words to write. The weather was foul, snowing and sleeting, and she sat in the parlor with Elizabeth and Matilda, drinking tea and making a brown challis dress for the St. Valentine's Day ball that would be held at the American House...annoyed because she still couldn't fit into last winter's ball-dresses even though the seams had been let out as far as they'd go. "It absolutely isn't fair," she declared archly, stitching lace to the low swoop of the corsage. "You eat *one* piece of cake and you get *enormously* fat, and then it takes *years* of nibbling on bread and water before all is well again . . . that can't be right, can it? Why don't we ever have a lecturer at the Mechanics Institute on why *that* happens?"

And both Elizabeth and Matilda—who appeared to be able to consume tarts and gingerbread all day without gaining an ounce—went into peals of laughter.

Lina appeared in the door. "Miss Molly? Dr. Henry's here to speak to you."

Shabby-looking as always, the angular physician bowed as he came into the room. Elizabeth rose graciously and said, "You must be frozen, Dr. Henry," in a voice that Mary had heard her use on other occasions when she was being gracious to people she considered beneath the notice of Todds. "Lina, please fetch another cup for Dr. Henry."

"Please don't trouble. . . ."

"It's not a bit of trouble. . . ."

He's here from Mr. Lincoln. Mary knew it, for Dr. Henry was, like Simeon, one of the closest friends Lincoln had in Springfield. Her heart seemed to shrink in her breast to the size of an apple-seed.

She wondered whether Speed would have come, if he hadn't feared meeting Matilda.

She set aside the yards of soft snuff-colored fabric and sat with folded hands, saying all the proper things in the long rigamarole ritual of tea and welcome and "Oh, Matilda and I can go sit in the front parlor . . ." which was freezing cold, no fire being kindled there on days when Elizabeth was not receiving company. . . .

And wanting to scream.

After byzantine maneuverings, Elizabeth and Matilda left the parlor for the kitchen. Dr. Henry sat quiet for a time in the upholstered velvet chair Elizabeth had vacated, and

Mary, hands still folded, waited, feeling as if the room echoed
with the hammering of her heart.

She knew she should make some further inane inquiry
about Dr. Henry's health, or how was dear Mrs. Henry...?
Or offer him sugar or a slice of gingerbread. No young
lady—as Betsey, and Elizabeth, and Mammy Sally had always
impressed upon her—ever came at things brashly with a
man, letting him know what you thought or wanted.

But she felt too lost to go on.

"How is Mr. Lincoln?"

"Not well," said Dr. Henry.

I will not cry.

"He is...in terrible torment of mind. And the body can
endure only so much, when the mind is torn, as his is, between scruples, and honor, and desire."

What a tidy formula, thought Mary bitterly. She shut her
lips on the question, *What is his desire, and exactly where does
he think his honor lies?*

"You should remember, too," Henry went on, turning
Elizabeth's silver sugar-tongs over and over in his thin fingers, "that for nine months now he has worn himself out
physically, campaigning. And the Legislature rescinding all
those motions and plans he fought so hard for, I think only
added to this crisis in him. You know how deep his passions
are, behind that bumpkin façade."

Mary nodded silently, remembering the power of his arms
around her, the naked hunger of his kiss.

"He is a man whose heart is stronger than his body." Dr.
Henry set the tongs down, finally met her eyes. "And it is
wearing him away. Speed looks after him as well as he can,
and his new landlady Mrs. Butler, but we are all concerned."

Mary drew a deep breath. "Does he want me to release
him from our engagement?" She wondered whose voice it
was that she heard saying those words. It sounded astonishingly calm.

Henry leaned forward, and took her hands.

That means yes, thought Mary, despairing, even before he replied.

"Miss Todd, Mr. Lincoln holds you in highest esteem. Too high to put you in the position you would be in, he says, were you to go through with this match. His debts weigh heavily on his mind, and the . . . the disapproval of your family. . . ."

"He says," repeated Mary, and looked helplessly into those kind and worried blue eyes. "What do you say, Dr. Henry?"

Did he tell you about Matilda Edwards?

Would you say so, if he had?

She remembered Lincoln telling her he'd written a letter, which someone—probably Speed—had put on the fire. Had he written because he knew that he couldn't face a woman's tears? Because he knew he was no good speaking without notes, and would end up giving in if she cried?

Or because, as she'd learned in their correspondence over the summer, he could write what was truly in his heart?

She remembered Speed telling her that Lincoln had broken up with his last fiancée—the portly Miss Owens over in New Salem—by letter. Had he seen her face-to-face—had she wept as Mary had wept on New Year's Day—would he be married now?

I'm twenty-two! she wanted to scream. *How much longer can I go on waiting?*

"I'm a doctor of people's bodies, Miss Todd," said Henry gently. "Not their minds, and not their hearts."

"His heart?" she asked, trying to keep the anger out of her voice. "Or mine?"

She wrote the letter sitting in the parlor before the fire, while Dr. Henry sipped his tea and Elizabeth and Matilda undoubtedly dissected Lincoln's character and prospects in the kitchen and prayed that Mary would come to her senses. Mary forced herself to pretend she was writing a practice composition at Madame Mentelle's: *My dear Mr. Lincoln, it is with deep sorrow (deepest sorrow?) that I take pen in hand. . . .*

Her usual method of writing was to write as she spoke,

tumbling, hurried, thoughts sparking other thoughts in a welter of ellipses, parentheses, and underlines. Now she forced herself to consider every word, to remain formal and contained. *I release you, I wish you well, but remember that my feelings toward you have in no way changed. I will always be . . . Your Mary.*

Her hands shook as she put down the pen and, contrary to Elizabeth's repeated admonitions of thrift, she thrust the three botched attempts into the fire. Let Elizabeth guess what she might have said rather than find it on the back of a sheet on which she wrote her grocery-lists.

She was still staring into the fire as Dr. Henry took his departure. "Is everything all right?" she heard Elizabeth inquire in the hall, and despair flared in her at the note of smug satisfaction she detected in her sister's voice.

Cold flowed through the room with the opening and closing of the outer door.

SPEED LEFT SPRINGFIELD QUIETLY BEFORE THE END OF January. Dances were held in the big common-room of the American House in honor of St. Valentine's Day and Washington's Birthday: Lincoln attended neither. There was a rumor—which Mary heard through Jamie Conkling, Mercy's fiancé—that the new President, Mr. Harrison, was considering Lincoln for chargé d'affaires of Bogotá, in return for the prodigious efforts Lincoln had put forth during the campaign. Mary's heart was sick at the thought of Lincoln leaving Springfield—leaving the country!—but it came to nothing. President Harrison died in April, and his Vice-President, former Virginia governor John Tyler, was a compromise nomination whom no one had taken seriously. Tyler took over as President, owing no favors to anyone.

Ninian and others, who had expected great rewards from a successful Whig candidate, were considerably miffed.

A more serious rumor—and one that Mary tried to push from her mind—was that Lincoln, in addition to wearing the willow for Matilda Edwards, was shyly courting his landlady's young sister: "A much better match, if you ask me," sniffed Elizabeth. "Though what a child of sixteen would want with marrying a man of thirty-two, I'll never know. Not that there's anything wrong with a young girl marrying a man of maturer years," she added hastily—she and Mary were in the ladies' cloakroom at the American House, Mary having been press-ganged into pinning up a torn petticoat-flounce at the Washington's birthday dance. "Was that Mr. Webb I saw you dancing with earlier, dear?"

"It was." Mary concentrated on pinning the stiff taffeta—not easy, between the uncertain dimness of the single oil-lamp, the arctic temperature of the cloakroom, and the shrieks of laughter from Mrs. Browning's daughters nearby as they compared notes about a friend's engagement. Her breath was a cloudy puff of gold. "Trying to be gallant and to pretend that he hasn't two darling little objections to any sane woman taking her place as the second Mrs. Webb."

"Now, dearest," coaxed her sister, "you know how you like children. You always said how you loved your little pupils at Ward's. And you're just a marvel, Betsey writes me, with the little ones at home. As for Mr. Lincoln, marrying the Rickard girl will do him no good politically. She's quite common, I understand, as one could expect. But then, for all Mr. Lincoln's undoubted virtues, his background and man-ner are such that no one can or would take him seriously for any post higher than the State Legislature." Disinterested as she was in politics, Elizabeth was still Ninian's wife.

Mary bent her face down over her sister's petticoat-frill, unable to trust herself to meet Elizabeth's eyes.

"Don't tell me he *fell* for that?" gasped one of the Browning girls, and the other said, "Darling, men have no idea how long it takes for a woman to know she's with child! They don't know what's happening when we get our monthlies, or anything about women, really. You can tell them almost any tale and they'll believe it."

I drove him away, thought Mary dully. *Not just to Matilda, who of course isn't interested in him, but to this...this sly little chit of a girl.* It was all she could do not to scream, to leave the American House that night and go at once to the Butler house, where Lincoln was boarding.

To throw herself, sobbing, into his arms again? To promise as she promised Elizabeth and Mercy and Julia and everyone else who knew her, at one time or another, that she didn't mean the things she said when she was in a temper? *I don't want to be this way...!*

Or to pull Sarah Rickard's hair out in black handfuls and fling it into Lincoln's face?

For an interminable year, she waited for the news that Lincoln was going to marry Sarah Rickard.

And wondered what on earth she was going to do if he did.

Through the bitter days of winter she did daily battle with her pride not to write to him, to engineer a meeting. Instead she systematically kept every other beau in Springfield on her string and tried not to remember that she was now twenty-two. Only in Springfield was it possible for her to remain a courted belle—in Lexington she'd have been on the sidelines years ago, hearing the Arabella Richardson Bodleys of the world say "Poor dear," in hatefully sweet sympathy.

There was Mr. Webb, of course, faithful and paternal as ever.

And for a time she toyed with the idea of detaching the handsome Lyman Trumbull from his growing affection for Julia Jayne. Two years ago, in Lexington, she wouldn't have hesitated about it for an instant.

But the grip of Lincoln's hands on her shoulders—the slow deep twinkle in those gray eyes when she picked a hole in Douglas's tirade on states' rights, or made some sharp observation on a third party that amused him...How could she forget those and make herself settle for someone else?

When spring came and people started getting about the streets a little more, Mary would see Sarah Rickard coming and going from the Butler boarding establishment, a slender

small girl with black hair and tilting dark eyes. It had hurt
her, that Lincoln had asked for release from her the moment
he knew that his best friend no longer had any claim on
Matilda Edwards, but in her heart she'd known that Matilda
was no threat. If Ninian frowned on Lincoln courting a mere
Edwards sister-in-law like Mary, even had Matilda been willing, he would never have permitted a match between
Lincoln and a full-blood Edwards.

But this black-haired sprite in flowered green calico was a
girl of the world Lincoln had left, a girl of the farms and the
backwoods, who sang the old ballads he loved as she went
about her work.

So Mary waited. She never saw them in company, and listen as she would, there seemed to be no other gossip about
them, one way or the other—where Elizabeth had picked up
her information Mary didn't know. Lincoln dissolved his partnership with Cousin John Stuart, who since his election to
Congress had been drifting further and further from him politically. Instead Lincoln went into partnership with Mary's
elderly and irascible cousin Stephen Logan. When April
opened the roads, Lincoln began riding the circuit again:
Tazewell County, McLean County, Livingston County,
DeWitt County, Champaign County, Logan County, Menard
County. She saw him little in company, and wondered if, having been told that he was no fit mate for a Todd of Lexington
and unwelcome in the Edwards family circle, he had withdrawn completely from the gay social circles of the town.

But ladies did not ask such things of their brothers-in-law.

In June, Springfield was shaken by the murder trial of the
Trailor brothers, William, Henry, and Archibald. The three
men had been seen entering town with the amiable and simpleminded Archibald Fisher, who had then vanished. The
town hummed with anger and suspicion, posses going out to
spend most of a week searching the brush along Spring
Creek and tearing down Hickox's milldam so the stream
could be dragged. Returning to town, Lincoln patiently
asked questions of everyone in sight, combed the country-

side, and eventually located Archibald Fisher in the care of a doctor who had found him wandering about the countryside after a mild head injury, much to the secret annoyance of everyone who'd come to the trial expecting it to end in a spectacular triple hanging.

Mary, personally, had to clap her hands over her mouth to keep from laughing when Lincoln rose to his full gangly height in the courtroom and said, in that high, rather hesitant voice, "Your Honor, I would like to call to the stand Mr. Archibald Fisher...."

On the way out a spectator muttered, "It was too *damned* bad, to have so much trouble, and no hanging after all."

Ninian's only comment was "Jackanapes."

But she could see how the production of the supposed victim, alive and smiling mildly, in open court before a townful of would-be spectators to a hanging, would have been more than Lincoln could resist. Seeing him from the back row of the crowded courtroom, she thought he looked exhausted, like a man burning up inside with slow fever. If he saw her, he gave no sign of it.

The courts adjourned for the summer. Lincoln left for Kentucky, to spend some weeks with Speed at Speed's family plantation near Louisville. Thus he missed Mercy Levering's marriage to James Conkling, and the sight of a somewhat thinner Mary bedecked in a new frock of pink and copper sprig-muslin—her father had come through with a special gift yet again. She wondered if Lincoln would have stood up with Jamie, had Mary herself not been present.

Were people saying, behind her back, "Thrice a bridesmaid, never a bride"?

During that long summer, she thought often of that tall shy backwoodsman, encountering for the first time the slow-paced luxury of a Kentucky plantation. Wished she could be there, or at least read a letter of his impressions of the world she knew so well. She pictured him, sitting on the porch of the Big House with Joshua—though most of those "Big Houses" were not actually so big—listening to the singing of the field hands as they came home in the twilight. How would it look to him, that strange double world of white and black?

Christmas came, and spring again, and summer's heat and storms. Matilda Edwards departed gracefully for Alton, having broken every heart, male and female, in Sangamon County.

Mary was twenty-three.

We can't stay forever in our fathers' houses....

She turned down another offer from Mr. Webb, put Mr. Gillespie off with smiles and dimples and eyelids fluttered behind her fan.

Elizabeth started to look at her with sharp sidelong glances, which did nothing for Mary's temper.

She was waiting. She did not know what she was waiting for.

"I would like to see him happy," she said, one afternoon in late August, when Bessie Francis, Simeon's stout motherly wife, came calling and found Elizabeth out. It wasn't often that Mary saw Bessie alone, but she liked the big woman, who shared her love of politics and, being Simeon Francis's wife, knew everything about everyone in Sangamon County. She asked Bessie to stay, and Eppy brought lemonade from the kitchen to the sweet-scented shade of the porch, for the day was grillingly hot. Among the things the two women laughed about was the anonymous letter Lincoln had written to the *Journal,* hilariously funny as all Lincoln's political satires were and signed "Rebecca of the Lost Townships," poking fun at the political policies of the dapper Jimmy Shields.

"He writes these pieces that leave everyone laughing.... He was the one who wrote the Sampson's Ghost letters, wasn't he?"

"Couldn't you tell?"

"Once I got to know him, yes. And all those other silly aliases he uses, like John Blubberhead. And yet with that, and with all his jokes and jests, every time I look at him I see this...this terrible sadness. A darkness... *It goes so heavily with my disposition that this goodly frame, the earth, seems to me but a sterile promontory.* Is he..." Mary hesitated. "Is he happier now?"

Bessie didn't answer for a time, but in her eyes Mary saw an understanding, and another question entirely. Before her younger friends, Mary was careful to chatter of beaux and frolics, for there was nothing so dreadful as to be seen wearing the willow for a man who'd made a spectacle of himself following Matilda Edwards all around town...

But Bessie, in her forties, wasn't a frolic or a gossip.

After a little silence the older woman sighed. "No," she answered, "I don't think he's happier. I don't think Abraham has had much experience with happiness in his life. I suspect he's always been too intelligent not to see farther than is comfortable for a man." Bessie—and Mrs. Butler, Lincoln's landlady—were the only people in town who called Lincoln Abraham. "Are *you* happier now, Molly?"

Mary mutely shook her head.

Bessie said nothing, only plied her fan of stiffened newspaper. Around them, bees hummed in the honeysuckle.

"I know I should get over him and move on." Mary tried to force her voice not to tremble. "I know it's absurd to...to turn down what Elizabeth calls 'good offers,' as if they were pieces of land come up for sale. She asked me last night what my plans were, and I don't *know*! But the thought of marrying anyone else is...is simply impossible."

Bessie smiled, with gentle teasing, "That's not what Mr. Gillespie seems to think. Or Mr. Webb. Or Mr. Trumbull..."

"Well, a girl must have beaux." Mary plucked a sprig of the honeysuckle, turned it in her fingers, as Mercy had done that evening, five years ago. Then she asked, "I heard...that is, someone mentioned to me...that Mr. Lincoln was courting Sarah Rickard." She glanced quickly at her guest, then turned her eyes out to the shadows of the lawn again, to the sporadic passersby on Second Street. "Is that true?"

Bessie sighed. "That was over months ago." She looked as

if she might have said something else, then held her peace, and said instead, "And since that time he's been on the road almost constantly, traveling between the courts."

Mary stroked the polished leaf in her hand, and said, "Indeed." Silence lay between them for a time, broken by the metallic throb of the cicadas in the trees.

"Well." The older woman rose to go. "Simeon tells me you speak and read French like a native—is that true? For he's gotten a box of the oddest old French books, and hasn't the faintest idea of what they are or what to do with them. Would you care to come over to dinner Saturday and help us look through them?"

"I'd love it!" Mary stood too, and walked her the few feet to the steps. "The one thing about Springfield that's the hardest to bear, is that I can never find a novel I haven't read before! It makes me glad I read French because that gives me that much more chance of finding *something!*"

"Well," smiled Bessie, "I hope we'll have something Saturday that will cheer you."

Accordingly, on Saturday evening Jerry harnessed the carriage and drove Mary the few streets to the Francis house. Though Springfield was still very much a frontier town, with woods and prairies only a few blocks from the new (and in places still unfinished) State House, Simeon Francis had a large and pleasant house, built of whitewashed lumber and surrounded by wide gardens of vegetables and flowers. Bessie was renowned as a cook, though like most of the housewives in Springfield she was in a constant quest to find and keep a servant girl from among the daughters of the itinerant population of Irish and Portuguese laborers. Guests of the Francises were just as likely to be pressed into service making gravy as entertained in the parlor.

Though it was nearly eight by the Courthouse clock, the sun had not yet set. The house was filled with the scent of boiled vinegar—Bessie had obviously been doing her pickling that day, even as Mary had spent most of the afternoon in the sweltering kitchen helping Eppy and Elizabeth put up preserves. Simeon greeted Mary on the porch and led her through to the parlor, where Bessie, red-faced and a little rumpled-looking, sat on a low pouf with a small box of books before her.

"Mr. Speed used to stock books at Bell's," the older woman said. "But that imbecile Irwin doesn't see the use in anything that isn't an almanac or a book on how to physic horses.... This looks like a novel."

"It's *Notre Dame de Paris*!" exclaimed Mary in delight. "Victor Hugo—the story of the hunchback and the gypsy-girl! Oh, put it aside for me...whatever it costs, I'll pay you...or I'll write Papa to pay you," she added with a laugh. "This one isn't French but Spanish: Lope de Vega. And *Manon Lescaut*...Oh, put this aside for me but don't *dare* tell Elizabeth.... Oh, and *Les Liaisons Dangereuses*!"

So absorbed was she in looking through the volumes—and trying to think of a way of getting *Les Liaisons* back to the house with her that evening without incurring Elizabeth's censure—that she didn't even hear Simeon leave the room until he returned. Then she only saw Bessie look up and smile, and turning her head to see who had entered, Mary—with her hair tumbled forward from its ribbons in her enthusiasm and book-dust all over her hands—found herself face-to-face with Lincoln.

"Simeon," commanded Bessie briskly, "I need help with the corn pudding." And she caught her husband's sleeve and dragged him bodily from the room.

CHAPTER TWENTY-ONE

"I'VE MISSED YOU," SAID LINCOLN BLUNTLY, INTO THE PRO-found silence that followed.

You knew exactly where a letter would reach me, surged to Mary's lips—anger, pique, love, humiliation...the scared pain of eighteen months.

She took a deep breath and said, "I've missed you, too."

She started to rise from the hassock where she sat and Lincoln said, "No, don't get up, I'll come on down there. What have you got?" He folded his long legs, to sit on the floor beside her hassock.

"Books," said Mary, blessing Bessie—the scheming matchmaker!—from the bottom of her heart. And, when Lincoln picked up *Les Liaisons,* she added with a quick grin, "I'll have to smuggle that one into the house. It's supposed to be most improper for girls to read."

Lincoln grinned back. It was almost as if all the past year and a half had never been. "Well, there's chapters of the Book of Genesis—and Judges, too!—that wouldn't pass muster by half the ministers in this town."

"Oh, tell me which!" Mary bounced on the hassock and clapped her hands like a child.

"Now, I had enough hard names called me campaigning for Harrison, I'm not going to have 'corrupter of young maidens' added to the list." A door closed somewhere in the house; Simeon's voice called back to the kitchen.

"...for goodness' sake, Bessie, there's only the four of us, unless you've got the Russian Army in the basement and didn't tell me about it...."

Bessie was famous for the quantity, as well as the quality, of the food she served.

Lincoln's eyes warmed with affection at the overheard words. Then he looked back at Mary, and the amusement died away. Gently, he said, "Miss Todd..."

"You may make that Molly," said Mary softly. "If you like."

Lincoln was silent, no doubt turning over in his mind what it meant to call her by her nickname again. Then, very quietly, he said, "Molly. All these months I've owed you an apology that I wasn't man enough to make. I know I hurt you. I am sorrier for that than I have ever been for anything in my life."

Mary said, "It's all right."

"And I made a fool of myself."

You certainly did! In front of all Springfield, too. And of me... What are you saying, Mary Todd???

She took a breath again, thanking God that for once in her life she hadn't blurted her first, fatal, unconsidered thought.

Why was it that in novels, girls who loved and who passed through pain were always afterwards in perfect control of their hearts and thoughts and their nasty, flaying, ungovernable tongues?

"People do." She looked into his face, so close, for once, by her own. "Goodness knows I've gone through most of my life making a fool of myself. Saying things that I later wish I'd cut out my tongue before I said. Because I do wish that, I can't tell you how often."

Simeon came in then, with the announcement that dinner was on the table. If Mary had had a gun then, she would have shot him. Over dinner she asked Lincoln about Kentucky, and they were able to compare their thoughts concerning the divided world of the South. "I'd seen slaves being sold on the block in New Orleans," Lincoln told her. "Right out on the sidewalks of Baronne Street, like so many cattle. And comin' down the river on the flatboat, we'd see 'em in the sugar-fields, an' hear 'em sing, strange songs, African they must've been, like nuthin' human. But this was the first time I've lived with house-slaves fetchin' whatever I needed, an' cleanin' an' cookin'; first chance I'd had to actually talk to Mrs. Speed's servants. A couple evenin's I walked out to the quarters. Though I don't imagine they'd tell a white man the truth about what they really felt, I did hear some remarkable storytellin'."

"Did they tell you about the Evil Mr. Jaybird, who takes tales of bad children to whisper into Satan's ear in Hell?" asked Mary with a twinkle. "My Mammy used to scare me to death with that one."

His eyes widened in alarm. "Lord, I guess it would! No, I didn't hear that one...though I did get to pretend I was a Democrat for an hour and a half, so Speed could have the time alone with the young lady he was courtin', while I kept her pa busy rakin' me over about politics."

"That," laughed Simeon, "is nobility beyond the common run, Lincoln."

And Mary said, as lightly as she could, "It's good to know other people besides myself have families like dragons, that have to be fought."

At the end of the evening Lincoln helped Mary on with her light lace shawl, when the jingle of harness announced the arrival of the Edwards carriage. Mary cast a quick glance through the front window, praying that neither Ninian nor Elizabeth had decided to go for a little ride in the cool night air. But as far as she could see—the quarter-moon had risen late and it was very dark beyond the tiny yellow spots of the carriage lamps—only Jerry was on the box, so there would be no need to fear that that unmistakable tall silhouette would be seen in the lamplight of the door.

"Is there..." Lincoln hesitated, his big hands ever so slightly brushing her arms as he settled the lace wrap in place. "Is there any chance that we might meet again?"

Mary turned, her heart pounding suddenly, and looked up into his face. "I'm sure Bessie and Simeon could arrange it. Couldn't you?" Her glance went past him to their hosts. Bessie was smiling. Lincoln looked grave, and a little un-happy—Ninian had been a friend too long for him to feel comfortable about carrying on clandestine meetings with a member of his household. Mary wondered again what her brother-in-law had said to Lincoln, that night the winter before last, and told herself firmly that she'd only be arrested if she went straight home and brained him with the fire-shovel.

Not for separating them, she realized. But for hurting a sensitive man already so cruelly uncertain of himself.

A week later, Bessie Francis sent a note to Mary asking for her help in making over a dress—a task both of them knew Elizabeth loathed—on a night when they knew Elizabeth would be out with the ladies of the Episcopal Church sewing circle. Again Bessie dragged Simeon away to "help with supper" for nearly an hour and a half, and Mary and Lincoln sat in the parlor, talking and more at their ease than Mary could remember at any time in their earlier courtship. Had his sojourn in the world from which she'd come, she wondered, changed his perspective on her? She recalled his diffidence in company—and their earlier meetings had nearly always been in company. Recalled, too, how she had flirted with other men.

"It's just what one *does,* Mr. Lincoln," she explained earnestly, when the subject came up, and to her relief he laughed, as if she were some titled French lady explaining royal court procedure to an American. "One *must* have beaux."

"So I hear tell," he replied, scratching his deplorable hair. "And I've always thought the ladies should have just as much right to wag their tails as us men."

They helped clear up after supper, and sat in the warm darkness of the porch watching the fireflies. When Simeon and Bessie went inside Lincoln kissed her, gently at first and then with hungry urgency. Mary returned home that night shaken to her bones and profoundly glad that the single lamp in Ninian's front hall was too dim to give Elizabeth much of a look at her face.

Love grew in her like weeds in a wet, hot June. Love, and passion, for his roving touch waked in her a reciprocal sensuousness. She no longer wondered how the blameless heroines of so many novels "fell." Had not Lincoln been scrupulous of her honor, even in the midst of their most fevered embraces, Mary guessed how easy it would have been for them to slip from caresses that teetered on the edge of danger into coupling like animals in the hot darkness of the parlor.

She found herself thinking, for days on end, of the strength of his arms and the smell of his flesh, with an intensity that made her blush. She was aware, as the first sharp frost of September silvered the grass, that Elizabeth was watching her more closely. But it was hard now to hide her thoughts. Did Lincoln think of her, too? Daydream about her? When he was in the State House, or the brick building where the courts met, did he count the hours and the days until Bessie thought up some other excuse to invite them both to dinner?

Even when they were alone together, he was deeply self-contained. When he spoke with passion, that passion was often directed toward politics, toward justice and the purposes for which men united to govern themselves or toward the law.

His own passions he seemed to fear, thrusting her away from him sometimes with trembling abruptness, as he had the first time he'd kissed her. It was as if, for him, any middle ground between the clearheaded comradeship of two Whig politicians—one of whom happened to be a woman—and the brute lust that she tasted in his kisses was unexplored territory, in which he did not know his way. When he held her in his arms he whispered, "My God, Molly, I love you," but at other times he held himself back. Not aloof, but simply deflecting the issue, as he'd deftly dodge answers about road-tax legislation by coming up with some absurd story or jest that would have everyone laughing so hard they'd forget that he hadn't made a direct reply.

Was that because he was a lawyer? she wondered. Or because somewhere, sometime, someone had taught him to keep every feeling to himself?

It was at Simeon's that he read out loud to her the second

of the "Rebecca" letters, describing, in an aside about Jimmy
Shields's honesty in office, "I seed him... floating from one
lady to another and on his very features could be read his
thoughts: 'Dear girls, *it is distressing,* but I cannot marry you
all. Too well I know how much you suffer; but do, *do* remember, it is not my fault that I am *so* handsome and *so* interesting.'" Mary, who had had enough of Shields's self-satisfied
courtship, nearly choked with laughter, and the following
week, when Lincoln disappeared into the case he was working on—something he was maddeningly wont to do—she
and Julia spent an idle afternoon in Mary's room, gigglingly
composing another letter from "Rebecca," enlarging upon
Shields's supposed courtship of the author of the letters.

*"I don't think, upon the whole, I'd be sich a bad match nei-
ther—I'm not over sixty, and am just four feet three inches in my
bare feet, and not much more around the girth. . . ."*

"Mary, you are *bad*!" Julia rapped her with the feather end
of her quill, and Mary said, "Oh, wait, wait, I've got an idea,
let's write a poem about their marriage!"

More suffocated laughter—goodness knew what
Elizabeth thought the two young women were up to behind
the closed bedroom door. But, Mary reflected, Elizabeth was
used to Julia coming up to visit, and they did giggle like
schoolgirls. . . .

Pardonably proud of their masterpiece, Mary presented
the completed composition to Simeon, and it duly and
anonymously appeared in the *Sangamo Journal* on Friday.

Reading it in Simeon's parlor at their next meeting, just
before his departure for the Tazewell County Circuit Court,
Lincoln only rolled his eyes and grinned. "You girls'll get me
in trouble yet."

"I always said Lincoln's a fool and a jackanapes," snorted
Ninian, over supper a week later. "It's one thing to call a man
a liar and a thief in print—you saw what Lincoln and
Douglas called each other during the election!—but it's another to make him a laughingstock, and he should know it.

Well, he went too far with that poem. Jimmy Shields has called him out."

"Called him *out*?" Mary set down her fork, aghast. Even Eppy, carrying the platter of corn pudding in from the kitchen, paused in startled alarm.

Elizabeth said, "Good heavens," and Mary knew that her sister saw what she herself saw in her mind: Mary Jane Warfield crumpled weeping on the sofa of her father's parlor, with the sunlight falling through the bow window onto her unworn wedding-gown and veil. Panic seized her, and with it terrible dread.... "Does Mr. Lincoln even know how to use a dueling pistol?"

"More like squirrel-guns at twenty paces, I'd say. Or bowie knives."

"This is no joke," reproved Elizabeth, with a glance at Mary's ashen face. Ninian sighed.

"This is just what we don't need, with the Whigs in the minority all over the country and elections coming up," he said sourly. "They'll be lucky if they aren't jailed, the both of them. This isn't Kentucky or Louisiana! I understand Shields and General Whiteside went down to Tremont where Lincoln's trying a case and issued a challenge."

"They aren't really going to *fight*?" Mary felt tears burn her eyes. In her mind she saw from a great distance the dream she'd had the night before Cash's duel, of the two men firing into the earth, and the earth bubbling forth blood.

"Lincoln's named a second," said Ninian. "I hope and pray they'll have the sense to go kill each other across the river in Missouri, but even so..."

Mary got up and ran from the table, shaking with terror. Later in the afternoon, in spite of the towering storm clouds gathering, she had Jerry drive her to Bessie's. "I'm afraid it's true," said Bessie. "You *were* a little rough on Mr. Shields, Molly—but he was already hopping mad over Lincoln's earlier letter. Don't take it to yourself."

"What happened?"

The older woman shook her head, unwilling to speak.

She'd taken off her apron and the day-cap that kept kitchen-soot and grease out of her hair, but the heavy folds of her skirt still bore the stains of boiled huckleberries. Looking through the open back door into the kitchen, Mary could see that she still hadn't found a girl to hire.

Then Bessie sighed. "Jimmy came flouncing over to the office last week, demanding to know who'd written the Rebecca letters. Simeon asked for twenty-four hours and went to Lincoln, and told him that Shields was ready to have blood for them. Lincoln said he'd written the four of them. I gather Jimmy went away and thought about it for a few days. Then he followed Lincoln down to Tremont with a second and demanded satisfaction."

"Dear God." Mary pressed her gloved hands to her face. For an instant she was thirteen again, standing at the foot of the stairway at Elizabeth's second-day party, caught in wrongdoing and aghast at what she had done. "Dear God, he will never speak to me again!"

I've lost him, she thought. *After we had just found one another. How could I have been so stupid . . . ?*

And then, *Dear God, what if he's killed?* Shields, for all his vanity, was an accomplished shot. Lincoln had told Mary of a youth spent in country wrestling-matches, but the only time he'd fought another man with weapons in his hands had been when his flatboat had been attacked by river-pirates on the way to New Orleans. He'd been twenty-two, and still carried the scar of that skirmish on his forehead.

Shakily, she asked, "When do they meet?" How could she get through the time, not knowing, hating herself, fearing that he would hate her for getting him into this mess . . . ?

"Wednesday," said Bessie. "Day after tomorrow. Lincoln came back from Tremont last night and left again for Jacksonville early this morning, with Dr. Merriman for his second, and Shields's second going along. He didn't want you to know."

"Does he . . . does he hate me?"

The older woman regarded her sharply for a moment, as

if debating whether to tell a comforting lie. Then she poked her graying hair back into its knot at her nape, and said, "Molly, I could as easily read what a wooden post feels about things, as I can that man. You'll have to ask him yourself, when he comes back."

If he comes back.

CHAPTER TWENTY-TWO

THERE WAS A THUNDERSTORM THAT NIGHT, CRASHING OVER the huddled town like the wrath of a God who knew exactly the mess Mary Todd had gotten her beloved into. After a night of covering, screaming, and sobbing in her bed, Mary had a headache all of the following day, and the next— Wednesday—as well. She crept sick and shaken about the house, avoiding Elizabeth, avoiding Julia—whose wild excitement at the drama of the whole affair caused Mary to lash out at her in screaming fury—and wishing there was some way she could avoid herself. She dreamed she stood on the dueling ground on the river's bank, with Jimmy Shields beside her, and pools of blood soaking the ground. Dreamed she saw Lincoln walking away from her toward a small boat on the river where a solitary gray boatman waited, to carry him to the far, dark shore. Lincoln's face, and stiff wild Indian-black hair, were covered with blood. He neither looked back at her nor spoke, and she knew he was dead.

Friday a note reached her from Dr. Henry: *The duel was called off; Mr. Lincoln has gone on to the Woodford and McLean Circuit Courts.*

She burned the note in her bedroom fireplace, lest Elizabeth guess she had more than a passing concern about whether Shields shot Lincoln or not. It wasn't until over a week later that she was able to stroll, unnoticed, over to Bessie's house.

Lincoln was there, warming his big hands by the parlor fire. The leaves that strewed the mud of the streets were brilliant reds and brilliant gold, and one of them, adhering to the heel of Lincoln's boot, made a bright splash on that spare dark figure, like a tiny wound. Mary stood in the parlor doorway feeling as if her heart had stopped.

Then he looked up at her, and held out his hand. "Molly, you are just more blame trouble...."

She caught his hand in both of hers, sank down onto the sofa beside him, certain her knees would no longer hold her up. He looked tired, his hair a wild tangle as usual, but he put his other hand on her shoulder and pulled her to him, kissed her hard.

"Oh, Mr. Lincoln, I am so *sorry!*" she sobbed, and began to cry. "I never, *ever* thought..."

He sighed. "Now, what am I going to do with you?" And dug in his pocket for a clean handkerchief—he was getting better about carrying spares. "Now, don't cry, Puss. It all came to nothing, like the raccoon that tried to wash a lump of sugar...."

"What *happened*?"

"Well, as the challenged party, I had choice of weapons," said Lincoln. "Now, back when I was in New Orleans, I heard tell how this feisty little Creole once challenged an American blacksmith to a duel. The American bein' about my size, he stipulated that the duel was to be fought with sledge-hammers in six feet of water, which would have put the surface about six inches over the Creole's head. I figured this sounded like a good idea, so since Jimmy Shields stands about two inches taller than Steve Douglas, I said we would fight with cavalry broadswords, each of us to remain on the far side of two lines drawn six feet apart...."

Mary's sobs dissolved abruptly into a hiccup of laughter. "Six feet apart? He wouldn't have been able to touch you!"

"And I'd barely have been able to touch him," added Lincoln. "It was the best I could do. I've had a little practice with the broadsword, with that fellow that teaches it over in the Delaney Building across from the State House, but I'd just as soon not have it on my record that I'd carved up a state auditor, even if he was a Democrat. That kind of thing gets around."

He shook his head, and gazed down into the fire. "And if that wasn't bad enough, it's like when two boys get into a fight behind the schoolhouse—boys run for miles to get their licks in. Now Shields has challenged Bill Butler to a duel. . . ."

"Your landlord? For what?"

"For laughing when he heard the conditions read off, I think, though Shields has it that it's something else—and *his* second is talking about challenging *my* second. . . . And of course all of this is all over the newspapers. I just wish everyone would forget the whole thing."

Mary looked down at his hand, still clasped in both of hers. Softly, she said, "Thank you. Thank you for saying you'd written all the letters. That was . . . very gallant of you. It was foolish of me, stupid beyond all measure. . . ." She looked up, and met his eyes, her own brimming with the tears of contrition that had always appeased her father.

He shook his head. "Molly, what *am* I going to do with you?"

There was a long silence. Then, hesitantly, she said, "I . . . I've been wondering that myself."

Bessie and Simeon, as usual, had disappeared to the back of the house. In the grate a log broke, sending down a whisper of glowing coals. Beyond the windows, the wind moaned softly in the trees.

Lincoln sighed, and put his hands gently on either side of her face. "Molly, I love you." It was the first time he had spoken the words in cold blood. "God help us both. But I would be the greatest scoundrel unhanged if I asked any woman to marry a bankrupt and a debtor, particularly a girl of your breeding, who's had ease and comfort all her life."

"You know money means nothing where love is true." Mary's hands came up to grasp his wrists. "I would love you if you were a beggar on the streets."

He smiled. "I don't doubt you would, Molly. But you'd also get darn tired of livin' on the few pennies I'd bring in. I love you," he repeated, as Mary opened her mouth to protest. "And one day, God help me, I shall be proud to look your brother-in-law in the eye and ask for your hand."

It was the most he had said on the subject, and so much did Mary burn with joy at the words that she said nothing more. But even as she threw her arms around him, even as they clasped one another tight by the sinking embers of the fire, she thought, *When?*

And what happens if you meet another slender young thing of sixteen before that time?

The mere thought of going through another eighteen months—or two years—or how much more?—like those she had just passed through made her breath come short. *And what if he died?* she asked herself, as Simeon drove her home through the cold darkness of the streets that night. *What if the glowing green rivers of cholera rose, even from this dry Western prairie? What if he fell sick, as my mother fell sick...? What if some other lunatic Democrat calls him out and refuses to be put off with broadswords at six feet?*

What if, what if, what if?

October wind rolled handfuls of leaves through the small glow of the buggy lamps, like skittering goblins. Ahead of her she saw the glow of windows, the house where she had a single room, on sufferance.

We cannot remain forever in our fathers' houses....

How old would she then be?

She was nearly twenty-four already. The belle of Lexington, the girl who'd collected beaux like they were buttons...would she really end as an old maid? With Bella Richardson Bodley saying sweetly, "Well, she let herself get so fat...and she never *could* learn to keep her temper...." and her friends pushing their brothers and husbands to dance with her out of pity?

Her body flooded with sickened rage and terror at the picture of that future.

She loved Lincoln as she'd never loved anyone else, as she couldn't imagine loving another man. The dread of losing him, of the twin terrors of desolation and humiliation, kept her staring at the ceiling in darkness until she heard the soft clatter of Eppy in the kitchen at dawn.

Lincoln left on Thursday, for the DeWitt County Circuit. He was gone for a month. Winter was coming, and the prairies around Springfield wore their drabbest robes, the grass bleached a ghostly gray by the summer sun, the riot of flowers killed by the autumn frosts. Lincoln came home on a rainy Sunday night; rain was still falling on Monday afternoon, when Mary got a note from Bessie inviting her to dinner. She told Jerry as she got into the carriage, "Simeon will bring me home." She knew that in fact Simeon would be down at the newspaper until past midnight—Bessie had told her this earlier in the week—and that Bessie never emerged from her kitchen once she'd finished clearing up the dishes and usually simply retired to bed.

She trembled with the thought of what she intended—hoped—to do, but the recollection of the previous twenty-two months of waiting, of wishing, stabbed her like a goad. *It isn't as if he didn't love me, or I him. . . .*

Helena's words from *All's Well That Ends Well* circled in her mind:

> *Why then, tonight*
> *Let us assay our plot; which, if it speed,*
> *Is wicked meaning in a lawful deed. . . .*

As Ninian's carriage jolted along Sixth Street through the gray world of falling rain, she closed her eyes. She wondered if she should pray, but knew not to whom or for what. She only knew she could not go on as she was.

Her heart felt very clear, knowing exactly what she had to do.

Lincoln was exhausted, and quiet during dinner. "It's nothing," he said, when Mary asked what troubled him. "I don't like to think of the rain fallin' on the grave of—" He hesitated . . . *over a name?* "—of those I've loved."

For a long time, after Bessie left them alone together, they sat on the couch before the fire, silent, in the circle of each other's arms. When Mary drew closer to him, and drew his head down to hers, he responded with a wordless gratitude, his big hands tangling in the thick coils of her hair. This they had done, many times before, this dance of passion, of kisses and touch, flirting with the heart-shaking borderlands of delight and need. She loved his strength, and he, she guessed, the fire of her response, holding him to her, gasping as he pressed her back against the arm of the couch.

It was nothing any true lady should do—no true lady should permit a beau more than a single chaste salute: Betsey, and Granny Humphreys, and Elizabeth had emphasized this, over and over.

Did they really, she wondered, believe it was possible to draw back from the seductive ambrosia of this? Sometimes it seemed to her that this was truly what she and this man sought: to see how deep they could sink into darkness and fire and still have the strength to draw back.

Always it was he who drew away, as if he could trust himself only so far and no further. When she felt him move to do so, instead of letting him go she clung tighter. He whispered her name, and she pulled him to her: "I want you. I want all of you."

"You don't know what you're asking...." His voice was hoarse and she could feel his body trembling as it bent over hers.

"Do you think I'm a child?" she breathed. "Do you think I don't know? I know that you're the man that I love." All those conversations with Frances, with Mary Jane Warfield, and Merce—all those came back to her, about those things that girls only whispered about at night. The things that Elizabeth, and Betsey, never guessed that she had learned. Her hands tightened hard behind his neck and she slid her body down beneath his in a crushed sigh of petticoats, so that through them her legs pressed against his thighs. "I know that you're the man that I will marry, the only man I've ever loved or ever will love. Ever *can* love. Don't turn my love away."

He looked down into her face, his eyes hidden by the shadows of the dying fire, with his tangled hair hanging down over them. But he breathed like a man who had been running.

"Life is short," said Mary softly. "We don't know what the future will bring. I don't want never to have done this."

When they lay together later on the couch, locked in each other's arms in a tangle of disordered clothing, she touched his hair gently, wonderingly. Wondering how anyone could have thought him ugly. In repose the bony, mobile face recalled to her some vision of a prophet sleeping in the wilderness, at one with the silence and the stones.

At her touch his eyes opened, relaxed and infinitely at peace.

"Molly." He brought up his hand to cup her cheek. Seven years as a clerk, and a lawyer, and a legislator had not eradicated the frontiersman's hardness from his leathery palm. "I swear to you that I will be your husband. That I will not forsake you."

"I had no fear of that." So strongly she felt his love, and saw the tenderness in his eyes, that she honestly did not know whether what she said, at that moment, was a lie or not.

Lying in her own bed later, after Simeon had returned from the newspaper, and driven her home through the lessening rain, Mary turned the matter over in her heart and in her mind. Her body ached—Mary Jane had warned her about that—and she knew she'd have to inspect her petticoats closely and wash out the telltale spots of blood. Would have to do it early, before Lina was finished with the breakfast chores. Wet and muddy as last night had been, it would be easy to drop wet stockings or wet shoes on them, to cover dampness where dampness would not ordinarily be.

Mary Jane had told her about the blood, too.

What Mary Jane hadn't told her—or Merce, or Frances,

when hushed questions and answers had been exchanged on darkened front porches during summer nights—was how profoundly the passage from girl to woman would alter her perceptions. How differently a woman looked at a man, once he became a lover instead of a beau.

Yesterday she had loved Lincoln with a girl's passionate yearning. Tonight, lying in her bed listening to the rain, she understood that with the fulfillment of that yearning, a new and wholly unsuspected dimension of love opened. She wanted him always, a part of her without which she was not—had never been—complete.

I will not forsake you, he had promised. *I will be your husband. . . .*

She wondered if, when the new day dawned, he would come to Ninian and ask for her in marriage.

In a novel, the lover would put aside his diffidence and his foolish concerns about money, and come striding up to the House on the Hill in the morning. *Your sister is of age,* he would say, *and you cannot hold her from her own course any longer. . . .*

Of course, in a novel, the lover wouldn't have spent eighteen months mooning after Tilda Edwards and Sarah Rickard.

Mary closed her eyes in the darkness, folded her hands on her breast over the remembered heat of his lips. *I will be your husband,* he had said, and her heart told her that once he had given his word, Lincoln was a man who could be trusted to the ends of the earth. She fell asleep not knowing whether she could carry through with what she had planned, or whether she would trust him and wait.

I will be your husband, he had said.

Only—an accident, or a lawyer's caution even in extremis?—he still had not mentioned when.

Lincoln did not come striding out of the raw mists at breakfast-time, to claim her from Ninian. Ninian wiped his mouth on his napkin and departed for the State House; Elizabeth disappeared into the kitchen in quest of a blancmange Eppy was making for Mrs. Irwin, who was down with *la grippe:* "You will come visiting with me, won't you, Mary? It's been an age since you did, and I'm sure everyone is asking where you've been. . . ."

The day passed in a blur and in the midst of an afternoon call on Mrs. Browning and her daughters at the American House, listening to their account of the negotiations with contractors over the marble floors of the new State-House lobby, Mary thought suddenly, *Dear God, what if I am with child?*

Even if he marries me as soon as I know for certain—three weeks from now—the baby will be early. Everyone in town will know! No one—nobody—will receive me in their houses again! We'll both be outcasts. And Elizabeth . . .

Panic filled her heart, blotting out all further discussion of how that particular contractor had come by his appointment. The faces of the Browning ladies, and of her sister, retreated to a dream, mouthing meaningless sounds. Mary debated feigning sick to return to the house but didn't dare—*What if Elizabeth asks just why I am sick? Can she read it in my face already? Did she not speak of it because we were just about to set out on her visits? Will Ninian send me home . . . back to Betsey?*

Dear God! Anything but that!

The visits seemed to last for months. The evening, after supper—waiting in the parlor while she and Elizabeth worked at their sewing—for decades. Mary's fingers trembled in the yellow light of the whale-oil lamp and she wondered again if Elizabeth was looking at her strangely, but she dared not plead a headache and go up to bed. What if Mr. Lincoln came by, and they said, "Oh, Mary has gone up to bed with a headache"?

At ten she knew he would not come.

In the morning, as early as she dared—meaning just after breakfast, and she flinched at Elizabeth's cheerful "You're up early, dear,"—she had Jerry harness the carriage, and drove to Bessie Francis's house. ("I was up all night trying to remember what I'd done with my coral bracelet, and I remember now I left it at Bessie's Wednesday...." Did that sound convincing?) She only meant—she told herself later—to ask Bessie what she should do, what she thought....

But Lincoln was there, having breakfast with Bessie and Simeon as he frequently did. She heard his trumpeting high-pitched laugh as she came up the porch steps. Try as she would she later had no recollection of any intervening process between that, and standing in the doorway of the kitchen, seeing the handwritten papers strewn on the table among the breakfast things, and Lincoln in his shirtsleeves rising, his face wreathed with delight at the sight of her.

"Molly..."

She took his hands, and drew him into the empty dining-room. Bessie and Simeon, as always, hung back to give them the time they sought with one another.

"I had to see you," she said, and Lincoln bent his tall height down, to kiss her lips.

"And I was plotting away with Simeon like Brutus and Cassius rolled into one, to come up with some reason Ninian would believe for you to come over here again soon, I..."

She squeezed his hands hard, shaking him a little; in the dimness of the curtained room, he looked down at her in consternation. "What is it? Did Ninian...?"

She opened her mouth, and the words that came out were: "Mr. Lincoln, I'm with child."

And the next second, she would have given everything she possessed never to have spoken those words; would have traded her life not to have them emerge from her mind into reality, the reality of the rest of her life.

Lincoln's eyes widened with shock, like a man who has stepped unthinkingly around a corner in a friendly place, and been run through the heart with a spear.

CHAPTER TWENTY-THREE

Bellevue 1875

BEYOND BELLEVUE'S WINDOW BARS, AND THE WHITE CUR-
tains that let in such maddening quantities of light, the summer day dimmed. Mary's head ached as she remembered the
appalled shock in Lincoln's eyes, and anxiety began to overwhelm her, as it so often did at this hour of the day—the
medicine she had had immediately after Robert left seemed
to have had no effect at all. She understood Mr. Wilamet saying that she mustn't give Robert the advantage by being
sleepy or forgetful, but Robert was gone now.

And she wanted to sleep, and forget the lie she had told,
and all that came of it afterwards.

"Amanda," she called out, and a moment later the young
woman was at the door of her room.

They both pretended Amanda didn't spend her days on
the other side of the barred and curtained interior window,
but Mary had only to get to her feet and walk to the door of
her room—not locked, these days, for where was there for
her to go?—for Amanda to meet her, smiling, in the hall.

"I'm still feeling quite ill," she told the younger woman.
"Please ask Dr. Patterson to give me another dose of
medicine."

"Of course, Mrs. Lincoln."

But it wasn't Dr. Patterson who came to her room, but
John Wilamet.

"There's no need to go on watering down the medicine
now," she said, at the first sip from the glass he gave her.
"Robert is gone, and good riddance to him! How *could* he—
how could *any* boy—do what he did...?" She stopped herself, shook her head, hearing her own voice beginning to
crack with anger and feeling her head throb.

"Robert is gone," she repeated. "And what I need now is to go to sleep." It was still afternoon, but what did that matter? The visit had exhausted her.

"Mrs. Lincoln," said John softly. "Do you know what's in the medicine?"

Mary blinked at him, startled at the question. His tone was the tone of a man who speaks to evade a request, and she'd had enough of that with her husband. She snapped, "What does it matter what's in it? Of course I don't know what's in it, it's a secret of the manufacturer! Manufacturers are entitled to their secret formulae. How else would they make any money? And what that has to do with—"

"This medicine contains opium," said John. "They all do."

"That's a lie!" Mary gasped the first words that came to her aching, buzzing brain. "I would *only* take opium under a doctor's advice, and then only a very little for my neuralgia!"

"You've been taking large quantities of opium for years," said John. "Your doctors have been giving it to you for years and you've been drinking twice, three times, five times as much on the side. Your whole system is habituated to it."

"What a thing to say!" Mary backed from him, her hand clutching the glass. "How dare you call me an opium-eater! Mr. Lincoln was the most strictly temperate man I knew. He would never have permitted my doctors to do anything so wicked!"

"Mrs. Lincoln." Patience and care tempered his voice far beyond the youth of his thin face. "May I ask you a favor? For old times' sake?"

Mary checked the fury rising in her, settled back into her chair. She remembered this young man as a boy in Camp Barker, remembered him driving her through the green trees of that hot foul city by the Potomac. Remembered laughing with him, in better times.

For old times' sake.

For the sake of times that had been sweet.

There were flecks of gray at his temples now and he

looked careworn in the last fading daylight from the window. It crossed her mind suddenly to wonder what road had led him here, to this place, and whether his mother and sisters were still alive. His mother had been a strange woman, like a wild black Medea, but his sisters, especially little Lucy, had been dear to her, like so many of the contraband children in the camps.

The memories stilled her, drew her back to earth out of her rage.

"Of course," she agreed. But warily. She wasn't an opium-fiend! And if he thought he could call her one just because she took a little more medicine than pious hypocrites thought proper in a woman...

"Would you listen to me for a few minutes," said John, "while I talk about medicine? I'd like your thoughts on this, before I decide what to do."

He's going to take my medicine away from me! She could hear it in his voice. *For my own good, they all say... Wicked. Wicked like all the rest...*

"Most of the patent medicines you've been taking," he continued, "the ones they sell in the drugstores already bottled, contain opium. I've worked with medicines, I know what opium smells like and what it tastes like. It's there. Sometimes a lot of it. I don't know how much. Most doctors prescribe small amounts of purer opium for coughs, or headaches, or intestinal flux. It's the only thing that works. Most doctors don't know, or don't want to know, how quickly a patient can become habituated. Many doctors I know are opium-takers themselves, and don't want to admit how harmful it is. Beyond that, nearly all those medicines contain alcohol as well."

"Well, a little bit, of course..."

"I don't think it's a little bit. They put in bitter herbs, or sweet syrups, to change the taste. But I think most of these medicines are stronger than saloon rum."

"What are you telling me?" Mary set down her glass on

the bedside table behind her, her black-mitted hands closed into fists. The headache behind her left eye gave a sudden agonizing throb—old Chief Lightning-Wires getting his tomahawk ready, she thought despairingly. Anger flashed through her on the heels of the pain. *I need that medicine....*

"That you think that as well as being insane, I'm a drunkard? An opium-eater?"

"Not of your own choosing..."

"Not under *any* circumstances or conditions! The very *idea* that because I have *occasionally* taken laudanum for my truly *agonizing* neuralgia and headaches, that I would... would *guzzle* such a thing of my own volition is an insult, the rankest implication that no gentleman would even consider in regards to any woman! I'll have you know that my husband was a member of the Washingtonian Society, that he was the most strictly temperate man who ever drew breath! And the kindest, and the best!"

Tears began to flow from her eyes and John reached out to her, but she whirled from him, strode to the window in the blind fury he recalled from other days. "I shall report you to Dr. Patterson. You will find yourself sweeping out saloons, where I daresay you belong! Now get out of here! Get out of my room or I shall scream!"

She was screaming already, and John, very quietly, got up and left. Mary rushed to the door as he closed it and pounded on the panels, crying, "And don't you *dare* lock me in!" She yanked on the knob and the door came open with such violence that she staggered. He was walking away down the corridor, where the lamps had not yet been lit for the night. She screamed after him, "How can I rest here if you keep upsetting me? How can anyone rest in this place?"

She slammed the door behind him, opened it and slammed it again.

Then she went to the table and poured herself another glass of the medicine he had left. The whole bottle had been watered. She could tell how weak was the bitter taste that she was long used to associating with the strength—the warming comfort—of whatever medicine contained it.

She drank most of the bottle, and fell deeply asleep.

SHE DREAMED SHE WAS ATTENDING HER OWN WEDDING, IN Ninian's house, on that night in early November of 1842.

She stood in the back of the big double-parlor, nearly out of sight in the shadows in her black widow's dress. She was astonished at how young Ninian looked, the mass of his raven hair unfaded, glowering like a bear staked for baiting as the small group assembled in the lamplight. Elizabeth in her rose-colored dress, her hair still black instead of gray, alternated between seething indignation that her advice had not been taken, and annoyance that the wedding had been arranged with barely four hours' notice, and no time to do proper baking.

There was a cake, but it was still mildly warm from the oven and the frosting wouldn't set. The smell of ginger filled the room.

And Mary herself...

How pretty I was! She felt a kind of wonder at it, for it was something she had quite forgotten. That plump, bright-faced girl in her best dress of embroidered white muslin, with the collar of Irish lace, dancing with excitement one moment, then turning, suddenly, to look up at her groom with anxiety that amounted almost to fright in her eyes.

Trying to tell herself that she'd done right.

Lawful meaning in a lawful act...

Trying to convince herself that love was enough.

Praying that the words she'd said to him in Bessie Francis's dining-room that morning had not killed once and for all the love he bore her.

Even in the orange lamplight, and the hot glow of every candle Elizabeth could place in sconces and branches on table and sideboards, Lincoln looked ashen. His dark brows stood out sharply above the adze-blade nose. But it was the only

sign he gave of whatever was going on inside. A politician—
and a good one—he was never at a loss in company, shaking
hands and chatting with the thirty-some friends and family
who had been hastily gathered by word of mouth: Old Judge
Brown and Lincoln's fellow-lawyer James Matheny, Frances
and Dr. Wallace, Lincoln's landlord William Butler and his
wife . . . But when the eddies of talk swirled away, and he
took the hand of that plump, pretty little partridge in white
to lead her to the Presbyterian minister, she could see that his
eyes were haunted, as if he were mounting the steps of the
scaffold.

He'd had a gold band inscribed that afternoon: *A.L. to
M.T. Nov. 4, 1842, Love Is Eternal.* He held her hand, and
spoke as if he'd memorized the words. "With this ring I thee
endow," said Lincoln, "with all my goods and chattels, lands
and tenements. . . ."

"Lord Jesus Christ God Almighty, Lincoln, the statute
fixes that!" boomed Judge Brown from the crowd. "Get on
with it!"

Everyone laughed, including, thank God, the groom
himself. With laughter he put the ring on young Mary's finger. With laughter, they kissed.

Laughing herself in the shadows in her secret corner,
Mary saw that young girl—for she *was* only a young girl, she
understood now, no matter what others said or she feared
about being an old maid of twenty-four—look up into the
face of the man she adored to distraction. And she thought,
*I'm glad I lied—if it was a lie. I'm glad I brought this about. I'm
glad we had the time together that we had.*

All of it, good and bad.

*Because good and bad, all put together, there wasn't so very
much.*

*And if I had not lied as I did, there would have been less of it, or
maybe none at all.*

But she turned her head and glimpsed behind the backs of
the crowd a young man in the natty gray suit of a different

era, his burly body held stiff, his face with its drooping mustache a cold mask that revealed nothing of his thoughts.

You lied, Robert Todd Lincoln's eyes said.

And because of your lie, my father never loved me with the whole of his heart, as the firstborn son has a right to be loved.

CHAPTER TWENTY-FOUR

Springfield 1843

THEY LIVED IN A SINGLE RENTED ROOM IN THE GLOBE TAVERN, at a cost of four dollars a week.

It took Jerry two trips in the carriage to bring five of Mary's trunks, plus hatboxes, valises, and books, to the plain two-story wooden boardinghouse on Adams Street. She spent the rest of the week going back and forth to Elizabeth's house, packing up what remained. Though Lincoln had left his room at William Butler's on his wedding morning without the slightest idea that he'd be moving in with a bride within twenty-four hours, he was able to walk over from Butler's the following morning with all his possessions crammed into two saddlebags and a cardboard box.

"Growin' up the way I did, I never did need much," he said, almost apologetically, as Mary, laughing, looked around the small room for places to put everything. The books—her novels, his law-books, and her volumes of Shakespeare and Burns—they stacked on top of the single bureau. There was no bookcase. "I see those big houses—your brother-in-law's among 'em—and they look so fine, an' I always end up wonderin', *what the blazes do them fill 'em up with?*"

"They fill them up," smiled Mary, turning back to her tall husband, "with the amenities of fine living. With the where-withal to make music—for one's friends and for one's own peace of mind. With the space to entertain and give parties, for the pleasure of the friends one already has and to meet one's business and political acquaintances. With a healthy and happy environment in which to raise one's children."

Lincoln hesitated fractionally before putting his big hands on her shoulders. His grin was rueful. "And dear knows what our poor little codger's gettin' himself into, arrivin' early this way," he said, and bent to kiss her. His black hair hung down in his eyes—never, to the end of their days together, did Mary see it brushed back for more than five minutes at a time. *If he's to go anywhere in politics,* she thought, *we're going to have to invest in a little pomade.* "But we'll deal with that as best we can, Molly, and I reckon we'll brush by somehow."

He kissed her again, and then—Jerry having departed—folded her in his arms and carried her to the bed.

He left the next day for Taylorville, for a one-day session of Christian County Court. Mrs. Beck, who owned the Globe, found planks that could be put together to form a rough bookcase: Mary and Lincoln had already formed the habit of reading to one another in the evenings, Mary in this case reading *Les Liaisons Dangereuses* and translating as she went. ("Lord, that Valmont's a scoundrel!" exclaimed Lincoln, as if the whole thing were happening in Springfield instead of the Paris of the *ancien régime.)* Mrs. Beck was less than pleased when Mary complained about the curtains—which were faded and limp—and responded to Mary's suggestion that they be at least starched and ironed with a tart, "Well, my lady, I'll certainly send one of the slaves to take care of it right away!"

Mary flushed bright red, but Mrs. Beck had already turned on her heel and strode off down the stairs; Mary spent the rest of the rainy day with the six additional trunks of dresses, shoes, underwear, and books that Elizabeth had sent over, trying to arrange them in such a fashion that two people could at least get from the door to the bed without turning sideways. Julia arrived with Mary's cousins Lizzie and Francy, to sweep her off for tea at Uncle John Todd's, but that first night alone Mary lay for a long time awake, listening to the clamor of men's voices in the common-room downstairs, to the clang of the bell that announced the arrival of the stages, to old Professor Kittridge's drunken harangues in the yard, and to the Bledsoe family arguing over money in the room next door.

Wondering how she, Mary Todd of Lexington, who could have been the wife of any planter in Kentucky and several states around, had come to be alone in this dreary place.

And trying to push from her mind the shame at her lie and the dread of what Lincoln would say if he ever found out.

He won't, she told herself frantically. *I can tell him I miscarried....* She'd heard Mammy Sally speak of slave women who'd done so. *Or is it different for darkies than for whites?* Who could she ask?

The thought of him finding out—of standing revealed in his eyes as a liar and a cheat—was more than she could bear.

"You really must talk to that woman," said Mary, when Lincoln returned late Wednesday afternoon. "She's insufferable, and a slovenly housekeeper. I had to starch and iron the curtains myself, and I had a headache all the rest of the day. And her cooking leaves much to be desired as well. If we were to move to the American House . . ."

"It would cost us half again as much," said Lincoln gently, drawing Mary to his side where he sat on the bed. "And that we cannot afford."

"Oh." Mary looked down at her hands, filled with shame that she hadn't thought of that before getting into a quarrel with their landlady.

"I told you, didn't I, that you'd be marrying a poor man—"

"As if that mattered a whit to me!"

"Well, if it's true I'm grateful for it. And if it's not quite as true on closer examination as you thought it was when you said it, I'm glad you're still willin' to stand by it."

Mary opened her mouth to protest, then saw the twinkle in his eye and retorted, in mock primness, "You're not the only person in this household who stands by his word, Mr. Lincoln. I can be patient in a good cause."

"That's my Molly." He tightened his big hand on her shoulder, and bent to kiss the top of her head. "As for Mrs. Beck, I heard all about your hoo-rah from her on my way across the yard, an' I smoothed her feathers a trifle. You got to remember, she runs this place with just the two servant girls, when she can *get* a servant girl, and most of the work she does herself. Of course she'll get cross, when somebody tells her to do more. One day I'll be clear of the National Debt that landed on me when I took over my partner's half of that wretched grocery in New Salem, and then we'll be able to live...well, if not like Brother Ninian and Sister Elizabeth, at least as well as common folks. You think you got enough flub-dubs in them trunks to last you till then?"

Mary put on a considering expression as she studied the trunks, then glanced at him, smiling. "If you're not too long about it."

When the times were sweet, they were very sweet.

Lincoln had grown up in a man's world, and for years had associated mostly with men. With his agonizing shyness around women went a curiosity about them that few men had—as he was curious about all things, and all people. In the same spirit that he'd listened to the Speed slaves telling stories in the quarters, he would listen with a slow grin, cracking his knuckles, when Mary spoke of the intricacies of the Southern family feuds that had carried from Virginia to Kentucky and on into Illinois, and the inflexible rules about who left cards on whom, and why. He hadn't been joking when he'd said a woman should have the same right to sexual freedom as a man—he was also inclined to let women have the vote. "But God help you if you say so in this state."

For her part Mary had never known a man like him. Her experience had for the most part been with men of her own class, townsmen who saw the world in terms of making a living, and connecting with other men—and peripherally with their families—who would further their own careers.

Lincoln's countrified earthiness, that had so repelled Elizabeth, drew Mary. She felt that she was dealing with a man from a different age of history, a woodsman at heart who saw the world in terms of simpler survival, and who thus saw through the persiflage of town life and town ambitions to the bone and bedrock of politics and law.

At night they would read to one another from her books or from the half-dozen newspapers that were the party organs of Democrats, Whigs, Locofoco Democrats, "the conscience Whigs," anti-Tyler Whigs, and all phases of opinion in between. Or they would simply talk until the bedroom candle burned out. Shortly after they were married, as she brushed her hair before bed, he asked her shyly, "May I do that?" and she smiled at him sidelong:

"You heard the minister, Mr. Lincoln, and you know the laws of the state. It is now *your* hair, and you may do with it what you wish."

But the sweetness of those times didn't make up for her constant dread of being found out in her lie, and the galling humiliation of being truly poor. And Mary quickly found how right Elizabeth had been. From the first she hated poverty—hated it and all that it meant.

During that freezing winter, when she would struggle through the mud of Adams Street on foot and see Elizabeth pass in Ninian's carriage, she didn't even have the consolation of sympathy. She knew what Springfield gossip was. She had proclaimed, again and again, to every one of her friends that Lincoln's poverty and debt mattered nothing to her. She knew how Elizabeth would look down her nose, if word reached her that Mary did not actually like to be cold in their little boardinghouse room (Mrs. Beck charged extra to keep fires burning during the day), or disliked the appalling sameness of Mrs. Beck's uninspired cooking. She could almost hear Elizabeth say it: *You have no one to blame but yourself.*

To be poor was to be branded wrong in the eyes of the entire town.

When, in years past, Mary had pictured herself as married, she had always assumed she would have a home—perhaps not as elegant as that of Elizabeth and Ninian, but at least a place of comfort, like that of Bessie and Simeon Francis. A place in which to be "at home" when friends came calling, a place where she could give dinners and put up preserves. But even with the little money from her mother's will that came to her on her marriage, Lincoln insisted that they had not the money for a house. So they remained at the Globe, where the noisy talk of the men in the common-room, the clang of the stagecoach bell, and the arguments of the Bledsoes next door kept Mary awake far into the nights.

What Lincoln had imagined marriage would be like, he did not say. Sometimes she wondered if he had ever pictured himself as being married at all. Or had he, she wondered, simply assumed that he would continue his bachelor existence of boardinghouses and courtrooms, arguing politics and swapping yarns with his male friends?

Whatever he'd been expecting—or not expecting—Mary found that Frances had been right in observing that at thirty-four, Lincoln was deeply set in his ways. She tried to remember this, when he'd stay out late at the law office, or the State-House library, or wherever it was he stayed until long after dark, leaving her to sit at the boardinghouse dinner-table with two dozen teamsters, laborers, clerks, and transients alone. Harriet Bledsoe and her six-year-old daughter Sophie were often the only other females at the table, and though some of the men were careful about their language, others weren't, and what Mary didn't learn about disgusting table-manners in that first winter could have been written on the back of a very small visiting-card.

Mary's resentment took the form of fits of rage; Lincoln's, of silence and absence, from which he'd return to apologies, embraces, and long sweet nights of lovemaking and talk. During the day when he was gone Mary would sometimes go calling on Julia or Bessie or Merce Conkling, but she found herself embarrassed, for they were now wealthier than she. They generally asked her to stay to luncheon or dinner ("Darling, everyone in town has heard about Mrs. Beck's cooking!") but she dreaded the thought that she was being looked upon as a cadger.

When she stayed at the Globe, she ran the risk of the equally idle Harriet Bledsoe knocking at her door, "for a chat." Harriet's husband was a new-fledged lawyer, just entering partnership with Lincoln's English friend Ed Baker, but Harriet herself read little but the Bible and had no conversation beyond her family back in New England and how much she missed the way things were done there. Mary's delight in dresses and jewelry she regarded as sinful; her newspaper-reading and interest in the question of Federal lands she considered simply bizarre. She'd bring Sophie to do her samplers in quiet beside the little fire—Mary sometimes suspected that Harriet was in the habit of letting the fire go out there, and brought her daughter over to Mary's room only so that the two of them could stay warm—at the Lincolns' extra expense.

"It seems like I saw more of you before we were married than I do now," Mary complained late one evening, when Lincoln finally came up the narrow wooden stair. It didn't help that she'd heard his voice downstairs in the common-room for a good hour already, talking to drunken Professor Kittridge and Billy Herndon. His high laughter was distinctive, and could pierce walls. She had waited, trying to read by the single candle that was all they could afford that week, with growing impatience—did the man have no concept of time?

Apparently not, because Lincoln looked mildly startled and said, "I'm only making hay while the sun shines, Molly. Mr. Logan's taken on more cases, with the Supreme Court sitting. . . ."

"Surely you can work on those while the sun is *actually shining,* and not leave me waiting for you alone in this wretched room in the dark!"

His face clouded in the candlelit gloom. "It's the work I do that will get us *out* of this room. . . ."

"*If* you do it! *If* you do it, and don't spend your days the way you've spent the past hour and a half, sitting around with those idlers downstairs while I waited up here!"

"Molly, I'm sorry...."

"You've said you're sorry and you always end up doing the same thing! Sitting around in the common-room with every drover and law-clerk and pettifogger in town...!"

"A man is entitled to his friends, I guess," retorted Lincoln, "as you're entitled to running about all day with yours."

At that Mary lost her temper completely and lunged at him, hands striking out blindly. He caught her by the wrists and held her off with the same brutal, easy strength that five years before he'd used to hold off Professor Kittridge, while she screamed at him, words that she later could not even remember, words of reproach and fury that she wasn't even sure were directed at him. She didn't know who it was, at whom she wanted to scream, *You are always gone, always! You always leave me alone!*

He finally shouted at her, in anger of which she hadn't thought him capable, "Any man would leave you alone if he could!" and thrust her down onto the bed. Then he strode from the room, shutting the door behind him. Mary staggered to her feet and yanked the door open again, screamed after him,

"Get out of here! Get out!"

She slammed the door, then slammed it again. Then she stumbled to the bed, fell on her knees beside it, and barely had time to pull the chamber pot out from underneath before she began to vomit, her body spasming agonizingly in her stays. For a long time after that she simply lay on the floor beside the bed, sobbing and too exhausted to get up, her head throbbing and the room spinning around her.

They had quarreled before, but not like this. She had read in his anger the bitterness of his frustration at being tied down, as his father had tied him. *He didn't even need to know I lied, to turn against me,* she thought in despair. *He was afraid to marry me, afraid of my temper, and now he hates me....*

She vomited again and sweat poured down her face, down her aching body....

What is wrong with me?

And she thought, *What I told him was true.*

It wasn't a lie after all.

I really am going to have a child.

Lincoln was out nearly all night. Mary lay awake, waiting—listening to the voices downstairs. She thought she heard his laughter before she fell asleep. He must have come up sometime after midnight, with such silent animal stealth that he did not wake her, for she was wakened in the darkness by his voice sobbing out, crying confused words of terror, and she felt his body struggling at her side.

"Mr. Lincoln," she whispered, reaching over to shake his bony shoulder, "Abraham..."

He came awake with a choked cry and she felt him half sit up, bone and sinew trembling like a whipped horse beneath the coarse linen of his nightshirt. He gasped, "I done my best!" It was the hopeless plea of one who knows that one's best is no extenuation in the face of Fate.

"I'm here," she said, touching his arm again. "I'm here."

With a sob he caught her to him, clinging tight with arms and legs, like a drowning child. "Don't leave me," he implored her, and Mary locked her arms around his ribs.

"Never, my love."

His big hands closed in the thick handfuls of her hair.

SHE PASSED A WRETCHED SPRING AND SUMMER. LINCOLN WAS gone all of April, for the circuit courts, and again for nearly three weeks in May and June. Her pregnancy was a difficult one, an exhausting cycle of migraines, queasiness, and alternating rage and tears. She quarreled repeatedly with Mrs. Beck, with Mrs. Bledsoe, and whoever else came within her range, including both Frances and Elizabeth. When Julia Jayne came to her, breathless with delight, with the news that she was going to marry Lyman Trumbull, Mary burst into hysterical sobs.

Mary tried to explain, but couldn't understand herself, the

blind rages that came over her, in which she would say anything and which left her ill with remorse. How could she explain, she wondered, to women who'd never felt the need for bright intellectual sword fights how dreary the feminized world of babies and pregnancy could be? After her quarrel with Elizabeth—from whose house she stormed back to the Globe on foot—she sent a note to her sister apologizing, but received only the briefest and coldest reply.

Only Lincoln seemed to understand. After that single outburst of frustrated anger he seldom lost his temper with her again. He'd do his best to talk or joke her out of her rages, but if he could not, he would simply leave. Sometimes he wouldn't come back till the small hours of the morning, though she would hear his voice, and his distinctive laugh, downstairs. Mary hated him at such times—she would infinitely have preferred a good fight—but the hatred vanished with her anger, clearing up the way her headaches cleared up, and she would apologize in the morning.

"I don't mean what I say," she promised anxiously, one hot June morning as Lincoln brought her up coffee, toast, and a copy of the *Sangamo Journal* from the dining-room before leaving for his office. It was her one consolation in the final stages of pregnancy, that even Mrs. Beck wouldn't expect her to come downstairs in her condition, and made up trays for her. If Harriet Bledsoe brought them up, the coffee was usually tepid and mouth-wringingly strong—the dregs of the pot—but Lincoln could always talk the landlady into making fresh.

Lincoln, Mary was finding, could talk just about anybody into just about anything.

"In fact I don't . . . sometimes I don't *know* what I say," she added, a little uncertainly, for this was something she'd never admitted to anyone else. "It's as if someone else is talking— someone I don't know . . . someone I hate. And I think, *Who's saying those terrible things?* And it's me." She leaned forward on the pillows, looked up at him as he rolled down his

shirtsleeves and fetched a sock from the over-jammed drawers of the hotly-contested bureau. "Do you understand?"

He smiled down at her. She'd heard him at dawn in the
yard, splitting Mrs. Beck's kindling for her—looking down
from the little dormer window at the end of the hall she'd
seen him in his shirtsleeves, handling the ax as casually as she
herself would wield a crochet-hook.

"I understand there's folks that are that way," he said.
"There was this feller in New Salem, used to pick a fight
with anybody, just about. Seemed to be nuthin' he could do
about it. He'd only do it once a month or every six weeks,
and you could tell he was spoilin' for it because he'd come
out of his house without his hat on, so everybody knew. And
everybody would just figgur, 'Here comes old Benson without his hat on, better get out of the way,' same as we say,
'Oops, it's rainin', better take an umbrella.'" He leaned down
and put his hand on her nightgowned side, where the child
that would be Robert slept within her flesh, and kissed her
on the top of her head. "He wasn't near as sweet as you,
between-times."

Then he was off, to the County Court or the Whig Party
meetings, and Mary had to get through another day alone.
Another day of wondering how she could possibly look after
a child—how she could have been so stupid as to get herself
"in a fix," as they said, and throw away comfort and friends.

She rarely felt well enough to go out, and few visited her.
When one is in no position to entertain, Mary discovered,
one gradually ceases to be invited. The gay Coterie of her
Springfield friends seemed to have forgotten her in the flurry
of picnics and dances and parties leading up to Julia Jayne's
wedding.

Bessie Francis came, brought her books and newspapers,
and helped her sew for the baby. Her talk of Legislative scandal and Locofoco enormities was the breath of life. But
Bessie had her own house to run and half of Simeon's newspaper as well. Mostly Mary was left alone, with her resent-

ment, her headaches, her swollen feet, and the everlasting, oven-like summer heat.

Twice she dreamed of crouching in the darkness of the upstairs hall at the old house on Short Street, listening to baby Georgie crying in the dark. Praying she'd wake up before the bedroom door opened and the men carried her mother's body out, her long dark hair trailing down to the floor.

Robert was born on the first of August, in the upstairs room of the Globe Tavern, with a midwife, Mrs. Beck, Bessie Francis, and Harriet Bledsoe in attendance. The labor seemed endless, the airless room filled with flies. Bessie closed the curtains on the wide windows, to cut down the grilling sun-glare, but the dimness was terrifying, and Mary, alternating between the bed and the birthing-stool that the midwife set up, lost track of time. Pain wrenched her, but no child came; only memories of the smell of blood and her mother's moans—and afterwards that terrible silence.

"Mammy Sally?" she whispered, clinging to Bessie's hands. "Where is she? Why doesn't she come?"

Bessie whispered, "Hush, dear. Hush."

Once, as if through a long tunnel of pain, she heard Lincoln's voice, and Bessie's replying, "Not yet. It's just taking longer. You go back downstairs."

"Is that the truth?" he demanded, his voice hoarse with raw fear. Then immediately, "I'm sorry, Bessie. Just—my sister died this way. Died because they wouldn't send for a doctor." From the bed Mary saw him in the doorway, framed by the gloom of the hall, sweat on his face and his black hair hanging in his eyes. Past Bessie's shoulder his eyes met hers, and Mary held out her hands to him.

"This is no place for a man," insisted the midwife firmly. "They only get in the way—and faint, like as not, at the sight of a little blood."

But Mary whispered, "Please," and in the end the midwife let him in. He might have no parlor conversation, but he held Mary's hands, stroked her hair and her back with the wordless gentle strength of a man encouraging a mare in foal.

"You'll be fine," he told her, and though she'd heard his fear about his sister's death, there was something in his voice that kindled belief, and Mary knew, then, that she would be fine.

A few hours later Robert was born.

Chapter Twenty-Five

Bellevue 1875

"IS IT TRUE?" MARY asked DR. PATTERSON, WHEN THE NEXT afternoon, sluggish and aching, she came down to the wide parlor of Bellevue Place. "Is it true that the medicine that I've been taking is mostly opium?"

"Oh, not *mostly*, Mrs. Lincoln." Dr. Patterson seated himself on the chair across from her, and peered intently at her face. "There's only a little, for medicinal purposes, and of course if it's properly taken there is no more harm in it than a sip of after-dinner sherry. How do you feel this morning? You look tired."

"I don't feel well," she said. "I . . . I slept badly, and I'm afraid my neuralgia is acting up again." Waking, she had hidden the empty medicine bottle. She guessed that John would get into serious trouble for leaving it in her room, though she was honest enough to know that she'd have done everything in her power—up to and including physical violence— to keep him from taking it away from her, when she needed it so. She had been appalled to find it empty. Surely, *surely* she hadn't drunk the whole thing? She couldn't remember. She should have saved it, hidden it for the next time they wouldn't give her as much as she needed. . . .

But she felt the woozy aftermath of one of her "spells" still on her, even as she'd had Gretchen help her dress, and the urgency of her instinct to hoard the medicine frightened her.

"Would you like a little medicine to get you through the morning?"

Mary met Patterson's gaze, trying to read his intent, but in his brown eyes she saw only kindness and concern. *He truly believes that giving me opium is the best way to deal with me.* Her glance passed over his shoulder, to Mrs. Hill and Mrs.

Johnston, who sat placidly near the window, gazing out into the grounds.

And what does he give to them?

"No, thank you, sir," she said. "I think a little walk in the garden will do me good."

"Splendid!" Patterson rose, and helped her to her feet. "Most of our troubles today arise out of irritated nerves, Mrs. Lincoln. Modern cities are no place for those of delicate constitutions. No wonder so many women find themselves prey to hysteria and delusions. All the hurrying and scurrying, all the clocks and traffic and noise! The best mode of life is quiet, without overstimulation. You do very well to take just a little mild exercise. Would you like Gretchen or Amanda to accompany you, Mrs. Lincoln?"

"Thank you, no. I'd like to be by myself."

He frowned at that, and gave her a grave talk about not permitting herself to fall into morbid reflection, but in the end let her go. As she walked out into the graveled terrace above the roses she could see Mrs. Wheeler and Mrs. Edouard sitting quietly on a bench beneath an elm-tree. Talking commonplaces, neatly dressed, just as if Rosemary Wheeler hadn't spent all day yesterday howling and pounding on the walls of her room, and Heloise Edouard hadn't been subjected to a "water treatment" every day for a week.

The best mode of life is quiet. *And if you're not sufficiently quiet yourself,* thought Mary, *a little medicine will make you so.*

Does Robert know?

Of course he does.

The smell of roses and grass washed over her, sun-warmed and soporific. Though it was high spring, the breezes from the Fox River flickered through the trees, cooling the blessed shade. It would be good, thought Mary, to stay here, to never worry about things again. To not be afraid; to not be sad; to feel neither humiliation nor grief— not for long at a time, anyway. The perfect life.

The resting-place she had been seeking for ten years.

"Live and lie reclined
On the hills like Gods together, careless of mankind.
For they lie beside their nectar, and the bolts are hurled
Far below them in the valleys, and the clouds are lightly
*   curled*
Round their golden houses, girdled with the gleaming
*   world . . ."*

She remembered reading Tennyson's "Lotos-Eaters" to her husband in bed, and the far-off look in his gray eyes as he savored the words. This was during the second winter of their marriage, which they'd spent in that tiny rented cottage on Fourth Street. Sleety wind howling outside the windows, Robert soundly asleep in his cradle at the foot of their bed. The lamp burning with a warm amber radiance and Lincoln crowded up close beside her under the heap of quilts: he was perpetually cold, and the room was freezing. One of the good times.

She'd set the book down on the counterpane, and they'd talked about that dreamy land, and what each would do, if offered the chance to live there.

"Surely, surely, slumber is more sweet than toil," he'd repeated, one big hand ruffling the fur of Lady Jane, the cat that lay on his stomach. *"The shore / Than labor in the deep mid-ocean, wind and wave and oar; / Oh rest ye, brother mariners, we will not wander more."*

AFTER A TIME MARY TURNED AWAY, FROM THE SUNLIGHT AND the roses of Bellevue's garden, and from that cherished memory, and circled the house, to the corner where the side door was hidden behind a little wall. That was where she'd seen John Wilamet, more than once, standing where he could look out over the garden without being observed from the house. As she walked, she was conscious of Amanda, watching her from the parlor windows.

She supposed that was something that one became used to. Part of the price one paid for this ultimate peace.

As she'd thought, John was standing near the side door.

He saw her come around the corner of the house and made to go in. She called out softly, "Please don't go, Mr. Wilamet," and quickened her step to reach him. "I wanted to tell you . . . I wanted to ask your forgiveness for my losing my temper at you yesterday. I . . ." She hesitated, looking up at him. His eyes were grave and tired behind his spectacles.

She realized he'd probably spent a worried night, wondering if she really would complain about him to Dr. Patterson, and what she would say. In her Washington days she'd seldom hesitated to complain of fancied ill-treatment. She swallowed, and drew a deep breath.

"When one . . . ceases to take opium . . . what else can one take, for pain? Because I do have genuine pain, you know. All my life I have suffered from migraines, and twelve years ago I was in a carriage accident, and suffered injury to my back and shoulder. I cannot . . ."

The memory of the empty medicine bottle returned to her, and her frantic thoughts of hiding medicine. The memory, too, of the medicine she *had* hidden, in every room she'd inhabited, all those years. She felt her face grow red. In a suffocated voice, she went on, "I cannot be without *something*."

She had turned her eyes down to her small chubby hands as she spoke. Now, looking up again, she saw respect and pity mingled in the young man's face.

"I'll see that you get only as much as you really need," he said. "But I promise you, you're going to think you need more. And I promise you, too, that you're going to feel terrible."

"It's so . . . *humiliating*," said Mary quietly. "To realize . . . to realize what one has become. In spite of oneself, one's best intentions. And you're quite right," she added, more briskly, "Dr. Patterson doesn't see any reason at all why every woman in this place shouldn't be opiated twenty-four hours a day. We're only lunatics, after all. I'm sure he considers it more restful for everyone concerned."

"It is," said John, and Mary stared at him, startled, before breaking into laughter. He laughed, too.

Of course it was. That was why Robert had sent her here.

It felt good beyond belief to laugh again.

Then she sighed, feeling the anxiety that was already beginning to gnaw at her grow stronger, the restlessness in hands and feet that at times could drive her to distraction. Remembering the migraines, and the nightmares from which she fled. The memories of guilt and shame. In a muffled voice she said, "I think I will need a great deal of help."

"I promise you," said John, "that I will give you all the help that I can."

THE REST OF THE DAY MARY spent in her room, and many days after that. In part this was because she feared that, if Dr. Patterson pressed medicine of some kind on her for her restlessness and pain, she would swallow it gladly—would swallow anything, to be rid of the physical malaise and the horrible darkness.

And in part, it was because the grief that descended upon her was so incapacitating that she thought she would die of it. It was as if everything that she had fled and pushed aside, all those years, was returning, distilled and fermented by time. Everything that she had been unable to cope with then assailed her now, a night ocean in which she was adrift in the most fragile of canoes.

Without John coming to see her—coming to talk, to hold her hands, to give her small amounts of watered laudanum to hold the worst of the physical symptoms at bay—she did not think she could have endured it.

He came every few hours, sometimes so stealthily that she was certain Dr. Patterson did not know of the frequency of his visits and would not have agreed with either his diagnosis or his treatment. Mostly he simply let her talk, about

Lexington, about Springfield—about Mr. Lincoln, and Elizabeth, and Betsey, and her boys. About the horror of her loneliness; about her anger that had all her life run like fire and poison in her veins.

But there were always those times at night, when all the house slept and she could not. When the door was locked and, far off, she could hear one of the other patients screaming. Then all she could hold on to was the memory of that windy night over thirty years ago, and Lincoln turning his head on the pillow to look at her:

"Would you go live in the land of the lotos-eaters, if you could, Molly?"

And she'd replied with the prompt optimism of twenty-five, "Of course not! It sounds flat dull to me."

His eyes twinkled. "You wouldn't notice how dull it was, you'd be so happy all the time." His hand stopped scritching Lady Jane's chin and the cat wrapped her paws protestingly around his wrist. One of the first things Mary had learned about her husband was that he always had a cat or two around him, and could never pass up even the straggliest stray. She'd fretted about one of the four currently in residence scratching the baby, but Lincoln had said, "Oh, I don't think they will," and so far they hadn't.

"Would you go there?" she asked. "To live where you could do nothing, and be happy all the time?"

"It's tempting," he admitted. "When I get the hypo—hypochondria, Dr. Henry calls it—it seems to me that if what I feel could be evenly distributed through the whole human race, there wouldn't be a smiling face left on the surface of the planet. But it's happened to me enough now for me to know that I won't die of it, and it *will* end—it always does. And it seems to me that if we were all to sit, every man under his own vine and fig-tree, we wouldn't do much to help those that need helping. And you notice, those lotos-eaters don't seem to have families, or children, or friends. Would you trade a whole bouquet of lotos-blossoms for Bobby, even when he's squalling his head off? Or for either of your sisters, even when they're hell-bound to tell you about what a mistake you made marryin' me?"

Mary feigned deep thought. "Ask me the next time Bobby's squalling," she said.

DESPITE HIS INITIAL DISMAY AT FINDING HIMSELF A HUSBAND and a father, Lincoln worked hard to do his best at both. He still had his periods of bitter resentment at the loss of his easy-going bachelor life—his silences, his absences, an occasional flash of volcanic temper. But he adapted—outwardly at least—more quickly than did Mary.

When Bobby was wailing, or Mary had to leave some all-too-rare gathering of her friends to go home and care for him, she reflected that Lincoln could adapt because there was less change for him to adapt *to*. It was far easier for a man than for a woman, to be somewhere else.

Perhaps because of the tensions in that cramped boarding-house room, Robert was a fussy, nervous child. He had been born, moreover, with a left eye that turned sharply inward, a deformation that Mary was sometimes able to ignore, and sometimes—to her abiding shame—was not. From the first heart-sinking moment she saw her son's eye, she felt certain that God had punished her lie by giving her a defective child. Every time she picked him up, in spite of all her will to feel something different, she was overcome by shame.

The infant felt it—she *knew* he felt it—and he would scream and would not be comforted.

But Lincoln had only to lift his son in his huge hands for the baby's cries to cease. With his great physical strength, and his calmly logical intelligence, he had a vast store of tender-ness, and an almost womanly patience. He likewise exerted himself in caring for Mary, whether during one of her mi-graines or merely in her simple day-to-day conflicts with the world; caring quietly and without fuss, as he had the night she gave birth to their son. He would have been, in fact, the perfect husband, if he'd been around most of the time.

But he wasn't.

A month after Bobby was born, Lincoln was back on the circuit, leaving Mary to deal with Mrs. Beck and those other inhabitants of the tavern who didn't appreciate an infant's screams at all hours of the night. Mary knew they were right, but her shame at agreeing with them made her defensive, and she found herself in a number of sharp quarrels even with Harriet Bledsoe, who took care of her following the birth.

Knowing Lincoln couldn't afford to live anywhere but at the Globe, when her father came to Springfield to see his new grandson she swallowed her pride and asked him for money to set up housekeeping. With what he sent—ten dollars every month thereafter—they were able to move to the cottage on Fourth Street. Elizabeth, to whom Mary was speaking again by that time, thanks to their father's patient negotiations, sent Eppy to help nurse Bobby and deal with the heavier indoor chores.

The smiling freedwoman had been given as a gift to Ninian's father when she was seven, long years ago. Eppy undertook to teach Mary—who was already accounted a good cook—the heavier skills of day-to-day plain cooking, things the daughter of Robert Todd—or the sister of Elizabeth Edwards—had always been able to relegate to a servant: gutting and boning, and how to judge the amount of kindling and the heat on various portions of the cottage's old-fashioned open hearth.

She initiated Mary, too, into the never-ending routines of keeping house—the first time that Mary truly learned the sheer physical drudgery of being a poor man's wife. As with the cooking, she had helped out in Elizabeth's house, and knew what had to be done. But she'd always known that if there were morning-calls to make, or a picnic to go to, someone else would sweep the floors, clean the lamp-chimneys, clear the ash from the kitchen hearth, keep the boiler topped up with hot water, make sure the family chamber pot was clean and scoured, air the beds to keep the ever-present bugs at bay, keep up the kitchen fire, and cut up

newspapers to furnish the out-house. This didn't even include the labor of washdays, and the tedious exertions involved in making sure that Lincoln had a clean shirt and her
own petticoats were fresh and starched.

Eppy came over to help on those days—it was appalling
how much linen a six-month-old baby went through in a
week—but Mary always felt behind. She was not lazy, and
when she felt well enough was perfectly willing to work, but
life did not stop when she had a headache.

Then Bobby would cry, and Mary would have to go attend to him, leaving the rugs half-beaten or the few lunch
dishes still sitting in their pan of cooling water. . . .

And at night, aching with fatigue, she would be too weary
to open a newspaper or to care whether President Tyler had
been drummed out of the Whig Party, or why. She would lie
alone and listen to the far-off thunder of the prairie storms,
trembling with panic and head throbbing with the onset of
migraine, tensely waiting for Bobby to start shrieking again
just when things looked to be finally settling into silence. . . .
And she would hate Abraham Lincoln.

That was her second secret, never whispered to a soul—
for to whom could she whisper it without admitting that
she'd been wrong?

She hated him as she had hated her father when he was
not there. And the shame of feeling what she felt was worse a
thousand times than that of the lie she had told. Then he
would come home, and the sweet times would return.

At winter's end, Lincoln started negotiating with Reverend
Dresser, who had performed their wedding. In May—
between the Champaign Circuit Court, the Moultrie Circuit
Court, and a convention of the Seventh Congressional
District Whigs in Tremont—they moved into Dresser's four-
room frame cottage on the corner of Eighth and Jackson
Streets: Lincoln, Mary, Bobby, six cats, Bob the Horse, and
Clarabelle Cow in the stable out back.

They played hide-and-seek, laughing, in the bare whitewashed rooms, and made love on the naked planks of the bedroom floor.

It wasn't Ashland—or even the House on the Hill—but it was theirs.

Then Lincoln disappeared on the circuit again, leaving Mary to her own devices.

He made arrangements with the neighbor, Mr. Gurney, to do the heavy work of cutting kindling, hauling water from the well, and milking Clarabelle. He also wrote to his cousin Dennis Hanks, back in Coles County, Illinois, offering to house Dennis's young daughter Hetty so that the girl could come to Springfield and go to school. Mary welcomed this arrangement, in part because she felt so completely unable to cope with the physical toil of running even a small house un-aided, and in part remembering what little Lincoln had told her of his own childhood—the hopeless childhood of the uneducated dirt-farmer.

If it had been so for him—like the snaggle-haired silent backwoods children Mary remembered from the Lexington Court Days, ill-clothed and illiterate as puppies—how much worse was it for a girl, who couldn't even leave her family's house to strike out on her own?

Hetty Hanks stayed for nearly eighteen months. Looking back on that time later, Mary supposed that if she herself had been more used to the demands of housework, less terrified about money, less resentful of Lincoln's absences, she and Hetty might have gotten along better than they did. Indeed, as it was she often enjoyed the company of this tall, quiet, skinny girl—as if Hetty were the daughter Mary one day hoped to have.

Elizabeth—and particularly the sarcastic Ann, who was now living in the front bedroom of the House on the Hill and cutting her own swath through Springfield's bachelors— rolled their eyes when they encountered this gawky back-woods girl in Mary's kitchen, calling a chair a "cheer" or saying she had a "heap sight" of chores. But Mary made the girl welcome, bought dress-goods at Irwin's and helped her make new clothes, bought her the first pair of shoes she'd ever owned.

Those were on her better days. But Hetty's ideas of "working for her keep" were very different from Mary's, and, like her cousin, she had a tendency to disappear when she didn't like what was going on. She also had an appetite like an anaconda (though she never appeared to gain an ounce, reflected Mary ruefully). In weeks when Lincoln had been too forgiving about his fees—or simply hadn't bothered to collect them—the perpetual theft of eggs, bread, butter, and sausages made a difference, particularly when Hetty would share them with her friends.

Quarrels were inevitable, and grew worse, rather than better, over time. Every time Lincoln would take his young cousin's side ("She treats me like she thinks I'm one of her daddy's slaves!"), Mary felt furious and betrayed. To her mind Hetty was simply lazy, as Lincoln was lazy. When he was away riding the circuit, as he so often was, there was no one to arbitrate at all, and there were days of silent sulking and resentment that defeated her best efforts to understand.

On days when migraine closed in on her, when Hetty didn't return from school till nearly suppertime and the kitchen fires went out, when Bobby's crying sawed at her pounding head, she would picture Lincoln as she knew he must be, arguing in some sweltering little courtroom about defaulting debtors or absconding seducers or divorcing farm-couples. Pictured him later repairing to the local tavern to sit telling yarns and talking politics with judge, opposing counsel, most of the jury, and upon occasion the defendant as well, before everyone went upstairs to sleep three to a bed and eight to a room, snoring and scratching like bears in wintertime.

And she would hate him, and every man who lived that way and left their wives behind with their babies and their silent slow-moving second cousin from Indiana.

It was not an easy year for any of them. At times during that miserable year of 1845 Mary would wonder, with tired amazement, how she who had been the belle of Lexington and the toast of half the Illinois Legislature had ended up here in a four-room cabin in last year's faded dress, washing greasy dishes. When she realized in September that she was with child again, she wept.

That despair was a low point, for Hetty was fascinated by the prospect of a new baby, and did her work more cheerfully thereafter. By the time Lincoln came home, full of enthusiasm at the possibility that had been discussed among the Illinois Whigs to nominate him for Congress, Mary had regained her good humor, and had begun to make plans for the new child.

But her pregnancy was accompanied as the first had been by devastating migraines. And as she chased the now-mobile Bobby around the house and through the vegetable garden in the back and out into the mud-wallow of Jackson Street, she could not rid herself of the feeling of being overwhelmed by events which she ought to have been able to manage, but was not.

CHAPTER TWENTY-SIX

LINCOLN WAS OF LITTLE HELP TO HER AT THIS TIME. IN ADDI-
tion to riding the judicial circuit—he'd acquired a buggy to
do it in, now, instead of simply going horseback with a couple of saddlebags—he was working the political circuit, and
was gone most of the fall. The choice of Whig candidates for
Congress came down to himself and Edward Baker, the
cheerful little Englishman who had been one of Lincoln's
partners in defending the Trailor brothers for the murder of
the not-quite-dead Archibald Fisher.

That summer Baker was a frequent guest at the gatherings
of politicians that took place in the little parlor of the Eighth
Street house.

It was at such times that Mary was happiest: the mistress of
her own house, however small, and a hostess whose burnt-
sugar cake and intelligent conversation were not soon forgotten. Listening to the talk of the growing Democratic
strength, and the threats of war with Mexico, Mary felt that
she'd finally earned her chair around the stove—even if the
stove was her own hearth and not the one in Speed and Bell's
store or the *Sangamo Journal* offices.

From such discussions, and reading the newspapers, she
was often able to help Lincoln hone his speeches—he would
reword his thoughts a dozen times, and practice them on
her: "Are you sure you want your prose to sound that purple?" she sometimes asked. Or, "Do you think it will help
your cause to make a personal attack that way?" She recalled
the aborted duel with Jimmy Shields. By Lincoln's thoughtful expression, so did he.

In his political dealings, Lincoln never forgot a face or
mislaid a name, always remembered something to ask about

family or acquaintances. He never told a lie, but, lawyerlike, committed himself rarely to any specific course of action. He never made a promise that he was not prepared to keep.

Even when, in the discussions of rotating the Whig Congressional seat among the several leading Whig Party members, he facetiously offered to name his unborn child after Baker if Baker agreed to step aside in his favor, he surprised Mary by holding to that promise when Baker did, in fact, decline the nomination. "I thought you'd want to name your son after Joshua Speed," she said, that evening after their guests were gone and he was helping her and Hetty clear away the coffee-things and brush the tablecloths. "He is still your best friend, isn't he, even away in Kentucky?"

"He is, and I do," he replied. "No, you sit down," he added, as Mary started to follow him into the little kitchen, "you been on your feet all evening." Mary sat obediently, in the chair that Baker had occupied. She had worked hard to set a good table, knowing from her own upbringing how good hospitality invisibly smoothed the edges of politics. This was probably the last gathering at the house before she began to show her condition to the point that it would be improper for a lady to appear in public.

Vexing, she thought resignedly, but it couldn't be helped. Betsey's pushiness in joining the men's discussions while visibly pregnant had always annoyed her.

"A rose by any other name is going to smell just as sweet," he said, and put his arm around her shoulders. "If Baker steps aside and I name my boy Joshua, that'll tell the entire state, Lincoln doesn't keep his promises."

Mary glanced up at him with a sidelong grin. "And if Baker steps aside and I have a girl, what are you going to do then, Mr. Smart Politician?"

"Name her Edwina," said Lincoln promptly. "Or shoot myself."

After that evening, as Mary expected, there were no further political suppers, but she felt satisfied in a way she hadn't, approaching Bobby's birth. She had learned, at her fa-

ther's knee and at Henry Clay's elbow, the difference between a small-time politician and one whom state leaders
and legislators took seriously. Her instincts told her that
when she had met Lincoln, for all his brilliance he had been
perceived as a backwoodsman, not only by Ninian and
Elizabeth, but even by his friends. A man doesn't tell a man,
*Don't say "ain't got" and don't wipe your hands down your front
after a meal.* He only thinks, *What a hick!* And passes on, to
vote for a man who looks like he knows what he's doing.

Teaching Lincoln the finer points of table-manners was a
little like teaching Bobby (or Hetty)—only Lincoln understood why he needed them. "No one," Mary had told him
once, "is going to campaign on behalf of a man who eats
with his hands. Not for Congress, anyway."

At least Bobby didn't have thirty-five years of eating with
his hands to unlearn.

But after that evening, though he was in town for the
county court session, Lincoln was seldom at home. He
opened his own law firm as a senior partner that year, with,
of all people, the chinless Billy Herndon, who had previously
been a clerk in Speed's store. As migraines added to the fatigue of advanced pregnancy and the exhaustion of trying to
keep up with a very stubborn and active two-year-old, Mary
noticed that Lincoln spent more and more time at his law office, often working on late into the night. More often, she
suspected, yarning with Billy—who worshipped him with
an irritating possessiveness—or stopping by Irwin's store to
talk politics around the stove. Of course the house was small,
she thought resentfully. And of course he could have no
peace there, for reading or for thought.... Did he think *she*
had any peace? Or was able to settle down with a newspaper
or a book?

On Christmas Day there was a final, resounding quarrel
with Harriet—with Lincoln caught in the middle as usual—
and the girl returned to Coles County. Mary and Harriet
made up before her departure and both shed tears as Harriet

and Lincoln got on the stage, but Mary felt, along with loneliness and disappointment, relief that she was gone.

Living with Lincoln was difficult enough without the
complications of a growing young woman in the house.

Even when he was home, Lincoln frequently wasn't
home. His self-absorption when his mind was abstracted
with some thought was absolute. Mary could stand a foot
away from him and say, "Bring in the kindling," and he
wouldn't turn his head, would simply go on gazing into
space. Piecing together tomorrow's arguments for Court, or
assembling points for a speech to deliver in Petersburg next
week. When she wasn't tired out from cooking and cleaning,
and when her head didn't ache, Mary was in awe of the
amount of information her husband could deal with solely in
his head.

But half an hour later, when after three more requests the
kindling box was still empty, she'd go over and give his hair a
hard twist, and he'd look up at her in surprise, as if he'd just
realized he *had* a wife, let alone a house, a kitchen, an old-
fashioned hearth that was wretched to cook on (unlike
Elizabeth's new, modern iron stove), a kindling box, and a
son whom he was supposed to be watching and who was
nowhere in sight with darkness falling. . . .

There were times when Mary wondered if marriage to
Edwin Webb—or the handsome Nate Bodley and the demands of running Indian Branch plantation with a staff of
slaves—would not have been an easier way to live.

Then some night she'd be tangled back in her old nightmare, of hiding in the dark hallway of her father's old house
on Short Street, of hearing baby Georgie crying in the terrible stillness. The smell of blood and sickness, lamplight falling
suddenly through an opening door. Her heart would hammer and she'd fight to wake up, fight not to be there when
they carried her mother out of the room and away down the
pitch-black hall—*If I scream maybe I'll wake myself up.* . . .

But no scream would come, only whimpering moans that
echoed those from that other room in her dream. . . .

Then big gentle hands would shake her, and she'd roll over and clutch at those hard arms, that iron chest, and he'd rock her like a child, singing some old mountain ballad under his breath until she slept.

EDDIE'S BIRTH PASSED ALMOST UNNOTICED IN THE DOUBLE IN-tensity of the Supreme Court sessions and the beginnings of a campaign for the Congressional Session of 1847, over a year hence. This time in addition to the midwife, Frances's husband, Dr. Wallace, attended, and both Frances and Elizabeth were there. (Ann was at a taffy-pull at Julia Jayne Trumbull's.) While Mary rested, panting, between bouts of pain, Elizabeth came in with a cup of hot tea for her, aproned and pink-faced from the heat of the hearth, a shirtsleeved Lincoln at her heels. In spite of her pain Mary had to smile, wondering how the two of them got along, sharing work in that tiny kitchen. Afterwards Lincoln came in, holding Bobby by the hand, a tubby little boy of two and a half with that revolting, inward-turning blue eye.

"There, you see?" Lincoln told the child softly. "Your mother's just fine. And now you got a little brother to play with."

Bobby only looked doubtful, and reaching over Mary's sheltering arm, gave the tiny red bundle a sharp poke—which resulted in a most gratifying yowl. Bobby looked startled, but pleased.

As soon as Mary was on her feet again, and not in the same room with Eddie's cradle and Bobby's little bed, Bobby repeated the experiment whenever he could, prodding his brother out of sound sleep for the pleasure of hearing the noise. Of course, by this time Lincoln was on the road again, meeting with the Whig leaders in Jacksonville. Mary tried reasoning with her elder son, but finally dealt with the situation by giving him a sharp slap the next time she was brought from the kitchen by Eddie's wails. It solved the Bobby-poking-Eddie problem—Bobby never did it again and indeed quickly came to feel protective of his brother—but thereafter Bobby developed the habit of simply disappearing.

She would be sweeping the floor—an endless task, in a town that was perpetually either fogged with dust or drowned in mud—or peeling potatoes in the kitchen, then suddenly turn in panic, realizing she hadn't heard the scurry of his steps since . . . when? "Bobby's run away!" she would cry, and pelt through the kitchen door, looking around the vegetable garden, the laundry shed, Clarabelle's stable. Jackson Street was often filled with wagons and horses, coming and going to the new construction of houses, offices downtown, the new church on Third Street. The thought of that sturdy little boy running into the muddy road, being struck, being carried home dead by strangers, sent her rushing into the yard. "Bobby will die! Bobby will die!"

She couldn't explain this fear, not even to Lincoln, any more than she could explain why thunderstorms turned her weak and sobbing. When Lincoln was in town she'd send whichever hired girl was working for them that week flying down to the law offices to fetch him. When he wasn't, she'd run next door and enlist young Jimmy Gurney in the search, and send out the hired girl, too. She lived in dread that she would be too late. That strangers would come to her and tell her that her son was dead, through her neglect. The son with whom she was never quite comfortable, whose deformed eye filled her with the double guilt of both responsibility and revulsion.

Hetty's presence at least had given Mary the illusion that she had "help," though she suspected her covert conflict with the girl hadn't helped Bobby's wary secretiveness any. Hetty's departure put Mary in the same position as every other woman in town she knew with the exception of Elizabeth: Frances, Julia Trumbull, Bessie, Merce Conkling, and all the rest were in constant quest for Irish or Portuguese girls who were willing to work and could be trusted not to steal silverware or entertain their boyfriends on the premises the moment their mistress's back was turned.

Yes, slavery was wrong, Mary reflected. Cash Clay, and Mr. Garrison of *The Liberator*, and the other abolitionists were correct when they said that the ownership of slaves destroyed the souls of the masters and eroded society from top to bottom....

But obviously neither Cash nor Mr. Garrison had ever tried to find someone willing to help with the cleaning for a price that wasn't extortionate.

It was all very well for Elizabeth to look down her nose and make remarks like, "Oh, you haven't yet begun your spring-cleaning?" in a voice that implied that anyone who hadn't finished spring-cleaning by mid-April was an irredeemable slattern. Elizabeth's husband was rich, Elizabeth had three house servants and a coachman, and Elizabeth wasn't laid up for three days at a time with migraines. At times Mary looked back on her days as a belle in Lexington, and on those gay excursions with Stephen Douglas and James Gillespie and little cock-a-hoop Jimmy Shields—looked back on herself, in her gowns of pink silk and rose-colored velvet ribbons—and wondered who that was that she was looking at, and what had become of that girl.

Wondered what had ever possessed her to marry a man who was poor and in debt.

Except that she could imagine living with no one else. On those rare occasions—*extremely* rare, that summer of 1846—that she *did* live with him, she reflected wryly, or have more of him than his name on the nameplate of the front door.

And then suddenly it was September, and Lincoln was striding through the brown leaves of the kitchen walk calling out, "Molly! Molly!" to bring her to the door in her apron. "We're elected! It's official! I'm junior Congressman for Illinois and we're going to Washington!"

CHAPTER TWENTY-SEVEN

✥

To Mary's intense gratitude, the Congressional term to which Lincoln was elected wouldn't start until December of 1847. She couldn't imagine trying to travel with an infant and a boy of three. "Are you sure you want to come?" asked Lincoln, once Mary's first spate of triumph, plans, and delight had run itself down. The current hired girl, Bridget, had joined them in the kitchen, leaning on her broom and beaming in vicarious delight. Bobby sat on Lincoln's knee, Mary being in occupation of most of his lap.

"Are you ashamed to be seen with a wife in tow, Mr. *Congressman*?"

"One so pretty, and dressed so fine as you? Never." He kissed her, something that always made Mary blush, for she had seldom seen Ninian kiss Elizabeth or her father kiss Betsey. It was one of the things Elizabeth considered ill-bred about her gangly, unwanted brother-in-law. "But we'll be living in a boardinghouse. Most Congressmen do."

"And what of that?" asked Mary. And, seeing a world of remembrances about Mrs. Beck in the lift of his brows, she added, "Pish, I was just a girl then, and didn't know how to go on. I hope I've learned a little more about the world by this time." She tousled Bobby's blond hair and kissed him, and leaned up to kiss her husband's hollow cheek. "To be able to attend Washington parties, to mingle with the makers of our country's law and policies, I daresay I could be happy living in a tent."

"And that's one in the eye for Mrs. Edwards," added Bridget—which of course had been the first thing Mary had thought, though she hadn't said it.

It seemed like there was so much to do, in the next year!

Winter and spring, and a blazing-hot summer that seemed never-ending...She went shopping at Irwin's with Julia Trumbull and tall Cousin Lizzie—now Lizzie Grimsley, where *did* the time go?—and the three of them spent happy weeks studying *Godey's* and sewing and furbishing up dresses that would be fit for Washington parties.

That spring of 1847 the newspapers were filled with the war with Mexico, whose bellicose President Santa Anna had begun arming the moment the Republic of Texas applied for inclusion in the United States. Fighting broke out in April across the whole northern segment of Mexico that Congress had been trying to acquire by negotiation for years. The United States claimed the Mexicans had crossed the border to attack. Torchlight rallies were held. Militia companies formed overnight and rushed toward the Rio Grande. Southern slaveholders and land speculators pricked their ears at the prospect of new cotton lands to replace the worn-out soil of Alabama and the Carolinas.

One minute it seemed like forever until the Lincolns' projected departure, and the next, they were packing to leave. Lincoln found a renter for the house, and spent all of one October day moving their furniture up into the north-ernmost of the little slant-roofed attic rooms while Bobby did his best to get underfoot on the narrow attic stair and kill them both.

Then they were all getting on the stagecoach, under gray autumn skies.

Despite the proud dome of the sandstone State House, Springfield looked very small across the golden swell of the prairie.

At Scott's Hotel in St. Louis they were met by Joshua Speed, plumper now with the first flecks of gray in his beard, but with the same cheerful sparkle in his eye. "What's this I hear about you naming *my* namesake after some pettifogging politico, Lincoln?" The two men embraced, and Mary shook hands with the sweet-faced, dark-haired lady introduced to her as Fanny Speed.

"Now, I won't have you raking poor Mr. Lincoln down," said Mrs. Speed. "Your husband is a brave man, Mrs. Lincoln. When Joshua was courting me, Mr. Lincoln pretended to be a Democrat, so that my father could lecture him on the evils of his party while Joshua spoke to me on the gallery. I doubt that even David did that for Jonathan in Bible times."

"David would have thought King Saul heaving spears at him was a good trade, after ten minutes with your pa," grinned Lincoln, and Mrs. Speed tapped him on the elbow with her fan.

"Oh, the little darling!" Mrs. Speed added, tiptoeing to look at Eddie, whom Lincoln was carrying on one hip. The boy was, at nineteen months, solemn and long-faced and worrisomely thin, and looked for all the world like a miniature version of Granny Parker, except for his gray Lincoln eyes. Bobby, with his round face and watchful blue gaze, cock-eyed as it was, was all Todd. And for that matter, thought Mary suddenly, panic clutching her, where was Bobby...?

She caught him just before he got out the hotel door and into the street. The traffic and bustle in St. Louis made Springfield look like a country village. The town was a river port, and the jumping-off point for the trading caravans that crossed the prairies and the Great American Desert to the Spanish colonies around Santa Fe.

Now with the Army to be supplied and militia companies streaming south, St. Louis jostled with merchants, bull-whackers, boatmen, and traders, in spite of the hardship of winter travel. In the crowded hotel dining-room Mary could barely make herself heard above the din as she gossiped with Fanny Speed over mutual acquaintances and kin all over Kentucky and Virginia. As for Lincoln and Joshua, immersed in discussion of the war, it was as if neither of their wives existed.

For some years, Mary knew, the two men's friendship had cooled—because of Joshua's management of his mother's plantation, she guessed, which put him in the position of owning and working slaves.

For all that Lincoln upheld the law of the land that permitted slavery to exist, on a personal level he both hated and feared it. She felt a pang of jealousy, watching them together now. Seeing there a past that she could never share.

From St. Louis all six of them took the steamboat to Louisville, and from there the Lincolns proceeded on to Frankfort. It required the efforts of all four adults to keep Bobby from coming to some kind of grief on the boat. The four-year-old proved just as prone to wandering on a boat of two hundred feet by forty as he had with all of Springfield to choose from, and Mary lived in constant terror of seeing him pitch himself over the rail of the high hurricane deck into the deadly swift currents of the river. Just above Cairo Bobby did disappear, and while Mary and Fanny Speed searched frantically among the boxes, bales, and crates of New Orleans merchandise on the fore-part of the lowest deck, Lincoln walked to the back along the promenades that ran along the sides of the boat, where coffles of slaves were chained, to be sold in Louisville.

Mary came hurrying aft with the news that she hadn't found a trace of Bobby, she was certain he'd gone overboard, to find her husband sitting on a keg of nails, their errant son at his side, talking to one of the chained blacks: ". . . couldn't take my eyes off the boat engines, even when we was flat-boatin' and these things was the enemy an' the invention of the Devil."

"They still is, sir," agreed the slave equably. "We crunched up a flatboat in the fog not ten miles below Vicksburg—why don't they never hang lights on them things? Fog was so thick the pilot couldn't see the river below him. . . ."

"Ain't that just like a pilot, to keep goin' in a blind fog?"

"You ever get crunched by a steamboat, Pa? Father," Bobby corrected himself hastily, seeing Mary approach.

"Lord, yes! I thought I'd drown, stayin' under till the paddle went by overhead. . . . Mother," Lincoln added, turning to her with a smile. "I found the rascal just where I thought he'd be."

"I just wanted to see the wheel," explained Bobby.

"You just wanted to get yourself killed leanin' over that rail, li'l Marse," corrected the slave. "*And* give your poor Ma a conniption-fit. He's fine, ma'am," he added. Bobby was covered head to foot with splashed-up river-water and the soot of engine-smuts. "We kept him back off the rail."

Mary gave each member of the coffle a quarter, for whatever small luxuries might be bought in Louisville, and hauled the protesting Bobby back to the higher decks of the boat. But that night when she waked in their little stateroom in the rear of the boiler-deck to hear the muffled singing of the men chained below, she saw the moonlight shining in her husband's open, listening eyes.

THEY WERE FIVE DAYS TRAVELING UP THE OHIO RIVER TO Carrollton, where the Kentucky River flowed down from the dense green forest, and another day and a half going up the Kentucky to Frankfort. From the upper deck of the smaller stern-wheeler on that leg of the journey Mary watched the scenery transform itself into home: the gray rock of the banks becoming more jagged and fantastic, the trees darker and thicker than any Illinois woodland. This was The Dark and Bloody Ground, the violent land that the Todds had settled in the wake of the Revolution in the East, worlds distant from the clean-smelling grassy spaces of Illinois.

The land where she had flirted, and danced, and been hailed as the belle of Lexington.

The land she had fled eight years ago.

The land in which she still walked, most nights when she dreamed.

When Pendleton opened the door to the front hall of the big house on Main Street, Mary cried, "Pendleton!" and clasped the servant's hands, almost before she saw the rest of the family. She led Lincoln in, keeping a firm grip on

Bobby's hand while Lincoln carried Eddie: The boys had nearly exhausted themselves running up and down the corridor of the train from Frankfort, and Mary, her head aching from the jolting and the noise of the train, was a little surprised that several of the passengers hadn't hurled the two obstreperous children out the windows.

And there they all were on the stairs, looking so changed. Her father coming down toward her, grayer even than he'd been four years ago. "Molly," he smiled, and bent gravely to take Bobby's hand. Mary braced herself, cringing, lest her father or Betsey draw back from Bobby's defective eye, but Robert Todd said only, "Well, now, sir, you've grown some since last I saw you. And got yourself a brother now, too, I see."

The others on the stair pushed forward. Betsey, so thin she looked like she'd break if she tripped, but still with that chill precise air: "What filthy things trains are, to be sure." She scrubbed at a smut of soot on Eddie's cheek, as if Mary should have been able to keep the boys clean on a conveyance that belched coal-smoke and churned dust with every yard it traveled.

Granny Parker, blue eyes still sharp though her hair was snow-white now: "Let the girl be, Betsey! You should have seen yourself last month when you came home on that thing from Frankfort!" Good heavens, was that stocky man with the receding hairline and red-veined nose *Levi*? And the shifty-eyed sallow malcontent beside him—smelling faintly of corn liquor—that couldn't be *George*?

They had to be, because the two young gentlemen of the ages Levi and George *ought* to have been—*were* still, in Mary's recollections—must be Sam and David, David, whose crying had nearly driven Mary crazy that horrible cholera summer of 1833. And the others were children she felt she'd never seen before: a coolly self-possessed girl of fifteen (not *Margaret,* surely!), a plump, vivacious girl a few years younger *(Mattie?!?),* a beautiful blond boy of nine who couldn't be anyone but Alec, Alec who'd been born while Mary was teaching at Ward's. . . .

"So you're my little sister?" asked Lincoln, looking down at the pretty golden-haired eleven-year-old who was the only one of them to come to him instead of hanging back.

Mary cried in delight, "Emilie!" and seized the little girl's hand as Lincoln picked Emilie up as easily as he'd have picked up a kitten, and gave her a kiss on the cheek. For years now Emilie had written to Mary—not often, but frequently and candidly enough to let Mary know that the child she'd taught her first samplers still remembered her with love.

The littler ones—Alec, Elodie, and Katherine—crowded around their tall new relative, clamoring to be picked up also and making the acquaintance of their rather overwhelmed small cousins, both of whom clung to their father's legs.

"That's going to be your President of the United States, is it?" Granny Parker folded her skinny arms beneath her shawl and stood beside Mary.

"He is," agreed Mary, a little defensively: Granny Parker had always been unpredictable.

"Not much to look at."

"On the contrary," replied Mary, "I think he's grand."

A door opened behind her. Warmth and familiar scents from the big kitchen enveloped Mary in a tide of the past so powerful that it brought tears. Even before she turned she knew who stood there, her smiling face more wrinkled than ever but her eyes as wise. "Mammy Sally!" Mary cried, and flung herself into the old woman's arms. "Oh, Mammy, I missed you! I missed you all!"

"Well, don't weep about it, child," said Granny Parker, both amusement and impatience in her voice.

"No need to weep, child," added Mammy Sally kindly. "You're home now."

YEARS BEFORE, WHEN LINCOLN HAD RETREATED IN EXHAUS-tion to Speed's plantation, Mary had pictured him in her home state, seeing close up for himself the conditions that so many Yankees fulminated against in self-righteous ignorance. In the three weeks they spent in the big front bedroom of her father's house that November, she had a chance at last to act as her husband's guide as he further explored the world of the South, this ambiguous double world of white and black.

Being Lincoln, of course, he would talk to anyone and listen to anyone, without the slightest sign that he even noticed whether they were white or black, male or female—he and Cash Clay were the only men she'd met in her life who had ever suggested that women as well as men ought to have the vote. She noticed that the house servants, who could be the sternest critics of "white trash" manners and pretensions, accepted him immediately—and not, she was sure, because he was a Congressman. They'd seen Congressmen before, and thought fairly poorly of some. One morning, waking early, Mary came downstairs and found Lincoln having breakfast in the kitchen, talking to Mammy Sally and Nelson. "You watch out for that one, sir," she heard Nelson's voice as she crossed the shadowy dining-room. "She get mad at Mammy Sally once, she put salt in her coffee—"

"Now, I can't *believe* my Molly would do a terrible thing like *that!*" gasped Lincoln, in such exaggerated shock that both servants burst into the good-humored laughter of those—Mary reflected with wry affection—who knew her all too well.

Then she heard Mammy Sally say, more quietly, "She look happy, Mr. Lincoln. I always knew she'd need a strong man to take care of her; you're good for her."

Elizabeth might have her doubts about what was due a Todd of Lexington, Mary reflected, her heart warmed by joy. But it was wise Mammy Sally who saw more clearly what Mary needed.

It was good to know.

On the second night of their stay, Robert Todd held a party in their honor, and in the midst of flirting with old beaux (Nate Bodley had grown sadly stout and reeked of liquor) and catching up news from girlfriends (Mary

Wickliffe had married the brother of Meg's husband, of all things), Mary glanced across the crowded room and saw Lincoln as usual in a knot of men, local politicians—listening with the air of a man who seeks to comprehend the place in which he finds himself.

He always listened more than he talked. She had heard him described as a jokester and a talker, but in fact he was more an observer. It was only that, when he talked, people remembered the tales and jests he told. She was intensely sorry Cash Clay was away—Cash had been among the first to volunteer, Meg Wickliffe (now Preston) had written her, and had gone with General Zachary Taylor to invade Mexico. He had been captured in January; "We just heard he's been freed," Meg now informed her breathlessly. Even without Cash's assistance, Lincoln and Robert Todd were engrossed in conversation hours after Betsey had gone yawning up to bed and the servants had cleaned up after the rest of the long-departed guests.

"I don't think you'll find a man in this country who'd argue that with Oregon settling up, we shouldn't have the rest of New Mexico as well," her father said. "Mexico can't hold the harbors of the California coast, for instance, and if we don't take them you know it's only a matter of time before Russia does."

After making sure Bobby and Eddie were tucked up in the trundle-bed in the corner of the guest-room, Mary crept silently back downstairs. The rear parlor was dim but for a single lamp, its amber light outlining her father's blunt features, Lincoln's long nose and jaw.

"I s'pose the average highway robber would make the same point about the contents of your pockets—that he's got a better use for 'em, an' if he don't take 'em the feller down the road will." Movement in the darker shadows of the front parlor, where Pendleton was loading the last of the abandoned punch-cups onto a tray. "But that aside, my question is: will the slaveholders in Congress try to make New

Mexico into slave territories? An' then admit 'em as slave states?"

Robert Todd laughed. "We haven't even taken those places yet, Lincoln, and here you're worrying about what their status as *states* will be?"

"I am, yes. That's a flaw of my character. Because as long as slavery has a legal foothold in this country, it's gonna be like an alligator in your bathtub: every time you turn around, there the blame thing is. And the more I look at the problem, the more it seems to me that it's beyond my ability to come up with *any* solution that won't cause more damage than it remedies."

Mary slipped through the door, and settled on the black horsehair sofa, content to simply listen to the talk of these men that she loved. Lincoln was smiling, cracking his knuckles, his eyes very bright. In the forgiving warmth of the lamplight, her father's face shed years; it was as she remembered it from her childhood.

She was, again, her father's favored child, listening to the talk as she'd always listened, included in that circle of friendship and power.

If there was greater contentment in life, she couldn't imagine what it might be.

THREE WEEKS OF PEACE. THREE WEEKS OF BEING ABLE TO LIE abed with her husband in the mornings, secure in the knowledge that Mammy Sally was looking after Eddie and that Bobby had been absorbed into the flock of younger Todds, playing noisily in the wide garden with Alec and Elodie, Mattie and Kitty. On the first day of their stay, she and Betsey had taken the children aside and ordered them on pain of death not to tease Bobby about his eye, and so far the threat seemed to be working. And even if Bobby ran away, Jane or Judy would find him, not she.

Three weeks of Chaney's marvelous cooking, of rides in the countryside with her father and her husband. Of watching Lincoln's utter bliss in browsing through her father's library and reading everything he could lay hands on, far into the night. Three weeks of listening avidly to talk of the war and the upcoming session of Congress. Of seeing the men of the district encounter Lincoln without the memory of the uncertain hick who had first come to Springfield in buckskin britches shrunken halfway up his shins. Here, he was, instead, a man who had been elected by the voters of his state.

A man who would one day have power.

And their approval shone back onto her, who had seen this man's promise and married him, when nearly everyone else had turned away.

They went to hear Henry Clay speak, first in the courtroom, then in the town's brick market-house while the rain pounded down outside. Thin and brittle-looking now, his hands stiff with arthritis, Clay blazed with his old intelligent fire as he denounced the war with Mexico, which had already claimed the life of his oldest son. Afterwards Mary fulfilled one of her deepest dreams by introducing Lincoln to Clay, beside the rough temporary stage that had been erected at one end of the hall. She flashed her old flirtatious smile at the statesman who had been like a second father to her: "And I promise you, Mr. Clay, he will be President one day. Though I'm still waiting for that invitation to *your* inaugural ball."

Clay laughed, "It may happen yet, Miss," and shook one long finger at her. His ginger hair was snowy now and this made his eyes seem pale as the wintry sky. He glanced across at Lincoln—there was not much difference in their heights. "I'm running for the Senate again this year—drives me crazy to see others making a mess of things up there."

"I'll try to keep things from going all to hell, sir," promised Lincoln, a little shyly, "till you arrive."

They took the stage to Winchester, Virginia, and from there the railroad to Washington City. They arrived late—the December night was bitterly cold and drizzly, the streets outside the depot swamps that rivaled the worst of

Springfield's hog-wallows. Lincoln found porters for their four trunks, free blacks or, Mary guessed, slaves "working out" and bringing their owner part of whatever they earned for the day. As they walked down the dark street toward Brown's Hotel—recommended by Lincoln's legal colleague Judge David Davis—Lincoln gazed around him, as if sniffing the air in this, the largest city he'd seen in his life.

Far down one street the dark bulk of the Capitol loomed, lost in a maze of scaffolding. Brick houses stood among trees, some of them mellowed and elegant with years. Here and there newer buildings, taller and bulkier, shouldered each other in modern blocks. The streets were extravagantly wide, and gold lights shone in a few windows, blurred with mist.

"So this is Washington," said Lincoln softly. He carried both his sons, Eddie on his arm as easily as if the boy had been a parcel and Bobby on his shoulders, looking out wearily over his tall black hat. Both boys, after darting crazily up and down the aisle of the train car all day as was their wont, had suddenly crumpled with exhaustion, and Eddie was snoring softly in the circle of his father's arm.

Mary drew a deep breath, trembling all over with excitement, anticipation, triumph. "Yes," she said, and her breath misted amber in the lights of the hotel as they approached its doors. "We're finally here."

Chapter Twenty-eight

Washington 1848

THEY REMAINED ONE NIGHT IN BROWN'S HOTEL. THE following morning Lincoln went out and found them quarters at Mrs. Ann Spriggs's boardinghouse on First Street, just down the hill behind the Capitol, where both Cousin John Stuart and E. D. Baker had stayed.

And Mary remembered all over again why—and how much—she loathed boardinghouses.

She had met already Mr. Washburne, Lincoln's plump and pink-faced Congressional colleague from Galena. The first night at Mrs. Spriggs's, Mary could see the two men making a great effort to keep the conversation general at the common-table, before vanishing into the parlor to the more serious endeavor of hashing through what kind of political horse-trading each had had to do to get here, and comparing impressions of just how the land lay in the House of Representatives. Mary longed to join them as she'd joined Lincoln and her father but here there was no Mammy Sally to make sure Eddie was tucked up warmly and to keep Bobby in his bed. By the time overexcited Bobby was finally asleep—he wanted both a song and a story—it was quite late. Slipping down the stairs, she found Lincoln and Washburne still beside the parlor stove, with an elderly, ascetic gentleman who'd been introduced to her as Mr. Joshua Giddings—a name she recognized instantly from the abolitionist papers that Cash still sent her.

"You'll find within a day how it is in this city, sir," Giddings was saying, jabbing a skinny finger at Lincoln. "Slave pens within a hundred yards of the Capitol Building. Aside from the sheer disgrace of it, the traffic in Washington City represents a constant danger to every free man and woman of color who tries to go about their business here, for the slave-dealers do not scruple to kidnap men and women of color on these very streets, drug them with opium, and sell them south to Virginia and Georgia under the name of law. How anyone can hesitate to take a stand against such doings . . ."

"It all depends on what kind of stand you're fixing to take," replied Lincoln in his slow, light tenor. "I'll do my utmost to bring about whatever change in the law will mitigate the situation, but I can no more oppose the Constitution as it stands, than I can plead in court that my client should be permitted to break a law which I—or he—privately considers to be unjust."

Giddings's pale eyes glinted behind their spectacles, but for a moment he said nothing. Cash, Mary reflected, would have been on his feet and shouting.

"If nothing else," put in Washburne, "God help any man hopeful of being elected to anything who says the blacks should be freed. There are few enough jobs for white men in Illinois. You speak to any laborer on the street in Galena and he'll tell you there are too many Portuguese and Irish and Italians coming in as it is. And that in Illinois, let alone what it's like in New York. It wasn't more than a dozen years ago they were burning colored orphanages and beating free Negroes to death in the streets. They won't stand for it, sir— and a man who doesn't get elected loses his chance to do any good whatsoever for anyone."

"That reminds me of a story," remarked Lincoln, stretching out his long legs to the stove—which barely provided enough heat to encompass the three sitting near it, much less Mary in the darkness of the stairway arch, with her shawl of pink cashmere wrapped around her shoulders. "You ever hear about the Continental soldier after the Battle of Bunker Hill who scouted on ahead to the British lines? First he put on a red coat, so the British wouldn't shoot him, then he picked up a British musket, because it would shoot straighter than his own old piece, then he put on a pair of British boots so the British pickets wouldn't identify him by his old moccasins, and then a powdered wig for the same reason. . . . He ended up looking so much like a redcoat that he was finally obliged to shoot himself."

Listening to him—watching his exaggerated gestures, the way his face changed to the voice of this character or that, Mary had to smile. They would love him here in Washington. This was his place . . . and she would be here at his side.

From upstairs, Bobby's voice called out fretfully, "Mama!"

Elsewhere in the house another voice replied, "Can't someone shut that brat up?"

Mary tore herself away from the glow of the fire, the three men's faces, the laughter and the talk, and hastily ascended the stair to her child.

She got Bobby settled—the room was freezing cold, and Eddie was coughing—and then got into her nightdress behind the dressing-screen, brushed out her hair, and got into bed. She fell asleep still waiting for Lincoln to come upstairs.

LIVING IN WASHINGTON, EVEN IN A BOARDINGHOUSE, HAD ITS compensations. Their first Friday evening in the city, Lincoln bribed Mrs. Spriggs to look after Bobby and Eddie, and took Mary to a "drawing room" at the White House. The hack let them off some distance down Pennsylvania Avenue due to the crush of other hacks and polished town-carriages, all vying for position in the black sea of mud. Picking their way along the edge of the unpaved street through the raw mists under the shelter of her husband's big black umbrella ("And you *will* fold that thing up before we reach the steps. . . . What a sight we'll present to the President, coming up like a . . . a greengrocer and his wife . . . !") Mary saw its windows glowing through the darkness, and it seemed to her that her heart turned over in her breast.

The Executive Mansion.

We will live there. I know it.

Her grip tightened hard on the bony arm linked through

hers and wild excitement shivered through her like a flame. In a way, she knew they were coming home.

"Whatever you say, Mother," Lincoln agreed, in his most placid bumpkin style, but she could tell that he was as excited as she. She glanced up at his face, saw the light in his eyes as he looked at the place, the hard eager folds at the corners of his mouth. He didn't speak much of his ambition—he didn't speak much, Mary knew, of anything that mattered deeply to him. But since they'd left Springfield under its gray prairie skies five weeks ago, she'd felt in his flesh and his bones and his breath the vibration of his exultation.

He was, at last, coming into the place where he could make some difference in the lives of men. Where he could use his abilities, and be recognized and heard.

And she was by his side, his partner before all the world.

She made a mental note to write Elizabeth all about "our evening at the Executive Mansion," "our conversation with Mr. Polk," even if Polk *was* a Democrat. That should teach her to call Mary's husband a hayseed.

The doors of the mansion stood open. Voices poured out, into the raw winter air.

The gathering, Mary realized with a pang of disappointment as they stepped into the lamp-lit hall, was not a select one. It seemed like everyone in Washington was there.

An endless reception line snaked from the front hall into the Red Parlor, where the diminutive President Polk and his dark-eyed imperious wife stood side by side, shaking hands with all comers. Mr. Polk smiled and nodded and spoke a few words of greeting to "our new colleague from Illinois," but passed on immediately to greet Mr. Washburne, in line behind them. Mrs. Polk expressed a polite hope that Mary was finding residence in the capital comfortable, while coolly evaluating: dress, hair, deportment, toilette, and jewelry in a single all-appraising glance. Ticked off on a mental list, filed for future reference, and the page turned. Mary wasn't even given a chance to say whether she was finding residence in the capital comfortable or not.

I'd like to see you try to put yourself together for a reception in a boardinghouse room with two boys underfoot and no one but your husband to lace you up, Mary reflected, looking back at the elegant, slim woman already exchanging affectionate greetings with a quiet-voiced Virginia lady, scion of one of the local planter families and—from the way everyone greeted her— hostess to half the government. Mary picked out the expensive sheen of Italian silk in the golden warmth of the chandelier, fabric unobtainable in Springfield, the tulle light as summer breath. The swagged double skirts made her own tiers of ruffles appear slightly dowdy and very much a remnant of last year or the year before.

Little Stephen Douglas came over to her, dandified as ever, and joked about old times. But he was drawn quickly back into the circles of the Southern Senators, whose wives all seemed to be cousins or schoolmates and have little interest in Illinois Whigs. Douglas had recently married the daughter of a North Carolina planter, and seemed to have been taken in as a brother by every slaveholding Democrat in Washington, she reflected.

Mary recognized at once who the influential hostesses were, around whom the men clustered; the talk was of politics, but politics as a closed club of who knew whom. The wives of the powerful Southern Senators, or of local bankers and landholders, had their townhouses here and could entertain such birds-of-passage as mere members of the House. They greeted Mary politely—when they noticed her at all— but spoke of politics in the context of long-standing personal alliances: who could be trusted and who could not, who was on the outside and who was on the in, and who was discreetly keeping a mistress in some little rented cottage in Alexandria across the river.

Five years of marriage had accustomed Mary—almost— to no longer being the belle of the ball, but in Springfield at least she was more and more being recognized as Abraham Lincoln's wife.

Here, no one seemed particularly to care what things were like in Illinois, or who her husband was.

Behind her, as she moved away from one chatty group in quest of her husband—who as the tallest man in the room wasn't hard to locate—Mary heard someone say, "Oh, she's from the West." She didn't know whether it was she whom the speaker meant or not.

In the chilly winter months that followed, she attended five more Friday "drawing rooms" at the Executive Mansion, and seldom spoke to a soul.

Dutifully, the day the family moved to Mrs. Spriggs's, Mary had gone to a printer's and had new cards made up: *Mrs. Abraham Lincoln*—gilt-embossed in the most handsome Germanic black-letter—and smaller ones with just *Abraham Lincoln*. She'd been warned by Cousin John's wife that Washington printers cost three times what Simeon Francis charged and were slow to boot, but there was no getting around them. With the most furious haggling Mary could do, she could not get any of the three printers she consulted to lower the cost by so much as ten cents on the hundred, and the dent they made in her monthly budget was painfully large.

When first Mary had married him, Lincoln had joked about morning-calls and visiting-cards as the flub-dubs of the rich, on par with President Van Buren's notorious golden spoons. He'd changed his tune, however, when Mary had started making morning-calls on the wives of those politicians who came to Springfield for the Legislative sessions, and the dinner parties she'd organized had smoothed the rough edges of acquaintanceship among men of power from different parts of the state.

He himself had commented—a little to his surprise—on how much difference it made, trying to talk a man into throwing his support to a road-building appropriation, whether you talked to him in a tavern's common-room or in your own comfortable parlor after a good dinner.

Leaving cards was another way of cementing ties—of

marking yourself as someone to be taken seriously by people of wealth and power.

Thus, by the time they reached Washington, Lincoln was willing to do what all Congressmen did: spend an hour or two between breakfast and the start of the Congressional sessions at eleven, two or three days a week, in attendance on Mary as she made the rounds of the homes of Washington's elite, leaving a trail of cards in their wake. Two of Mr. Lincoln's (for Senator Useful and Mrs. Useful) and one of Mary's (for Mrs. Useful—God forbid even the implication that a lady should call upon a man!), with a corner folded down to indicate that Mrs. Lincoln had called in person. Mary deeply enjoyed this ritual, whether Lincoln accompanied her or not. If the hostess was "at home," it was a way of learning news and rumor, of getting the name Lincoln known, and of talking—if she was lucky—of something other than servants and children for fifteen minutes.

Many Congressmen made calls on Sundays as well, but Lincoln drew the line at that, preferring to take the boys down to the steamboat wharves on the Potomac while Mary attended St. John's Episcopal Church, or to take his sons to look at the ragged mudholes and heaped masonry where contractors were preparing to rear a granite obelisk as a monument to George Washington. As the winter advanced these outings became less possible. Washington was cold with a damp, clinging chill entirely foreign to the hard iciness of the Illinois prairies or Lexington's upland frosts. Few streets in the city were paved, and like Springfield's humbler ways, the vast and splendidly named avenues of the capital turned from aisles of dust to rivers of mud.

Now and then Mary would be invited to the handsome house Stephen Douglas and his wife had taken—with his father-in-law's money, she suspected—but few Washington ladies returned Mary's calls. It didn't seem to matter that so many of them—including the doyenne of them all, Dolley Madison—were connected in one way or another with the Parker/Todd clan. Mary left cards on everyone, from Mrs.

Polk and the wife of the wealthy banker William Corcoran, on down to the Congressional wives in other boarding-houses. Although she knew that, naturally, one's own scope for entertaining in a boardinghouse parlor was sorely limited, she expected invitations, or at least the courtesy of returned visits.

But everyone seemed to be so busy laying cards on the ta-bles of the great themselves that there was no time to so much as drive by—or send a servant by—Mrs. Spriggs's. Those who did visit, she gathered almost at once, were the wives of junior Congressmen, like herself, without power or influence. It would not do to be seen too often with them.

And indeed, with Bobby and Eddie to look after most days—and most nights, while Lincoln was out in informal after-session colloquies with his male colleagues in eating-houses, taverns, or other boardinghouse "messes," as they were called—Mary would have been hard-pressed to re-spond to an invitation from even Dolley Madison herself. She'd see the famous hostesses drive by in their carriages on the icy streets, or in the Capitol rotunda on those days when she could bribe Ann Spriggs to look after the boys so she could sit in the galleries with the most astonishing mélange of Congressional wives, town prostitutes, men-about-town, and what appeared to be half the colored population of Washington, slave and free, to listen to the debates. Like every other Congressional wife, Mary learned to recognize Dolley Madison, in her stylish gowns with her paint and powder fighting a rear-guard action against the years, or her queenly young niece Adele Cutts; heard the admiring whis-pers as people pointed out the Blair ladies—almost royalty in Maryland—or William Corcoran's wife Hannah.

Mary thoroughly enjoyed those rare visits to the Capitol itself, its lobby like a fair with journalists, spectators, *nymphes du pavé*, hawkers of hothouse oranges, and candidates for government pensions or government jobs lying in wait to ambush their Congressman the moment he put his head out the Chamber door. The United States had captured Mexico

City, and terms of peace were being wrangled. Already abolitionists like Giddings were beginning to protest that slavery
must not be allowed to spread. The atmosphere of power, influence, and rumor that tingled in the hallways and galleries
filled her with delight and a sense of her own importance,
and she reveled in writing knowingly to Elizabeth and
Ninian, *They're all saying at the Capitol* . . .

One of her greatest triumphs was the evening when
Lincoln brought John Quincy Adams to dinner at Mrs.
Spriggs's "mess." The former President's wife entertained
very little in the house they rented on Thirteenth Street.
"Mrs. Adams has never quite gotten over the degradation of
my choice to serve in Congress, after being President of the
land," remarked the old gentleman, with a dry glance at
Lincoln under his shelving white brow. "I cannot induce her
to see that no man is degraded by seeking service in the government of his country—or in being elected as selectman of
his hometown, for that matter."

Adams spoke in French to Mary, of Paris in the days before the Revolution, and of London and St. Petersburg in its
wake. Mary recalled what Henry Clay had told her father
about cold, stuffy, reserved, and charmless Adams: that he
was like a very dry wine, that repels on first mouthful and
only reveals its complexity to the thoughtful.

She made sure to include the quote in her next letter.

But most days she spent alone in the boardinghouse
room. The damp climate went to Eddie's chest, and the little
boy was often sickly. Bobby, forced to remain indoors, was
bored, noisy, and sullen, and Mrs. Spriggs referred to both
boys as "those tiresome apes." By Bobby's increasing silence,
and unwillingness to play with the few local boys he encountered, Mary suspected that the local boys called him "Cock-
Eye," as a few of the Springfield children had.

Lincoln, as usual, was preoccupied. Though Mary tried to
be patient, a good partner to him in his responsibilities, his
habitual abstraction sparked stormy quarrels: "I'm here to do
a job of work, not play dry-nurse to the boys!" he flared at

her on one sleety Sunday afternoon, and Mary shot back with, "We'd be able to get Mrs. Spriggs to watch them more often if you'd act like a father and teach them a little discipline!" Lincoln went silent after that, and when Mary flung herself down on the bed in tears, he took Bobby and Eddie for a walk despite the cold. They came back just before dark, all three spattered from head to foot with mud and full of tales of seeing the war-hero Jefferson Davis's new towncarriage, driving up to the White House gates.

Just before Christmas, Lincoln enraged most of Congress with a resolution condemning the war with Mexico. Despite this, he confided to Mary, on one of the rare evenings that they spent reading in the warm downstairs parlor while the boys played at the hearth, he was being asked by other Whigs in Congress to support General Zachary Taylor for President.

"It'll mean a speaking tour, after Congress shuts up shop in summer," he told her, a little apologetically. "Through New England, they say. Now, you can go on back to Springfield with the boys, Molly—I'm sure Washburne would be glad to escort you. . . ."

"If you *dare* to go traveling through New England without me, Mr. Lincoln," said Mary, lowering her novel and regarding him with sparkling eyes, "after *martyring* myself in this *dreadful* city all winter, you'll come home to find the doors locked against you and all your clothes in a cardboard box on the porch."

Mrs. Penfold, the literal-minded and evangelistic lady who had the room next to theirs upstairs, looked up from her knitting, shocked. But Lincoln merely smiled and said, with deep satisfaction, "That's my Molly."

Eddie had a cold again after Christmas, and another in February. Lincoln would come in from sessions of the House, or meetings of the Postal Committee—to which he'd been appointed apparently on the grounds of his year's stint as postmaster of the village of New Salem—and would sit up nights with the feverish toddler so that Mary could get some sleep. Waking from a troubled doze—she seldom actually slept even when she could—Mary would see him, sitting on the edge of the trundle-bed with Eddie in his arms, rocking him and making the little rusty growls under his breath that passed, for him, for a lullaby:

> "The water is wide, I cannot get o'er,
>   Nor do I have the wings to fly;
>   Give me a boat that can carry two,
>   And we both shall cross, my love and I. . . ."

Had the mother he never spoke of sung him that, she wondered, when he was ill?

He was up all the night, and gone in the morning to meet with Giddings on a bill to outlaw slavery within the District of Columbia, after going down to the yard in his shirtsleeves to chop kindling to keep Mrs. Spriggs sweet. So there passed another day, Mary reflected despairingly, that they couldn't make calls or set up connections, and that she would have no adult conversation and no time to read. How anyone could get along with Mrs. Spriggs she couldn't imagine, but Lincoln would do errands for her, and sweet-talk her out of extra firewood—for which she usually charged five cents extra, or ten if she had to cut kindling—or boiling water for poultices and tisanes.

Eddie was on the mend—and getting fractious—when Lincoln came in, late that night, with the news that John Quincy Adams had been felled by a stroke during the session, and was not expected to live. "The poor old gentleman!" exclaimed Mary, sitting on the edge of the trundle-bed. She'd been trying to get Eddie to eat, but the child refused the porridge that was the only thing Mrs. Spriggs would cook for him.

"He had an apoplexy not long ago, and got over it," replied Lincoln, sitting on the other side of Eddie on the bed, with his big hands hanging down between his knees. Bobby, who'd been underfoot all day, ran to his father's side to be taken up on his knee. Lincoln hugged him, but absently, his mind still on the picture of that white-haired old gentleman toppling from his chair to the House floor, gasping for air. "They carried him into the Speaker's room, and there set up a cot; Douglas went to fetch a doctor. They say he'll stay there till he's fit to be moved, but myself, I think he'll end his life in the place where he spent it, in the house of service to his country. And that is not such a bad way to end," he added softly.

He sat silent, gazing into the shadows. How long he might have remained thus, oblivious to his surroundings, Mary didn't know; she'd seen him lost in one of his moods for hours. But Eddie seized the porridge-spoon from the bowl and whacked his father on the arm with it, leaving a long sticky smear. And, when Lincoln made no response whatsoever, piped up, "Papa, *nasty*!"

Mary pulled the spoon from him. Lincoln, roused from his thoughts, looked down at the boy, amusement flickering in his eyes: "I should say it is nasty, son—and you're bound to spread the nasty around until something gets done about it, aren't you?"

As Mary darted to the water-pitcher for a rag—her husband was perfectly capable of going into a debate on the floor of Congress with a smear of oatmeal on his sleeve—Bobby said, "Mama told Mrs. Spriggs to make Eddie a blancmange and Mrs. Spriggs said—"

"Never mind what Mrs. Spriggs said," snapped Mary, tears constricting her throat again at the recollection of that bitter exchange of personalities. Her head throbbed, with hunger as much as anything else, for in the wake of the quarrel with the landlady she'd been too exhausted to go down to supper. "Mr. Lincoln, that woman is impossible! I merely asked—a most *reasonable* request—that she make a blancmange for Eddie, or permit me the use of her kitchen to make one myself. In a most *disagreeable* voice she informed me that she could not spare the maid to help me or to go out for the almonds, of which she *said* she had none in the house.

Though how any woman calling herself a cook could be without them..." She caught herself up, hearing her voice growing shrill. In the calmest tone she could, she added firmly, "We simply must find another place to live."

The light of the single lamp on the bedside table picked out the surge of jaw-muscle as Lincoln clenched his teeth. Resentment flooded through her, anger not only at the petty and avaricious Mrs. Spriggs, but the chewed-over details of the quarrel that she'd been waiting until nearly nine o'clock at night to present to her errant husband.

At the same time she saw his eyes travel to her—her hair loosened from its pins with Eddie's fitful pulling, the oatmeal-stains on her own dress and shawl, her eyes swollen with tears and headache. And past her, to the room, stuffy, cluttered with the boys' things, smelling faintly of mildew and chamber pots, two cans of the morning's wash-water still not carried out and a huge damp stain on the rug where a third can had been overturned by Bobby. The day had been rainy and Bobby bored to distraction and petulant. Mrs. Spriggs and her own husband were the only adults she had spoken to since she'd waked that morning.

Her eyes burned again and she felt the frustration blossom in her, turning her sick.

Very gently—in the same voice he'd used to try to conciliate her in her quarrels with his cousin Hetty Hanks— Lincoln said, "Mother, the town is as full as it can hold, with Congress sitting. But I will look—"

"When?" retorted Mary bitterly. "If you can't even come in time for supper, or to spend an hour with your wife and sons..." That hurt him—she saw him flinch like a man struck by an arrow—and felt a hateful spurt of pleasure that she'd at least gotten his attention. Did he realize that while he was politicking with his men friends and laying plans to elect Zachary Taylor President—on God knew what platform, since the man had no opinions on anything that Mary had ever read!— his wife was cooped up in a twelve-by-fourteen room with two squalling children, waiting for a word with him?

"I'm going back to Lexington," she said.

Lincoln's eyes widened, stricken, but he said nothing.

"I'm writing to my father tomorrow. You don't care if I'm here or not...."

"Now, Molly, that's not true...."

"It is," she cried hotly, "and you know it is." The instant guilt in his face confirmed her words. Fury blinded her: at the mighty Washington hostesses who had no time for the wife of a mere Representative, at Mrs. Spriggs, at the other boarders who slurped soup through their whiskers or cleaned their ears at the table, at the poverty that would not let them take a house here, that for five years now had reduced her to the status of servant and drudge. Bobby and Eddie, as they generally did during their parents' quarrels, clung closer to Lincoln, making themselves invisible in his bony shadow. "You don't care...."

Trembling, she forced herself to stop, hiccoughed, and stood, fumbling at her skirt pocket for a handkerchief.

Lincoln silently fished a clean one from his coat. Years of living with Mary had taught him to carry them.

She took it from him, feeling surprisingly, suddenly clear in her mind and heart. The poison-pain of resentment dissolved; it was as if a door had opened, in her life and in her mind. The words, flung at him in anger, showed themselves now as an actual solution, and it was as if an iron bond broke from around her chest.

She stretched out her hand, and laid it alongside his face. He looked up at her in surprise that was almost comical.

"You know Eddie hasn't been well," she said softly. "And poor Bobby is bored frantic, aren't you, darling?"

Bobby regarded her for a moment with those wide-set, mismatched blue eyes, gauging what she wanted him to say. Then he nodded.

Lincoln shut his eyes, drew in his breath, and let it out. Then he looked up at her again, and took her hand between both of his. "You truly don't mind?"

"Of course I mind." She bent to kiss his cheek. "And I'll

be *miserable* away from you." The old rallying tone crept back into her voice. "But we're both miserable now. And if we're *both* going to be miserable anyway—and you had *better* be miserable while I'm away, Mr. Lincoln, and I'll write to Mr. Douglas and ask him to make *sure* that you are—at least the boys will have their cousins to play with, and be happy, and you'll get some work done without worrying about us."

Not, she reflected, that Lincoln *did* worry about her, much, when he got talking politics with his cronies. . . .

But he knew he ought to.

"You are a saint and a martyr, Mother." He scootched Eddie aside, to make room for Mary on his knee.

The following morning at breakfast he managed to sweet-talk Mrs. Spriggs into making a blancmange, too.

CHAPTER TWENTY-NINE

INQUIRING AMONG HIS CONGRESSIONAL COLLEAGUES, LINCOLN found a respectable middle-aged clerk named Shepperton and his wife who were traveling to St. Louis via Lexington on family matters early in March. Mr. Shepperton proved a reliable and helpful traveling companion: laughing indulgently at the boys' obstreperousness, keeping track of the trunks and parcels, tipping porters just the right amount, and deferring to Mary in all things. Mrs. Shepperton adored him and agreed with everything he said, stupid or not, in the course of the four-day journey. She herself talked of nothing but the superiority of honey and onions for the cure of every ailment from catarrh to leprosy and Mary suspected that if, like Petruchio, he'd called the sun the moon his wife would have cheered his perception, but the couple were otherwise perfectly friendly and pleasant to travel with.

Mary was simply ecstatic at the thought of going home.

Chaney, Pendleton, Nelson, and Mammy Sally crowded to embrace her. Margaret and Mattie, Elodie and Emilie, gay young Alec and little Kitty, and the rest engulfed Bobby and Eddie into their midst; even Robert Todd beamed and Granny Parker gave her dry acerbic smile, and Betsey tried to look as if she were pleased.

It was heaven to be in Lexington again.

This was a true homecoming, she felt, coming home to be again someone she hadn't been in a long, long time. The woman she had become in Illinois—the poor man's wife who washed her own dishes and cowered from thunderstorms—faded almost at once. She felt, if not like a belle again, at least like her former self.

It was wonderful simply not to have a headache,

something she'd suffered every spring she'd been on the
Illinois prairies. It was wonderful beyond words not to be
tied to the drudgery of housework. Wonderful, too, to know
that the work of the house was being done by reliable slaves
who knew their business instead of facing the daily exasperation of trying to explain to a sulky fourteen-year-old Irish
girl that the *entire* floor of the parlor needed to be swept, and
not just the parts that showed.

With Mammy Sally to look after the boys, Mary found
her irritation at them dissolved. She could laugh and play
with them, sympathize with Bobby's attempts to adopt a kitten (Betsey's hatred of the whole cat tribe remained as viru-
lent as ever), and take the time to read to them each night. As
Betsey's notion of bedtime didn't include bedside candles,
much less chapters of *Young King Arthur,* the group around
the trundle-bed in the guest-room rapidly expanded to include Kitty, Emilie, Elodie, and Alec—Betsey sniffed and
clicked her tongue, but said only, "Well, just one chapter, and
no talking afterwards." Sometimes, when he was home,
Mary's father tiptoed in to listen, too.

With the improvement of the railway to Frankfort,
Robert Todd was home most weekends, and that spring of
1848 was the most Mary had seen of him in her life. In the
long mellow twilights, while the children dashed madly
about the wooded lawns behind the house and down to the
spring, she would sit with him on the gallery overlooking the
garden, and talk of the upcoming election, and Lincoln's
plans, and how to revive the flagging Whig Party in the face
of the Democrats' war-time triumphs. He listened atten-
tively to her descriptions of Washington, and spoke to her of
his worries and doubts concerning the vexing issue of slavery: "The abolitionists are going to drive this whole country
straight to perdition, with their disregard of facts as they are.
Yes, slavery is wrong, but it exists! And there's no way you're
going to keep it out of the territories. You can't just legislate
it away, poof—and devil take the hindmost!"

Sometimes Betsey would join them, and Mary was surprised at her own ability to get along with her stepmother, now that she was no longer the unwanted stepdaughter who refused to marry the first man who would take her off Betsey's hands. They even laughed together about the Spider Incident, though Betsey never spoke of why Mary had been angry with her—Mary pretended she no longer recalled. That was all past and done now, and Mary was married to a Congressman, a fact, she knew, that made her father enormously proud.

Granny Parker and Emilie joined them too, those soft twilights when the air was filled with the smoke of lemongrass smudges. On several occasions Cash Clay and Mary Jane came, their own rowdy band of offspring joining the shrill-voiced shadows chasing back and forth among the trees beside the stream. Cash was full of descriptions of Mexico, and of its capital where he'd been held prisoner, like a gaudily-colored island in the midst of its shining lakes. He had, for over a year before the war, operated an abolitionist newspaper in Lexington, the *True American*. At the mention of it, Robert Todd rolled his eyes. "You could have got yourself killed," he said.

"If I had," declared Cash, leaning forward impetuously and jabbing with his finger, "I would have taken many a man of the forces of iniquity with me." With his black hair tumbled over his forehead, he seemed unchanged from the wild young man who'd smuggled Mary copies of *The Liberator* at Madame Mentelle's. He had, he related, reinforced with sheet iron the doors and windows of the *True American,* and installed two brass cannon on the table inside, pointed straight at the doors. To this he'd added a trapdoor on the roof and enough kegs of powder to blow the building and any invaders thereof sky-high. Mary knew this was not braggadocio: Abolitionist editors had been murdered before this, and their presses and offices wrecked.

"And I'd have stood them all off, and died in the attempt," he vowed, with a vast sweep of his arm, "had I not come down with typhoid fever, and had them destroy the newspaper in my absence."

Mary laughed, but in the dim light of the lamps and mosquito-smudges, she saw Mary Jane's glance slip sideways to her husband, and in her eyes there was no mirth. Cash was still, thought Mary, as ready to get himself killed without a moment's thought about how his wife and children might fare without him, as he had been when he'd accepted the challenge to a duel on his wedding-eve fifteen years before.

More than at Cash's egoism, Mary was shocked at the violence with which the town's slaveholding faction had greeted Cash's newspaper. She had always feared the readiness to lash out, that lay beneath the surface of Southern manhood; their willingness to destroy life or property to make a point. She remembered too vividly Elliot Presby's blood in the ditch of Main Street, and the men who had seen nothing wrong with beating him only for speaking to them of the evil of holding slaves. According to her father, the Legislature was increasingly in the hands of slaveholders, men whose factories, plantations, livery-stables, or sawmills simply could not operate without unpaid black labor.

Spring waxed warm. Eddie's sickliness abated, and with Chaney's cooking, his thinness filled out to pink-cheeked strength. Though he tired easily, her younger son was treated as a sort of beloved mascot by the other children, and showed signs of Bobby's—and his father's—insatiable curiosity, coupled with a sweet-tempered friendliness to all. Bobby— whose speech had picked up a marked Kentucky flatness of vowel—had become his protector and minor god.

Mary and Emilie spent long evenings together, talking of dresses, of hope, of love. Letters came from Washington, letters that brought pangs of loneliness, of longing to lie curled up against that long leathery bag of bones—longing for those endless wonderful talks after the candle was blown out, longing for the touch of those big callused hands, for the passionate strength of his kisses.

Pangs of guilt, too, because she hadn't the slightest wish to rejoin him in that horrible boardinghouse in that miasmic swamp of a town. Lincoln wrote of missing her terribly, wrote with longing of his sons, but she knew that if she were with him he'd go on his absentminded way just as before, not coming back from the House of Representatives until midnight, not giving a thought (or much of one) to what she might be doing all day, cooped up in a boardinghouse room with two small boys.

And sometimes—though she would never have admitted it to a soul—it was so good simply to have the luxury to sleep alone!

So she visited Mary and Margaret Wickliffe—now both Preston—quietly, because her father was engaged in a lawsuit with their father over a cousin's inheritance that was being claimed by Old Duke—and walked out to Rose Hill to have coffee and to laugh with Madame Mentelle. Her old teacher was as sharp as ever, and full of cynical comments about the new phenomenon that was sweeping the East, the conviction that certain persons could communicate with the dead.

"A mishmash of Swedenborgianism and plain superstition," Madame pronounced, and refused to participate when the Wickliffe-Preston girls, Mary, Emilie, and Madame's daughter Maria—who had married one of Henry Clay's sons—organized a séance in the Rose Hill parlor to communicate with the spirit of George Washington. The result was inconclusive, but everyone giggled and had a spookily good time.

There was talk, in May, of Mary going back to Washington, but in the end she decided to remain in Lexington. In June she went with the rest of the family out to Buena Vista, the summer home that was Betsey's property, riding and walking in the countryside as if she were a girl again.

Congress would adjourn in August—by which time, Mary knew, Washington City would be a sweating hellhole smothered in dust. Nevertheless, when Lincoln wrote her

that he was going with the other Whig leaders to New
England to campaign for Zachary Taylor, Mary wrote back
immediately that she would come. *I look forward to being with
you again on the sixth of September,* Lincoln wrote back; and in
spite of the tediousness of the promised journey, and the wet
heat of the capital, Mary found herself looking forward to
it, too.

In the end, her desire to see him again got the better of
her. She packed up her sons and her trunks (it was astound-
ing how much extra clothing and luggage she'd accumulated
over the summer!) in late July, and prepared to take the stage
to Winchester, in company with her brother Levi, and
thence to the weary succession of trains that would eventually lead to Washington.

In the dark before dawn on the day of departure old
Nelson hitched up the carriage, and everyone except Betsey
came down to breakfast by lamplight. Emilie hugged Mary:
"I'll write to you, I promise. Tell Mr. Lincoln I hope his
side wins." Robert Todd rode with Mary, Levi, Bobby, and
Eddie to the Courthouse square, where the stage took its departure:

"You take care of those grandsons of mine, you hear?" he
smiled, and gave Mary a hearty bear hug as he helped her
from the carriage. In the dove-gray quiet of the square the
six brown horses shook their heads, snuffing at the air and
jangling their harness; black hostlers from the stage company
held the leaders' heads. Two slaves belonging to Mr.
Blanchard the silversmith sloshed buckets of water on the
plank sidewalk and the smell of wet wood was strong in the
warm air. "And tell that husband of yours not to let another
seven years go by, before he brings you back here to call."

He pressed a roll of banknotes into her hand, and leaned
down to kiss her. Then Levi helped her into the stage—Eddie
and Bobby were already poking each other and the other passengers were starting to get annoyed—and the grooms sprang
away from the horses' heads. Mary leaned out the window

and twisted around backward, all her bonnet-ribbons fluttering, to get a last glimpse of her father's tall, burly shape, waving to her before he turned back to where Nelson waited with the carriage.

It was her last sight of him alive.

Chapter Thirty

Although her experience with Washington City had been ghastly—and Mrs. Spriggs hadn't improved any in the August weeks that Mary and the boys were back in the upstairs room on First Street—she hugely enjoyed the speaking tour. The weather was hot, but at least the boys weren't cooped up in hotel-rooms by rain and cold. She would take them sightseeing in the daytime in whatever town they were in—Boston, New Bedford, the small New England hamlets where the Yankee half of the Revolution was born.

In Illinois, and later in Washington, she'd grown accustomed to Yankee accents and the self-righteous pushiness of Yankee so-called manners, enough to deal with having them around her all the time, though at the hotels she sorely missed the gentle reliability of her father's slaves. The money her father had given her made it possible for her to pay hotel maids to look after the boys in the evenings, so that she could hear her husband speak.

Growing up where Henry Clay set the oratorical standard, she knew Lincoln was good. Even had he been a stranger to her, she reflected, looking up at that beanpole figure in the tin-sconced glow of the oil-lamps around the halls at Cambridge, at New Bedford, at Dorchester and Boston, he would have held her enrapt. And looking at the faces around her, listening to the murmur and stillness of the crowd that was like the sough of wind through leaves, she knew she wasn't the only one who thought so. She bought all the local newspapers and scanned them while riding the trains or the stages: *"He spoke in a clear and cool, and very eloquent manner . . . carrying the audience with him. . . ."* *"The Hon. Abraham Lincoln made a speech, which for aptness of illustration, solidity of argument, and genuine eloquence, is hard to beat." "It was a glorious meeting."* In the hotel-rooms she clipped the articles out. Bobby and Eddie helped her file them away in envelopes, to be later pasted in albums.

In those few evenings when he was not meeting with local Whigs, or speaking, Lincoln and Mary would talk late into the nights, analyzing what those newspapers had said, as if through those journals they listened to the voices of the people in the crowd. As he had in Springfield, he practiced his speeches on her, and listened thoughtfully to her advice.

Mary had always loved the thrill and confusion of Presidential campaigns. Now she felt as she had during Harrison's campaign, when she and Merce and Julia had all gone to rallies wearing their banners, and cheered for hard cider and log cabins.

"Yes, and the cryin' shame of it is that we're runnin' another man on log cabins an' hard cider, or the next thing to it," sighed Lincoln, as the train chuffed out of New Bedford for Boston. Bobby and Eddie crowded to the window, craning to get a last sight of the harbor with its forest of masts: prairie boys, both had been riveted by their first glimpse of the open ocean the previous day. Despite his speech, and his meetings with the local Whig bosses, Lincoln had made the time to go with Mary and the boys to the harbor, where the whaling-ships stood in port, and the streets were filled with strange dark-faced men with savage tattoos. It had been, Mary realized, Lincoln's own first look at the sea—and hers as well.

"As good a man as Old Zack is," Lincoln went on, stretching his neck to look through the window for a final glimpse, "he doesn't stand for anything, much. People all over the country know his name and will vote for him, which they wouldn't for someone like Mr. Seward." He named the aristocratic former New York governor, who would share the platform with him at a huge mass meeting a week hence in Boston. "And Seward is by far the abler man. *He's* the one we should be electing." He drew about him the vast skirts of the brown linen duster he wore, against the smuts and fluffs of soot that floated through the car.

"And if the committee had nominated Seward instead of Taylor, he could make his own speeches, and not have me and the other local worthies do it for him. But you ask Mr. Gurley next door to us, or the Reverend Dresser or any of our neighbors in Springfield who William Seward is, and they won't know, nor any reason why they should elect him over Lewis Cass, who fought the British for the freedom of our nation back in 1812...."

"I'm still sorry," said Mary softly, "that the committee didn't stand behind Mr. Clay. He would outshine a dozen of Seward and Taylor put together." Past the window, the sea vanished behind the ghostly line of dunes. Then the train swayed, swinging westward, and that long gray shining promise vanished from view.

Lincoln sighed again, and settled back into his seat. "I too," he said. "Clay is a man I'd make speeches for gladly— not that I grudge a word of what I say for Old Zack. But Clay's made enemies. Too many people only remember that fool accusation of selling out his supporters in trade to be made Secretary of State. And he's old," he added quietly. "Seventy-one, older even than Cass."

Mary nodded. She recalled having a fight with one of her schoolmates at Ward's over who was handsomer, Andrew Jackson or Henry Clay ... or Mary's father.

In her heart she knew Clay would not run again for the Presidency that he had so deserved.

"Taylor at least is hale and healthy," said Lincoln, and she thought she caught a trace of the same sadness in his voice. "He can be trusted to live out his term and put men of caution and principle in places where they can do some good."

"Yourself included." Mary squeezed his hand.

She saw the echo of her pride—and her hope—glint briefly in his eyes, but he only shook his head.

"But it is a chore," he added with a comical grimace, "coming up with reasons to vote for the man besides the fact that he'll appoint men who *do* know what they're doing. I certainly wouldn't vote for a man on those grounds alone, no matter what a great soldier he was. For that matter, *I* was a great soldier, too. I looked courageously behind every bush in northern Illinois for Black Hawk and his braves—who hid from me, knowin' how ferocious a fighter I was, so I never saw hide nor hair of 'em—not to mention sheddin' my blood to a thousand mosquitoes...."

Mary clasped her hands over her heart in a burlesque of passion. "What woman could resist a Hector, a Hercules, a warrior such as you?"

Bobby and Eddie poked each other and giggled as their parents embraced and kissed, and the starchy Boston couple in the next seat tried to pretend they hadn't seen such shocking goings-on.

Lincoln made his final speech in Boston—clear and lucid arguments as to why votes for the Free-Soil splinter groups and so-called Conscience Whigs were in reality votes for the Democrats—and then they were en route for the home they had left nearly a year before. In Buffalo they booked a cabin on the steamer *Globe,* bound for the bustling little lumbertown of Chicago over the succession of canals and waterways that crossed the peninsula of Michigan. But before it steamed out into Lake Erie, the little ship took the occasion, to Mary's joy, to go upriver to Niagara Falls.

The sight of the water, pouring down endlessly, torrents of it, curtains of it, a world of vapor and rainbows, silenced even the boys. Lincoln stood on the deck of the little tourist steamer, openmouthed with shock, awe, and the most utter delight Mary had ever seen on his face. Not even the sight of the ocean had filled him with such wonder. "It's been falling like that—just like that—when there weren't even white men on this continent," he said wonderingly, as the *Globe* chuffed away back toward Buffalo. "When Christ walked the earth it was like that—thundering in the silence here, unseen by anyone but the Indians and God. It'll be falling like that when all of us are gone." He shook his head, trying to grasp the largeness of Time, with the mist of the falls beaded like raindrops in his hair.

In Chicago, they took a room in the Sherman Hotel. Mary was unimpressed by the city. It seemed to have been built and populated entirely by Yankees—pushing, mannerless, and valuing money before all other things. Balloon-frame houses of roughly sawn boards lined streets so deep in mud that there were signs posted on particularly soupy intersections: THE SHORTEST WAY TO CHINA. Regiments of pigs whose numbers would have put Springfield's swine population to blushing shame rooted vigorously for garbage or lay in wallows in alleys. Lincoln chuckled all the way to the hotel at a story the train conductor had told him, about a Chicago citizen who saw a man's head and shoulders sticking out of a mudhole at the intersection of State and Lake: "Can I help you, pilgrim?" "No, thanks," the mired man said cheerfully. "I've got a horse under me."

And it was crowded, frantic, jostling with activity. Mary remembered how, ten years ago, Stephen Douglas had spoken of his trips to Chicago to speculate in land—when she'd taken tea with him and his new wife in Washington, he'd told her that lots he bought for five thousand dollars were selling now for twenty thousand. Irish, Polish, Portuguese, and German immigrants slogged through the muddy streets or along the very few crude board sidewalks; the air stank from privies, sewage, and coal smoke.

Yet there was money here, business, power. Mary might wrinkle her nose, after all these years, at Northern accents, but from her years of poverty she understood what the Yankee way of life could bring. At the Sherman Hotel, while Mary took the boys out and doubtfully tried to find something in the overwhelming confusion for them to sightsee, Lincoln met with the leaders of the Chicago Whigs, businessmen who made her father's leisured graciousness seem laughably naïve. When she came back that afternoon Lincoln told her the Chicago bosses had asked him, at six hours' notice, to speak that night at a rally at the Cook County Courthouse.

They spent the rest of the afternoon in the hotel room together, drinking vile tea and working out what he'd say.

The rally turned out to be so huge that it adjourned to a nearby public square, where crowds stood in the mud by torchlight and listened for nearly two hours. The cheers when Lincoln finished were deafening; Mary stood near the stage, jostled by strangers who reeked of sweat and tobacco, looking up at her husband in the torchlight, transformed and seeming to blaze with his cold intelligence as he always did, when carried away by speaking before a crowd.

He will be President. In her bones she knew it. *Taylor will be elected, and will give him something, some office, that will get him known, and he will be on his way.* She longed to throw her arms around him as he descended the platform, to embrace him in her wild delight. But he was surrounded at once by men, those clever, crafty businessmen, lawyers, speculators, politicians who governed things. There was the florid-faced Mr. Judd, who was building railroads with Irish and German labor; their rosy friend Congressman Washburne from Mrs. Spriggs's; plus old friends from Springfield, Edward Baker and Lyman Trumbull...

And all of them, Mary observed with an inner smile, Lincoln greeted as if each was his special friend, his close confidant. She knew this did not spring from calculation or hypocrisy, but from genuine interest coupled with a very clear idea of how anyone, from lowest to highest, could help; could be knit together into a single fighting unit. It was as if he said to each, *I need you . . . I need you all.*

Around them in the square the crowd was still shouting, talking, a yammer of noise and torchlight in the cold October night. It was the sound of victory. Lincoln had fought the good fight for "Old Rough and Ready" Zack Taylor, and in time his reward would come. Douglas might have made a fortune here in this mudhole town and be the fair-haired boy of the slaveholding Senators, but Lincoln would have something more.

Around the narrow shoulder of Isaac Arnold—a skinny,

bearded, watchful fellow lawyer—Lincoln caught Mary's glance, and the corners of his eyes crinkled in a smile.

RETURNING TO SPRINGFIELD ON OCTOBER 10, LINCOLN TOOK their old room in the Globe Tavern, rather than put the Ludlum family out of the Jackson Street house. "Ludlum has asked me if you were intending to come back to Washington with me in November," Lincoln told Mary, on a windy night a day or so later, after they'd settled the boys to sleep in the trundle-bed. He'd spent the day with Billy Herndon, catching up all the legal business of the past year—tomorrow, Mary knew, he'd spend with Ninian, and Simeon Francis, and Cousin Stephen Logan, and Dr. Henry around the stove in the office of the *Sangamo Journal,* conferring about the recent state elections—which had been disastrous for the Whigs—and how they were going to organize to secure victory for Taylor.

But at least, she reflected, now she could visit Bessie Francis, and Julia, and Cousin Lizzie . . . and Elizabeth, who had Ann still living with her, and those two certainly deserved each other. . . .

She heard the query in her husband's voice, and glanced over at the sleeping boys. Eddie was sleeping, anyway. Bobby was pretending to sleep, as he usually did so he could listen to his parents' voices.

She paused, hairbrush in hand. Lincoln was sitting up in bed with the quilt over his knees, a book on his lap, and Charlotte, Mrs. Beck's calico cat, asleep on his feet. It didn't take more than a few hours for every cat in the house to make Lincoln's acquaintance and decide to sleep on his bed—at Mrs. Spriggs's there'd been four of them.

Lincoln went on, "Ludlum said he'd be pleased if he could rent the house until March, when the Congress adjourns again. I said I'd talk to you. I know you weren't much happy with Washington."

November to March. It wasn't much longer than he was

gone when riding circuit. Mary thought about the little cottage on Jackson Street, about trying to deal with that horrendous succession of sulky Irish girls. Bobby and Eddie were older, and past the stage of disturbing everyone with squalling and crying, but they were still young enough to need constant minding, when she'd hoped to be attending sessions of the Congress or paying calls on the town's hostesses. During the weeks of August before the speaking tour, she'd been able to go to Congress only twice.

"I thought, Molly, that maybe you'd like to stay here at the Globe. I know you get along all right with Mrs. Beck these days." Which was true. Not being pregnant or exhausted, Mary had found, did wonders for her ability to deal with the Globe's no-nonsense landlady.

Mary felt as if a key had been turned, releasing her. Felt as she had when she'd finally said, *I'm going back to Lexington....* "Will you be all right on your own?" she asked him.

And saw, by the lightening of his eyes, that he, too, had suffered while the four of them were trying to live together in the Washington boardinghouse. That he'd felt guilty over leaving her to her own devices, torn between his ambition, his duty, and his love for and protectiveness of her. "Well," he replied gravely, "since I'll be sending my whole salary here to pay Mrs. Beck, I won't have enough left to go chasing around bad women in Washington...."

"Mr. Lincoln!" Mary swirled over to him in a flurry of white nightgown and unbraided hair, to rap his arm smartly with the hairbrush she held. "I have *never* been so shocked in all my life! Do you mean to tell me that *actual members* of the *government of the United States* even *know* what bad women *are*, much less chase around with them...?"

"Only the Democrats," Lincoln assured her gravely, and pulled her giggling into bed at his side.

He was gone two days later, stumping the southern part of the state with Dr. Henry in a last-minute effort to rally the Illinois Whigs to Zachary Taylor's banner—a successful effort, for the General won the election handily. Mary was elated, and saw him off on the stage a few weeks later with a glow of pleasure, knowing there would be good things ahead. If he was given an appointment in Washington it would be for three or four years, longer than a single session of Congress. They could take a house there, and *then* she could be one of the hostesses, and not a petitioner leaving cards for other people's servants. One could get decent help in Washington, too, since it was possible to rent slaves or hire freedmen, who were *far* more reliable than the wild Irish. . . . Her deepest regret about not accompanying Lincoln was that she couldn't be at Taylor's inaugural ball at her husband's side. He left early, he wrote her, and in the shoving and confusion of the gentlemen's cloakroom lost his hat, and had to walk back to his boardinghouse bare-headed in the rain.

While he was gone, that winter of 1848, Mary enrolled Bobby in school. She was beginning to feel deep concern about her older son, and hoped the schoolmistress could do with him what she herself could not. But the boy was forever in trouble with his schoolmates, partly because he was teased about wearing patched breeches, but mostly because the other children called him "Cock-Eye." When he wasn't in trouble he would simply run away, and even with Mary, his secrecy and his silent defiance were getting beyond what she could handle. After his fifth truancy, she took him to Dr. Wallace's small consulting-room behind the drugstore.

"It's a relatively simple problem." Dr. Wallace straightened up, gave Bobby a piece of peppermint, and drew Mary to the far corner of the office. "The muscle on the inner side of the eyeball is too short. It's a fast and easy operation to cut partially through it; in most cases the eye will return, if not to a completely normal position, at least to one that is barely obvious. There's a specialist here in town, Dr. Bell, who should be able to do it. Bobby will have to do eye exercises to restore the balance of the muscles, but I think that should solve the problem."

When Lincoln returned to Springfield in March, Mary told him what Dr. Wallace had said—told him, too, about

Bobby's increasing quarrelsomeness and truancy at school. "If he's to get any education he mustn't be always fighting," she insisted. "Dr. Wallace promises that the earlier the surgery is done, the more normal his eye will appear when it heals."

She tried to keep her anxiety out of her voice, to sound matter-of-fact. Try as she would, she could never completely push from her heart the ugly fact that the boy's inward-turning eye repelled her. Every time she saw her son's face, she heard the whisper in the back of her mind: *Mary Todd played the harlot. Mary Todd lied to get a husband. This is God's punishment.*

She could speak all she wanted about what was best for Bobby, but in truth, she would have done anything not to have a child whose imperfection trumpeted her shame. She wanted to love him wholeheartedly—to be *able* to love him wholeheartedly. With the defect gone, at least her lie would not be literally staring her in the face.

Lincoln nodded, though he didn't look happy at the thought of putting his son through the agony of surgery. That was the day they moved back into the cottage on Jackson Street, the boys dashing from room to echoing room in an atmosphere of soap and ironing and fresh paint. Lincoln carried the familiar furniture down from the attic room where it had been stored, reassembled their bed and put together small beds in the low-ceilinged attic bedroom for Bobby and Eddie ("Now, you boys remember I can hear every sound you make!" Mary warned). Eddie was dancing with joy at the prospect of sharing a room with his protector.

The surgery was set for June, when Lincoln would have built up his much-neglected law practice again. The eye specialist, Dr. Bell, would perform it, with Dr. Wallace assisting. Mary felt reassured by Wallace's presence—she trusted Frances's husband as if he were her own brother. For a month and a half Lincoln was busier, as he said, than a one-armed paperhanger, writing letters for men to whom he owed political favors on top of his legal work, juggling what little influence he had acquired in Washington.

Then in May he became entangled in what turned into a ferocious three-way tug-of-war over the one patronage office he truly desired, that of United States Land Commissioner. Though the flurries of letters and negotiations with Cyrus Edwards—father of the lovely Tilda, now long married to her handsome Mr. Strong—and other Whig leaders kept him preoccupied and absentminded, Mary understood, and followed the proceedings eagerly. As Land Commissioner, Lincoln would be able to dispense offices on his own and build up a network of influence that would lead to votes.

A few days before Bobby's surgery, word reached them that a Chicago man named Butterfield was being seriously considered for the post. Wrought up and torn between his complex negotiations and the day-to-day demands of his practice, Lincoln lost his temper, one of the few times since the early days at the Globe that Mary had seen him in a real rage.

"When I was sweating blood to get Taylor elected Justin Butterfield was all for Clay; when I was making speeches here, there, and yon he was sitting home with his feet on the fender! There isn't a Whig from central Illinois that's received any office, not *one*! Did someone forget to count our votes?"

After more letters—more nights of coming home late, of the dining-room lamp's glow dimly seen under the shut bedroom door—Lincoln packed his bags and took the stage for Indianapolis, whence the railroad cars would bear him to Washington. "You want to have Wallace put off the surgery?" asked Lincoln, the night before his departure, as Mary washed up the supper dishes.

She shook her head, aghast at the thought of further delay. Bobby had run away from school again that morning, after Lyman junior had taunted him, and the schoolmistress had informed her in private that one more problem and he would be dropped from her class. With Eddie down with another cold, and constantly underfoot, Mary couldn't imagine teaching her defiant elder son his letters herself at home. "We'll be all right," she said. "The longer we delay, the worse it will be."

But when Bobby was strapped down to the padded table in Dr. Bell's surgery—when Dr. Wallace gripped his head, and Dr. Bell pulled back the eyelid to expose the mucous membrane, and Bobby started screaming in terror and pain—her nerve failed her. She fled the room, sick and fainting. Crumpled on a chair in the empty outer office, she heard the little boy's screams through the open door; pressed her hands to her ears, knowing she must go back into the surgery to be with him but knowing that if she did she would start screaming, too....

Before she could gather her strength to stand, Dr. Wallace emerged, spots of blood dabbling his clothes. "We're done, Molly." He gave her a few sips of brandy and then led her into the surgery and she held the sobbing, half-fainting boy in her arms, dizzy herself and terrified by the greenish pallor of his young face. But at least she was able to keep her composure. Dr. Wallace walked them home and Mary put Bobby to bed, then went to bed herself, trembling and shivering.

In the weeks after the bandages came off, Bobby did his eye exercises with diligence strange in a six-year-old, and after that time he was quieter, less quarrelsome but also far less communicative, even with Eddie.

He never spoke to either parent about the surgery.

As far as Mary could tell, he never mentioned it to a soul.

Chapter Thirty-one

On the third of July, Lincoln was home again. "Butterfield got it," he said, as Mary came into the lamplit kitchen from the dining-room where the boys were having their supper—as usual Lincoln had come in through the side door into the kitchen, dusty and tired from riding in the Indianapolis stage since dawn. He hugged Bobby—"Your uncle tells me you were a brave boy. Are you all right?" Then he turned to Mary. "I read the papers in Washington."

Mary nodded, though her head ached. She knew she looked terrible, haggard with sleeplessness and night after night of nightmares since first she'd read the news in the *Journal* a week earlier that cholera had broken out in Lexington. "Emilie wrote me," she said as Lincoln gently folded her into those long arms. "What a sweet child. She said she knew I'd be worried about Papa, and she says they're all well. They're out at Buena Vista, the house Betsey owned at their marriage, you remember. It's five miles out of town. Even Levi and his wife and their children are there. Catch Betsey thinking to write."

"News in Washington was that Mr. Clay was down sick."

"Emilie says he's better. Both he and his wife were ill. She says Papa's still campaigning for the Senate, in spite of the epidemic. He lived through one epidemic perfectly well," she added, a little shakily. "Of course they'll all do fine through this one."

Lincoln smiled, and kissed her on the top of the head. "That's my Molly." Bobby, his eye covered with a bandage, ate his soup and said nothing.

That night she dreamed of the cholera. Smelled again the thick choke of lime and gunpowder in her throat, and heard baby David crying, crying like an endless, steady machine-whistle. Dreamed of hearing thumping in the darkness, and of creeping out of her bedroom into the dark upstairs hall, to see Nelson and her father bringing down trunks from the attic to give to old Solly the gravedigger, because there were no more coffins to be had in the town.

And in her dream, both Nelson and her father were dead. Their faces were green with decay and their hair and clothes smelled of the mold of the graves. Outside in the streets the green, glowing essence of the cholera flowed like fouled water through the streets, shining sickly in the night.

Lincoln shook her awake in the darkness and she rolled over and clung to him, pressing her face to his bony chest, sobbing as if her heart would break. When she slept again she was back in the Winchester stagecoach, twisting around to get a final glimpse of her father as he stood waving to her in the Courthouse square.

But he wasn't there.

Two weeks later she got a letter from Emilie, telling her that her father was dead.

MARY WEPT UNTIL SHE WAS SICK. THE DEATH HIT HER DOU-bly hard, for the same day she received Emilie's letter, Julia Trumbull's five-year-old son, Lyman, died as well, from scarlet fever. Lying in the dark of her bedroom, head throbbing with migraine, she was only dimly aware of comings and goings in the house. Lincoln would sit beside her for hours in the darkness, or stretch out next to her on the bed, quiet as one of the cats, and hold her as he did during a thunderstorm.

None of it seemed to touch the bottomless core of her grief.

Fanny and Dr. Wallace came in and out often during the daytimes. They'd taken Bobby and Eddie to stay at their home—Mary heard later that it was there that Lincoln ate, when and if he ate. Sometimes she would sleep, and would dream of her father. In her dreams she was still sitting on the porch with him in the mosquito-humming darkness, smelling the smoke of his cigars. Then she'd wake and remember that he was gone.

And she would weep again, as if she did not know how to stop.

Even when she was up and around again she felt dazed, and her father's image haunted her. Fanny, Merce, Cousin Lizzie, and Bessie Francis took it in turns for weeks to come calling, as they were taking it in turns to call on and care for Julia. They were almost the only outsiders she could stand to see, and sometimes she could not even endure being with them. She emptied the little chest of trinkets her father had given her—pearl earbobs, silver combs, the sapphire pendant that she hadn't even unwrapped in years—and gave them to her friends, unable to look at them without seeing her father's face. During the days Lincoln took the boys to the office with him, and later she heard that Bobby and Eddie both came very close to driving Billy Herndon into murdering them and pitching their bodies into the street.

Mostly she simply couldn't believe that her father was gone. When Lincoln told her that he'd been offered the governorship of the Oregon Territory, she could only shake her head tearily and whisper, "No...no..." The thought of leaving her friends and family again, of months on a ship around Cape Horn and years of living in God knew what wild conditions in the forests, filled her with horror. Lincoln nodded—by the look in his eyes she could see he didn't think much of the idea himself—and no more was said of it. But she noticed that he was offered nothing else.

She was only beginning to believe her father was actually dead—only beginning to adjust—six weeks later, when her sister Ann came flouncing into the kitchen in red-faced fury with a letter in her hand and announced, "That *imbecile* brother of ours is trying to get Papa's will thrown out of court!"

Mary didn't need to be told which imbecile brother Ann

meant. Levi was a sulky tosspot, but like his father tended to deal with problems by simply not being there. George—a young man who also, as they said, had a spark in his throat—was volatile and temperamental and generally in debt, and loathed Betsey perhaps most of all Robert Todd's "first children." Mary paused only long enough to instruct Ruth—the current "girl"—in getting dinner into the Dutch oven (God knew whether she would, or what would come out), then took off her apron, collected Eddie and Bobby from the yard, and followed Ann to Elizabeth's, where an indignation meeting was in progress in the parlor. The upshot—after several hours' free exchange of personalities about George and Betsey—was that when she returned home that evening, it was to ask Lincoln to go with her to Lexington, to safeguard the interests of the four Todd sisters when George's challenge of Robert Todd's will came to court.

They stayed with Granny Parker, in the big house Mary remembered so well from childhood. Long residence in Lexington had given her a front-row seat on the almost unbelievable viciousness of family quarrels in the large clans of the county, once the terms of some patriarch's will emerged. She herself had personally expected that Betsey would bag most of her father's money for herself and her children—that was what Betsey had all her life maneuvered to do—and had resigned herself to letting that happen rather than causing the kind of storm that had torn apart the various branches of Wickliffes, Bodleys, Crittendens, and Breckenridges over the years.

In this she'd guessed correctly. The bulk of the money—and all seven slaves—were to go to Betsey, with the surprising exception of Nelson. Nelson, it turned out, had bought his freedom years ago at a nominal fee and had simply continued as the Todd coachman because manumitted slaves were legally obliged to leave the state, and Nelson had too many friends in Lexington. The rest of the money was to be "equitably divided" between the "first and second children."

Which left only a pittance for George. With the invalidation of the will, and the resulting forced sale of all Robert Todd's property—including the slaves—all proceeds would be equally divided among all the heirs, Betsey and the fourteen Todd children getting equal shares. Even with six of those children's shares put in trust under her administration, this would leave Betsey barely able to continue housekeeping at Buena Vista and could entail the sale of Buena Vista itself.

"I always hoped the woman would get a comeuppance somehow," stated Granny Parker, folding her clawlike hands over the ivory head of her cane. "But damned if I don't feel sorry for her."

The situation was further complicated by the lawsuit Mary's father had been embroiled in against Old Duke Wickliffe at the time of his death. At issue had been the large estates of Duke's second wife, one of Mary's Russell cousins. "I never seen so much dirty laundry washed in public in my life," muttered Lincoln, turning over the forty pages of the closely written document defending Old Duke's right to the estates.

"Does it mention that octoroon boy, that was Mary Russell's only grandchild from her first husband?" demanded Granny Parker, who was having tea with Mary and Lincoln on the porch as Lincoln thumbed through the document. The autumn sun splashed the frowsty lawn between the old house and the small brick dwelling on Short Street where Mary had spent her first thirteen years. Levi and his wife lived there now, and their two older children dashed back and forth with Eddie and Bobby, with Elodie and Kitty and Alec, shrill laughter ringing in the hazy air.

"Oh, Molly knows all about it," stated Granny Parker, when Lincoln glanced over at Mary, with a gentleman's hesitancy about going into the whole sordid story in front of his wife. "Everybody in town knows Old Duke blackmailed his wife into conveying her property to him, under threat he'd sell that boy and his mother, who'd been mistress to Mary Russell's only son."

Lincoln lowered the document and stared at the old lady, baffled. "And there are still people in this state who claim that the institution of slavery is . . . is *beneficial*? That it doesn't corrupt everything and everybody it touches?"

Granny Parker let out a sharp crack of laughter, her eyes bright. She'd taken to Lincoln at once, and the gracious wealth of the Todds be damned. It might have had something to do with the number of his Lincoln cousins she'd encountered over the years—one of them had been Sheriff of Lexington for a time. But Mary guessed that the old lady saw in Lincoln the kind of men who'd come out to Lexington with her in her youth, back in 1790 when the only thing there had been a blockhouse in the canebrakes. "Thousands of them, boy, thousands of them." She nodded thanks as her elderly maid, Prudence, came out with more hot water for the teapot.

"You all right, Mr. Lincoln?" asked Prudence, holding up the pot, and Lincoln said,

"Yes, ma'am, thank you."

"The only reason I haven't freed Pru, Annie, and Cyrus so far," said Granny Parker as Prudence departed, "is that then they'd have to leave Kentucky, and I can't do without 'em. Besides, where would they go, that they wouldn't be in danger of some slicker like old Robards trapping 'em back?"

She jerked her head toward Short Street, across which the wall of Robards's slave jail was visible. As usual this time of the afternoon his common stock was out on benches beneath the awning, as Pullum's had been before, the men dressed in new blue coats and plug hats, the women and children in clean calico. Mary knew from Cash that Robards kept "choice stock"—coincidentally all of them light-skinned girls under the age of twenty—inside, where buyers could look at them in private.

Lincoln folded his hands and said nothing for a time, but his face was harsh with disgust. Mary knew he hadn't forgotten.

It took three weeks to draw up the documents for the

division of Robert Todd's property, and to make sure that
Betsey and her younger children would be comfortably settled at Buena Vista until such time as the estate could be
sorted out. This process was made no easier by George's constant carping that his stepmother, as executrix of her husband's will, would cheat him out of his due share and had
"poisoned our father's mind" against him and his siblings.
Mary marveled at Lincoln's calm patience in pointing out to
his brother-in-law that most of the slaves had been Betsey's
personal property and not her husband's—or were Granny
Parker's, and not subject to sale for George's benefit. George
and Mary got into more than one screaming-match, which
ended with George storming out of Granny Parker's house in
a fulminating rage.

During that time Lincoln also spent a number of days at
Judge Robertson's office, taking depositions about the affairs
of Old Duke Wickliffe and his wife amid a storm of conflict-
ing testimony, character witnesses, and hearsay dating back
twenty years. He said little about the squalid tangle of concu-
binage and blackmail, but Mary could tell, when they finally
boarded the train for Frankfort and the long journey back to
Springfield, that the whole business had left as sour a taste in
his mouth as it had in hers.

"I never thought I'd live to feel sorry for Betsey," she
sighed, as the depot and the last houses of the town gave way
to the lush dark landscape of rock and trees that cloaked the
hills. "And as for George—Bobby, stop it! Now, come sit
down.... I don't fly into rages like that, do I?" She looked
worriedly up at her husband, who was gazing out at the
trees, still absently fingering the last late-blooming rose that
thirteen-year-old Emilie had given him for a buttonhole. "I
mean, not *that* badly?"

"Never," Lincoln assured her, with amusement deep in his
eyes. "But at least now I see you come by it honestly—or
would come by it honestly, if you ever was to do so."

"Well, I—Eddie, now, leave that lady alone...!" She
sprang to her feet, to recapture her roving offspring.

Winter had settled in on Springfield when they returned. Iron-cold winds slashed across the gray prairies, bringing first rain, then snow. Lincoln returned to a stack of accumulated mail saved for him by Billy Herndon, a depressing agglomeration of criticism for his speech against the Mexican War, newspaper articles misquoting and misrepresenting everything he'd said, and the accumulating evidence that his recommendations for positions were being steadily ignored in Washington. Eddie, who had seemed to perk up in Lexington's warmth, came down sick again early in December. Mary and Lincoln moved his little cot back into their room, and took turns through the nights applying poultices and giving him the saline draughts and spikenard teas prescribed by Dr. Henry and Dr. Wallace. In the mornings Lincoln would walk to the law office in the dreary darkness on only a few hours of sleep, and Mary would return to the closed-up, stuffy room with mustard compresses for the boy's chest, or boiling water to make steam for him to breathe.

Bobby would sit with his little brother after school, reading stories from his primer or playing games. Now and then Mary would hear Eddie's thin voice speak to his brother in barely a whisper.

On the thirtieth of January, a letter reached Mary from Emilie telling her that Granny Parker had died. She was so exhausted from looking after Eddie, and so frightened by the child's worn-out weakness, that she could only retreat to the parlor, where she sat weeping by the fireplace while Ruth moved quietly about the kitchen, preparing dinner for Bobby. When Lincoln came home he listened to her news, read Emilie's letter, and said softly, "She was a fine lady, Mother, and had lived a good long life. You lie here on the sofa, and rest a little. You look done in."

He looked done in himself, but Mary leaned back and he went into the kitchen to get her a cup of what Mammy Sally had always called "headache tea." Her eyes closed, she heard him speak to Bobby, asking the boy about his day, and how his brother did. Bobby had grown very silent through that tense and worried Christmas as his brother grew no better. Then Mary heard Lincoln go quietly into the bedroom where Eddie lay. He moved with that catlike soft-footedness that was always so astonishing in so tall and loose-jointed a man.

Hours later—she never knew how many—she woke chilled, her neck cricked and aching from falling asleep in her corsets. It was nearly pitch dark, and only the tiniest glow of embers writhed on the unbanked hearth. The house was profoundly silent. Someone had laid a quilt over her, and she gathered it around her shoulders as she limped, stiffly, through the parlor door and across the hall to the bedroom. She opened the bedroom door carefully, so as not to introduce a chill or draft.

The single candle's flame had not been snuffed or trimmed and was smoking badly. By its juddering light she could just make out her husband, sitting on the edge of the bed with one hand pressed over his mouth, the other closed around the tiny clawlike fingers of their child. Eddie's breathing was a horrible, pain-wracked rasp, and beneath the little boy's lashes Mary could glimpse the wet glimmer of half-open eyes. Lincoln's eyes were closed. She could see his shirtsleeved shoulders tremble, and realized he hadn't been able to force himself to get up and fetch her.

Or he hadn't dared to leave his son's bedside.

She crossed the room silently and knelt beside him, put her hand on top of his and Eddie's.

About an hour later Eddie died.

Chapter Thirty-two

Bellevue June 1875

"LOOKING BACK, I REALIZE I BARELY EVEN THOUGHT AT THE time how terrible Eddie's death was for my husband." Mrs. Lincoln raised her forehead from her hand, turned to regard John Wilamet with tired eyes in the close gloom of her room. "I knew he grieved—sometimes in the night I would wake and hear him weeping. But he was always a man who would retreat with his griefs, like an injured animal. And I was...not much able to help."

For the fourth day in a row she had kept to her room, requesting the carriage only to feel too ill and depressed to take it. Every time John came in to check on her she clutched at his sleeve, talking, sometimes for hours, as if words could cleanse her mind of the shadows accumulated there.

He'd told Dr. Patterson that he was encouraging Mrs. Lincoln to put aside her delusions and to resign herself to a quieter life. She seemed to trust him, he said tactfully, because they'd known one another years ago.

Patterson had agreed, after a wise little lecture on the inadvisability of telling patients about the composition of their medicine: "I've never met one who didn't believe she knew more than a trained doctor, about what was best for her."

But in fact John only listened.

Sometimes he wondered what his mother would have said, if ever she spoke of her life instead of simply absorbing patent medicines in an effort to hide from its injustices.

But he couldn't imagine to whom his mother would speak.

The curtains were closed against the summer sunlight. Outside, the air was redolent of cut grass, of roses and warmed earth. This room, where Mrs. Lincoln sometimes lay all day in bed—though she had risen and had Amanda dress her both yesterday and today—was stiflingly warm, dim and enclosed as a womb. It could have been any room, in any year: bed, chairs, table, armoire. Nothing to tell whether it was 1875 or 1855 or 1835, except the tired lines in Mrs. Lincoln's face.

"I was . . . shattered," she went on softly. "I never knew such grief was possible. Coming on top of my father's death, and Granny Parker's . . . For months I caught myself wondering, in unguarded moments, why my father didn't write to me anymore. Wondering if he was angry or just busy . . . I'd look out the window and see Bobby playing and I'd panic, thinking Eddie was lost. . . . And he was." She shook her head sadly, wonderingly still, after all those years, that the too-thin child she'd chased down the aisles of so many train cars was not in the world anymore. "He was."

She folded her hands, plump soft hands that looked as if they'd never quite become accustomed to housework. The gold band placed there long ago by a diffident backwoods lawyer glinted through the somber lace of her house-mitt.

"So deep was my grief that it never crossed my mind what his death did to Mr. Lincoln. How it broke him. Changed him." Mrs. Lincoln's voice was calm, as if she looked on the events now from a great distance, from some shaded place of safety. "He never spoke of what moved him—of what hurt him, or what mattered most deeply to him. I think maybe when he was a child growing up there was no one to listen, the way Mammy Sally would always listen to me. And of course that winter—Eddie's death—followed hard on that terrible debacle in Washington. But for—I don't know, four years? five years?—he seemed to lose much of his interest in politics, and holding office, and the ambition that had all his life driven him. As if, like me, for a little while he simply couldn't see a reason to go on."

ON A DAY-TO-DAY BASIS IT WASN'T AS PROFOUND OR DRA- matic as that, of course. Lincoln continued to argue cases in court, to write up bills in chancery for clients, to send patient letters recommending political supporters for government jobs that seldom materialized. While Mary lay in bed for days, so sick with weeping that she could not even emerge for her four-year-old son's funeral, Lincoln managed the house as well as he could. He took Bobby to the office with him—a silent, withdrawn seven-year-old who seemed not so much dazed by his brother's death as simply puzzled. Dr. Wallace, and the ever-faithful Dr. Henry and his wife, made sure that someone dropped in on Mary several times a day, and there were many nights that Bessie Francis came over to cook supper for Lincoln and Bobby, and to make sure there was food in the house for breakfast.

The Reverend Dr. Dresser came too, and spoke of God's inscrutable mercy and of the joys of Heaven. But the words were like the food the fairy-folk were said to serve travelers who wandered into their realms: shining and aromatic, but providing no more nourishment to Mary's weeping heart than handfuls of twigs and leaves. She knew Lincoln had gone to speak to Dr. James Smith, of the Presbyterian Church, who had conducted Eddie's funeral, and found some comfort in the little Scot's simple faith. Sometimes, when she lay alone in the dimness, she heard Dr. Smith's voice in the parlor, and Lincoln's hesitant replies.

Sometimes Lincoln would read to her in the evenings from Smith's book, *The Christian's Defense*. The words helped a little, mostly while he was reading them—while he was there to speak to her of his own groping, painful thoughts concerning destiny and death. But always the darkness would return.

She would wake in the night, thinking she heard Eddie's gasping breath. She would hear Lincoln's footsteps on the steep attic stair as he went up to comfort Bobby—Bobby who never wept during the day. When Lincoln returned to bed she would grasp him frantically in the black hollow of the darkness, sometimes making love with a fierce desperation, as if the joining of their flesh would somehow negate the shadow of inevitable loss.

By March she was with child.

The newcomer was a Christmas baby and they named him William Wallace, after Fanny's husband. From the moment she knew she had conceived, Mary began to feel better, and Lincoln, too, seemed much more himself. But all that year, and in the years that followed, it seemed to her that Lincoln's heart was less in politics, and far more deeply involved in the raising and the care of his sons.

Maybe he understood, she thought—as her own father never had—that the time given to one had to be stolen from the other.

He was still gone for weeks and sometimes months at a time, six months out of the year. He was still maddeningly absentminded when he was present, retreating into that unreachable fortress of his thoughts to the exclusion of chores that needed doing, kindling that needed splitting, children who had fallen out of a toy wagon that he might continue to haul, oblivious, down Eighth Street.

But he was undeniably home more, and could not get enough of holding his new baby son, singing to him (if you could call the noise he made singing), changing his diapers and shirts. From the moment of his birth Willie was a sunny child, rosy, healthy, laughing and looking around him alertly. It was as if, Mary thought, God had relented at last, and given her a perfect infant to love.

Lincoln spent long hours at the office on the State House square. He would leave early in the morning, in his rusty black suit with a big gray shawl draped around his shoulders if the day was chill, and sometimes not return until late in the evening, having stopped to yarn with his cronies down at Dillard's store. On such occasions Mary—stranded at home with baby Willie and trying as usual to keep the house clean, the meals cooked, everyone's clothes washed and ironed, and the hired girl (if they had one that month) up to her work—frequently lost her temper with him, giving vent to her frustration in shrill vituperation that she barely recalled later. Afterwards, when he took Bobby with him to eat at a café downtown, or simply wrapped his old shawl around his shoulders and vanished into the night, she felt sick with remorse.

But she didn't know how to stop herself. Literally didn't know how to do it. And he would say, when she came to him weeping with apologies, "Everyone does the best they can, Mother." And he'd tell her some absurd story to make her laugh.

Part of her anger came simply from exhaustion. The small sum that finally came to her from her father's estate meant they were able to keep a hired girl more steadily—Ruth remained with them for some years. And after Willie's birth, when Lincoln devoted the whole of his time and attention to his law practice, money came a little easier. But Mary, for all her willingness to make a good home, had not been raised to housework, and never really got used to the endless physical labor involved. For many years she actively resented her sister Elizabeth, with her servants and her big house, her wealth and her tea-parties, her modern stove and her carriage which was so much finer than the dilapidated Lincoln buggy. Even Ann, who'd married one of the town's wealthiest storekeepers, had a finer house and did only the lighter housework.

Mary would sometimes see one or another of her sisters as she came and went to the market, afoot and sometimes with Bobby at her heels. She'd note the velvet bands on Elizabeth's wide bishop sleeves, or the vast extent of Ann's crinolines, or even Julia Trumbull's stylish rice-straw bonnet, and look back wonderingly on her days with the gay Coterie of the House on the Hill and the warm endless security of peaceful Lexington. Though her own dresses were neat and pretty, there was no denying their housewifey cotton fabric. No denying either that she made them herself, rather than paying a sewing-woman to do it.

Then when Lincoln would come home—two hours late to dry and shriveled chicken, or a week and a half later from the circuit court in Tazewell—her anger would boil over, not at him, but at the fact that she was no longer the daughter of a wealthy man, but only the wife of a poor one. Lincoln did what he could, for her and for the children, but this involved riding the entirety of the Eighth Judicial Circuit, something only the circuit court judge did—the fat and wealthy land speculator David Davis. Lincoln would come back, after three weeks or a month, with tales of cheap inns and moldering bedclothes, of sharing a bed with opposing counsel *and* the adjudicating justice—"We're lucky we didn't have the defendant and the clerk of the court in there with us"—with lawyers from half the state snoring in a pile on the other side of the room.

Mary would laugh, but those were nights she would spend alone, with insomnia or nightmares for company. Every few weeks, and sometimes oftener, she would be laid up with migraine: blinds drawn, sick with pain in semi-darkness, while Ruth whipped up meals for Bobby and Willie or took them over to the neighbors'. When the huge summer thunderstorms rolled across the prairie Mary would huddle under the sheets, sick and sweating and sobbing, pressing the pillows over her face so that Bobby wouldn't hear her scream.

Praying that Lincoln would come home.

Visions obsessed her that would not be argued away. Visions of Bobby being struck by lightning, of the house being struck and catching fire and Willie perishing in his cradle in the blaze. Of Old Buck being swept off his feet by a sudden rise while crossing some stream, and of Lincoln being swept away, drowning far from her.

Leaving her without a word of farewell.

Then her fear came out as anger, as fears often do. In her rage she would accuse Lincoln of leaving her, of not loving her, of pushing off onto her shoulders all the raising of their sons. He would disappear for a long walk or return to his office—sometimes past midnight, or in the driving rain, sometimes rubbing his forehead if she'd thrown a book at him or hit him with a piece of firewood—and be back with a joke or a story for her when she emerged, exhausted, from the spell of her rage in the morning. Often after he left she would sleep, and wake up filled with fear that he wouldn't return at all. At such times she couldn't imagine why he continued to love her, but in her heart—in the marrow of her bones—she knew he did.

There were compensations. They were sweet years.

Deep winter and early spring, and the hushed stifling heat of midsummer during the State Supreme Court session, Lincoln was hers, as much as he ever was anyone's. As often as he would spend sitting around Dillard's with his friends talking politics—and even in those years he was never completely separated from politics—there would be evenings when she would step out the side door and see him coming down Eighth Street with half the boys in the neighborhood tagging at his heels.

Lincoln was endlessly fascinating to the boys of the town, probably because he spoke to them exactly as he spoke to adults, except—Mary hoped—he kept his jokes a little cleaner. With a frontier boy's blithe estrangement from the entire concept of clocks and time, he would stop to spin them stories, to talk about his unsuccessful attempts at Indian fighting or his trips down the Mississippi to New Orleans on a flatboat, to listen to their speculations and opinions about the way their own small worlds worked.

On Sunday afternoons he'd take Bobby—and Willie, as soon as that intrepid little soul mastered the art of walking—and upwards of a dozen local boys of all ages, and, resplendent in his old Conestoga boots and rough wool pants with one suspender, would walk with them out onto the prairies, looking for birds' nests and lizards and June bugs. On Sunday evenings he and Mary would sit on the kitchen porch in a couple of broken-down cane-bottomed chairs, while the boys dashed madly up and down the rows of the vegetable garden and the luminous miracle of the prairie sky gradually lost its brilliance, and the stars appeared overhead and despite

whatever smudges Mary could concoct they both got bitten
to pieces by mosquitoes. When Bobby had gone up to his little attic room and Willie fell asleep—and Willie would always drop off as if he'd been hit over the head, within
seconds of murmuring "G'night, Papa, g'night, Mama"—
there would be long winter evenings of lying wrapped in
each other's arms, sometimes reading, sometimes cuddling,
sometimes only softly talking, with anywhere from one to six
cats snoozing on their feet.

Sweet years.

Though the dinners she gave weren't instruments of politics anymore, there were still friends to entertain. Old friends
departed: Julia and Lyman Trumbull for Alton, Dr. Henry
for the far-off Oregon Territory. During Lincoln's second
year in Washington, gold had been discovered in
California—it seemed for a time that the whole of the country was on the move. New friends appeared. When she
could, Mary sewed with the other ladies of the Episcopal
Church, or hosted birthday parties or taffy-pulls. Their talk
didn't have the intellectual headiness of local politics—which
sometimes annoyed Mary—but they were far from stupid
and seldom dull. In the summers they all helped each other
bottle and pickle and preserve the bounties of the gardens.
Willie would assist in these efforts from the moment he
learned to walk, as cheery and open as Bobby was secretive,
toddling into the kitchen with his arms full of tomatoes and
squash.

When Willie was two and a half, Tad was born—Thomas,
named after Lincoln's father, who had died, after years of
whining letters asking for money, in Coles County, Illinois,
in 1851. Mary felt, almost from the moment of Tad's con-
ception, that all was not as it should be. Her pregnancy with
Willie had been easy, or as easy as pregnancies ever were with
her, for she suffered migraines sometimes for weeks at a time
and her temper became more uncertain than ever. Dr.
Wallace examined her and agreed that she carried a bigger
baby than Willie had been.

Labor was an agonizing nightmare, to produce the longest, thinnest baby with the biggest head she'd ever seen: "Sort of like a tadpole," Lincoln told her later, when she woke up after falling into exhausted sleep. He was sitting beside her bed, the new-wrapped bundle of infant in his arms. Tad squalled and fussed when Lincoln gave him back to her, and was never, after that, really quiet except in his father's arms. Lincoln spoke to her gently and humorously, and addressed his new son as "Tadpole," but she could tell he'd been badly frightened.

It didn't stop him from leaving a week later for the McLean Circuit Court.

He was gone two months.

During those months her smoldering anger at him resurfaced, for she knew she'd been hurt by her son's birth, and she was a long time healing. Even when she was on her feet again, and able to get around, the pains and the cramps stayed with her, and the internal weakness that got her up a dozen times a night to use the chamber pot redoubled. After the birth, she suffered an agonizing infection of her bladder and privates that was months in easing: months of tepid sitz baths in her bedroom, while Bobby was at school and Willie called repeatedly for her from the parlor and Tad howled in his crib.

After Tad's birth, she never felt quite well again. It was nearly Christmas before she and Lincoln lay together as husband and wife, and then—probably at the advice of Dr. Wallace—Lincoln was careful with her, drawing back from anything that would get her with child again.

They both knew that this was not to be.

She missed the rough-and-tumble intimacy of their earlier relations, but with the internal troubles that followed on Tad's birth, she was grateful for Lincoln's understanding. And in many ways it was enough, just to lie with her head on his shoulder, quietly talking in the shadows.

Dr. Wallace prescribed Battley's Soothing Cordial for her, with the strict instructions that no more than a teaspoon of it be taken at a time, and never more than twice in any one day. The medicine was a lifesaver, dulling the throb of migraines and letting her drift into sleep, or taking the edge off the worst of her cramps and letting her tend to Willie or get out with her sewing circle or do whatever her work was that day.

She didn't like the sleepiness that followed on a dose—she had far too much to do. In addition to her work in the house, she had friends to visit with and neighbors to see, Cousin Lizzie or the Widow Black, and Mrs. Wheelock a few houses along Jackson. Though she still saw Merce and Julia, most of her friends were not the same bright gay crowd she had gone buggy-riding and picnicking with in her early days in Springfield. Instead they were neighbors, women who shared her current life of housewifery and children, and who certainly didn't look down their aristocratic Edwards noses at her because her husband was poor.

Then in June of 1854 Lincoln came home from the circuit with two-week-old copies of the *Chicago Herald* in his pocket, which had reached him in Urbana: "Congress has struck down the Missouri Compromise," he said, when Mary—with Tad on her hip and Willie orbiting her skirts— came across the deep grass of the yard to the stable where he was unsaddling Buck.

"I read that." Mary set Tad down but kept firm hold of his hand. The child would get into literally anything and she was trying to keep him away from large quadrupeds as long as she could. "They can't do that, can they?"

"No, they can't." Lincoln dropped the saddle over its sawbuck, slipped the bridle from his horse's head. He'd already shed his jacket—the rough corduroy one he wore for riding the long prairie roads—and in the shadows, in his shirt-sleeves, with his black hair tumbled and standing up as usual in all directions, he looked like the hayseed storyteller who'd diverted old Professor Kittridge from her in the Globe Tavern's yard. "But they did. It's like every slaveholder in the South who wants to move into the Territories—and take his slaves with him—has been just waiting for Henry Clay to die, and Daniel Webster to die, and all those men to die who sweated to hammer out a compromise that would let this nation grow without tearin' ourselves apart over rich men ownin' slaves who run poor men out of work." He snatched up the currycomb and rucked it across Buck's back where the saddle had rested, working swiftly and automatically, the way Mary crocheted while concentrating on some piece of gossip with Cousin Lizzie. "So there *are* no free states or slave states anymore. Anytime some group of slaveholders wants to bring in slave labor to farm Illinois, they can do it, if they can get enough legislators to back them. And you bet the first man to do *that* is going to be *your* beau Mr. Douglas...."

"He was not my beau!" cried Mary indignantly. "Not for very long, anyway. Oh, I was just a simple country girl." She put her knuckles to her forehead in imitation of every pure-hearted heroine in every play they'd ever seen, in Washington and Boston ... even after sixteen years, Springfield still didn't have much in the way of theaters. "That Democrat blackguard broke my poor heart and went on to pass the Kansas-Nebraska Act...."

"You're still a simple country girl." Lincoln came around the horse's hindquarters and out of the stall, one long arm extended to embrace her. Mary ducked aside with a squeak, since her husband was now covered with horsehair, road-dust, and sweat. He smiled, looking down at her; then his smile faded. "And in pushin' that Act through Congress, Douglas is goin' to be responsible for a lot more broken hearts than yours, Molly, before this is done."

He scooped out oats for Buck, retrieved his sons from under Clarabelle's feet, and, with Tad under one arm like a parcel and Willie on his shoulders, walked with her through the bean-rows and the tomatoes back toward the house.

All that summer, they followed the newspaper reports of what was taking place in Kansas. Thousands of squatters from slave-states—chiefly Missouri—flooded the huge territory, driving back the thousands of immigrants being sent to the state by abolitionist organizations in New England. In July,

Cash Clay came on a speaking tour to Springfield, and under the spindly trees of the State House square spoke for two hours about what the forces of slavery would do in the way of intimidation, ballot-box stuffing, and outright bloodshed, to vote into Kansas a state constitution like Missouri's, under which no word against slavery could be legally spoken and under which the penalty for aiding a slave's escape was death.

For those two hours, Lincoln lounged on the ground under a tree whittling—Mary had never managed to teach him to use a chair, and even at home, if there was no company, he'd sit or lie on the floor. But afterwards he went to Clay, and Mary introduced them. Following supper at the house on Jackson Street, and after the boys were put to bed, she sat in the parlor with the two men, talking until far into the night.

Chapter Thirty-three

By fall Lincoln was campaigning again, on behalf of anti-Nebraska candidates for the Legislature.

"He's only making a fool of himself," declared Ninian, when Mary encountered him in the parlor of the House on the Hill as she waited for Elizabeth to come downstairs. "The Constitution defends the right of every man to his property, wherever that man may be or go within the country's boundaries. That's all the Kansas-Nebraska Act upholds. The right of every man to his property, and the right of self-government, which is why we fought to free ourselves from the British in the first place. Your husband has let his passions about slavery get the better of him, like far too many other-wise intelligent people in this country. He's going to find himself caught short."

"My husband," said Mary coolly, "*never* lets his passion about *anything* get the better of him—which as I recall was one of the arguments you and Elizabeth used against my marrying him. That he was *cold*."

"Don't chop logic with me, Mary." Her brother-in-law frowned down at her from his tall height. "The matter is too serious for that. If we want to preserve the Union we must find grounds upon which to end, once and for all, the bick-ering about slavery. The Kansas-Nebraska bill provides that."

"The Kansas-Nebraska bill truckles to Southerners who will not give up their slaves," she retorted, "and who hold the Union hostage in their demands to be allowed to keep them."

"Maybe." Ninian's face was hard, and sad; Mary forced herself to remember that this man had, like herself, walked daily past the Lexington whipping-post and auction-block. "The men who run the Legislatures of the cotton states are all slaveholders: it's not only their livelihood, it's their way of life, and they will not give it up. Is it worth giving up the Union, so that the abolitionists can congratulate one another on how righteous they are?"

Elizabeth came down then, and Ninian bowed and departed. With some difficulty Mary turned her mind back to the matter that had brought her to the House on the Hill: the letter she'd received from Emilie, now eighteen years old. "I wrote and asked her to come and make a long stay with us," she told her sister, unfolding the much-crossed sheets. "Since you'll be too much involved in matchmaking for Julie this season..."

"Julie is only seventeen," protested Elizabeth primly. "*Far* too young to be thinking of marriage."

"Of course!" Mary clasped her gloved hands before her bosom and nodded gravely. "And you were how old when you married Ninian?"

"Thirty," replied Elizabeth, who'd been seventeen. "Which makes me fifty-two now...and are *you* undertaking to find Emilie a husband?"

"Darling, I wouldn't *dream* of it." Mary winked. In fact, once Ann had married, Elizabeth had lost all interest in assisting any further sisters into Springfield matrimony. She maintained a polite interest in the affairs of Margaret, Mattie, and the rest of the Todd half-siblings back in Lexington, but it was Mary who wrote to them, not Elizabeth. Loyal and infinitely patient with her blood-sisters, Elizabeth—like Granny Parker whom she was more and more coming to resemble—never regarded Betsey or her eight children as anything more than interlopers.

"Well, with Mr. Lincoln back in politics," remarked Elizabeth, "at least Emilie won't be able to complain of having a dull winter."

By the end of an autumn of campaigning for various Whig state legislators opposed to the Kansas-Nebraska Act,

Lincoln was beginning to talk about campaigning himself: for the United States Senate. The repeal of the Compromise that, thirty-four years earlier, had averted the breakup of the Union troubled him deeply. And the prospect of slavery spreading—and with it, the bloody conflicts between slave-holders and abolitionists—filled him with foreboding. When Lincoln entered a public debate over slavery at the Courthouse, Mary, in the audience, heard beneath his usual calm logic and clear, precise arguments a power that hadn't been there before. Over the years, she knew he'd improved. Partly at her urging, he'd discarded much of the clownish-ness and personal satire that had characterized his earlier speeches. Now he renewed his ties with anti-Nebraska politicians, both Whigs and Northern Democrats. There were many nights when he and Mary would sit in the parlor reading newspapers from all over the country until the fire burned low in the grate; many more when she would go to bed, only to wake hours later alone and come across the hall in her wrapper to find him still staring into the glow-ing ash.

In September he challenged Stephen Douglas to a public debate on the subject of the Kansas-Nebraska Act. Douglas, in the midst of his own campaign to get another pro-Nebraska Democrat elected to the Senate from Illinois, re-fused to meet him. When most of the countryside was in town for the State Fair, and pouring rain turned the fair-grounds to glue, Douglas spoke in the State House, defend-ing the Act and his own part in pushing it through, in terms of the sacred right of self-government for each state. When after Douglas's three-hour speech the crowds began to dis-perse, Lincoln shouted from the stairway outside the hall that he would rebut Douglas at the same time the follow-ing day.

Lincoln and Mary stayed up most of the night, Lincoln scribbling madly to incorporate the notes he'd taken into a rebuttal of the Act on which he'd worked long and thought-fully since the summer. Mary and Emilie fixed supper, and

Emilie got the boys to bed, reading Willie a story while Mary came into the parlor to listen to Lincoln practice it through. "That's a long introduction to your main point," she remarked.

"I have to show each link of the chain, Molly, for men to see how they've been bound by it."

"I understand," she agreed. "But it sounds less like the rebuttal you promised, and more like a polemical diatribe."

Lincoln said, "Hmmn."

The following day, Mary left the boys with the Wheelocks and joined the crowd that pressed into the Legislative assembly-room, watched the lanky figure take the rostrum.

He was almost like a stranger to her, seen that way by the unforgiving afternoon light, with his face running with sweat in the heat and his hair like a dark haystack. Was that really the man who would lie on the parlor floor propped on his elbows, arm-wrestling gently with the boys? The man who had told her that silly story about the old lady and her cat over breakfast that morning? The man she'd hit over the head with a stick of firewood only a few weeks ago?

"When a white man governs himself, that is self-government; but when he governs himself, and also governs another man, that is more than self-government, that is despotism. . . .

"Nearly eighty years ago we began by declaring that all men are created equal; but now from that beginning we have run down to the other declaration, that for some men to enslave others is a 'sacred right of self-government.' . . .

"Our republican robe is soiled, and trailed in the dust. Let us turn, and wash it white, in the spirit, if not the blood, of the Revolution. . . . If we do this, we shall not only have saved the Union, but we shall have so saved it, as to make, and to keep it, forever worthy of saving. . . ."

There was talk of forming a new free-soil party in opposition to the Nebraska Act—the Republican Party. Lincoln, who mistrusted splinter parties, remained a Whig, and began aligning and rallying his old connections among the Whigs. He was on the road again all October and most of

November, meeting with this or that party leader, in between his appearances in the circuit courts. He started out running for the Legislature as well, but in his letters to her—some of them barely notes—Mary could tell he was more and more inclined to seek instead a Legislative nomination for the Senate.

"However you slice it, the Legislature is local," he said, on one of his rare visits to Springfield—she hadn't even known he was home until she'd looked out the front window of their neighbor Reverend Miner's house to see her husband, with his usual pack of boys trailing along at his heels, walking up Jackson Street in the icy twilight. "Any good I can do here is only local good."

He held out his hands to the kitchen fire, red and chapped. Mary, who'd run breathlessly across to the house, saw the gloves lying on her scrubbed kitchen table would have to be mended again. It was nearly impossible to find gloves for those immense hands. Eleven-year-old Robert was already dipping tea-leaves from the caddy into the pot, having, she saw, maneuvered the kettle on its gallows-hook over the fire. He moved with an economical neatness that was an echo of his father's movements, quiet-footed as a shadow.

"In the Senate I can do something that can actually help this country out of the mess it's heading straight for—the mess it's already in, if you read the newspaper reports from Kansas."

"Can you be in the Legislature and the Senate at the same time, Pa?" asked Robert, diffident as he always was around the father he seldom saw. His eye had completely healed and there was hardly anyone who even remembered that he'd been called Cock-Eye. But either the teasing he'd endured—or the hideous ordeal of terror, betrayal, and agony at the doctor's hands—had left a permanent wariness in him, a chilly barrier that Mary was never able to break.

"No," said Lincoln. "No, I can't... and if I'm elected I'll

have to resign. But at least if I'm elected," he added with a grin, "the rest of the folks in the State House will remember my name."

He was elected, and he did resign—and, Mary learned a few days after the election, so did Lyman Trumbull, who had just won the Congressional seat for Alton. A Democrat, Trumbull had split with Douglas over the Nebraska Act— "He's the one we have to beat," growled the fat Judge Davis, when Lincoln held a strategy session in the parlor one sleeting December evening. Mary greeted the men at the door and made coffee and cake, enormously grateful that Emilie was keeping the boys out of the way in the kitchen.

Emilie, with her piquant face and beautiful red-gold hair, had only a passing interest in politics, but she was lively and funny and all three boys adored her. She had no trouble inventing a word-guessing game that interested both an in-quisitive four-year-old and an eleven-year-old who con-sidered himself too grown-up for such "baby" things, leaving Mary to listen quietly from the kitchen to the talk of the men.

Politicians, yes, but different from the drawling wealthy landholders and bankers who had thronged her father's par-lors and argued about the National Bank over juleps. Different, too, from the smoothly powerful transplanted Southerners of Ninian's clique. These were lawyers and busi-nessmen, harder and, Mary thought, shrewder than her father's friends or Ninian's cronies.

Judge David Davis was wealthy, but that wealth was self-made in land speculation. Immense and opulent, he occu-pied most of the sofa, plump hands folded over acres of subdued waistcoat—his eyes snapped with the single-minded attentiveness of a predator waiting to pounce. Ward Lamon, too, was massive, but instead of being fat like Davis he more resembled a grizzly who could kill with a swat—a lawyer from Danville, where he'd partnered Lincoln on any number of court cases. Lamon would play the banjo and tell jokes to the boys, when he'd come with Lincoln to

Springfield, but Mary knew Elizabeth would never have had him in her parlor. Nor would she have had canny Simeon Francis—she had never forgiven the editor for fostering Lincoln's courtship of Mary and, in Elizabeth's eyes, making a fool of her before all Springfield. Stringy Leonard Swett reminded Mary of Cassius in *Julius Caesar,* too lean and hungry-looking to be completely trusted, and little Stephen Logan—the eccentric of the Todd-Edwards clan—was not a man who had patience with anything that was not life and death.

Mary understood that in the matter of the Kansas-Nebraska Act, they were, indeed, facing the possibility of the life or death of the United States. She knew instinctively she would not be welcome in their strategy session. They were like soldiers closing ranks for battle, wary of any outsider and of women most of all.

"Trumbull's got the Chicago Democrats behind him." Davis turned toward Lincoln, who—she was glad to see—sat in the chair nearest the fire, even though he sat with his long legs drawn up so that his knees were under his chin. "Norman Judd and John Palmer, railroad men."

"The Democrats are split," said Lamon dismissively. "Pro- and anti-Nebraska—half of them will waste their votes on Jimmy Shields, of all people. I hear Governor Matteson supports him."

"The one we need to watch out for," said Lincoln softly, "is Matteson himself. He runs his supporters like Wellington running the Battle of Waterloo. I watched him horse-tradin' all over the state. He's pro-Nebraska and pro-Douglas, and he'll support Douglas up to the steps of the White House... over the smokin' ruins of this nation."

Watching their faces from the door of the dark little dining-room, as Lamon waved aside the chances of Matteson being nominated and Davis outlined who should approach which legislators for support, she was reminded of men playing chess, or poker for high stakes. Gone was the camaraderie of the gentry who ran the countryside because they were the landowners and it was their taxes that supported the state. These were men gambling for position, for the control of patronage that would allow them to do favors for those who would help them to more power.

With the possibility of slavery spreading to all new states—and flowing back like blocked sewage into the established old ones—the stakes were too high for hesitation or mercy. Lincoln's face in the firelight was hard, almost a stranger's face to her. The face of a lawyer whose client stands in grave peril of hanging.

In the days that followed, Mary and Lincoln made endless lists of supporters, tallying whose votes in the Legislature were assured, and whose would require more work, more promises, more convincing. Mary pulled together her neatly organized envelopes of newspaper clippings: not only Lincoln's speeches, but records going back years of who supported whom and why. It was clear that Lincoln was the strongest of the anti-Nebraska contenders.

"We'll win this time," breathed Mary, as Emilie fixed her hair and laced her up for the New Year's Day reception at the House on the Hill. "We'll win.... This time we *will* take a house, for we'll be there six years...at the very least! One simply cannot do *anything* from a boardinghouse.... Of course Lafayette Square is the most fashionable, but it's quite expensive.... Though the neighborhood along Thirteenth and Fourteenth Streets is perfectly genteel.... You will come visit us for the Congressional season, will you not?"

On the twentieth of January a blizzard dumped over a foot of snow on the town and hammered the small neat houses of clapboard and the brick mansions of the wealthy alike. Trains were stranded on the prairie, the rails buried under snow, trapping most of the Legislature and delaying the voting. Lincoln came in from chopping wood or milking Clarabelle shivering and half-frozen. He plowed his way across the knee-deep snow of the yard half a dozen times a day to make sure Buck and Clarabelle were warm enough in their snug stable, and dug out the path to the outhouse three and four times. On the third day of this he came in with something tucked in the front of his coat—

"What is it, Pa?" asked Robert, as Lincoln knelt by the kitchen stove, and Willie cried ecstatically, "It's a *puppy!*"

"Oh, the poor thing!" Mary knelt beside the wet ball of shuddering yellow fur. "Where did you find it?"

"In the stable." Lincoln tugged off his gloves and unwound his scarf. "Must have wandered there to get out of the wind—Bob, maybe you can break off a chunk of this morning's milk and heat it up for our little friend?"

Robert laughed—the milk had been thawed earlier in the day. There wasn't much of it, but Mary knew better than to protest that it should all be saved for baby Tad. The puppy lapped weakly and Willie, with great presence of mind for a four-year-old, fetched a clean towel and hung it in front of the hearth, to heat up as a bed for the newcomer. Emilie said, "One of those split-oak breadbaskets will do, won't it, Mary dearest?" and from beneath the kitchen table Sheba, Cinders, Little, and Bigger sneered as only cats can, as if to say they'd seen more impressive rats.

That night, while the wind screamed around the eaves, little Fido crept across the hall and scratched at the bedroom door, whining to be let in—which of course Lincoln did. He settled the pup on the foot of the bed by his feet, despite Mary's protests—"Those cats are bad enough. He's warm enough in the kitchen, surely?"

"He'll be no trouble," Lincoln promised, with the blitheness of one who hasn't had a cat spit up a hairball into his braids. He slithered back under the covers, shivering. Mary felt the pup curl itself confidingly as close to her feet as he could, and heard, from somewhere, one of the cats growl warningly. "Now, girls," her husband admonished. Then, to Mary, "The poor little fellow's probably lonely in the kitchen. When he's bigger he'll be fine there."

Mary sighed, knowing she'd acquired yet another bedmate

for life. "You'll be sorry when he follows you into the Senate chamber, Father."

"I'll sic him on the Democrats," came Lincoln's voice out of the darkness, and strong arms wrapped around her waist. "I think even he could take on Jimmy Shields, don't you?"

Chapter Thirty-four

JIMMY SHIELDS GOT FORTY-ONE LEGISLATIVE VOTES ON THE first ballot when the Legislature finally assembled, after twelve snowbound days—Lincoln got forty-five. In the gallery of the Legislative chamber, Mary hugged her cloak around her and shivered with apprehension. All Lincoln needed to win was fifty-one votes.

Definitely, F Street between Thirteenth and Fourteenth. Or possibly Capitol Hill? For her first reception she'd serve quail, with the béchamel sauce M'sieu Giron had taught her the secret of, and perhaps a few touches of her good Kentucky specialties....

She glanced beside her at Julia Trumbull, whose face was pink with the cold within the black fur of her coat-collar. Lyman Trumbull got exactly five votes. Mary squeezed her hand in sympathy, and on her other side, Emilie pressed her elbow in discreet congratulation.

The balloting began again. The crowd in the gallery up under the Legislative chamber's dome reminded her of the Washington Congressional audiences, only without the brightly dressed contingent of prostitutes. It certainly was as good as a theater—better, in some ways, because you knew everyone.

She watched from above as wizened little Cousin Stephen Logan moved among the legislators; watched his faded red head, his hands move as he spoke. A ladies' cloakroom had been set up off the lobby for the convenience of the spectators who'd come to watch the vote—ordinarily, of course, the building had facilities only for men. On her way downstairs, breathless so as not to miss the moment when Lincoln's victory would be announced, Mary saw Simeon Francis talking to big-shouldered Ward Lamon in the lobby. He tipped his hat to her and she came up to him and asked, "How goes it?"

"Sewn up," declared Lamon, and Mary clapped her hands in triumph.

"I'll be the first to tell Elizabeth. That will teach her to call Mr. Lincoln a bumpkin. She's just *torn,* you know, between admitting she was wrong about him and having a Senator for a brother-in-law. But pride won—it always does, with Elizabeth. She's doing the handsome thing, though, and is holding a victory reception for Mr. Lincoln at the House on the Hill tonight...."

Simeon's eyes narrowed. "I think it'll be closer than your sister's counting on, Mrs. Lincoln. Governor Matteson's working to bring back Democratic votes, like your husband said he would...."

"Matteson's had *one vote!*"

"He picked up support on this last ballot...."

Drat, thought Mary, *I did miss the count....*

"And Judd and Palmer say they won't vote for a Whig under any circumstances."

"They're afraid Mr. Lincoln won't pass along contracts to Democrats, is what they're afraid of," retorted Mary, and Simeon raised his grizzled brows.

"That's exactly what they're afraid of, Mrs. Lincoln," he answered. "We've got some of the anti-Nebraska Democrats voting for Lincoln now, but they're doing it looking over their shoulders, hoping they haven't guessed wrong."

By the sixth ballot most of Jimmy Shields's supporters had switched their allegiance to Governor Matteson. Mary saw Billy Herndon—chinless and self-important as ever, though nowadays he wore the dignity of the Mayor of Springfield— scuttle from the Representatives' chamber for the third or fourth time, hurrying, she knew, down the State House steps and across the trampled snow of the square to the office he and Lincoln shared. Lincoln would be there, she knew, pacing the worn carpet or stopping by the iron stove in the long room's center to warm his hands, his shabby shawl pulled close around his shoulders, waiting and listening for someone's step on the stair. Willie had protested at not being allowed to stay with his father while he waited—the two younger boys were at the Wheelocks' house, where Robert would go for supper when he got out of school. But Mary for once had been firm. The day would be nerve-wracking enough for Lincoln. At least he shouldn't have to play nursemaid as well.

On the next ballot, a number of Lincoln's Whig supporters—who on the whole either liked Matteson's non-committal politics or hoped for public works contracts—voted for the governor.

"Why doesn't Lyman throw his votes to Lincoln?" demanded Mary, leaning over to tweak Julia's sleeve. "That would end this, and it would still get an anti-Nebraska candidate into the Senate. That's what Mr. Judd and the others want, isn't it? What difference does it make to them who it is?"

Julia's dark eyes avoided Mary's as she replied with forced lightness, "Good heavens, Molly, I don't know why politicians do what they do! I'd certainly never dream of asking Mr. Trumbull. Besides," she added, with a touch of smugness in her voice, "Mr. Trumbull is picking up votes, as you can see."

"I wonder if that could be because Mr. Trumbull is a rich man, and my husband a poor one."

Julia stared at her for one moment as the implication of that sank in; then her face turned crimson within the frame of dark hair and dark fur, and she whispered, "Oh—!" and turned away.

Mary scarcely noticed, because the tally had just been read out: Governor Matteson *(Another rich man,* thought Mary in fury, *with patronage to give out....)* forty-seven, Lyman Trumbull thirty-five—she could not imagine how she had once thought he was so attractive! Abraham Lincoln, fifteen.

Billy Herndon left the chamber again. Mary knew exactly how long it took, for him to cross the snowy State House square, to climb those two flights of stairs. To come back, including a brief stop in the lobby to take a drink from his hip-flask, if he wasn't swearing Temperance this week . . .

She saw Logan, Francis, and Lamon huddled around the tall fair paunchy Herndon in a corner of the chamber, Logan shaking his head again and again. Her hands clenched hard, unbelieving, knowing what she saw, as the three men moved among the milling figures below, speaking now to one man, now to another... speaking only to those fifteen who still supported Lincoln.

No, Mary thought, NO...

Tears flooded to her eyes; she clung to the support of Emilie's hand.

On the tenth ballot, Lyman Trumbull was appointed to the United States Senate.

"You said yourself, what difference does it make who it is," said Julia.

"None, I suppose," retorted Mary, hot with fury for her husband's sake, "if both men are *honest.*"

She turned and flounced down the gallery stairs, brushed past Bessie Francis's extended hand of sympathy, strode out across the lobby to the icy night beyond the huge bronze State House doors.

The party at Elizabeth's that night was still held, in Lyman Trumbull's honor. "I know how disappointed you must be," sympathized Elizabeth as Lincoln entered the lamp-lit parlor, with Mary and Emilie on either arm. Lincoln smiled and shook his head.

"Not too disappointed to congratulate my friend Trumbull," he replied, stepping forward to shake the new Senator's hand. Afterwards he kept everyone at the party in a roar of laughter for hours with stories.

For her part, Mary could not bring herself to be so forbearing. She cut Julia Trumbull dead, and never spoke to her again.

THROUGHOUT THE FOLLOWING YEAR THERE WAS INCREASING bloodshed in Kansas, as Missouri squatters forced a slave-owner's constitution and government on the state, and Free-

Soilers set up their own, rival government in Topeka. Mary avidly read newspaper accounts all spring, of intimidation, ballot-stuffing, and outright fraud, while Lincoln was on the circuit and away in Chicago. More and more often he was called in on patent-infringement cases for the McCormick Reaper company, or for Norman Judd's Illinois Central Railroad. Meanwhile—according to Cash's letters—the Free-Soilers of Kansas began to import guns.

She found her time fully occupied, even had she not been giving small dinners for Lincoln's political friends, and introducing Emilie to every eligible bachelor in Springfield. To her despair, it was becoming clearer to her that Tad, like Robert, had been born with a deformity, in Tad's case a speech impediment that rendered his words nearly incomprehensible. Having seen what her distaste for imperfection had done to Robert, she worked hard to be patient in teaching the child, who in addition was nervous and cried at the slightest provocation.

Only Willie made up for her frustration and occasional despair, and Willie—perhaps because she was relaxed with him as she could not bring herself to be with his brothers—quickly took on himself the role of her protector, when his father was away.

In the spring Emilie returned to Lexington unbetrothed, and promptly fell in love with one of Mary's Hardin connections, a young lawyer named Ben Helm. Excited letters passed back and forth, Elizabeth temperately approved....

But both Mary and Lincoln were aware that, in a sense, Lincoln was only marking time until the next Senatorial race.

Marking time, and praying that the sectional conflict would not explode before then.

When he returned to Springfield, they would talk of the bloody raids by one Kansas faction against another, of the horrors of retaliation and blood-feud. "It's like watchin' a fuse burn down," said Lincoln one night, dropping an armful of newspapers on the parlor table, "an' us sittin' on the keg." Billy Herndon—who to everyone's surprise had made an excellent Mayor—joined the antislavery forces with his usual headlong enthusiasm, arguing that any means, "however desperate," should be used against the enemies of freedom. Lincoln, who as his longtime partner was inevitably tarred with the same brush, was hard put to calm the radicals.

"We're fighting for freedom and for our country," he said to Mary later. "We can't do that by breaking our country's laws."

Billy, being Billy, signed Lincoln's name to a call for a meeting of Sangamon County anti-Nebraska supporters while Lincoln was away in May. Mary stormed over to the law office and screamed at him that he would ruin Lincoln with the more moderate voters, and—when Billy only looked down his nose at her and intoned, "This is politics, ma'am, and not something to discuss with ladies,"—went to Cousin John Stuart, who reprimanded Billy himself. By year's end, the anti-Nebraska Whigs had been absorbed into the Republicans: the more radical abolitionists, who objected also to foreigners and Catholics, formed the American Party, also known as the Know-Nothings.

By the middle of the following year—1856—Lincoln received over a hundred Republican nominations for Vice-President, to run in tandem with the flashy adventurer and hero of the Mexican War, John C. Frémont.

Lincoln was forty-seven, and seemed older—but then, even as a backwoods bumpkin there had always been something patriarchal about him. Mary was thirty-eight, a fact which surprised her. Lincoln still called her "my child bride" and though, to the boys, she referred to him as "Father," she sometimes caught herself thinking of him as exactly that: the father she still so sorely missed. He smiled when she called him that, and called her "Mother," which made her laugh. She pictured them sometimes as an old white-haired couple, surrounded by grandchildren...being invited to tea at the White House and pointed out in Washington society, as Dolley Madison was pointed out in her carriage, with love and respect.

In the same week as the Republican Convention, news reached Springfield that Missouri "border ruffians" had raided and sacked the free-soil city of Lawrence, Kansas. In retaliation the abolitionist John Brown and his men murdered and mutilated five pro-slavery men on Pottawatomie Creek, and reading of it Mary shivered, as if at the sound of summer thunder.

Frémont and his eventual running-mate—a New Jersey Senator named Dayton—were defeated.

Mary felt no regrets at this. Though the victory of "Free Speech, Free Press, Free Soil, Free Men, Frémont" might have brought patronage, she believed that the cost would have been too high. In every newspaper that came to the house on Eighth and Jackson—and there were dozens, now—Southern Congressmen and Southern businessmen spoke angrily against the consolidation of anti-slavery forces into a single, Republican, party.

It was clear to her that if a Republican were elected President, there were those in the South who would demand that the Union be dissolved. The handwriting was on the wall. Only thus could they protect the institution upon which not only their economy, but their very society, was based.

Mary herself tried to talk Lincoln into voting for the Know-Nothing candidate Millard Fillmore, Zachary Taylor's Vice-President, who had filled out the end of "Old Rough and Ready's" incomplete term, and who had visited Lincoln a few years ago in Springfield, and spent a half-hour discussing roses with Mary.

She had other concerns that year. The Springfield town lot her father had left her finally sold, and to her immeasurable relief, Lincoln agreed to use the money to enlarge the house. Emilie's stay in the only spare nook available—Mary's sewing-room—had brought home to her the need for more space, particularly as Tad was old enough now to move into the overcrowded second attic with his brothers. The attics were transformed into a full-fledged second story, and—God be praised—a modern stove was acquired for the kitchen in place of the old assortment of roasters, gallows-hooks, Dutch ovens, and boilers on the kitchen hearth.

Robert got his own bedroom—suitable to both his fourteen-year-old dignity and his impatience with Tad's restlessness—with Willie sharing a smaller room with Tad. Tad adored Willie, who never treated him as a baby, as Robert often did. Imperious even at four, Tad would choose the games, and the easygoing Willie would fall in with whatever schemes his mischievous brother would devise.

Carried away with the joy of the new house, Mary bought new carpets, and a suite of parlor furniture, considerably over-running her budget. Lincoln's anger when he got the bills surprised and frightened her—she hadn't seen him that angry since the early days of their marriage. She'd far rather he'd shouted at her, as her father or brothers would have, rather than the cold silence that preceded his leaving the house. She half-guessed that he distrusted his anger, as he distrusted his sexual passions, and would pull away from it as he had pulled away from her during those feverish nights in Simeon Francis's parlor, after Bessie had gone to bed.

He was gone most of the night, and though he accepted her tearful apologies as always, she mentally swore never ever to spend money without telling him again.

One of the things Mary loved best about the new shape of the house was that she finally had the luxury of *her* own room, connected by a door to Lincoln's smaller bedroom where, if he had a case, he could stay up half the night writing without disturbing her often-fretful sleep.

She missed him sometimes waking her if she had a nightmare. But many times he would do so anyway, for he was a light sleeper himself. Hearing her whimpering in her sleep, even through the closed door, he would pad through in his nightshirt to gently shake her, usually climbing into bed beside her to hold her till dawn.

For her part she loved the luxury of sitting up reading by lamplight late into the night, without having to worry about whether Lincoln would be disturbed or when he might come in from his office. And though she didn't say so to him, she particularly enjoyed not having to sleep with Fido and six cats. Many nights he'd come in and sit in the chair beside her bed, reading the newspaper, with the dog curled confidingly at his feet.

Billy Herndon of course put the story around that Mary had had the second story put on without Lincoln's knowledge, because when Lincoln came home from the circuit and saw the second story had been completed, he'd facetiously asked a neighbor where the Lincolns lived: he didn't recognize the house, he said. It was the kind of thing Billy *would* take seriously. He'd gone around for weeks telling everyone that Lincoln had no appreciation for what he called the "Sacred Beauty of Nature" because Lincoln had replied, deadpan, to Billy's inquiry about Niagara Falls, "I just wondered where all that water came from."

CHAPTER THIRTY-FIVE

In March of 1857—only days after the elderly Democrat James Buchanan was inaugurated President—the United States Supreme Court handed down its decision that Dred Scott, a Missouri slave, had no right under the Constitution to seek his freedom because, as a Negro, he was not a citizen of the United States. Scott's master, an Army surgeon, had taken his slave first to Illinois, then to the Minnesota Territory. On his master's death, Scott had sued for liberty—as hundreds of other slaves had, over the years—on the grounds that he'd been resident of a free state and then of a territory from which slavery was banned.

Residence in a free state or a free territory meant nothing, Supreme Court Chief Justice Taney ruled, because Congress had no right to exclude slavery from either states or territories. The Missouri Compromise, over which fighting still continued in what men now called Bleeding Kansas, was in fact unconstitutional. The Founding Fathers had never intended blacks to be included in their definition of "liberty," since they had mentioned them neither in the Declaration of Independence, nor in the Constitution.

"Taney's wrong," said Lincoln softly, when he got back from the Clinton County Court, where he'd heard the news. "And there will be hell to pay."

Mary could almost feel sorry for Stephen Douglas, as the Senate race of 1858 drew near. As the architect of the Kansas-Nebraska Act, he was obliged to defend it, like a man trying to put out a prairie-fire with a teacup.

In the North.

In the South, Douglas was praised as a defender of the rights of states to govern as their people demanded, and as the friend of those who feared the abolitionists' increasingly strident demands. More and more, Southern slaveholders were proclaiming that slavery was the only condition suitable to the Negro race. It was beneficial to them, they insisted: it would be cruel to thrust inherently primitive and childlike intellects out into the cold, cruel world.

As Mary's father had once said of Frances's canary.

"And it isn't cruel to let people like that horrible Mrs. Turner back home in Lexington own them, I suppose?" fumed Mary. "The one who beat so many of her slaves that her coachman eventually killed her in self-defense? And was hanged for it?" She handed her husband a cravat. He'd come back to the house for an hour's rest and some supper, which he hadn't eaten, after a day spent at the State House, where the Republicans of Illinois had gathered to nominate their candidate for the Senate.

Norman Judd—of the "we won't vote for a Whig" group two years ago—had opened the convention with a banner saying, COOK COUNTY FOR ABRAHAM LINCOLN.

The papers that lay on Lincoln's small desk—Robert had twice kept Tad from shuffling them into a different order—were Lincoln's acceptance speech.

This time, thought Mary, he would win. He had to.

"Or that awful woman in New Orleans, back when I was a girl?" she went on. "I spent half my evenings in the kitchen, listening to Nelson and Mammy and Chaney talk. I know how everyone in town treated their darkies, and something tells me people haven't changed that much over the years. Some people—like Papa—treated them well...."

"Except that they could be sold," reminded Lincoln softly, "to people who wouldn't treat 'em quite so well."

Mary was silent, thinking about Jane's tears, all those years ago when Saul had been sold to help pay Uncle David's debts. Remembering Pendleton, and Chaney, and Patty, sold as part of her father's property in the settlement, just because George didn't think he was getting enough of his father's money. Of Jane and Judy, sold too to help clear up Robert

Todd's debts. When Emilie had come here—good God, was it four years ago already!—she had spoken of the financial hardship in which Betsey and all the younger ones were living; her latest letter informed Mary that Betsey had gone to live in Alabama with Mattie and her husband.

What had happened to Saul? To Jane and Judy? To Pendleton, whom Betsey had nursed through the cholera; to grouchy old Aunt Chaney, who'd made such wonderful pastries; and the timid, good-natured Patty? Mary hadn't the faintest idea.

"Papa never would have sold them," she said at last.

But as President of the State Bank of Kentucky, Papa had sold hundreds of slaves when other men had died in debt, with as little thought as George had had, for where they went or what became of them.

"No," agreed Lincoln. He started to turn from the mirror—Mary handed him a hairbrush. As usual his hair was too long and looked as if a hurricane had passed across his head. "The Founding Fathers did what they had to do to make the Union, and I'm not about to undo their work. But they knew the evil they dealt with, and tried to limit it. And that we must do, or make a mockery of all they strove for."

Robert, Willie, and even Tad, who was just five but already knew the difference between the State Legislature and "We-uh Gongweth," as he called it, had wanted to go with their mother to hear their father accept the nomination. Mary had told them that children weren't allowed in the State House galleries, which was partly true—mostly, she wanted to hear Lincoln speak without worrying about Tad slipping away and ending up dancing a jig on the podium. Lincoln walked the three blocks to the State House square alone, through the falling summer twilight, to meet with Judd and Davis and the others before the convention re-convened at eight. She got the boys settled and followed later, taking her place in the crowded gallery with Cousin Lizzie,

Dr. Wallace, and a new friend, Hannah Shearer, the lovely sister of their neighbor the Reverend Miner. The night was hot and smelled of far-off storm; Mary's head throbbed a little, and the itching discomfort of her old female complaint was back, but she'd forborne to take the usual two spoonfuls of Battley's Cordial: she wanted instead to savor every moment of triumph.

Lincoln stepped to the podium, and his voice cut the molten lamplight of the room like a silver knife. *"If we could first know where we are, and whither we are tending, we could then better judge what to do, and how to do it. . . ."*

In his black suit and black silk cravat he looked, if not exactly like other men, at least like a man of respect and education, not like some shambling backwoods lawyer. Mary had never quite taught him to sit in a chair when he wasn't being observed, and she despaired of ever breaking him of the habit of answering the door himself, in his shirtsleeves and like as not with a hammer in one hand and a mouthful of nails. . . .

But tonight he looked like a man voters could take seriously. He looked like a Senator.

And he spoke like a prophet whose God was justice.

"A house divided against itself cannot stand. I believe this government cannot endure, permanently half slave and half free.

"I do not expect this Union to be dissolved—I do not expect the house to fall—but I do expect it will cease to be divided. . . ."

"He should have cut that out." Dr. Wallace leaned across to Mary. "Lamon and the others told him to. He's going to lose any chance of getting into the Senate if he alienates all the Southerners living in the south part of Illinois."

"I think we've had enough of candidates who won't talk about what we're actually voting for," retorted Mary, whose opinion had been—Lincoln had asked her—to leave it in. "At least he's honest enough not to try to sell voters a pig in a poke."

Wallace raised his eyebrows, and shook his head. "Whether he's just won the election or cut his own throat," he mused, "you've got to admit he's come a long way."

. . .

A month later, with the campaign heating up, Lincoln issued a challenge to Stephen Douglas, for seven debates on the issue of slavery. Mary held her breath for the week it took Douglas to make up his mind. Ever since the days of hearing secondhand of Lincoln and Douglas arguing in Speed's store—"Like two gods throwing lightning at one another,"—she had longed to see these intellectual warriors meet.

Knowing Douglas, she knew exactly why he hesitated. Like Ninian, he would rather simply that the issue go away; he didn't want to alienate one side or the other. The object was to get into power first, *then* implement policy.

Maybe he suspected that his own position was false. That of the rights of states to choose their own path was less easy to defend than the biblical and patriotic echoes of that single word "liberty."

Maybe Lincoln's challenge was simply too public for him to back down.

Banners, posters, cartoons in newspapers spoke of the "Little Giant"—with his awe-inspiring presence and his voice of bronze and thunder—meeting the challenge of the "Giant Killer." There was much talk of David and Goliath, though newspapers differed on which combatant was on this occasion fighting on the side of the Lord. Through those seven weeks of campaigning Mary followed the debates in the *Illinois Journal,* with Robert reading over her shoulder and Tad, Willie, and Maria Francesca—the latest of the "girls"—listening eagerly, as if for news of a battlefront. When Lincoln came home—a day here, two days there—he was mostly occupied with the Republican leaders in Springfield, or in conference with newspapermen whose presence was increasingly a part of any major campaign. One of them, a young German named John Nicolay, became something of a fixture around Lincoln's law office and a fast friend of the new law clerk, dapper and supercilious John Hay.

In addition to debating Douglas, Lincoln crisscrossed the

state, addressing meetings, rallies, audiences large and small, sometimes in towns he himself had staked out while a young surveyor struggling to make a living in New Salem. He remembered everyone's name, and the circumstances of previous meetings—Mary knew well his prodigious capacity, not only to recall everyone he had ever met, but to take a genuine warm interest in their doings, as if each man was a friend encountered across the stove of some country store.

Douglas was campaigning hard, too. But whereas he traveled by special train with an entourage including his second wife, Dolley Madison's niece the regal and beautiful Adele Cutts, Lincoln always rode the public cars, shaking hands with and listening to everyone he encountered. When at last Mary took the train to Alton to see them meet—when she finally stood in the heatless October sunshine of the Alton Courthouse square—the difference between the two candidates was even more pointed. Douglas radiated wealth and power, resplendent in a new blue suit and immaculate linen, every inch the respected Senator with offices in hand to bestow and bowing as gracefully to applause as he'd bowed to Mary, years ago in Elizabeth's parlor. Lincoln, following him up alone, looked like he did on any day in court, in his rusty black suit with the sleeves too short and the pants-hems hovering several inches above his worn black shoes.

She heard the cheers for "Old Abe," "Honest Abe," and her heart glowed—though she knew Lincoln hated the nicknames. He smiled and lifted his hand and the cheers swelled to a roar. A man who'd cut wood and slaughtered hogs for his living, a man who understood what it was to be poor. Last night at the Franklin Hotel, Lincoln had recounted how, during his first long-ago campaign for the Legislature, en route from one small village to another, he and Cousin John Stuart had passed reapers in a field, getting in the last of the wheat. The workmen had said they had little use for any candidate of either party, but would vote for any man who could do his share of the work; Lincoln had promptly climbed

down from Cousin John's buggy, borrowed a scythe, and led
the crew on a full round of the field.

"You can't pretend, with a scythe in your hands, Mother,"
he'd said to her. "Thank God they wasn't makin' shoes. It
was as good a campaign speech as I ever made."

Mary, looking up at the platform now, couldn't imagine
Stephen Douglas reaping wheat.

But it had been a fierce campaign. She saw it in Lincoln's
lined face, heard it in Douglas's hoarse and nearly inaudible
voice. Douglas started out speaking in defense of his
policy toward Kansas: "... the signers of the Declaration of
Independence... did not mean Negro, nor the savage Indians, nor
the Fejee Islanders, nor any other barbarous race...."

He spoke for an hour, before Lincoln got up and replied.
Mary had, in her luggage, transcripts of all the previous de-
bates, from the ferocity of Douglas's first accusations that
Lincoln had been "in conspiracy" to form an abolitionist
Republican Party, through later baiting that he intended the
Negro race to be either (a) extinguished or (b) amalgamated
into the white race through interracial marriage.

Lincoln rose, with the sunlight slanting now, blinking a
little in it with that deceptive bumpkin slowness that had
fooled so many rival attorneys. But there was nothing of the
bumpkin in the penetrating tenor that rang out over the
crowd; nothing of the bumpkin as he spoke of the conflict
"on the part of one class that looks upon the institution of
slavery *as a wrong,* and of another class that *does not* look upon
it as a wrong."

All his awkwardness, all the slightly comic effect of the
scarecrow height and mud-fence ugliness, seemed to melt
away, until only the voice was left, speaking words of silver
and steel.

"*That is the issue that will continue in this country when these
poor tongues of Judge Douglas and myself shall be silent. It is the
eternal struggle between these two principles—right and wrong—
throughout the world. They are the two principles that have stood
face to face from the beginning of time; and will ever continue to*

struggle. The one is the common right of humanity and the other the divine right of kings."

Mary closed her eyes, listening to the roar of applause. *They must elect him,* she thought. *If only they could elect him outright, and not put everyone through that horrible balloting in the Legislature. . . .* Hard to remember that neither Lincoln's name nor that of Douglas was anywhere on the ballot.

Only the names of men who would go to the Legislature, who would be favorable to one or the other.

On the second of November, in the pouring rain, Democrats won fifty-three percent of the seats in the Legislature. Much printer's ink was expended in accusations that illegal voters were brought in: "Thousands of roving—robbing—bloated pock-marked Catholic Irish were imported upon us," was how Billy Herndon put it. But in the end it made little difference.

At home, Lincoln was silent and deeply depressed, though he smiled when Willie presented him with an execrably spelled homemade "newspaper" article about the debates, complete with drawings. By the end of the week he was back in his office, with Billy and young John Hay—something for which Mary was deeply grateful, since an autumn on the campaign trail instead of the court circuit had reduced the household finances terrifyingly, and she'd overrun her credit at every shop in town. On the fifth of January, when the Legislature voted for Senator, Lincoln was in the Supreme Court chambers, arguing cases Herndon had filed.

By that time, the wildness of the campaign seemed a thousand years ago.

It was a winter of penny-pinching. Mary groaned with remorse every time she crossed those beautiful flowered rugs, sat on the new parlor chairs. She would wake in terror from dreams of being back at the Globe Tavern, hearing the clanging of the stagecoach bell, her heart hammering and her mind filled with desperation and the echoes of the Bledsoes arguing in the next room: *We have to get out of here! We have to get our own house. . . .*

"Things will be fine," Lincoln soothed, gathering her into his arms. "I just need to get back to real work, and God knows there's plenty of it out there...."

"I should never have had the house enlarged!" Mary sobbed. "We could use that money now, and we don't need a place this big...."

"Well, if you really feel that way," said Lincoln worriedly, "I'll start tearing it down tomorrow, but I think it might be better to wait for spring."

He could always make her laugh.

During one of their debates in Freeport, Lincoln had come out and asked Douglas if Popular Sovereignty meant that the people of a territory could *exclude,* as well as permit, slavery? Since that was what Popular Sovereignty was about, Douglas had been forced to answer yes...and had immediately begun losing support, not in Illinois, but in the Southern states that had looked to him to carry their banner to the White House.

By summer, Douglas was courting the Republicans to form a third party to elect him President in 1860. Between cases, between journeys, Lincoln worked to heal the rifts that his own defeat had left in the discouraged Republicans, juggling speeches against Douglas's still-catchy doctrine ("If one man chooses to make a slave of another man, neither that other man nor anybody else has a right to object") with vicious internecine squabbles between the wealthy Mr. Judd and Mayor Wentworth of Chicago about whose candidate (and whose pet newspaper) was going to wield power in the Republican Party. He went campaigning in Ohio, Indiana, Wisconsin, and Iowa, for Republican candidates and to strengthen the Republican Party. Mary and the boys went with him on one such journey, to Cincinnati and Indianapolis.

Mostly he went alone. In his absence her fears of poverty—of losing their home, of having to return to the nightmare of boardinghouse living—would return, and she found herself nervous, depressed, and easily angered. This anger frequently took the shape of quarrels with Robert, who, with one eye on his college education, would put forward tidy plans of how the family finances could be regularized.

Robert was a tall, big-shouldered boy of fifteen now, with blue Todd eyes, given to chilly silences and measured opinions. He did not appear to possess any sense of humor—Mary wondered how something that was so much a part of both parents had managed to be left out.

When Willie obtained, from God alone knew what source, four long, fat, black cigars, and talked Tad and two playmates into "blowing a cloud" behind the barn, it was Robert who was shocked. Mary took one look at the four green-gilled experimenters and nearly collapsed with laughter.

Robert, now a member of the Springfield Cadets, was applying to Harvard, with the intention of becoming a lawyer like his father—and a millionaire, he said. Mary grieved at the thought of losing him, but after Robert's carefully worded criticism of how she ran the household (*and let him try to keep five people decently clothed when his father forgets to collect his fees!* she thought) she sometimes had the despairing sense of never having known her oldest son at all.

After Robert's stinging criticism it was always Willie who would pull her out of her blues. Willie was as happy and open as his older brother was self-righteous and withdrawn. Willie, like his father, could always make her laugh. Like his father, Willie always knew when she needed arms put around her. It was Willie who'd come to sit beside her, when the prairie thunder hammered and his father was away.

"Really, Mother, it's no wonder Tad's a bundle of nerves, the way you take on," Robert would say, impatient, from the bedroom door.

And after he'd leave, Willie would tighten his small grip on her hand and whisper, "I'm here, Mama. Everything will be all right." It was he who'd make her "headache tea" when she had a migraine, or would hold her hand when she'd taken a couple of spoonfuls of Atkinson's Female Cordial and lay quiet in the dark, waiting for the pain to subside.

Robert took the train east to Massachusetts and failed—spectacularly and humiliatingly—in his Harvard entrance examinations. "I told him he wasn't working hard enough," fumed Mary, when they got the letter. "But he never would listen." She bit back the accusation, *If you'd only been around more* ... "He just freezes on me and won't say a word."

"He's shy." Lincoln folded the letter and tucked it into the inner band of his hat, where he stowed most of his notes for speeches and the letters that had to be answered soonest, as if by proximity with his brain they'd remain "on his mind." He set the hat on the porch-rail beside them and settled back on the cane-bottomed chair, lifted a hand to wave at the minister's wife, Mrs. Smith, walking down Jackson Street in the summer twilight. Only last week, he'd helped her nail a new step on her back porch.

"There are preparatory academies back East. I know Douglas has influence with the President of Exeter. He'd write Robert a recommendation." Despite the drubbing they'd given one another on the campaign trail last fall, Lincoln and Douglas remained good friends, an attitude Mary found difficult to understand.

"And how much is that going to cost us?"

"Not more than we can afford, Mother."

"He should have studied harder...."

"And maybe I should have campaigned harder," said Lincoln with a grin. "Then I'd be a Senator now."

Mary said nothing, torn between her worry about money—her worry that Lincoln would find out about the cost of her latest dress, the expense of the dinners she'd given to make an impression on Messrs. Judd and Palmer when last they'd been in town—and her genuine wish for Robert to get the kind of education his intelligence deserved.

Between campaigns and cases, Lincoln had given Robert what time he could. But there was always that wall around the boy, from behind which he would regard his parents with haughty, slightly accusing eyes.

Because his father left him home to deal with his mother's temper?

Because his mother had betrayed him into those moments of agony under the surgeon's knife?

Because he was old enough to remember Kentucky, and what it was like to live in a wealthy house with slaves instead of one in which pennies were counted when his father— again—let his law work slip in favor of political speeches?

Because Lincoln and Mary had spent the first year of his life resentfully adjusting to the loss of familiar comforts, familiar freedom?

Because, after all these years, he still missed Eddie, for whose loss Mary had been too grieved herself to give him comfort?

Mary didn't know.

In November, newspapers began to suggest that Abraham Lincoln might be the appropriate candidate for the Republicans to run for President in 1860.

"Me?" Lincoln roared with laughter that made Mary lower the paper—it was the *Sandusky Commercial Register*— and regard him across the kitchen table in miffed dignity. The day's rain had stopped, but the early-falling darkness was bitterly cold. Fido and the cats had called a temporary truce so they could all make space for one another in front of the stove.

"And why wouldn't you make a good President? A *great* President?"

"And what are they gonna run me on?" Lincoln grinned. "My Black Hawk war record, or the bang-up job I did on the House Post Office Investigatory Committee back in '48? 'Why, Mr. Secretary of War . . .'" He steepled his long fingers in mock conference with an imaginary Cabinet official, "'I seem to recall just sech a problem back when I was on the Post Office Committee. . . . Only instead of bein' invaded by Britain, France, and Russia all at the same time, we had to

investigate postmasters passin' mail free along to their
friends....'"

"You're being silly," said Mary severely, her own heart
beating hard at the thought of what Elizabeth would say to
the news that her "bumpkin" brother-in-law had been
elected to the highest office in the land.

"Anybody who would elect *me* to the Presidency,"
Lincoln rose and fetched his old jacket from the cupboard
behind the door, "is the one's bein' silly." But as he turned to
go out into the dark yard to feed Buck, Mary saw the glint in
his eye, like a traveler topping a rise of land, and looking out
into new territory ahead.

Chapter Thirty-six

In February of 1860 Lincoln went to New York, to speak at a gathering of the Young Men's Central Republican Union—some of those "young men" being fairly venerable, like William Cullen Bryant, who was sixty-five, and Horace Greeley of the *Tribune,* New York's most influential Republican newspaper. Cash Clay would be speaking, too, and other anti-slavery luminaries. Already Mary could see, in the various journals that came to Jackson Street, the jostling among the men who sought power, like jockeys edging for position at the post. Chief among them was William Seward, senator and former governor of New York, a wily extremist whom she judged—and Lincoln judged—would scare off more voters than he'd draw in a national contest. Salmon Chase, the Republican governor of Ohio, was a less controversial but far less colorful contender: nobody knew ill of him because he really didn't have much to say. John C. Frémont was in the running, too, and an assortment of lesser fry, including an Associate Justice of the Supreme Court named MacLean, and the indefatigable Cash Clay.

None of them, she thought, could come up to Lincoln.

And Lincoln, she was well aware, wasn't unknown. He'd just had his debates with Douglas published in book form and they were selling smartly.

It was, of course, unthinkable that a man should campaign openly to become President. No man who boldly strove for the office was regarded as quite trustworthy. But Mary knew her husband well, and she knew he'd spent hours perfecting his New York address, and that he'd paid a hundred dollars for a new suit to give it in.

She later heard from Robert about his father's visit, how

the other boys at Exeter had looked at each other in appalled astonishment at the sight of the immaculate and gentlemanly Robert's scarecrow progenitor. But when Lincoln rose to speak at the Cooper Union, when he passionately denounced the spread of slavery to new territories while upholding the Constitution that provided for it in existing states—when he argued for Union and compromise against the radicalism of either side—Robert's classmates could only whisper to him how proud he must be, that that man up there was his father.

What Robert himself felt, he did not say.

And by the time Mary got her son's account of the address—which was followed by a speaking tour of New England—she already knew that Lincoln had told his supporters to put his name in. He would run.

ALL SPRING THEY WATCHED THE NEWSPAPERS. AGAIN THEY made lists of supporters, spoke far into the night of what points to emphasize to whom. Mary clipped every article about Lincoln—or about Douglas, who was bidding for the Democratic Presidential nomination—that she could find, sticking them into a scrapbook with Willie's help. (Tad's "help" had resulted in large portions of Fido's fur being clipped off to get the glue out of it—thereafter part of Willie's job was to keep meticulous track of the glue-pot and of his younger brother.) Hannah Shearer and Cousin Lizzie came by nearly every day, to catch up on the latest word or speculate about Lincoln's chances. The whole town, it seemed, was watching and listening.

In April the Democrats met in Charleston, South Carolina, and roundly rejected Douglas—the question Lincoln had forced upon him in Freeport had had its lethal effect, like a slow-killing wound. The northern Democrats stormed out in a rage and set up their own convention in Baltimore. Without the necessity of nominating a Westerner—Lincoln—to counterbalance Douglas, William Seward pushed forward his

Republican claims, or rather had his chief handlers push him forward ("Blushing and protesting all the way, I daresay," Mary sniffed) for President.

Lincoln was home for a week in March and another in April, between making speeches and arguing cases for the Illinois Central Railroad in Chicago. Those weeks, he spent much time at his law office and more writing letters or conferring with Judge Davis while Billy and John Hay dealt with his legal correspondence. As always, when he turned his energies toward politics instead of legal work, the family finances suffered. At other times, his absences would have been maddening; now, Mary scarcely noticed whether he was there or not.

It only mattered that he be nominated.

It only mattered that he win.

Mary recalled Henry Clay, one of the men who, thirty years before, had saved the Union through diplomacy and compromise, passed by again and again for President. Of all the statesmen she had ever heard of, he had deserved the Presidency most: *"For all of his running,"* the old song went, *"he never arrived. . . ."*

"Whoever gets the nomination in Chicago in May will win," said Lincoln softly, on one of those rare nights when he was home. "The Southern Democrats are for John Breckenridge, the Northerners for our friend Douglas—now here's a third Southern Union candidate stepping up, Bell. If the Republicans can pull *all* the anti-slavery votes together, they can take the election."

In Decatur and Chicago, "wigwams" were built—huge ramshackle temporary halls with canvas roofs—for the Republican Conventions, first the state and then the national a week later. Lying in bed reading, Mary would see Lincoln through the bedroom door in his own room, writing by lamplight at his little desk: letters to Norman Judd, letters to Judge Davis, letters to fellow attorneys and political supporters Ward Lamon, Leonard Swett, Isaac Arnold. Letters to the editors of every Republican newspaper in Illinois, and to the

German-language papers that served that powerful minority. Even letters to Lyman Trumbull, whom she still considered perfidious and untrustworthy. Now and then he'd lean down to scratch Fido's silky yellow head, or would move aside whichever of the cats chose that moment to sit on his papers.

When he was finished with his work he'd come into Mary's room, and sit on the foot of the bed and talk until he'd tired himself out enough to sleep. On other nights, she fell asleep to the soft scratching of his pen.

He went to Decatur for the state convention: "Blamed if some band of fools didn't carry in a couple of fence-rails, all done up with streamers and flags, that I was supposed to have split down in Macon County thirty years ago, and put up a painting of me splittin' 'em." He shook his head, but Mary could see he was pleased, and moved closer to him on the sofa. He'd come home that evening on the train—the days when he'd ridden in the saddle all over the central portion of the state were long gone—and Tad and Willie and Fido all crowded as close around him as they could, as if like a fire he radiated both light and warmth.

"Does this mean you're going to be President, Pa?" Willie looked up into his face, gray eyes sparkling. Lincoln's eyes, Mary reflected, without that haunted shadow of sadness, the eyes of the child Lincoln had never been.

"Not yet, son." He ruffled Willie's thick, chestnut-brown hair—gold-flecked, like Mary's and Robert's. "It means I get to put my name in the hat, and if it gets pulled out of the hat, it means I get to stand on the starting-line and run the race."

"Oo gowa bead Dougwath?" Tad's combination of lisp and slur made any attempt at communication from him problematical—something that infuriated the boy in dealing with his playmates—but neither Lincoln nor Willie seemed to have the slightest problem understanding.

Lincoln smiled. "I'll beat him if I can, son. And that's *Mister* Douglas."

"And then will there be no more slavery?"

Lincoln and Mary exchanged a glance over Willie's head.

"That," said Lincoln softly, "is what remains to be seen."

Thanks to the skillful maneuvering by Norman Judd and David Davis—and a little judicious chicanery about the advance seating of Lincoln supporters in the Wigwam—the Republican delegates in Chicago nominated Lincoln on the third ballot. Seward was said to be seething, but in fact, Mary thought Lincoln was right when he said Seward would lose the moderate votes to Douglas in the Presidential race itself. "Seward's an abolitionist," he said, when he and Mary met briefly in his bedroom, where he repaired to put on a cravat, after the editor of the *Illinois State Journal*—none other than his old friend Edward Baker's son, now married to Elizabeth's Julie—brought the news to the house. "If Seward were elected, the whole South would secede from the Union. They're not about to sit still for a man who claims there's a Higher Law than the Constitution."

The booming crash of guns made Mary startle. She'd had a migraine the previous day, out of sheer nervousness, and her usual springtime headaches made her jumpy. She wished they could have gone up to Chicago, instead of remaining in Springfield pretending that election to the Presidency was of only minor concern to them. "That's for you, Lincoln!" cried young Mr. Baker, when Lincoln and Mary came down the stairs. "They're firing off the cannon at the Courthouse for Illinois's first Republican candidate for President!"

The gunfire went on all afternoon.

Nobody seemed to think it was an omen.

Henry Clay, Mary thought, remembering again that tall red-haired man in her father's parlor. Counting back the elections, the four-year wildness like a national quartan fever, the elation and the dizzy sense of power. Henry Clay, and old Hard Cider and Log Cabins Harrison... Then the intoxication of campaigning through New England for Zachary Taylor, who owed Lincoln so much and who died before any patronage could be dispensed.

And now it was Lincoln—her own husband—whose name would be on the ballot.

In a way she couldn't believe it.

In a way, there was nothing else real in her life.

Elizabeth was full of faint praise and sidelong remarks about what would happen to the country if an avowedly anti-slavery candidate were elected. Ninian was a Douglas man, despite Mary's twits about certain conversations back in the days when the Little Giant was her beau. Cousin Lizzie Grimsley spent evening after evening in the kitchen with Mary, drinking tea and playing that agonizing, marvelous game of "What if...?" Lincoln remained at home all the summer and fall, doing nothing, it seemed, but writing letters, endlessly. Everywhere his supporters made speeches, rallied voters. He took on young John Nicolay—the German-born journalist who'd helped get his name in so many southern Illinois papers—as a secretary, and still he'd spend all day at his office with correspondence, and into the night.

Mary chafed and fretted, kept up her books of clippings, gave dinners several times a week for Lincoln's supporters and struggled, with Maria Francesca's help, to keep the house spotless in between. In these days Lizzie was her mainstay. Bessie and Simeon had gone away to Oregon the year before—the *Illinois State Journal* being only a new name for the old *Sangamo Journal*—and her other close friend Hannah Shearer had moved to Pennsylvania with her ailing husband. Mary liked John Nicolay, and was inclined to like Lincoln's clerk John Hay, Nicolay's inseparable friend. Even more she liked the effervescent Chicago youth named Elmer Ellsworth who'd also come to work as Lincoln's clerk. Ellsworth had organized a prize-winning regiment of Zouave militia, who marched and drilled with nimble élan at pro-Lincoln rallies. Ellsworth was a born knight-errant, like an older version of Willie, and seemed to include in his clerkly duties that of looking after Mary and the boys when Lincoln was out of town.

Journalists came that fall too, like swarming bees. Sometimes they were polite, sometimes obnoxiously demanding. All wanted to see the man called "The Rail-

Splitter" at home. Mary greeted them warmly, though she'd already begun to mistrust them; she refrained from remarking tartly that her husband hadn't split fence-rails in thirty years and hadn't liked doing it even then. They were delighted when they caught him in his shirtsleeves chopping kindling. Journalists in the South called him an ape and speculated that he had Negro blood in his own veins, since he loved that servile race so much.

Then it was November.

Lincoln's name wasn't even on the ballot in a number of Southern states.

He spent most of Election Day at the State House, in the small room off the rear hall usually reserved for the governor. He'd been there for days—coming out on the day before the election, he'd been stopped by a journalist who'd demanded how he was going to vote. "By ballot," Lincoln said—which he did, after cutting his own name off the card so that it could not be said that he had voted for himself.

All day she waited. Lizzie came in the morning, and helped her play hostess to a steady stream of callers, with occasional breaks to retrieve Tad from the polls, where he was standing outside waving an American flag and exhorting citizens—rather incoherently—to vote for his father. Darkness fell, though she could see the torchlight around the State House and the polling-places when she and Lizzie walked to the corner.

"Do you think there'll really be trouble with the Southern states, if Mr. Lincoln is elected?" asked Lizzie worriedly, pulling her shawl close around her shoulders. She was a big girl, taking more after the tall Todd men than the women of the family.

"I can't imagine why." Mary looked up at her quickly. "It isn't like Frémont running on a Free Soil ticket. Mr. Lincoln is a moderate. He's never been an abolitionist, in spite of what all those Southern newspapers keep insisting. He's *always* said that since the Founding Fathers permitted slavery to exist in the South he's not going to end it there, only keep it from spreading into the territories."

Yet she shivered. Emilie had written her from Lexington: *I think you ought to know what they're saying....* And she received enough of the Lexington papers to feel a deep foreboding, deny it though she might.

Politics was a vicious business. She knew the lies that were being printed, and believed. She knew there were those in the South who'd scream that their rights were being violated by even the election of a Republican President. From the day she'd seen Nate Bodley cane Elliot Presby in the street, she'd known that the merest breath of criticism toward slavery could rouse some Southerners to bloody violence.

Like dark voices whispering in a dream, it came to her that if he won, Lincoln would have to face a hundred thousand Nate Bodleys.

That there was something beyond victory, other than a procession in triumph to the White House with Elizabeth gnashing her teeth in the background.

But he'll win, she thought, pushing that qualm aside with a rush of excitement. *He must win....*

What came after could be dealt with then.

Lizzie and Maria Francesca helped her put Tad and Willie to bed. The boys were wild with excitement. It was impossible, in their eyes, that their father could be defeated.

Or that evil would come after victory.

She thought of Lincoln in the telegraph office, surrounded by the men who'd supported him through the campaign—Davis and Lamon, Swett and Arnold, hatchet-faced Lyman Trumbull and dapper little John Hay scuttling around like a banty rooster...Elmer Ellsworth as excited as her two sons and Billy Herndon running in and out with cups of coffee. Papers on the floor, telegraphic scrap, newspapers from here and there...

The atmosphere reminiscent of the days of argument around the stove at Speed's store—the political hearth tacitly forbidden to women. After all she had done, she was shut out of that, and her heart twinged with resentment and anger that had no place to settle.

Lizzie was still at the house at midnight when Mary heard Lincoln's stride on the kitchen steps. She sprang to her feet and the next instant heard his voice, high and clear in the night, "Molly..."

She and Lizzie dashed into the kitchen—of course he'd come in that way, he never used the front door....

"Molly!" He stood in the kitchen door, breathless, beaming, cravat askew, smiling like the rising of the sun. "Molly, we're elected!"

She flung herself into his arms, Lizzie crowding to their side, Fido yapping excitedly around everyone's feet.

President, she thought.

President of the United States...

Even then, it crossed her mind that this was the end of their days of peace.

CHAPTER THIRTY-SEVEN

Bellevue July 1875

"MRS. LINCOLN." DR. PATTERSON PUT ASIDE HIS NAPKIN, and folded his hands. "Now, is it true that you sent a letter out of here to a Dr. Swenson in New York?" He took a folded paper from beside his breakfast plate, crossed and re-crossed with Mary's blotted handwriting, held it up in the hot butter-colored sunlight of the family breakfast-room. Beside him his wife regarded Mary with a sad frown, as if she'd caught her urinating on the floor of her room as Mrs. Johnston was wont to do.

Mary could only stare, open-mouthed as much at his tone of gentle reproof—like an adult chiding a willful child—as at the postman's betrayal. "I am not in the habit of lying, Dr. Patterson, any more than I am in the habit of seeing my private correspondence in the hands of a person to whom it was not addressed."

"Now, Mrs. Lincoln," said Patterson soothingly. "The postman has orders to give me any letters that my guests send out without my knowledge. You are here to rest, and that means not overtaxing your nerves. I don't think that's so unreasonable, do you?"

"Not unreasonable!" Mary's hands clenched in her lap and the leaden ache that had settled on her head and belly for weeks since she'd cut down her medicine tightened its hold. "You forbid me to send letters—"

"But I don't, Mrs. Lincoln." Patterson's voice never wavered from its friendly warmth. "Don't you think you're being a little unfair to us here? I only ask that you limit your correspondence to those known to me. We must have rules. You can see how so many women write wild and unthinking letters to people who haven't any idea of their condition...."

"I wrote Dr. Swenson, sir," said Mary, through gritted teeth, "because he *has* an idea of my condition—and his idea of my condition might not agree with those brutes my son bribed to declare me insane!" She had met Dr. Swenson at the Spiritualist camp on the shores of Lake St. Catherine, a few years before. He was a dreamy New Englander whose high-paying practice of medicine had been interrupted by his daughter's death.

Patterson merely looked mildly grieved, as if he heard no more than the further ravings of the insane. Behind him, Jenny the housemaid came in and cleared away the plates to the sideboard. On the other side of the table, Young Doc sat with folded hands, watching the scene between his father and Mary as if observing some clinical demonstration in a class-room. Only Blanche seemed to think there was something improper in the scene being played out before the family: she looked frightenedly from her brother to her father to her mother—like Fido would during Mary's quarrels with Robert back in Springfield—but said nothing.

"Mrs. Lincoln," said Dr. Patterson patiently, "you have to admit that you did agree not to correspond with people not known to myself and to your son, when you came to live here."

"What choice had I—?"

He held up his hand against her hot protest. "Now, you admit that you agreed. You are here to rest. Your son, as your legal conservator, is merely trying to see that you do so. Can't you see that your untruthfulness, your willfulness and lack of cooperation are only evidence of how badly you *do* need rest? All this changing your mind—" He gestured at the basket of cornbread still on the table before her, untouched. "This ordering cornbread at breakfast and then wanting to eat only rolls, or asking for griddle-cakes at supper which you then don't touch... Is that the activity of a sane woman?"

You obviously never met my sister, thought Mary savagely, recalling Ann's capacity for ordering food that was never eaten. Cornbread and griddle-cakes, the foods of her childhood, sounded so comforting, yet with her stomach still gripped by the periodic nausea that was the aftereffect of reducing her medicine, in fact rolls were all she actually wanted to eat.

"You order the carriage, then delay and delay...say you're going to go out walking and then stay in your room..." Patterson shook his head and sighed. "It is all part of your nervous condition, rebelling against the irritations of daily life. And of course I understand that much of the time you're not able to see it." He said it as if his understanding were a wise and forbearing favor. Mary wanted to fling her coffee-cup at him, though she supposed that, too, would be interpreted as willfulness and lack of cooperation.

"Your entire nervous system is like the most fragile of plants, which cannot withstand the shocks, the chills, the storms of the outside world, Mrs. Lincoln." Patterson rose from his place and came around the table to her, holding out his hand to help her up. "What is so bad about remaining with us and resting? We only want to help you."

"By reading my correspondence?" She pulled her hand from his gentle grip. "By having me watched every moment? By barring my window and forbidding me to seek the comfort of the spirits with my sisters in faith?"

"Now, you know that's only your insanity speaking. You know the spirits don't *really* visit people. What is so difficult about accepting the inspired authority of Scripture? You must learn to control your willfulness, and your tendency to deceit, Mrs. Lincoln. I fear you will be with us for a long time."

SITTING IN HER ROOM, MARY STARED OUT THE WINDOW. A jaybird dove through a shaft of sunlight, wings a flash of sapphire against the green velvet of lawns and trees. The July heat brought her the scent of the roses, and the thick intoxication of the grass.

It brought her other things as well.

It brought her the memory of that sweltering Chicago

July, four years ago now... four years almost to the day. The fifteenth, she thought, her heart beating fast—as it had been the fifteenth of April, that night in Ford's Theater....

It brought her, with heart-tearing exactitude, the baking, breathless dryness of that summer of 1871, the way the air had pressed suffocatingly on that dark little furniture-cluttered room in the Clifton House where Tad sat, propped in that inquisitorial horror of a "therapeutic" chair, gasping for breath.

It brought the very feel of those worn impersonal hotel sheets over his emaciated body, their starchiness as she gripped them, as she crouched on her knees at Tad's side. Brought her the feel of that enormous hand, soft instead of callused but like Lincoln's down to the very shape of the bones. A young hand, a boy's hand. Tad was only eighteen....

He squeezed her fingers gently, responding to her frantic clutch. Tried to smile.

"The doctor says he cannot live," Robert had said to her softly, in the hall outside the room. His voice was low and urgent and his grip on her arms had tightened, as if he would have put a hand over her mouth to keep her from crying out in grief. "The doctor says he cannot live, so please, please, Mother, don't make it worse for him!"

How like Robert, she thought bitterly, *not to understand.*

Yes, of course Tad, so sweet, so completely devoted to her all his short life, would be upset by her tears.... But Robert didn't understand what it meant for Tad to die! On her knees by the bed Mary had stared into her youngest son's face, twisted with the pain of struggling to breathe. In those bones she had seen so clearly another face, just emerging: the jutting nose, the high cheekbones, the heavy brow, and the sad gray eyes. Lincoln must have looked like that at eighteen, she thought. Or he would have looked like that if he'd had a decent home to grow up in, a proper education, someone who loved him....

When Robert left the room to fetch fresh water in the pitcher, she had fallen to her knees beside the chair, gripped

Tad's hand. "Don't die, Taddie!" she whispered, frantic tears streaming down her face. "Please don't die! Fight! Fight to stay alive! For me, for your mother! Taddie, I shall die without you, I shall die if you go too...!"

Tad had wept, and tightened his hand on hers. He had still been holding it a few hours later, when his life slipped away.

MARY CLOSED HER EYES, TEARS BLINDING HER AT THE MEMory, as if it had happened yesterday. She wanted to close the curtain, to retreat to her bed, but she wanted more than anything else to blot out that grief, with laudanum, Godfrey's Cordial, Nervine, chloral hydrate, anything....

Tad was gone. Sorrow covered her like cindery darkness, familiar and comforting. She opened her mouth to call for Amanda, to say she had a headache—which she certainly did—and ask Dr. Patterson to give her an extra drink of medicine. He would, of course, and John would never know.... John was away for a few days, on business in New York.

Then she sighed, and closed it again. The jaybird was perched on the back of a bench beside the harsh gravel of the drive, visible around the corner of the house. *He will carry word of my weakness to Robert,* she thought, *and I will be that much further from getting out of here.*

I should have sent the letter to Dr. Swenson with John. Or does he, like the postman, have "instructions" to turn over all correspondence to Dr. Patterson?

Probably. What a fool she'd been, to think that women before her hadn't tried to suborn the postman, or bribe one of the attendants, to get letters out to their friends. One of the things Robert had taken when he'd cleared out her room at the Grand Pacific—one of the things he hadn't brought to her here—had been her memorandum-book which contained the addresses of friends. She'd met so many people over the years, and she couldn't call the addresses of more than a few dozen to mind. Of those, some were people who had no power, who obviously couldn't help her. What she needed were doctors, whose testimony would overturn those monsters Robert had bribed, or Congressmen, who could ask questions in the government, force those in power to make Robert—and Patterson—turn her loose.

Voices drifted to her through the window; she opened her eyes. Violet Goodwin and Olivia Hill were strolling along the gravel path, trailed by the ubiquitous Gretchen. Mrs. Goodwin was talking agitatedly, gesturing with her thickly gloved hands. Probably about the shortcomings of cleanliness in Bellevue, or Dr. Patterson's remissness in some detail. Mrs. Goodwin dwelled in a world of constant horror, of catastrophe held at bay only by the most rigid adherence to a thousand small rituals of her own invention, and was most tedious on the subject. Mrs. Hill nodded understandingly—her reaction to everything, Mary had discovered—and put out a hand to pat her companion, despite the fact that Mrs. Goodwin hated being touched and everyone at Bellevue knew it.

Mrs. Goodwin pulled away from her, shrilled, "Filthy slut, don't touch me!" loudly enough for Mary to hear her from her window. Gretchen sprang forward and seized Mrs. Goodwin by the arms, Mrs. Goodwin began to struggle in earnest at the contact, Gretchen shouted for assistance, Mrs. Hill—whom Mary had discovered had no common sense—waded in to try help "calm" the thrashing, sobbing woman....

And Dr. Patterson, Young Doc, Zeus, and Peter came running.

"Just don't touch me!" Mrs. Goodwin kept screaming. "Get your dirty hands off me! My God! My God!"

"Now, as soon as you learn to cooperate...," began Dr. Patterson, and Mary closed the window. In a sort of dumb show she watched Mrs. Goodwin dragged back to the nearest door of the house, to the inevitable hydrotherapy and chloral hydrate. Last night Mrs. Munger had waked screaming from nightmares and was still slumbering under a combination of opium and chloral hydrate, something that happened several times a week.

The jaybird on his bench cocked his head and seemed to smile.

Mary pulled the curtain, walked back to sit on the end of her bed, hands gripping each other in the diffuse gloom.

How long will it be before I really lose my temper, and have Dr. Patterson decide that my "condition" is getting worse? Before I'm force-fed anodyne until I forget what freedom is or why I want it?

She remembered standing in the doorway between her room and Lincoln's, in that comfortable little house on Eighth and Jackson—the house that she could never bring herself to go into again, that she could barely bring herself to recall. It was the evening he'd been nominated for Senator, he was about to walk down to the State House in the misty gloom of evening. They'd been speaking of slavery, the key issue between himself and her old friend Stephen Douglas, the rock on which the Democratic Party had split... "Papa treated them very well," she'd contended.

And Lincoln had replied, "Except that they could be sold to people who wouldn't treat 'em quite so well."

And she had remembered her father's death, that had condemned so many of his slaves—so many of her friends—to the block and the coffle, to be shipped away to serve strangers, never to see those they loved again.

Robert was mortal.

If he dies while I'm in here, what then?

To whom would custodianship pass?

She understood now, exactly, why John Wilamet and his family had fled from Virginia, why Lizabet Keckley had humbled herself before her white friends, had begged and worked and borrowed money to obtain a freedom which offered her no guarantee of anything except more hard work.

She hadn't thought of Lizabet in a long time. Now she remembered the dressmaker's melodious alto voice saying, "I find helping others eases my grief."

Helping others, thought Mary. *Not "resting," as Dr. Patterson calls it.*

Without John there to talk to it was hard sometimes to remember why she shouldn't simply call for medicine. The thought *He'll never know, after all* crossed her mind with a frequency that horrified her.

But the memory of the time when she had been well enough, and free enough, to help others let her lie down on her bed in all her clothing, and close her eyes. To take her mind off the nagging ache in her heart and in her flesh, she counted up the addresses she knew—doctors, Congressmen, any man in power who might possibly owe her a favor from her days of success.

But if all of them had deserted her then, what made her think any of them would be of help to her now?

In her dream she was in the Cook County Courthouse in Chicago again, the heat so thick that she feared she would die. Her head pounded, her heart felt sick, her flesh itched like fire, and her mind reeled woozily. In a half-daze she looked from face to sweating face of those respectable citizens on the jury. "I am of the opinion that Mrs. Lincoln is insane," said Dr. Danforth on the witness stand, and beside her, her lawyer Isaac Arnold said, "No questions."

"On one occasion she spent $600 on lace curtains; on another, $450 on three watches which she gave to me, for which I had no use. . . ." Robert's mouth moved under his mustache, his eyes fixed at some spot on the cornice-molding above her head.

"No questions," Arnold said, and in her dream she leaped to her feet, screamed at them, "Cowards, blackguards and cowards!" They took no notice of her. Robert went on spouting prices and dates and opinions of her sanity. The jury—which included Dr. Patterson, now, and Young Doc, and President Grant and Nate Bodley—all nodded their heads wisely.

A firm hand took her elbow and drew her down into the chair. Turning her head she saw Lincoln beside her, dressed in the rather shabby black suit he wore on the circuit courts, his black hair rumpled and hanging in his eyes. He had a couple of legal briefs in front of him and his saddlebags lay on the floor beside his chair. "Do something!" she hissed. Lincoln was the best lawyer in the state. He'd argue rings around Ayers and Swett.

Lincoln listened to Robert for a few minutes more—"She spent $700 on jewelry last month, $200 on soaps and perfumes, though she has no home in which to hang curtains, trunks full of dresses which she never wears...."

He leaned close and whispered, "I think you're going to have to get another lawyer, Molly."

"Why?" she demanded. "Who?"

But before he could reply there was the crack of a gunshot, hideously loud in the enclosed heat of the courtroom, and his arm jerked convulsively, wrenching away from her hand. Mary caught him as he slumped, smelled the gunpowder and the horrible hot smell of blood....

SHE JERKED AWAKE, GASPING, HER WHOLE BODY TREMBLING. The smell of blood lingered in her nostrils, on the shoulder of her dress. She could swear the smell of gunpowder gritted in the air. Her whole body ached for the comfort of the medicine, the comfort of darkness.

You're going to have to get another lawyer.

She knew exactly who he meant.

Someone whom she would not even have met, save for the long Calvary that followed the election of 1860: the Calvary that ended in nightmare.

CHAPTER THIRTY-EIGHT

Springfield January 1861

THE PICTURE WAS CRUDELY DRAWN, AND SO VICIOUS THAT IT took Mary a moment to realize what it was.

It was her husband's nude body, hanging by the neck from a dead tree. His flesh was splotched with tar and feathers and his features were drawn so as to be almost Negroid, but there was a sign around his neck saying *Old Abe,* in case there was any question of identity. Under it was scrawled in brownish fluid that had powdered away in the paper's creases, SAY YOUR PRAYERS NIGGER–LOVER.

Mary recoiled in shock. Beneath that folded paper, on Lincoln's small desk beside his bedroom window, there were others, some of them drawings, some of them letters. She glimpsed only a word or two, but the hatred seemed to rise off the paper like a stench. *"Nigger-lover." "You are bound for Hell and we will send you there." "Liar." "Ignorant ape." "You will never live to reach Washington." "Word has reached us that there is an organization forming in New Orleans for the express purpose of your murder." "Say your prayers."*

"Molly."

She turned, breathless, to see Lincoln framed in the doorway of the hall, one of Sheba's new kittens in his huge hand. Her terrified face told him at once what she'd seen. He set the kitten on the bed in passing, strode to her side.

"It's all right," he said.

"All right? *All right?* Those—those *things . . .* that *filth . . .*" She stared up into his face. His battered trunk from his Congressional days stood open beside his dresser—he still owned little besides a few shirts and his books. He could almost have moved to Washington with his saddlebags, the way he'd come to Springfield twenty-five years ago. The

new suit he'd purchased to go to New York in lay spread out
on the bed, already acquiring a faint speckling of cat-hair. A
dozen newspapers strewed the carpet.

"Why didn't you tell me?"

"I didn't think you needed to know."

"You didn't think I needed to know?" she screamed, her
terror flaring into rage. "Someone threatens to murder my
husband, calls him—"

"Mother!" He stepped close again, and she slapped his
hands aside. "Mother, not so loud."

Sturdy footsteps shook the stairs. "Who's going to murder
Pa?" Willie came tearing into the room, snow flecking his
dark hair. Lincoln immediately scooped up the letters and
slipped them into the drawer of his little writing-table.
"Seceshes?"

On Willie's tenth birthday, four days before Christmas,
news had reached Springfield that the State of South
Carolina had voted to take itself out of the Union.
Mississippi, Florida, and Alabama were all reported to be on
the verge of secession as well, and President Buchanan—an
elderly diplomat whose election four years ago had owed a
great deal to the fact that he'd been in England during most
of the sectional squabbling of the Fifties—had responded
only by setting up various Congressional committees to look
into compromise.

Lincoln grinned, and ruffled his son's hair. "They'll have
to catch me first."

"Oh, my God," Mary whispered, as Willie went to the
narrow bed to gather up the kitten. "I can't leave you at a
time like this...."

Her own six trunks were already packed in her room,
preparatory for departure for New York. For weeks—
between visits from Congressmen and Senators, men whom
Lincoln hoped to forge into a Cabinet—Mary had been trying to organize which of their furniture and possessions were
to be sold, and which put in storage in the attic box-room for
four years, until their return. When Philadelphia political boss

Simon Cameron—to whom David Davis had promised a Cabinet position in return for Pennsylvania's votes, to Lincoln's outraged disgust—came to Springfield, he had spoken to her over dinner about the White House furnishings. Some things, like dishes, belonged to the house, but Presidents brought their own linens, bedside lamps, "everyday" dishes, small furnishings for the personal parlors upstairs.

A quick review of most of the contents of the house at Jackson and Eighth had convinced her that a shopping-trip to New York was in order. Since Ann's husband, the jolly and diffident Mr. Smith, was about to embark on a buying-trip to New York for his store here in town, he'd offered to escort her and her sister. Mary still recalled, from their passing visit in '49, all those beautiful shops in New York, places she had barely glimpsed.

She recalled, too, with vivid envy, the hostesses of Washington: the glittering Mrs. Corcoran, the haughty Mrs. Clay of Alabama, the vivacious Varina Davis—the way those stylish uncrowned queens had looked down on the outdated ruffles of a Western Congressman's wife. She would not give anyone the opportunity to do so again. ("Definitely Stewart's," Cameron had purred, to her question. "I shall send a letter telling him you're coming.... And look in at Laurent DeVries's as well. Laurent's silks tend to be more à la mode, though *never* tell Alec Stewart I said so.")

But if anything should happen to Lincoln while she was gone...

"I'll be all right, Mother. You know you want to go and I think the change'll be good for you. Besides, Bob is expecting you to come back here with him. I'll be in a little more danger without your protection—" He dodged aside as she slapped at him. "—but I'll manage."

"We'll protect Pa." Willie's face was radiant at the prospect of standing guard. "Me and Tad and Fido." To demonstrate his readiness to die in his master's defense, Fido half-woke from his doze in the corner, sat up, and yawned.

Mary left two days later, nagged by the thought of what

other threats her husband might be hiding from her, but
elated to be gone. Since the election she had seen almost
nothing of Lincoln, except when he came home, preoccupied and exhausted, from his makeshift office in the governor's room of the State House. Every few days he would
have someone to the house, and Mary and Maria Francesca
would put together a dinner to entertain them.

After reading about them for years in the newspapers,
Mary felt she knew them all, even those who hadn't been
pointed out to her in Chicago. Supporters like square-built
Norman Judd, or men like myopic former Governor Chase
of Ohio who had vied with Lincoln for the nomination.
Lincoln spoke to Chase about a Cabinet post, which Mary
thought a mistake: how could a rival be trusted? Simon
Cameron thought—and had broadly hinted—that he would
like to be made Secretary of the Treasury, despite the fact
that his Philadelphia political machine was corrupt from top
to bottom and he himself couldn't be trusted with twenty-
five cents.

And elegant little William Seward, whom Lincoln wanted
as Secretary of State, clearly envisioned himself as ruling the
country with Lincoln as a mere figurehead.

Lincoln conferred with them all, patiently, keeping his
thoughts to himself so well that none of them seemed to realize that he *had* thoughts. Which suited Lincoln just fine.

If Mary had thought the reporters were bad before the
election, now they flocked like vampires in some Gothic
novel. What would Old Abe do if President Buchanan sur-
rendered the U.S. military installations in Charleston Harbor
to the new South Carolina government? *(Do you think the secessionists don't read your newspaper, sir?)* Is the Rail-Splitter going to free the slaves? *(I suggest you review his speeches over the
past fifteen years. . . .)* Mary would exert herself to be polite
and gracious when she really wanted to chase them out of
the house with a broom, and they'd smile and tip their hats
and then go back to their home cities and print the most hor-
rifying misquotations, misrepresentations, and outright lies.

Worse than any of these pests were the candidates for government jobs, great and small. "I voted for you and got all my friends to vote for you, now you make me assistant secretary of Nevada Territory...."

It was her dream of patronage and power transformed to nightmare by sheer volume. It seemed as if everyone in the United States were making a pilgrimage to Springfield to talk to Lincoln, as if, with other states threatening to pull out of the Union, he had no more important things to deal with. And during all this, Tad and Willie ran wild with excitement, trying to make their own shrill voices heard by their distracted parents and refusing to be fobbed off with Aunt Lizzie or Lincoln's young clerk Mr. Ellsworth.

Mary felt intensely disloyal about the relief that filled her as the train pulled away for New York. For the time being, she could be away from the aggravation of the situation, and could revel in her dream of the future. Her dressmaker in St. Louis—Madame Blois to whom she'd begun going when Lincoln started working for the railroads—had been ecstatic when she'd heard, as she'd written to Mary: so much to prepare for, such a great office to fill.

True, Mary reflected, but though she'd have to start with several gowns appropriate to the wife of the President, she wasn't entirely certain that Madame Blois was up to the very latest styles. She'd have to see who the really elegant ladies of Washington—Mrs. Corcoran, and Mrs. Clay, and General Davis's wife—went to. Her luggage included an envelope of swatches: it was a certainty she'd never find jewelry appropriate to her new station anywhere but in New York.

She closed her eyes. Journeys were a world of their own, in which everyday care didn't exist. In the first-class car, with its plush seats and gold-trimmed hardware, she felt bathed in the old wild excitement of her girlhood. Her brother-in-law Clark was a bore, of course, and she couldn't imagine how she'd get through two days on a train with Ann without pulling every lock of her hair out, fistful by fistful, but...

"Mary!"

She looked up as Clark returned along the swaying aisle, a newspaper in his hand.

Wordlessly he held it out. Ann snatched it. "Good God," she cried. "Alabama, Mississippi, and Florida have seceded!" And she glanced at Mary in sisterly malice as Mary seized the paper back. "It looks like you won't be First Lady of the land after all, dear, but only First Lady of the North."

RUMORS SEETHED IN THE AIR OF NEW YORK. FOR THREE DAYS Clark—and Mr. Dorsheimer, the Treasurer of the State of New York—squired Mary from shop to shop, where, as Mr. Cameron had promised, even the great merchant prince Mr. Stewart bowed as they showed her silks, shawls, earbobs, trim, shoes of the very latest styles. In the evenings reporters came calling on her at the Astor House, and if it had occurred to any of them that she wasn't the wife of a "complete" President, nobody said anything.

Though in her heart Mary never forgave Ann for that "First Lady of the North" remark—and vowed to un-invite her from the Inauguration on the strength of it—she still felt pleased that Ann was there to witness this triumph. Everyone deferred to her—everyone asked questions and listened closely to her answers. Slick-haired young gentlemen from the *Times* and the *Tribune* and the *Herald*—even the London *Times*—leaped to their feet when she entered the lobby, and laughed heartily at her wit. It was like being the belle of Lexington again, without Betsey around to spoil her enjoyment.

"For the Lord's sake, Mary," said her brother-in-law, when she came down to breakfast in the hotel's handsome dining-room on their last morning in town, "did you have to go tell them Old Abe appointed Seward Secretary of State?"

"Nobody informed me that it was a state secret." Mary spread out her enormous skirts—twelve yards around the hem and rustling deliciously with taffeta—to take a seat at the small table that Mr. Astor himself had set aside for her and her party. Robert, across from her, looked uncomfortable. He'd come in last night, while she was still talking with the journalists, and they'd hailed him boisterously as "The Prince of Rails," a nickname by which he was known everywhere now and which he loathed quite as much as Lincoln hated "Old Abe."

He'd grown, in his eighteen months in the East. At seventeen and a half he was nearly six feet tall, his thick shoulders rendered less overpowering by the immaculately cut tweed of his suit and the subdued elegance of his collar and cravat. There was no trace of mis-alignment in his eyes, except a slight immobility when he was tired. He looked like he'd lived in Boston the whole of his life. He would be, she thought, an impressive man.

"Seward's an abolitionist," complained Clark peevishly, shaking out his napkin. "What are the Legislatures of Georgia and Virginia and Kentucky going to think, except that Old Abe means to abolish slavery after all?"

"Now, I'm sure if the legislators of those states read Mrs. Lincoln's remarks," soothed Mr. Drosheimer, "they'll also read the President's statements that he's only against the *extension* of slavery, that he won't touch it where it already exists. Are you feeling quite well, Mrs. Lincoln? It will be a long journey today." Throughout the journey—in fact since the day of the election—Mary had felt in jaggedly unequal spirits, torn between elation and anxiety without the steadying balance-wheel of home, neighbors, family.

The gaiety of travel enraptured her—the reaction, when it came, was crushing. The thought of Lincoln, alone and unprotected in Springfield, had preyed on her mind through a half-sleepless night. The images of those hateful letters and pictures returned to haunt her in terrible nightmares. New York was gorgeous, glittering, sophisticated—her new friends were delightful—but she found that at times the crowds frightened her, and she would return to her hotel room nervous and weepy. Sally Orne, the wife of a wealthy

Philadelphia merchant to whom Simon Cameron had introduced her, recommended Uhrquart's Pacifying Indian Bitters for her nerves, and swore by its results. It did seem to help.

"I'm quite well, thank you for asking," Mary replied now to Mr. Dorsheimer. "As for the Legislatures of Virginia and Kentucky, you name two of the most loyal states of the Union, sir. I think we need hardly worry about a few radicals there, whatever the people of Georgia may choose to think."

"We'll need to worry about a few radicals in Maryland," said Robert grimly, "if they decide Father's going to interfere with *their* property. We have to cross *through* Maryland to get to Washington. There might be trouble with those Plug-Uglies they write about."

Mary shivered, and drew her new pink cashmere shawl from Stewart's more closely around her shoulders. Despite the two fireplaces in the Astor House's dining-room, the morning was cold. To no one in particular she murmured, "I shall be glad to get home."

At home, when they got there ten days later—three days late due to inclement weather, but free of charge from Buffalo to Springfield, thanks to a very friendly magnate of the State Line Railroad—the confusion was even worse. According to Lincoln, who met them at the railroad station, a tall black shadow in the falling snow, he had played host to delegation after delegation, from Indiana, Illinois, California, Pennsylvania; Cameron's supporters, Cameron's detractors, petitioners that he provide Cabinet posts for everyone from the Governor of Maryland to Cassius Clay. He looked exhausted, when he and Robert and Clark brought Mary's trunks into the house. The lines in his face had deepened, and he didn't look like he'd been sleeping well.

Or shaving.... "Really, Mr. Lincoln, you haven't been meeting all those delegations that way! You look like a savage!"

His old smile returned and he rubbed his stubbly jaw. "I had a letter from a little girl named Grace Bedell," he said.

"She was of the opinion that I'd make a more impressive President if I had a beard."

Mary's mouth dropped open in disbelieving shock.

"An opinion shared by Davis and Trumbull and the others. Not to mention," added Lincoln in a lower voice, with a glance through the kitchen door to where Robert was exchanging mock cuffs with his two younger brothers, "it might be that on our way through Maryland to Washington, it would be better if quite so many people there weren't as able to recognize me."

"*I* think it looks swell," added Willie, coming into the kitchen—which was, she was relieved to note, still warm and orderly, in contrast to the shadowy glimpse of stacked boxes and half-wrapped parcels visible through the doors of dining-room and parlor. Lizzie and young Ellsworth had promised to make sure Tad and Willie stayed fed, warm, and out of trouble, and had, with the help of Lizzie's brother Lockwood, and the free colored valet whom Lincoln had recently hired, been organizing the furniture to be stored or sold. The much grander personal furnishings that she had bought in New York City were going to be shipped straight on to Washington. "He looks like a pirate!"

"Oh, thank you," sighed Lincoln. "Just the thing to give confidence to the South." But his eyes twinkled. "Looks like we're going to Washington the long way," he went on, pulling off his gloves and moving the gently steaming kettle to the front of the stove, to heat up for tea. "People need to be reassured, Mother. They want to see me and they want to hear everything's going to be all right—and God knows I need to see *them*. When a man asks help of someone," he added, "it comes better face-to-face."

He ran a hand over his jaws and through his hair, and she wondered despairingly how she was going to get him through four—or with luck, eight—years of the Presidency without letting him appear before the Prince of Wales or the Czar of Russia with his hair like a canebrake. "I've got invitations to stop and speak in half a dozen cities already—Cleveland and Cincinnati and Harrisburg and Honolulu for all I know—and more coming in all the time. It means leaving early, the eleventh...."

"Of *February*? But I'll be in St. Louis! I've made an appointment for fittings for my dresses! That's two weeks from now! Madame Blois will never be able to have them ready...."

"You and the boys can meet me in Indianapolis. The sale of the furniture's on the ninth—I think Mel Smith's buying most of it. Then we'll be staying at the Cheney House till we go."

"Good." Mary liked the Springfield druggist and his wife. "That gives us time for one last reception here, before we leave." She looked through the dining-room door and into the parlor again, seeing how dark the house was, and how cold and musty it already felt. Fido, curled up by the kitchen stove, raised his head worriedly, sensing that the world as he knew it was coming apart. Henry Rolls, whose yard backed the Lincolns', had already agreed to take the little yellow dog for the four years the Lincolns would be gone; she wondered if the boys would miss him.

If they would miss this house, as she would.

The reception was a splendid one, and lasted far into the night. Lizzie, Mary, and her two older sisters all turned the house upside-down, cleaning and sweeping and scrubbing. Elizabeth lent her Eppy and Lina, and came over to take charge of the baking herself. Then all the Todd girls turned out in their finest, to bid an official good-by.

Everyone in town put in an appearance—Merce and Jamie, the Reverend Smith, who'd spoken so kindly at Eddie's funeral; the ladies of the Episcopal Sewing Guild; Cousin John Stuart and Cousin Stephen Logan; the Gurleys and the Wheelocks and Mrs. Dall, whose infant Mary had nursed right after Tad's birth.... The house was crammed from parlors to attics and there was barely room for Eppy, William the new valet, and Maria Francesca to move about the kitchen. Robert, stiff and shy in his natty Eastern tailoring, stood with his parents, shaking hands and making sure to speak to everyone who filed in. Lizzie as usual tried to keep track of Tad and Willie and as usual succeeded only about two-thirds of the time.

To Mary's intense relief, Lizzie—who was accompanying her brother Lockwood, Elizabeth, the young Julie (now Baker), and Young Bess (as everyone called Julie's sister) to Washington City for the Inauguration—had promised to remain for a time as a guest in the White House and keep an eye on the boys until Mary found her feet. Harrison Grimsley shook his head over the plan and warned Lincoln, "I promise you, if my wife stays on with yours, you're going to have your hands full with the pair of them."

Lincoln grinned and ducked his head. "The boys'll keep 'em busy." He'd just returned from three days in Coles County. In all the time she'd known him—even when his Cousin Hetty was living in her sewing-room—she had seldom heard Lincoln speak of his family, though she was aware of the steady stream of ill-spelled and whining letters he'd received over the years, mostly asking for money. She remembered how he'd rushed down to Coles County when his stepbrother had written him that his father was dying: which had turned out to be a false alarm, but while he was there, could he loan them twenty dollars?

He had declined to rush down, the next time his stepbrother wrote. His father had died.

He had come back from this most recent visit to his stepmother sad and thoughtful: "They don't treat her well," he'd told Mary. "Like she was nothing, because she's of no use to them anymore."

She guessed, since they would be in Washington four years—if not, as she already hoped, eight—that Lincoln and old Mother Sarah would not meet again.

The reception was scheduled to last until midnight, but it was closer to two in the morning before the last guests finally left. Many of them were office-seekers, who had wangled their way into the party to speak to Lincoln. Toward the end of the evening, Robert, Ellsworth, and John Hay—like boisterous young Musketeers—were acting as discreet chuckersout. Lincoln spent the next morning at the State House, but returned, exhausted, in the afternoon; she heard him lie down as she moved quietly about her own room, packing up the last of her things. In addition to Elizabeth, her daughters, and Lizzie, Dr. Wallace was going to be part of the Lincoln party—Frances was no longer healthy enough to undertake so long a journey—and her half-sisters Margaret and Mattie would be meeting them in Washington, to see her triumph *(and request government jobs for their husbands,* she reflected) as well.

Downstairs she could hear the boys—*too loud,* she thought, *they'll wake their father*—and Ellsworth's light, free laugh. But the house seemed strange, half-empty in the gray winter light.

From the next room she heard Lincoln call out, "Molly?" and there was fear in his voice.

She thought, *Nightmare,* and hurried to open the connecting door. *And no wonder . . .*

He was sitting up on the edge of his bed in his shirtsleeves, hair all tousled on his head, staring across the room at his shaving-mirror on the wall. "Look in that mirror," he said. "Do you see one reflection in it, or two?"

She angled her head, for the mirror was set high. "One." It looked, in fact, pretty much as it always had. "Are you all right?" His unshaven face looked waxen with shock.

"Yes. I guess." He shook his head, ran a hand through his hair. "It must have been a dream—one of those dreams when you dream you wake up."

"And you saw two reflections?" Her voice wavered a little—she knew from Mammy Sally the evil of seeing one's own face in a mirror in a dream.

Lincoln nodded. "One looked pretty normal—'cept for the beard, that is. But the other, the one behind it, was white, like a ghost's face. Like a dead man's. And it come to me—almost like hearin' someone say it—that was because I'd be elected twice."

She whispered, her heart like ice in her breast, "Elected twice—but you won't live through your second term."

He stood, and took her hands in one of his. "We don't know that." And his grip tightened a little when she tried to pull away. "It's only a dream, when all's said."

But he didn't believe it. She could hear that in his voice. And neither did she.

SHE DREAMED OF HIM HERSELF, A FEW NIGHTS LATER, WHEN she lay asleep in the Wide Missouri Hotel in St. Louis after a day of fittings and shopping and chatter with Lizzie and with Madame Blois. Dreamed first of herself, burning her old papers the day before yesterday, her last day in Springfield. All those old letters, those quick-scribbled notes he'd sent her while on the circuit or in Washington. *Just cleaning house,* part of her said casually, and part of her admitted her fear that some journalist would get hold of them, and use them for God knew what. His views had changed over the years—in his letters he had not always been discreet.

In her dream she turned her head, to see Lincoln standing in the back door of the house, watching her as Mr. Smith the druggist and his men moved the last of their furniture away. Fido sat next to his boots, raised a worried paw to scratch his knee—*Will everything be all right?*

Then she dreamed of the bedroom at the Cheney House—the elegant bridal suite, the best in the hotel, where Tad and Willie had shared the trundle-bed and Robert had slept on the couch. Saw in her dream Lincoln there alone, roping up his single small trunk by himself: books, papers, a few shirts, and his new suit. Robert was already gone—*down to the station?* Robert was fanatically punctual and lived in terror of missing a train.

Outside the windows, the sky was bleakly dark, just staining with morning gray. Lincoln took one of the hotel's cards

to the little marble-topped desk, wrote on the back, A.
Lincoln—White House—Washington, and stuck it in
the leather label-holder on the trunk. He carried the trunk
downstairs himself, a tall man alone in the cold stillness of the
morning, to join Robert and Ellsworth, Nicolay and Hay
and the others waiting in the lobby. To go to the train station
and start for Washington, not knowing when, or whether, he
would return.

CHAPTER THIRTY-NINE

Philadelphia February 1861

"MR. LINCOLN?" ABOVE THE HUBBUB IN THE BALLROOM OF the Continental Hotel in Philadelphia, Mary wasn't sure how she heard Norman Judd's murmur, but she did. She turned her head to see the railroad magnate touch Lincoln's sleeve, and the look on Judd's face was the iron look of a man who has received the worst kind of news.

Lincoln saw it, too, and knew it for what it was. He'd been shaking hands since eight-thirty with the cream of Philadelphia society, telling funny stories, remembering the names of everyone who was introduced to him and remembering too whatever contributions they'd made to Whig politics back twenty years. He bowed a little to a banker and his wife, with whom he'd been chatting under the chilly white glimmer of the gasoliers, and said, "If you good folks will excuse me, I think there's another crisis brewing." He kept his voice droll, so that the stout banker and his stouter wife both laughed. Mary, delightedly renewing her acquaintance with the vivacious Sally Orne, saw his tall black form edge away through the crowd toward the gilt-trimmed ballroom doors.

"Excuse me," she said, and began to thrust her way through the crowd after him.

There were times, during the ten days since they'd begun their journey to Washington, that she wondered if they were ever going to reach the capital at all. Every city they passed through, it seemed, had invited Lincoln to stop, to speak, to receive the local dignitaries—dignitaries whose support would be desperately needed, if the seceded Southern states should refuse to compromise or to return to the Union. Needed still more, if loyal and powerful Virginia, or worse yet, Maryland, should decide to join them.

Since meeting the Springfield party in Indianapolis, there had been days when she had barely spoken to her husband at all. Certainly she had not spoken to him alone. As if to remind the new Chief Executive of his obligations to Illinois Central, Norman Judd had provided them with a special Presidential car, decorated like a plush hotel suite with crimson curtains and gold tassels. Even in its privacy Lincoln was always surrounded by his supporters and advisors, that group of handlers she was coming to hate. It was as if the group around the stove at Speed's had taken over his life, leaving only crumbs of him for her. When he talked politics, he talked now with them. Judd was always there, and fat David Davis, the gigantic Ward Lamon, and crafty Orville Browning. Hay, Nicolay, and young Ellsworth added some lightness to the party, rushing about like squires to the political champions.

More than ever she was grateful for the company of Elizabeth and her daughters, and of Lizzie, and Lizzie's brother Lockwood. The atmosphere of alternating tension and elation, wearing enough on her, had turned her younger sons—never the quietest of souls to begin with—into frantic little dynamos. Frustrated at being shut out of the men's councils, Mary would slap the boys or shriek at them, something she knew did not help the situation but which she could not seem to keep herself from doing. What a blessing to have Elizabeth or Julie Baker, or Lizzie, scoop Tad up and say, "Your Mama's tired now, Taddie...," and bear him screaming into another part of the car.

Moreover, she knew there were things she wasn't being told. Telegrams reached them at all stations, and Lincoln would go into conference with the men again, leaving her like a child shut out of her father's study.

She had heard of it, however, when Lamon came in from the train platform in Westfield, New York, with the news that Senator Jefferson Davis—hero of the Mexican War and fixture of Washington society and politics—had been sworn into office as President of the Confederate States of America. "Looks like they mean business," Browning had said, and Lincoln had only looked grim and sad.

Mary reached the door Lincoln had just passed through, to one of the smaller anterooms of the Continental's ballroom. John Hay stood beside it, smart-looking in new evening-clothes. The New York newspapers had had such a field day describing Lincoln as a hick, a bumpkin, an uneducated baboon who would make the United States ludicrous in the eyes of the world, that everyone, Lincoln included, was being very careful to be absolutely correct in all things.

"I'm sorry, Mrs. Lincoln," Hay said. Though he'd read law in Lincoln's office for over a year, he'd been officially taken on only days ago as John Nicolay's assistant. "Mr. Lincoln asked that he not be disturbed by anyone."

"What is it?" she demanded. "What's happened?"

Hay's dark eyes shifted. "It's nothing serious."

"Tell me!"

"Mother . . ." Robert appeared at her side, gently took her arm. "It's nothing serious. Everything's fine."

He was lying. They both were lying.

Trembling, she went back to the reception. She wanted to scream at them, to weep, to force them to let her into their secret councils. But she knew that with Lincoln out of the ballroom it was up to her to smile and greet all those Biddles and Mifflins and Rittenhouses. Elizabeth glanced over at her with warning disapproval for even inquiring about masculine business: Mary raised her chin defiantly and stared back. But when she finally returned to their suite and Lizzie unlaced her from the exquisite gown of lilac silk, she had a pounding headache and was so nervous she was ready to scream.

In Harrisburg the next day Lincoln went to the State House to address the Legislature. Mary was reading to Tad and Willie in the hotel parlor when she heard them return. Outside the door she heard Judd's deep voice, "Do you think it's wise?" and Lincoln's, "She'll wonder where I am, and there'll be no quieting her unless she knows what's going on."

The words went through her with a sickening jolt. She felt just as she did when thunder began to growl in the distance. She shut the book and got to her feet as the door opened. They were all around him: Judd and Davis, Browning and Robert and Ward Lamon, looking as grim as Judd had the night before. There was another man with them whom she vaguely recognized as Mr. Pinkerton, a solid little man like a knot of hardwood, with watchful dark eyes that never relaxed. Lincoln said, "It looks like there's definitely a plan to ambush me in Baltimore, Molly, while the railroad car's being hauled from one depot to the other to get on the Washington line. Fred Seward brought word last night that the local Plug-Uglies plan to rush the car, and Mr. Pinkerton here—he's Mr. Judd's railroad detective—says he's got proof."

The hate-letters flooded back to her mind: the vile drawing, the writing that had looked so much like blood. She put out her hand to steady herself on the chair and Willie stood up, protectively, at her side.

"Mr. Pinkerton," Lincoln went on, "says he's got it worked out for me to go into Washington by another train, alone, without fuss. . . ."

"Without fuss?" She felt panic rising in her. "What do you mean, without fuss? Alone? Without a guard?"

"If nobody knows it's me, nobody's going to attack me."

"And what if someone guesses?" She looked from one to the other of them—Judd, Pinkerton, Robert, Davis, fools, all of them, who were going to get her husband killed! She began to tremble, thoughts surging into her mind of rushing at them, striking them with her fists, with a broom, with a whip. . . . "It's all very well for you to grow that stupid beard, Mr. Lincoln, but you've been seen with it by thousands and thousands of people in every city along our way. What if someone's overheard your precious plan?"

"Molly—"

"Don't you 'Molly' me!" She jerked her hand from his touch. "What if you're murdered? What will happen to me, to our boys? What if *we're* murdered? Or doesn't that matter to your precious committee? What if we're caught and held for ransom?"

"I have to get to Washington," answered Lincoln quietly, "to be inaugurated as President...."

"Don't leave me!"

"Molly..."

"Don't leave me!" She felt as if she would suffocate with terror. "Don't be a fool! You're protected here, with an escort—they're not really going to attack with Mr. Buchanan's soldiers on this train...."

"Mrs. Lincoln," intervened Pinkerton, "believe me, they are. There are only twenty soldiers, and our reports indicate that there are hundreds in this plot. And with you and the boys and this whole..." He gestured impatiently, as if Elizabeth and Julie, Lizzie and Lockwood and Dr. Wallace, were all present as well. "...traveling road-show trailing along after him, those Baltimore secessionists are going to know exactly where to look for him."

"So you're going to send him out away from any protection and hope that nobody's going to notice a six-foot-four-inch man pussyfooting his way through Baltimore!"

"I've got that all arranged, ma'am. He'll be on a sleeper car, in a berth, as my sick relative. Nobody'll see him on his feet—"

"Well, that's a brave way to commence your administration!" She whirled on Lincoln, hearing her own voice rise to a termagant's shrillness. Any words, anything to make him change his mind..."Sneaking into your own capital city in disguise because you're afraid of a rumor—"

"It's not a rumor," snapped Judd.

"Don't you talk to me!" Mary screamed at him. "Don't you say a word to me!" Whipsawed by eleven days of travel, exhaustion, and uncertainty, she burst into frenzied tears. She struck at Lincoln's hands as he led her to the back of the parlor, tried to fight free of him, to flee. . . . Only there was nowhere to flee to. She was dimly aware of the men glancing at one another, of Robert's face wooden with embarrassment, of Willie coming up on her other side:

"It's all right, Ma. Things will be all right."

Of Lizzie's arms around her, gently easing her away from Lincoln, to whom she perversely clung the moment he tried to draw away and go back to his precious advisors—*may they all burn in Hell for eternity.* . . .

"Go back to them!" she screamed at him, shoving him suddenly away. "Go back to them and leave me! You don't care a thing about me and you never did! You'd sooner be inaugurated President than keep us safe, me and your sons!" And she flung herself, weeping, into Lizzie's arms.

Their suite at the Jones House Hotel included several bedrooms, though Governor Curtin had asked Lincoln and herself to spend the night at his house. Lizzie led her into the nearest one—assigned to Robert, Hay, and Nicolay, to judge by the leather gripsacks dumped on the beds and the scent of bay rum—and eased her into a chair. "So I won't disturb his precious advisors?" cried Mary resentfully. But it was good to be away from the men to weep, with Lizzie patting her hands and Elizabeth and the two girls hurrying back and forth with cold compresses and hartshorn. At least, she thought, *someone* cared. . . .

But the childishness of that thought tore her, as her paroxysms of tears subsided. *I've made a fool of myself,* she thought, bitterly, *and in front of them.* . . . Trembling, she blew her nose, and got to her feet.

"No," she said, when Lizzie tried to stop her. "I'm fine now. Let me go."

She could hear the voices of the men still in the parlor. Talking about her, she knew. About the scene she'd just made. About how right they were to keep her out of things. Her face grew hot with shame as she stepped past Lizzie and opened the door.

They all turned, faces wary—manlike, dreading another scene. Lincoln started toward her immediately but she said in her steadiest voice, "Mr. Lamon?"

The bearlike lawyer stood at once. Like Lincoln he was a frontiersman turned lawyer; in the plush comfort of the Presidential railroad car, he'd whiled away hours of travel playing the banjo and singing for Tad and Willie's delight.

"Please go with him, Mr. Lamon." She turned to Mr. Pinkerton, regarding her with suspicion in his reptilian eyes. "I understand your point, sir, about not drawing attention to my husband by a large entourage, and I apologize if I . . . if I let my feelings overcome me. But I beg you will allow at least one bodyguard, in the event of . . . of the unexpected."

Lincoln looked down at Pinkerton, then over at Lamon. "That's not a bad idea. I allow I'd feel a little better about it myself, knowing there's two of you."

"That's a good point, Mrs. Lincoln, and well taken." Pinkerton sounded like the admission cost him an effort to make. "Thank you."

"I won't leave his side, ma'am." Lamon opened his coat, to show her the two bowie knives he habitually wore at his belt. "You can count on me, Mrs. Lincoln."

SHE SLEPT LITTLE THAT NIGHT. AFTER SUPPER WITH THE GOV-ernor, Lincoln, Lamon, and Pinkerton took their departure. She lay awake most of the night fighting visions of the anonymous sleeping-car being stopped en route, being over-swarmed by shouting men with clubs, ropes, tar and feathers; men who all had Nate Bodley's face. Then she would wake to hear the soft voices of Robert, Hay, Ellsworth, and Nicolay, continuing their endless card-game in the parlor.

Coming out to the parlor to breakfast the next morning she found Ellsworth beaming over the coffee-cups: "This came in around six, Mrs. Lincoln." He held out a telegram, unopened—an open one lay beside Nicolay's plate.

Reached Washington Safely—Willard's Hotel

But it was a bad start, she thought, dropping sugar into her coffee, when a President could not enter his own capital city in triumph, for fear of being murdered by the very people he was taking an oath to protect.

CHAPTER FORTY

THE WHITE HOUSE HAD CHANGED GREATLY SINCE MARY LAST
had entered it for James K. Polk's receptions. Five days after
her arrival in Washington—five days in which she barely saw
her husband for more than a few minutes while he distract-
edly gulped down an egg and a cup of coffee for breakfast in
their parlor at Willard's Hotel—she was received in the Blue
Parlor by Harriet Lane, President Buchanan's niece.

Buchanan was a lifelong bachelor; Miss Lane, violet-eyed
and beautiful and just edging past the final frontiers of even
the most diplomatic definitions of "youth," had acted as
hostess in his household since the death of her parents when
she was a child. She had a slight British inflection to her
voice and the well-schooled perpetual smile of a longtime
member of the diplomatic corps, but behind it she watched
Mary warily from the moment the gangly Irish doorman
showed her into the Blue Parlor.

The newspapers—particularly the Democratic ones like
James Bennett's *New York Herald*—had been merciless about
the "Illinois gorilla" who was about to take over the
Presidency, and his fat loud-mouthed vulgar wife. Mary had
closely quizzed her escort that day—the white-haired Mrs.
McLean, whose husband was an Associate Justice of the
Supreme Court and had been one of the contenders for the
Republican nomination—to make sure that her gown of ma-
genta taffeta, with its flowing Isabeau sleeves, was, as
Madame Blois had assured her, of absolutely the most fash-
ionable style.

It apparently was, to judge by the infinitesimal relaxation
in Miss Lane's cool greeting. The President's niece unbent a
bit more at Mary's firm, polite handshake and quiet voice,

and Mary silently blessed Madame Mentelle for schooling her, all those years ago, out of all but the slightest Bluegrass inflection in her speech. The Blue Parlor had at some time in the recent past been completely refurnished—she also noticed that the old glass-and-wood screen in the front hall that she remembered had been replaced by a new one of glass and iron—but the furnishings had a shabby look to them already; the brocatelle upholstery was worn and the brightly figured rugs threadbare.

"Housekeeping here is the most *appalling* challenge," drawled Miss Lane, with a gesture at the gaily painted blue ceiling, which was already peeling slightly over the fireplace and around the medallion of the Roman-style gasolier. "Rather like a cross between a palace and a hotel, with a subscription ballroom thrown in. Nothing really prepares one for it."

"I'm sure I'll manage," said Mary, detecting the patronage in the younger woman's light voice.

"Well, of course with so many of the town's hostesses leaving now over this horrible secession, goodness knows what your entertaining will be like. I understand the Corcorans left last week for Paris—that's their house across Lafayette Square, they gave the most astonishing parties—and the Taylors will be gone as well. And of course the Davises."

"I am sure," said Mary thinly, "that Washington will not suffer for lack of entertainments."

"Of course not," agreed Miss Lane, with the words *But who in their right senses would want to associate with the Republican riffraff coming in to take their places?* unfurling like an invisible banner in her restrained little smile.

Mary itched to slap her.

After tea Miss Lane showed her over the house and introduced her to the servants—"The doormen and the gardeners are the only ones employed by the government itself, you know. Will you be keeping on the rest of the staff? Mr. Vermereu, the butler, is a Belgian, but the rest are British.

Uncle is a great believer in the British system of training servants, and I've found them quite reliable."

"Certainly I'll keep them on for the time being," replied Mary, determined to yield nothing to this flawless haughty woman, with her air of speaking to a country cousin.

If the downstairs of the house was shabby, with its tobacco-stained rugs, torn upholstery, and window-drapes that bore the scissor-marks of souvenir-hunters, the upstairs resembled a down-at-the-heels boardinghouse. Her heart sank. The long central corridor was bare and gloomy, with gray filtered light leaking into it from the open doors of the bedrooms on either side. At the east end, through ground-glass doors, the shadows of men were visible in the vestibule of the President's office; the murmur of their voices and the vibration of their feet served as an uneasy reminder of those delegations that arrived, one after the other, at Willard's Hotel, demanding of Lincoln what he was going to do about the new Confederate States. Trunks were open in several of the bedrooms. A valet was packing one of them, a maid another.

In three days, this will be mine.

The wife of the President.

The First Lady of the land.

"Thank goodness, Mr. Pierce had all the plumbing modernized." Miss Lane's plummy voice broke into her private ecstasy. "Not that it works, half the time. But at least you have it. America does have *some* advantages over Britain— Uncle's house in St. James had only the most *primitive* bathing facilities and was absolutely *glacial* in the winters. The bathroom here has allegedly hot water piped in. . . ." She opened a door off the small private corridor in the southwest corner, to reveal a handsome dressing-room papered in imitation oak-graining, and floored with oilcloth printed to look like tile. "And there's another water-closet off the secretary's office, at the other end of the house. *Ghastly* number of bedrooms here to heat, but then you have quite a large family, haven't you?"

"I married young," lied Mary sweetly, with a glance at Miss Lane's ringless finger. *You old maid.*

"That's usual out West, isn't it?" *Where they haven't anything better to do with their lives, do they?* Miss Lane gathered her rustling skirts, and preceded her down the wide stairs.

Three days of delegations, of debates, of sitting beside Lincoln at dinners during which he was preoccupied in talk with political hosts. Suite Six at Willard's Hotel was besieged by office-seekers, whose determination and persistence made the jostling madness that had plagued him at Springfield look like a Presbyterian Church tea. Lincoln took to waking early and going for long walks before sunrise with Robert or Nicolay. Often he'd breakfasted before she woke, and was closeted all day with Congressmen trying frantically to reach a compromise to conciliate the Confederacy. "I will not extend slavery into the territories," he said, over and over, and the delegates went away.

In those days she received few calls from Washington hostesses, at least partly because the parlor of Suite Six was constantly in use by her husband. "The President's wife is never obliged to make calls," Adele Douglas informed her, when she invited Mary and her sisters and nieces for tea to the beautiful house she and Mary's old suitor owned on Lafayette Square. "It's a pity that all the really powerful hostesses were Southerners and slaveholders—which stands to reason, Washington being situated where it is. And of course nearly everyone else in Washington is here only temporarily."

Everyone but the Cuttses, who were related to the late and much-mourned Dolley Madison. Mary wondered, wryly, if one reason Douglas had fought so hard for re-election was because his wife didn't want to surrender her position as one of Washington's social leaders. "For the past seven years now everyone has agonized over their guest-lists, so as not to have fights breaking out over every dinner. Even before the election Mrs. Clay of Alabama would refuse to go in to dinner with anyone who'd been elected on an anti-slavery ticket, and she knew who they all were. Goodness knows what this season will bring."

"I daresay if Maryland secedes," replied Mary, "we'll all have other things to think of besides our guest-lists."

In fact she was far more interested in the horrors of the crisis that loomed over Washington—the desperate attempts to find some grounds of compromise between the Union and the secessionist states—than she was over the niceties of Washington's social scene. But as ever, she was excluded from the men's councils, and relegated to the task of forming the necessary social network with the wives of Cabinet members and influential Senators.

William Seward, whom she had distrusted from the days of the Chicago convention when the hawk-nosed little New Yorker had tried to take the nomination from Lincoln, had left his ailing wife in Albany. But Salmon Chase's daughter Kate—the ranking Cabinet hostess in town—made clear from her first visit that she intended to establish *herself* as the center of Washington society in her father's rented house, as she had been center of society in Columbus during her father's gubernatorial days.

Kate Chase was young, red-haired, breathtakingly pretty, highly educated, and keenly intelligent, and Mary loathed her at sight. To Mary's gracious invitation to call at the White House, Kate had replied, with an air of great innocence, "And I hope that *you* will call on *me*," a slap in the face given the Washington custom that the President's wife did not make calls. Mary could not believe it wasn't calculated.

It did not help that it was obvious to Mary that both Seward and Chase regarded Lincoln as an uncouth barbarian who had to be "handled" as a pawn for their greater wisdom—though how much wisdom there was in Seward's plan to start a war with both Britain and France so that the Confederacy would leap back into the Union again, she was at a loss to determine.

The morning of the fourth of March dawned cloudy and raw. Rumor had flown around the previous afternoon that there would be an attempt to assassinate Lincoln during the inaugural parade, inflaming all Mary's fears anew. It had taken Willie and Lizzie hours to quiet her before the dinner that Lincoln was giving for the men he'd selected for his Cabinet. In addition to the hated Seward and the oleaginous Cameron, there was the sanctimonious Mr. Chase of Ohio; Mr. Welles, Secretary of the Navy, a newspaperman who sported a bad wig and had a beard like a holly-bush; Mr. Blair, whose extensive family had been virtual royalty in Maryland for generations; Mr. Caleb Smith, yet another of David Davis's political debtors; and Mr. Edward Bates, who had been appointed mainly because he came from Missouri and had political connections to every Democrat in that barely loyal tinderbox state.

On Inauguration Day, Army sharpshooters lined the parade route, and were stationed in the windows of the Treasury Building as well. She remembered the young Lexington blades of her youth, shooting apples off fenceposts at a hundred yards, or two hundred.

Any one of them could have sent that drawing, those letters. *"Say your prayers...."*

She stood in the crowd of the diplomatic gallery, clinging to Lizzie's hand in the bitter cold of the day, waiting for the sound of a shot.

At one, James Buchanan and Abraham Lincoln emerged from the Capitol, followed by Mary's old friend from Lexington, John Breckinridge—Buchanan's Vice-President, whose wife hadn't called on Mary because Breckinridge was so violently opposed to the limitation of what he called "the rights of property"—and by swarthy, stocky Hannibal Hamlin, the Maine politician who'd been elected Lincoln's Vice-President.

Lincoln looked out over the crowd—as usual, he was the tallest man present—and removed his hat, looked around for somewhere to put it while he spoke. Behind him a man stepped out of the crowd, and held out his hand. "It would be my honor to hold that for you," he said.

It was Stephen Douglas.

"Apprehension seems to exist," Lincoln read, in a voice that seemed to carry like the note of a chime over the now-silent crowd, *"among the people of the Southern States, that by the accession of a Republican Administration, their property, and their peace, and personal security, are to be endangered. There has never been any reasonable cause for such apprehension. . . ."*

Mary closed her eyes, seeing again the vile drawings, the scribbled threats. Hearing in her mind Old Duke Wickliffe's voice thundering about the "damn abolitionists wanting to steal our property"; seeing Nate Bodley's cane rise and fall, splattered with blood.

Reasonable cause, she thought, has never had the slightest thing to do with politics.

Print a lie in a newspaper—whisper it across a Washington tea-table to your society friends—and there is no catching up with it.

And Lincoln knew this.

". . . there needs to be no bloodshed or violence; and there shall be none unless it be forced upon the national authority. . . ."

No mention of secession, or of the Confederate States of America. He was being a lawyer, always leaving the door open, pretending for as long as he could that he did not see. *No wonder people call him a fool,* Mary thought. *They don't see that until something is made official, it's possible to go back and pretend it all never happened.* That was a piece of politics she'd learned at her father's knee.

"One section of this country believes slavery is right, and ought to be extended, while the other believes that it is wrong, and ought not to be extended. This is the only substantial dispute."

No, Mary thought, and shivered. *One section of the country believes that neither the Federal government, nor any other section of the country, has the right to tell them what should be legal and what should not be legal.*

And one section of the country believes that it is their right to withdraw from the compact of Union that they entered willingly, eighty-five years ago.

And they are willing to fight for that right.

This, too, Lincoln knew.

The sound of his voice brought gooseflesh to her arms, though it had been so familiar to her for so many years. In courtrooms or in the State House, or across the kitchen table, laughing over Billy Herndon's latest fad. The words made her heart beat faster, even on this second hearing—despite the desperate press of business he'd made time to go over it with her. It was one of his best, and she knew it would not alter one single Southern heart.

Cold air breathed across her face, and with it the scent of rain. The murmur of the crowd was the echo of a thousand political-speakings of her girlhood, as they listened to Henry Clay or Old Duke Wickliffe or her father, so familiar that it was a part of her blood.

But everything was different now. It was no longer just arguments over patronage, bonds, whether or not the state would pay to build a railroad or dig a canal.

If compromise was not reached, blood would be shed.

"We must not be enemies," said Lincoln. *"Though passion may have strained, it must not break our bonds of affection. The mystic chords of memory, stretching from every battlefield, every patriot grave, to every living heart and hearthstone all over this broad land, will yet swell the chorus of the Union, when again touched, as surely they will be, by the better angels of our natures."*

Mary opened her eyes as Chief Justice Taney—the man who six years before had told Dred Scott that because he was black he had no right to seek his freedom—held out the Bible, for Abraham Lincoln to swear that he would uphold the Constitution and the laws of the land.

HARRIET LANE MAY HAVE THOROUGHLY DISAPPROVED OF A family of Illinois hicks moving into the house that she had considered her own for four years, but she knew her duty as a hostess. Upon their arrival at the White House after the Inauguration, Mary found—to her intense gratitude—a hot dinner waiting, hot water in all the guest-rooms, and all the beds made up with fresh sheets. Young Ellsworth rose with glowing eyes from his place between Elizabeth's daughters and offered a toast: "To the President of the United States!"

Lincoln inclined his head, raised his glass—which contained water, Lincoln having seen, as he'd once said, enough drunkenness in his youth to last him a lifetime—and replied, "With the permission of all of my family, I will take this opportunity to say nothing at all."

Laughter, and thunderous applause from those around the table—Hay and Nicolay, Ellsworth and Lizzie, Lockwood and Mary's three sisters Margaret, Mattie, and Elizabeth, Dr. Wallace, the husbands of Mattie and Margaret, Elizabeth's daughters...all those who had come to see their kinsman and employer and friend put in charge, as Willie phrased it, of everything.

The windows were dark when they finished, bade a temporary *au revoir* to those of the party who were staying at hotels, and crossed through the hall for the first time, to climb the grand staircase, and seek their respective beds for what rest they could get before preparing for the Inaugural Ball at eleven. Large as the White House was, it was going to be a tight squeeze.

"I've put you and the girls in the Prince of Wales's bedroom," said Mary to Elizabeth, with rehearsed lightness. All her life, it seemed to her, she'd been waiting to say that with just the right degree of insouciance.

Elizabeth, being Elizabeth, said only, "I hope the sheets are properly aired."

Her girls at least looked deeply impressed.

But as they reached the landing and Mary fell back to ask Lincoln about the carriages to take them to the so-called Muslin Palace of Aladdin—set up for the occasion behind City Hall—he held up a folded note and told her, "This was handed to me as I came in. It's from Major Anderson at Fort Sumter. He says unless supplies get to him within the next few days, he'll have to surrender the fort to the government of South Carolina."

"What are you going to do?" she whispered, as they reached the top of the stairs, the family scattering before them down the dark central corridor with firefly candles in hand.

He sighed. "God knows, Mother."

Chapter Forty-one

Ever since Lincoln's nomination at the Illinois state convention, ten months previously, Mary had pictured in her mind what it would be like, to be the wife of the President. She had remembered the elegant and commanding Sarah Polk, standing at her unassuming husband's side; remembered the crowded reception rooms and the fashionable Washington hostesses, and the gossip of receptions, at-homes, dinners, evening parties that had trickled down to her at Mrs. Spriggs's.

And she had seen herself in command of it all.

Nothing had prepared her for the reality.

During the first week she only saw her husband at breakfast—if she rose early enough for it, which on most days was nearly impossible. When they found themselves together at a reception for the diplomatic corps—held at the rambling stone cottage that had once belonged to the governor of the Soldiers' Home on the high wooded ground on the outskirts of Washington—Lincoln tipped his hat to her and inquired straight-faced, "Do I know you, ma'am?" And her slow-steaming resentment dissolved into laughter.

They were together again for an hour at church. In Springfield Lincoln had been a lackadaisical church-goer; in Washington he was either more conscious of appearances, or felt a greater need of guidance and prayer. Perhaps he simply recognized that at the New York Avenue Presbyterian Church, not even the most persistent candidate for office would come up to him demanding to be made Minister to Belgium, and he would have a chance to spend a little quiet time with his children and his wife.

"I feel like an innkeeper," groused Lincoln at one point,

"who is trying to live in one wing of his establishment while trying to put out a fire in the other."

Office-seekers had besieged him at Willard's Hotel, but in those first weeks, the White House was never without a line of men, in all stages of elegance or inelegance or downright odiferous decrepitude of person. They waited from dawn till long after nightfall in the office reception room, the outer office, the dark little vestibule at the top of the office stairs, and trailed in a line down the stairs themselves to the front hall, waiting to see the President, whom each one of them considered to be personally in his debt for his election. Only a set of ground-glass doors separated the vestibule from the upstairs hall. Occasionally one or two office-seekers would wander through in quest of a lavatory or a glass of water, or merely to "have a look at the house," as one furry-eared Missourian put it when he peered through Lizzie's bedroom door.

Between conferences with delegates from Maine, Oregon, Massachusetts, and California—between half-clandestine meetings with representatives of Virginia in a frantic attempt to keep that wealthy, powerful, and perilously nearby state from following South Carolina and the others out of the Union—between hectic arguments with the Cabinet about whether to supply Fort Sumter or abandon it to the rebels—Lincoln saw all these men.

Mary quickly came to hate them. She understood that Lincoln was now a public figure, and had his responsibilities to his constituents. *She* was now a public figure—it was what she had all her life wanted to be. But not *this* public. The lack of privacy—and of respect—made her nervous, knowing as she did that any one of those men might be a secessionist with a derringer in his coat, and the fact that they took Lincoln away from her, all day, every day, filled her with resentment.

That first month, though Margaret and her husband went on to Italy at the end of the week and Mattie and her husband returned to the rebel state of Alabama, she had

Elizabeth, Lizzie, Lockwood, and the girls to keep her company and help her settle in. Elizabeth's undeniable talents for organization went a long way toward smoothing the transition from Harriet Lane's ways to Mary's, and it was good, when she gave her first reception on Friday night and her first "at-home" Saturday morning, to have her family around her, their elegant clothing and quiet demeanor a visible rebuke to those who called her a loud-mouthed and vulgar Westerner.

It was comforting, too, to know that she was undeniably the most elegantly dressed woman in the room. Adele Douglas gave her the name of the best seamstress in Washington ("She worked for Varina Davis, you know"), a tall and lovely mulatto woman named Lizabet Keckley. Mrs. Keckley arrived on Mary's first morning in the White House—Tuesday, with the reception looming Friday—took Mary's measurements with speedy competence, reviewed all the silks from Stewart's and Laurent's and selected a deep rose moiré, and promised to deliver it Thursday. In fact the dress wasn't ready until Mary was pacing the floor Friday evening in her petticoat and wrapper: it shouldn't have taken that long, Mary fumed, for Mrs. Keckley to make the alterations in trim that she had demanded at the fitting the day before. But after that initial hitch of nervous hysterics, apologies, and a contrite note from Mary the following morning, she settled in well with the dressmaker, who certainly had a better eye and a more up-to-date sense of fashion than Madame Blois.

But few Washington ladies came to her at-homes.

And most of those who did were lavish in their praise of Kate Chase's at-home the Wednesday before. When they spoke of the younger woman's lovely house and stylish furnishings, Mary writhed. The White House in its current run-down condition was an embarrassment, not only to the Lincolns personally (reflected Mary) but to the nation. What on earth would the French ministers think, or the British, who were openly negotiating to help the rebel government? One of the first to call on her was Mrs. Taft, wife of the

Chief Examiner of the Patent Office, who had left her card on Mary at Willard's. She had, it transpired in the course of the conversation, two sons, twelve-year-old Bud and eight-year-old Holly: "You must send them over to play with my boys," said Mary, consciously drawing back her envious attention from Mrs. Taft's extremely stylish blue velvet bonnet. "Poor things, Tad and Willie have been terribly lonely, now that all the excitement is dying down. I haven't yet had time to find them a tutor." The thought of sending them to school, even a private school, filled her with dread. What was to stop the same men who'd written those terrible letters to Lincoln from lurking outside the school, stealing his children?

Consequently Bud and Holly Taft—sturdy fair-haired boys accompanied by their pretty and excruciatingly well-behaved sister, Julia—appeared the following day, and immediately gave Tad and Willie the measles.

Dispatches continued to come from the besieged government forces in Fort Sumter—a tiny islet in Charleston Harbor still held by the United States—and Fort Pickens, off Pensacola in Florida. Gouty and ancient General Winfield Scott—Old Fuss and Feathers, Lincoln called him in private, on account of the gorgeousness of the older man's uniforms—recommended the forts be abandoned, and turned over to the Confederate government. Frederick Blair of Maryland, the father of the new Postmaster and patriarch of the most powerful family in that critical border state, retorted that such an action would be treason on Lincoln's part. Cash Clay turned up and accepted Lincoln's offer of the post of Minister to Russia—Mary suspected that the Russians were just insane enough to get along well with him, though she wondered how poor Mary Jane would deal with St. Petersburg winters.

The Cabinet met late into the night.

Then at 4:30 in the morning of Good Friday, the twelfth of April, the Charleston garrison opened fire on Fort Sumter. Lincoln became even less visible than usual that day, and the next, except for a brief appearance at a gathering in the big oval family parlor upstairs. But though he looked grim and preoccupied, Mary could also see a springy lightness in his movements, as if a band of iron had been unlocked from around his chest. Coming up beside him, she whispered, "They fired the first shot, didn't they?"

And he grinned down at her, hearing the perfect understanding in her voice. "They certainly did," he replied. Mystic chords of memory and the better angels of Jefferson Davis's nature notwithstanding, she guessed that he had known all along that it would come to bloodshed. And since she had seen the hate-letters in his desk, she had known, too, that it was the South that would strike the first blow.

On Monday Lincoln issued a proclamation calling for seventy-five thousand militia troops for ninety days. Three months seemed long enough, everyone thought, to take care of the trouble. Effervescing with enthusiasm as usual, young Ellsworth quit his job in the War Department and hied off to New York to raise, he declared, a troop of volunteers among the city's fire companies.

Two days later Virginia voted to secede from the Union and establish its own government, and all eyes in the city turned north, to the railway lines that crossed the slave-state of Maryland.

The week that followed was one of the most nerve-wracking of her life. Militia troops were stationed around Washington, but even Tad could tell that they would be no match for a Confederate army. In the dark before dawn one morning, Mary overheard Lincoln say, "If I was Beauregard,"—he named the commander of the troops in Charleston—"I'd be on my way to take Washington now." He was speaking to Hay and Nicolay, in the chill, dark, and drafty upstairs corridor. *He probably thinks I'm asleep,* thought Mary, lying in the dimness of her bedroom, staring at the tall rosewood bedposts by the flickering whisper of the night-light in its painted glass shade. *As if anyone could sleep.*

She closed her eyes, vainly seeking the rest that had

eluded her all night. *They'll kill him.* Earlier, she'd been wakened by Hay's soft knocking on Lincoln's door; had heard the
young secretary tell him that yet another plot against his life
had been uncovered.

Who knows what soldiers will do, if they burn the town?

Her head throbbed, as it had since the previous evening.
She heard their steps fade down the hallway, to the office
where Lincoln would read dispatches and write letters until
the first of the endless delegations started to arrive. She heard
Hay's lovely baritone voice, "You think Colonel Lee will accept your offer? He's a Virginian...."

"I pray he does," answered Lincoln. "I'd hate to have to
put our trust in Old Fuss and Feathers."

Aching for sleep, she crept from bed and dug in her cupboard for her bottle of Indian Bitters. She didn't like to take
it—it sometimes left her drowsy in the morning and if she
was absent from breakfast she wouldn't see Lincoln again all
day—but at least it let her sleep.

General Scott ordered the strongest and largest of the
government buildings to be fortified, as miniature redoubts
to which the members of the government could retreat and
hold off attackers if necessary. Mary could not keep from
thinking of the men of the Texas Revolution, back in 1836,
when she was still at Mentelle's, holding off a Mexican army
for nearly two weeks in an old church, waiting for relief that
never arrived.

Six hundred Kansas volunteers camped in the White
House's huge East Room. Tad, Willie, Bud, and Holly pil-
fered cookies from the kitchen downstairs and took them to
these uncouth guests, and spent most of their time among
them, learning how to disassemble and clean rifles, how to
cook on campfires on the lawn, and hearing tales of the
bloody internecine warfare that had torn Kansas apart for the
past seven years.

Night after night she would hear the shaggy young ruffians moving about downstairs, as she sat with Lizzie and
Elizabeth in the oval parlor, waiting for Lincoln to return

from conferences, delegations, meetings in the big office beyond the ground-glass doors. The clatter of boots vibrating
the old bones of the mansion, the rough voices raised in occasional song, reminded her that morning might see rebel
troops pouring across the river. Confederate flags could be
seen flying over Alexandria, at the other end of the Long
Bridge. It was a struggle not to give way to fear, and to the
anger that fear always fuelled.

Without her family there she didn't know what she would
have done. Elizabeth's steely level-headedness always had a
calming effect on her, and Lizzie did what she could to keep
Tad and Willie entertained and out of everyone's way.

Not that they needed it, of course. When not in the East
Room learning God-knew-what rude ditties from the
Frontier Guards, the two boys had established a bastion on
the White House roof—with a log for a cannon—and spent
hours watching the hills of Virginia. Mary listened, through
strained nerves and the renewed agonies of female itching,
for shouting in the streets, for the crack of gunfire, for the
running feet and the outcry that would herald inevitable
disaster.

On the twenty-third of April, the Dominion of Virginia
formally allied itself with the Southern Confederacy.
Through the night Mary listened to Lincoln's footsteps, pacing his bedroom, or the corridor outside. Any troops coming
to guard the capital must pass through Maryland, through
which only two months ago Lincoln had had to be smuggled
in disguise. Coming back indoors after he'd talked to General
Scott in the White House drive—the elderly commander of
the Union forces was so gouty he couldn't climb the stairs to
the office—she overheard him say quietly to Nicolay, "I begin to believe that there is no North."

Then on the twenty-fifth, the Seventh New York
Regiment arrived, marching through the rain down the
muddy unpaved streets. Mary ran with the boys and Lizzie to
join Lincoln on the White House steps to watch them pass;

afterwards she went up to her room and burst into tears of relief.

Washington became an Army town. Regiments of ninety-day volunteers, hastily organized, camped on the swampy Mall between the Capitol and the White House, and the reek of their latrine-trenches hung like a permanent miasma in the air. The Seventh New York set up shop in the House Chamber of the Capitol. Cash Clay showed up with a battalion, and strutted through the White House halls adorned with three pistols and an "Arkansas toothpick"—a bowie knife as long as Mary's forearm—and for days her younger sons tried to imitate his walk and his extravagant drawl.

Lincoln wrote to Ben Helm, Emilie's young husband, who'd come to Springfield with her on her most recent visit. Since their weeks at the Todd house on the way to Washington in 1848, she and Lincoln had regarded Emilie as a daughter, and during her stays in Springfield Lincoln had come to treat her more as a younger sister. He had confided to Mary that he planned to offer Ben a good military post. *Please, please,* Mary prayed, *let Emilie come here, be here with me.* Lizzie and Elizabeth were both talking of returning home, and the thought of being left alone in this hostile town filled her with dread.

But when the young lawyer came down the stairs and into the Red Parlor where she was having tea, she saw the sadness in his dark eyes and knew it was not to be.

"Excuse me, please," she said to her guests—Elizabeth, the girls, Adele Douglas, and sixteen-year-old Julie Taft. Ben stepped with her into the hall: a slim man, darkly handsome as the hero of a Gothic novel.

"Your husband has just offered me the chance at a career," he said quietly. "Paymaster in the Army, with rank of major. It's something it would take me years to get to on my own. I've told him how much I appreciate it, beyond what words can say."

"But you won't take it."

"I asked him to give me a few days."

She saw the answer in his eyes. "Kentucky is still in the Union." She spoke sadly, as if to one standing already on the deck of a departing ship.

"Your husband is an honest man, Molly," said Ben in his soft voice. "I respect him, and you, too much to be less than honest with either of you." He put his hands on her shoulders, and bent a little to kiss her cheek. "I'll give your love—and his—to Emilie."

"I'd hoped to have you both here in Washington." Tears filled her eyes—of disappointment, and something far deeper. "You know Emilie would have been the belle of the town."

"Nobody's going to be the belle of this town more than you, Molly." Ben smiled, and pressed her hands in his. "Good-by."

She never saw him again.

That same day Colonel Lee—Lincoln's hoped-for choice for Commander in Chief—resigned his commission in the U.S. Second Cavalry, and crossed the river to Virginia, the land of his birth.

Washington waited for what was to happen next.

Simon Cameron, Secretary of War, reveled in the sudden influx of troops and started handing out plum contracts to all his supporters, regardless of the quality of the uniforms they were selling or the cost to Congress.

Salmon Chase met with Lincoln in frantic sessions to arrange financing for a war. Suddenly bankers—from New York, Philadelphia, and several European banking houses—became a part of Washington society.

The masses of office-seekers, which had begun at last to thin, redoubled. Good Republicans felt entitled to positions supplying the troops or selling things to the government or acting as clerks or marshals or quartermasters. Tad would trot up the stairs past them, greeting them in his almost incomprehensible lisp, on his way to finding some horrendous mischief to get into with his brother and the Taft boys.

With everything else that was going on, Mary tried desperately not to worry about Tad. From being a relatively normal seven-year-old, except for his speech, he now reverted to old, babyish behaviors, refusing to dress himself or pay the slightest attention to his beleaguered tutor. Lincoln said mildly, "He'll get over it," and Mary did her best to believe him.

On one occasion the four boys explored the attic and found the bell-wires that connected every room in the house with the servants' quarters in the basement. Lincoln, who was curious about things like bell-wires himself, tracked them down, amid servants scurrying up and down the stairs and unimaginable chaos. John Nicolay threatened to break their necks and throw them out the window—a sentiment that was heartily seconded by several members of the Presidential Cabinet but which did nothing for the feud that was beginning to smolder between Nicolay and Mary—but Lincoln only laughed. Another expedition to the attic yielded the cardboard boxes where all the visiting-cards of everyone who had ever crossed the White House's threshold were stored: the boys played "sled on the snow" and came downstairs filthy and dropping from every cuff and seam little squares of pasteboard engraved with the names of long-departed Washington luminaries: Dolley Madison, John Randolph, Aaron Burr.

"You want to watch your boys, goin' up to the attic that way," warned Johnny Watt, the smooth-faced Irishman who was head groundskeeper. "The house is riddled with rats, you know. Big ones, some of 'em, and worse now the Army camps are so near. We got one big tycoon up there I swear has been in office since Jackson's day, and Miss Lane not holdin' with cats." He shook his head, watching Mary with bright blue eyes.

Though Tad was the youngest of the four boys he was usually the ringleader in their enterprises. Alexander Williamson, the young Scotsman who came in every morning to tutor the boys, said that Tad's wild misbehavior and sudden, flaring rages might stem simply from frustration that no one understood his combination of mumble and lisp.

Willie and Tad were the only two people in the house—perhaps in all of Washington—who weren't afraid constantly during that tense, waiting month of April 1861.

"Pa won't let anything happen to us," Willie said to Mary, one afternoon when anxiety and sleeplessness had driven her back to bed with an excruciating headache. He took her hand—it was another of those days when she had slept late and slept poorly, and so had missed seeing Lincoln even at breakfast. The constant murmur and grumble of men's voices from beyond the glass doors at the end of the corridor was a reminder that she probably wouldn't see him until late that night, if then.

"Ee'a bead-a sececheth," added Tad. "Ooo thee."

Mary sat up in bed, though the movement brought nausea and a dreamlike tickling sensation in her mind, as if she were about to start speaking in tongues as people did in the Bible. She hugged the boys close to her, praying they were right.

At the end of the month, when no one had yet attacked Washington and Federal troops had occupied Maryland to protect the railroad north, she came to the conclusion that a trip to New York could not be put off longer. The occupation by Federal troops of the East Room had ended, but it had reduced the already shabby carpet and draperies to mud-crusted and tobacco-stained rags.

And with the onset of hot weather, Mary found herself prey to "Potomac malaria," bouts of chills and fever that plagued many in the low-lying capital marshes.

What really spurred her on, however, was an editorial in the *Charleston Mercury:*

If Washington was offered to us for nothing, the offer should be rejected. With a new Republic we should have a new Capital, erected in the heart of the South. Let Washington remain, with its magnificent buildings crumbling into ruin, a striking monument to future ages of the folly and wickedness of the people of the

North. It would teach a lesson, in its silence and desolation, all the nations of the earth should learn and understand.

Fuming, she showed the paper to Lizzie, and that evening to Lincoln, when for the first time in days he put in an appearance at the family dinner-table rather than simply foraging around at midnight in the kitchen.

"We cannot let it be said, *anywhere,* that the Union suffers *any* diminution of its state or power," she pointed out, thrusting the paper into his hands. "On the ninth, as you know, there is to be a reception for the officers stationed here in the capital and their families. Though the servants have done wonders cleaning up the East Room I *cringe* to think of anyone going in there."

Least of all—as she didn't say—Kate Chase.

CHAPTER FORTY-TWO

THE THOUGHT OF LEAVING LINCOLN AND THE BOYS IN A PLACE of danger—the nightmare of reading in some newspaper that Beauregard had attacked unexpectedly after all, that the city was in flames and the President hanged—tormented her, but the recollection was stronger still of the way Kate Chase had surveyed the Red Room curtains and run her gloved fingers along the top of the mantel when she thought Mary wasn't looking.

Or perhaps when she thought she was.

By this time Adele Douglas and Mary Jane Welles—the kindly wife of the bushy-bearded Secretary of the Navy—had relayed to Mary some of the things the elegant Miss Chase had said about the President's wife at *her* at-homes.

A special session of Congress had been called for the first of July, and Mary knew that would entail a good deal of entertaining. There was the winter season to be thought of, too; truncated perhaps (as longtime Washington hostess Mrs. Eames pointedly lamented when she compared present-day Washington to the brilliance of that city under Buchanan and Pierce—"But of course you weren't here then, were you, Mrs. Lincoln?"), but critical.

After two more fittings with Mrs. Keckley, Mary, Elizabeth and her daughters, Lockwood Todd, and Lizzie—escorted by the very charming Federal Commissioner of Public Buildings William Wood—left by train for Philadelphia. Mary was ashamed of the relief she felt. Relief to be away from Washington. Relief to be on a journey again, under the different rules that applied to journeys. Relief not to be constantly terrified.

She was ashamed that she was *not* constantly terrified. She had, after all, left her husband and two of her sons in a city that (the *Charleston Mercury* notwithstanding) might be sacked and burned at any moment. But she loved traveling, and once they had bypassed Baltimore she found herself feeling better, and sleeping more soundly, even without the assistance of Atkinson's Cordial.

And New York City in the springtime was so lovely.

Alexander Stewart, white-haired and regal, met them himself at the train station and escorted them in his own carriage to the Metropolitan Hotel. For six days, Commissioner Wood conducted Mary and her relations through the shops and warehouses of New York, examining wallpapers, carpeting, furniture, crystal and dishes, dress silks and trim. The terror and stench of Washington seemed mercifully far away, as if the United States and the Confederacy (though Mary loyally refrained from referring to the rebel states as a separate nation) were two mythical lands about to do battle in a legend, like Greece and Troy.

The hurry and crowds of the New York streets had little to do with soldiers, artillery, preparations for invasion and death. Well-dressed businessmen strode along the paved flagways, coat-skirts flapping in the breeze from the river. Rough laborers in soft caps and corduroy jackets shouted to one another in Gaelic or German; well-dressed boys rolled hoops in the grassy lawns of Washington and Union Squares.

Reporters crowded about her every time she passed through the Metropolitan's lobby, tipped their hats to her, laughed at her imitations of Cameron and Seward. Commissioner Wood winked and flirted with her, and Mary flirted right back, despite Elizabeth's sharply whispered admonitions.

For the first time since her marriage—other than the months spent in Lexington—Mary felt truly young.

After all those years of counting pennies, of worrying what Mr. Lincoln's income might be, of wincing at the cheap lampshades and cheap upholstery and the patches on Robert's breeches that screamed failure to her and to anyone of decent breeding (like Elizabeth) who entered her house, Mary was finally able to relax and enjoy the exhilarating peace of knowing that she was buying the best. She conscientiously bought only American-made goods, even when she was purchasing for herself—except of course when there were no good American products, as with silk. She dickered endlessly with the merchants to make sure she was getting the best prices, and felt a warm surge of triumph each time she scored a victory.

So she reveled in her happy duty, weighing the relative merits of Wilton and Axminster carpeting (Sally Orne in Philadelphia gave her good advice there), or deciding whether pristine white china with a gold rim would be more impressive than rich-toned solferino, and picking which of several grades of fancy straw matting would be best for the halls. The White House, when she was finished with it, would be truly the handsomest house in America, a palace that would proclaim the Union's confident strength to the British and the French.

And would, incidentally, put paid once and for all to those accusations of uncouthness and vulgarity that were still circulating in Washington and—via the *Herald* and its fellows— throughout the country.

The days were wonderful, the evenings exciting, as Commissioner Wood escorted her to the theater and restaurants. Men made much of her, and gave her presents, with the understanding that she'd "put in a good word" for them with her husband. Aside from the welcome sensation of being young and attractive again, this soothed the hurt of being shut out of the planning and politics she so enjoyed. She did, indeed, have a place as a shaper of policy—at least, these men seemed to think so.

Only at night would her fears return, the agitation and headaches and, twice, those strange spells of disorientation, as if she were in danger of becoming detached from her body and forced to watch herself doing and saying alien things.

She telegraphed Lincoln daily at the War Department, shaking her head over the memory of how long it had taken for letters to pass between Columbia, Missouri, and all those small Illinois towns, once upon a long-ago time.

At the end of the week Elizabeth and her daughters took the train for Springfield under Lockwood Todd's escort, and Lizzie, Mary, and Commissioner Wood went on first to Boston, then to Cambridge to visit Robert, a very grown-up Robert with a new fuzz of pale mustache and much talk about "the men" of his hall and year. "There's a troop of them forming, if more volunteers are called up," he said, as he walked across the commons with Mary in the humid twilight after supper in the Hall.

She flinched, and put out her hand quickly to take Robert's. She had to force her voice into what she hoped was a semblance of normalcy. "Oh, darling, I'm sure that won't be necessary."

"It won't be necessary for my country to fight when it has been fired upon by an enemy?" Robert stopped, and looked gravely down at her. "Or it won't be necessary for *me* to fight for my country?"

"Let's not talk about it now, dearest." In her heart she saw young Ben Helm, walking out of the White House's marble-floored vestibule and down the steps in the sunlight. That night, in the cozy little Cambridge hotel, she dreamed of the White House, with black crape wreathed on its doors and all its windows darkened; dreamed of seeing it afloat in poisonous greenish mists that flowed up out of the ground.

All the way back to Washington two days later she struggled with a rising sense of dread, that she would return to find some terrible event had taken place. She chatted mechanically with Lizzie and Mr. Wood to take her mind from her fear, but every time the train slowed, her mind filled with confused visions of it stopping, of an officer in the blue uniform of the Army coming down the aisle to her: "I'm sorry, Mrs. Lincoln, the train can't go any farther. Washington has been taken...."

John Nicolay met them at the station with the news that Virginia had officially become a part of the Confederacy, not merely an ally. Union troops had crossed the two bridges to the little town of Alexandria and had established bridgeheads there. The President, he told them, had been closeted with his Cabinet pretty steadily since the news had arrived on Tuesday.

Mary said, "Thank you," and settled her enormous, spreading crinoline over the carriage seats. It was Adele Douglas's carriage, on loan to the Lincolns. Mary could hardly wait to tell Lincoln of the beautiful open barouche she'd chosen, for which the businessmen of New York had agreed to pay! Nicolay asked politely after the journey, then dropped into conversation with Commissioner Wood, for which she was glad, for she had begun to see how deceived she had been in the thin young journalist with his faint German accent. Her blossoming dislike had flared into furious resentment when she'd been told that Nicolay, not she, would be in charge of social arrangements at the White House.

"It'll be more for consistency than for anything else," Lincoln had told her, when she'd gone storming into the parlor at Willard's—this had been a few days before the Inauguration—to demand why the State Department's point-by-point description of etiquette had been delivered to the young secretary instead of to herself. "You know how your headaches lay you out, Mother, and you've told me yourself there's never any knowing when you'll be struck by one. You wouldn't want, nor could we afford, for the purely mechanical arrangements of diplomacy to be put off by your illness."

"You think I can't be trusted?" she had demanded. "Is that it?" And, having no real argument against Lincoln's reasoning, had raged at him in a fury of tears fuelled by the exhaustion of that interminable journey from Springfield. The memory still rankled, against Nicolay, whom she suspected of putting himself forward with the argument and the suggestion, and against

Lincoln himself, though her grudge had been mostly sub-
merged in the tensions of the past few months. Riding back
to the White House now through the streets of town, already
thick with rising clouds of dust, she reflected that her husband
probably wouldn't even take the time to separate himself from
his precious Cabinet to greet her. And the boys would be off
somewhere with the Taft children....

Tears of weary self-pity stung her eyes, and she took
Lizzie's hand for comfort. Even in the twelve days she'd been
gone, Washington had grown noticeably hotter, and the
stench was incredible. Rows of tents covered the open Mall
that stretched from the Capitol to the river. The reek of the
latrine-pits vied with that of the horse-lines and the victualers' pens of cattle and swine.

More herds blocked the streets, en route to their destinies,
and there seemed to be teamsters and wagons everywhere.
Men in uniforms swarmed, no two companies arrayed
alike. Blue, gray, young Ellsworth's gaudy scarlet-trousered
Zouaves... country boys in twos and threes gawking about
them as if Washington were a real city instead of the provincial Southern town that she knew it was. Bowery toughs
from New York swaggered and cursed at the free blacks of
the town, the first blacks that many of them had ever seen. In
New York and Philadelphia Mary had seen for herself what
she'd read of in the papers for years: the virulence of the hatred white working-men bore against the free blacks.

They would fight to preserve the Union, but newspapers,
street-corner orators, broadsides all vociferously proclaimed
that they would not fight to flood the Northern cities with
men more impoverished—and willing to work for lower
wages—than themselves.

And among the ninety-day militia soldiers, strode warriors
of that secondary army that had followed on the first since the
Greeks sat down before the walls of Troy: teamsters, sutlers,
victualers, laundrywomen, harlots, bunco-artists, thieves. All
coated with Washington's impenetrable dust, all waiting for
the fighting to begin.

Two members of the Cassius Clay Battalion stood by the gate off Pennsylvania Avenue. The carriage-wheels crunched on the gravel of the circular drive. She glimpsed wizened Mr. McManus in the doorway, and the next moment the tall thin shape of her husband emerged from the dark hall behind him.

At least, she thought with relief, he wasn't in his shirt-sleeves. Gladness swept her. Tad and Willie shoved past him and ran down the steps, followed almost at once by young Ellsworth, handsome in his Zouave uniform, ready to escort her up the steps. Bud and Holly, and young Julia in her white dress, grouped around Lincoln like a second family; Julia held a bouquet of welcoming flowers.

Home, Mary thought.

But the house itself, looming up behind them, even in the hot spring sunlight seemed to her to be shadowed, like the terrible house of mourning in her dream. *It's only because it's so shabby,* she thought, as Commissioner Wood helped her from the carriage. *And only because I'm tired.* Her head throbbed and she thought with longing of a few quiet hours in her room. *When the new furniture arrives, and we get a new coat of paint on it, it will be the finest in the city, in the nation....*

Yet as she walked toward the steps, her sons romping around her like puppies—*Tad couldn't possibly have grown taller in less than two weeks!*—she shivered at the sight of it, as if, like the house in her dream, it was filled, not with the bustle of business and the noise of life, but with poison, and darkness, and the stench of death.

CHAPTER FORTY-THREE

TWO NIGHTS LATER SHE WAS WAKED FROM UNEASY SLEEP BY the tramp of men marching. Hair hanging down her back, she crossed to the window and put aside the curtains: dark figures, dark banners, gun-barrels catching cold dark gleams of moonlight. They were heading down the Mall toward the Long Bridge, which joined Washington to Alexandria. Only that day she had been driven past it in the carriage on the way to review the flag exercises of the Seventh New York Regiment, and Lincoln had pointed out how the planks of the bridge had been taken up to prevent rebel cavalry from charging across it.

The night was stifling, the window-glass tepid against her cheek. She had a horror of mosquitoes, and even with netting draped around the bed, the mere sound of one in the room was enough to keep her awake. The nights here were thick with them, like dust-motes around the lanterns of the guards by the White House gates.

She watched until the columns gave way to ambulance-wagons, supply-carts, remounts, and reserves. Still sitting beside the window an hour or so later, she heard the distant crackle of musket-fire, that told her the fighting had truly begun.

Because of being waked she slept late, until the day's heat woke her, sweating and itching. Her maid was just hooking her into one of her new dresses of pale-blue muslin when there was a knock on the door.

It was Lizzie. Her eyes were red and swollen and sick panic struck Mary to the heart, even before she spoke.

"Oh, darling, I'm so sorry," Lizzie whispered. "It's poor Ellsworth."

The two women went into the hall. Mary could see, beyond the ground-glass doors, Lincoln's tall shadow, struggling to get through the press of men in the vestibule without visibly thrusting them aside. She was familiar with this sight. It would take him an hour sometimes to get from his office to the doors that separated the business part of the White House from the family quarters, maybe another to get past the line between the doors and the stair. On this occasion, as had happened many times before, two men who evidently felt their affairs simply couldn't wait followed him down the hall, talking all the while: "... seein' as how it was me that got you the vote in Jackson County, you understand that I traded a lot of favors for it, and it's only right that I be given a quartermaster's post in return..."

She didn't hear what he answered. It seemed to take a long time. Why didn't that horrible man from Jackson County drop dead of the palsy as he spoke? When the man and his friend disappeared back through the ground-glass doors—nearly colliding with another office-seeker who was trying to come through into the hall and take advantage of this near glimpse of the President as well—Lincoln took Mary and Lizzie aside and drew them after him into the parlor. His lined cheeks were streaked with tears.

"The Zouaves were part of the force that took Alexandria last night." He spoke as if setting facts before a jury. "There was little fighting. Ellsworth and his men took the telegraph office first thing, to keep news from spreading farther south. They hoisted the flag there. When it got light they could see a rebel flag flying on top of the Marshall Hotel. Ellsworth led his men to pull it down—they were coming downstairs with it when the owner of the hotel shot him." His voice broke and he pressed his hand, very briefly, over his mouth.

Then he looked at his hand, as if he could see his friend's blood there, and said, very softly, "What have I done?"

"Exactly what you swore you would do," replied Mary steadily, though her own mind stalled on the fact that she would never see that ebullient young friend again. "Upheld the Constitution against those who would tear this nation apart."

And Lincoln sighed, like a man who feels the full weight of the cross settle at last on his shoulder, to be carried up the hill.

They were driven in the carriage to the Navy Yard that afternoon, to see the body. Someone had washed Ellsworth's face and covered him with a sheet, but some of the blood still soaked through. Spatters of it still clung to his hair and the gallant mustache he'd grown. Looking down at him, Mary saw him when he'd first come to Springfield, brimming with plans and enthusiasm for Lincoln's election; saw him all those evenings when he'd come home for supper with Lincoln and help with the dishwashing afterwards.

And looking down at him, she saw, as if with horrible double vision, Robert's face, waxy, bloodless, and flecked with gore.

She closed her eyes, and gripped Lincoln's arm until the wave of dizzy horror passed.

They held the funeral at the White House, a bier erected on the trampled and boot-scarred carpets of the dilapidated East Room. Lincoln wept again, as Mary placed a wreath and Ellsworth's photograph on the casket, that would be taken to the railroad station for the long journey back to his parents in New York. Feeling the convulsive grip of her husband's black-gloved hand seeking comfort in hers, she knew that guilt still tormented him.

His election had triggered the secession of the Southern states. His policy that the Union was indissoluble—that the Confederates were in fact rebels and no legitimate government at all—had dictated that they should not be let go in peace.

He had known there would be blood.

Even that of a young man who had, for a year, been like a son to him.

Not Robert, thought Mary frantically. *Never Robert . . .*

Robert arrived two days later from Harvard, wearing a

black armband for the friend who had been like a brother. He was very quiet and made the time, between his father's conferences concerning the appointment of a Quartermaster General and long discussions with Seward, to have an interview with his father in his office. The following night, as Mary was getting ready for a Presidential levee, Lincoln came into her room and told her quietly, "Bob asked if he might leave school, and join the regiment some of his classmen are forming."

"You told him no!" She seized his sleeve in a death-grip. "You told him no!"

"I told him no," agreed Lincoln quietly. Mrs. Keckley, who had arrived to make sure her handiwork was most pleasingly arrayed on Mary and had remained to help her dress and fix her hair, retreated with soundless tact into the hall.

"He's too young," Mary gabbled, as if she had not heard him. Panic filled her, the same panic that had driven her, frantic, into the yard on Jackson Street screaming, *Bobby's run away! Bobby's run away!* "He isn't even eighteen. And he must finish his schooling, if he's to have any position, any hope of success, in the—"

"I told him no," Lincoln repeated, taking her hands. He'd written to Ellsworth's parents, she knew, trying to compose what words of comfort he could to people who had lost a son, when his own son of military age still lived.

It was the start of a nightmare, like a tour of Hell that only got worse the further they went, and from which there was no turning back.

When she looked back on it afterwards she wondered how she ever lived through it at all.

Less than ten days after Ellsworth's death, Stephen Douglas died in Chicago, where he'd been on tour to raise support for Lincoln's decision to fight for union against those who would divide the country. Ill before he started, he'd worn himself out in the campaign, tirelessly speaking in behalf of the man he'd battled so bitterly and known so long.

He was a hard drinker, and his health had not been good for some time. When an attack of rheumatism hit, he had had nothing with which to fight the complications that followed.

Mary felt shocked, bereft. Even as she kept expecting to hear Ellsworth's footfalls leaping up the Grand Staircase two at a time, she could not imagine—literally could not form in her mind—that she'd never see those sparkly brown eyes again, or hear that gorgeous baritone voice dispensing his practiced compliments. She had herself driven to Adele Douglas's house—only a hundred yards away across the square—and wept with the widow, clinging to her in the red velvet dimness of the parlor.

He could have been my husband, Mary thought, dazed. The lovely Adele had known him first as a Congressman in Washington, a man famous already for the Kansas-Nebraska Act. But Mary's memories of the man went back to Springfield, and being swept along in that surprisingly strong light grip in cotillion dances at the American House; to his rolling laughter in the long prairie twilights as he drove her back from a picnic.

He couldn't be dead. It all had to be some terrible mistake.

In the evenings, when Lincoln could tear himself from the constant tormenting swarms of office-seekers, he sat in silence in the parlor. Remembering, Mary thought, those winter nights around the stove at Speed's store, hurling at one another the lightning-bolts of their minds.

And still troops poured into Washington. Volunteer companies on ninety-day enlistments from Massachusetts, Philadelphia, and New York, in all their varied uniforms or no uniforms at all. Companies composed entirely of Irishmen, or Germans, or of the inhabitants of single villages in Connecticut or Maine, all cousins and brothers and schoolmates. Camps sprouted up all around the perimeter of Washington, reinforcing its single old stone fort on the Potomac. Soldiers occupied the grounds of the old Custis mansion of Arlington on its bluff across the river, where the kindred of George Washington had once lived; the rattle of gun-limbers and ammunition wagons sounded in the streets day and night. Rumors proliferated about everything and anything. Half the population of Washington seemed to be secessionist spies, sending information nearly unchecked to the enemy via relatives in Maryland and Virginia. Nearly every permanent inhabitant of the town was related to someone in the rebel army.

Barrooms proliferated, many of them makeshift dispensaries of liquor under canvas tents. Fights proliferated, too, and all of a sudden, when Mary and Lincoln were driven to military reviews or the dedication of new camps, they saw women openly strolling the streets in gaudy dresses and hair of hues not found in nature.

Mary went abroad little in those days. She found solace in the conservatory that Buchanan had had added to the Executive Mansion, a fascinating indoor garden whose glass walls and steep-sided glass ceiling provided a comforting privacy. Roses grew there, and a hundred varieties of fern; camellias red, pink, and white; bougainvillea in hues to match the newest shades of fashion; peonies and fuchsias from China and Japan. Johnny Watt, the head groundskeeper, showed her around the long aisles of heavy, green-painted tables and told her stories of this plant or that, the bronze chrysanthemums that had been a gift from the Tycoon of Japan, brought back by Mr. Perry from his famous voyage; the intoxicating white jasmine that had been given, it was said, by Dolley Madison to Mr. Adams—the *first* Mr. Adams—and had now grown as thick as a man's arm.

Sometimes she would send down to the conservatory for bouquets, to be sent to Mrs. Taft or to Mrs. Fox, the sister of Postmaster Blair—her husband was helping to organize the coastal defenses. Sometimes she and Lizzie went to sit there in quiet talk, and at such times Watt would putter about with his shears or his watering-can, invisible as the bees that flew in when the hinged ceiling-panes were open. Far off the voices of her sons could be heard, riding their ponies in the rough ground between the house and the White House stables—cavalry-charging the Taft boys, who invariably got the task of being rebels.

Sleeping poorly, Mary almost never rose in time to encounter Lincoln at his spare breakfast. Lizzie would usually eat with her, when she came down mid-morning, but by that time the boys would be at their lessons and Lincoln would be in his office—with a long line of men stretching down the office stairway, across the vestibule, and out the front White House doors. Or he would be out with Seward, visiting the Army camps, shaking hands sometimes with every member of a newly come regiment and returning in the afternoon with fingers so tired and swollen that he could not hold a pen. When she did see him she could see that he was exhausted, distant, and preoccupied.

She didn't feel able to tell him how badly she needed him, but she did need him: for comfort at Douglas's death, for reassurance against her terror that Robert would steal away and enlist and be killed in another foray. When he went out for long walks through the streets of Washington alone, late at night or early in the morning, her temper would snap, for she knew the city was Southern in sympathy and even its Unionist citizens resented the government that had brought soldiers in to make the streets unsafe and raise the prices of everything.

Then there would be a scene, and Mary would retreat, weeping, to her room, and to Lizzie's comfort. By the time Mary had calmed down again and would have gone to him as she had in Springfield, he had returned to his office, where he would sit writing until late in the night. She would promise herself that she would keep her temper better, as she had promised herself—and him—a thousand times before.

He doesn't need this. His tasks are hard enough. Then some piece of Nicolay's officiousness or a bad day of itching would set her off again.

Congress met on the Fourth of July. The town was fuller, but because of fear of invasion most legislators did not bring their wives. It made for dull—and humiliatingly small—

at-homes at first, but Mary had always preferred and enjoyed the company of men. One of her earliest and most welcome callers was the dandified bachelor abolitionist Senator Sumner of Massachusetts, with whom she could talk about slavery or Chinese silk brocades with equal enthusiasm. It was he who told her of the wrangling going on in Congress, how everyone there was calling for action, for a strike at the rebel armies, though the Generals themselves protested that their men were green recruits who could not keep discipline under fire.

"It's because of the enlistments, you see," Sumner explained. "On the fifteenth of July, the ninety days are up. The men will begin to go home, without a blow being struck."

He glanced toward the Blue Parlor's long windows, through which—past the low hedge and the stables—could be glimpsed the gaggle of tents, flags, corrals, and cook-fire smoke of the camps along the Mall.

"It will expose the capital to danger again, since you can be sure the rebels aren't going home. And it will make us, and our demands, look ridiculous, Mrs. Lincoln. Whatever state the soldiers themselves are in, you know that no politician is going to stand for that."

Chapter Forty-four

ON THE NINETEENTH OF JULY THE ARMY MARCHED INTO Virginia under the command of Irvin McDowell, one of the few West Point officers who'd remained with the Army of the North. Their goal was the rebel force camped at Manassas Junction, where the railroad went down into the Shenandoah Valley and the heart of Virginia.

Mary woke in the small hours of the twenty-first, hearing what she first thought was distant thunder. But though the night had been close and hot, and the threat of storm seemed to hang in the air, she sensed that this was different even before she heard John Hay's step in the hall, the cautious whisper, "Mr. President?"

She opened her door a crack and saw the pair of secretaries, trousers pulled on over their nightshirts and braces hanging, Nicolay's Prince Albert beard a ruffle of disarray. The two young men shared a bedroom down at the end of the hall, near the glass doors.

Lincoln appeared in the dark of his bedroom door, still dressed, shirtsleeves and bare feet with his black hair standing out in all directions. He must have lain down and slept in his clothes, too exhausted to undress.

Nicolay said, "McDowell's men engaged the rebel forces just outside Manassas, sir, on the banks of Bull Run Creek."

"Too soon for any word, I suppose?"

Nicolay shook his head, but Hay grinned and said, "Anybody who can get a pass through the lines is heading out there in carriages with picnic-lunches, to watch the battle."

Lincoln stared at him, openmouthed. "Here I thought bein' a lawyer for twenty years I'd heard everythin'. Guess I was wrong."

He ducked back into his bedroom and returned a moment later with his coat, cravat trailing from his pocket and boots in his hand. He was back for breakfast, however, as Sunday church-bells began tolling over the city: "You heard, I guess?" he asked, after one glance at Mary's anxious expression.

"C'n 'ee go oud 'ere, 'oo?" demanded Tad, his face a single blaze of excitement, and Willie added eagerly, "We can ride our ponies. That's faster than the carriage."

"Nope." Lincoln dropped a kiss on top of Mary's head, then sat beside her. "It's comin' on to rain and all them Senators and their ladies in their carriages is just goin' to get wet." He turned to her again, asked softly, "You all right, Mother?"

Mary nodded. All she could see was Ellsworth's bloodless face, and the dark stains on the sheet that covered him, and, across the table, the discontented eagerness in Robert's blue eyes. In the morning stillness, with the windows open, the guns could be heard.

Lincoln went with her, Lizzie, and the boys to church, where she heard not a single word of the sermon, which she assumed to be on the subject of the battle being fought. She was conscious only of Robert beside her, and of her prayer, *Let the fighting end quickly, quickly, before he goes....*

After church Lincoln went back to the War Department, to wait for telegrams that were, Hay reported, coming in at fifteen-minute intervals. A small company had captured a nearby telegraph office in Fairfax. In the evening he drove out to the Navy Yard, and while he was gone Seward arrived, breathless and grim-faced.

"The battle's lost," he said.

Rain started before Lincoln returned. Throughout the night he was in his office, while rain pounded on the windows and carriages arrived under the portico of the northern doors. Senators and Congressmen who'd driven out with picnic-baskets came in, bedraggled and shaken and scared. McDowell's men had been slow getting across Bull Run

Creek itself; the rebel forces had rallied behind a Virginia colonel named Jackson, "as behind a stone wall," they said. Then more rebels had showed up, God knows from where—"Johnston's men, Mr. Seward thinks," John Hay told Mary, on one of his trips down the hall past the parlor where she and Lizzie sat up with the boys. "They could have come by train from the Shenandoah Valley."

The retreating Union forces had gotten tangled up in the rout of carriages, buggies, sightseers on horseback, panic spreading across the countryside under the driving rain.

"Are the rebels on their way here?" Lincoln kept asking. Nobody seemed to know.

Robert and John Hay acted as go-betweens, hurrying from Lincoln's office to the oval parlor, where Mary and Lizzie drank endless cups of tea and tried to keep Tad and Willie from running down the hall to join the Cabinet meeting. From the windows she could see torches and lanterns in the camps, and if they crossed the hall, from any of the bedrooms on that side—the guest-room where Lizzie slept, or Tad and Willie's—knots of wet, exhausted men were visible, limping weaponless down Pennsylvania Avenue, uniforms soaked with rain.

At two in the morning she heard the footsteps of many men: Lincoln, Seward, gouty General Scott hobbling on his cane. She stood as they came into the parlor. "I've advised the President that you and your sons be sent north, before Maryland takes it into its head to rise up and throw in their lot with the Virginians," the General told her. Red-faced, white-haired, fat, and lame, he had fought the British in 1812, and Santa Anna in '46. "Once the railroads are cut there'll be no getting you out, ma'am."

"There's no getting me out now, General." Mary put her arm around Tad's shoulders—Willie was sound asleep on the sofa. "My place is with my husband, and with the government that he represents."

"Told you so," Lincoln murmured.

"Are you leaving?" She looked across to meet his eyes.

He ran his hand through his hair, and shook his head. "Like the preacher said when the widow's house burned down and he came runnin' out in his nightshirt, this kind of thing doesn't look good."

She turned back to the old soldier. "Then I am staying, too." Hay and Nicolay traded a glance—expecting another scene like that in the Jones House Hotel in Harrisburg?

But Lincoln said, "I think that settles it, gentlemen."

He was up all night, and most of the following, talking with Charles Sumner, who was of the opinion that immediate emancipation of the slaves would both cripple the South and win hundreds of thousands of new soldiers to the Union cause. "To make up for the hundreds of thousands of men who'd desert if I did it, I suppose," he sighed to Mary the following day. "Not to mention bein' the last straw for Maryland." The city was in feverish tension, waiting for an attack from across the river or, worse yet, to hear news that Maryland had risen in revolt and that they were cut off.

Throughout that week Mary and Lincoln visited the wounded, in the makeshift hospitals set up all over Washington in the wake of the battle, in churches, in public buildings, and in private houses. She had to steel herself to see them, to walk between the beds through wards that stank of blood, of filth, of unwashed bodies, and of the horrible sweet rottenness of gangrene. The face on every dirty pillow was Ellsworth's. Or Robert's.

Still, the rebels did not attack. By seizing near-dictatorial powers as Commander-in-Chief, Lincoln put Maryland under what amounted to martial law and began systematically silencing the pro-rebel press. Sumner shook his head over this when he took tea with Mary in the Blue Parlor.

"It scarcely looks well, my dear Mrs. Lincoln, for a man who's declared war to uphold the Constitution to be so blithe in his disregard of the First Amendment."

He would have been a slightly ridiculous figure, with his long curly mane and extravagant waistcoats, to someone who didn't know his history: his fierce support of abolitionism in the Senate had gotten him caned—nearly fatally—in the Senate chamber in 1856.

"And in order to defend a Southern capital, his alternative is...?"

Sumner pursed his lips, and held out his cup for more tea. "Shutting down rebel newspapers isn't going to silence criticism of his policies, you know." He regarded her for a moment in silence, then added, "Nor of you."

Mary stiffened. "If you mean that tiresome piece in the *Times* about me 'making and unmaking the political fortunes of men...'"

"No," said Sumner. "I mean the rumors that you're sending information about troop movements to your three brothers in the rebel army."

Mary was silent, feeling as if her whole body were balling itself into a single fist. "Where heard you that?" she asked, very quietly. But her eyes must have had a dangerous sparkle, for the Massachusetts Senator raised his brows, and kept his tone light.

"Where does one hear anything, Mrs. Lincoln? It's being said around the town."

"You mean it's being said in Kate Chase's parlor." Mary heard the shrillness of anger in her voice and couldn't modulate it away. "By a woman who hopes to discredit my husband through me, so that her father can be elected. And it's being repeated by men who're looking for some reason besides themselves, that their lives and their country are a mess." She set down her cup, which was spilling. Her hand was shaking.

WITHIN A WEEK TENSIONS EASED ENOUGH FOR THE PRESIDENT to give a reception, and within two, to hold a formal dinner in honor of the visiting Prince Napoleon of France. Later Secretary Seward was quoted all over Washington as saying that he had given an exactly similar banquet for half the cost.

Robert made arrangements to return to Harvard, with

Mary and Lizzie accompanying him north as far as the beach resort of Long Branch, New Jersey. After Prince Napoleon's dinner Lincoln came to her bedroom to unlace her and brush her hair, looking, for the first time in those hectic weeks, relaxed and in good spirits, though tired. He looked, in fact, very like the man she had known in Springfield, except for the beard.

"I saw you flirting with those hussies at last Friday's reception," she said severely. "That Mrs. Eames, and that General's wife, whatever her name is."

It had surprised her a little in the past weeks to see the number of ladies who flirted with Lincoln—surprised her and annoyed her. She knew better than anyone the strength of the desires that ran beneath the exterior of homespun humility and cool logic: she much preferred Lincoln when he was too shy to flirt back.

"I expect you to telegraph me every day while I'm away, and you can be sure I'll get a complete report on you from my spies."

"Why not you?" sighed Lincoln. "I'm sure Jeff Davis is."

It was good beyond words to be away from Washington. Good to know that Robert was going safely back to Harvard—good to feel healthy again, and to be fêted and fussed over again by reporters in New York. In Washington she felt invisible, like that child in Lexington, ignored among all the others, or, worse, pointed at and gossiped about. Robert of course looked down his nose and said, "You want to be more careful at what you say to the papers, Mother," but she merely laughed at him, giddy with relief at being able, finally, to laugh.

She'd written to her old Springfield friend Hannah Shearer, begging her to join them at Long Branch, promising anything, if only she would come and keep her company. The thought of losing Lizzie was hard to bear. "I've been away from poor Harrison for six months already, dearest." It didn't seem like six months, reflected Mary, as she boarded the train to return to Washington in September. Sometimes it seemed like years. Six months ago there had been no war.

Six months ago the sisters she'd helped raise, the brothers she'd played with, were not adherents to a cause that had sworn death to her husband and ruin to all he stood for.

Six months ago it wasn't being whispered all over town that she was a traitor.

Six months ago Ellsworth—and Stephen Douglas—had both been alive.

Returning to the White House was almost worth it, however. In the weeks she'd been gone, Lincoln had stayed at the little stone cottage at the Soldiers' Home by Rock Creek, where it was cooler, and the arrangements with the painters and decorators that Mary had made for the White House had all been carried out. She stepped across the threshold of the big mansion with a sense of exhilaration. The smell of fresh paint and plaster, the brightness of new wallpapers and carpets, made her spirits soar. The East Room was gorgeous, restored from the tattered wreckage of military occupation, the new carpet like a lake of soft green cut pile floating with pink roses.

She felt as she had at parties at her father's house, when she'd had a new dress to show off: the effervescent desire to rise on her toes and dance.

This, thought Mary, was truly the appropriate setting for the President and his Lady. The place to which she could have, with pride, invited Henry Clay.

Lincoln himself looked ill and tired, though he was glad to see her home. In Mary's absence Secretary Seward had made him and the boys a present of a basket of kittens, all of which had promptly gravitated to sleeping on Lincoln's bed when they should have been hunting rats in the White House attic. Sometimes when she couldn't sleep, or would steal down the hallway to the water-closet in the dressing-room, she would see, by the light of her candle, Lincoln stretched out on top of the sheets in his too-short yellow nightshirt, with kittens on his chest, pillow, and feet.

She worried about him a great deal, in that first fall and winter of the war. He would be in conference, with Generals and Cabinet members, sometimes until midnight; there were nights when she heard him pacing the floor of his room until she drifted off to sleep. With more and more troops assembling under the cocky little General McClellan—the Napoleon of the West, the Democratic newspapers called him—there were equipment and provisions to be decided on. Lincoln, fascinated as he was by gadgetry or machines of any kind, would go to the rifle-ranges to test new guns himself, or steam down the Potomac to watch demonstrations of new sorts of electro-mercury lamps.

With more and more troops—on enlistments of three years now, not three months—came fresh waves of rumor about rebel spies. During the summer the Mayor of Washington City had been arrested on suspicion of sympathy with the rebelling states, and one of Adele Douglas's aunts, the beautiful Rose Greenhow, was discovered to be running a ring of spies who passed information about troop movements to the rebel forces across the river. Mrs. Greenhow was incarcerated—along with many others—in the Old Capitol Prison, but the passing of information didn't cease. Half of the city's prostitutes engaged in a lively secondary traffic in military information, and newspapers blithely continued to print whatever plans and projections their reporters could learn.

More than one anti-Lincoln journal, in addition to snide editorials about *"entirely abolishing the Constitution of the United States, and substituting instead a naked philo-negro despotism,"* pointed out that Lincoln's wife, as yet another Southern lady, could not but be engaging in the same informational trade.

Reading the papers daily, Mary would be sick with anger, and with grief that she could not even speak of her fears for Ben Helm, for her half-brothers Alec, David, Sam.

Cold weather drew on. Rains laid the dust of the unpaved streets, then transformed it to mud. Congressmen came back to town and their wives left cards at the White House; Mary hugely enjoyed sorting through them to decide who should be invited to entertainments, and who not. With her long experience and strong instincts for social arrangements, it still infuriated her that John Nicolay would be in charge of the White House invitations and seating arrangements rather than herself. It angered her still more that Lincoln would not back down from this position: "Now, Mother, you know you couldn't have gone to Philadelphia, or New York, if you'd had to stay here and manage things."

"You don't trust me!" she shouted at him—this was on one of the rare evenings that he'd come into the oval parlor before eleven, when she retired to bed. "After the way I worked to make our home respectable, so you could get ahead...if it wasn't for *me* you'd be living in a cave and throwing bones on the floor for the dogs! And this is how you thank me!"

She stormed into her room and slammed the door, weeping—she found she wept far more easily now than she ever had in Springfield, and she had been, she knew, overly sensitive then. *It's the War,* she thought. *The War and this terrible house...*

But more than that—and in her heart she knew it—the source of her constant sense of panic these days was the bills that had begun to flood in from the merchants of Philadelphia and New York.

The bills! Mary's stomach churned when she thought of them. How could she *possibly* have spent over $5000 on up-holstery fabrics? On the *fabrics,* not even counting what Mr. Alexander had charged to re-cover the furniture that years of hard wear and those dreadful Guards had spoiled. Seven hundred dollars for crystal glasses? But what would the French ambassador, the English minister, Prince Napoleon, say about being served in those old chipped ones that had been in the house when the Lincolns had arrived? Of course she'd spent a great deal at Stewart's on silks and dress-goods for herself, but no one, *no one,* was going to sneer at her....

No one was going to say that the President's Lady was some countrified Westerner who didn't know how to dress!

I had to do it, she thought in despair. *I had to, and no one understands!*

She herself didn't understand how she could have spent that much. They must be cheating her, she thought. . . . But she remembered overspending when she'd bought furniture for the remodeled Springfield house, remembered not being quite aware of how that had happened, either.

Why couldn't money be like it had been for her father? Something you had and something you spent, a comfortable golden vagueness which no gentleman—and certainly no lady—ever discussed in specific terms. As a girl Mary had never had the slightest idea of what her clothes had cost. She'd just gotten what she wanted, and the shopkeepers sent their accounts to her father.

Why couldn't it still be that way?

Through the wall of her bedroom she heard Lincoln's footsteps in his own small bare chamber, and the faint creak of the bed as he lay down. Much later, in the dark pre-dawn, she heard him get up again, and go padding down the corridor to the bedroom where his secretaries slept. When the soft tread faded, she slipped on her wrapper and went to the door of her bedroom, and out to the main corridor, dark and terrifying and cold.

A faint stain of yellow lamplight showed through the secretaries' half-open door, and she could hear Lincoln's voice, reading aloud:

"What a piece of work is man! How noble in reason! How infinite in faculty! In form, in moving, how express and admirable. . . ."

And Nicolay's, answering, she couldn't hear what. Relaxed talk, of anything and nothing—of anything except the War that was tearing the country apart. Like the talk around the stove at Dillard's, or among the lawyers in those primitive country inns on the Eighth Judicial Circuit.

Lincoln's laughter: "That reminds me of a fellow in DeWitt County who married two wives. . . ."

The gentle talk that he'd come into the parlor that evening seeking, thought Mary, when she'd flown at him with demands about why she wasn't in charge of White House invitations, when she knew perfectly well that it had something to do with her refusal to invite that scheming hussy Kate Chase to dinner when Kate's father was a member of the Cabinet.

She stole quietly back into her room, her head throbbing, took a spoonful of Indian Bitters, and returned to her cold bed.

~~~~~

Chapter Forty-five

MARY BEGGED LINCOLN'S PARDON, SICK WITH DREAD THAT he would simply turn cold on her—or worse, bring up the subject of the bills—and was forgiven.

But the matter of invitations still rankled, and John Nicolay still remained in charge of White House official entertainments.

There were so many people in Washington to whom one had to be polite, no matter what one knew they were saying behind one's back! "You're the President of the United States," said Mary, half-playful and half-earnest, over breakfast. "Surely that gives you the right to not have to put up with schemers and liars and hypocrites who would just as soon do you a dirty turn as not!"

"I surely wish it did," Lincoln sighed. Even the egg that was usually all he'd have for breakfast curdled untouched on the plate before him in the chilly sunlight. "But in fact it takes that right away."

Willie looked up at him, baffled. "Then what *do* you get, Pa, for being President?"

"I get to have an eagle embroidered on my napkin," replied Lincoln promptly. "And I get to have the band play when I come into the room."

Mary supposed he was right—that as President, he did not have the right to pick and choose whom he entertained. But the knowledge that Kate Chase's at-homes were better attended than hers—and that the Treasury Secretary's daughter lost no opportunity in advancing her father's chances for the next Presidential nomination by spreading gossip about Lincoln and Mary—made it difficult for Mary to be polite to the younger hostess.

She began to hold regular unofficial drawing-rooms in the Blue Parlor on her "off" afternoons, and, later, on Saturday nights as well, so that she could invite whom she chose. The company was mostly male, though Ginny Blair Fox was often present, and Sally Orne, when she was in town.

It was good to talk of literature and art as well as politics, to hear stories of foreign cities and the fashionable world outside the provincial circles of government. It was good to have a few hours in which she didn't have to worry, or watch what she said. It was good to feel that she was important—to push aside the troubling sense that Lincoln was avoiding her, and making plans and decisions in which she had no part.

Senator Sumner was a regular attendee, always ready to top her stories with his own or to give her pointers on the absolute newest styles in hats. Ben French was another, a gray-whiskered, fatherly man whom Mary had originally met back when he was a Democrat in 1848 and he'd come by Mrs. Spriggs's. He was a Republican now, and had replaced William Wood as Commissioner of Public Buildings, though he liked to say that the real Mr. French, dwelling like a little doll inside his skull, was a famous composer, trying to dig his way out. He played the piano beautifully in the Red Room, and wrote poems.

The Byronic General Dan Sickles came often, though there were some in Washington who frowned on him because of the scandal in his past, when he had shot the man who'd seduced his wife; the brooding darkness of that murder seemed to burn in his eyes, like a character from one of the novels Mary so loved. And for European dash and fashion there were Jacob and Henry Seligman, bankers from Frankfurt-am-Main.

Most fascinating of all was Chevalier Henry Wikoff. An American, Wikoff had moved like a graceful shadow through European courts for many years. The Chevalier seemed to have met everyone and to know amusing and slightly scandalous stories about them all, and his judgment on matters of etiquette and social usage was as impeccable as the cut of his waistcoats. He had a terrible reputation (Lizabet Keckley said), though to Mary he was never anything but gallant and deferential, and Mary—who'd developed her own hatred of the "vampire press" over those calculated innuendoes of Southern sympathy—was inclined to disbelieve half of what she heard. Even men who disapproved of him, like Charles Sumner, had to laugh at his tales of what the Sultan of Turkey had done with the French Minister to the Sublime Porte, and how the transplanted court of an Indian Royal Prince had comported themselves in a London bathhouse. It was Wikoff who gave her private entertainments and menus the last touch of Parisian elegance, the European flavor that made the diplomats nod approvingly. It was he who told her of what was being read in Paris, and what gossiped about in Madrid.

It was Wikoff who started calling her the "Republican Queen," a title swiftly picked up by the press.

Mary found it soothing beyond words to be treated like a belle again. When she looked in the mirror, although she dressed with great care, she was burningly aware that she was now forty-three, that her figure had thickened and her face had not only aged, but hardened. She looked forward eagerly to her salons in the Blue Parlor, where for a few hours she could forget that her husband spent fourteen hours a day talking to office-seekers and Generals, and preferred the company of his secretaries in the dark watches of the night.

In October word reached them that Lincoln's old Springfield friend Ed Baker—who had resigned from the Senate to take up command of the volunteer company he had raised in Oregon—had been killed in action at Ball's Bluff, and for a time her nightmares and grief returned. Willie wrote a poem about his father's friend, and it was published in the *Washington National Republican*.

> No squeamish notions filled his breast,
>   The Union was his theme,
> "No surrender and no compromise,"
>   His day thought and night's dream.

Meanwhile cocky General McClellan drilled his troops on the banks of the Potomac, asked for more men, and didn't go out to fight.

Late in November Lincoln proclaimed a national Day of Thanksgiving, and invited Josh Speed and his wife to the White House for turkey dinner. In the end they had Army beef instead, since Tad and Willie had taken to playing with the enormous turkey that the cook kept penned behind the stable to fatten; two days before Thanksgiving the boys appeared in Lincoln's office with a pardon for Jack the Turkey, asking him to sign, which of course he did. The cook complained to Mary about having to change the menu, Mary complained to Lincoln, and Lincoln—who didn't have much to laugh about those days—only laughed.

Mary also had very little to laugh about, as the New Year approached and bills poured in like a hemorrhaging wound. Fifteen thousand, one hundred and ninety-eight dollars from Carryl Brothers in Philadelphia. Three thousand dollars from Houghwont and Company in New York. That was the solferino and gold dishes. Thousands more for Brussels velvet for new draperies in the Red Room. "This can't be right!" Mary sat back, aghast, her hand going to her throat; the next second she glanced up at young Mr. Stoddard, the assistant clerk who had been assigned to deal with her correspondence.

"I couldn't say, ma'am," replied the young man. "I can get Mr. Nicolay to double-check the bill with Alexander's—"

"No!" She reached as if to physically catch him, keep him in the parlor, then drew back her hand, ashamed. She made her voice light, the coquettish tone of a belle, denying something was important even as it burned a hole in her heart. "No, don't trouble Mr. Nicolay with it... or my husband. I... I will write to Mr. Alexander...."

It couldn't possibly have cost $1700 to have new wallpapers in the East Room and the big State Dining Room downstairs! Why didn't she remember it costing that much?

Her hand began to shake as she looked through the other

bills Stoddard had given her. Her mind simply blanked out the sums, dissolving them into a buzzing vagueness. There had been enough trouble over the $900 the dinner for Prince Napoleon had cost—the thought of going to John Nicolay for money to cover the overrun turned her sick to her stomach with dread.

The thought of what Lincoln would say was unthinkable.

"You can go, Mr. Stoddard. I will deal with these. I . . . I'm relying on your discretion. You know how the newspapers get hold of things."

"Of course."

I can't deal with this now, she thought, as the clerk's footsteps retreated down the cavern of the upstairs hall. Tears flooded her eyes.

Lincoln, she knew, would be beyond furious. Manlike, he had no idea how much redecoration cost, and no notion of the difference in appearance between the best materials and inferior goods. It was the Springfield house all over again. Few men she knew understood that one never knew how much work would cost until it was actually done. *Nor should he have to worry about this,* she thought wretchedly. He was already obliged to entertain hundreds of people several times a week out of his own salary.

She couldn't let anyone know.

Even as she couldn't let anyone know of her grief and fears for Ben Helm and her brothers.

Alone in the curtained dimness of the parlor, she could hear the voices of the men beyond the glass doors. Careless voices, loud and coarse. Cursing sometimes, as if they didn't even realize that the President's wife and children might be within earshot; or talking about the women who had swarmed to the city in such numbers, following the Army, women with names like Short Annie and Lucy Twenty-Three.

He didn't need this evidence of Mary's fecklessness, on top of everything else.

She thrust the bills into her secretaire and locked it. Her

head ached and she fled the dark room, seeking someplace where there wasn't a chance that Nicolay or Hay would walk in on her as she wept.

Like a fugitive shadow, her silk taffeta skirts rustling, she descended the wide stair, slipped through the dining-room where servants were already laying the table for dinner, and down the short corridor of glass that led to the conservatory. Even in the corridor, the humid warmth of the greenhouse enfolded her in its comforting embrace. Southward through the wavy panes of the corridor's glass Tad and Willie were visible on their ponies, galloping back and forth across the cropped grass of the paddock. Their tutor, Mr. Williamson, sat on the fence and watched them good-naturedly. It was he who'd named the ponies Caesar and Napoleon (though Tad pronounced his mount's name "Teeda"—and Williamson still hadn't had the slightest success in teaching the boy to read).

Silence and sweetness, and the thick scents of greenery and earth. She sank down onto one of the heavy green benches, pressed her hands to her face. Five thousand dollars! And another $3000 . . . plus that bill for the rose-colored silk for the new gown for next week's reception . . . but she could just imagine what the newspapers would say if she made an appearance in the same gown she'd worn to entertain Prince Napoleon!

But this was all her fault, nevertheless. She always swore not to spend any more money and this always happened. She didn't quite know how or why. She lowered her head to her hands, and began to cry.

"Now, then, Mrs. L.," said a gentle Irish voice, "we can't have you makin' those lovely blue eyes red."

She raised her head. Johnny Watt stood before her, in his rough boots and mud-stained shirtsleeves, his honest countenance grave with shared sorrow. The groundsman had a trowel in one hand and hanks of string dangling from his pocket, for tying up vines. Gossip attributed him with years of corrupt bookkeeping and chicanery, but Mary couldn't believe that was true any more than some of the vile rumors being circulated about the elegant Chevalier Wikoff. Certainly no more true than the abominable absurdities ascribed to *her*. A quiet and unalarming presence, Watt was always willing to take time from his work to show her the new blooms.

"Sure, Mrs. L., it's no great thing to run over the amount you was given," he said, when Mary had sobbed out her trouble to him. "Why, Congress does it all the time, and you don't see them fine gentlemen in tears over it, not that nine-tenths of 'em would know what a tear was if they was to drown in an ocean of 'em.... All they do is shift over money from some other fund."

Mary blew her nose, folded her handkerchief, and looked across into those bright, understanding eyes.

"It's like a man shiftin' change from one pocket to the other, that's all," Johnny went on encouragingly. "Nothing to grieve yourself over, or to go showin' a long face to poor Mr. Lincoln, and him with so much else to worry him nowadays. Why, it's what Congress does payin' that stuck-up laddybuck Hay to be the secretary of your husband's secretary, when he's on the books as a clerk in the Department of the Interior."

He snipped a pink rose from the bush nearby, neatly trimmed off the points of the thorns with his shears and wrapped the stem in a square of tissue from the box on the bench.

"Now, what's to keep you from turnin' that smooth English scoundrel Goodchild out, that was Mr. Buchanan's steward, who's been sellin' the food you pay for out the back door? You could do his books yourself, and have Mr. Nicolay pay over his salary to you. I'm sure you'd run the place better than Goodchild ever did." He grinned his leprechaun grin. "It's what you do, after all, when you've over-spent your dress allowance back home. You turn off the cook and do your cookin' yourself for a month or so, till the dibs get back in tune."

She laughed shakily. "So it is! Not that half of those wretched cooks we had in Springfield could make a sauce as well as I. I think Mr. Lincoln always ate better in their absence."

"That's the spirit, Mrs. L.!" Johnny gave her a boisterous thumbs-up. "A few months of old Goodchild's salary, and things will be right as rain."

But Nicolay regarded her with frosty suspicion when she suggested that she keep the departing steward's salary herself, and the interview ended—as had so many with the secretary—with her temper snapping, and Mary screaming vituperation at him and then fleeing back to her parlor in tears. Nicolay distrusted Watt, and believed every tattled rumor of his raising produce on the White House grounds to sell to the local grocers. He claimed the groundsman was a Southern sympathizer, though Mary guessed he'd have claimed anyone a Southern sympathizer who didn't sympathize with John Nicolay.

When turning off the steward didn't produce enough of a surplus to cover the bills, and Watt offered to order several thousand dollars' worth of trees and roses for the garden and hand over the allotted money to her instead, Nicolay began to make investigations—"Not that it's any of his business, the schemin' German," muttered Watt. "It's all money for the house, after all."

At last, when the creditors became insistent, Mary sent a note to Ben French, begging him to come at once. Instead he sent a note saying he was otherwise engaged—it being Sunday afternoon—and that he'd wait on her first thing in the morning. She passed the rest of the day in panic and tears, and retired to bed with Indian Bitters and a headache, to be roused with difficulty by her maid Mrs. Cuthbert the next morning at nine with the news that Mr. French was waiting in the Red Parlor.

It was on the tip of Mary's tongue to demand just who he thought he was, to arrive at this hour of the morning and expect a lady to see him all of a crack. . . . But the memory of the bills drove her out of bed. "Just get me my wrapper," she instructed, stumbling groggily to the vanity to brush her hair, "and ask him to come up to the parlor."

"Mrs. Lincoln . . . !" The maid was scandalized.

"Just tell him, and hurry!" Her head still throbbed from last night's headache, and she felt woozy. "I'm sure I'm perfectly decent in my wrapper." It was new, silk velvet, and of a sumptuous burgundy hue. "Certainly it covers more of me than an evening gown."

Mr. French half-rose from the parlor sofa as she rushed into the room, the bills in her hands. Merely the sight of that stocky, heavy-shouldered gentleman, and the thought of confessing, released another flood of tears: she could barely get the words out. "Please, please tell the President that it's a common thing, to over-run appropriations. Everyone does it! The money can be taken from some other place, like a man shifting his coins from one pocket to the other, but he must sign to have it done."

French's eyes bulged slightly when he saw the bills. He shuffled through them, as if hoping that some of them were duplicates, then looked at Mary again with startled awe. She sniffled, and wiped her eyes. "Please," she whispered. "Please, I shall be ruined if you don't get him to sign—but don't tell him that I spoke to you! Don't tell him that I asked you to help me! Swear it! Promise me!"

When French was gone, she sank down on the sofa, trembling with remorse and humiliation. She heard the Commissioner's footfalls traverse the hall. Heard the glass doors open, and close.

He will hate me, she thought, her hands tangling in her long hair. *He will hate me forever.* The thought of Lincoln's coldness, his silence, was more than she could bear. How could her life have changed so drastically, when she had achieved her lifelong goal? What had she done wrong?

In time, when French did not return, she summoned Mrs. Cuthbert, dressed, and went down to the conservatory again. As she crossed through the hall she saw Lincoln's thin form silhouetted against the daylight of the open front doors, descending the steps to where his horse waited. Hay and Nicolay stood on either side of the door until he was gone. Then Hay whistled, and rolled his eyes: "What a blow-up! I don't think I've ever seen the Tycoon that mad! What was it about? Did you hear?"

"The Hellcat's spending," replied Nicolay grimly. "An elegant, grand carpet for $2500...."

"Did anybody tell him what that pink-and-green monstrosity in the East Room cost?"

"He called me in and asked who let that upholsterer Carryl into the house. I said I didn't know at first, then said it has to have been Mrs. Lincoln...."

"Who approved it in the first place?"

"That idiot Wood, who went to New York with her."

"You think there was ever anything really between them?"

Standing behind the doors of the Blue Parlor, Mary clenched her hands in fury. How *dare* that puppy insinuate that there had been anything in Mr. Wood's escorting her to New York? Was that what the newspapers were saying, too? What Kate Chase was whispering in her so-fashionable parlor? The man was gallant, that was all. God knew Mr. Lincoln was gallant enough to the ladies to make Mary want to tear his hair out.

"The man's an imbecile, but he's not crazy." Nicolay shrugged impatiently. "And of course Frenchie would swear he'd never seen a requisition for so much as a teaspoon. 'It will never have my approval,' Father Abraham said. 'I'll pay out of my own pockets first—it would stink in the nostrils of the American people to have it said that the President had approved a bill over-running an appropriation of $20,000 for flub-dubs for this damned old house, when the soldiers cannot have blankets....'"

Their voices faded, up the office stairs.

CHAPTER FORTY-SIX

WORSE WAS TO COME. CHEVALIER WIKOFF TOOK HER ASIDE during the next Saturday evening soiree and murmured, "Please forgive my mentioning this, Mrs. Lincoln—only the wish to be of assistance to a lady in distress would prompt me to so much as mention a matter which must be extremely painful to you. But it happens that I might be in a position to help you. I have friends...."

His voice dipped discreetly—he'd already mentioned and hinted at his connections with the French embassy, and his work for the English government in India and Turkey. "Friends who would pay a good deal for advance notification as to what your husband intends to say in his message to Congress next week. Nothing to do with our friends south of the river," he added hastily, as Mary opened her mouth to protest. "And nothing to do with anything that would come out in this country. Purely for internal consumption only. By the time it reaches Eng—the home country," he corrected himself modestly, "the address would have been given here already."

He glanced around him, though the groups in the oval salon were all engaged in animated talk: General Sickles bowing over the hand of Ginny Fox. Sumner and the Seligman brothers laughing over one of Sumner's stories.

"They offered me eight hundred dollars," Wikoff murmured. "I told them I no longer played that little game. But when a mutual friend spoke of your need, I realized at once it may be a way out of your difficulty. And it's surely no crime to 'spoil the Egyptians,' as Moses says, and carry away money from a rival government who wants to hear things the day before they come out in the newspapers anyway. I only offer it for your consideration."

And Mary thought, *Eight hundred dollars!* As if she'd been tossed a rope in a stormy sea. There was the traditional New Year's reception to be thought of—which had to impress diplomats and Senators alike—and her cherished hope of holding a grand private ball in the White House—perhaps for Lincoln's birthday?—one to which she would have to invite no one but those who supported and honored her husband.

And it wasn't as if his Congressional message contained military plans, or anything that would aid the Secessionist rebels if it leaked out. Surely there was no harm in showing the text, "for internal consumption only," to some domestic department in England? In the back of her mind, all the way over to the government printing office on an invented errand a few days later, some small voice kept screaming, *You know he would be furious—he would hate you for this. . . .*

But Lincoln's scrupulous honesty, particularly where money was concerned, was one of the things that had always annoyed her about him, especially when they needed the money so badly. Wikoff had recently sold her a quantity of stock in the Nevada silver-mines, and had proven himself honorable in that transaction. He could be trusted.

And it was Lincoln's fault, really, for refusing to consent to sign an appropriations bill. . . .

How often, in their Springfield days, had he neglected his practice for politics, but objected when Mary prevaricated with storekeepers over credit unredeemed? He simply didn't understand.

When the text of the Congressional message appeared in the *New York Herald* two days before Lincoln delivered it to Congress, it was as if someone had set off a bomb in the White House. Wikoff—probably because of his former reputation, thought Mary indignantly—was immediately suspected and called before a Congressional Judiciary Committee; she was sick with dread until word came back to her that Wikoff claimed that Johnny Watt had stolen the address. Watt, to Mary's astonishment and relief, assented to the lie, and in heartfelt gratitude she wrote a letter furiously denouncing those who claimed the gardener was a Confederate sympathizer.

Something must have gone wrong, she thought, *with Wikoff's transfer of the information to his contacts in the British Ministry. He must be trying to protect his sources. Or perhaps he, too, is afraid of retaliation . . . ?*

Wikoff was put in the Old Capitol Prison for a month, with the notorious Mrs. Greenhow and the other rebel sympathizers. He sent Mary a thoroughly amusing note apologizing for his inattendance at the New Year's reception. The *Evening Star,* the *National Intelligencer,* the *Boston Advertiser,* the *Telegraph,* all had a field day, trumpeting corruption and inefficiency, and segueing into speculation about Mrs. Lincoln's extravagance and parsimony, including a ridiculous tale that she was cutting up the outworn White House sheets to make drawers for "Old Abe" and her family.

Further and far juicier rumors circulated by mouth, spread, Mary was certain, by the servants she'd discharged and fanned by Kate Chase's malicious gossip.

Lincoln accepted the story of Watt's responsibility, and asked Mary nothing of the matter. But his chilly silence terrified her more than shouting ever could. The rainy nights passed sleepless, or clouded with dreams of trying to explain to him that she'd needed the $800 to pay Carryl of Philadelphia for a sapphire pendant.

"My dearest, dearest Mrs. Lincoln, can you ever forgive me?" whispered Wikoff, when, on the first of February, he appeared again in her Blue Room salon. He looked not a hair the worse for his month of incarceration, immaculately turned out as usual and resplendent in a new waistcoat of yellow silk. He fell to one knee in front of the chair where she sat, and kissed her hands. From the other side of the room General Sickles and Senator Sumner looked shocked. "I was aghast, horrified. . . . I'd warned the Minister over and over about a certain one of his clerks. . . ."

"It wasn't you who sent the address to the paper?"

"Good God, no!" Wikoff gazed up at her with dark, ardent eyes. "How could you suspect...? Except of course that it is what everyone *did* suspect...."

"I *knew* there had to be some mistake!"

Wikoff shook his head solemnly. "Never make a social misstep, Mrs. Lincoln. Even those mistakes one makes in the passion of one's youth, the world never forgives, nor ever again regards your actions with anything but suspicion! All I could do was keep quiet—and trust to Watt's good nature. What," he asked suddenly, peering into her face. "Not crying?"

Mary dabbed quickly at her eyes.

"My dearest Mrs. Lincoln, staying in the Old Capitol Prison wasn't pleasant, but I'd go back there for another month rather than cause you pain...."

She half-laughed, turned her face aside. "No, it's just that my son has come down sick—Willie—and I'm worried about him, a little...."

And my husband barely speaks to me, much less reads me his speeches anymore. And the young men he spends his days with—and his nights—call me "Hellcat" behind my back....

And I'm so alone.

She drew a deep breath, and called on all those years of hiding her heartaches from her old Lexington nemesis Arabella Richardson. "I'm quite all right. I'm doing what I can for Mr. Watt, for of course he cannot be simply turned out of his job here. I've written to—"

The door of the Blue Room opened. Lincoln stood framed in it, wearing his coat but no tie, the way he often worked in the evening. His face was grave, but she instantly saw the anger burning deep in his gray eyes.

"Mr. Lincoln," she said, rising, a welcoming lilt in her voice. "To what do we owe...?"

Lincoln quietly crossed the room, nodding to Sumner and Sickles, and bowing deeply to Ginny Fox. He got close enough to Wikoff so that no one else could hear except Mary, and said softly, "Please come with me, Chevalier." In

the doorway she glimpsed Nicolay watching, and beside him
another one of the reporters who were around so often—
Smith or Jones, she didn't remember the name, only that he
wrote for a Boston paper....

Lincoln took Wikoff by the elbow and walked him out of
the room. The whole of the salon flooded after them at a discreet distance into the vestibule, hanging back behind the
glass windscreen that shielded the doors, to see and not be
seen. Mary heard Nicolay's voice behind her: "... of course
he's a spy! Smith showed the President the evidence—
Wikoff's been in the pay of the *Herald* all along...."

At the outside doors, Mary heard Lincoln say quietly,
"Chevalier, I don't want ever to hear of your coming into
this house again."

Wikoff started to say, "You wrong me, sir...." But Lincoln
had already turned away. McManus, the Scots gnome who
kept the doors, closed them in the Chevalier's face.

Lincoln paused beside Mary in the gaslit front hall, the
other members of her salon crowded around and staring,
aghast. With great gentleness—considering how furious she
could see he was—he bent down from his height and kissed
her cheek, then walked across the hall, and disappeared
through the doorway of the servants' stair.

THE GRAND PRIVATE BALL THAT SHE HAD COAXED AND
scrimped and maneuvered for—and, some said, committed
minor treason for—took place four nights later, and was one
of the most splendid in the history of Washington. Since it
was private, and not official, the invitations were out of
Nicolay's control for once. She had given a great deal of
thought to the guest-list. The Marine Band played, and
Washington's finest restauranteur, M'sieu Gautier, outdid
himself on the provision of refreshments at the midnight supper: sweetened replicas of Chinese pagodas and the Goddess
of Liberty; a sugar Fort Pickens and an edible frigate *Union*,

guns, smokestacks and all; pâté de foie gras and beehives full of charlotte russe.

But for Mary the night had a hollow, unreal quality, like attending a party in a dream. Even Lincoln's gentle teasing, as Lizabet Keckley put the finishing touches on Mary's scarf, gown, and hair, had a subdued note, as if he were trying to resume the old lightness of their conversations, before he'd thrown the Chevalier out of the house. "My cat's got a long tail tonight," he said, smiling at the length of her white satin train, and Mary tapped at his elbow with her fan. "Maybe if some of that tail were up around the head it would have a better appearance," he added—he always professed to be shocked at the low cut of her ballgowns, though they were certainly no lower than, for instance, those of Harriet Lane or Kate Chase.

She had also noticed he didn't animadvert on the propriety of other women's dresses.

Mostly, as they descended the stairs and crossed through the wide State Floor corridor to the East Room, her thoughts were with Willie, lying sick upstairs. He'd seemed to feel a little better that day, when Lincoln came into the guest bedroom to tell him about the offer he'd had from the King of Siam of a corps of elephants for his army. ("C'n 'ee hab un?" demanded Tad at once. " 'Fraid not, Tadpole," said Lincoln gravely. "It'd scare your ponies if we kept it in the stables, and we need the East Room for your mother's fandango.") But the pale skin of the boy's forehead had still felt feverishly hot to Mary's lips, and today he'd seemed worse, tossing restlessly between sleep and waking.

Between Lizabet Keckley's ministrations, Mary had gone back to the guest-room a dozen times to see him, and had always found Lincoln there. He'd reached out to her and taken her hand, and the shadow of the Chevalier—and of the eighty couples who had returned their invitations as inappropriate in days of war—retreated before the shadow of still greater fear.

That shadow followed them down to the East Room, like

an uninvited guest. The great reception hall glittered with gaslight, the air redolent with the masses of hothouse flowers with which it was decked. Through the evening Mary was torn between concern for Willie and bursting pride in the beauty of the place. She and Lincoln made the promenade of the room, shaking hands with officers, diplomats, Senators. The midnight supper in the State Dining-Room was admitted to be superb, even by the fussy old Lord Lyons, the British Minister. But Mary excused herself two or three times, and, gathering her vast skirts in hand, hurried up the stairs, to where Lizabet Keckley sat by Willie's bed.

The next day Willie was worse, and by Saturday the doctors were saying that it was typhoid fever, the same disease that had some ten days ago killed Queen Victoria of England's Prince Consort Albert. The usual Saturday reception at the White House was canceled, and Mary spent all the day sitting beside the bed, changing the cold compresses on Willie's head, and reading to him when he woke. Lincoln hired an Army nurse—a Quaker lady named Mrs. Pomeroy—to look after Willie and take some of the burden from Mary's shoulders. He himself came in as often as he could, and Lizabet was there every night. Bud and Holly Taft also spent much time in the sickroom, and young Julia brought flowers—Holly went to play with Tad, but Bud remained beside Willie's bed. Lincoln had a cot moved into the guest-room, so that he could be with his son at night.

On Monday Tad came down sick. Lincoln spent most of the day sitting beside one or the other of the boys, though Hay and Nicolay brought telegrams from the War Department about the fighting now raging in Tennessee. Willie's throat was so swollen that he could eat little, and it seemed to Mary, when she came into the room over the course of the next week, that her son was wasting away before her.

As the days went by she forced herself not to see the looks the doctors gave one another, when they thought her back was turned.

He can't die! she thought frantically. *Not Eddie and Willie too!* His delirium terrified her, when he would mumble fragments of games, or call out for his Springfield friends, Jimmy Gurley or Delie Wheelock, or for Fido. Bud Taft was there almost constantly, holding his hand.

"He'll get better," said Bud, rubbing the waxy little claw in his grip. "My uncle was sicker than this last year, and he got better."

Bud looked exhausted; he had been there most of the night, and come back again that morning. But he only shook his head when Lincoln came in and said gently, "You should get some rest, Bud." The afternoon light was beginning to fade from the windows, and by its pallor Willie's face looked gray against the pillows, like a tired little old man's.

"If I go he'll call for me," said the boy. "I want him to know I'm here."

Mary, who had sat up most of the night also, let Lincoln ease her into her room, loosen her stays and take the pins from her hair. "We'll call you," whispered Lizabet, "if there's any change."

Lincoln drew the coverlet over her, and bent to kiss her. "He'll be fine," he said.

For an hour Mary lay, listening to the mutter of the petitioners for office who, even at this time, still lined the hallway and the stair. Once she heard Nicolay's voice, asking how the boys were; now and then Lizabet's step in the hall would have her sitting bolt upright, heart pounding in panic. When the twilight shadows began to gather she heard Lincoln's step in the hall, and coming to the door of her room, saw her husband emerge from the sick-room, carrying the sleeping Bud as lightly as a baby in his arms. He took the boy across the hall to his own bedroom and laid him on the bed, then went back to stand in the sick-room doorway, framed in the wan silvery shadows.

Mary wrapped her shawl around her shoulders, went to slip her arm around his waist. Beyond the doorway, Lizabet wrung out a towel with lavender-water, mopped Willie's face; no lamp had been kindled, but the remaining daylight showed up the glitter of the tears flowing down her face. She looked up and said, "He seemed better about an hour ago, ma'am. Stirred a little, and smiled, and held Bud's hand. Now...."

Astonished at how calm her own voice sounded, Mary said, "Go lie down, Lizabet. Mrs. Pomeroy will be here at six. I shall watch until then. You look all in."

Lizabet embraced her silently, and Lincoln led the seamstress down the hall to the cot that had been fixed up for her in Mary's room. Mary heard his steps retreat toward his office; she drew her shawl more closely about her, and sat in the chair that had been Lizabet's, beside the bed with its drapings of purple and gold. Her little protector, she thought, looking down at his face, her champion, whose faithful presence had gotten her through all those years of Illinois thunderstorms.

He'll be fine, Lincoln had said. She repeated the reassurance to herself—he had to be fine. She could not imagine... Her mind hesitated over even forming the words. She could not imagine anything else.

She supposed she should light the lamp, for the room was growing dark, but could not bring herself to turn away from the bed, or to let go of her son's fingers. She was still sitting there, holding that thin little hand, about an hour later when Willie died.

CHAPTER FORTY-SEVEN

New York and Washington   July 1875

THERE WERE VERY FEW PLACES IN THE WORLD WHERE JOHN Wilamet felt safe, and New York City wasn't any of them.

His initial contact with Irish teamsters on his first day in Washington during the War had been followed by a hundred potentially similar incidents in his years with the Medical Corps. Whole regiments of the Union Army had been Irish, and the Irish, in general, had no use for black men, free or otherwise. New York had always been an Irish city, and as far as John could see, as he came down the granite steps of the Grand Central Depot on Forty-second Street, it hadn't changed.

The city was as squalid now as it had been just after the War, the streets clogged with the dung of a hundred thousand horses and humming with flies in the sweltering heat. He left his grip at the railroad hotel Zeus had told him about—it catered mostly to the colored waiters and railroad porters—and took the elevated train up Third Avenue, glancing repeatedly at the address on one of the two letters in his pocket. The city had grown, spreading above Forty-second along both sides of the wild green woodlands of the Park. Rows of neat brownstones were broken by occasional giant blocks of European-style apartments. Did squatters still camp in shacks on the broken ground around Harlem Heights? Once upon a time there'd been hundreds of them, black and white, eking a living from vegetable-patches, free-roving swine, and theft.

The address he'd been given, however, was a respectable small wooden house on East Ninety-second Street, set high above the street and brightly painted. Dr. Jacob Sunderhof registered only the slightest surprise to see that the John

Wilamet who'd written him about his "Guaranteed Cure for Drug and Alcohol Inebriety" was a black man. He stepped around the desk in his consulting-room and shook hands with John warmly, and if he looked surprised at least his face didn't fall into that expression of disappointed annoyance with which John was so familiar in dealing with Americans.

"It is so difficult to convince doctors in this country that there is any *need* for a cure for inebriety," sighed the German doctor, gesturing him to a chair. "They point out—quite correctly—that as long as an opium-taker continues to take opium in moderation, there is no problem. His symptoms are suppressed, and laudanum is inexpensive and easily obtainable. A patient can live for decades, for the rest of his life, in fact, with no ill effects whatsoever." He shrugged. "So where, they ask, is the problem?" He was a little ginger-haired man of about fifty, with a Prince Albert beard that was darker than his hair. His consulting-room, with its matched suite of blue plush chairs and its charts of physiognomical regions and "types," spoke of a prosperous practice.

"Where the problem always lies with alcohol and drugs," said John softly. "With those who don't take them moderately. Who seemingly can't take them moderately."

"Exactly." Sunderhof nodded sadly. "They would like to stop, but their bodies have become so habituated, and their characters so degenerated, that the physical effects of withdrawal drive them back to their bad habits. It is a much more widespread problem than you would think, especially since the War. Men come to me all the time, men who were wounded, or who contracted the flux, which was terribly prevalent in both the armies of the North and the South...."

"I know," said John. "I was in the Medical Corps at Crown Point and at Richmond."

"Were you?" Sunderhof's eyebrows shot up. "I didn't know.... Well, then you understand whereof I speak."

"All we had was opium," agreed John. "I don't think anyone even thought about how difficult it was to quit."

"But now," beamed the doctor, reaching into his desk,

"the problem has been solved." He opened the little rose-wood box with its mountings of brass. Within was a glass-and-steel hypodermic syringe and needle, and a vial of clear liquid. "My system is simple, and makes use of regular injections of morphine. It works for both drunkards and opium-takers. No patient who has been treated with this system has shown the slightest inclination to return to his old ways."

John shut his eyes, trying not to imagine what his mother would do if given access to regular injections of morphine. Then he looked at Sunderhof again. "And they are able to quit using morphine, too?"

"Dear heavens, why should they?" asked Sunderhof, gen-uinely surprised. "Morphine is part of the treatment. While undergoing my morphine treatment, I have never had a pa-tient relapse."

FROM NEW YORK IT WAS A HALF-DAY DOWN TO WASHINGTON by train—the capital had changed, if anything, more than New York.

Both cities seemed to John not only bigger, but heavier, more clogged with stone and brick and humanity. There were more buildings in downtown Washington, and the streets in the center of the city had been paved. Gaslights and sidewalks gave the place more the air of a true city than it had had during the War. But as John walked away from the cen-ter of town toward the streets above K Street, he was con-scious of more grime, of more loafers both white and black along insalubrious streets, of a deeper sense of desperation and poverty.

During the long ride down from New York that morn-ing, he'd tried to digest his disappointment, and the cold tiredness that settled on his heart. Maybe there was no an-swer for his mother, no way to break her desperate predilec-tion for the drunkenness of gin or paregoric. As the handsome houses of downtown gave way around him to run-down cottages and weedy ditches, his mind roved back to his childhood. To his mother's constant quarrels with the other women in the quarters at Blue Hill, to her inexplicable rages that alternated with periods of childlike sweetness.

Maybe there was no answer for him, or for any of those who had to live with her.

Lizabet Keckley still lived in the same neighborhood where she had before the War, but the neighborhood itself had deteriorated. The wooden cottages of the free colored servants and artisans were dilapidated and mostly needed paint. Porches and porch-roofs sagged. The streets were unpaved, and nobody had bothered to clear dead dogs, dead cats, dead rats out of the gutters. Flies glittered in the hammering heat.

But the big wooden house from which Mrs. Keckley's letter to him had been addressed was as spotlessly neat as any John had been in, painted fairly recently, the porch in good repair, although laundry hung prominently in the yard. As he came up the steps to the porch Mrs. Keckley rose from the wickerwork chair where she'd been watching for him, setting aside her sewing. She took his hands in hers, kissed his cheeks, and smiled her familiar smile.

"Mrs. Keckley," he said.

"John, you're a grown man now and you can certainly call me Lizabet."

"I wouldn't dare," he said, and they both laughed. When he had first read Dr. Sunderhof's article about a cure for drunkenness and drug-taking, he had written to Elizabeth Keckley, telling her he was coming to New York, and asking if she would see him.

She occupied two rooms at the back of the house. She had lived with the owners—the Lewises—in half a dozen successive boardinghouses that they had owned, and the rooms were spacious, airy, and as comfortable as any rooms could be in Washington in the summer. From the wide windows they could look down on the yard, which though weedy and hung with still more laundry, at least hadn't degenerated into a trash-pile the way so many did in this neighborhood, where the demands of making ends meet took precedence above the time required to keep some absentee landlord's property neat.

As they drank lemonade by the open window he answered her kindly questions about his mother's health and mental state as well as he could, and about Clarice and little Cora, Cassy and Lucy's children, and what it was like in Chicago. He found himself, a little to his surprise, telling far more than he'd meant to. There was something about this calm, strong woman that engendered trust. She listened without putting in any opinions, any remarks—listened gently and givingly.

No wonder the wives of two rival Presidents had taken her into their confidence.

While they talked she kept working, stitching tiny jet buttons on a bodice of pink silk and black flowered net, her strong, supple hands quick and neat as machines. Her parlor was her workroom—there was a recent-model Singer sewing machine by the window where the light was best, and the silks draped over racks and hangers were as elegant as anything Dr. Patterson's ladies brought with them to Bellevue in their copious luggage. Beside the fireplace—which had been re-modeled to accommodate a little heating-stove—hung photographs of Abraham and Mary Lincoln, and of two little white boys whom John guessed were Willie and Tad. On the other side hung a larger one, of Frederick Douglass, the black runaway who had been abolitionism's spokesman for twenty years.

"I heard Mrs. Lincoln is at your sanitarium," said Mrs. Keckley, and her soft voice was sad. "Poor woman."

"Do you think she's insane?"

She regarded John in surprise over her reading-glasses. "You're the doctor, John. And you've seen her. I haven't seen nor spoken to her since 1868."

"Was she insane then? Or when you knew her first?"

She was silent, neatly whipping thread through the shank

of the button, watching him from her beautiful dark eyes. "Why do you ask?"

"Is she insane?"

"Yes." And then, "No. Not really." She tied off her thread, snipped it with small gold scissors shaped like a crane. "Crazy," she said. "But not insane."

He smiled wryly at the distinction. "Did she get worse, after her son died?"

Lizabet Keckley sighed, and sat still, the needle and scissors motionless in her hands. "I think any woman goes crazy for a time when her child dies, John. I know I did. You keep thinking there was something you could have done, or done differently. And mostly there wasn't."

She brought the pink and black gown around in her lap, with a gentle rustling of silk taffeta, and threaded up her needle again. Her hair was graying at the temples, and the lines in her face were more pronounced than they'd been ten years ago: there were more shadows of weariness accumulated in her eyes. She positioned a flounce of black lace, and spoke as she sewed, neat and perfect.

"Willie's death struck her down like she'd been hit with a two-by-four. She was never the same after that. She told me that it was all her fault. That it was God's vengeance on her for holding such a splendid reception the week or two before."

"That's common," said John, thinking of all the hundreds of women he'd encountered—at Dr. Brainert's clinic, at Lake Forest and Jacksonville—who were convinced there was something they could have done. It no longer surprised him.

"From the day I met her," Lizabet said, "—the day before the Inauguration—she could be so sweet and genuinely thoughtful some days, and other days would fly into rages or take pets over anything. She'd make all kinds of threats and say anything that would hurt you, and later she'd come back apologizing in tears. And she'd be truly upset, truly sorry, not pretending just to use you. I think she genuinely couldn't help the things she said. That was how she was."

John nodded, remembering the woman who'd held his shoulders through paroxysms of sickness that first day, with the tender firmness of a mother—and like no mother John had ever had—and the next moment had been shrieking like a harpy at the ladies of the Freedmen's Relief Association for not keeping better order in the tents.

It crossed his mind to wonder whether Lizabet Keckley got along so well with Mary Lincoln because at some time in her life, Lizabet had learned to deal with someone even more abusively capricious, from whom she was not free to walk away.

"And she was inconsistent," Mrs. Keckley went on. "She had such lovely manners, the kind they teach in young ladies' deportment classes. Yet I've seen her—"

She laughed softly, ducking her head. "Oh, dear, I shouldn't tell this story on her.... One day Mrs. Taft, the mother of Tad and Willie's little friends, came calling wearing a new bonnet, straw trimmed with purple ribbon, embroidered in black. Mrs. Lincoln thought this was the prettiest thing she'd ever seen, and went to the same milliner—Willian's on Pennsylvania Avenue—and asked for another just like it. Mr. Willian told her that he had no more of the purple velvet ribbon with the black figures, so Mrs. Lincoln went to Mrs. Taft and asked her to give her the ribbon off *her* hat."

It was exactly the kind of thing John's mother did, when she'd had a drink or two, or a nip too many of "pain medicine." Not drunk enough to be noticeable, but not quite paying attention to what she should be doing.

"Mr. Lincoln knew there was something wrong." Lizabet returned to her sewing, and her eyes filled with tears at his name. "She'd always been temperamental, but this was different. He knew it. He knew there was something wrong, and he knew it was getting worse. He was frantic over it. But he didn't know what the problem was, and there wasn't even anyone he could talk to."

No, thought John. Not in the riven world of Washington

politics, with every newspaper in the country watching and waiting for him to fail.

"The President didn't have clerks and aides and a staff the way he does now. Just his secretaries. They lived as part of the household, and all of them working together in that same big room like a shoemaker and his apprentices in the same shop. Every decision about the War had to come to him—nobody else could make it. Four years, I don't think the man had a full night's sleep. He could see there was something happening to her, but he didn't know what he could do and he couldn't spare a minute of his attention from taking care of the country and running the War. He was like a sentry on duty, that no one remembered to relieve."

She sewed in silence for a time, and in the little garden behind the house, two children ran back and forth among the laundry, screaming with laughter.

"So she was alone," went on Mrs. Keckley. "And when you're alone like that, in as much grief as she was, it's terribly easy for the unscrupulous to take advantage of you. You'll believe anything they tell you. She was never one who could endure the deaths of those she loved. She was a faithful church-goer, but her faith wasn't strong. And when the blows fell on her, there was nothing to ward them off."

She hesitated, looking up from her work, as if there were something else to be said that she was uncertain about trusting him with. Her eyes went to a corner of the room, where a framed daguerreotype hung, a young man who looked almost like he could have been white, but for a suggestion of fullness in the lips. He wore the uniform of the First Missouri Volunteers—not a colored regiment—but John was long used to the subtle signs identifying those who "passed."

A small vase stood on the table before the picture, with a fresh-picked rose.

"And in this world," finished the seamstress in her soft voice, "if you seek the solace that the dead offer to the living who reach out to them anyone will call you insane."

· · ·

MARY HAD NO RECOLLECTION OF SUNLIGHT AT ALL, IN THE spring of 1862.

For a month after Willie's death she kept to her room, with the curtains tightly drawn. Sleep and waking blurred together in a long, confusing haze. She had memories of waking in darkness, head throbbing, eyes hurting—remembering, and weeping afresh.

Willie was gone.

Sometimes Elizabeth was there, or Lizzie or her nieces Young Bess and Julie Baker—blessed, blessed comfort of having women she knew around her, women she trusted, before whom she did not have to even think about keeping up the façade of politeness or restraint. For many nights Lizzie slept in bed beside her, so that when Mary woke from her suffocating nightmares she had someone to cling to, someone to hold.

Sometimes Lincoln was there, exhausted and haggard. She had a confused impression of shoving him away, of screaming at him things that her mind refused to bring back when she thought of it later...maybe the whole incident was a dream. Surely she would never, ever say to him, *He would not have died if we'd stayed at home.... You killed him, bringing him here so you could be President....*

Surely *that* was a dream. And in any case it was *her* fault, *her* whose pride and vainglory God was punishing. If it wasn't a dream, would he have, in other fragments of recollection, cradled her in his arms as he did, rocked her on his knees like a child?

It was only later that Elizabeth told her how sick Tad was, during those days of mourning. Between the crushing demands of Cabinet meetings, conferences with Generals, and diplomatic consultations, Lincoln spent hours with his youngest son, who had emerged from his own fever to be told that the brother he cherished was dead.

Mary knew she should have gone to Tad, should have come out of her room to comfort her husband. But the thought of emerging even into the hallway filled her with dread. The thought of speaking to anyone was both frightening and confusing, as if for a time no one was real anymore.

She could not imagine living without Willie.

When, in moments of self-pity, she had in the past pictured her own deathbed, she had always imagined that it would be Willie beside her, clasping her hand as he'd held it against the terror of prairie thunder. It was Willie with whom she would spend her old age, after Mr. Lincoln—who was after all a decade older than herself—passed on.

Now Willie was gone.

The newspapers resounded with Union victories at Fort Donelson, Tennessee, and in Missouri: *15,000 Prisoners Taken. Missouri Cleared of Rebels in Arms. The People Disgusted with Secession.* But though Mary was as aware as Lincoln was of how critical those victories were, they felt unreal to her. She knew she should care, but couldn't.

Willie was gone.

It was Lizabet Keckley who first told her that those who had passed the veil of death could speak through it to the living who were willing to hear. Mary had sobbed, "He's gone... he's gone..." as she had sobbed for days—weeks, maybe—in the dim, stuffy room, while Lizabet held her, her scented cheek pressed to Mary's hair. "He's gone and I'll never see him again."

"But he's so happy where he is," Lizabet said gently. "Happy in the Summer Land. He wants you to be happy, here on earth."

She spoke with calm confidence, the first person, of all those who'd come to her in her bereavement, who seemed to have anything to say besides *I'm so sorry* and *You must be brave....*

"They all want us to be happy, for the few seasons that we're on opposite sides of the Veil that divides this world from the next."

And Mary raised her head and looked at her, remembering things Lizabet had said, when in the course of fittings, or while the seamstress dressed her hair for parties, they'd spoken of griefs passed, and of the sons each of them had lost. Mary whispered, "Is it true? You told me once you'd... you'd spoken with George." George was the son who had died in battle in Missouri, at the age of twenty-one, having enlisted as a white man since men of color were permitted in the ranks only as ditchdiggers and teamsters.

Lizabet nodded mutely. Mary had listened with interest at the time that she had first spoken of the "Circles" that met in darkened parlors by candlelight, to hear the words of the dead through the lips of mediums, but it had been like hearing about the ceremonial customs in the court of the Tycoon of Japan. She recalled the giggling séance in the parlor at Rose Hill, the summer Lincoln was in Congress, and how she and the Wickliffe girls had all jumped a foot every time the old house creaked.

Remembered, too, Granny Parker's acrid opinions about the famous Fox sisters of New York that summer, and their spirit-rapping ghosts.

Indeed, it had been Meg Wickliffe Preston who had, on a recent visit to Washington, introduced Mary to a "trance-medium" named Cranston Laurie: "His control has revealed the most astonishing things about the future," Meg had assured her.

Like the clear metallic click of a key in a lock, Mary thought, *I can talk to Willie again. Hear his voice.*

I can ask him to forgive me....

It was as if a paving-stone of granite laid over her heart cracked, revealing beneath the first green shoots of spring.

LIZABET KECKLEY WENT WITH HER TO CRANSTON LAURIE'S house in Georgetown for that first séance. Mary told Lincoln she was going to spend the evening with old Jesse Newton, of the Department of the Interior, and his wife. Lincoln expressed only deep gratitude that she was feeling well enough to go out. Elizabeth, Lizzie, and the girls had returned to

Illinois by that time, though Lincoln, Mary knew, had begged at least Lizzie to stay. Though chilly, the air was beginning to smell of warmth renewed.

Mary was obsessed with the thought of meeting someone who could possibly communicate with Willie, with the thought of speaking again to her son.

Of asking his forgiveness, for her vainglory and her pride.

She had dreamed of him, over and over, in the month of darkness in her room. Dreamed of being back in the house in Springfield, of hearing his footsteps running up the stairs ahead of her, of hearing his laughter, only to open the door of his room and find no one there. From these dreams she would wake weeping, her head throbbing and all her limbs seized with painful restlessness. She knew she was taking more of Dole's Cordial or Indian Bitters than Dr. Wallace would probably approve, but she knew too that they were the only solace she had. She would, she vowed, reduce her consumption of them when her sadness had passed and she was feeling better. Lizabet bought them for her, and brought them to her in her sewing basket . . . and Mrs. Cuthbert and Ruth Pomeroy, each ignorant of the other two, did the same.

But the thought of speaking to Willie swept away any need for oblivion, and she stepped down from the carriage in front of the small Georgetown house with her heart pounding in anticipation.

Cranston Laurie was a man of quiet, silver-haired dignity. He and his wife welcomed Mary with gentle goodwill, and the others gathered in the candlelit parlor—how sweet candle-light seemed, after the cold modern White House gaslight!—greeted her but kept their distance, respecting the grief that was as clear on her face as it was in the sable crape of her dress. The Lauries' daughter, Mrs. Belle Miller, spoke of her own experiences with the spirits: "My spirit control loves music, and will sometimes take me over when I'm playing. Everyone tells me that at such times my playing is completely different, strong and unearthly." She laughed a little and waved at the shiny black grand piano that filled a quarter of the parlor. "I wish I had been acquainted with the spirits when I was a girl and forced to have lessons!"

Her parents laughed as well.

"Just as well you weren't, Puss," smiled Laurie. "You'd have sent your music-teacher running. When Belle is seized by her spirit control—a French nobleman named Ramilles, who studied with Mozart and was later guillotined in the Revolution—the strength of the spirit music will sometimes lift the piano bodily from the floor!"

"What is it like?" asked Mary timidly. "When the spirits come?" She thought of Mammy Sally's ghost-tales, and of the stories Meg had heard from her mammy and whispered in their room at Rose Hill, of haunts that followed people back from cemeteries in the darkness, to pluck at the covers of their beds.

Young Mrs. Miller frowned. "I can't really say. Once Ramilles enters into my body, I remember nothing. Only a deep sense of well-being and peace." She smiled, her face lit with the memory of ecstasy. "Of course you understand that in forming a Circle, we pray and sing hymns, and surround ourselves with a shell of pure thoughts, so that no evil or angry spirit can enter. Please do not think that there is any danger in what we do!"

Mrs. Laurie exclaimed in denial of the very thought, but Mr. Laurie said gravely, "Please, Mrs. Lincoln—we would like to share with you the comfort that we partake of during our Circles, but if you have the smallest doubt or mental reservation, by all means withdraw. We would not for the world wish you to do anything you were not comfortable with."

"No," said Mary slowly, "no, what you say is . . . is familiar to me, in a way. As if I half-knew it already. I would like very much to see a medium in action."

Mr. Laurie beckoned. From the shadows near the fire-place a young lady rose, diminutive and childlike in her white schoolgirl dress and hair-ribbons. "Nettie, dearest," said Mrs. Laurie, "this is Mrs. Lincoln. Mrs. Lincoln, Miss

Nettie Colburn. She's come to Washington to be closer to her father and her three brothers. All of them have enlisted in the Army. Nettie has been receiving visits from the spirits since she was quite a tiny girl."

Nettie curtseyed gravely, and regarded Mary with childishly wide-set blue eyes. "It's a gift God has given me," she said. "They want so badly to come, to comfort those who weep for them—and to bring messages from the Other World."

The half-dozen other people in the parlor assembled around the table in its center, Belle Miller going to the piano. There she played "Shall We Gather at the River," and Mary felt both self-conscious and uneasy as she sang, wondering what Dr. Smith back in Springfield would say—or her sister Elizabeth, for that matter. Yet the atmosphere was soothing, and the prayer Mr. Laurie invoked to "The Highest Lord of the Universe" unexceptionable. Glancing sideways, she saw Lizabet Keckley's face relaxed and serene, eyes closed, waiting in confident joy.

Nettie Colburn sat with bowed head for a few moments, then looked up suddenly and gasped, "She's coming...!" and her head dropped over sideways, exactly as if she had fallen asleep. In the candlelight her face seemed suddenly older. At her side, Mr. Laurie breathed to Mary, "It is her spirit control, an Indian spirit named Pinkie."

"Many spirit here tonight," said Nettie—Pinkie—opening her eyes, and her voice was different, a deep contralto instead of the girlish soprano in which she'd spoken before. "Many spirit cry out to be heard; cry out to welcome wife of Big Chief."

It's true, thought Mary, shocked, staring across the table at the girl's transformed face. *The spirits do come....*

"Is my son one of them?" she demanded breathlessly, and Nettie—Pinkie—regarded her with an infinity of compassion.

"Big Chief lady lose two son," she said softly. "Both here—both so happy. Little boy, bigger boy... big boy say he came to take the little one's place. Two men, one short, one tall . . ."

"Father . . ."

"Two women," said Pinkie. "One old, old—she wears a shawl. And one young, so pretty. So sad. She hold out hand, she say *'My little girl. My little Mary Ann.'*" Then the medium shuddered, her head jerking, and her face altered again. She closed her eyes, and when she opened them, looked straight across the table at Mary and said, in what seemed to Mary to be exactly Willie's voice and expression, "Mama?"

Mary began to sob, barely conscious of Lizabet's comforting fingers squeezing her hand. She did not know exactly what had happened, there on the other side of the table, in Nettie Colburn's thin body. But she knew the terrible weight of loneliness eased and lifted, as if light had shone through the Veil from the Summer Land beyond.

CHAPTER FORTY-EIGHT

SHE WENT BACK, AGAIN AND AGAIN, TO THE HOUSE IN Georgetown.

She did other things in those weeks. She visited the wounded and the sick in the Washington Army hospitals.

A battle was fought at Shiloh Church on the Tennessee River, fought for two days, leaving almost 24,000 men wounded or dead on the blood-soaked field—a quarter of all the soldiers involved. Wounded poured into Washington, and Mary, like nearly every other woman in town, went to visit them, to write letters home for them, to fetch water for them in the heat of the hospital wards. To bring them fruit and keep their spirits alive in the face of exhaustion and pain.

With Lizabet Keckley's guidance she became involved in the work of the Freedmen's Relief Association. Upon occasion she rode out in the carriage with Lincoln to the Navy Yard to watch the testing of new guns, and even received a few private callers. But in truth she lived from séance to séance, and the days between were often a blur.

All of Willie's things she gave away, except his pony, Napoleon, which Tad refused to part with. She found herself unable to even look at the Taft boys, or Julia, and sent Julia a note asking her to stay away. Tad himself went into hysterics at the sight of the girl who had been his and Willie's friend. Tad's behavior worried and frightened Mary, for the boy missed his brother frantically, and his tears would trigger in her fits of uncontrollable weeping. Lincoln could deny the boy nothing, and let Tad sleep in bed with him, to still the child's nightmares. Many nights Lincoln stayed in his office until two or three in the morning, conferring with Generals or debating in agony over the military pardons of which he was the final judge of life or death. Tiptoeing down the dark hall, Mary would see the skinny, pale-faced child asleep in Lincoln's bed, waiting for him, his black hair sticking up stiffly in all directions like his father's, surrounded by a half-dozen slumbering cats.

She felt paralyzed. She knew there was something she should do, for her husband and her son, but could not bring herself to face their pain as well as her own. The spring heat advanced, and she began to suffer again from chills and fever, and from agonizing recurrences of the female infections that had plagued her since Tad's birth. There were days now when she could not get out of bed without a spoonful or two of Indian Bitters, Braithewaite's Patent Nerve-Food, or Dole's Quaker Cordial.

Lonely and confused, without even the Taft boys for company, Tad refused to proceed with his lessons, and poor young Mr. Williamson was reduced to simply keeping the boy occupied and amused for a few hours a day. Even what little Tad had learned, he seemed to have forgotten in his distress. She could see the boy retreating daily into a world peopled by his father and by animals—a Philadelphia merchant had sent him a family of white rabbits, to which had been added Nanko and Nanny, a pair of enterprising goats. Always outgoing, Tad had a lot of friends, especially among the White House military guard, but there was no one, it seemed, to whom he now gave his heart.

And piled on top of all of the grief and worry, there was the continued nightmare of the bills. They poured in without cease. Though Mary dismissed more servants, and even appointed Johnny Watt's twenty-one-year-old wife, Jane, as White House steward in return for a portion of her salary, it did not seem to help. The newspapers were relentless, running articles about how the President's wife was buying cashmere shawls and carriages for her relatives out of taxpayers' money, while soldiers starved and shivered in their camps on the Potomac.

There was a poem someone had written, about the ball

she'd given in February... the ball during which she'd been frantic with worry over Willie lying sick upstairs.

What matter that I, poor private,
    Lie here on my narrow bed,
With fever gripping my vitals
    And dazing my hapless head!
What matters that nurses are callous
    And rations are megre and small,
So long as the beau monde revel
    At the Lady-President's ball!

The condition of the soldiers, at least, was no exaggeration. Trainloads of wounded were pulling daily into Washington—wounded men, and men who had come down sick from the diseases of the camps: typhoid, pneumonia, measles. Houses and churches all over Washington were converted into hospitals, including that of Adele Douglas on Lafayette Square. Simon Cameron's system of favoritism, contracts, and bribery was having its inevitable result in mismanagement and shortages of which the ultimate victims were the men.

Men—and boys no older than Robert—lay tossing on those narrow bunks, waiting for someone to change crusted bandages or soiled sheets; delirious, sometimes dying before anyone ever saw them. As the spring advanced and the weather turned hot, flies tormented them, and such was the dirtiness of most hospitals that sickness spread among the men like fire in old straw.

Fighting now raged up and down the Shenandoah Valley of western Virginia, as Stonewall Jackson outflanked and outfought three Union armies at Cross Keys, at McDowell, at Strasburg. In addition to thousands of casualties, the rebel forces supplied themselves happily from captured Union depots.

Though Mary did no actual nursing, she was aware that merely the presence of the volunteers, and the members of the newly founded Sanitary Committee, cheered the wounded. Some of them laughed with her over Lincoln's brief foray as actual Commander-in-Chief, when he'd gone down to Fort Monroe in May. General McClellan had been "too busy" to see him, so Lincoln had looked around him and enquired if anyone had thought to take the rebel-held Navy yard at Norfolk—something that had evidently never occurred to McClellan. Lincoln had personally supervised the reconnaissance for landing-sites, and had the Navy start a bombardment. The rebels had cleared out in a matter of days.

"Service is the best cure for grief that there is," said Lizabet, one afternoon in the full heat of spring, as they carried water in from the big water-butts in the center of the hospital camp at Mount Pleasant among the trees on Fourteenth Street. In the tent wards they, and a woman from the Sanitary Committee, dipped up water from the pail in tin cups and carried it to the men who lay on the cots, moaning softly with pain or murmuring under the influence of the opium pills the surgeon had handed out.

There was no banter, no joking in this ward. Most of the men didn't even know who she was.

This was the ward of men newly brought in, where their field dressings would be cut off and from which they would be taken for surgery in their turn. Mary shivered at the smell of blood and dirt, at the smell of gangrene. Minié balls did savage damage, literally disintegrating the bone within the flesh; these men would return home minus an arm or a leg, if they returned at all.

Yet strangely, these days she did not often find herself thinking, *Not Robert*... as she moved from bed to bed with her dripping cup. In the bearded—or pitifully beardless— faces, she saw other women's husbands, brothers, sons, men who had thrown themselves into battle for those things that Lincoln himself would have fought for: for the Union, and the right of the government to say to the individual states, *I don't care if it's what the majority of your citizens find most profitable, some things are simply WRONG.*

When she visited the hospitals—and, more and more now in Lizabet's company, the growing number of contraband camps—she found sometimes even her dread and terror of the mounting bills in her secretaire didn't torment her. There were now days when she was even able to put her grief aside.

"You're right about that, Madame." The woman from the Sanitary Committee looked up from the letter she was writing for a scared-looking young soldier: a tall, stout, fair-haired woman with a hooked nose and a decided chin. She, too, wore the deep black of mourning, her sleeves turned back over stout forearms. She laid one broad, soft hand comfortingly on the wrist of the man in the bed, and said to Mary, "If we cannot ask why those we love were taken from us, at least we can demonstrate our trust in God's goodness by doing His work. And goodness knows," she added, with a quick flash of humor in her hazel-gray eyes, "with the amount there is to do around here, one is simply too tired to grieve."

She rose from her stool beside the cot: "We've met before, I think, haven't we, Mrs. Lincoln? In Chicago, during the convention? My name is Myra Bradwell. I'm one of the organizers of the Sanitary Committee."

Mary remembered her, a schoolteacher, she'd thought, and probably a proponent of women's rights. But the black of her clothing touched Mary's heart and she said, "Bless you for what you're doing—especially in the face of your own loss."

The look of briskness—of running her life and everyone else's with maximum efficiency—faltered for a moment in the taller woman's eyes. "Thank you," said Myra softly. "I was so sorry to read about your son. Your brother, too, wasn't it?" And Mary nodded, surprised that the woman would have read newspapers so closely to have picked up that small an item.

"Sam was my half-brother," she said. "We weren't close...." Her throat closed hard, thinking about the fair-haired child at the breakfast-table in Kentucky, all those years ago. Thinking about the other brothers who *were* close—Alec and David, and Emilie's husband Ben, all of them somewhere being shot at by these broken and bloodstained soldiers in blue. Angrily, she added, "I suppose that was one of those articles that said I was sending him—or one of my other brothers—secret papers that I'm stealing out of my husband's desk?"

"Considering the number of people in Washington who *are* sending information across the river to the Confederates," remarked Myra, "I can only wonder that they'd think you were sending anything General Lee didn't already know about. But from the time of Jezebel on, men will point fingers at a foreign woman married to their chief. It's a good way of proving how patriotic and vigilant you are without actually putting yourself in danger."

Mary laughed, surprised at the sound of her own laughter, and instantly guilty. She thought, *Willie* ... she had not, she thought, laughed since he'd fallen ill.

She gave Myra Bradwell a card, and invited her to call. The Blue Room salons were less glamorous without the presence of the Chevalier, and Mary still felt humiliated over the way Lincoln had ejected him, without so much as an inquiry, and in the presence of all of her friends. Sometimes Watt—whom Mary had talked her fellow-Spiritualist Jesse Newton into giving a job as special agent in the Department of the Interior—would send her up a message that Wikoff wanted to meet her, and would let the Chevalier into the conservatory, to which he still kept a copy of the key. Both Wikoff and Watt lent Mary money, not once but several times, never asking a thing in return.

Wikoff may have been a bit of a rogue, thought Mary resentfully, but at least he treated her like a beautiful woman. At least he talked to her, instead of retreating into her husband's guarded silences. At least he asked her opinions, instead of—silently but firmly—relegating her to receptions, to ordering books for the White House library, to bearing gifts of flowers and fruit to the hospitals which they both visited.

It's because my health isn't good, Mary told herself, when he'd gently change the subject away from war plans or politics, when he'd put off her questions with a story that made her laugh. *He keeps me out of important decisions because I so often don't feel well.*

But in her heart, she suspected that this was not true, and the suspicion was like powdered glass in her clothing, inflaming her at every move.

All those things were her daylight life. Mostly, she lived for the darkness of Cranston Laurie's parlor, and the soft voices singing hymns in the candlelit gloom.

There was a medium named Colchester, the illegitimate son of an English Duke, through whom Willie spoke to her as well. Colchester's séances had a stronger emotional charge than Nettie Colburn's, for under his mental summons the dead would actually take ectoplasmic form. Often, in the darkness, she heard voices murmuring behind her and in the corners of the room, and felt the brush of unseen hands on her shoulders, hair, and face. When the blurred shapes of drifting light formed up in the darkness, Colchester described their faces and clothing. On several occasions the glowing shapes walked around the table, while the distant music of horns and tambourines breathed in the shadows.

It was at one of Colchester's séances that Mary, a little to her surprise, encountered Myra Bradwell. "I only want to know that my girl is happy," whispered Myra, startlingly different from the bustling woman she had encountered at the hospital camp. "She was only seven when she was taken away last year. It's cold comfort, being told by some minister that it's the Will of God. And why should we not speak to them, if God allows it?"

Mary couldn't speak, but hugged Myra like a sister, and in her dreams now she sometimes saw Willie and little Myra playing together in the Summer Land.

Predictably, Nicolay had nothing good to say about either Nettie Colburn or Lord Colchester. "The man's a fraud and a fake," the secretary stated, on one of those rare occasions on which he came to the Lincoln parlor—in general, these days she and Nicolay kept as far apart as possible. "He's certainly not the son of an English Duke, though he may be illegitimate for all I know. . . ."

"Oh, *Heaven* forfend that a man not of legal birth be able to speak to those on the Other Side," snapped Mary, throwing up her hands in mock dismay.

"Heaven forfend," countered Nicolay grimly, "that every Spiritualist and medium in the country take it upon themselves to advise the President on how he should conduct the War. Or ask him for government posts for their relatives and friends."

Mary colored hotly, because, in fact, both Nettie and Lord Colchester had at times received information from the spirit world about rebel troop movements and intentions, which she had naturally relayed at once to Lincoln. And of course, her gratitude for contact with Willie again was such that she couldn't let their friends and family go away empty-handed, when they needed jobs and money so much.

"Now, the spirits have as much right to tell me what to do as anyone else does," put in Lincoln mildly, looking up from the papers Nicolay had brought him. "May be God's way of tellin' me that even killin' some of those office-seekers won't get 'em off my back."

But a few weeks later, when Mary had invited Mrs. Laurie, her daughter Belle, and Nettie Colburn to a small "circle" in the Red Parlor, hardly had Belle gone under the influence of her control and begun to play the piano when the door opened quietly and Lincoln stood framed in the darkness of the hall.

The music faltered and stopped. The gaslights had been turned off—spirits having a far more difficult time materializing in the harsher blue emanations of such illumination—and only three candles cast their glow across the dark-crimson wallpaper. "So this is our little Nettie, is it?" Lincoln asked, looking down at the thin young lady in her schoolgirlish white dress. Nettie nodded.

"Do you mind if I join you? Mother?" He looked across at Mary. Beside her, General Sickles and Mr. Newton of the Department of the Interior had the air of schoolboys caught out in mischief.

Hesitantly, Belle Miller said, "You know the spirits don't often materialize in the presence of a skeptic," and glanced across at Mrs. Laurie, but Nettie Colburn said firmly, "No, that's quite all right, Mr. President."

They didn't make a circle that night: Lincoln sat silently on the sofa beside Mary, watching and listening as Nettie went under the influence of the spirit Pinkie. Willie did not materialize, though he was there, Nettie told them, and was happy to see his papa. Turning to Lincoln with her blank, enchanted eyes, she said, "The spirits call to you, beg you, to go through with what you are considering, about freeing all the slaves. God and the angels will support you in this, you will be doing His work...."

Mary glanced quickly sidelong at Lincoln's face. It was something she'd heard rumor of, but since the Wikoff affair he'd spoken to her so little of any plans or thoughts. His face was impassive, as it was in court, but he smiled a little.

Chapter Forty-nine

By May the heat was nearly intolerable, the dust choking, and the stench of the camps a foul miasma that cloaked the city. Tad was ill again, which threw Mary into a panic of migraine and tears. In July she took him and went north, with Lizabet Keckley as a companion. Anything was better than staying on in a city rank with damp and sickness, and hideous with memories of her lost son.

New York, as always, cheered her, even in the agony of her grief. It was a real city, with bustle and activity, paved streets and beautiful stores, not like the provincial filth of Washington. Though there was no opera or theater at this time of year, merchants invited her to lovely parties and bowed to her when she came through the doors. She missed Lincoln desperately, but she felt on the whole less lonely than she did trapped in the dark parlor of the White House, knowing he was at the far end of the hall and she wouldn't see him until nearly eleven at night and maybe not then.

She slept better when she was away from Washington, though she still woke in tears and there were many days on which she simply could not get out of bed. It was good only to be away from the constant disapproving presence of Nicolay and Hay, away from servants who pried and told tales. It was so comfortable to be able to take medicine when she needed it, instead of worrying about whether the two secretaries would somehow find how many bottles she had hidden away.

Not that she needed medicine nearly as much, away from Washington. She had Lizabet to keep her company, the best of companions, and Tad, and Robert, who met them in New York. She even had John Watt, who had decided to try his luck outside of Washington—Mary had agreed to help him get settled in gratitude for his silence in the Wikoff affair. It was Watt who introduced her to Republican cronies of his, Simeon Draper—a real-estate developer—and Abram Wakeman, who promised "assistance" in paying some of her debts. "No, no, it's all for the good name of the President," purred Draper. "We're all good Republicans here. But if you could put in a good word for me, when your husband is seeking a good man to become customs collector for the port of New York...."

For a time she had Myra Bradwell, too, in New York raising money for the Sanitary Committee.

Money was needed. After seven days of fighting around Richmond, General McClellan had limped back to Washington. Sixteen thousand of his men—almost a sixth of his force—were dead or lay wounded in the Washington hospitals. McClellan called for 100,000 more.

Leaving Tad with Lizabet at the hotel, the two women attended the séances of Lord Colchester—in New York also—at a neat brownstone on Fifty-second Street near the river, where the spirits warned Mary to beware the lies of slanderers, who would cast stones in their ignorance at men of the spirit.

"Meaning himself, I take it," said Myra, as they climbed back into the carriage which Lord Colchester had himself sent to bring Mary that evening. "Covering his back in case of scandal. My husband's a judge," she added, intercepting Mary's shocked, inquiring look. "I've studied a great deal of law in order to help him with his cases—when this War is over I'm thinking of seeing if I can pass the Bar. So I've learned to watch and listen, I think a lot more than some of these poor souls do, who come seeking anyone they think will help them with their grief. And Colchester doesn't ring true to me."

"You're not a feminist?" asked Mary, appalled at this revelation in her newfound friend. It was one thing for a woman to know about politics, and to utilize the power of patronage behind the scenes. Ladies did that, although of course no lady would ever let the gentlemen know. It was quite another to put on men's trousers and make men stay home and take care of the children, the way the newspapers said—not that it wouldn't have done Mr. Lincoln a great deal of good to know what Mary had to go through, in their early Springfield days.

Myra shot her a slantways glance, then laid a reassuring hand on her wrist. "That's a word men like to throw at any woman who won't do what they expect her to. The same way they'll tar every medium with the brush that a few crooked ones have mucked up. But just because some men lie," she added, "doesn't mean Truth doesn't exist."

Myra must have heard rumors—or been prescient herself—for shortly after that, before Mary returned to Washington in mid-July, a young California newspaper reporter named Noah Brooks attended one of Colchester's Washington séances under the guise of a seeker after truth, and seized one of the ghostly, glowing apparitions around the waist. The apparition was solid enough to struggle like a tiger and give Brooks a smart blow to the head, after which Colchester left the country rather precipitously.

Brooks, to Mary's grateful surprise, didn't use the incident to attack her credulity, as most reporters would have, but merely had a good laugh about fraudulent mediums in general. His name began to appear regularly in Lincoln's letters to her, and she gathered that the good-natured young journalist and the President were becoming fast friends.

When she returned to Washington, Congress had risen and the city was somnolent under a blanket of heat, filth, and dust. Elections were approaching, with men dying and money being spent on battles the Union did not win.

A few days before her return Lincoln moved out to the stone cottage on the grounds of the Soldiers' Home again, and it was there that Tad and Mary joined him. She slept better there, and felt better: the water of Rock Creek tasted cleaner, for one thing, than the murky Potomac liquid that issued from the White House pipes. She and Lizabet could walk in the wooded grounds without feeling spied upon. Tad still cried at night, and on most nights insisted on sleeping with his father. Mary had hoped to cure him of this, but Lincoln only shook his head and said, "He doesn't take up much room, Mother."

On nights when Lincoln worked late at the White House, to which he rode horseback in the pre-dawn cool of every morning, Tad slept with Nanko and Nanny instead.

The journey to New York had helped, and not being in the White House helped. But simply the return to Washington brought back recurrences of Mary's blinding grief. These would come on her suddenly, in debilitating waves, and there were days when it was as if Willie had died only the day before. Her grief lifted a little when she worked with Lizabet, at the hospitals or at the contraband camps that were springing up all around Washington, but her spells of grief were still so intense that Lincoln once took her to the window, and showed her the walls of the building where the mental cases were housed. "Try and control your grief," he begged, "or it will drive you mad. . . ."

Often after that she was aware of him watching her with worried eyes.

When the rumor circulated that Lincoln was going to proclaim an end to slavery—when the Northern Army refused to return Southern slaves who escaped across the frontier between the two enemy countries—runaways poured into Washington. They camped in sheds or under blankets, or simply beneath the stars. They surrounded every fort of the city's defensive line, clustered in trashy and disorderly zones around every military camp.

Nearly all of them were field hands, untrained for any other kind of labor, illiterate due to the nearly universal application of Black Codes throughout the slave states, and unaccustomed, most of them, to fending for themselves in any fashion. The Freedmen's Relief Association did what it could, to find them food, blankets, places to live, jobs, but the absorption rate was painfully slow. The Irish teamsters who worked for the Army—and for the civilian merchants who were making fortunes off the concentration of soldiers—hated them. Mary's newfound young friend John Wilamet was far from the only one who was beaten and left in a ditch.

"They understand what this war is about better than any of your husband's Generals, Madame," commented Frederick Douglass, the acknowledged leader of the freedmen, as he walked with Mary and Lizabet through the messy snaggles of shelters that spread around Camp Barker. Douglass, whom Mary first met through the Freedmen's Relief Association, was a tall, harsh-faced somber man who had not been content with merely escaping to freedom himself, but who had worked, for the twenty-four years since his flight, to free the whole of his people. "They know it's about their freedom, whether your husband will admit it or not."

She looked around her at the camp, at the ragged men and women clustered around the rough marquee where Mrs. Durham—a green-grocer who doubled as a midwife and who had taken a dozen fugitives into her own small house—was dishing out what meager rations of corn and beans had been passed along to the Association by the Army. Compared to the wise Nelson, the starchily well-mannered Pendleton, and the competent Chaney and Jane, most of these contrabands seemed to Mary hopelessly primitive and ignorant.

Yet Pendleton, Chaney, and Jane had all been sold, when her father had died, to pay his debts and satisfy those of her brothers who needed cash money quick. As had the tall man beside her, dressed in his immaculate dark suit and cravat. As had Lizabet, beautiful, understanding, strong Lizabet... Even young John, following behind them with another box of blankets, would have been sold before he was very much older, separated for all time from his mother and sisters.

Quietly, Mary replied, "I tell him that. He says if he proclaimed the Negro free he'd lose three states and half his Army."

"For every fool Irishman who quits in disgust," said

Douglass, "there will be seven black men striding forward to fight for their brothers, their wives, their children whom they left behind in bondage. Would you not fight, John?" he asked, turning to the youth who'd become Mary's messenger in the camps.

"To be free?" The youth looked up at the tall man with his large nearsighted eyes. The scar he'd taken on his forehead from a gang of teamsters on the day of his arrival was still a raw welt. "To know they couldn't come after me, couldn't take me back because there's no place to take me back to?" He grinned, a shy sweet flash of a smile quickly put away. "In a minute."

"Your husband is a lawyer." Douglass looked down at Mary again. "He keeps his mouth shut, and waits. He's doing all he can to re-settle us elsewhere, to send us back to Africa or down to Central America—to offer money to the Southerners for our release. Anything to avoid unilateral abolition by proclamation. He can afford to do all that. He's white. White men have been arguing and bartering and delaying, trying not to offend other white men, for fourscore years and six, while the black man has waited in chains, and seen his children grow up and grow old in chains, and die. Tell him to put aside his fear. Tell him to take up the sword whose hilt God has been thrusting at his hands for all these months. He will not regret it."

Mary answered something—she didn't know what. In her mind she saw Saul come into her father's kitchen, and put his arms around Jane: saw the way Jane relaxed into him, stealing the preciousness of love from the realities of other men's property rights.

In her mind she saw Jane weeping in Mammy Sally's arms, hugging herself as if to keep her heart from tearing itself out of her body with grief, at the news that Saul had been sold.

And superimposed on them both, she saw the foul drawing, the letters written in blood. *Make your peace with God, nigger-lover. . . .*

If he frees them, she thought, *those who wrote that letter will have his life, whether the Union wins the war or not.*

And he knows it.

IT SEEMED, IN THE LATE SUMMER OF 1862, THAT THE RUMORS of Lincoln's plan to emancipate the slaves gained strength and force. It was as if, as Douglass had said, everyone knew that slavery was the true issue, though Lincoln continued to speak only in terms of Union, and of not letting slavery spread to new territories. Lincoln continued to seek the alternatives of colonization and recompense, seeing the contraband camps and fearing the influx and dislocation that outright emancipation would bring.

And meanwhile the swaggering General John Pope led the Union Army of Virginia against Manassas Junction again in the hopes of taking that vital gateway to the rebel heartland.

He lost a fifth of his men—14,000 wounded or slain.

At a séance at the Soldiers' Home just before that battle the Indian spirit Pinkie spoke through Nettie Colburn, urging Lincoln to use the dictatorial powers he had already taken as a result of the War, and give the slaves their freedom.

Sitting in his rocking chair in a corner of the parlor, Lincoln made no reply, though afterwards, when the guests had departed, he commented to Mary that it seemed a little hard for the spirits to be taking a stand on the matter, too. "Though I don't see why they shouldn't, I suppose," he added resignedly. "Everyone else in the country tells me what I should do about it, from Governor Seward on down to the little old Quaker ladies who come to my office to tell me how God wants this War to be run."

He sounded tired, barely more than a tall shadow in the gloom of the vine-covered porch. Even here above the creek, the night was uncomfortably warm, almost too warm to sleep. General McClellan had been in the field—though not making the slightest effort to actually attack the rebel capital—and Lincoln and his new Secretary of War, the neurotic Edwin Stanton, had essentially been in command in Washington. Frustrated, Lincoln had telegraphed his chief General, *If you are not using your army, might I borrow it?*

It was obvious to Mary that McClellan was either a rebel sympathizer, or simply had his eye on the 1864 elections as a Democratic, Northern peace candidate—a curious goal for a General.

"But I can't issue any proclamation now, Mother. Not while we're being beaten all hollow in Kentucky. It would do the slaves no good, if we scream *'You're free!'* over our shoulders while we're high-tailin' it for cover in Washington—and it'll turn the whole issue into a joke. Maybe the spirits don't see that."

Now she said, hearing the defensiveness in her response, "And why shouldn't the spirits have a concern, for a matter so close to the true destiny of humankind? They have given you warnings before."

"Like the warnings that Seward, Chase, and Stanton are all traitors?"

Mary colored in the darkness, for she was the one who'd relayed the warnings to him. Even before Nettie Colburn had given her Pinkie's warning, she had hated and mistrusted the former New York and Ohio governors, as she mistrusted the new Secretary of War.

"I can't sack my Cabinet on the word of..." Lincoln paused, then went on, "...of spirits." He stroked the ears of the curly-haired brown puppy he'd brought back from the Army camp, picked up stray outside a mess tent; the little animal was already inseparable from him.

"You sound like you don't believe that the dead can speak." Mary tried hard to keep her annoyance out of her voice, that anyone, even he, would question that Willie—*his* son, too!—had spoken that night.

Sometimes she felt a great deal of sympathy for the chubby, long-departed Miss Owens back in Illinois, who had refused to marry this stubborn man.

"I never said that," answered Lincoln quietly. "I think the dead can speak, if they wish. But whether they speak through the likes of Nettie Colburn or Lord Colchester is another matter, Mother."

IN THAT SAME HOT AUGUST, REBEL FORCES INVADED KENTUCKY, and raised the Stars and Bars over Frankfort. Mary shivered when she read of the fighting around the Kentucky city of Richmond, of the savage small-scale conflicts between neighbors, and the devastation of the countryside she had known. Was Rose Hill still standing? she wondered. Were Cousin Eliza and the sisters of Mary Jane Warfield Clay still all right? Shortly after Second Manassas word had reached her that her youngest brother, handsome little Alec, had been killed in battle outside of Baton Rouge.

France and Britain, Mary also knew, were both close to officially recognizing the rebelling states as a separate nation—a nation that would sell unlimited amounts of cotton to English mills, and wink at the French control of Mexico. And once that precedent was set, that states *could* resign from the Union, how long would it be before California got annoyed and pulled out, or some New England coalition that didn't approve of an election or a future President's policies?

They were only waiting, she knew, for a Southern victory.

In September, Robert E. Lee led his army across the Potomac into Maryland.

On the seventeenth, McClellan's army met Lee on the banks of Antietam Creek. After fourteen hours of fighting, a third of Lee's army was wounded or dead, and a third of McClellan's men who'd fought, almost 23,000 men, the population of a city. Whole regiments had ceased to exist. Whole generations of the young men of certain towns, certain families, who had enlisted together to fight side by side.

Unpursued by McClellan, Lee withdrew silently over the river.

Three days later, on the twenty-second of September, Lincoln signed a Proclamation that set aside the original intent of the United States Constitution. Unless the Southern states rejoined the Union, it said, by the first of January, 1863, all slaves in those states would be "then, thenceforward, and forever free."

CHAPTER FIFTY

LETTERS OF CONGRATULATION AND PRAISE POURED IN FROM abolitionists, writers, Quakers, ministers.

Letters of abuse poured in, too, from abolitionists who carped that slavery had only been ended in the rebel territories—that men and women in the border states, and in the conquered areas of Louisiana and Virginia, were still as unfree as ever. Just how they thought Lincoln would have kept the border states from joining the Confederacy if he liberated *their* slaves, they didn't say.

Workingmen who volunteered to fight for Union ceased volunteering in droves. They also ceased subscribing to government securities to support the skyrocketing expense of the war.

Southern Unionists felt betrayed. Slave-holders in Maryland, Kentucky, Missouri muttered, seeing the day coming, inevitably, when their human property, too, would be taken from them—tens of thousands of dollars' worth, shattering their ability to continue agricultural production as they had known it. Moreover, as Frederick Douglass had pointed out, the fact that free territory existed close by meant that more and more slaves would run, knowing that no one there would return them to their owners.

"It doesn't matter." Mary flung down the *New York World* and reached across the lunch-table to clasp Lincoln's hand. "In a hundred years—or a dozen—people will recognize this for what it is. Thousands and tens of thousands who live in slavery in the South already recognize it."

"If they know of it." Lincoln sounded tired; he'd been up most of the night dealing with plans for the raising of additional forces in rebellious eastern Kentucky and querulous letters from slaveholders in Maryland. Several columns of comments about his being *"adrift on a current of radical fanaticism"* and *"an act of Revolution"* that would render *"the restoration of the old Constitution and Union impossible,"* were not what he needed.

"They'll know." Mary remembered those shadowy forms slipping through the darkness of her father's yard, those cryptic signs written on the alley fence. "Davis and his government may forbid anyone to tell them, but they'll know."

MARY WENT BACK TO NEW YORK FOR THE SENATORIAL elections. Between the numbing horror of casualty statistics, the workingman's outrage at Emancipation, and Lincoln's unilateral decision to suspend the right of *habeas corpus* in the interests of security, these were an unmitigated disaster for those who supported Lincoln, Union, and the war. She remained there or in Boston through most of November, unable to bear the thought of moving back into the White House with the coming of the Congressional and social winter season.

Her official year of mourning was up. Indeed, most women mourned only six months for a child. She knew she would have to resume entertaining, receiving visitors, acting as hostess at receptions and balls...which would still be planned by that supercilious cold-fish Nicolay. Returning Congressmen and their wives were already leaving cards at the White House, and there were very few of them Mary actually wanted to see. The hollow inside her ached, not only for Willie, but for Sam, for handsome little Alec who had played with Robert in her father's garden on Main Street. Through a Boston medium her youngest brother had said to her, "Tell your husband I forgive...."

She returned to Washington in a state of soul-sick dread. Rumors were flying again, exacerbated by the wild undercurrent of excitement among the contraband and free colored communities as they watched the days count down to January the first, and the confusion and indignation among the slave-owning population of Washington City about the status of their bondsmen. A Union attempt to capture the rebel capital at Richmond resulted in a resounding defeat at Fredericksburg and yet more trainloads of shattered men poured into Washington early in December. Lincoln visited them whenever he could in the dozens of hospitals around the city; Mary resumed her quiet work among them, often with only Lizabet or John Wilamet for company.

One December evening, as she and her Spiritualist friends Mrs. Dixon and Jesse Newton were putting on their cloaks in the White House hall to leave for an evening at the Laurie home in Georgetown, Lincoln stepped quietly out of the half-hidden door of the servants' stair. "Where are you bound for, Mother?" He'd been in a Cabinet meeting since before supper—Mary had expected him to be closeted with them most of the night. She could hear Seward's extravagant voice upstairs still, as the men descended the main staircase: Lincoln had early acquired the habit of coming and going by the servants' dark and narrow stair.

"To Georgetown," she said guardedly. "To a Circle."

"Hold on a moment," said Lincoln, "and I'll go with you."

Her eyes widened, but she wasn't nearly as startled as Cranston Laurie and his wife were, twenty minutes later, to see the President's tall form unfold itself from out of the carriage in the wintry darkness. Lincoln shook hands with the Lauries, bowed to Belle Miller and Nettie Colburn, then retired to a rocking chair in the corner, still wrapped in his gray shawl with his big hands folded over his waist.

One of the things people forgot about Lincoln was that, for all his skill with words and sounds—he could imitate bird-calls, as well as every member of his Cabinet, with equal ease—he had the frontiersman's quality of silence. In the dim glow of the single candle that burned on the table, Mary was conscious of him watching. The others, she was almost sure, nearly forgot his existence, as one forgets the presence of a sleeping cat. The faces around the table gradually relaxed, as Belle Miller played the triangular grand piano—Mary could hear when the spirit control Ramilles took possession of the slight young woman's body. As the chords gained in strength and manliness, crashing like waves on the rocks, the piano itself began to rock and sway, lifting from the floor and moving to the music, like a ship at anchor in a heavy sea.

Nettie spoke, in the thick voice of one of her several spirit guides, this one old Dr. Bamford: "Well, I sees we got us a new guest here tonight. Troops a little low these days, Abe, on account of that spat out in Tennessee?"

Silently, Lincoln got to his feet and walked over to the moving piano. Mary had told him of how the spirit of Ramilles would enter the piano itself, lifting and rocking it with the force of his unearthly music. The piano at the Soldiers' Home had moved a little, when Belle had played it there, but it had stopped within moments. This instrument showed no signs of stopping. Even in the darkness she could see its back foot lifting far off the floor. Lincoln put his hand on the piano, then under the back of it, while Belle played on, her eyes blank, her face filled with the passion of the French musician's spirit, so that in the dense gloom it seemed in fact to be a different face entirely.

Mr. Laurie seemed about to protest, but the spirit Dr. Bamford called out jokingly, the words eerie in the mouth of the slender blonde girl, "Hey there, Abe, you want a good look at that-there pi-anny? Ramilles, old friend, why don't ya just step back an' let the man see?"

Face like an automaton's, Belle Miller rose, her hands still sweeping, crashing over the keys. Lincoln ran his hand thoughtfully beneath the keyboard, then placed a hand on one of Belle Miller's, while her other hand continued to play. Then, as the piano rose and fell again, he said, "Well, let's see if we can manage to hold that thing down," and with a light move, like a boy hopping up to sit on a fence, he swung up and perched on the piano's lid.

The piano rocked like a bucking horse, then rose and fell again. Even when Lincoln was joined by two other gentlemen of the Circle, the powers of the spirits were unaffected.

Mary didn't know whether to feel fascination, triumph, or mortification that her husband—the President of the United States!—would so make a fool of himself.

"I told you," she said, as Burke the coachman drove them back to the White House an hour later. "Now do you believe that the spirits of the dead come? That they are capable of crossing the boundaries of the world to speak to us?" Her voice trembled a little, with earnestness and desperation to believe. "Do you believe that that piano was raised and moved by invisible forces?"

The carriage was dark, the city around them sinking into slumber. Only the faintest gleam of the carriage-lamps, and the glow of sentry-fires near the Treasury Building, cast threads of gold on Lincoln's eyebrows and beard as he looked down at her. He drew in his breath to speak, then let it out, and put his arm around her. When he did speak, his voice was gentle. "I do allow that that piano was raised and moved by unseen forces," he said. "And I am sorry, Molly, that you were not able to speak to those you longed to hear from tonight."

Although Nettie had professed them present, neither Willie, nor Mary's father, nor Alec had spoken directly to Mary that night.

They never did, on those occasions when Lincoln was in the room.

AFTER THE DEBACLE AT FREDERICKSBURG, IN JANUARY LINCOLN replaced the affable and inefficient General Burnside with General Hooker, hoping against hope that the change would do some good.

It didn't. In early May Hooker marched south in yet another attempt to take Richmond and was surprised one afternoon, while sitting on a farmhouse headquarters porch near Chancellorsville, by Stonewall Jackson's forces charging out of the near-by woods. The general had somehow entirely missed the fact that they were in the area.

Eighteen thousand perished or were wounded at Fredericksburg. Almost twice that, at Chancellorsville.

Every night after supper Lincoln would slip out by the servants' stair, and walk through the bitter-cold darkness of the President's Park to the War Department to read the dispatches as they came in. Many nights he'd fall asleep on the sofa in the telegraphers' room, to be waked by the clerks an hour before dawn so that he could return to the White House in time to wash, shave, change his clothes for another day.

Other nights, wakeful herself, Mary would hear the thump of boots in the downstairs vestibule, the hushed voices of Stackpole the doorkeeper and messengers—or more often the Generals themselves. Then the boards in the hall would creak and going to her door, Mary would see Nicolay and Hay, nightshirted and bedroom candles in hand, at Lincoln's half-open door. And Lincoln would go padding down the hall barefoot in his yellow nightshirt, with his long legs bare as a stork's and Jip trotting faithfully at his heels, to confer with Generals on the landing in the dark.

Mary tried to get him to eat, tried to make sure he slept. His dreams after Fredericksburg and Chancellorsville were fearful.

The Union held Kentucky and Tennessee with a sliding grip. The rebels, although they had lost New Orleans, still kept their hold on the middle of the great Mississippi River valley, laughing to scorn the Union forces that besieged Vicksburg. Across the country men muttered against the draft, and those who could afford to, hired other men to take their places in the ranks.

Every day brought hundreds of wounded into Washington's hospitals. After a few editors were summarily arrested, the newspapers were quiet, but Mary knew that privately printed fliers circulated the city about her rebel sympathies—some of them even handed around in Congress—and rumors continued to fly.

Late in June word came over the wires that rebel forces under Robert E. Lee had crossed the Potomac again. They were marching through Maryland, and on to strike into Pennsylvania.

Mary had taken Tad to Philadelphia the week before, to escape the pestilential stink of Washington in summer. Sally Orne was delighted to see her, and her undemanding friendship was a great comfort. Through the winter season and into the spring, Mary had presided over official receptions and her private salons in the Blue Room, though large gatherings of strangers filled her with dread. By the end of March, she had discontinued the receptions.

At the news that a rebel army had invaded the state, the city of Philadelphia went into a panic. Lincoln telegraphed Mary, "I do not think the raid into Pennsylvania amounts to anything at all," but she returned to Washington anyway, to the cooler precincts of the Soldiers' Home. There Tad could ride, accompanied by William Crook, a soldier specially appointed to guard him. Washington was still alive with rumor about plots to kill Lincoln, or to kidnap him, to ransom in exchange for the thousands of Confederate warriors languishing in prison camps. Mary was obsessed by the fear that some rebel sympathizer might take it into his head to kidnap Tad instead.

She saw as little of Lincoln as ever. He would leave before dawn, riding horseback with Nicolay and Hay to the White House through the cool twilight. Some nights he didn't return at all. He'd send messengers—and occasionally flowers from the White House gardens—but Mary guessed he was sleeping on the sofa in the telegraph office, Jip at his feet.

"God knows what Hooker's intelligence is up to," reported Charles Sumner, who called with flowers—Mary suspected it was Sumner who reminded Lincoln to send the bouquets she received. "Nobody seems to know whether Lee's still in Pennsylvania or not, or what he's doing there."

Days later word came that the enemy was only a few miles from Harrisburg, where the railroad ran down to Washington.

Lincoln dismissed Hooker, and put a man named Meade in command.

On the last day of June word came that Meade had met Lee's army, near the Pennsylvania town of Gettysburg.

For two days Mary saw nothing of her husband. Sumner and Ginny Fox came to the Soldiers' Home with snippets of news. "Your husband has barely stirred from the telegraph office," said the Massachusetts Senator, taking the plate of gingerbread that Mary handed him. "The clerks get him sandwiches, but I don't think he eats them, which is probably just as well, considering where the food has come from. He goes back and forth to his office, and that mob of imbecelic petitioners and office-seekers there makes me want to go up and down the hall with a whip, like Jesus in the Temple, and drive them out so the poor man can get some sleep. You know if Lee wins, it will mean we'll have to sue for peace."

Mary said, "I know." Sumner too looked haggard—it had taken him two years to convalesce from his caning by a Southern Senator and in some ways he'd never completely recovered. She guessed that he could see as well as anyone else, what would become of Emancipation, if the North could not put down the rebellion in the South.

All those young men dead, at Antietam, at Chancellorsville, at Shiloh. Ellsworth and Alec and Ed Baker. The Republican Party, fissured already among moderates and bloody-shirt radicals, would turn on Lincoln like wolves, to save their own votes in the North.

"Is he all right?" she asked after a time. "Mr. Lincoln? Would it help him if I at least visited and got him to eat?"

"I think that's a splendid idea, Mrs. Lincoln." Sumner smiled his beautiful smile. "At least they'd have to let him alone for an hour for that."

Mary returned it with a little sideways twist of her lips. "I think you underestimate the forbearance of the average office-seeker, sir. They would not let him alone if he was dying. We can but try. If nothing else," she added, "I can hear for myself what's going on, rather than get everything second-hand."

 · Not, she reflected, that she actually would. Lincoln seldom spoke to her of matters either political or military these days.

Nevertheless she sent the cook over to the White House the following morning to make a light lunch, and a little before noon had the carriage brought around, and drove down Pennsylvania Avenue through grilling heat and a choking fog of dust. Though opening the windows of the family dining-room let in the stinks of the camps, the river, and the stables, it was better than suffocating. She even visited the greenhouse for a small cluster of roses to put on the table.

Lincoln looked like ten miles of bad road, but smiled when he came into the dining-room—half an hour late— and saw lunch ready. "What's the news?" she asked him, and he shook his head.

"Nothing good. It can't go on much longer, they've been at it since Sunday...." He passed a hand wearily over his face, as if trying to clear from his mind the darkness of the future. "We can only hope, and pray."

He spoke no more of the battle, but she knew he was thinking of it; he was preoccupied and silent, and excused himself early. "I must go," he said. "Word usually comes in about this time."

"Of course." She told herself that if she'd given him a glass of water when he was thirsty, he was no less grateful even though too tired to say, *Thank you.*

He walked her to the door, and handed her into the carriage. The dust, and the supply wagons and artillery moving through the streets, kept the carriage to a walk along Pennsylvania Avenue, but once they reached the road along the Rock Creek bluffs, Mr. Burke whipped up the horses.

The team sprang forward into a trot....

Mary heard Burke yell in shock and surprise at the same instant that she saw the high driver's seat of the barouche jerk, sway, and drop at one end. Burke snatched at the railing for balance and Mary screamed, and at the same instant the horses, panicked at the unfamiliar noises, the jerk on the reins, leaped and bolted. The carriage-wheels jarred on the road-side. She thought, *The creek-bottom* ... as the carriage reeled and teetered. ...

Almost without thinking she caught up her skirts and flung herself over the door and out. ...

SHE CAME TO IN THE DARK, THINKING, *CHOLERA. THERE'S cholera in the town and we'll all die.*

Her father and Nelson were getting down trunks from the attic, to give to old Solly to bury the dead.

Pain went through her skull like white-hot daggers, her whole body hurt as if she'd been wracked by the Inquisition. *I must have caught the cholera after all.* ... She listened for baby David crying, but heard nothing.

David must have died. ...

No. It's Willie who died.

Someone came over to her, when she started crying. "Mrs. Lincoln?"

Ruth Pomeroy, who had been Willie's nurse. Mary had the confused impression that there had been something else after Willie's death ... a trip to New York? A battle? Why did the image come to mind of Lincoln sitting on a piano in a darkened room, with his long legs dangling over the edge?

Or had she only dreamed it?

"Mrs. Lincoln, how do you feel?"

She managed to whimper, "Hurts," and Mrs. Pomeroy gave her a glass of something that had the swoony bitterness of laudanum. She drank it gratefully, hoping it would fore-stall the preliminary lightning-flashes she could already see in the corners of her vision. Sometime later she heard Sumner's voice, muffled and distant, as if in the hallway.

"What happened?"

Through her shut eyelids, she saw them clearly, the tall

Senator and the homey Quaker woman framed in the dim glow of the single oil-lamp in the hall.

"The carriage-seat came off," said Mrs. Pomeroy's voice. "They took her first to the military hospital nearby, and sent for Mr. Lincoln...."

She tried to recall Lincoln being with her, and failed.

"An accident?" asked Sumner—in her dreamlike vision she saw Mrs. Pomeroy shake her head.

"The bolts that fastened the driver's seat were removed, and the seat fixed up with glue, that would hold just until the carriage picked up speed. The carriage was in the stable. According to Governor Seward, nearly anyone could have got at it. They must have thought Mr. Lincoln would be returning with her. She's lucky to be alive."

SHE FELT WELL ENOUGH THE FOLLOWING DAY TO CONFER with young Mr. Stoddard about the details of the White House Fourth of July reception, but remained in bed. The migraine retreated, but for months afterward she had the feeling that those burning jagged lines, those rains of fire wavering in her vision, were never far away, lurking behind the curves of her skull-bones. On the night of the Fourth she heard the fireworks at the White House, far off toward the center of the town. When she drifted off into half-sleep she would jerk awake, thinking they were gunfire and wondering if Lee had marched south from Gettysburg, to seize the capital. Would they fortify the Treasury Building again, were soldiers camping in the East Room on her new sea-green-and-rose carpet? In dreams she saw Lincoln lying dead on the White House steps in a pool of blood.

She woke to the sound of Lincoln's footsteps, and Tad's shrill cries of welcome.

The door of her room flew open, Lincoln's face radiant in the light of the branch of candles he held.

"Lee's retreated!" His voice shook with relief. "He's on

the run. Meade should have him surrounded by the end of the week. Dear God, and then it will be over."

AT THE SAME TIME THAT NEWS REACHED MARY THAT HER friend General Dan Sickles had been severely wounded in the battle, a telegram came to Lincoln from General Meade: *We will drive the enemy from our soil.*

"We don't *want* to drive the enemy from our soil!" fumed Lincoln, when he came to visit her at the Soldiers' Home. "We want to *capture* the enemy and his whole army and then the war will be *over.* I've got a good mind to go up there and take over command of the Army myself."

"Ca' I gum?" asked Tad promptly, enthralled at the prospect.

Lincoln sighed, and shook his head, and laid a reassuring hand on Mary's wrist, for she had started up with panic in her eyes. "The office-seekers wouldn't let me get ten feet outside the city limits," he said regretfully. "Plus, if I led the Army, sure as check we'd come to a gate someplace and I still can't remember the order to file 'em through it."

Mary laughed shakily, and settled back among the pillows. Though at first she had thought she'd taken no more hurt from the carriage accident than sprains and bruises, the cut on her head had become infected, leading to great pain and fever. For days she lay tossing—and weeping with pain at every movement—in the grilling summer heat, between fever and laudanum only vaguely aware of where she was. Mrs. Pomeroy was kind and gentle, but in her fever Mary hated the sight of her, for it brought back to her the recollection of Willie's death.

When she came out of her delirium, it was to the news that General Sickles would recover, though he had lost a leg—

—and that the city of Vicksburg, that controlled the Mississippi River and with it the whole center of the

Confederacy, had been taken, by a Western General named
Ulysses S. Grant.

Lincoln's face fairly glowed in the light of the bedside
lamp as he gave Mary this news. The stream of food supplies
from Texas—and of European arms, textiles, ammunition,
and machinery coming to the Confederacy through
Mexico—was now cut. Grant was on his way to assume
command over the Union forces fighting for Chattanooga,
the major junction of the South's network of railroads whose
heart lay in Atlanta.

"We got a wedge in the log," he told her. "We have the
chance, now, to split 'em wide open.

"A delegation of Gospel ministers came callin' on me in
my office today," went on. "They said, 'You can't appoint
General Grant to command at Chattanooga—he drinks.' I
asked if they knew what his brand is—I wanted to buy a barrel apiece for my other Generals."

CHAPTER FIFTY-ONE

As soon as she was well enough to travel, Mary left for New York with Tad and Mrs. Pomeroy. She tried not to complain to Lincoln, for she knew he had troubles enough for any man, but she felt that the carriage accident had injured her far more severely than the doctors knew. Her headaches had redoubled, not only in ferocity but in frequency. The fear of the pain prompted the habit of taking a few precautionary spoonfuls of Female Elixir to stave them off before they began.

She suffered, too, from agonies in her shoulder and back, so that on some days she felt unable to get out of bed at all without the assistance of a good deal of medicine. She disliked it—it made her sleepy sometimes, and at other times she heard herself saying things that she knew she shouldn't, but anything was better than the pain.

Her nightmares worsened, nightmares in which Robert ran away and enlisted, nightmares in which Mary walked down endless lines of cots, crying his name. Sometimes she found him on a bloodstained plank at the Navy Yard, where Ellsworth had lain, his face wax-yellow in death and flecked with blood. Sometimes she saw him sitting up, alive, in a chair, like General Sickles, but instead of having a single leg as a bandaged stump, it was both legs and both arms, and his blinded eyes wrapped with a bandage beneath which blood flowed down like tears.

From this she would waken screaming, and fumble for the bottle on her nightstand, to drown the image from her mind.

It was after such a nightmare—such a remedy—when she sank back dazed onto her pillows, that she first saw Willie step through the wall. Later she wondered if it were a dream, for she felt very strange and detached from herself. She didn't think so. Wondering, trembling with joy, she saw her son come through the wall, not only Willie but little Eddie, shining faintly blue in the darkness. Both boys smiled joyfully and reached out to her. She woke weeping, though with joy or sorrow she didn't know.

Robert joined the little party in New York, and escorted them to Mount Washington, one of the dozen quiet summer resorts in the White Mountains of New Hampshire. It was a relief to have Robert with her, for she knew Tad would be well looked after by his brother. For all his tendency to nag, Robert cared deeply for his brothers, and in his gentleness with Tad, she saw the memory of his own loss of Eddie. With this worry lifted from her, she was free to meet other women who sought, in the White Mountains, to escape the pressure and heat of the cities. Wealthy women, most of them. And many of them women who, like herself, had suffered crushing losses.

When her headaches, and the pains in her back, permitted, she took refuge in the comfort of séances with a medium who lived in Mount Washington, a hollow-eyed woman named Mrs. Guinan, whose controlling spirit could raise and lower the table in the center of her parlor while the music of harps and tambourines drifted bodiless through the dark.

"Poppycock," said Robert irritably. But it was Robert's disbelief, and not Mary's faith, she thought—and said—that was poppycock. Robert spoke to her again about enlisting: "The Army is desperate for men," he said, which was true. There had been riots in New York against the draft, a week before Mary's arrival there. "And I look about me at the men who are left at Harvard, and I'm ashamed."

But the thought of losing him threw Mary into hysterics: "If anything were to happen to you I should die!" she sobbed. Tad, frightened, began to hiccough and cry, and

Robert took him away for a walk in the woods while Mary retreated to bed with a few spoonfuls of Indian Bitters.

The subject was not spoken of again.

She lingered in New Hampshire for almost two months, where the air was pure and the war far away. Only when the leaves turned red and gold, and Robert had to go back to Harvard, did she return to New York, terrified to the last that Robert would steal away secretly and enlist. Even in her days of pain, or of dreamy lassitude when she would not stir from the sofa, Mary had followed the progress of the war through newspapers. There had been horrific fighting all around Chattanooga in Tennessee, with tens of thousands wounded and dead. But she was in New York when Lincoln's letter reached her, two days before her return to Washington, that her sister Emilie's husband, Ben, had received a mortal wound, fighting against Grant's men on the banks of Chickamauga Creek.

EMILIE WAS PASSED THROUGH THE UNION LINES AT FORT Monroe, Virginia, early in December, with her two children. Betsey, thin and weary in home-dyed mourning, her fair hair nearly white, escorted her. All her sons by Robert Todd were dead by Yankee bullets. With the blue-coated soldiers standing around the freezing-cold depot in Fort Monroe, Mary held her frail stepmother in her arms and wept.

Betsey took Emilie's younger girl on to Lexington, which had been captured twice in rebel raids but was now back in Federal hands. Emilie and her dark-haired little daughter Katherine boarded the military train for Washington with Mary, and moved into the big bedroom at the northwest corner of the White House's second floor. At twenty-six, Emilie seemed like a shadow of the gay girl with the red-gold hair who'd sat beside Mary in the gallery of the Springfield State House, upon whom Robert had developed his first eleven-year-old case of calf-love. She was almost literally a shadow: food was no easy thing to come by, in a countryside ravaged by war. Though Mary was sick with grief at Ben's death and Emilie's sorrow—Emilie was with child, too, from Ben's last furlough—it was good beyond words to have her little sister there. Good to have someone to talk to who knew Lexington, who had visited Springfield.

If Mary could not return to those peaceful places, those joyful times, the next best thing was to know that Emilie remembered them, too. In a way, her memory made them that much more real.

Emilie refused, however, to swear allegiance of any kind to the Union—Tad and Katherine came close to blows one evening in the library, over who was the real President. And Emilie refused, with a stubbornness that irritated Mary in spite of her love for the girl, to come with her to the Circles at the Laurie house: "Ben will be able to speak to you, I know he will!" Mary cried, but Emilie only burst into tears and shook her head.

When Mary told her about the visits she received—almost nightly, some weeks—from Willie and Eddie, and sometimes her brother Alec, Emilie stared at her as if she heard the ravings of a madwoman.

Emilie remained at the White House for over a month. She received no visitors and refused to join in the rare family excursions to various Washington theaters. On the day of Kate Chase's wedding—to a wealthy Rhode Island Senator and political General who promised to be of maximum assistance to her father's upcoming Presidential campaign—Mary and Emilie remained ensconced in the oval parlor, drinking tea and indulging themselves in recreational slander.

But word got out. The newspapers published that one of Mrs. Lincoln's Confederate relatives had been foisted onto honest Father Abraham at the White House—that there was a spy in place in the government's heart. In November, shortly after Lincoln's return from the dedication of a new cemetery on the Gettysburg battlefield, General Sickles arrived at the White House to visit while Mary and Emilie were having tea in the Blue Parlor with Cousin John Stuart, who was in Washington on business.

With Sickles was New York Senator Ira Harris, red-faced and belligerent with drink. Sickles, thin from privations in the Army hospital and limping on two canes, was resentful and bitter at the loss of his leg: Mary guessed almost at once that the men had only come to be able to say they'd seen Mrs. Lincoln's rebel guest. She supposed allowances could be made for Harris—his only son was in the Army—but the New York Senator seemed to think that rebel women merited nothing in terms of gentlemanly behavior: "I see the rebels are running like scared rabbits from Grant in Tennessee."

"I'm sure they were only following the example the Yankees set for them at Bull Run, and Manassas, and Chancellorsville, and Fredericksburg." Emilie dropped a lump of sugar into her tea and returned his hostile glare with a Southern belle's sweetly merciless calm. "Will you have bread-and-butter, Mary, dearest?"

"They could be mopped up in a week," went on the Senator, "if we had the men to pursue them. What about your son, Mrs. Lincoln? How is it that he isn't in uniform? He's old enough, and strong enough, to serve his country. . . ."

"Robert is . . . is making his preparations to enter the Army," Mary faltered, praying that this wasn't in fact the case. "He is not a shirker, as you seem to imply. If fault there be, it is mine. I have insisted that he should stay in college. . . ."

"I have only one son," thundered Harris, rising from his chair. And, returning his glare to Emilie, he added, "And if I had twenty sons, they should *all* be fighting rebels."

"And if *I* had twenty sons," retorted Emilie, coolly dabbing butter on her bread, "they would all be fighting yours, sir."

As gatherings went, reflected Mary, this one ranked right up there with the fatal first of January, 1841. Emilie rose from the sofa and glided from the room with no appearance of hurry, but Mary heard her break into a run the moment she was in the hall: "Excuse me, sirs," Mary said quickly, and hurried after her. She caught up with her in the stygian gloom of the upstairs hall, while Emilie was fumbling with the knob of the guest-room door. "Darling..."

Emilie stiffened like a ramrod, nearly invisible in the shadows in her black dress, but a sob broke in her voice. "It's all right, dearest. I know he's nothing but a damn Yankee."

Mary folded her sister in her arms, and for a time the two women clung together in the dark, refugees alike from a world that was no more.

The clump of crutches on the stairs. Sickles passed them without seeing their sable clothing in the gloom of the hall, turned in to the little corridor that led to Lincoln's room. "Oh, now that is too much!" whispered Mary furiously. Lincoln had come back from Gettysburg with a high fever and was still listless and exhausted. She started to go toward the bedroom but Emilie's arms tightened around her. "Probably thought of some really juicy lie to tell him..."

Sickles's voice rose to a trumpet, and there was an emphatic slap, as if he'd struck the table with his hand: "...and it is unwise of *you,* sir, to have that rebel in this house!"

"General Sickles..." Lincoln's voice was dangerously soft. "My wife and I are in the habit of choosing our own guests. We do not need from our friends either advice or assistance in the matter."

Beside her in the gloom, Emilie whispered, "Oh, Molly, I should not have come."

"Nonsense! We need you here, both Brother Lincoln and I. You are good for us...."

"It was kind of you to ask me, and to take me in," her sister murmured. "But I see that I will have to go."

CHAPTER FIFTY-TWO

EMILIE LEFT FOR LEXINGTON IN DECEMBER. MARY WAS DESO-late. She pleaded with Lincoln to put in his word with her sister, and he said, "I have asked her already. She has made up her mind. Let us not make departure harder for her than it already is."

Mary went with Emilie as far as Philadelphia, where she stayed for a day or two with Sally Orne, yearning for the younger woman's friendship to ease the hurt of her isolation. She felt her loneliness more sharply now, for a few months previously she had had a falling-out with Elizabeth over Ninian's dismissal from the Army commissary post that Lincoln had arranged for him. Both Ninian and Ann's husband Clark Smith had been accused of corruption. Neither Elizabeth's letter, nor Ann's, had been forgivable.

The nation was tired of war. Tens of thousands of men had died—torn apart by minié balls, wasted by pneumonia, measles, and dysentery in the camps, eaten up by gangrene in the hospitals. There was no end in sight. In the darkened parlors of Cranston Laurie and the other Spiritualists, Mary met more and more black-clothed women, women who had lost their husbands or their sons, women who spoke with bitterness of the bloodshed that would surely resume again in spring. Across the Potomac, General Meade and Robert E. Lee maneuvered and skirmished in the thick woods of the wilderness that lay between Washington and Richmond. Meade was cautious: "Like an old lady trying to shoo a flock of geese across a stream," muttered Lincoln. Lee—with half the Union numbers, ill-fed, ill-armed, ill-supplied—eluded them.

Lincoln was facing re-election with almost no chance of

winning it. Salmon Chase electioneered tirelessly for the
Republican nomination, backed by Sumner, who had decided that Lincoln was doing nothing for the slaves he'd
promised to free. The various wings of the Republican Party
scrambled to dissociate themselves from Lincoln's failure.
McClellan was running for the Democrats on a promise of
peace.

"Which doesn't surprise me," mused Lincoln, when he
came into Mary's bedroom to bid her goodnight, the night
of her return from Philadelphia. "When he was General of
all the armies he purely did his best to avoid sheddin' anybody's blood."

"The tide has turned," insisted Mary, sitting up sharply in
bed. She was glad to see him, though the sight of him filled
her with guilt. She'd done some shopping in Philadelphia
with Sally, and though many businessmen of the city—including the ex–Secretary of War Simon Cameron—had gen-
erously promised to help her out with her debts, she was still
very much afraid of what Lincoln would say if he found out
how much she'd spent. Even she wasn't clear what that sum
was, but she knew it was bad.

"With the Proclamation of Emancipation there has been
no more talk of Britain or France entering the War on the
rebel side," she went on, not liking how beaten his face
looked, in the glow of the gaslight. "Their people would not
stand for it! Nor, with the victories we have won, will our
people simply . . . simply whistle down the wind the men
who have already died, the blood that has been shed."

"The blood that has been shed," repeated Lincoln softly,
and turned his hand over, looking at the palm as he had that
day in the Navy Yard, when he had seen the corpse of his
young friend Ellsworth brought in from the first skirmish of
the war. *"Will all great Neptune's ocean / Wash this blood clean
from my hand? / No, this my hand will rather the multitudinous
seas incarnadine / Making the green one red."*

He turned his head, and gazed for a time at the mirror
over Mary's cluttered dressing-table, where his own reflec-

tion could be glimpsed, chalky blurs of face and shirt-front standing out from the dark of hair and beard and coat, and the darkness all around.

"You are right, Mother," he said, after a long time. "I shall run, and if General Grant wins another victory I may just win. And then, I suppose, we shall see."

He came over and kissed her, but she could see he was exhausted, and she told him to go to bed himself. She heard his footsteps on the floorboards of the hall, and heard them pass his own little bedroom and go on instead to the main corridor, that led to his office.

It was only many hours later that Mary, waking from inchoate and frightening dreams, remembered the vision he had had, before they left Springfield, of the doubled reflection in his mirror: his living self, and a ghostly afterimage that whispered of death in his second term.

ROBERT ARRIVED IN JANUARY, AND FORMALLY REQUESTED HIS father's permission to join the Army: "With McClellan seeking the Presidency, it looks worse than ever, for you to order every man in the nation to give up his son, and hold your own out of the fray."

Mary wailed, "No!" when Lincoln came into the parlor and told her of Robert's request—Robert, fearing a scene, had consulted his father in his bedroom. She sobbed, "Don't let him go!" and sank to her knees. "Please don't let him go!" Robert's dour glance at his father was full of a world of *I told you so.*

"I shall die if anything happens to him! Are you trying to take away all my boys?" It took Lincoln hours to comfort her, while the winter rain hammered on the parlor windows. She wept herself into a blinding headache, but when Robert returned to Harvard, it was with the understanding that he would enroll in law school there the following year.

A week or so after Robert's departure, she was reading to

Tad in the parlor after supper when he looked up sharply and said, "W'at dat?"

Fire blazed red in the dark beyond the parlor windows. As she dropped her book and sprang up she heard running footsteps crash in the hall. She caught up her shawl, ran downstairs, hearing someone shout, "The stable's afire!" Hay and Nicolay passed her on the stairs. Stumbling out the kitchen door, Mary saw in the wild glare of the flames Lincoln dash for the stables, clear the boxwood hedge that lay between as if it hadn't been there. Servants were pelting after him; she could already hear the horses screaming inside. Beside her, Tad yelled desperately, "Teeda! 'Poleon!"

Lincoln yanked open the stable door. Flame billowed out to meet him and he fell back, shielding his face with his arm. Tad screamed the names of the two ponies and made a lunge down the steps—Mary snatched at him, and Stackpole the doorman grabbed the boy in his arms. Tad promptly bit him, drawing blood, but the big Irishman held on.

The men around the stable were falling back. Lincoln made two more tries to find a way inside—Nicolay took his arm, pulled him back toward the house. Mary put her shawl over her ears, to keep out the screams of the burning horses inside. When Lincoln reached the house again he was weeping. "It's 'cause a N'poleon," said Tad softly, calm now, to Mr. Brooks, one of the journalists who'd been in Lincoln's waiting-room when the fire started. "He wa' Willie's pony." Then Tad himself burst into tears, grieving the final link with his brother that was gone.

IN MARCH, WITH MUTTERINGS OF DISCONTENT SWEEPING THE country, Lincoln called General Ulysses S. Grant from Chattanooga and offered him supreme command of the Union forces. "The man's a butcher," protested Mary, as she and Lincoln descended the Grand Staircase to the reception in Grant's honor. "As well as a drunkard." Thanks to the "vampire press" she felt that she knew most of the Generals as well as their own wives did, if they had wives. "The casualties among the men fighting for him have been appalling!"

She had spoken, too, to men who'd served under Grant, as she'd made the rounds of the hospitals. "He don't care how many men he kills," had said one soldier. "Just so he gits where he's goin'."

"I can't spare that man," said Lincoln quietly. "He fights. Him and his pal Billy Sherman, they're a team of fighters."

He laid his gloved hand over Mary's, which lay on his elbow. Below them, the murmur of diplomats, Congressmen, officers rose from the hallway outside the East Room like the soughing grumble of the sea.

"If we don't have victories by November—if the war doesn't look to be ending—McClellan will let the Southern states go. It will be for nothing: Emancipation, Gettysburg, deaths . . . all the suffering and the compromises and the wars we have fought so far, for the Union to survive. Then God knows what will happen. Once the principle of Union is breached, there is nothing to hold either the North or the South together, and we will destroy ourselves piecemeal, or be eaten up by the first aggressor strong enough to take us on one at a time."

As Lincoln shook hands with a seemingly endless stream of guests, someone near the doors shouted "There he is! The man who took Vicksburg! Let everyone have a look at you, General!"

There was a rowdy confusion, then several Western Congressmen half-lifted General Grant up to stand on the nearest sofa, to Mary's fulminating indignation—she knew exactly what that crimson brocatelle had cost. She and Lincoln were forgotten as people crowded around Grant, fighting to get a sight of him, to get near him, to touch him. Anger at the slight—and her own growing suspicion that Grant was probably eyeing the Presidential nomination himself—turned her heart to unforgiving flint.

Ulysses S. Grant turned out to be a medium-sized, scruffy, shy man in a rumpled dress-suit, his newly trimmed beard redder than his hair. Since the formal reception-line seemed to have disintegrated anyway, Lincoln breasted through the crowd to the sofa, leaving Mary and Nicolay to keep what order there remained. When Lincoln finally brought the General over to meet her, Mary inquired with cool politeness, "Ulysses—what an interesting name, General. And what does the S. stand for?"

Grant replied expressionlessly, "Hiram."

He looked like a man who craved a stiff drink.

His wife, Julia, who came to Washington later and called at the White House, was in Mary's opinion worse: buxom, common, cross-eyed, and, Mary suspected, ambitious.

But Grant got things done. He and General Sherman—Uncle Billy, the soldiers called him, and said quite seriously that he was not entirely sane—went after the rebel forces like war-dogs unchained. Grant proceeded to cross into Virginia and attack Robert E. Lee in the tangled nightmare of the wooded peninsula that guarded Richmond; Sherman went south through Tennessee, following the rails to the Confederacy's supply-depot and manufacturing heart: Atlanta.

And Lincoln turned to the agonizing task of fighting a war that after three years nobody wanted anymore, and getting himself re-elected in whatever spare time was left to him.

Receptions were held twice weekly at the White House: Congressmen, diplomats, Senators, Generals, and their wives. Mary put off her mourning to attend them, standing at Lincoln's side as he shook hands until his right hand was so swollen he needed Hay's help getting his glove off. But the crowds of petitioners grew gradually less, and several nights a week he was able to escape from the White House completely.

While the armies were in winter quarters he took Mary, and sometimes Tad, to the theater often. Lincoln loved the theater deeply, and in the carriage on the way home they would talk of what they had seen, *Faust* or *Der Freischutz* or the gorgeously romantic young John Wilkes Booth in *Marble*

Heart, and Mary could pretend a bit to herself that they were courting in Springfield again.

But not entirely like Springfield. Lincoln no longer talked to her of politics, or the conduct of the War or the country, the things that illuminated his life and hers. On nights when he was tired, having very little in the way of small-talk anyway, he barely spoke to her at all. She sensed him walking on eggs around her, and it maddened her.

She knew her temper had grown not only short, but uncertain as well since the carriage accident. Things angered her, or terrified her, for no reason. She knew that those spells of disorientation—of feeling herself about to do or say something unthinkable—were more frequent, and that they had been joined, usually in the evenings, by episodes of dreaminess, as if she were about to disappear.

She knew, too, that she was taking more medicine than was probably good for her, but why not? The pains in her head and her back were almost constant. She could usually pull herself together for the receptions, but often she found herself looking at the faces of the men and women around her and wondering, *Who are these people? And why am I here?*

And almost worse than the pain, almost worse than her continuing grief at Willie's death, pervasive as darkness or summer dust, was her growing guilty terror about the bills.

Above all, she sought relief from that shame.

They never stopped coming in. Mary knew she couldn't *possibly* be spending as much as they said, but each individual bill could be checked. Every purchase she made was only after haggling down the original price. She simply didn't understand how it happened. Shopping itself, which filled her heart with restful delight, had become such a pleasure that she could not forgo it. It was one of the only joys she had. She would sort through her purchases as she'd once sorted through her father's presents, obscurely warmed by their beauty and by their reassurance that as the President's wife, she now owned the best. She sometimes found things in her luggage, returning from a trip, that she barely recalled purchasing at all.

But she knew that if Lincoln didn't win the election in November, all the bills would be presented—and he would no longer be so caught up in petitioners and testing new rifles and arguing over increased draft quotas that he did not notice.

Then he would suffer disgrace, as well as she: for who would believe, once the newspapers got hold of the matter, that he hadn't known?

Shame scorched her at the thought, shame and terror. He cherished his honor—his reputation for honesty—above all things. *He never wanted to marry me,* she thought in despair. *If all this comes out, he will turn from me . . . and then I will die.*

"He has to win," she said one afternoon to Lizabet Keckley, as the dressmaker was fitting the bodice on a glossy gown of eggplant satin. "He must, Lizabet!" Her voice shook—she had had a headache earlier in the day, and still felt strange, from its aftermath and from the extra Cordial she had taken. The words came tumbling out of her mouth as they so often did at her Blue Parlor receptions, things she had planned never to tell a soul.

But of course Lizabet could be trusted.

"Moreover, if McClellan and his lackeys get hold of my debts, they'll use them against my husband—use them to defeat him, and it will all be my fault! I have a good mind to go to those politicians who've been making a fortune off Mr. Lincoln's patronage. It is only fair that *they* should help me, Judd and Lamon and Mr. Weed in New York, and that fat toady Davis. *If* they could be trusted not to tell."

When she went to Philadelphia for a few days in spring to visit Sally, and again in the summer, she met with Cameron, and with the German bankers the Seligman brothers, promising to use her influence should Lincoln win. She had long become adept at political deal-making, and at least in the past Lincoln had taken her advice. Anything, anything to keep Lincoln from finding out! She reached home again only days before a rebel force struck up past Grant's army and bore like a band of devils straight for the capital.

In the sticky July heat the few servants at the Soldiers' Home packed what they could of the family's clothes, and Lincoln, Tad, and Mary moved back to the White House, its reception rooms under sheets, its mirrors swathed in gauze. "If Washington is taken, might it even have the effect of uniting the country, of stiffening resistance?" asked Mary, fighting panic as the carriage joggled through the early-morning streets of Washington. "It might even help your campaign...."

"Washington won't be taken," said Lincoln. But he, like Mary, was listening. In the morning hush, she could hear the spatter of rifles.

Two days later they all went out to Fort Stevens, on the perimeter of Washington's ring of fortresses, where the rebel forces under Jubal Early were trying to break through. Fort Stevens, like most of the other forts in the defensive ring, was a square of rammed earth walls, surmounted by a parapet and occupied by rough plank buildings crowded together: sutler's store, artillery park, powder magazine. Beyond the wall, a trashy ruin of scrap lumber, filthy blankets, and trampled or burned spots in the ground showed that there'd been a con-traband camp there, whose inhabitants had fled.

From the woods a hundred yards away, rifle-fire cracked out. Mary remained in the carriage in the middle of the en-closure, her hands locked around the protesting Tad's arm in a death-grip—there were two young boys barely a year older than her son, drummers, running along the wall fetching ammunition or water for the men crouched behind the para-pet. Lincoln climbed the rough wooden steps to the parapet itself and walked along it, stopping now and then to speak to this man or that—a soldier close by him jerked back suddenly and fell.

Lincoln turned, startled, and a soldier crouching near yelled, "Get down, you imbecile!" and grabbed the skirts of his black coat. "You'll get your fool head shot off!" Lincoln sprang down from the parapet to the walkway behind it where the men crouched under cover. He was still head and shoulders over the parapet and, cursing, the soldier shoved him completely behind cover.

Already soldiers were carrying away the dead man, crouching as bullets whined overhead. Mary closed her eyes, feeling as if she were going to faint.

Any of her soldier brothers would have shot that tall black figure, killed him. . . .

Had any of her three soldier brothers been left alive.

By Sunday, two corps of Grant's men had filed into Washington's defensive ring, marched double-time from the siege camps before Petersburg and Richmond. General Early was forced to withdraw. The band of rebel horsemen went on to elude their pursuers and burn Harrisburg, Pennsylvania, increasing the cries for the war to be stopped.

Which, she supposed, was the point of the whole raid. The summer was one of agony. Grant returned to the siege-lines before Petersburg, unable to break through to capture Richmond. Lee, undermanned and starving, held him in a death-lock. Patiently, Lincoln negotiated with Republican politicians about what promises could be made for treatment of the seceded states once they were conquered, *if* they were conquered. And all the while, wounded men came back from the fronts by the trainload.

Through it all she visited hospitals, distributing fruit and flowers to the sick men and reporting on the conditions— still horrible despite all the Sanitary Committee could do— in the vain hopes that Lincoln might be able to have changes made. She met Myra Bradwell again, working indefatigably among the wounded, and had her and her English-born husband to supper one evening. Lincoln and Myra talked about law and women's suffrage until past midnight, and Mary was much taken with Myra's big, slow-moving, gentle husband: the Judge, she called him.

But the heat, and the stink, and the miasma of sickness hovering over Washington in the summer proved too much, and in August Mary took Tad and fled to the cool mountains of Vermont.

It was there that she read that Uncle Billy Sherman, Grant's fellow butcher, had taken Atlanta, dealing the Confederacy a crippling blow.

The bloody tide had turned.

Mary—and everyone else in the country—could see that victory was only a matter of time.

CHAPTER FIFTY-THREE

THE SUMMER OF 1864 WAS A STRANGE TIME, FRIGHTENING and dark. She remained in Vermont until late in the autumn. Sometimes she spent whole days lying on the sofa in a haze of migraine and paregoric, surrounded by newspapers. They were filled with editorials and letters about Lincoln's call for Negro regiments: jeers from white men in both North and South who scoffed that a servile race—a people who had submitted to slavery for generations—would be useless as soldiers.

They were swiftly proven wrong. Black men flocked to the Union standards with a kind of angry joy, and fought with courage and ferocity at Port Hudson, Louisiana, in South Carolina, and in the Crater before the fortifications at Petersburg. When they were captured by Confederates they were generally slaughtered out of hand, for violating the cardinal law of the slaveholding states: that no black man carry arms against a white. Reading accounts of the battles—or letters from Lizabet Keckley, or Frederick Douglass, or even from her young friend John Wilamet, now with the medical corps in Grant's camp before Richmond—Mary wondered if Lincoln's hesitation in using the black troops more frequently was because he feared to further alienate the population of the South.

The reactions of the Northern soldiers were bad enough. "I'd rather be a private in a white troop than the General of a nigger regiment" summed it up.

On days when she felt better she would write long letters, to Mercy Conkling, or Cousin Lizzie, or to Lincoln. She had tried to get Lizzie the job as postmaster for Springfield, for which Mary considered her cousin far better qualified than most men she knew, but did not succeed. She tried again to get Lincoln's permission for Emilie to sell her cotton without taking the loyalty oath, in order to avoid destitution, but Lincoln refused.

Mary didn't know whether she should feel anger at his wretched stubbornness about honor, or pity for the pain she knew he felt. Both Margaret and Mattie—Emilie's full sisters—made similar requests, and Mary's pity dissolved when it came to her ears that in the expectation of receiving the coveted permit, Margaret had purchased hundreds of bales of other people's cotton at dirt-cheap prices, with the understanding that the profits would be split.

To make matters worse, when Mattie visited the White House briefly that fall, she had obtained an exemption from Lincoln to having her luggage searched. She had immediately bought up enough medical supplies—mostly quinine and opium—to fill several trunks and had borne them back in triumph to the Confederacy, along with a new uniform for Robert E. Lee.

With Atlanta taken, and victory assured, Lincoln was easily re-elected in November. His Vice-President this time was Andrew Johnson, a dour and self-educated War Democrat from Tennessee. There was now little talk of making peace. When Mary returned to Washington late in November, she saw the ranks of the blue-clothed, dark-faced soldiers march past at military reviews, singing: "Mine eyes have seen the glory of the coming of the Lord. . . ."

And she wondered if somewhere, Saul, Nelson, and Pendleton were listening, and any of those men chained on the deck on the Ohio River steamboat who'd kept four-year-old Robert from falling into the paddlewheel, all those years ago.

She found her husband deeply withdrawn, exhausted, like a man running completely on nerves. Tad was wilder than ever, charging the flocks of petitioners on the office stairway a nickel apiece "for the benefit of the Sanitary Committee," or harnessing Nanko the goat to a laid-down kitchen chair and racing this improvised chariot up and down the White House halls. He still slept with Lincoln every night, and visited his father in his office a dozen times a day through the "secret passage" Lincoln had had built that fall, a short hallway cut out of one end of the office anteroom that led directly from his own office to the parlor. Tad had a special knock: Lincoln would even interrupt Cabinet meetings to let his son in.

"You're spoiling him rotten," snapped Mary, during one of those sharp-tongued squabbles that she'd initiate in the hopes of breaking through the wall of her husband's silences.

Lincoln didn't mention the weeks she'd take Tad to Philadelphia and the White Mountains with her, and let him run wild, buying him anything he asked for. He said only, "He'll grow out of it," with a patience that made Mary, her nerves in shreds, itch to pull his hair out by the roots.

He wasn't well, either. On those rare occasions when she saw him in full daylight it was obvious to her that he'd lost nearly thirty pounds over the past four years, and his color was not good. But to her questions he merely replied, "I feel fine, Mother. Just tired."

And he looked at her with a gaze as probing, as questioning, as worried as her own. She sometimes wondered whether he knew about her debts, or about the deals she'd made with businessmen and politicians to cover them. She didn't think so. She knew him well enough to know that his devil-take-the-hindmost honesty would not have tolerated the situation, if he knew. But the fear that he might guess created still more silence between them, a silence she had no idea how to break.

With Atlanta taken, and the broken-down nexus of the South's railway system in Union hands, the end came rapidly. Without shipments of supplies, the Confederate troops were starving. They fought without boots and sometimes without guns or ammunition, running forward under fire to snatch the weapons from the hands of the enemy dead. Still they hung on, maneuvering with dwindling strength in the tree-clogged swampy country around Richmond.

Unable to sell their cotton, Confederate civilians were starving, too. Mary dreamed one night of Arabella Richardson Bodley, her girlhood nemesis, sitting alone in the echoing shadows of an empty house, weeping in a faded dress of home-dyed black. That fall Emilie wrote to them of her brother Levi's death, from the physical hardships of starvation on a constitution undermined—Mary strongly suspected—by drink. Still, Emilie's accusation hurt, that they had contributed to his death. "The last money I have in the world I used to make the unfruitful appeal to you... I request only the right which humanity and justice always gives to widows and orphans. I would also remind you that your minié bullets have made us what we are."

Lincoln did not afterwards mention his "Little Sister," but Mary could read the grief in his face.

Dozens of women now waited among the petitioners in Lincoln's office, to beg for the release and reprieve of brothers, husbands, sons imprisoned for military crimes, usually desertion or dereliction of duty. Mary always regarded these women with suspicion, as she regarded any woman who came close to Lincoln. In her more reasonable moments she knew perfectly well that she had not the slightest cause for mistrust—Lincoln would no more betray her than he would betray the Union.

But he had never lost his liking for women. And with his neglect of her—his maddening distance from her—her jealousy festered.

In January of 1865, against Mary's pleas and sobs, Lincoln finally asked General Grant if he might have room on his staff for Robert, who was commissioned as a Captain early the following month. The Army was still camped before Petersburg, twenty-five miles from Richmond on the Appomatox River. Mary lived in an agony of apprehension, expecting every morning that the day would bring her news of her eldest son's death.

When Lincoln told her, early in March, that he was making a trip to Grant's headquarters, she said at once, "You cannot leave me behind."

"Ca' I go doo?" demanded Tad in the next breath—Alexander Williamson, though he still couldn't entice the boy back to his studies, had at least worked with him on his speech, with the result that he was becoming slowly more intelligible. "I wanna see dem rebels—ca' I day my gun?"

So a party was organized: Mary and her maid Mrs. Cuthbert, Tad and his bodyguard Billy Crook, traveled downriver on the small steamboat *River Queen,* which was anchored below the bluff at City Point. Though Lincoln was quite clearly ill he asked to be taken to see the fighting. Mary wept again and pleaded, remembering the soldier who had fallen only feet from him on the parapet of Fort Stevens. "These men are shedding their blood—giving their lives—for my principles and my decisions," replied Lincoln quietly. "The least I can do is let them know how I value them."

She absolutely insisted that Tad remain with her on the *River Queen,* however, and even the boy's subsequent tantrum and tears would not move her. She posted Lieutenant Crook to keep an eye on him and keep him busy, and spent the day pacing, nervous, and endeavoring to be polite to Julia Grant. The train back from field headquarters was late and she sent a dozen messages to the telegrapher's tent, demanding to be told why. When the reply came that it was hauling several cars full of wounded, and thus forced to travel slowly, she was convinced that this was only a lie to calm her, and got into a quarrel with Julia Grant on the strength of it.

Lincoln got off the train silent and pale. "Did you see fighting?" demanded Tad, as he seized his father's hand.

"Only the field afterwards," Lincoln said, "and the burying of the dead." He went to his cabin and closed the door.

In the morning he looked a little better, and set out on horseback to watch General Phil Sheridan's men coming in across the river. The plan was that he would meet Mary and Mrs. Grant at General Ord's camp at Malvern Hill in the afternoon to review Ord's troops. Mary alternated between annoyance that she was relegated to following in a mere ambulance wagon, and agony that Lincoln's party would be overwhelmed by rebel cavalry, a situation which wasn't helped by Julia Grant's matter-of-fact "Nonsense, the rebels haven't either the horses or the men to take on a bodyguard."

"That's exactly the kind of lie I expect *your* husband *would* tell you," snapped Mary as Colonel Porter helped her into the wagon.

Julia Grant's square face reddened. "Just because your husband managed to get himself re-elected, you think you know everything about soldiering," the General's wife retorted. "But let me tell you, if it weren't for *my* husband's victories, McClellan would be in office now!"

Colonel Porter began hesitantly, "Ladies, now, it's a long ride...."

But Mary ignored him, ignored everything but the rush of uncontrollable fury that filled her. "Oh, and you're just waiting until the next election, aren't you, for you to move into the White House!"

"Ladies..."

"Well, if we do I *certainly* wouldn't be able to come up to *your* standard of balls and receptions, even if it's *not* wartime...."

"Of *that* I haven't the smallest doubt!" Mary shot back at her. "But what the diplomatic community might think of being served whiskey punch and cookies instead of more customary hors d'oeuvres I shudder to imagine, even if you *do* manage to get yourself a decent dress!"

Mrs. Grant stared at her in shocked fury, and then turned her face away, breathing hard. Mary whirled at once upon Colonel Porter and demanded, "Can't your driver go any faster? The review shall be over by the time we get there."

"The going is very difficult over corduroy roads like this one, ma'am," replied the officer nervously. He nodded out the front of the wagon, past the driver's rigid blue-clad back, to the band of felled trees laid side to side over which the ambulance wagon was cautiously bumping. "It's swampy country from here to Malvern Hill, ma'am. This's the only kind of road—"

"Don't you think I know about the kind of terrain that justifies a corduroy road?" shouted Mary. "Don't treat me like a child! And just because the road's bad doesn't mean your driver has to stop and make a separate decision at each log!"

Porter swallowed. "See if you can't speed 'em up a little, Tim," he said to the driver, and Julia Grant said icily, "I ought to warn you, Colonel, that I am an absolute martyr to seasickness in a swaying vehicle!"

"Well, in that case, I suggest that you stay here," retorted Mary, "and I shall *walk* to Malvern Hill. Stop this cart."

"Mrs. Lincoln, it's a sea of mud between here and there...."

"I'm sure the mud will part for her, as the sea did for Moses," put in Mrs. Grant.

"I said stop this cart and let me out!" Mary shrieked at the Colonel. "Or else make your man move those horses a little!"

"Ma'am, I don't—"

Mary swung around on the driver. "Speed those horses up!"

"Ma'am—"

Her head gave an agonizing throb—really, Carrington's Nerve Elixir was nearly useless in keeping headaches at bay... "I said speed them up or stop them and let me walk!" she screamed, tears suddenly bursting from her eyes at the thought of missing the review—missing the chance to stand by her husband's side at a time when it really mattered—at the thought of having the moment spoiled by a headache.

"Do it, Tim," ordered Colonel Porter, and Tim laid on the whip, starting the ambulance forward with a brutal jolt that flung Mary against the back of the wooden seat and caused Julia Grant to cry, "Oh, my God!" The next jar flung both women up off the seat entirely, cracking Mary's head on the bow of the ambulance's roof.

But because Julia had already begun to moan and whine about the jolting motion, Mary only said, "Well, if *you're* not interested in seeing *your* husband—and I can certainly sympathize!—I am interested in seeing *mine*." And clung grimly to the back of the seat, as those horribly familiar barbed lines of fire began to crawl across her vision, and the pain in her back and shoulder blended with the pain in her head into a jagged symphony of agony.

When, nearly two hours later, the ambulance finally rocked to a stop at the camp, the review was already in progress. She heard the music of the bands while they were still bouncing and hammering through the woods, and screamed at the driver for yet more speed. Julia Grant was sobbing and threatening to be sick, a ploy Mary herself had used far too many times to take seriously. She held out her hand peremptorily to Colonel Porter, and as he helped her down from the wagon, the first thing that met her eyes was Lincoln, mounted on a tall bay horse, leaning over to speak to a very pretty blonde woman riding beside him to review the troops.

Mary saw red. For a moment it was as if she'd finally surprised Lincoln courting Tilda Edwards, or lingering in the woods with his landlady's young sister, all those years ago. When he turned the horse her way, and started to dismount, she screamed, "How *dare* you...!" and lunged at him, so that he had to catch her wrists to keep her from physically striking him. "How *dare* you send me by that roundabout way, in that *heinous* vehicle, with only a few soldiers for guard, so that I could have been captured by the rebels at any moment, while you put up another woman to ride with you before the Army, as if she were your wife instead of *me*!"

The blonde woman, still in her sidesaddle, reined away, startled, as from a snarling dog. General Ord rode over quickly and put an arm protectively around her—his wife, thought Mary. Or his doxy—she looked like a designing slut...!

"Molly..."

"Don't you 'Molly' me! Don't you treat me as if I haven't eyes, as if I count for nothing! Without me you'd still be scratching out a living trying land disputes in the backwoods! The closest you'd have gotten to real politics would be arguing them around the cracker-barrel in Irwin's store!" His face and the faces of those around him appeared and disappeared behind floating slabs of yellow light. She lost track of what she was saying, until she turned away in fury. Someone took her arm—she didn't know who—and led her toward the tents. Looking back, she saw Lincoln still standing, one moment surrounded prosaically by half a dozen blue-clothed and embarrassed officers, and the next, it seemed, alone and wreathed in an aureole of incandescent flame.

Chapter Fifty-four

MARY DIDN'T EVEN KNOW HOW SHE GOT BACK TO THE *RIVER QUEEN,* or for how many days after that, on and off, her migraine lasted. She had dim recollections of Secretary Seward escorting her back to Washington—recollections of chattering to Illinois Congressman Carl Schurz, who accompanied them, about military dispositions and her opinion of Grant's armies. Between burning clouds of migraine agony and the blessed haze of Nervine, excruciating nightmares intruded. She hadn't *really* shrieked at Lincoln in front of the entire General Staff...

... had she?

Or demanded that he dismiss "that drunken butcher Grant"?

Or called Julia Grant a cross-eyed whore?

Dimmer still was the recurring image of her husband riding in review of troops at the side of a beautiful blonde woman, who sometimes had Mrs. Ord's face and sometimes that of Tilda Edwards. All the men saluted, salutes that should have belonged to her, Mary....

Had he sent her in the ambulance because he hadn't wanted her at his side? Had Colonel Porter had orders to make her late? When she asked Mrs. Cuthbert, timidly, if Mr. Lincoln were back from the headquarters yet, her maid said he wasn't. The President had sent word he would be delayed another two days.

A lie?

He doesn't want to come home to me, thought Mary bleakly. *He doesn't want to see me....* As soon as the maid had left she stumbled to her feet and found her bottle of Nervine. It wasn't a headache remedy—at least, it didn't say so on the label—but she'd found it worked as well as paregoric.

But the following day the shame and guilt and horror and pain were swept away like yesterday's tracked-in mud by voices in the corridor, by Mrs. Cuthbert bursting into the room: "Ma'am, it's true. The news is confirmed by dispatch, it'll be in the papers tonight. Jefferson Davis and his government have abandoned Richmond."

Mary blinked painfully in the curtained twilight. "Abandoned..." For a few moments the words had no meaning.

Then, "Abandoned *Richmond*? You mean, left it? For our troops?"

The maid nodded, her face flushed with nearly disbelieving joy. "They're marchin' into Richmond today, ma'am, and your husband with them. He's sent you a telegram...."

Mary sat up with a jolt that made her head feel like it was coming off her shoulders, almost grabbed the yellow envelope from the maid's hand. "I should be there," she said. "I should be beside him, when he rides in!"

Was Mrs. Ord at his side?

ENTERING RICHMOND TODAY. MILITARY ESCORT
WAITING TO BRING YOU IF YOU ARE FEELING
WELL ENOUGH.

"What time is it? Draw me a bath, and have Peter get out my trunks.... Tell Mr. Hay I'll be going to Richmond tomorrow." She fumbled herself into the wrapper Mrs. Cuthbert held for her. "He should have waited for me!"

"I don't expect General Grant would have let him bring you when they all first went in," said the maid tactfully. "Not till they'd made sure all the rebel troops were really gone."

"I'll believe that when I hear Grant didn't have that cross-eyed cow of a wife with him." She shook back her hair and settled it into place with a pair of jeweled combs that had been a gift from the Seligman bankers. "Not that he'd care. He looks like the kind of man who takes more thought for his horses than he does for a mere *wife*. Especially that one.

Put in the dark-green velvet, I'll need to look like the President's wife when I ride in. I should ask dear Senator Sumner to accompany me, and Secretary Harlan's sweet daughter. Robert is so fond of her. . . ."

She paused, as it crossed her mind who would most rejoice in the news. Who would most long to enter the ruined capital of the Confederacy, to see the chief city of the slaveholding states crushed in final defeat? "And bring me my lap-desk, please," she added. "And tell Mr. Hay that I'm going to ask Mrs. Keckley to accompany me."

"IT WAS ONE OF THE KINDEST—AND ONE OF THE GREATEST—things anyone ever did for me," said Lizabet Keckley softly, gazing out the window into the laundry-hung yard of the Lewis boardinghouse, as if she could see back across the ten years that separated that hot April from this sweltering July of 1875.

Ten years, thought John.

It was not so very long a time.

"I'd heard the day before, that Richmond had fallen. I gave all my girls all the day off." She laughed a little, at the memory of the time when her business had been large enough to support a little workshop of "girls."

"We took the *River Queen* down to City Point the next morning, and the military train on into Richmond. Mr. Lincoln met us there."

She shook her head wonderingly, and John knew exactly what she was recalling, for he had been there too. The burned buildings, the charred bricks of chimneys like the pillars of ancient Roman ruins—the fires lit by the rebel forces to destroy the bridges, the tobacco works, and the military warehouses had run wild, destroying nearly a third of the city. Some women watched them, silent and gaunt in home-dyed mourning. The slaves—ex-slaves—crowded the streets to watch the soldiers march in. . . .

"She was like a little girl," said Lizabet. "She was wild. She glowed. It was *his* triumph, *his* vindication. But I think it was more for her than that. She'd spoken to me many times about her father's slaves, people she grew up with, parts of her family. I know slavery in Kentucky—at least for the house-servants—wasn't what it was farther south, but she hated it. Hated that people she cared for could be taken away like that. I don't think she ever got over that."

"I know *I* never did," remarked John drily, and Lizabet glanced over at him, and laughed.

"Under it all she has a good heart, you know. She was so much a lady of the South, but she saw what slavery was, and what it did to us. One of the first things she did was take us into the Legislature, where all the desks and chairs were tumbled around from the Confederate Congress leaving so fast, and papers still scattered on the floor. She brought me up to the front of the room and had me sit in Mr. Davis's chair. I picked up some of the papers lying on the floor—one of them was the bill saying free people of color would not be permitted to enter Richmond. I still have it."

Her smile turned reminiscent and a little weary. As if she looked further back still from that high seat in the Confederate Legislature, backward down the long road she'd trodden, the road they'd all trodden. As if she saw straight back to her days in the unceiled cabin in Virginia, to the first time she was whipped at the age of four, and to her parents, weeping over the news that her father's master was moving West, and taking his human chattels with him. To the beatings of a mistress determined to "break her insolence" and the rape that had given her her only child.

For years, John knew, Lizabet had "worked out" so that her wages might support master, mistress, their family, and others. She had humiliated herself, begged, and negotiated with her circle of white customers in St. Louis to help her buy her freedom. When she'd begun working in Washington, she had paid them back every penny of what her freedom had cost.

"She gave a dinner that night in Mr. Davis's mansion," Lizabet said after a time. "And she had a lot to say about Varina Davis's taste in wallpapers and clothing, I remember, and none of it good, though it was so close to her own that you could barely have told them apart. I remember her friend Senator Sumner at that dinner, in his fancy vest, and Robert so handsome in his uniform, with Mary Harlan, whose father was a Congressman and in Mr. Lincoln's Cabinet—and both the young people more caught up with holding hands under the table than with the fact that the Union had broken the back, not only of the rebellion, but of slavery for all time. Which was as it should be." She smiled again, at that long-ago sight, of new love like the first blossoms on the black ruin of war.

"She must have apologized to Mr. Lincoln, and begged his pardon, as she always did. When she and I went out to Richmond in the train she was shivering and wound up like a clockspring, but at the dinner they were friends again.

"They were sweet together, you know?" Her eyes softened, rueful and kind. "Him so tall and grave, and all in black, for he never really came out of mourning for Willie. And her fussing around him in a circle with all her ribbons fluttering, making him bend down so she could slick his hair for him, and always watching him out of the corners of her eyes, worried whether he was all right. Which he wasn't," she added. "He was sick by then, and always tired. His hands and feet were always cold, he said, and his color was bad. But he'd go to the hospitals with her, and shake hands with thousands of men."

John nodded, remembering those two figures in the moonlight on the deck of the *River Queen*. Remembered how Mary had reached out her hand for her husband's; remembered Lincoln taking off his tall hat, and bending down to kiss the small, plump woman in her costly black silks.

Remembered the love and partnership in that kiss, and the unspoken knowledge that the other would always be there.

EIGHT DAYS AFTER THE FALL OF RICHMOND, ROBERT E. LEE, wearing his last good uniform—probably the one Mattie had smuggled him from Washington—rode up to Appomattox Courthouse and handed his sword to Ulysses Grant.

And it was over.

Lincoln read a speech, to the thousands who assembled by night on the White House lawn. It became one of Mary's clearest memories of him, standing in the window, with Tad beside him holding a lamp. Lincoln's face was cruelly gouged with weariness but very calm, as he spoke of his plans for rehabilitating the secessionist states back into the Union. His strong tenor voice carried out into the sticky darkness against the roar of the cicadas in the trees.

She had a headache that day. Even Robert's return the following day—Thursday—to the White House from Appomattox, or the prospect of seeing *Our American Cousin* on Friday night, didn't cheer her. Only when she went on her carriage-ride Friday afternoon with Lincoln did her spirits lift, with the fresh air and sunlight, and the chance to be with her husband alone, if one discounted the presence of fourteen cavalrymen clattering their sabers all around.

It was the first time they'd been alone together since the disastrous review at Malvern Hill, which he did not mention at all. When he referred to the trip, he spoke of the tortoise he and Tad had found beside the railroad track, and she of Varina Davis's gowns which had still been in the house at Richmond—"Most of them could have stood a stitch or two," she sniffed, which made him laugh, as she hadn't heard him laugh since Springfield.

"The War is over," he said, leaning back on the carriage-seats in the dogwood dapple of slanted evening sunshine. "All but the shouting—of which there'll be plenty, when the Legislature hears that I don't plan to hang every Democrat politician in sight. But it's over, Mother. And you and I are free."

The carriage turned up the last stretch of Pennsylvania

Avenue, still damp enough from winter and spring so as not to be dusty. The White House seemed to shine ahead of them through its sheltering trees. She closed her eyes briefly and took Lincoln's hand, then smiled up into his face as his immense grip returned her squeeze.

The last sunlight warmed her face, and made her feel alive again, after all those years of darkness and terror and unsurvivable grief.

Willie was gone. All her brothers—except the obnoxious George—were dead.

The world of peace and beauty that had been the South—the world of black and white in which she'd grown up—had vanished, its passage marked by blackened walls and the black clothes of widowed belles who, like her, would never forget what they had lost.

But she was here, and the spring evening was sweet. She and Lincoln had survived the War together. She felt as if they'd spent a long hideous night both clinging to opposite ends of a shipwreck spar adrift in a stormy ocean. Unable to speak to one another, unable to do anything but hang on and pray their strength would last till daylight.

Now they'd been cast up together on an unknown beach. What would lie in the land beyond she didn't know. But somehow, after four years of grief and confusion and separation, she had her husband back.

SLEEPING IN THE AFTERNOON, IN HER ROOM AT BELLEVUE Place, Mary dreamed that she was in the dream that Lincoln had had, a day or two after his return from Richmond.

She dreamed of the White House, its long upstairs hall utterly dark. The air felt stuffy and silent, as of a house long deserted. She saw Lincoln, asleep with the sleep of exhaustion in that small spartan bedroom. Saw his eyes snap open, saw him look around. It was dark in the room and cold, but she heard now—as he heard—the sound of someone weeping, somewhere in the house, weeping jaggedly . . . as if he or she had been crying for hours but could not stop.

He sat up, and ran his hand through his hair. He was dressed in shirtsleeves and trousers, barefoot as if he'd lain down too tired to even completely undress. For a time he listened, then got to his feet and went to the door, listening in the darkness. Mary watched him pad soundlessly through the empty halls, looking into the rooms, first upstairs and then down. Beds empty and stripped of their sheets, his office bare in the ghostly moonlight, no papers. No charts on the long battered pine tables, only a tattered map of the Union and Confederacy still pinned to the smoke-defaced paper of the walls and that stained old picture of Jackson above the fireplace. He looked into her room, and Tad's. Both were empty and cleared out. Even the cats had gone, and little curly-haired Jip.

Downstairs the East Room was a cavern of darkness, in which candles burned like constellations of fevered stars. A huge dim shape reared in its center, a black canopy shrouded with black curtains; every window was hung with black. Here alone were people—men, soldiers, standing around a black-draped coffin. Now and then one would shift his feet and the creak of boot-leather and the clink of a buckle were loud as cymbals in the deathly silence of the house.

Lincoln crossed the thick green carpet with its pink roses, from Carryl's of Philadelphia. Stood for a moment looking up at the sable canopy, the coffin that it sheltered. Distantly the sound of weeping began afresh. He stepped forward to one of the guards, the soldier tired, like a picket after a long night's watching.

"What is it?" asked Lincoln softly, and looked at the coffin in the shadows. "Who is dead in the White House?"

The guard answered, "The President. He was shot by an assassin. He's dead."

CHAPTER FIFTY-FIVE

"SHE GAVE AWAY EVERYTHING HE OWNED," LIZABET KECKLEY said. "She told me she could not bear the memories they held."

Late-afternoon sunlight glared on the waters of the Potomac, glimpsed through the ragged screen of trees. Closer, pools and puddles that studded the Mall's unkempt grasses flashed like silver. At the far end of the long park, closer to the Capitol, some effort was being made to transform the open land into the sort of *tapis vert* that its designers had originally envisioned, but at the moment it was pretty much as John remembered it from a decade ago: a swampy strip of ground where people grazed their cows. The granite monument to George Washington didn't look any further along than it had been when the money to build it ran out in the late 1850s.

Beside him, Frederick Douglass nodded. Though his hair was whitening he still stood tall and regal, his hard, almost frightening features relaxing into a rare expression of personal grief. "She gave me a pair of his spectacles," he said, in his deep, beautiful voice. "And one of his canes—one that I think he actually used once or twice. People were forever presenting him with canes, and of course he had about as much use for a cane as I have for a pink silk petticoat. At fifty-five he had the body of a twenty-year-old. You have his coat, don't you, Lizabet?"

The seamstress shook her head. "I forget who she gave his coat to. She gave me his brush and his comb, because I'd often comb his hair, the last thing before they went down to a reception. I cut it, once or twice—he was always letting it get too long. I wish I had kept the cuttings."

"We don't think," said Douglass softly. "Not until it's too late." He paused in his long stride as three little boys dashed across the path with their hoops. "She gave the rest of the canes—and a number of his other things, like waistcoats and gloves—away to people who she thought might pay some of her debts."

"Was it true, that he left her in debt?" asked John.

"You know what they say, about how you find a cobbler in a village?" asked Lizabet wryly. "You look around and see which children have no shoes, and you follow them home. He'd gone bankrupt once, for trusting a feckless partner in that store he ran back in New Salem—I think he was twenty-three. The sheriff sold his surveying-tools and horse at auction. His friends clubbed together and bought them back for him, but I don't think he ever got over it. When he died his estate ran to something like eighty thousand dollars. . . . But he left no will."

John blinked, not understanding, and Lizabet smiled with a kind of reflective irony. Few who had been slaves had ever even thought of making wills, for what was there to leave? Legally, until January of 1863 neither John nor his mother, nor the kingly man who walked now at his side, had even owned their own bodies.

"When a man doesn't leave a will," Lizabet explained, "it means his wife and his children can't touch a penny of his money till the estate has been probated. Sometimes that takes years. Mr. Lincoln knew better. He was a lawyer—he'd spent twenty years cleaning up the affairs of men who hadn't left wills. And it wasn't that he didn't know his life was in danger, from the moment he was elected to office. People turn strange, when they think about death." Her eyes strayed toward the dazzling river again, and John saw in his mind the burned-down candles, the fresh flowers, before the picture of her nearly white son.

"I think it might have been a blind spot for him, the way money was for her," she said. "Or maybe he was just more frightened than he ever let on."

"So what happens," asked John—who had never encountered or much thought about this aspect of the lives of the white and rich, "—while the courts are probating a man's estate? What do his wife and children live on?"

Lizabet and Douglass exchanged a glance, then Douglass said, "Nothing. I don't know how the ancient Hebrews arranged such matters, but when Jesus of Nazareth urged charity to widows and orphans, he was *not* talking in generalities. Mostly they go live with their families... only Mrs. Lincoln had managed to have a fight with two of her sisters and wasn't speaking to them, and the rest had been on the wrong side of the War. When Lincoln died, Mrs. Lincoln had managed to personally insult most of *her* family and *his* Cabinet—I think at one point about two weeks after the assassination she called Secretary of War Stanton to the White House and accused Andrew Johnson of being part of Booth's gang. Then over the next few weeks she made a clean sweep of it and alienated everyone else she'd formerly missed."

John saw in his mind Cassy and Clarice haul Phoebe back from physically assaulting Lionel—Phoebe spitting at their big, good-natured housemate, screaming insults and threats and lashing out with her nails.... He lived in daily dread of hearing that the whole family had been evicted from their half of the broken-down dwelling because his mother had attacked the rent-collector again.

Mrs. Lincoln accusing her husband's successor of having compassed his murder—he could just picture her leaning forward in her creaking corset, could hear her high, sweet voice breathlessly gasping the words behind the crape screen of her veil—seemed laughably mild.

Through the whole of the afternoon, until late-falling summer darkness cloaked the park and mosquitoes drove the three former slaves back to the omnibus and Mrs. Keckley's stifling room at the Lewises' again, John listened to his friend's recollection of the black nightfall of Mary Lincoln's life. And while Lizabet would speak calmly of those weeks of sitting in the darkened guest-room in the White House—for Mary could not bear to enter even her own room there, much less sleep in the big carved bed in which she had on rare but treasured occasions lain with the husband she'd adored—he could feel the suffocating gloom of that curtained chamber, and hear the woman's keening, like an animal howling in a trap.

Mary had been brought back to the White House that wet morning of Holy Saturday by Secretary Welles's wife, Mary Jane, and by her fellow Spiritualist Elizabeth Dixon, the only friends who could be located at short notice. Throughout Easter Sunday, she had been forced to listen to workmen building the towering black catafalque in the East Room to enthrone his coffin. Lizabet had arrived late Saturday morning and sat beside her, holding her hands when Mary would let her.

"She wept until she was ill." Lizabet shook her head, as if across the dark river of years she could still look straight into that cramped little room with its closed curtains, could still hear the hammering downstairs. "I've never seen a woman in such grief. She said, many times, that she wanted to die, that she'd rather Booth had shot her as well. We were all of us worried—Dr. Henry who'd been in town from Oregon, Mrs. Welles, Mrs. Lee that was one of the Blair family and sister to Ginny Fox, Mr. French that had helped her out with her debts, Senator Sumner. . . . Those were the only ones she'd see. Mr. Stanton, the Secretary of War, was running the country, since the same night Mr. Lincoln was killed his Secretary of State, Mr. Seward, was attacked by another of Booth's gang, and stabbed so badly that his life was despaired of. That's something almost no one seems to remember about the assassination."

"They would have got Johnson, too," said Douglass in his velvety bass. "Only Booth's man turned coward at the last minute and went and got drunk instead."

John reflected privately that it was astonishing the would-be killer hadn't encountered the Vice-President in the tavern to which he'd fled.

"Mrs. Lincoln never stirred from that room for six

weeks," said Lizabet softly. "Sometimes sleeping—she slept a great deal. Sometimes only sitting and staring. Sometimes screaming and wailing, like a woman in an opera or a play. We all made sure she was never alone. I must have heard her recount that last evening, detail by detail, three hundred times in that month and a half, sometimes twice and three times in the space of a few hours, until I was ready to scream myself. Even Dr. Henry, who was the most patient of men, said to me once in the hall, 'Isn't she aware that the rest of us have lost a dear friend, too?' "

"You would be, and I would be...I hope," said John. "But Mrs. Lincoln isn't like that."

"No." A wry and reminiscent expression tugged the corner of Lizabet's mouth. "No, she isn't."

Certainly no one is like that, he added mentally, *who's had four or eight tablespoons of Battley's Cordial or Indian Bitters, three or four times a day for years.*

And who would deny a woman so bereft the comfort of medicine for her pain?

Lizabet went on, "She felt that it was somehow her fault, as she did when Willie died. She was always one to see misfortune as God punishing *her,* for something she had done. She kept trying to see what could have been done differently, as if she could go back and take another path, so that he could live. Poor Mr. Johnson stayed in his boardinghouse—with a pack of children and grandchildren and his poor sickly wife—and Secretary Stanton ran the country. I think Mrs. Lincoln couldn't face the thought of coming out of that room. Of emerging into a world that she wouldn't share with him."

In his mind he saw again that lanky silhouette against the evening sky of Virginia, taking off his hat and bending down to kiss the plump little figure at his side.

"Where did she go when she did come out?" he asked. "Back to Springfield?"

Lizabet shook her head. "It wasn't that easy."

And John thought, *No. Nothing was ever that easy with Mary Lincoln*.

Give her a difficult situation, and she was bound to make it worse.

In between paroxysms of grief, Mary had managed to quarrel with every single friend and neighbor in her adopted hometown of Springfield over the resting-place of her husband's body. (*What else?* thought John with an inner sigh.) She could not bring herself to attend the funeral, but when Robert returned from Springfield with the news that its town fathers had lovingly formed a Lincoln Monument Association, and spent $5,300 on property for a magnificent tomb at the center of town, she had flown into blind rage that the tomb would not include a family crypt.

"I don't know whether it was because she truly couldn't endure the thought of eternity not spent at his side," said Lizabet, "or because she wanted, once and for all, to be recognized as the wife of the martyred hero, the way she'd always wanted to have everyone know she was the President's wife. Probably both," she added, with a touch of sad affection for her friend. "Probably both."

"After all the mud that had been flung at her in the papers for four years," mused John, "who can blame her for wanting to claim her place?"

"She wrote back to Mr. Conkling—who was the husband of her best friend in the old days—that Mr. Lincoln had expressly wished to be buried in Oak Ridge Cemetery in Springfield, in a family vault," said Douglass. "I gather from something she said to me later that he'd only said once that he wanted to be buried in someplace 'green and quiet'—not a description of downtown Springfield, whichever way you look at it. For all that he became a lawyer, and a politician, and the servant of his intelligence and his destiny, I think he was always a bit of a backwoodsman in his heart."

When first he'd come to the cities of the East, wondered John, had Abraham Lincoln found them as confusing and noisy as he himself had found Washington, that first autumn of his freedom? Did he dream of the woods, as John dreamed of them, over and over in the stinking South Side slums?

"So of course she couldn't go back to Springfield."

Douglass raised his eyebrows. "Not after threatening to have her husband's body buried in Washington if the Monument Association didn't do things her way, she couldn't."

Lizabet chimed in, "She claimed also that Lincoln had intended to move the entire family to Chicago after the end of his second term, because, she said, he couldn't face returning to the house where his beloved Willie had lived."

"Hadn't they lost another child already in that house?" asked John, remembering Mary's rambling account of her life.

"Of course," said Lizabet. "And in my hearing he spoke a number of times, about when they would be able to go back to Springfield. It was she who couldn't face it. Her friend Myra Bradwell and her husband lived in Chicago—still live there, in fact—and Mrs. Bradwell was part of the community of Spiritualism there. I know Robert wanted to return to Springfield, where they owned the house at least and he could be apprenticed to practice law. But Mrs. Lincoln... had her way."

Of course she did, thought John, recalling his own mother's wild rages and arbitrary demands. *Of course she did.*

"It was nearly summer by the time they left the White House," said Mrs. Keckley softly. "The day they left was the day before the Army of the Potomac was to return to town, after the final surrender of the last Confederate troops, and the capture of Jefferson Davis. Carpenters were building a reviewing-stand in front of the White House for General Grant and President Johnson—hammering filled the halls, as it had when they were building the canopy for Mr. Lincoln's coffin. The place looked as bad as it did when Mr. Lincoln and Mary had first moved in, because after the funeral sightseers went through the lower floor and helped themselves to nearly everything. Silverware and dishes were showing up just weeks afterwards in pawnshops from Washington to Boston, and of course the papers all said she'd made off with them, in all these trunks.

"And after all that," she sighed, "it was just Robert and Tad and I, and the two White House guards Tom and Will, who loaded up the luggage. I know she'd angered some people with her hysterics, and turned others away with how she'd go on and on. But when it came to it, I nearly cried that there were so few, to see her on her way."

CHAPTER FIFTY-SIX

MARY, ROBERT, LIZABET KECKLEY, AND TAD RODE TWO DAYS and two nights by train to Chicago, where they lived first in a downtown hotel, and then in a cheaper hotel in Hyde Park, at the end of the new streetcar line, seven miles south of the city on the shore of the lake. John Wilamet remembered Chicago in the Sixties, before the fire: wealthy neighborhoods of fine brick houses along Michigan Avenue and on the lakefront, surrounded by wide grounds and trees, interspersed with ragged shantytowns called "patches"—Conley's Patch, Goose Island, Little Hell, and Ogden's Island—where the Hungarians, Poles, Germans, and Irish lived in rickety sheds or minuscule rooms subdivided from the upper floors of commercial buildings.

There were few blacks in the town in those days. They lived in unbelievable squalor south of Maxwell Street. He remembered the trains that would roar through the crowded neighborhoods of the poor without slowing down; remembered the stench of the river that was an open sewer for the lumber, soap, and packing plants all along its banks. Remembered rats fed so fat on slaughterhouse offal that a trap wouldn't kill them. You had to listen for the noise of the bar slamming down, then go out and finish the job with a hammer.

Remembered the tangles of alleyways where the poor kept pigs, cows, chickens in tiny yards, along with fodder, stored hay, coal oil, and kindling for stoves. No wonder the place had gone up like tinder.

It had been Hell, waiting only for the touch of the Fire.

Lincoln's estate had been put in the hands of Judge David Davis, his old friend of his circuit-riding days. While all over

the country Lincoln was being apotheosized from a shrewd
jokester into a saintly martyr, Congress was refusing to vote
so much as a dollar toward a pension for his wife and children. This was partly because Mary had managed to personally insult and offend nearly everyone in the government,
and partly because, quite simply, no Presidential widow had
demanded one before.

William Henry Harrison and Zachary Taylor—log cabins
and hard cider notwithstanding—had both been wealthy
planters. Congress had paid their elderly widows the remainder of their husbands' first-year salary, and they had retired to
the family plantations in ladylike dignity, surrounded by adult
children and hosts of grandchildren to care for them.

The Re-United States, moreover, had been facing the
debts of four years of ruinously expensive warfare running to
hundreds of millions of dollars. In the midst of dealing with
martial law in a conquered rebel territory—and hundreds of
thousands of former slaves who had no idea where to go or
how to make their livings—Congress had not wanted to listen to a middle-aged, abrasive widow demanding at the top
of her lungs and in every "Letters to the Editor" column in
the East, to be paid at least the balance of her husband's salary
for the year 1865, and a pension on top of it.

"She was entirely justified," remarked Douglass, as he,
John, and Lizabet walked through the cobalt twilight past the
red-brick towers of the Smithsonian Castle, toward the park's
edge. "It was Lincoln's election that started the War, and
Lincoln was its final casualty. She was owed at least the pension that any soldier's wife would have had, for giving a husband to an enemy bullet."

"Not that a soldier's pension was what she asked for,"
mused Lizabet. "But in her mind the principle was the same.
And then of course in those days both the country as a whole
and every wealthy Republican in sight were showering gifts
on General Grant—including two houses, horses, carriages,
and everything from ornamental swords to gold-rimmed dinner service for a hundred. They could all see that he was go-

ing to be the next President, and wanted him to remember them kindly. Mrs. Lincoln was furious that she had been 'forced' to live in a common boardinghouse. Judge Davis— and Robert, I'm sure—would point out that she had a perfectly livable house in Springfield, but she wouldn't hear of living in it ... nor of selling it. Through all her letters to me during 1866 and '67, I don't think she ever once mentioned selling the Springfield house."

They crossed Constitution Avenue, walked along Seventeenth Street where it bordered the President's Park. Through the trees, lights could be seen, though John couldn't imagine President Grant and his family were still in residence at this grisly time of year. Without the War, and in the deeps of summertime, Washington had subsided into what it had been all along: a hot, sticky little Southern city floating on a marsh.

Was Mary Lincoln sitting this evening in her window back at Bellevue tonight, he wondered, as he so often saw her, looking out at the gathering dark? Was she keeping consumption of opium down in his absence? Or would they have to go through the whole heartbreaking process of illness, depression, restlessness, pain again?

His heart ached for her, as it ached in spite of himself when his mother would sit weeping on the rear porch of the house, rocking like a child for hours with her arms around her knees.

Give them shots of morphine every few hours. Why not?

He shook his head, his mind returning to Lizabet's words, and to Mary's account of her Washington years. "She was still in debt, wasn't she?" he asked. "The debt that she'd never told Lincoln about?"

Lizabet's lips drew tight.

"You have to understand," she said, after a time of silence, "that for Mrs. Lincoln, spending money was a sickness. Shopping was how she spent her days, how she got out of herself ... how she rested. Many were the days she'd spend hours, showing me all she'd got. She hoarded up treasures like a drunkard drinks, almost without thinking. And she couldn't stop."

In March of 1867 (Lizabet said), she received a letter from Mary Lincoln, pleading—in her usual imperious fashion—with her to meet her in New York between August and September of that year, to assist her in selling up her wardrobe. *I cannot live on $1,700 a year,* she wrote, and would be forced to give up the house that she had so recently bought—the house that she had hoped to make her permanent home—and return to living in a boardinghouse.

December would see the opening of Congress and by October the local Washington hostesses would be putting in orders for new gowns . . . but Lizabet went.

"I'd heard from her twice, maybe three times after I left them in Chicago," said the seamstress, as they left the gaslights of Pennsylvania Avenue, entered the darker and shabbier precincts beyond. "I'd read in the newspapers about the subscriptions to raise money to pay her debts. She claimed Judge Davis was undermining these efforts by telling everyone she'd be perfectly able to pay her own debts once he got done probating Lincoln's estate. I don't know what the truth was, but Washington is worse than a girls' school, for gossip. But Mrs. Lincoln was my friend, and she needed me. So I went."

Mary's original plan was that Lizabet should go to New York first and procure rooms for them at the St. Denis Hotel, a plan conveyed in a letter written after Mary must have left Chicago, so there was no chance for Lizabet to write back suggesting any other scheme. Annoyed and filled with trepidation—Mary had a habit of proposing schemes that were abandoned at the last minute—Lizabet closed up her business.

She found Mary, however, at the shabby-genteel establishment near Union Square, as directed, and after an argument with the manager over the hotel's policy of not renting rooms to people of color—something Mary hadn't even thought of—they were given adjoining triangular chambers on the fifth floor, barely larger than cupboards.

"How provoking!" Mary sat down on Lizabet's bed, panting a little from the climb. "I declare, I never saw such unaccommodating people. I shall give them a good going-over in the morning."

The next morning, however, Mary knocked on Lizabet's door at six and urged her to come with her out to breakfast—since the St. Denis refused to serve persons of color in the dining-room, and it hadn't occurred to Mary to send for dinner in their rooms the night before—and to sit in the park and discuss the situation.

"That fat blackguard Judge Davis, who I daresay wants to keep the interest for himself, still hasn't made a distribution of my Sainted Husband's estate." Mary's face was pink with anger in the black frame of her turned-back veils. "I have written and written to those ungrateful Republican politicians whom my husband helped to positions of power, begging them—and *threatening*! For they are *all* scoundrels—to contribute *something* of what they owe to His memory, to my support. That young Mr. Williamson, that was Tad and Willie's tutor, has *supposedly* been acting for me in this, but he is a most *dilatory* young man!"

Lizabet couldn't imagine what influence a Scots schoolteacher would have on the gang of hard-line radical Republicans currently in control of Congress, but didn't get a chance to speak, which was probably just as well.

"I managed, by the most *terrible* sacrifices, to pay off some of my debts, with the niggardly *pittance* Congress gave me—only the first year's salary of my Dearest One's second term, after taking out six weeks' portion *and Federal taxes*! I was able to purchase a house in Chicago for Tad and myself, on the same street as my dearest Myra! But without money to keep it up, I have been forced to rent it out, and live once more at the Clifton House on the proceeds, a most *plebeian* atmosphere, when one considers the glory that once I knew."

Tears filled Mary's eyes, and Lizabet put her arms around

those plump shoulders. For all her pretensions, her rages, and her blithe conviction of entitlement, Mary Lincoln had a sweetness to her, a genuinely good heart whose warmth drew Lizabet in spite of what she'd learned over the years of this strayed Southern belle. In the bright morning sunlight of the park, Mary looked somewhat better than she had that hot May day when she'd left Washington. She had noticeably put on weight over the past two and a half years, and she moved as if every gesture gave her pain, but there was, at least, a little of her old sparkle to her eyes.

But it was brutally clear to Lizabet that her friend had lost the mainspring of her life. This beaten quality closed Lizabet's mouth on any remark she might have made about those who at least *had* a house, who were able to get their debts paid by others instead of having to work with thread and needle themselves. When she spoke, it was only to ask, "What did you have in mind?"

"Say what you like about Mrs. Lincoln," sighed Lizabet, as she threw open the windows in a vain attempt to lessen the day's accumulated heat in her boardinghouse rooms, "she wasn't one to sit quietly on the sidelines waiting for events to take their course. Will you have coffee, Mr. Douglass, or tea?"

WILLIAM BRADY AND SAMUEL KEYES, DIAMOND MERCHANTS of 609 Broadway, assured Mrs. Lincoln that the gowns she'd worn while the President's wife, the furs in which she'd wrapped herself and the jewelry that had glittered on her throat in the midst of those terrible days of war, would bring in somewhere in the neighborhood of a hundred thousand dollars. Lizabet had distrusted those two smooth-talking gentlemen, when they came to call at the St. Denis, but had held her peace. "The people will not permit the widow of Abraham Lincoln to suffer; they will come to her rescue when they know she is in want."

For several days Lizabet walked around New York City in quest of dealers in secondhand clothing, and drove with

Mary to various stores on Seventh Avenue with the dresses worn during her four years as the Republican Queen. Afterwards, Lizabet tried to push the squalid bargaining, the polite dismissals, the barely concealed contempt, from her mind. Brady insisted that Mary write letters to him, purportedly from herself in Chicago, which he would then, he said, show to prominent politicians, forcing them to buy or be exposed as abandoning Lincoln's widow to her fate.

When these letters were roundly ignored, Mary threw up her hands, turned the whole business over to Brady and Keyes, and returned to Chicago—with the request that Lizabet remain in New York as her agent, continuing the quest and overseeing Brady's exhibit and sale of the dresses, shawls, and jewels.

"I DON'T KNOW WHAT SHE THOUGHT I WOULD LIVE ON." Lizabet shifted the kettle onto the single burner of the iron heating-stove, knelt to puff the coals beneath it to flame. "She'd already borrowed six hundred dollars from Mr. Brady, not a penny of which she gave to me. I was angry— and the results of Mr. Brady's 'exhibit and sale' I think you already know."

The newspapers had been merciless in their criticism, both of the sale itself and of the dresses: . . . *they are jagged under the arms and at the bottom of the skirt, stains are on the lining . . . some of them are cut low-necked, a taste which some ladies attribute to Mrs. Lincoln's appreciation of her own bust. . . .*

As a rider, one or two journals brought up again the gossip of wartime Washington, the accusations of spying or bringing in relatives to spy in the White House, the tales of financial chicanery and cutting up the Presidential sheets for drawers. They spoke of her "good Republican" friend Simeon Draper, whom she'd recommended for the highly lucrative post of customs collector for the port of New York after he'd paid $20,000 of her debts.

One newspaper spoke of her as "a termagant with arms

akimbo, shaking her clenched fist at the country, and . . . demanding gold as the price of silence and pay that is her due
because she was the wife of a President." Another spoke of
"conduct throughout the administration of her husband . . .
mortifying to all who respected him . . ."

People had stared—people had whispered—but few
bought.

"AT THE SAME TIME AS ALL THIS WAS GOING ON," said
Douglass, from the faded brocade sofa, "Lizabet was making
the rounds among the free colored of New York like the
hero she is, trying to get up a lecture series whose proceeds
would go to Mrs. Lincoln. I agreed to lecture. So did the
Reverend Henry Garnet, and other men of color who had
led in the abolitionist movement before Emancipation. But
Mrs. Lincoln declined . . . for reasons best known to herself."

It had been years ago, thought John, but the bitterness of
the rebuff still tinged Douglass's voice.

"And all that time," the flame-glow of the lamp warmed
Lizabet's features as she measured out tea from a slender
stock, "she wrote me, urging me to keep after Brady and
Keyes—as if a pair of white diamond-merchants would pay
the slightest attention to anything a woman of color said—
and to remain in New York to look after her interests. I had
to go back to sewing just to pay my rent. Naturally I'd abandoned the Union Place Hotel the moment Mrs. Lincoln was
gone, and was boarding with a private family. When a Mr.
Carleton contacted me about writing a memoir, I should
have suspected something. Maybe I was too angry to care."

From the street below, musical with distance, rose the
voices of children playing, and the sing-song cry of the
candy-seller making a final round.

"I'd just heard, through a mutual Spiritualist friend, that
she'd finally got the distribution of Mr. Lincoln's estate, and
was fairly well-off. She never offered to send me so much as
a dollar. Mr. Carleton's people interviewed me, and pub-

lished the book under my name. But they'd re-written it, to make her look foolish—not that she wasn't completely capable of making herself look foolish when she tried. The chapter about the sale of the clothes was . . . nastier than it needed to be." She hesitated, then sighed again. "And I sold them the letters she'd sent to me. They promised they'd only use a few excerpts. I can't imagine why I was stupid enough to believe them. Of course they published them in full. She never forgave me for that."

"While you forgave *her*," Douglass pointed out gently, "for stranding you in New York, for causing you to lose your very profitable business in Washington, for treating you like a servant, while she went back to where she had friends, a house on whose rental she could live, and a pile of government bonds?"

Lizabet shook her head. "It wasn't an easy time for her either," she said. "That was just after Mr. Lincoln's old law partner, Mr. Herndon, began lecturing about Mr. Lincoln's life—claiming that Mr. Lincoln had only married Mrs. Lincoln in the wake of losing the single, great, true, and *only* love of his life . . . a New Salem girl named Ann Rutledge."

"Was that true?" John had read Herndon's biography a few years before, and had found it a welcome relief from the mawkish torrent of hagiographical idealization of Lincoln that had deluged the country immediately after the assassination. He couldn't imagine what the real Mr. Lincoln would have said of those awful paintings of George Washington welcoming Lincoln to Heaven while Liberty herself held a halo of stars over the Emancipator's neatly brushed hair.

On the other hand, he reflected, Mary Todd Lincoln would have bought every print of those she could get her hands on.

"That he loved Ann Rutledge?" Lizabet gazed for a moment into her tea, as if the truth might be divined in its slow-settling leaves. "I think he did. That she was the only woman he ever loved with the whole of his heart? No. Did you ever see them together? Mr. and Mrs. Lincoln?"

John nodded, remembering again those two disparate figures, silhouetted in the twilight.

"I don't think anyone ever knew the whole of Mr. Lincoln's heart," said Lizabet slowly. "I never met Mr. Herndon, but Mrs. Lincoln loathed the man—in the whole time he was Lincoln's law partner she'd never have him in her house. It isn't surprising he couldn't imagine that his friend would or could really love her. But whatever Mr. Lincoln felt about Miss Rutledge when he was twenty-five, he loved Mary. For all her faults, he told a visitor once—I forget who—that 'my wife is as handsome as when she was a girl and I a poor nobody.' He fell in love with her then, he said, and had never fallen out."

"Did you ever see her again," asked John, "after that trip to New York? After your book came out?"

Lizabet set her tea down, and folded her hands. Older and grayer, thought John, but still with that rock-strong calm that had struck him first in the provision tent at Fort Barker, all those years ago. That same patient affection for her volatile friend. "After I read the book—my book, I mean—and saw what they'd done with my story, I wrote her asking forgiveness. I don't know if she ever got my letter. She may have been taken up with Robert's preparations for marriage—I'm pleased to say his young Miss Harlan, the daughter of the Senator from Iowa, stayed faithful to him even when he ceased to be the President's son and became just a law clerk in Chicago. And after that, of course, Mrs. Lincoln left the country. I never saw her again."

Chapter Fifty-Seven

Bellevue July 1875

"We've been all over this before, Mother." Under his heavy fair mustache, Robert's mouth was starting to pinch up. "Dr. Patterson says that you need rest, and you certainly wouldn't get rest living with Aunt Elizabeth."

Mary immediately lowered her shoulders and cast down her eyes, an old trick of her belle days that she'd remembered. She couldn't think when she'd stopped doing it, but knew she hadn't done it in years. "Of course you're right, Robert," she made herself say, in a tone of contrition she was far from feeling. Betsey would have been proud of her. "It's been many years since your aunt and I have seen eye-to-eye, if we ever did. But Elizabeth still is my sister. And time heals many wounds. It would be a blessing and a comfort if I could at least write to her."

She tucked her chin and raised her eyes to his, hoping she looked as timid and hopeful as she had when she'd been trying to wheedle a new gown out of her father. Much as it scorched her with humiliation to realize it, she had to admit that John Wilamet was probably right about the medicine. Since she'd cut herself down to two watered spoonfuls a day—come headaches, hell, or high water—she'd found that in between feeling anxiety and depression, she was thinking much more clearly. The memories of her younger days were bringing not only pain and regret, but the awareness of how she'd manipulated gentlemen to get what she wanted.

Like permission to write letters.

She could just hear Mammy Sally's voice, *Now, child, you know you catch more flies with honey than you do with vinegar....*

"Very well." Mollified, Robert reached across the space between her sofa and his chair, to take her hands. "I know what a comfort it is to you, to write to *responsible* friends who have your best interests at heart—who know not to excite you with trifles. I'll speak to Dr. Patterson before I leave."

But Mary made sure to follow Robert to the carriage, and, when he simply started out the door, ducked her head into Dr. Patterson's office to call out gaily, "Oh, Doctor, my dearest, *dearest* son has said that I might now write to my sister!" She threw all the gladness of which she was capable into her voice, and Robert, instead of looking annoyed, merely smiled indulgently. "Whoever had a more thoughtful and generous son?"

You treacherous, unnatural blackguard, I will thwart you if I can.

"My mother seems to be so well recovered, I don't see the harm in it for her to write to her sister Elizabeth Edwards in Springfield," said Robert. "And to . . . Who else would you like to write to, Mother? Perhaps Mrs. Conkling? Or Mrs. Wheelock?"

She nodded with an expression of joy, though she had had no contact with either of her former Springfield friends since the bitter quarrel over the Lincoln Monument and didn't want any. The things those wicked traitors had said! But one didn't waste possible opportunities that might be needed later.

After two months in Bellevue she knew better than to suggest permission to write to any of the Spiritualist friends who'd given her such understanding support.

After Robert got into the Patterson carriage to be taken to the train-station, Mary went to gather a handful of stationery, an inkwell, and an envelope from the desk in the parlor: "I want to write my sister a nice *long* letter," she explained, beaming at Mrs. Patterson as the doctor's wife came in from the garden. "We have so much to catch up on! It's true we've been estranged for many years, but Elizabeth raised me, you know, and in so many ways stood as a mother to me. I hope and pray that she will at least let bygones be bygones, and be my friend again."

Her heart was pounding as she sat in the gloomy parlor,

conscious of every person passing through the room. When John Wilamet—just returned from his trip to New York— came in and asked if she were well, she nearly jumped out of her chair with guilt. But she folded her hands in a most natural way over the letter, and asked after his trip: "Did you speak to the nerve-doctor that you said you wished to consult there? Was the result as you hoped?"

The minute the young man's back was turned she slipped two more envelopes from the desk into her skirt pocket.

And, the next time the parlor was empty, two more.

She folded the five written sheets, in her jagged, closely crossed handwriting, sealed them in an envelope, and addressed it to Elizabeth. "Could you ride with me to the post-office?" she asked Mrs. Patterson, when that lady returned to the parlor. "It's such a lovely afternoon, now that it's growing cooler. Perhaps Blanche would like to bear us company?"

Gratified, Mrs. Patterson fetched Miss Blanche from her room. The simpleminded girl's face was bright with pleasure at the prospect of a drive into town. And indeed, though Mary's heart hammered as if she were back at Rose Hill hiding copies of *The Liberator* under her mattress again, she found the sultry evening air pleasantly sweet.

Mrs. Patterson—as Mary had hoped—remained in the carriage with Blanche. Mary tripped up the Post Office steps, and once inside that gloomy little lobby pulled the four stolen envelopes from her pocket and broke the seal on Elizabeth's letter.

She left only one sheet—the one actually to Elizabeth—in that envelope. Working fast, she addressed three others to the most politically prominent men whose addresses she could remember, and the fourth to Myra Bradwell. It took most of her little money to post them. . . .

"Dear, they must test those postal clerks for slowness," she laughed, as she hurried, panting a little, down the steps to the carriage. *"What, she sold a single stamp in under five minutes?"* Her voice flexed to mock an imaginary inspector's outrage. *"No job for her!"*

And Blanche crowed with laughter.

In the carriage riding back to Bellevue, Mary was hard put to keep from trembling, had to fight the waves of agitation that welled almost sickeningly behind her sternum. *I'll never get to sleep tonight,* she thought. *Surely this justifies another little teaspoonful. . . .*

She thrust the thought from her mind, barricading the mental door with the image of the self-satisfied expression on Robert's face.

One of them has to come, she thought desperately. *One of them has to help me; has to bring a real doctor here to testify to my sanity.*

And when he, she, or they did, Mary realized, the game would be up, as the children would say. Patterson would be furious. This was "will to insanity" with a vengeance. He might lock her up in earnest—he would certainly consult with Robert. What legal rights, exactly, *did* Robert have over her? As a convicted lunatic, Mary knew that she no longer had any rights at all. *The madwoman's family may do with her as they think best. . . .*

And anger flooded her, almost swamping, for a moment, her terror. Rage at the Pattersons—despite her gay chuckles at Mrs. Patterson's tale of some petty victory over the laundress—blind fury at Robert.

At her father.

At God, for ripping Lincoln from her and leaving her to face all this alone.

She took a deep breath, and looked away, over the side of the carriage, at the pleasant white-painted shops, the blue shade of elm-trees, that made up Batavia's small downtown along Union Street. *I can't let her see me tremble. I can't let her see my tears.*

Tears of bitterness and rage.

One of them has to answer. The men—General Farnsworth and the others—she put no trust in. She never had known a man who hadn't betrayed her. She realized the next moment that that statement included Lincoln, but didn't change it in her mind. She knew it was illogical, but she could no longer pretend that she didn't feel it: deep anger at him, that he was gone.

But Myra would come.

Myra who had come to her in the most terrible hour—save only for the nightmare of Ford's Theater—in her life.

WHEN JUDGE DAVIS FINALLY DISTRIBUTED LINCOLN'S ESTATE in November of 1868—and it still rankled with Mary that Lincoln had never bothered to make a will, for in that case instead of the legal one-third she'd probably have inherited everything, enough to keep house on—she began making arrangements to go to Europe. Robert came over to the Clifton House, where she and Tad were living, and put his foot down firmly. "You will not take my brother to live like a Gypsy in a succession of cheap German watering-places. He needs a proper education and he can get no better one than here in the United States."

"Tad is my son!" Mary put her arm around the skinny fifteen-year-old's shoulders, pulled him to her with a fierce grip. "He is all that I have left to me, since *you* have chosen to make your home apart from us!"

She almost spit the words at him, and Robert's lips tightened. The Clifton House, though respectable bordering on genteel, was, when you came right down to it, a boarding hotel, and the two rooms she had occupied there since the previous March were the cheapest and dreariest in the place. Like every boardinghouse room she had ever occupied, they were jammed with trunks, boxes, and chests of her possessions—with packages of newer purchases piled higgledy-piggledy on top—and this increased their stuffy gloom. When first they'd come to Chicago three years before, Robert, then twenty-two, had elected to get his own rooms rather than share crowded quarters with his mother and Tad.

She'd never quite forgiven him for that, either. Financially it would have made better sense for the three of them to remain together, instead of dividing the small income that Davis had paid them yearly from the estate.

"Don' worry about me, Bob." Tad's voice was just beginning to break. It would be light, as Lincoln's had been. "Last I heard, there were schools in Europe." And he grinned, bringing an answering smile from his older brother.

Three years in Chicago had altered Tad drastically from the restless hellion he'd been in Springfield and in Washington. At Robert's insistence, Tad had been sent to a number of elocution teachers, and as a result could speak and be understood by even those outside his immediate family. Perhaps because of this—or perhaps because of the terrible changes after his father's murder—much of Tad's wildness and anger had dissipated. He attended school regularly now, and had begun to catch up with the boys who were so far ahead of him. He had Lincoln's gray eyes, and coarse black hair. From beneath the softness of childhood, craggy familiar features were beginning to take shape.

Mary supposed that Tad would have learned more quickly still, had he been sent to boarding schools. But without her boy—without wondering when he'd be home that day, and what he'd been up to—her life was nearly unbearable, and she'd turned away from several that Robert had urged her to investigate.

Robert's mouth thinned to an ungiving line. "I forbid it."

Mary, her face beginning to pinken with anger, retorted, "Pooh! It's my money now, and I shall do with it as I please. You only want me to stay so you can borrow my money and get in on Judge Davis's real-estate schemes."

And Robert, stonily silent, made no reply.

The distribution of Lincoln's estate had freed Robert, too, from having to live solely on his earnings as a newly fledged attorney. That November he was making preparations of his own, to purchase a home on Wabash Avenue—in a considerably better neighborhood than Mary's now-rented house on West Washington, she reflected resentfully—and to marry Miss Harlan. In an atmosphere of chilly tension he took the train to Washington and formally proposed: the wedding was set to take place in Washington at the end of September. Mary and Tad would depart two weeks later on the *City of Baltimore.*

When Mary had left Washington, workmen were tearing down the last of the black draperies from the White House windows, left from Lincoln's funeral.

She and Tad stayed in Baltimore. She never ventured from her hotel room. She hated this city that had plotted Lincoln's murder before he'd ever arrived in Washington, but she did not think she could bear more than a necessary few hours in the capital itself. They took the train to Washington only on the morning of the wedding, Mary heavily veiled in black and fortified with Indian Bitters and Ma-Sol-Pa Herbal Infusion and leaning on Tad's arm. "Don't leave me, Taddie," she whispered, clinging to his elbow as they mounted the steps of James Harlan's rented town house, as she saw the moving host of beautifully dressed Cabinet members, Senators, family friends. "Stay right beside me every minute and don't leave me." Though almost six months had passed since Lizabet Keckley's infamous book had appeared, and over a year since Herndon's lectures on Ann Rutledge, she felt every glance, every whisper, as if they were burning coals being applied to her flesh.

Her veils were the only armor she had, her only means of keeping the curious at bay. Like a black opaque cloud amid the puffs and bows, satins and silks, fashionable pale pinks and blues, Mary spoke her briefest greetings to even her old friends like Ginny Fox, Jacob Seligman, and Charles Sumner. She wished only to be gone.

Robert's bride—also named Mary—was a fair, pretty, and ethereal-looking young lady in a gown of white satin, everything a well-bred young lady should be. She smiled sweetly as Mary took her hands.

"*How* I have always wished for a daughter! My dearest child, I have *so longed* to see this day!"

Other than that she recalled little of the reception, beyond an overwhelming sense of dread that she assuaged by a couple of surreptitious sips of Indian Bitters in the cloakroom. For nearly a year after Willie's death she had found herself unable to bear large groups of people, particularly strangers or semi-strangers. After Lincoln's death, the presence of anyone other than a few well-loved and well-known friends (which had included, alas, the *perfidious* Lizabet Keckley!) had filled her with a sense of nearly unendurable alienation from the whole race of humankind. She longed for comfort, yet when Charles Sumner came over to speak with her she found herself on the verge of tears.

Few others approached her. In three years, the cast of characters had changed in Washington, and people had heard enough about her battles with Congress over a pension.

She spent much of the ensuing three weeks in Baltimore in her room at Barnum's Hotel, emerging only for carriage-rides with Tad, or to visit a medium named Gibson, whom Cranston Laurie had recommended. Mr. Lincoln was present in the room, Gibson assured her, and disavowed any knowledge of any Ann or Nan Rutledge. There was no such person there with him in the Summer Land, nor had he known anyone of that name in his life.

But he did not materialize, nor speak to her. The night before the *City of Baltimore* was to depart she dreamed of him, in the dappled sunlight of the Land that lay beyond Death's Veil—dreamed of him walking hand in hand with the red-haired girl that Herndon had so eloquently described.

CHAPTER FIFTY-EIGHT

TAD AND MARY WERE IN EUROPE FOR THREE YEARS.

And if she could not be happy—and she could never be happy, she reminded herself every morning when she woke, when her Beloved One had left her here alone—at least she felt at peace.

She took a room in the Hotel Angleterre in Frankfurt, intending to stay for a week. Jacob Seligman had highly recommended Dr. Hohagen's Institute on the nearby Kettenhofstrasse, and it was here that she enrolled Tad. But from the first night, the friendly and un-curious camaraderie of the English and American expatriates who lived at the Angleterre drew her in and made her welcome. These were people who had not been raised with the rending questions of abolition, who had not gone through the horror of war firsthand; people who had the distance to be objective, and the pleasant good manners that Mary craved.

She stayed another week, and then another. After all, she could not abandon Tad. On his single day off each week they would take a carriage along the zigzag paths of the park where the city ramparts had once stood, or cross the bridge to Sachsenhausen and so to the green and peaceful country-side beyond. Sometimes they would take the train to Weimar, to see Goethe's house, or take a little excursion steamer down to the Rhine at Mainz.

And when Tad was in school, to her surprise she found the days were not as long as she'd feared they'd be. The little group of Americans in the hotel called on her and invited her to visit their rooms, and her circle of acquaintance widened to their American and British friends in other parts of the lit-tle city. They were a lively group, the ladies always willing to get up excursions or day-trips to the spas of Wiesbaden or Marienbad, or to hold afternoon teas. Even after Mary removed to the less expensive Hotel Holland she retained a number of friendships, and would go to the Angleterre's reading-room to keep up on the American papers.

This was partly to follow how her old friends and enemies were doing—Charles Sumner was still in the Senate, and Mr. Seward, recovered from the wounds he'd received on the night of Lincoln's assassination, still ruled as Secretary of State. *(What a pity it was not he who had died that Terrible Night, if one must have died and the other be spared. . . !)*

And partly, to follow what was being done about her battle for her pension in Congress.

During her first summer in Frankfurt, she went for several weeks to Scotland, where she visited dear old Dr. Smith from Springfield, whom Lincoln had made a consul. On her return she encountered, of all people, Sally Orne from Philadelphia at one of Frankfurt's summer spas. It was good beyond words to talk American politics again with someone who truly knew Washington, who'd been through the War. The two women chattered non-stop for several nights—completely disturbing everyone in the hotel-rooms around them—and the upshot was that Sally, who'd been traveling in luxury with maid, valet, and daughter in tow, agreed to put pressure on all her political connections once again to have Mary's pension put through.

"It's a disgrace—an absolute disgrace!" Sally cried, looking around the dreary fifth-floor chamber of the Holland, carpetless and crammed nearly to the ceiling with trunks and packages. "Your husband gave his life for his country, as surely as any of those poor soldiers did! You deserve no less than they!"

In point of fact—as the American newspapers shortly pointed out in a succession of blistering satires on Mrs. Lincoln's requests for her pension bill to be passed by Congress—the average widow's pension was about twelve dollars a month, and Mary was asking for three thousand a year. "My case is entirely different!" she insisted to Sally, when that lady and her entourage were preparing to continue on their journey to Italy. "Those young men, though I say not a word in their disparagement, at least had respite and sleep at night—which my poor husband *never* had, in four years of war. And moreover I was very much his partner in his task of governing, for which I deserve at least some credit!"

Between shopping for Robert's Mary—Young Mary, she called her—and for Baby Mamie, who was born in the fall of 1869—and writing streams of letters to Congressmen, Mary felt herself revive.

The American consul, Mr. Murphy, called now and then with his son (*To keep an eye on me for that traitor Seward, I'll wager*). There were several American and British gentlemen—not to mention several more of the Seligman banking clan—who would squire her for Sunday drives. Her special friends from her days at the Angleterre, the Mason family, still included her in their circle as if she were an aunt. Two British ladies from the Angleterre—Mrs. Culver and Mrs. Blaine—were Spiritualists, and it was a relief to Mary to be able to talk of matters concerning those who had passed over the Veil. Twice they held séances, and though no spirits materialized or spoke on those occasions, she left them filled with a deep sense of calm.

More than anything else, she wished Lincoln could be here with her, to see the cathedral in its old-fashioned square, to pass the dark rocks where the Rhine maidens were said to guard their hidden gold.

"But he is here, don't you see?" asked Mrs. Culver, setting her teacup down—Mary had invited her up to her room at the Holland to take tea and look at the needlework vests, the blue- and white-silk wrapper, that she'd bought for Robert's bride. "When a soul passes to the Other Side, they can come and go here as they please, like the angels of God. When you walk down the Zeil looking into shop windows, be sure that he's there at your side. When you stand in the cathedral and look at the arches and tombs and stained glass, you are sharing that moment with him, as you would have in life had God so willed."

"Of course," responded Mary instantly, "of course. But knowing that somehow, sometimes ... just isn't the same."

But it was close to that, when she was with Tad.

At Dr. Hohagen's, her son seemed to recover some of his old mischievousness, tempered now by European manners and the school's firm discipline. As the weeks and months floated by she was amazed and delighted at Tad's growth from boy to young man. He was beginning to read on his own, and talk to her like a man, and not a child, about the things he read. He took the lead in their excursions, escorting her to places his friends at school had said were *wunderbar*! From speaking only a few halting words in German— inculcated with enormous labor by his teachers in Chicago— Tad rapidly became far more fluent than Mary.

He was a comfort to her, too, when the American newspapers published indignant criticisms of her campaign for a pension. "They don't know you, Mama," he soothed, when she met him in front of the school brandishing the latest, a sarcastic account of how a fictitious German count was courting her in the hopes of getting hold of Old Abe's pension. "They're politicians. They'll say anything—they have to."

A later article pointed out that $27,000,000—nearly ten percent of the nation's budget—went to pensions already, and the widows of officers were content with $600 a year, not $3000: "poor needy widows who do not already have fifty or sixty thousand dollars." Another excoriated her for taking Lincoln's "brilliant boy" to be educated away from "American institutions." "They must have been talking to Robert," fumed Mary. As 1869 wore into 1870, the debates—duly sent on to her by Sally Orne—became more vicious, dredging up yet again the old rumors of her extravagance, her Confederate sympathies, and speculation of improper conduct with, of all people, the charming Commissioner Wood who had escorted her on her first buying-trip to New York.

Her headaches worsened. She wrote reams of angry letters to Sally, to her Spiritualist friend Ella Slapater in Pennsylvania, to Robert and his wife. Her neuralgia grew more frequent and painful as well, tightening the damaged muscles of neck and back and starting yet another round of sleepless nights, Godfrey's Cordial, Indian Bitters, and as many visits to spas as she could afford. Now fifty-two, she began to have night sweats, and her copious monthlies became erratic, until she never knew when they'd begin or how long they'd last. Sometimes it felt to her, looking back on those days, that she was angry all the time.

But in a curious way the anger made her feel alive. She was fighting, she told herself, for Tad's future—fighting, too, to be recognized for who she was: Abraham Lincoln's widow. The wife of the Great Emancipator. The woman who had stood by him through the terrible years of the War, the woman he had married—and loved, no matter what Billy Herndon said.

Just as she had been the legal keeper of his body, in the fight with the Monument Association, so now she was the keeper of his memory, and his son. She still lived for him, though he had gone on to the Summer Land; still managed his affairs in this world.

They could not deny her without denying him.

In July of 1870, President Grant signed the bill giving her a pension of $3,000 a year. This more than doubled her income, added to the $2,500 interest from the bonds Lincoln had left her and the rent from the Chicago and Springfield houses. She celebrated by buying pillowcases, a watch, and an evening dress for Young Mary, and several tiny bracelets for little Mamie, and by taking Tad, who was on summer holiday, to Austria.

In Austria, word reached them that France and Germany had gone to war. On their return to Frankfurt, the consul,

Mr. Murphy, called on Mary at the Hotel Holland and warned her to leave—the French troops were advancing on Frankfurt, which controlled Germany's railroads as Atlanta had the South's. While she was still trying to organize her trunks and luggage—really, it was *astonishing* how much she'd accumulated in her travels!—one of the generals she'd met in Washington, little Phil Sheridan, who stood shorter even than she did—called to reiterate the warning.

"I didn't flee from Washington in the face of the rebels, sir, and I will not flee from here like a scared rabbit," she retorted. "The French were always America's allies. Surely they will offer us no harm." And she pulled Tad, who'd come that day to help her pack and label, closer to her side.

"No, ma'am," replied Sheridan, who Mary had always thought looked like a schoolboy dressed up in a false mustache. "But they may shell the town. And if there's a siege, I wouldn't like to see the pair of you caught up in it."

Tad's gray eyes brightened, and he said, "It wouldn't be our first." He was, Mary guessed, within an ace of asking Sheridan if he could go along with him and observe the upcoming battle, so she caught his hand and said crisply,

"We shall be quite all right, General. Thank you for your concern."

As it was, before she managed to arrange transport for all of her many trunks and crates, the battle was fought and over, and the German forces under Von Moltke—with Sheridan along as an advisor—were besieging Paris. Still, the pleasant little city of Frankfurt had become an army town, as Washington had been in the War. Too many soldiers, too many horses, skyrocketing prices of food and very few of her friends remaining. She would wake in the night hearing marching men in the street, and for an agonized moment she would be back in Washington, with torchlight flaring on the ceiling of her bedroom, and Lincoln's steps padding restlessly down the hall to confer in his nightshirt with Generals on the landing.

It was time to go home.

THEY LEFT FRANKFURT IN THE FALL OF 1870, FOR ENGLAND, intending to remain there—as Mary had intended to stay at the Hotel Angleterre—only a few weeks. But the journey, and the tensions of travel, were hard on Mary. Her headaches multiplied and she broke her journey at Leamington, which like Marienbad and Baden-Baden was a hydrotherapy spa. The solicitousness of the doctors there, and the friendliness of the English, soothed her. Though Tad was wild to return to America, she lingered in Leamington until nearly Christmas, then moved up to London—again, for a short time only, she said—to visit her Hotel Angleterre friend Mrs. Culver.

She and Tad remained in London for another three months, at a boardinghouse in Woburn Square. With Mrs. Culver, she attended a number of séances among the Bloomsbury Spiritualists, but winter in London depressed her and brought on migraines and back pain again, accompanied now by the agonizing hot flushes of the change of life. The doctors—she could afford the best, these days—suggested a warmer climate for the remainder of the winter. Tad offered to take ship for America after Christmas, and she could follow after a few months of recuperation in Italy. But the idea of the young man facing the dangers of winter travel on the Atlantic brought her nightmares.

"I could not bear it, if anything were to happen to you, my darling!" she sobbed. "I could not bear it! Oh, do not do this to your mother!"

That said, she paid Tad's board in Woburn Square for the next few months, engaged a tutor for him, hired a nurse-companion for herself, and went to Italy. For two months she dreamed in the sun, marveled at the *David* in Florence and the multi-towered Cathedral in Milan. It was in many ways a dream come true. Growing up in that overcrowded house in Lexington, she had longed to see these things, to walk in the glittering Italian sunlight where Byron, Shelley, and Napoleon had walked.

Would she have chosen this path here, she wondered, had she been told through what griefs and pain it would lead?

She didn't know. But she got out more, and made a few friends. Her consumption of Female Elixir and Godfrey's Cordial declined as her health improved—it was in any case nearly as difficult to find them in Italy as it had been in Germany.

She and Tad returned to New York on the *Russia* in May. The weather was rainy and nearly as cold as winter. Tad caught a cold, and Mary nursed him assiduously in their tiny stateroom. In the dining-room, she had her own private table where she sat, heavily veiled in black; on the first evening of the voyage she was greeted by, of all people, little General Sheridan, on his way back from the German war.

She had never known the young commander well during the War, though since he was Grant's protégé she mistrusted him. But Sheridan was politely deferential to her, and on their arrival in New York he included her and Tad in his party that went ashore on the pilot's launch and avoided the three-day quarantine.

Thus, in contrast to their quiet leavetaking, she and Tad came ashore to bands playing "Hail to the Chief," and to re-porters crowding around—mostly around General Sheridan, to be sure. But one at least came up to her, and asked—impertinently, she thought—how she liked to be home.

"I like it very much," replied Mary, and glanced back at the launch from which she had just stepped, bobbing in the dirty water at the dock. "So far."

CHAPTER FIFTY-NINE

IT SOMETIMES SEEMED TO MARY, WHEN SHE LOOKED BACK ON her return to America, that the *Russia* had taken a wrong turn somewhere and had deposited her and Tad on another planet, some world other than the one they had fled three years before.

Everything was different. While Europe had dreamed in its centuries-old walls of stone and forest, in three years America had barged ahead into an era of railroad barons, monumental industries, get-rich-quick schemes, patent stoves, patent vegetable-slicers, bustle dresses, and bicycles, a world inconceivably distant from the America of the War.

Still further off, like the landscape of a dream, lay the world she remembered so clearly, the world of Lexington in the Thirties, of shady alleys and Mammy Sally's kitchen, and flirting with young gentlemen under the locust-trees of Rose Hill. No one even talked about that vanished world anymore.

No one talked about slavery, either, or secession, or the rights of the states. It was as if it had all never happened. They spoke instead of money, of Progress, of new places to go and new things to see and buy: of railroads, homesteads in the West, and the foolishness of women who campaigned for the vote.

It was a Yankee world now, and Mary despised it.

New York—where she stayed for some weeks—had spread north on both sides of the Park, and its crowded Irish slums had been invaded by Jews and Italians following the demands of factory labor. There were more buildings, higher buildings, walling the narrow streets into grim canyons of red and gray. When she returned to Chicago the noise of the railroads and the stench of the stockyards and packing-plants hung over the brand-new mansions and the filthy "patches" like a pall.

The thought of surrendering the rent from the house on West Washington made her shudder. Her years of scrimping and saving, of the humiliation of seeing her Springfield friends ride by in their carriages, and later of fighting for the pension and for her inheritance, had left their mark. Everything cost so much more these days. She couldn't imagine running a household, even on $5,500 a year. With her ill-health and the migraine agonies of menopause, she calculated she would have to hire at least two servants, maybe three.

"That's quite sensible of you, Mother," Robert said, escorting her from the train to the rank of taxis and casting a resigned eye back at the army of black porters with the trunks. "You know there will always be a place for you in my home."

"Always" lasted all of about a month.

Robert's house on Wabash Avenue was modest, with three bedrooms, a neat double-parlor, and a tiny yard behind it. Tad—still suffering from fits of coughing that he could not seem to shake off—had a small room in the attic, Mary the guest room adjoining little Mamie's nursery. Young Mary, who in her letters had expressed such graceful gratitude for her mother-in-law's advice about child-rearing, pregnancy, fashion, and household economy, proved to be, in person and out of her white satin wedding-gown, nervous and, her mother-in-law judged, hypocritical. Mary recognized the embroidered pillowcases she had sent from Germany, but saw no trace of the several lovely plaid dresses she'd sent, nor of the needlework waistcoats she'd bought for Robert.

"Surely I thought you must have loved them," she commented over supper that first night. "They are all the fashion, you know."

She saw the glance between Robert and his wife: "They

were so handsome, I thought I would save them for best," said Robert after a moment. "As a young lawyer just starting out, I've found it pays to dress more plainly."

"And that 'falling-leaf' color was the most elegant to be had." Mary heard the defensiveness in her tone, as she turned to Young Mary. "I spent quite fifty dollars on the silk, plus the cost of having Mr. Popp make it up. He sewed for the Princess of Prussia, you know, so the style must have been impeccable."

"It was," said her daughter-in-law quickly, setting down the soup tureen. The cook had laid out the dishes on the black walnut sideboard which badly cramped the inadequate dining-room—there didn't seem to be a maid to serve. "Only the dress didn't quite fit...."

"And you haven't altered it in *three years*?" Mary recoiled a little from the soup: "Dear heavens, that isn't *beef*, is it? In weather like *this*? Beef makes me quite bilious...."

Robert took the streetcar north into the city every morning, to the offices he shared with his law partner, Mr. Scammon. Tad, though he was still coughing and in Mary's opinion should have remained in his bed, went with him. The Lincolns kept no carriage, not even a buggy: "It's a ridiculous way of economizing, if that's what you're trying to do," protested Mary, after two days of being trapped on Wabash Avenue watching her daughter-in-law assist the maid-of-all-work in dusting knickknacks and sweeping floors. The thought of being stared at on the streetcars filled her with horror. "When Mr. Lincoln and I were first married, I assure you, we were *quite* poor, but we *always* had a buggy."

"I rejoice to hear it." An edge like glass glinted in Young Mary's voice. "As it happens, just now we do not."

"And it's equally ridiculous that you should be doing a servant's work," added Mary. "Surely for the money you're paying that cook, and that scullery-girl, you could get a couple of good parlormaids who know their way around the kitchen and can take care of Mamie as well. Why, times cannot have changed so much that you can't get a good girl for a dollar a week...."

Robert's wife, Mary found in very short order, was also given to fits of tears. She suspected, and said to Robert after four days, that Young Mary drank as well. Within the first week they had two vicious arguments about the housekeeping money, steely-voiced on the younger woman's side, with Mary flying into rages which escalated into tears and migraines that laid her up for two days. Her daughter-in-law and Tad were forced to care for her with tisanes, quiet, drawn shades, and Nervine. Robert looked haggard when he came into her room to hear her side of it—through the closed door Mary had already heard Young Mary's twisted accounts of the quarrels the moment the young man walked into the house—and began to stay later and later at the office, as his father had before him.

As they all did, thought Mary in a fury of resentment. *Anytime any man doesn't want to deal with his women at home, he disappears into "business," and gives that shopworn excuse, "I'm the one who supports the household, I have the right to a little peace...."*

At the end of a month came the worst quarrel of all, which ended in a screaming-match between the two women. In a way this gratified Mary, for generally Young Mary grew maddeningly quiet and spoke her unforgivable accusations in a calm voice that made her want to box her ears, as she had on many occasions done with her sister Ann when they were small.

When Robert came home—late—Mary was lying in her room with a pounding headache and the sick swoony dizziness that so often followed the taking of several tablespoons of Godfrey's Cordial. She'd heard Young Mary moving about her room for some time. It was full summer, breathlessly hot and unnaturally dry. The air felt electric, pressing her skull like a tightening iron band. Far off, thunder growled over the lake, only a few streets from Wabash Avenue on the other side of the small park. Her old sense of panic filled her, of the frightening approach of some crushing doom.

She heard Robert say, "Darling, what is this?" and Young Mary's voice, quiet as ice.

"It's a suitcase, Robert. And that smaller one is for Mamie. Your mother apparently doesn't consider me an adequate keeper of the household on your income...."

I did not say that! thought Mary furiously. *Not in those words, anyway... And in any case, it's true!*

"...though I can't imagine where she gets her advice from, having no experience herself in running a household within a budget. She saw fit to dismiss Mrs. Phelps today—for theft, she said, to her face...."

"Darling..."

"So I thought it best, if she thinks she can make a better home for you than I can, to get out of her way and let her do so."

"Darling!" Robert sounded desperate. *As well he should,* thought Mary resentfully, *if he's been married for three years to that whining little harpy.* "You must remember, my mother isn't quite right in her head."

It was the first time she had heard Robert say it out loud, though in the newspaper flurry that had surrounded what was now called the Old Clothes Scandal the awful word *insane* had been applied to her before—and reportedly, by Robert. Anger blazed up in her like matchwood and she staggered from her bed, catching her balance on the bedpost.

"She says things she doesn't mean. Since my father's death..."

"I have heard, every single, solitary day, about your father's death," replied Young Mary in a voice like overwound violin-strings. *"And* how your mother has suffered since. And with all due respect to Mr. Booth, I would not at all be surprised if I heard that your father had *arranged* to have himself shot."

"That is *infamous!*" Mary shoved open the bedroom door and strode down the stairs. "How *dare* you say such things?"

Sitting among the pillows of the blue plush sofa, tiny Mamie—not quite two—began to wail, staring anxiously from face to face in the gas-lit gloom. Tad, who'd retreated up the attic stairs at the beginning of the quarrel, came down looking as if he might start crying, too.

"I have a good mind to leave this house," cried Mary, "and to take that poor little child away with me, to get her out of the care of an ungrateful, whining, drunken—"

"Mother!" Robert thundered, as Young Mary's eyes overflowed with silent tears and she reached down for the handle of the small wicker suitcase at her feet.

The rest of the evening passed in a blur, first of shouted words that Mary barely remembered on waking the next morning, then of migraine agony and lurid dreams. It was nearly noon, and suffocatingly hot, when Tad came into her room and said gently, "If you meant what you said last night about finding a place to board, maybe I could take the street-car into town and make some inquiries? Mr. Scammon and Mr. Trumbull both speak very highly of Clifton House these days."

She had no recollection whatsoever of saying she would look for a place to board, but felt too exhausted and sick to argue. She said, "Lyman Trumbull is a lying blackguard," forgetting entirely that Trumbull had been one of her chief supporters during the pension fight and at one time—many years ago in Springfield—her favored beau. She remembered only how he had refused to step aside during the Senate race in 1856, and had taken the office from Lincoln.

If he had not done so, she thought, tears flowing down at the memory of Lincoln—alive, breathing, present, caring for her—among that little band of supporters in the parlor of the Jackson Street house, *how much would have been different....* "And his wife is a treacherous hussy. Any place that he would speak well of must be a den of infamy."

Two days later, she and Tad moved into the Clifton House.

They occupied two modest rooms on the second floor,

and at Mary's insistence ate their meals in Tad's room rather than going down to join the other boarders in the dining-room. Tad's cold was worse, and she occupied herself in making poultices, steaming herbs, coaxing him to take a wide variety of patent medicines. When he was better, he said, he would begin clerking with Robert at Scammon's.

But he didn't get better.

Within two weeks he was so seriously ill that she sent for one of the best pediatricians in Chicago, though Tad was eighteen. "It isn't consumption, sir," she insisted, as Dr. Smith tapped the young man's thin chest. "It *cannot* be consumption, for I have taken very good care of his health. He is Abraham Lincoln's son!"

Tad, who like Robert had for the past ten years heard himself described in terms of his father, winced slightly and traded a sleepy glance with the doctor; Mary had found that Godfrey's Cordial not only eased her own neuralgia well, but was also a marvelous suppressant of coughs.

At Dr. Smith's suggestion, Tad was propped up to sleep, so that he could breathe better. First this was done with pillows on his bed, and then, as the suffocating dry heat of July deepened and his breathing labored harder against the edema in his lungs, in a specially made chair with a rod across the front, to prop him up when he fell asleep. Even a shaky stagger down the hall to the toilets exhausted him, and Mary carried chamber pots, made medicines, rubbed eucalyptus balm on her son's chest and back. Her world—so wide and pleasant only a few months ago in Italy—shrank to a single curtained room, a single other person, a young man whose face was so like Lincoln's that sometimes in her dreams she wasn't sure whether she was dreaming of one or the other.

Then the sound of his gasping would jolt her out of her catnap sleep, the thready weak voice—identical to Lincoln's in its lightness—would gasp, "Mama..."

Robert would come, after a day of writing briefs and taking depositions, and stay with Tad until long after dark, so that she could sleep. It was Robert who told her that Tad was dying, Robert who insisted that she face the fact and not exhaust his brother with selfish demands that he live on for her. "You know nothing about it!" she sobbed, "nothing...!"

And when Robert finally departed, at close to midnight when the final summer twilights had faded out of the burning sky, she would cling to Tad's hands and whisper frantically, "Don't leave me, Taddie. Don't leave your mother all alone! I shall die if you leave me, I shall die...,"

Toward the end she didn't even know whether he heard, though sometimes tears would flow down from his closed eyes.

CHAPTER SIXTY

TAD DIED ON THE FIFTEENTH OF JULY, 1871. THE ANNIVERSARY of her father's death. A haggard Robert arranged the funeral at his home and afterwards took his brother's body down to Springfield. Tad was put to rest in the tomb in Oak Ridge Cemetery, with Willie, Eddie, and Lincoln himself. On his return Robert departed for one of the new resorts in the Western mountains, to seek rest of his own. He left his mother at his house: "Surely you will find it more comfortable than boarding, at this time." Young Mary and Mamie had gone back to Iowa, to care for Young Mary's ailing mother.

At any other time Mary would have responded to the news of Ann Harlan's illness with cynical suspicion that her daughter-in-law was simply fleeing from her, and thus deliberately depriving her of her only grandchild. At another time she might have queried why Robert didn't take refuge with his wife.

But she felt literally stunned, as she had in the days immediately following her carriage accident. Her memories of the days between July and October were little more than a blur of grief and cloudy dreams. Myra Bradwell came to the house daily, mercifully bustling and efficient, though she had, of all things, begun publication of a small legal newspaper and frequently brought long ink-smelling galley-sheets to read while Mary lay in numb silence on the sofa in her room.

Mary later was sure that it was Myra who made certain that one or the other of the Spiritualists came to sit with her, to make her meals that she did not eat, to sometimes brush her hair.

Mary did remember the heat, for like an obscene

afterthought it exacerbated the tormenting itches of her female parts that had begun with Tad's birth. Twice or three times thunder tolled over the lake, but no rain fell. The river sank, and the stench of it crept over the city. The shacks and sheds filled with cow-fodder and firewood, the wooden sidewalks and the wood-block streets, all cracked and bleached in the slow-baking heat. The curtained guest-room at Robert's house was like a dark oven, where she would lie in silence, or talk in feverish broken sobs to whoever happened to be with her that day.

Ella Slapater, a woman she had met through the New York Spiritualists surrounding Lord Colchester, came from Pennsylvania to be with her for almost a month. Robert, when he returned from Colorado, got that tight, wooden expression in his face whenever Ella spoke of the comforts of speech with the dead, but forbore to argue the matter. On an evening when Robert was out—Young Mary still remaining in Iowa with her mother—Mary, Ella, and Myra formed a Circle in the parlor, sang a hymn, and asked the spirits to come for their comfort.

If any came, they did not speak, and Mary went to bed uncomforted.

Mostly, in those autumn days, she felt nothing but a sense of vast confusion.

Tad was gone. Robert had been stolen from her by that treacherous hussy of a wife.

She could not even imagine where she would live now, or how. The whole of her life stretched before her, a bleak process of going someplace and waiting to die. Elizabeth sent a letter inviting her to live with her in Springfield—Mary tore it up and threw the pieces on the floor.

Never would she go and live again as a pensioner in Ninian's house.

September turned to an October equally hot, equally dry. Desiccating winds breathed over the prairies from the southwest, like the exhalation of Hell.

ON SATURDAY, OCTOBER 8, A FIRE BROKE OUT ON THE WEST Side. The insurance men called that neighborhood "The Red Flash": a crowded maze of wooden shanties, lumber-yards, saloons, and cheap frame houses. By morning the blaze had been put out, the stink of smoke adding to the city's multifarious stenches and the grit of it burning Mary's eyes when Myra came by, to have coffee with her on Sunday morning while Robert was at church. Mary spent the day in her room, while hot prairie winds rose and scoured the town.

"Will you come out with me for a walk in Lake Park?" asked Robert, when he brought her lunch.

The thought of the crowds in that small patch of greenery on a blistering Sunday like this one made her shudder. "Robert, how *can* you?"

"You cannot sit in a room for the rest of your life, Mother. You must come out sometime."

She merely covered her face with her hands, and turned away. "You don't understand! You cannot understand! If you did you would not demand that I ... I *parade* myself for people to stare at ...!"

When Robert said nothing she swung around to face him again, and noticed that he had left off wearing his black arm-band for Tad. His father, she recalled resentfully, had never worn anything but black, from the day of Willie's death to the day of his own.

Robert's mouth had a compressed look to it under his mustache, as if asking himself how he could put up with this woman. Mary lowered her head to her hands as a wave of heat swept over her, nauseating her. "Leave me alone. You want me out of here, so that little coward wife of yours will dare to come back!"

He did not reply. It was only later, after Mary heard the outer door of the house close, that it came to her that in fact he did understand—*as well as Robert could understand anything,* she thought. He had lost his last brother, as she had lost, now, all but one of her sons.

The howl of the wind and the smell of smoke followed her into her dreams. She dreamed of fire, of the smell of smoke—of the screaming of her sons' ponies as they burned to death in their stable—and waking, pulled her wrapper close around her and stumbled to the window. But she saw nothing, only the flat sleeping faces of the houses on the other side of Wabash Avenue.

Going downstairs she found Robert by the front door, still dressed, even to his jacket.

After his father's habit of walking around in his shirt-sleeves—and barefoot half the time—Mary had worked all her life to inculcate proper dress and manners in her son, whom she had never seen half-dressed in all the years since he'd left Springfield for Exeter School in 1859. Looking out, she saw red staining the northern sky.

"It appears to be on the other side of the river." Robert's voice was calm. "The river should hold it." Far off, a dim clamor came to her, too indistinct to be clearly identified but terrifying, a whisper of primal chaos. "There's nothing to worry about, Mother. Go back to bed."

She obeyed, but lay awake. Even at this hour the heat was oppressive, parched wind screaming around the house-eaves. When at last she slept, her dreams were dreams of horror. The cities of the plain were burning, as they had in the Bible—she saw them, two of them, with flames a hundred feet high dyeing the lake-waters blood-red. Then she found herself in the streets of those burning cities, whose wooden sidewalks, crisped with the summer's heat, roared up into lines of fire. The streets themselves burned, for they'd been paved with blocks of wood, and wooden fences carried the blaze as wires carry an electrical charge. Men and women poured along the streets, dragging wheelbarrows or trunks, or clinging to the reins of terrified wagon-horses whose heads were wrapped in coats to keep them from running mad in the blaze.

But the fire roared up before them, blocking their way. There was nowhere to flee to.

She woke, trembling, to the sound of shouting, of wagons passing in the street. Running to the window she saw the fugitives from her dream: men and women, young girls or what looked like shoeshine boys and newsboys, pushing handcarts, dragging boxes, carrying sheets or tablecloths filled with papers or books or silverware. Dozens of them, hundreds of them, running and stumbling as they looked back over their shoulders up Wabash Avenue. She leaned out the window and shouted, "What is it? What's happening?" but no one paid her heed. She threw a shawl around her nightdress and ran downstairs with streaming hair, out the front door to the sidewalk. "What is it?"

She grabbed a man's arm, a fat laborer whose jowls were blue with beard. He yanked free of her grip and ran on, as if he feared the Devil would catch him if he halted for so much as a second.

And Mary, looking back, gasped in horror, for it was true.

The Devil was right behind them.

Flames poured skyward far up the street. Smoke made a pall over the city, so that it was impossible to tell what time it was, or whether dawn had come. Flame lay across Wabash Avenue, many blocks away yet but sweeping closer, driven by the wind, devouring the wooden houses, the wood-framed brick buildings, the woodpiles and coal-heaps and sheds full of fodder and kindling and lamp-oil and firewood. Flames rose above the buildings, licking in the rolling masses of smoke, a wall of flame stretching west and east, like the front of an advancing army. From that wall the wind threw showers of sparks, igniting everything they touched. The noise of it was a fearful bellowing, unlike anything she had heard in waking life—it dwarfed the roaring of the White House stable fire to a titter.

And above it rose the clamor of those who fled.

"It's jumped the river," gasped an older man, like Mary in his nightclothes and barefoot, his garment black with soot.

"They're lootin' and robbin'—the firefighters can't stop it, it's got away from 'em, it's too big...."

From the crowd a woman with streaming hair screamed, "Davey!" and the man ran to her, the two of them instantly swallowed up in the mob.

Mary turned back to the house, crying, "Bobby! Bobby!" and ran up the stairs to her son's room. She expected to find him dressing, putting his legal papers into a valise, readying himself in his usual methodical way to make an escape.

But he was gone. She stood in the doorway of the bedroom, shocked numb, staring at the neatly made bed—Myra used to joke that Robert made his bed *before* he got up—the empty clothes-stand.

He had left her. *He had left her!*

Mary's jaw dropped. Never in a lifetime had she thought that Robert would desert her.

In the street a woman screamed.

Mary shrieked, "Bobby!" and ran downstairs again, to the dining-room, the parlor, the study.

But he was indeed gone.

Panic gripped her.

She tore upstairs, breathless and gasping at the exertion, pulled on a skirt over her nightdress and buttoned the highest button she could without a corset, stuffed her feet without stockings into shoes. Clutching the shawl about her she fled down the stairs, ran into the street. People were shoving and thrusting, shouting and coughing in the smoke. The air was filled now with flying cinders; through the oily clouds she could see that it was daylight, early morning, grilling hot.

She thought she was fighting her way along Mitchell Street toward the lake but wasn't sure. The neighborhood was unfamiliar to her, and the street was jammed with carriages, struggling figures, horses, cows, and dogs running wild in panic.

A fat woman carrying a cage full of finches slammed into her, screamed as she struggled past. Two little girls in nightdresses darted by, barefoot and clinging to each other's hands.

Smoke blinded her; she sprang out of the way of a man in a policeman's uniform who was riding a wild-eyed horse down the center of the street, then she turned and ran blindly....

The fire was ahead of her. The fire was roaring toward her, vomiting sparks that lit on the wooden roofs of the buildings all around her, kindling them like touchwood. She had missed her way and was among the shops on State Street, near the Michigan & Southern depot. Mingled with the crowd of terrified fugitives were others shoving and struggling in the other direction, their barrows filled, not with household possessions, but with crates of liquor and bolts of gleaming silk.

Someone shoved her aside, throwing her down against the hot bricks of a wall. Three rough-looking young men smashed a shop window beside her, rushed in and emerged moments later with their hands full of necklaces and earrings that flashed in the light of the advancing flames. Across the street a man and a woman, roaring drunk and shrieking obscenities, dove into a deserted tavern and came out with bottles of whiskey in their hands. Others—they looked like laborers, men wielding clubs while their girlfriends hauled a barrow—stopped those who fled and wrested away from them whatever looked valuable, silver candlesticks, their jewelry boxes. The pavement glittered with shattered mirrors, trampled underfoot, with a smashed rummage of bedding, crockery, a broken guitar. Looking down, she saw the street was littered with paper money, trampled in with all the rest.

A spark caught her skirt, setting the black crape instantly ablaze. She screamed, struck at it with her hands, and ran on again with the scorched hole in the fabric still smoking. The mob carried her along, she could not struggle against it. She tripped, and found herself next to the corpse of a man sprawled in front of his looted store, his skull cracked open and bright blood leaking into the gutter.

The shattering roar of an explosion split the darkness;

someone yelled, "They're blowin' up the buildin' for a fire-break!" Gunfire cracked; she couldn't tell from where or why. A girl ran past her shrieking, long blond hair blazing—one of the ruffians by a looted wine-store hurled a glass of liquor over her, and she ignited like a blue-burning torch.

Flame was all around them. She screamed "Abraham!" hoping against hope—against all logic and sense—that he'd come striding out of the smoke and the blaze of this hell, that he'd take care of her, lead her to safety....

They reached the lake, hundreds, thousands crowding into Lake Park, running across the rails of the Illinois Central line to the water's edge. Fire towered in the blackened sky, north and west of them; ash and cinders rained down. Children screamed in terror and pain; women slapped wildly at their burning hair. The heat was infernal, as if the fire reached out to devour them, and Mary, stumbling with hundreds of others into the waters of the lake, thought desperately, *What if the fire comes to the lakeshore? What if the trees in the park, the grass that's been drying to tinder all these weeks, catch fire as well? What then? Will we all be driven deeper into the water, to drown?*

The world shook again with explosions. She saw fragments of masonry hurled high into the sooty maelstrom overhead.

Her wet skirt dragged on her, her wet nightgown sodden on her uncorseted breasts. Men and women shoved against her, pushing further into the water as they were pushed by terrified newcomers. The weeping voices, the frantic cries rose on all sides as women tried to find their husbands or children, as men shouted for their families. The sounds were like the lamentations of Hell.

Someone fell against her—a boy of nine or ten, carrying a baby. Mary caught him as he stumbled. Without her grasp, he and the sobbing infant would have simply slipped below the surface, for his soot-black face was blank with shock. The lake-water that came up to her hips came nearly to his shoulders and others were thrusting them both out deeper. She took the baby from his arms, cradled it against her breast with one arm, and steadied him with the other.

"Are you all right?" she asked, and the boy stared up at her with uncomprehending eyes. *"Bist du verletzen?"* she asked, guessing from his fair hair he might be one of the immigrant children from the filthy patches back of the stockyards, and he clung to her skirt and sobbed, *"Wo ist Mutti?"*

Where's Mama?

Mary tightened her arm around the boy, for it was a question she'd asked all her life, and had never gotten a satisfactory answer.

For hours they stood there in the water, the crowds pushing tighter and tighter around them. Mary felt that she would faint, but knew that to faint was to drown. No one would catch her, no one would hold her up. Through the jostling rank of shoulders between herself and the shore, she could catch glimpses now and then of the park and the trees in the sickly glow of daylight.

The trees were yellow and limp, but still unburned. The lawns swarmed with huddled shapes.

Beyond them, the first houses—the handsome houses of the lakeshore—stood deserted but intact. Now and then gangs of looters pulled carts up to them, helped themselves to rugs, clothing, jewelry in full view of the onlookers, and went unhurriedly on their way.

Gradually, the red wall of flame diminished. Smoke continued to pour skyward, but Mary heard—like the tramp of the New York regiment down Washington's silent streets—the voices of men, the clatter of fire-wagons. They, too, were soldiers. It wasn't just her memory. She saw flashes of Union blue coats. Northward the flames still scraped the sky.

Feeling she could stand no longer, she began slowly, stumblingly, to push her way ashore. The crowding in the water wasn't so bad now. Others were creeping out of the lake, falling to their knees on the wet cinders between the railroad and the park's edge. The baby in her arms began to cry again, weakly, and she felt a surge of joy—at least the poor little thing wasn't dead—and the boy beside her helped her to kneel on the land. She could still see nothing but a wilderness of knees, a sodden wilderness of slumped shapes under the hellish yellow glare of smoke-stained day, but someone said the fire was burning itself out at the Rock Island and Chicago tracks.

She held the whimpering infant in her arms and relayed the information to the child's brother in German. "My mother is lost," said the boy in the same language, and she said reassuringly,

"The Army will find her for you, once they get the fire out."

He put his head on her thigh and slept.

They remained there, through the whole of a hellish day. Exhausted, starving, and thirsty, Mary dozed sometimes, and in her dreams she wandered through the contraband camps around Washington during the War, where shattered men and women huddled, who had left their old lives behind. Now and then explosions sounded across the city, and the sullen clouds rained burning cinders.

Dark fell, and a few hours later real rain began. Those few who had remained—Mary couldn't imagine how—standing in the lake-water throughout the eternity of that hideous day finally waded ashore and collapsed on the mud and cinders. Someone took the baby from her arms—she didn't know who, or whether the little German boy ever found his Mutti. Men and women started coming through the darkness of the park bearing lanterns. Some of the men wore the blue uniforms of Union soldiers, and the women were of that indefatigable breed who had throughout the War made up the Sanitary Committees and the Volunteer Nurses associations.

By that time she was too shattered to be much aware of what was going on around her, staring before her in exhausted shock, numb with fatigue and the horror of the things she had seen. But she heard a familiar voice cry, "Mary!" and looking up, saw Myra Bradwell standing a few feet away, a lantern and a sack of blankets over her shoulder.

By the shock in her eyes it was clear she'd barely recognized her, wet, disheveled, covered with mud and soot and ash. "Good God—*Mary*!"

And Mary held out her arms to her friend, and burst into tears like a child.

CHAPTER SIXTY ONE

Bellevue July 1875

MYRA BRADWELL.

Mary didn't think she'd ever been more grateful to see anyone in her life—not even Mr. Lincoln when he'd met her again after eighteen months in Bessie Francis's parlor—as she was to see that tall, sturdy figure stride to her through the smoke-black sodden limbo on Lake Michigan's edge.

Lincoln—though it was years since Mary had admitted this, even to herself—was just as likely to forget he was supposed to fetch the boys from school, or that he'd said he'd get fish from the market on his way home, or that Frances and Dr. Wallace were coming to supper (though, she had noticed, he never forgot appointments with his political cronies—that was just how his mind worked).

Myra, however, was like a rock.

From the window of her bedroom at Bellevue Mary watched the driveway under the sharp summer sunlight, praying that Myra would come.

ROBERT, MYRA HAD TOLD HER, THAT RAINY MONDAY NIGHT as she guided Mary back to the little house on Wabash Avenue, had heard at about daybreak Monday morning that the fire had jumped the river, and was moving south swiftly through downtown. Without waking his mother, he had set out on foot up Wabash Avenue for his office on Lake Street—no horse could be induced to go in the direction of the fire. The roof of the Crosby Opera House, in which he had his office, was already in flames when he reached the place. Opening his office safe, he'd piled his father's papers into a tablecloth, and with this tied up on his back had strode out of the burning building and through the inferno of looting, flames, and dynamited firebreaks for home.

Once out of the region of the fire he had encountered the dapper John Hay, who was also living in Chicago these days. The two men had stopped for breakfast at the Terrace Row house of Charles Scammon, Robert's law partner. Robert had advised Scammon's family against evacuating their home and clearing out its furniture and treasures. It might, he warned, affect later insurance claims, and in any case he thought the fire was slowing down.

After Robert and Hay left, the Scammons cleared out their possessions anyway and by noon the house was smoking rubble.

Robert was, of course, furious with Mary for leaving the house: "You were perfectly safe the whole time!" The fire had been stopped three blocks away by General Sheridan, Mary's erstwhile traveling companion on the *Russia,* who had ordered his men to blow up every building in its path. Every tree and bush in Robert's garden had been withered by the heat.

Later she learned that her dream had been accurate. Not only Chicago had burned that night. Baked tinder-dry by the same rainless autumn and fanned by the same scorching prairie winds, the town of Peshtigo, Wisconsin, across the lake—the depot for the whole of the Chicago timber trade that funneled building-wood from the northwest to the woodless Great Plains—had burned, too. Its destruction, unlike Chicago's, was complete.

LEANING HER ARM ON THE BARRED WINDOWSILL OF HER ASYlum room, Mary closed her eyes, saw again the red infinities of fire, the black curtains of smoke. Heard the noise it made—good God, that sound! Like the bellowing of an all-devouring monster. Saw a blonde girl run screaming past her with her flaming hair...saw the drunkard hurl his glass of liquor...

Nightly, for years, those scenes would replay against the lids of her shut eyes, and she would wake crying, thinking, *The city is on fire . . . !*

The city is on fire, and Bobby is gone, and I am alone. . . .

Mary opened her eyes just as Myra Bradwell and her tall husband climbed from a train-station hack and rang the bell at the iron gates at the end of the drive.

Her heart lurched, then triphammered with wild joy. *I knew it! I knew she'd come!*

Argus opened the gates, stood for a few moments talking to the pair. Myra hadn't changed much since the last time Mary had seen her—*good God, it can't be four years!* A little stouter, maybe, and she hadn't—*thank Heaven!*—started wearing "rational costume" of Turkish pantaloons and knee-length tunic as she'd been threatening then to do. Her neat dress of navy-blue chintz was perfectly plain, and being without a bustle—something Myra had steadfastly refused to wear—now put her, almost accidentally, into the very forefront of the mode.

Not, thought Mary, scrambling to her feet and calling for Gretchen, *that Myra would care.*

Myra's husband followed her up the walk, fair and bespectacled and still very English-looking in spite of half a lifetime spent in the United States. If she had not been married to Abraham Lincoln, Mary had frequently thought, she'd have liked to be married to Judge James Bradwell.

"Gretchen!" she called frantically. "Lace me up again . . . !" That morning General Farnsworth had come, making a lot of vague promises and telling her how much more rested she looked—*Of course I'm more rested, you imbecile, I've been locked up for two and a half months!* Returning to her room, she'd had Gretchen unlace her and had eaten a little lunch, meaning to remain indoors and rest. Though most of the physical pains of withdrawal from opium had abated, she still had bouts of queasiness, and without warning the darkness of depression would rise over her in smothering clouds.

"Get me dressed," she panted when her attendant entered, "at once, now. Someone has come to see me...."

YOUNG DR. PATTERSON WAS STANDING AT THE HEAD OF THE stairs when Mary, trailed by Gretchen, came hurrying down the hall. She could hear Myra's strong, clear voice below: "Couldn't I see her, Doctor, in the presence of her attendant? My only object in coming here was to see her."

"Not without a paper from her son." Patterson senior's voice from the parlor had the air of one who has reiterated the statement several times. "She may be out in a few days, Madame. Then you can see her to your heart's content."

"Is it likely that she would be," responded Myra reasonably, "if you don't even consider her well enough to receive visitors?"

Mary attempted to step past Young Doc, who put a hand on her arm. "I'm sorry, Mrs. Lincoln," he said softly. "No one is permitted to go down into the parlor this afternoon."

"That's ridiculous!" she gasped. Gretchen came up on her other side, quiet but tense. Ready for trouble. "You have no right to keep me from seeing my friends!"

"As your doctor," replied Young Doc thinly, "we have every right to keep you from doing things that will only worsen and exacerbate your condition—as you well know, Madam, in your saner moments."

Mary opened her mouth to lash out in protest, her face hot with anger. But his last sentence stopped her, as if she'd glimpsed Robert looking at her from around a corner—looking at her and waiting for yet another fragment of evidence that she was insane.

"I understood from your letters to the public that she is allowed to see her friends," Myra went on, in the voice of reasonable inquiry that Mary knew meant she had an unsheathed sword hidden behind her back.

"Well, Madame, she is no better"—Patterson's voice had an edge of impatience to it—"for meddlesome people come here to see her, calling themselves her friends, when in reality they come out of self-interest only, like that dreadful Mrs. Rayne from the *Chicago Post*."

"Doctor, please don't attribute such a motive to me!" Myra sounded as if she'd never heard of a newspaper in all her life. "I assure you my visit is only out of pure kindness to Mrs. Lincoln. She is one of my oldest friends. As you are not willing to let me see her, will you allow me to leave a note for her?"

Pressing forward—Mrs. Patterson had joined Gretchen and Young Doc in the hall and there was now no chance whatsoever of getting past them without a fuss—Mary could see Dr. Patterson's back below. He glanced at his watch, a habit he shared with Robert's lawyer friend Swett, a way of signalling that his time was far more valuable than theirs....

"There is no necessity for that, Madame. It would only disturb her mind. While she is under my care, I shall not permit her to be disturbed either by visitors or letters."

"If she is only permitted to see such persons as you choose, and is not permitted to receive letters except from such, she is virtually a prisoner, is she not?"

"No more so than other patients I have under my care." He glanced at his watch again, as if to say, *When will you take yourself out of here and stop wasting my precious instants, each more valuable than gold . . . ?*

"I quite understand," said Myra, in a cheerful voice that, Mary knew, presaged a serious skewering at some time in the future. "Doctor, it is some time until our train leaves—might my husband and I remain for a little time in your parlor, rather than sitting in the public depot?"

"Mrs. Lincoln," said Mrs. Patterson firmly, "Dr. Patterson has asked that no one be admitted to the parlor this afternoon. Now, you had one visitor this morning already, and I think we all agree that all he did was stir you up and make you uncomfortable. If your son thinks it's appropriate, you will be able to receive a visit from your friends on another occasion."

Mary made her face impassive, fighting not to burst into either tears or a tirade of abuse. *You smug hag, if you had a single friend in the entire world you would know what it means to be separated from them, when you have no one else!*

But as she had with Robert, she lowered her shoulders and her eyes and said, "Yes, of course. I quite understand."

And immediately Mrs. Patterson relaxed.

Down in the parlor, Myra was chatting with Dr. Patterson, inquiring about the difficulties of running a "rest home," as she called it, and pretending deepest fascination with the methods of "coaxing troubled minds back to sanity." All of which information, Mary was certain, was being mentally jotted down by the silent and self-effacing James. She heard Dr. Patterson say, "Mrs. Lincoln is quite a difficult case, very much troubled in her mind. As you know, she was sent here after an attempt to take her own life...."

That isn't true!

Heart pounding, Mary walked back along the hall to her room. Did Myra actually believe her to be insane? Had she come only to learn how serious her aberration actually was?

No. No, she believes me....

Does she?

Panic filled her, at the recollection of that expression of specious understanding in General Farnsworth's eyes that morning. What had that one-time abolitionist politician said to Patterson, after she had returned to her room? That she was insane but seemed sane most of the time, as Robert always said of her? That she "looked rested" as a result of her incarceration, so therefore her imprisonment ought to continue?

As Mrs. Patterson, young Doc, and Gretchen stood waiting for Mary to enter her room again, she saw John Wilamet turn the corner.

"Oh, Mr. Wilamet," purred Mary. "Perhaps before I lie down I could speak to you for a moment about..." *About what?* Her mind groped frantically for a convincing lie,

"...about that poem your dear mother recommended that I read. Mr. Tennyson's 'Lady of Shalott,' was it not?"

John faltered slightly at the mere thought of his mother reading or recommending any sort of poem whatsoever, but Mary locked eyes with him, mutely pleading with him to understand. He nodded amiably, and replied, "It was indeed," and paused. In the face of a discussion of poetry, both Pattersons and Gretchen went on their ways.

"You must go after Judge and Mrs. Bradwell when they leave the house—they're down in the parlor now—and tell them that I am not insane!" Mary whispered desperately. "That I attempted to commit suicide *after* I was tried and condemned to perpetual imprisonment as a madwoman, not before! Please, please, John, let them know the truth as you have seen it! Mrs. Bradwell is a lawyer—her husband is a judge! They will know how to undo the law that has made me a prisoner here!"

John looked down at her gravely for a moment. *If he tells me that I'm too excitable or shouldn't be "stirred up," I shall kill myself indeed....*

But he said, "And what will you do with your freedom, if they should undo the law?"

She almost cried, *I'd live!* But instead she said quietly, "That's no more your business, John, than it would have been my business to ask that of you, before my husband signed the Proclamation which set you free."

"Touché, Mrs. Lincoln. A palpable hit."

And turning with a smile, he hurried down the stairs.

JOHN WAS LOITERING WHEN DR. PATTERSON FINISHED HIS tea—and his lecture on Moral Treatment—and called for Zeus to harness the carriage, to take Judge and Mrs. Bradwell to the station. "I can drive them," he said, stepping into the parlor at precisely the right moment, as Mrs. Bradwell was shaking cake-crumbs from her skirts. "I need to stop in at Beck's Pharmacy. We're low on ipecac and salts."

"Thank you, Mr. Wilamet." Patterson smiled benignly. "Judge Bradwell—Madame—you have no objection to Mr. Wilamet driving you? Excellent . . . Mr. Wilamet is my assistant here. John, if you'd be so good as to ask at the receiving-office, we're also expecting a shipment of chloral hydrate—a very much more effective and modern inducer of sleep than laudanum," he added, addressing Myra. "We believe in a minimum of drugs here, only those that are necessary to restore the balance of the patient's mind. We have been working a great deal with sleep therapy, sleep being the greatest natural restorer that there is. . . ."

Even if you have to induce it with enough chloral hydrate to knock out a bear, thought John, as he led the way down the front steps to the carriage in the gravel drive. The previous September one of Dr. Patterson's patients, a Mrs. Harcourt, had died of "exhaustion" after an episode of mania, during which she'd been force-fed 110 grains of chloral hydrate over the course of a few hours. Patterson still sincerely believed it was the mania rather than the drug which had ended her life.

As they got in the carriage Mrs. Bradwell—whom John had met briefly during the War, though he doubted she remembered a mere member of General Ord's medical staff—said to her husband, "Well, what do you think, Judge?"

"Other than that the fellow's a self-important bore?"

Only when he'd driven through the gates and Argus had shut them behind the carriage did John draw rein, turn on the box, and say, "Please excuse me for interrupting, Judge, Mrs. Bradwell. . . ."

The older man regarded him with sharply raised brows—no Englishman of the upper classes ever quite got used to being addressed by a servant. It was as if, just for that first moment, one of the carriage-horses had spoken.

"Mrs. Lincoln begged me to speak to you—begged me to let you know that that suicide attempt of hers was after that . . . that farce of a trial. And she asked me to tell you anything you might wish to know about her condition." And, seeing—to his surprise—that Mrs. Bradwell was regarding him closely, he added, "We've met before, ma'am, briefly, during the War...."

"You were with Ord, weren't you? At Crown Point?"

"I was, ma'am."

"And you've been caring for Mrs. Lincoln while she's been here?"

"Yes, I have, ma'am." He flapped the reins, guided the team over to the shade of an elm at the side of Union Street, and drew rein again. Far off the Illinois Central whistled, but none of them paid any attention. There would be, he knew, another train in two hours.

"And do you consider Mrs. Lincoln is insane?" Mrs. Bradwell's shrewd gaze remained on his face. He had never in his life heard of a woman lawyer, although he'd encountered a couple of women doctors in his time. But he could easily believe this stout, motherly-looking woman was one. There was something in her gaze that he wouldn't have wanted to try lying to.

"I consider Mrs. Lincoln is crazy," he replied, paraphrasing Lizabet Keckley's quite accurate summation. "I don't think anybody who knows her would argue that. But insane?"

"In the newspaper accounts of her trial the doctors say she was delusional." Judge Bradwell spoke for the first time. He had a big man's deep, mellow voice, with a trace of English accent in his vowels and r's.

"I suspect they were hallucinations rather than delusions, sir," answered John. "I believe that was the fault of some of the medicines she was taking, medicines that she has been weaned off of now.... She has certainly not had delusions of any kind since she's been at Bellevue. Dr. Patterson doesn't agree with my diagnosis. He says she needs rest...which I think she does. I think she's needed rest for a long time."

"Do you think she would be able to deal with life in the world?" asked Mrs. Bradwell quietly. "I'm very fond of Mary—Mrs. Lincoln—but I'm not blind to her faults. And I don't think anyone would argue that she was not doing a particularly good job of dealing with life in the world in the years between her son's death, and that last disastrous trip to Florida. I don't think there was one of her friends who did not fear for her sanity and her health."

CHAPTER SIXTY-TWO

~

FOUR YEARS.

Mary stood by her window, looking out at the iron palings, the elm-shaded fragment of Union Avenue, where the carriage had passed. Just the sight of Myra's sturdy blue-clad form—of James's reassuring bulk—brought back to her how long it had been since she'd seen them.

Brought back the makeshift Rock Island depot, a shelter of crude lumber hastily erected amid the scorched ruins of downtown Chicago, visible like a blackened battlefield through the building's open sides. Brought back the stench of ashes, and memories that she could not put out of her mind.

How long she'd remained at Robert's house after the Fire, she no longer recalled. She thought it was several weeks.

Conditions weren't good in Chicago that autumn. Ninety thousand had lost their homes, and every surviving house was jammed. Boxcar-loads of food were being shipped in from all over the country but prices were sky-high. The city fathers in charge of such things ruled that the wealthy who had been left homeless be given first priority in the assignment of shelter, since the poor were more used to hardship.

Winter winds blew cold across Lake Michigan.

With nowhere in Chicago left to move to—and with Robert not about to offer continued residence under the same roof with himself and his still-in-Iowa bride—Mary wrote to Spiritualist friends in St. Charles, not far from Batavia, asking for recommendations of good boarding hotels near the Spiritualist congregation that was forming in that town. Anything was better than the nightmare stench of smoke and ashes that still hung over Chicago's ruins.

The community of Spiritualists in St. Charles had welcomed her. In the flickering candlelight of their darkened parlors she had sought, again and again, to hear Tad's voice, or Lincoln's, or to catch a glimpse of Willie's glimmering form coming toward her out of the gloom with outstretched hands. But it seemed to her she had lost all capacity or desire to make friends with the living.

Thus, the next three years were years of travel: Boston, the resort spas of Wisconsin, upstate New York, where Spiritualism and so many other odd movements had their birth. For a time she went to Canada, to another Spiritualist camp on the edge of Lake St. Catherine. Tad's inheritance, equally divided with Robert, made it possible for her to hire a nurse-companion. She found these women for the most part as grasping, irresponsible, and impossible to deal with as she'd long ago found the Portuguese and Irish girls of Springfield, and she went through them almost as quickly. Though she had hated slavery, she found herself longing for the good-natured reliability of Mammy Sally or Granny Parker's old Prudence.... Were there no such people left in the world anymore?

Even when she had a companion to look after her, she was alone.

"I DON'T KNOW IF YOU CAN UNDERSTAND," SAID MYRA Bradwell softly, "the...*familial* quality of the Spiritualists. Not the charlatans, or the fakes like that absurd 'spirit photographer' in Boston—the one who 'miraculously' produced a photograph of her with the ghostly shape of Mr. Lincoln standing behind her. She went to him incognito, but of course he'd seen a dozen likenesses of Mrs. Lincoln and knew her the moment she walked in his door. She bored everyone to distraction with the story of how Lincoln had projected his image on the photographic plate without the photographer knowing. Poor Mary. She had the maddening quality of never letting anyone's grief be more important or deeper than her own. . . ."

She frowned a little, her sharp hazel eyes losing some of their focus, as if she looked again, from her seat in the Patterson carriage, into the dim recesses of a parlor lit only by candle-flame. As if she listened for spectral knocks, or saw a name being spelled out, letter by letter, by a planchette.

Then she glanced up at John again and her eyes were bright.

"Everyone who comes to Spiritualism does so because they're in grief—a grief that's too deep for them to endure with the 'holy resignation' that unimaginative preachers recommend. So whatever her faults—or theirs—Mary sought other people of like experience. To her—as to me—it was a blessing beyond compare, to be able to talk to others who have passed over that same terrible road."

John recalled the sweetly reasonable Olivia Hill, whose steadfast Spiritualism was accompanied by an equally steadfast conviction that a squadron of demons was invisibly pursuing her and had to be destroyed at all costs. Remembered, too, the framed picture garlanded with flowers in Lizabet Keckley's sitting-room.

He asked, "Do you really speak to the dead?"

Would Lucy hear, if I called her name?

Myra smiled thinly. "I think the real question is, Do I really believe that the dead have spoken to me? Is it less reasonable to speak to the dead than it is to speak to an invisible Entity which created everything which is? At least we know who the dead were. We know they existed, once upon a time. Yet people—mostly men—present company excepted, Judge—claim every day that the theoretical Architect of the Universe takes time off from wars and famines to give them specific instructions about how people should behave, on whom they should love and how they should dress if they wish to please Him.

"Yes," she said firmly. "To answer your question, Mr. Wilamet, I believe that my daughter Myra has communicated with me, both through rappings, and through the movement of a pen held in a medium's hand. I do not believe that *all* communications purported to be from her were in fact from her. I certainly don't believe some of the ghostly white figures drifting around the parlors of such gentlemen as Lord Colchester were anything but Colchester's confederates draped in cheesecloth washed in a dilute phosphorus solution. But then my faith that little Myra lives on the Other Side, and loves me, is stronger than poor Mary's. She wants so desperately to believe. And she had—has—nothing else."

Two women strolled by, artificial flowers bobbing on their stylish bonnets. They glanced idly at the carriage, and John knew he would have to deposit the Bradwells at the station and return to Bellevue soon. He wasn't sure, but he thought Patterson was asking a little too frequently about his dealings with Mrs. Lincoln, and not because the doctor was interested in the progress of her case.

"Do you mean to help her?" he asked.

"I mean to see her, if I can." Grimness glinted in Myra Bradwell's voice. "If, as I suspect, she's been railroaded into that place, as so many women are railroaded for being Spiritualists if they happen also to be inconvenient to their menfolks—yes, I mean to help her. But an insanity verdict cannot be overturned for a year in this state. It will do her little good to be released from one asylum if she's only going to return to her son's house and her son's care...though it would serve him right," she added with a half-smile, "if it comes to that. Would you be willing to go down to Springfield with me tomorrow, to consult with Mrs. Lincoln's sister Mrs. Edwards? To see if we can convince her to open her house to her sister, as she offered to some years ago?"

"My day off is Wednesday. But nobody will question it if I trade it for Friday. I'll go down with you then."

"Excellent. Thank you. Could you meet me at the Galena Depot at noon, or as soon after noon as there is a train from Batavia? They must have shopper's trains in the morning."

"I'll be there. As to your getting in to see Mrs. Lincoln, that may be more difficult. Mr. Lincoln has said many times that his mother must be kept from Spiritualists, since they only feed her mania, as he puts it. As you found out, he's arranged with Dr. Patterson—"

"Robert knows perfectly well that I was a friend of his father's while Robert was still a schoolboy—or nearly so." A combative light flickered in Myra's eye. "As for Dr. Patterson, he'll find I'm not easily gotten rid of with two cups of tea, a lecture on Moral Treatment, and a piece of yesterday's cake."

CHAPTER SIXTY-THREE

Springfield July 1875

JOHN WILAMET TOOK THE FIRST TRAIN INTO CHICAGO THAT Friday morning, and by two in the afternoon was stepping off, with Mrs. Bradwell, in the depot in Springfield within a stone's throw of the handsome sandstone State House with its graceful dome.

Though he'd lived in Chicago for almost six years, John had never visited the state capital. After the insane scramble of people rushing through the lakeside city's streets, the jack-hammer noise of the trains, the jostle of wagons, drays, carriages, the overwhelming stench of the yards, Springfield seemed rustic under the crushing summer heat. As they walked along Second Street toward the Edwards residence, the hotels and boardinghouses around the State House—hushed and half-deserted during the summer's Legislative recess—quickly gave way to handsome frame residences surrounded by gardens, where cats blinked sleepily from under hedges of jessamine and yew.

"Did Mr. Lincoln live in one of these houses?" He tried to picture the man he'd seen riding through the burned streets of Richmond—the tall form silhouetted in the evening moonlight on the steamboat's deck—walking these board sidewalks and mud-wallow crossings, as Mrs. Lincoln had described, a marketing-basket in his hand.

Myra Bradwell shook her head. "They lived over on Eighth Street. In a place much less fine than any of these— just a simple frame house. No better than most, though Mary did furnish it up fine. I'll take you by there and show it to you. It's still rented out, and getting shabby these days. Most of their furniture—and Mr. Lincoln's books—were up in Chicago, at a museum I think, or some Exhibit Hall, and burned in the Fire. Mary told me when they first lived here you could walk a block from their house and be on the prairie. But it's much the same as it was."

Mrs. Ninian Edwards was taller than her sister and didn't resemble her in the slightest. With her long jaw and firm mouth, she more closely resembled Mary's descriptions of her fearsome Granny Parker. But about her clung the old-fashioned formality, the steely strength, of a Southern lady. And John found that like many Southern ladies, she was far friendlier toward him as a black man than women like Mrs. Patterson. The doctor's wife seemed to regard him as an archetypal Representative of his Race rather than an individual man.

If she believed in her heart—and she probably did—that he couldn't be trusted with certain tasks and was of a species wholly foreign to herself, at least Elizabeth Edwards was friendly, and believed him capable of being a doctor.

"I'm glad to hear she's doing better," she said, bringing in tea—for the three of them, a tribute to her fine-graded evaluation of social niceties. Had Myra not been there, John guessed, there would have been no tea. "I was most distressed when Robert wrote to me saying Mary's mind had broken down at last under the griefs she had suffered. And God knows, the sorrows she's seen would be enough to drive anyone raving mad. Your Dr. Patterson must be a very wise soul."

"He is," agreed John. He had spoken to Myra of Mary's misuse of medicines because he knew from years on the South Side that it was plain stupid to lie to your lawyer and because, as a professional, he trusted Myra Bradwell's professional ethics. But it wasn't anything Mrs. Edwards had to know. Even had he not been bound by his position of trust, Mary's shame and humiliation about being a habitual opium-taker would have been enough to keep him silent.

There was gossip enough about her.

"The problem is that now that she is better, Robert still wishes her to remain at Bellevue," said Myra. "I think you'll agree with me, Mrs. Edwards, that even if she wished to remain there—which she emphatically does not—a lunatic asylum is scarcely an appropriate place for a lady, however eccentric, of good family."

Elizabeth's breath blew out in a sigh and she made a gesture that in anyone less well-bred would have been a dramatic up-flinging of hands. "Precisely what I told Robert! My sister is—and always has been—an eccentric, particularly since poor Mr. Lincoln's death. But my nephew has never had the patience—or, I am sorry to say, the sympathy—to deal with her. All his life she has been an embarrassment to him, and when I heard of her incarceration the first thing that went through my mind was to wonder whether she had in truth crossed over the line into insanity, or whether Robert had convinced himself she had because he didn't want her to be out running about the world in a position to embarrass him still further by her antics. Particularly if he aspires to go into politics. But then of course I read in the newspaper that she had attempted to take her own life. There is no further danger of that now, is there?"

"No," said John. "But she is ... most unhappy at Bellevue, deprived as she is of her liberty. As any sane person would be."

"It is a pity," interposed Myra, "that she felt herself unable to come and live with you here four years ago, where she would have the quiet and regularity of life that she needs."

Elizabeth sighed again, and shook her head. "I thought it was, though I confess ... Have you ever tried to live under the same roof as my sister, Mrs. Bradwell?" The affection in her crooked smile—suddenly extraordinarily like Mary's—was mixed with wry wisdom and a lifetime of exasperation.

She went on, "But a few years ago was ... not a good time for Mary to come to Springfield. I would have preferred to see her do so, but 1872 was the year that oaf Billy Herndon chose to publish *his* biography of Mr. Lincoln—as if the world needed another one—and Mary was incensed. And since my sister is seldom incensed quietly, there was the usual shrieking-contest in the newspapers, with accusations of drunkenness on one side and insanity on the other, and everyone taking sides—mostly taking Mr. Herndon's side, because of that ridiculous quarrel over the Monument. All the wartime scandals were raked into the open again, and after all was said and done Mary felt that she could not come to the only family that she has."

"Did you read Mr. Herndon's book?" asked John curiously.

"Read it? I was in it. Billy came here—sober, for once— and asked a great many impertinent questions about my sister and Mr. Lincoln. And while I'm delighted that someone finally pointed out to the nation that Mr. Lincoln put his pants on one leg at a time like everyone else, Billy does tend to take straws and make trees of them simply because he likes the look of trees.

"The true problem was, I think," she continued, "that both Billy and my sister want to be the Keeper of the Flame, the True Authority on the National Martyr. The one that everyone else has to come to. The same way they both wanted to be first in his affection while he lived. But while Billy wanted to portray Mr. Lincoln as a man among men, Mary wanted to purge out all those unpleasant human details that showed him to be less than incomparably perfect—and that, incidentally, might reflect badly on her. And really, when it came to Billy claiming that Lincoln's mother was illegitimate—which true or false is taking realism a little far— or that Lincoln was an Unbeliever, I can understand Mary's point, though I do believe berating him like a fishwife in public print was not the best way to deal with the problem.

"The shouting seems to have died down now, though." She set her teacup down with a precise click. "I think that were Mary to come live in Springfield, she could do so without undue animosity."

"WHAT DO YOU THINK?" ASKED MYRA, AS SHE AND JOHN took their seats once again in the train for Chicago late that afternoon. At no time was train travel in summertime enjoy-able, for smoke and cinders blew in through the windows every time anyone opened them in an effort to mitigate the stifling heat, and the Illinois Central, like other lines, tended to relegate its oldest rolling stock to duty as "colored" cars. The hard wooden seats and battered paneling gave off a smell of ground-in dirt, tobacco smoke, and the sweetish reek of tobacco expectorate; the window-sashes were either broken or loosened and rattled like castanets with every jolt of the wheels; and the floors were clearly not swept as frequently as elsewhere on the train.

In the other seats, mothers hushed sleepy children, and men talked of prospects for work, in Springfield and points west, in quiet, beaten voices. Some glanced curiously at the well-dressed white woman in her striped summer skirts and parasol, but no one commented, and the boy who came through selling peanuts and bottled lemonade gave her a friendly grin when she bought some of his wares.

"About Sister Elizabeth? Allow me." John gestured Myra to put away her coin-purse, and handed the boy a silver quarter. The boy dug in his pocket for the nickel change from two bags of peanuts and two bottles of lemonade, and John waved it aside. With another smile the boy opened the bottles for them in a great fizz of carbonation, and went on his way wiping his hands on his apron.

"About Mary." Myra settled back on the scarred old seat. "In your opinion, is she well enough to be released into her sister's home?"

"Yes. Although whether Dr. Patterson would agree with me—"

"You leave Dr. Patterson to me." She sounded like a very businesslike knight referring to a very old and toothless dragon. "I must see her myself to be sure, of course, before I commit myself to any course of action. Or are you one of those who believe that such matters are best judged by physicians?"

John was silent for a time, cradling the lemonade bottle in

his gloved hands. Thinking about Mary Lincoln. About the fragile and melancholic Mrs. Hill. About women he'd known in Jacksonville, women who'd been put there years before by husbands or fathers who found them troublesome, sowers of discord, constantly angry for no reason that those husbands and fathers thought justified...

Slowly he said, "No. Dr. Patterson doesn't agree with the law in this state that a jury trial is necessary—he's been working for years to have it overturned, to permit commitment on the signatures of two physicians. But in my years of working with the insane, I've met far more than two physicians I wouldn't want as judges of *my* sanity. The more I deal with the insane—the more I realize I just don't know. I don't think anyone knows."

He fell quiet again, gazing out the window at the green-gold wheat-fields streaming past the windows, baking in the lengthening light of the evening sun. Birds flew up along the track, their calls drowned by the hammering of the wheels.

Peace and silence and stillness. The "rest" that Patterson kept advocating for the women under his charge, because their "systems" could not take the stress and noise of the cities...much as, before the War, John had heard it argued by his master's friends that to free black men and women from the joys of sixteen-hours-a-day agricultural labor would be no kindness.

He remembered that Abraham Lincoln hadn't liked agricultural labor sixteen hours a day, either, and had gotten out of that business as quickly as he could.

And for none of them—neither himself, nor Mary, nor Mr. Lincoln—had there been any going back.

"Do you know"—Myra Bradwell's voice broke into his thoughts—"how the law in Illinois came to be made, that a woman had to be tried by a jury to be committed insane, rather than simply locked up on the testimony of her husband?"

"Because of Mrs. Elizabeth Packard," John answered.

"When I worked at the state asylum in Jacksonville I met guards who'd known her."

At the time that the Reverend Theophilus Packard had had his wife kidnapped and locked away for disagreeing with his doctrine of the total depravity of mankind, John had still been picking tobacco-leaves and wondering what would happen to his mother and sisters if his master sold him to one of the slave-dealers going down to New Orleans.

"At least four physicians," said Myra, nodding, "testified that Mrs. Packard was insane, on such grounds as claiming to be older than her actual age, being an abolitionist, and refusing to shake hands with one of those examining doctors when he left. I read the transcripts. She was also a Spiritualist, and had the temerity to argue, in public, with her husband's religious opinions. It doesn't take much for a woman to be adjudged insane. Most doctors believe that women are more or less permanently insane anyway."

He opened his mouth to protest at this generalization and then closed it, remembering Dr. Patterson's strictures on women's mental and emotional derangements due to "the cycles of the female system"—i.e., menarche, menstruation, pregnancy, lactation, periods of sexual abstinence, menopause, and post-menopausal "drying of the womb." He'd wondered frequently what Mrs. Patterson thought of her husband's convictions.

Did she simply accept her husband's word as law, like a good wife should?

"Before the War," Myra went on, "like Mrs. Packard, I was an abolitionist. I broke with the mainstream of abolitionists when they decided to concentrate all their energies on freedom for the slaves, rather than freedom for *all* those whose lives and liberty can be disposed of at the whim of others. Though I rejoiced when Mr. Lincoln got up the courage and resolution—and the political timing, I might add—to liberate the slaves, I think that a great opportunity was missed. In many ways we're still trying to save a people, soul by soul. And in the course of the battle, I hear many of the same arguments.

Only in this case the whole nation is what the South was—and every man is a slaveholder who fears the loss of what he."

The train rocked as it slewed around a curve. At the front of the car in which they sat a child cried, fretful in the heat. Its mother murmured, "We be home soon, Sugarbelle, I get you some water then. We got no money for lemonade."

John got to his feet, and walked down the narrow aisle, catching his balance on the ends of the seats. He handed the mother the half-bottle of warm lemonade. She looked up at him, torn between the pride that spurns charity, and her child's thirst: John said gravely, "I didn't spit in it or nuthin'," and she laughed, her child laughing with her.

"You say thank you to the nice man, Sugarbelle."

Sugarbelle hid her face in her mother's skirts, giggling.

When John returned to his seat he told Myra, "Dr. Patterson spends Saturdays in town, seeing clients—he has an office on Washington Street. He leaves on Friday afternoons. If you came by the last train on Friday, I'd let you in. You could speak to Mrs. Lincoln in her room, or out in the rose garden without him watching over your shoulder."

Myra was silent for a time, her face unreadable, save for the look of dispassionate calculation in her eyes. Like Cassy, John thought, when his sister was figuring out how to get money or food for the family when there simply wasn't any money or food to be got. Then her attention seemed to return to the here and now, and she said, "Thank you, Mr. Wilamet. That should do very nicely."

"From there..." He shook his head. "Even if Mrs. Edwards were to invite her sister to come live with her, we still have to contend with Mr. Lincoln. As Mrs. Lincoln's legal conservator, he has the right to dictate what Dr. Patterson does. And Dr. Patterson will obey him—he needs every patient he can get at Bellevue these days."

"Does he?" Myra raised her eyebrows. "How many women are there?"

"About twenty. More than a quarter of the rooms at Bellevue are empty. It's been that way since the banks crashed

in '73. Of the families who are wealthy enough to afford
Patterson's prices, many more would sooner hire an attendant for Granny or Auntie and send her to Europe, rather
than admit to society that a family member is in an asylum."

"Hmn." Myra sniffed, and sipped her lemonade. "Rather
than admit to the parents of potential sons- and daughters-
in-law that there's insanity in the family, I daresay." She held
the bottle away from her as the train rocked. "Yet he's supposed to give excellent care."

"He does," agreed John. "But it isn't cheap. And I know
he's recommended incarceration to more than one of the
gentlemen who bring their wives to him for treatment for
their nerves. He isn't venal," he added earnestly, seeing the
calculating look return. "He would never recommend a
treatment that he thought was harmful. But he's like my master, back at Blue Hill Plantation in Halifax County, Virginia,
where I was born. He honestly believes that what he's doing
is best. I think Mr. Robert Lincoln is the same way. That's
hard to fight."

"Robert is certainly the same way," murmured Myra.
"He spent a part of his childhood in the Todd family in
Lexington, while his father was in Congress. I suspect he was
always a bit of a Southern gentleman in his heart, one of the
old-style Southern gentlemen who *knew* they were the lords
of creation. And growing up in a fishbowl the way he did—
it absolutely *blistered* him to have the newspapers call him the
'Prince of Rails'—he's always been excruciatingly sensitive
about his mother's newspaper donnybrooks. But it doesn't
give him the moral right to have her locked up, whatever his
legal rights might be.

"Yes," she said briskly, "we're going to have to deal with
Robert. But as for Dr. Patterson..."

She set her lemonade aside, and withdrew a newspaper
from her satchel.

It was the Bloomington, Illinois, *Courier,* folded open in
the middle.

MRS. LINCOLN

Is the Widow of President Lincoln a Prisoner?
No One Allowed to See Her Except by
Order of Her Son
An Account of a Remarkable Interview with
Her Jailer and Physician

"As I said, Mr. Wilamet, you leave Dr. Patterson to me."

CHAPTER SIXTY-FOUR

Bellevue Place   August 1875

"Springfield, 30 July, 1875

My dearest sister,
   This afternoon Mrs. Bradwell was kind enough to pay
me a visit, at which the subject of your health and happiness
was discussed. . . ."

Mary set the letter down and sat for a time looking out the
window of her room, scarcely seeing the emerald of the
lawn, the pale gravel of the drive glaring in the brilliant sun.
Sunday stillness blanketed Bellevue, and the thick scent of
cut grass. Like a jewel, the note of the church-bell in town
touched the morning air.

   If Robert is agreeable, Ninian and I would be more than
happy if you would come and make your home with us."

She drew a deep breath, feeling as if she had stepped into
a torrent, was being swept off her feet. Carried away by feelings she could not separate or name.

She should, she knew, feel relief and gladness. Myra was
fighting for her, taking steps to free her.

Why did she feel disappointment and rage?

Why did she suddenly smell again the honeysuckle of
summer twilight, and hear the retreating creak of Jimmy
Shields's buggy-wheels along Second Street, and the quiet
rustle of Merce's lavender muslin skirts? "They just want you
to be happy," Merce said. "We can't stay forever in our fathers' houses."

Our fathers die. Handsome Robert Todd, and the lover, the

husband, the friend I called Father. They abandon us. Can't we stay in our own houses?

Her eyes burned with tears as she thought of the brick-fronted house on West Washington Street, that she'd so briefly lived in but had not been able to keep up... *thanks to that lover, husband, friend being bone stupid enough not to make a proper will!*

I had the chance to live in my own house—my own place—for four years after Taddie's death, she thought.

And what did I do instead?

She squeezed her eyes tight, the tears sliding down her cheeks, and pressed her hand to her mouth as the final nightmare rose to her mind.

SHE RETURNED TO CHICAGO IN THE FALL OF 1873, NOT BE-cause she wanted to, but because she could think of nowhere else to go.

In the first weeks after the Fire, businesses had reopened amid black mountains of charred brick in downtown Chicago while other areas of the town still smoldered. Within months of the fire, handsome structures of steel-reinforced stone went up along the great avenues. Houses were rebuilt on the lakeshore for the rich. Beyond the packing-yards, stock-pens, and railroad yards, miles of tiny cottages of wood and brick were built for the workingmen flooding into the city from the East. From a distance, in Waukesha and St. Charles and St. Catherine, she had read in the newspapers and in letters from Robert and Myra of how the city was leaping back from its ashes like a vulgar phoenix.

It was two years before she could bring herself to return.

Nightly, in her room in the new Grand Pacific Hotel, she would wake in panic, thinking she smelled smoke. Would rush to the window, heart hammering, fearing to see the wall of fire advancing, men and women fleeing before it like deer from a forest fire... A man on the sidewalk with his head bashed in. A drunkard hurling liquor on a young girl's flaming hair.

In her dreams she would be standing again in the black waters of Lake Michigan with the crowding, sobbing damned, watched the flames advance. In her dreams the waters rose over their heads, and burned like oil with the flame advancing across them, to destroy them all.

But Robert was in Chicago. Robert, her only living son, her only link now with the life that she'd lived. The only proof that she'd been loved. Robert was Lincoln's son; Robert had played in the big garden of the house on Lexington's Main Street, with Alec and Emilie, with Sam and David. Robert was all that was left to her of those days.

She visited him when she felt well enough, though the sight of Lake Park and the streets around his house filled her with panic that was not lessened by her knowledge that it was unreasonable. Young Mary was "out with friends" when Mary called, more often than not. Robert refused to speak of her, or to answer the probing questions she asked about her daughter-in-law's housekeeping and child-raising habits.

But the servants, she guessed, looking around the neat, plain parlor, weren't being kept up properly at their work. And five-year-old Mamie, though perfectly dressed and exquisite as a tiny princess, seemed to her to be growing more timid by the day.

"She isn't treating that child rightly!" she stormed at Robert one Sunday afternoon, when his daughter burst into tears at spilling the sugar. "She's punishing her too harshly, isn't she? I daresay she slaps her for a trifling thing like that. Now, dearest, there's no need to cry, it's only a little sugar...."

It was, in fact, about a half cup of sugar spilled into the blue-and-yellow Wilton carpet, and Mamie ground her small pink fists into her eyes and rushed from the room in confusion. Robert said, "It is not my habit to interfere in my wife's sphere, Mother, be the question one of servants or one concerning my daughter. Mary has shown herself to be a loving and willing helpmeet—"

"How would you know that?" demanded Mary, stung. "If you spend all your days in your precious law offices and the courts, how would you know the first thing about what happens under your roof? That poor child isn't getting enough to eat and clearly is being mistreated, and I have a good mind to come here some day when your precious Mary is 'out with friends' and take her away with me! I daresay your wife would scarcely miss the child until it came time to put her to bed and maybe not then!"

Mary spent that night—and the remainder of the week—so sick with migraine that Robert sent a doctor to see her. Throughout the wretched Chicago winter Mary was ill, lying in the darkness of her curtained room with her head feeling as if the mad Indian shaman who ruled her headaches were trying to twist the bones of her skull apart. Her back and shoulder throbbed where the long-ago carriage-accident on the day of Gettysburg had jammed and wrenched the nerves. Some days she would leave the room only to go to the pharmacy for medicine, or down the hallway to the toilets, a dozen times in the day and again and again in the night, peering furtively through a crack in the door until the hall was clear, then darting along in her wrapper and shawl, her long graying hair lying like a heavy cloak over her back.

Outside, the winds screamed across Lake Michigan in unbroken fury straight down from the wastes of Canada. In her room the stuffiness of the gas heater, the stink of the fishtail burners, made her head hurt worse. She spent her days dreaming on the sofa in wrapper and shawl, surrounded by newspapers and magazines, sending for her meals to be brought up to her and bribing the maids to get her medication for her pain. She tried dozens of patented cordials, balms, and elixirs that winter, sometimes individually and sometimes mixed. It didn't seem to matter. She was aware of long spells of dizziness but many days she had little sense of being in her body at all.

The winter was one long, sickening blur.

Sometime during the spring—and the days, by this time,

were mostly the same—she was roused by some small sound in the night to find herself on the sofa where she'd drifted off in the midst of reading *The Moonstone*. It was late in the night, and the hotel deathly silent; only the hissing of the gas jet broke the stillness, and its cold small flame gave the room a frozen air, as if it could be anytime, day or night, outside the shut velvet curtains.

Lincoln stood in the room, ghostly and blue, shining as Tad and Willie shone when they would come to see her. His eyes had the bruised and sleepless look they'd had toward the last days of the War, but his face was the face of an old man, gouged with the lines of an age he had not lived to achieve. His beard, which flowed down over his chest now, was nearly white, as was his hair. He looked exhausted, and infinitely sad.

He looks as he would look today, thought Mary, shocked. *Like the husband I would have today.*

Dear God, I have aged too!

Their eyes met, and she thought, *It has been nearly ten years.*

I am fifty-six, and in February I will be the same age that he was, when he was killed.

How the years have crucified us both!

She tried to say, *My darling,* but her tongue felt thick as wet cotton. Lincoln smiled at her, that old familiar smile that lighted up the whole of his tired face, and said, *I look forward to being with you again on the sixth of September,* a sentence from one of his letters, written to her when she was at her father's in Lexington, getting ready to rejoin him in Washington for his speaking-tour of New England.

Waking, she thought, *Dear God, are those truly the length of my days? Will we truly be together, at last, in the Summer Land, on that date?*

Did he really come to me, to tell me, warn me?

In a way, it was as if the whole of the year, from that spring night until September, she was waiting. Waiting for him to come for her.

In her dreams, she would picture that scene, herself laid out on her bed in a darkened room. Once she'd imagined Willie kneeling by her bed. Now she saw Robert and Mamie there, weeping bitterly (Young Mary was "out with friends" and good riddance to her). The shining doors would open in the dark of the gaslit room, and Mr. Lincoln would come in, with Willie and Tad—Tad so tall, carrying little Eddie on his hip—trailed by all the others, her father and Ben Helm and Granny Parker and that glowing, radiant woman whose face she remembered in the tiniest detail, her mother, as lovely as she had been. . . .

Robert would look up and see them and sob, "I see them! I see them! Oh, Mother, I was so wrong. . . ."

(Or maybe Mamie would see them first, point and cry out, "Papa, shining angels!" And *then* Robert would look. . . .)

Mr. Lincoln would hold out his hand and smile. "Mother, I've come to take you home."

And she would sit up, young and pretty again as the girl in the pink ruffled dress, who'd perched in Ninian's carriage in the Globe Tavern yard, looking around her with wrinkled nose at the dusty pig-infested streets of Springfield.

As if her body were preparing, she was ill much of the year. There were wars with Indians who refused to give up their lands, and struggles in the Army-occupied South against the corrupt administrators that imbecile Grant had seen fit to put in charge, but it mattered almost nothing to her. She read of the events with a vast sense of detachment.

I look forward to being with you again. . . .

But she did not die in September. She couldn't understand what went wrong. Mr. Lincoln couldn't have been mistaken. She sat up all night on the fateful eve, with the gaslights flickering in her little room at the Grand Pacific, wondering what Robert would say when Mr. Turner the hotel manager contacted him in the morning, brought him to her chamber (she'd paid the maids specially to have it tidied that day) to see her lying cold and still on her bed. . . .

It was a windy night, not the great terrifying thunderstorms that sent her shuddering under the bedclothes, but a dry howling gale that filled her with the dread that she would smell smoke upon the wind.

At dawn she poured herself a glassful of medicine and drank herself to sleep.

Winter was coming on.

She had nothing to live for, not even, it appeared, death.

Throughout the year of waiting, dread, and illness she had gone out so seldom, and seen so few people. There was a lively circle of Spiritualists in Chicago, including Myra Bradwell, but they lived mostly in the northwest suburbs, and Mary did not feel herself able to deal with a streetcar, and grudged the expense of a cab. But she had kept up a correspondence with her friends, and Ella Slapater in Pennsylvania wrote warmly recommending that she journey to Florida, rather than endure another winter of Lake Michigan's brutal snows.

"There is a woman named Delia Crane in Jacksonville, of true spiritual power, in whose parlor I was at last able to speak face-to-face with my beloved mother once again. . . ."

So Mary packed her trunks, put more trunks into storage in the Grand Pacific's basement—after detailed instructions to Mr. Turner about their safety in case of another major fire—and took the train to Florida.

Robert did not see her off.

He had intended to, but when he'd come up to her room to help her pack, he'd discovered one of the special petticoats she'd made for herself, with pockets sewn in them so that she could carry money and bonds.

"Dearest, you know you cannot trust servants in these places these days," she'd explained, to his expression of horror. "The only safe place is to carry one's money about one's person."

"*Safe?*" Robert was aghast. "You refuse to invest your money—where it would actually *be* safe—and you carry it around with you, where any scoundrel could take it. . . ."

"They don't know I have it." Her anger rose at the disapproval tightening her son's brow. "Honestly, they haven't a pair of magic spectacles to see through a woman's petticoats—I *hope*! And as for investing it, or putting it in a bank, one has only to read a newspaper to see what comes of *that*! You only want me to do so because *you* want to collect the interest... *and* to borrow it to invest in land yourself!"

He turned bright red. "That's the most absurd thing I've ever heard! I want you to invest it so you won't spend it on idiotic silver-mining stock like you did during the War!"

"It was not idiotic! Mr. Wikoff's advice was always good—"

"Mr. Wikoff was a scoundrel and a spy and the stock he got you to buy was trash! You should invest in land because it's safe and profitable—"

"You want me to invest in land because you want to inherit it when I die!" stormed Mary, and Robert stalked in silence from the room.

Thus she and her nurse-companion Catherine Foy took a cab for the station and boarded the train alone.

It was the first time she'd trodden Southern soil since she'd been driven in the carriage through the burned-out streets of Richmond, to sit in Varina Davis's parlor and watch Lizabet Keckley walk about the shambles of the Confederate Senate chamber. From Mrs. Tucker—the owner of the Stephenson House, where she had stayed in St. Catherine—she had heard much of the outrages and injustices of the occupying Union troops after the war (Mrs. Tucker and most of her guests being expatriate Confederates), but she saw little of this in Jacksonville.

In many ways it was as if the bloodshed which had so nearly torn the country apart had not touched the small town on the St. Johns estuary. The servants at Mrs. Stockton's boardinghouse were colored, well-trained, quiet-footed, and respectful, the kind of domestic help Mary had longed for in vain for years. She and Mrs. Foy took the steamer upriver to

Green Cove's sulphur springs, where her arthritis improved with heat and mineral baths. For the first spring in several years she did not suffer from devastating headaches.

But Jacksonville, though certainly more pleasant in December than Chicago, was just as hollow, like a better-heated room of the same empty, echoing house. She spent a desolate Christmas with Mrs. Stockton's family—three War-widowed daughters and their teenaged children, who treated Mary like a beloved and eccentric aunt—and passed many days thereafter in the dimness of laudanum, chloral hydrate, migraines, and cloudy dreams. Mrs. Stockton seemed to understand.

"The voices you hear in your spells are the voices of the spirits, speaking beyond the Veil," she assured Mary, one March afternoon on the gallery when the two ladies took tea together. "I hear them often myself." She took a bottle of Indian Bitters from her reticule and poured a hefty dollop into her tea, following it up with three spoonfuls of sugar: she had, Mary well knew, female complaints as severe and agonizing as Mary's own.

Her black-clothed eldest daughter—who actually ran the boardinghouse—paused on the way back to the kitchen to cast a glance of patient exasperation at her mother, then went through the side door. Her husband, like Emilie's Ben, had died at Chickamauga Creek. A balmy breeze drifted in off the estuary, bringing with it the perfumes of salt-water and orange-blossom.

"Do you hear music also?" Mary remembered the séances at St. Catherine and the Spiritualist camps along the Fox River.

"Oh, dear, yes. The Colonel—my husband—used to play the fiddle, and often I'll hear it, coming from the bedroom door as I go up the stairs."

She spoke cheerfully, but Mary shivered. The voices that seemed to exude from the walls or the floor when she was having one of her spells had been angry voices, voices of malice, whispering of evil and death.

Spy, they said. *Hellcat. Limb of Satan. Liar.*

Perhaps it was the little bit of extra Cordial she drank at tea with Mrs. Stockton that brought them back that night, because as she lay awake in her room, staring at the amber pool of the night-light's tiny gleam, she heard them again.

Sometimes it was a hissing whisper. Sometimes merely a low mutter that she could almost make out—this she feared with all her heart, for it sounded like the muttering of the men in the hallway of that awful little house across from Ford's Theater on that terrible spring night. *Get that woman out of here. Who gets to tell her he's dead? Can we find some woman to take her back to the White House without a scene?*

Ten years ago. In two weeks it would be ten years exactly.

Desperately she sat up in bed and cried, "Tad! Taddie, darling, where are you?" And then, hopefully, praying the next moment that she'd see her middle son, her sweet-faced boy, her little champion, with his hands full of flowers from the White House conservatory, she called: "Willie?"

Were those two glowing shapes taking form there by the wall her cherished boys?

She saw their faces, their eyes and their hands, appearing and disappearing in a shining cloud. Saw their mouths forming words, their hands reaching out of the light toward her...

"Bobby," Willie said, his voice echoing Mary's own. "Bobby is lost. Bobby is lost. Bobby will die...."

And she saw, as if through a window, Robert crossing his own tidy parlor back in Chicago. Saw him stop, cough, soundless as a dumb show, clutch at his chest, knees slowly buckling as he collapsed to the floor. Saw Mamie run in, shaking her father frantically by the shoulder, sobbing in wild terror, her mouth moving mutely, *Papa! Papa!*

Where Young Mary was—where the servants were (if there were any that week)—Mary didn't know. But she heard Tad saying, "Bobby will die. Bobby will die."

Bobby will die.

She screamed, *"No!"* and the dream exploded like shattering glass.

Mary wired frantic messages from the telegraph office in Jacksonville the following afternoon: *My belief is my son is ill telegraph me at once without a moments delay,* she scrawled, addressing her wire to Robert's new partner, Edward Isham. *On receipt of this I start for Chicago once your message is received.*

And also to Isham, with instructions to deliver it to Robert on his sickbed: *My dearly beloved son Robert T. Lincoln rouse yourself and live for my sake All I have is yours from this hour. I am praying every moment for your life to be spared to your mother.*

She spent the night feverishly packing. Mrs. Foy tried to talk her out of returning—"Sure, you'll get to the station to find word that Mr. Robert is flourishing"—but Mary shook her head.

"He will lie to me," she snapped. Her hands trembled with agitation and she fumbled the cap from a bottle—she didn't care which bottle. They were all the same. "And that scoundrel Isham will lie. They don't want me near my son. Isham is thick as thieves with that mealy-mouthed hussy. She wants to keep me away from my son, away from my granddaughter. . . ."

Upon reaching the train station she tore up unread the telegram that was waiting for her. It would only be Isham's lies.

Start for Chicago this evening hope you are better today you will have money on my arrival.

Anything, anything to get him to live. To keep him at her side.

All the way to Chicago, three endless, nerve-shattering days on the train, she thought, *If he leaves me, too, I shall die.*

Three days in a bone-shaking train car, her arthritis and neuralgia racking her like the Inquisition's den of torments. Three days of tension and terror feverishly reading newspapers and magazines without the slightest awareness of the words. Three nights of lying on her narrow bunk, waiting for Catherine's breathing to deepen so that she could slip one of her bottles of Godfrey's Cordial or chloral hydrate out of her bag or her petticoat pockets, to take the few extra mouthfuls that would give her blessed sleep.

Three nights of sitting beside Tad's chair in the Clifton House, listening to the agonized gasping of his breath.

Of sitting beside that immense rosewood bed in the White House, with its ostentatious hangings of purple and gold, looking down at Willie's still face.

Of lying on that stiff horsehair sofa in Petersen's parlor, hearing men's voices muttering in the hall . . .

Dear God, let him live! she prayed as the train jolted and shook her aching bones. *Dear God, let him live until I get there! Preserve his life. . . .*

But she knew too well that God never answered such prayers.

The train reached Chicago on a leaden evening. After Jacksonville's balmy warmth, the chill of the half-constructed train-station cut her flesh like a knife. She stumbled from the train car, catching Catherine's arm, shaky as a drunken woman.

After the peace of Jacksonville, the noise of Chicago was like being beaten with a thousand iron hammers, the stench—of smoke, of soot, of packing-yards, of horse-dung, of unwashed humanity streaming along the platform all around her—was like one of the lower circles of Hell.

"You have to fetch a cab," she gasped to the nurse. "Put the luggage into storage here. I must get to Robert's immediately. I'll worry about a hotel later—after we get to Robert's, I'll send you to the Grand Pacific to make arrangements. I pray I'm not too late. . . ."

Catherine turned her head in the direction of the waiting-rooms, at the end of the long gloomy platform. The gas-lamps made splodges of yellow in the thickening twilight; the figures crowding and pushing toward the train cars and away from them were also hellish, a confusion of smelly tweeds and crowding shoulders, demon-faces leering from shadow.

The sturdy Irishwoman said, "I don't think you need worry about being too late, Mrs. Lincoln."

Jostling his way through the crowds on the platform, in obviously flourishing good health, his face flushed with annoyance, was Robert.

CHAPTER SIXTY-FIVE

Bellevue Place   August 1875

"I THINK FROM THE MOMENT I RETURNED TO CHICAGO IN March," said Mary softly, "Robert intended to have me incarcerated as insane."

She reached across the short distance that separated her chair from the one John had filched from the hallway for Myra, and clasped Myra's gloved hands. Even through the shut curtains of her room, the sunlight leaked in brilliant bars. The house was hushed, for dinner was served in the afternoon on Fridays, with only a small cold supper at night, so that Dr. Patterson could have a good meal before getting on the Chicago train at four. Myra had come walking up the drive at just after four, only a few minutes after Mary had taken her post at the window to watch for her: Mary's heart had pounded so hard with relief, with joy, with apprehension that even now her friend would be turned away, that she'd had to sit down to still her trembling.

She was still trying to get her breath when John had knocked on the door, and shown Myra in.

She hadn't heard what he'd said to Amanda, in the next room with the communicating barred window, but before she had even dried the tears of relief that streamed from her eyes at the sight of Myra she had heard the attendant's footfalls whisper away down the corridor carpet.

John brought in the chair from Amanda's room, and sat quietly in a corner while Myra and Mary talked.

"John has told you, about...about how I slid into... *misuse*...of my medicines." She could scarcely get the words out. She couldn't think of a soul besides Myra to whom she would even mention the possibility of such behavior, much less confess to what it had caused her to do. "I didn't think he could possibly be right, but since I have followed the regimen that he outlined for me, I have not had a 'spell,' nor any of the...the *delusions* that plagued me so."

She broke off, biting her lips and feeling tears sting, and Myra squeezed her hands encouragingly.

"Nevertheless, I did sometimes have dreams—*long* before I began taking medicine—that foretold disaster. Mr. Lincoln had them, too. So when I dreamed that Robert was dying, it seemed to me..."

She shook her head. It was impossible to rid her mind of the stony-eyed fury and suspicion in her son's face under the harsh gloom of the station gaslight.

"Well," she said, "he wasn't dying. Then I believed for a time that the dream had presaged some terrible accident, and of course he would not listen to me. And I admit that I acted like a crazy woman. Much of it I don't even remember, so I must have been taking...well, a great deal more Cordial than was good for me.

"I obtained rooms again at the Grand Pacific, and Robert took one next to mine. But as usual, we quarreled—over my money, which he wanted to borrow to invest, and over my going about the city by myself, and over my shopping. Yes, I know I spend too much money, but I *never* pay full price for things anymore....I will *only* buy after I have argued the shopkeepers down. And what harm does it do, to me or to anyone? Except of course to Robert, who views every trinket I buy as that much less he will inherit."

She heard the anger in her voice, felt the familiar deadly heat of it flush her face, and bit back the several other animadversions that rose to her lips about her only living son's determination to control her and her money.

Far easier to berate Robert, she thought, than to talk about the weeks she had spent, living in Chicago alone.

"I had...such terrible dreams. Dreams that the city was burning again. Dreams that Robert was planning to kill me for my money. I remember dreaming that he'd cut a door between his room and mine, and was going to creep in at midnight and smother me with pillows—I ran from the room into the hall, where he seized me.... I must have been sleepwalking, or still dazed from the dream, for I *did* scream that he was going to kill me, or at least he claims that I did. I—I may have. I honestly don't remember.

"He sent Dr. Danforth to visit me, and I remember almost nothing of the visit. He said—Dr. Danforth said—that I claimed that someone had tried to poison me at a train-station in Georgia on my way up from Florida. Again, I have no recollection of saying anything of the kind, but I do remember reading a story in a magazine—the *Saturday Evening Gazette,* I think it was—that involved the heroine being given poisoned coffee, and drinking a second cup in order to make herself sick enough to purge her system."

Her fingers tightened around Myra's, as if the sensibly gloved hands were a lifeline that would draw her from this deceptively sunny, quiet maelstrom of helplessness.

"Then Robert had me followed. He claimed it was because of the money I carried around with me in my petticoats, which he said would make me a target for robbers. But he gave the men instructions to make note of who I talked to, and who came to see me at my hotel. That tells me that his intention was not entirely disinterested, and that he was planning this for some time."

"They certainly must have told him what time you could generally be found in your room," commented Myra thoughtfully. "They were right on the spot when you returned from your shopping that morning, you know. And the judge—a busy man with schedules to keep—and jury were *waiting,* already empanelled, in a courtroom that was held ready. The witnesses all have to have been contacted at least a day in advance. It was nicely planned."

"I suspect that was Mr. Swett." Mary almost spit the name. "He never approved of me, not even when my dearest husband and protector was alive! I told Robert that I was planning to leave Chicago again, to go to California. He was horrified, of course, and forbade me to go, as if I was his child rather than a grown woman! But after he left the Grand Pacific and went back to live in his home again—we quarreled over my poor little Mamie, too, and how that dreadful mother of hers treats her!—I saw no reason to go on staying in that horrid room, with nothing to do day after day but visit the shops. Mr. Lincoln had spoken of going to California, and Mrs. Stockton in Jacksonville set me thinking of it again, telling me that it is a marvelously healthful climate, and now that the railroad runs there even a poor widow like myself can travel and live there safely."

"When was this?" asked Myra, and Mary shook her head.

"I don't remember. It was sometime after the first of May, because I know I wrote to Ella Slapater's cousin in San Francisco on the first. Robert urged me to go back to Springfield and live with Elizabeth—where he could keep an eye on me, I daresay."

She closed her eyes. All those quarrels—in the Grand Pacific's red plush lobby, in Robert's painfully neat parlor, in the kitchen of the house on Eighth and Jackson Streets back in Springfield—blurred into a single nightmare, of Robert's voice growing colder and colder....

Only it wasn't Robert's voice. And it wasn't Robert, who drew away from her, who walked out of the room.

"And within ten days," said Myra thoughtfully, "you were locked up."

WHEN JOHN ESCORTED MYRA DOWNSTAIRS AN HOUR LATER, to confer with Young Doc, Mary sat for a long time in the dimming twilight of her room.

Thinking about living again in Elizabeth's house.

Thinking about Robert.

Thinking about Lincoln.

All those quarrels with Robert, the cold reasonableness of his voice...she knew now why they triggered in her such rage.

He sounded exactly like Lincoln. The Lincoln she had screamed at, during those years of loneliness during the War. The Lincoln she had tried again and again to hurt, when he would shut her out, when he would meet her attempts to play her old part in his political life with such impenetrable evasiveness. He would listen to her spitfire rages, then walk away down the hall to his office, to fulfill a destiny in which she had no more place.

It had all come down to that: that he'd left her behind.

In a way, she realized, she'd known it even then. It was as if he saw further than she did, some larger plan beyond the day-to-day trading of influence and jobs that had been politics for her father and for every other man she'd ever known. As if he'd been looking down from above on a maze in which she wandered, only able to see a few feet before her. He'd gone ahead of her to where she could not follow. Had slipped from their earlier partnership, and abandoned her to the consolations of shopping and the gossip of her Blue Room salons.

In some corner of his heart he had to have known it, too, she thought. He was kind, but in his indulgence and care, had there been some element of guilt as well? Guilt that he had left her out, that he had run on ahead to become what he must be, leaving her to be what she was?

But at least, she thought, *he was kind. He cared for me, made sure—in the best way that he could—that I was all right.*

Does Robert tell himself that's what he's doing?

And now she would return to Springfield. To live again in Elizabeth's house. To walk on those streets once more, to pass by the market where she and her beloved had shopped for fish—with Lincoln stopping every three paces to talk to some crony... To be perpetually waiting to see him round some corner, straining to hear, in any crowded room, that crowing silvery laugh...

I can't do it!

To meet those other ghosts on every muddy street, on

every dusty pathway in the countryside... on Ninian's porch...

Dapper Stephen Douglas, bowing as he handed her up into his buggy.

Intelligent, gentle Dr. Henry, listening in that perfect peaceful quiet by the fireside to anything she had to say. Returning from Washington only weeks after Lincoln's death, Dr. Henry's ship had gone down off the California coast. News of it had reached her during that first hellish summer in Chicago.

Simeon Francis's bright blue eyes peering over the tops of his spectacles in that freezing, ink-smelling newspaper office.

Edward Baker's chiming laugh.

Eddie's quick pattering footfalls across a kitchen floor... Willie emerging from between the rows of the vegetable garden, covered with mud and his hands filled with wildflowers... the look on Tad's face as he sat in the parlor window, watching for his father coming up the street.

I can't do it.

Does that mean you'd rather Myra didn't try to get you out?

That you'd rather live here in the land of the lotos-eaters forever?

She laid her head down on her crossed wrists on the windowsill, too tired even to weep.

MYRA BRADWELL SPENT THE NIGHT IN THE WATCH-ROOM ADjoining Mary's, where Gretchen and Amanda generally took turns sleeping. Mrs. Patterson even had the cook send them up supper on a tray. John, lingering in the parlor while Myra talked to Young Doc in the office, had to marvel at the way the woman maneuvered the younger doctor, agreeing with everything he said, nodding and regarding him with an expression of awed respect that John hadn't believed her square, pleasant features capable of assuming.

"Of course poor Mary is insane," he overheard—Young Doc seldom shut the office door. "Good heavens, Doctor. I've known her since Mr. Lincoln was President, and I sa this coming for years. The improvement you and your father have wrought in her is absolutely marvelous...."

John could only shake his head in amused wonder.

"Of course, I'm not sure that a lunatic asylum is the proper place for her, when she does have family to stay with...."

"I would agree with you, Mrs. Bradwell"—Young Doc always started out by agreeing with everyone—"if Bellevue Place were indeed a lunatic asylum. But it is not. It is merely a haven for those whose nerves are distraught, as Mrs. Lincoln's most certainly are...."

And it was still Robert, thought John, who was calling the tune.

Something told him that it would take more than entreaties from family and doubts concerning propriety, to gain that tall young lawyer's permission for his mother to leave Dr. Patterson's care.

At about ten the following morning, when Young Doc was starting his rounds, Myra Bradwell came downstairs—having breakfasted with Mary in her room—and sought John out in the rose garden. "Would you keep an eye on the front of the house after noon or twelve-thirty," she asked softly, with a watchful glance at Zeus and Gretchen, who were helping Minnie Judd to a comfortable seat on a bench in the sunshine. Miss Judd had woken in a sobbing fit last night, screaming out that she had committed the Unpardonable Sin and must be punished—she was still visibly woozy from the chloral hydrate that had finally quietened her into sleep.

"There's a young gentleman coming to visit Mrs. Lincoln, with whom I'll be working to secure her release. I would appreciate it if he could come in to confer with us both in quiet."

Lawyer, thought John immediately. Though Myra ~~ll~~ was barred from practice herself—no woman being ~~e~~ to enter into independent contracts—after their ~~ing~~ he had found and read copies of the *Chicago*

Review of Law, which she edited and published. She undoubtedly had at her beck and call a score of hopeful newcomers to the profession.

If not a lawyer, a tame doctor.

"I'll be waiting," he promised her.

When she returned a few hours later—from the train-station, presumably—he guessed the brisk young man in the tobacco-colored suit who accompanied her was a lawyer, rather than a doctor. He was far too flashy to engender confidence in a patient. She introduced him as Mr. Wilkie, and John guided them around the house to the small door of the family wing, then checked to make certain Mrs. Patterson was nowhere in sight before letting them in with his key.

Wilkie and Myra left together at about four. After seeing them to the end of the drive, John returned to Mary's room, and found her still sitting by the window, the curtains half-open, as if she had watched them pass across the yellow-gold triangle of visible gravel.

"Do you feel all right?"

When she glanced up at him her face answered his question. It was calmer and more relaxed than he had seen it, he thought, since her arrival three months ago. Her eyes had a perpetually bruised look, from sleeplessness and weeping, but within the puffy flesh it pleased him to see that they were alert, as they usually were these days.

"I am," she said, in her small, sweet voice. "Thank you for asking, John. You seem to be the only one these days who's genuinely concerned about what my answer to that question might be. You and Myra, and Myra—well, once she sees a solution to a problem she goes at it like a bull at a gate, and doesn't ask what one feels about it, so long as it gets done."

On the corner of her dressing-table he saw the pages of Mrs. Edwards's letter from Springfield, and a half-dozen sheets, scribbled and crossed out, in Mary's erratic hand.

"You'd best not let Gretchen find those in your room and tell Mrs. Patterson that you have pen and ink," he warned.

"I'll keep them in my room for you, if you'd like." And seeing her mouth pucker with weary anger at being always observed, always forbidden, like a schoolgirl, he added, "Or I'll help you pry up a floorboard under the bed, like prisoners do. You can wait till Amanda goes down the hall to the toilet, then whip out your pen and write a few lines. . . ."

And her puffy face broke into its sidelong smile. Leaning close, she whispered, "Amanda *never* goes to the toilet. Nights when I lie awake, I can hear every sound. . . . I believe the woman is made of iron. Or is solid all the way through, like a carrot. . . . Dear God, what it is, to laugh again!" she added, as John gathered up the scribbled sheets, corked the ink-bottle securely, and slipped it into his pocket. "I don't think I've had a laugh since . . . since my friend Sally Orne came to stay with me at that *dreadful* little hostelry in Germany, and we kept every other traveler on our floor awake all night with our giggling and carrying-on!"

"I take it the interview with Mr. Wilkie went well?"

Mary hesitated, the joy wiped from her face, her tired eyes filling with tears once more. "Do you know, I dare not even think about it? That *equal poise of hope and fear* that Milton speaks of . . . it all seems so . . . so hopeless. And yet I cannot give up hope. I *will* not give up hope. I will *banish squint suspicion*. . . ." She fished in her drawer for a clean handkerchief. Every one had black borders an inch deep.

"Will you walk with me a little in the garden, Mr. Wilamet? It has been a long and tiring day."

I⊤ was almost a week before Mary wrote back to Elizabeth. During the scorching, humid August days, as John assisted Dr. Patterson or Young Doc with Mrs. Wheeler's hydrotherapy or in force-feeding Miss Judd, he overheard the comments of Mrs. Patterson: comments that sounded less ⸻ ⸺ like the observation of symptoms and more and ⸻ backstairs tale-telling.

Lincoln ordered cornbread again for breakfast and

then refused to eat it. Mrs. Lincoln asked for the carriage to be brought around and then delayed for three hours, ultimately deciding to spend the day in her room. Mrs. Lincoln had her room changed back to the first floor and then complained about having a different set of bedsprings, even though the new ones were of the same pattern as the old.... When he saw her during those days, to walk in the gardens or to talk in the parlor, he read the nervousness that lay behind her capriciousness, the tension that brought on headaches, the recurring waves of hope and fear.

She spoke to him many times about Springfield: about having been sent there by her stepmother, "in the hopes I'd land a husband and wouldn't be on her hands for the rest of my life, God forbid!" About what the town had been like in the 1830s and '40s, with muddy streets and a hog-wallow the size of a small lake occupying one corner of the State House grounds, and the green prairies blanketed with flowers, two blocks' walk from the little brown house on the corner of Eighth Street and Jackson. About buggy-rides in the countryside with one or another of her many beaux, and picnics in the shade along the Sangamon River; about political-speakings in the State House square and the crying of crickets in the long blue twilights, when she'd sit on the porch with Merce Levering or Julia Jayne and chat about friends or fashion or politics when politics was still a game....

"I never thought I would have to go back to living under Ninian's roof."

On Wednesday John took the train to Chicago, melting and stinking and scorching on the shores of the lake. Most of Cassy's customers had gone out of town, leaving the family broke but with a little breathing-room. By dint of burying small sums of money under the floor the way they used to as children in the quarters at Blue Hill, Cassy had saved enough for a family picnic on the lakeshore, and for once everything went well.

His mother was feeling well, and when washed and dressed and with her hair put up was still the wildly beautiful woman he had worshiped as a child. She talked and laughed and made jokes that had the children whooping with delight, and joined them in their hunt for fireflies in the bushes of Lincoln Park as the sun went down. He watched them from the bench where he sat with his arm around Clarice, loving the touch of his wife, the scent of her flesh and her hair, glad to be alive.

When times were bad they were bad, he reflected, smiling at Selina as she sat with baby Cora on her blanket, weaving a chain of daisies from the grass. But when times were good, there was nothing sweeter than these long summer twilights, other loving couples walking along the path in the park, the tall bronze shape of Lincoln's statue standing against the luminous cobalt sky.

Robert Lincoln came to Bellevue Friday morning, rigid with outrage. Though John was fully occupied with Mrs. Wheeler—who had spent the night screaming and pounding on the walls of her room, and had had to be sedated and, in the morning, forcibly gotten up and walked in the gardens to restore her "vital system"—he caught snatches of the lawyer's furious voice through the open windows:

"...the woman is a pest and a nuisance, the queen of a gang of Spiritualists, whatever you might say! I've warned Aunt Elizabeth against her—and against whatever henchmen she may choose to employ in this self-serving campaign to give you back control of your money!"

And later, as John guided the still-groggy and weeping Mrs. Wheeler through the hall to her own room again,

"Mother, I've gone to considerable trouble to find you a place where you will be safe, happy, and well taken care of! Now, thanks to your table-tapping friend, Dr. Patterson is in a panic, terrified of what bad publicity will do to this entire establishment...!"

"Well, God forbid that the jail where I have been locked in by my own child—where other women are locked up as well!—should have *bad publicity*! Oh, get me my smelling salts lest I faint with chagrin!" Mary's voice was shrill with sarcasm.

And when John emerged from Mrs. Wheeler's room after turning her over to Gretchen, Zeus passed him in the hallway and whispered, "Mr. Lincoln's gone to talk to Dr. Patterson. He don't look like a happy man."

Robert Lincoln was just coming out of Patterson's office when John came down the stairs to the parlor—Mrs. Lincoln was nowhere in sight. Through clenched teeth, Robert said, "I quite understand your position, Dr. Patterson, but please consider mine. In spite of appearances my mother is *not* competent to live on her own, at my Aunt Elizabeth's house or anywhere else! You can have no idea how difficult it is, to deal with someone who is insane in one area and appears normal in other respects...."

"I can," replied Patterson drily, "and believe me, Mr. Lincoln, I do. I have been in touch with the Bradwell woman this week, too—all these Spiritualist harpies are alike!—but I am in an extremely difficult position, both financially and, to be frank, legally. Laymen who have no understanding of the workings of the deranged mind and the feminine nervous system are more a nuisance than anything else, for all they see are the rights of the sane and the normal. But those, unfortunately, are the laws that bind us!"

"Please," begged Robert. "Please do not do anything until you hear from me. This matter will be straightened out— it *must* be straightened out. The thought of my mother rambling about at large with the whole of her fortune stuffed into pockets in her petticoats—going off to California or God knows where to get into God knows what kind of scandal...! Though trying to convince any of the Bradwell woman's gang of Spiritualists of anything may well be beyond any *man's* abilities. But I will try."

Patterson saw him to the door and paused, turning back, as he glimpsed John passing through the parlor. "John," he said, "I want a word with you." And to Robert, holding the door, "If they threaten to publish, there is not much that I can do."

"What you can do," replied Robert, "is get anything—anything at all—to support a diagnosis of continued insanity in my mother. We both know she is insane. What more do we need? It is, after all, for her own good."

And he strode down the brick steps, to where his cab stood in the graveled circle of the drive.

Patterson turned back, and stood for a moment, regarding John with tired and angry eyes.

Without a word being spoken, John felt his heart sink and turn cold.

"Mrs. Patterson informs me, John, that you were the one who admitted Mrs. Bradwell's friend Mr. Wilkie to the house last week, in my absence, to visit Mrs. Lincoln."

"Yes, sir." He wondered who Mrs. Patterson had heard it from.

"Did you inquire who Mr. Wilkie was?"

"No, sir. Mrs. Bradwell said he was a friend of Mrs. Lincoln's."

"She was lying," said Patterson quietly. "Something she does rather readily." In his mind John heard Mary's voice: *Myra... Well, once she sees a solution to a problem she goes at it like a bull at a gate, and doesn't ask what one feels about it, so long as it gets done.*

And Myra's voice, as she handed him the newspaper on the train: *You leave Dr. Patterson to me.*

No, he thought, seeing what was coming.

No.

It was as if he stood in a burning house, looking up and watching the ceiling collapsing down upon him in an avalanche of flaming debris.

"Mr. Franc Wilkie is a reporter for the Chicago *Times,*" said Patterson. He drew a deep breath. "I know you and I haven't agreed on the diagnosis of Mrs. Lincoln, John. And I have made countless allowances for your lesser experience and for the flaws in your education, as well as, perhaps, your prejudice concerning the widow of the Great Emancipator. But I did trust that you would be professional enough to consult with me, rather than taking matters into your own hands. I am very sorry that I am going to have to dismiss you."

CHAPTER SIXTY-SIX

Chicago August 1875

ALL THE WAY BACK TO CHICAGO, JOHN KEPT THINKING: *What amI doing going back so soon? I just rode this train....*

He felt numb with shock, as if he'd offered his hand to help a child who'd fallen on the street, and the helpless tot had produced an ax and chopped off his arm.

Not just the pain of betrayal—the question of how he was going to get through life missing an arm.

He'd have to tell Clarice.

He'd have to tell Cassy.

He could just hear his sister's scathing voice: *You lost your job over helping a white woman? A crazy woman? If you gonna lose your job helping a crazy woman, how come you don't help Mama?*

The fact that Mary Todd Lincoln was Abraham Lincoln's widow wouldn't cut any ice with Cassy. And in fact, John had not helped Mrs. Lincoln with any thought in mind that assisting her toward liberty was in any sense a payment for his own freedom.

She was eccentric, and in need of help, which he had given her as far as he was able. But once she ceased being delusional—and had apparently learned to control the cause of her delusions, at least for the time being—she did not deserve to be locked up simply so that Robert Lincoln would not be embarrassed.

John leaned his head sideways against the jolting wooden wall of the "colored" car, and stared out at the yellow wheatfields streaming by under black-floored mountains of gathering clouds.

Would he have helped Mary Lincoln if he'd known that assistance was going to cost him, not only the job that supported his family, but the career toward which he'd striven the whole of his adult life?

He didn't know.

Myra Bradwell.

He closed his eyes, and felt the anger rise through him, like pain coming on as the numbness passed away.

A reporter. The man she'd brought in was a Goddamned reporter. And it had never even occurred to her to ask John what the repercussions of that would be.

Even in his fury and despair, he had to admire the cleverness of the maneuver. It completely circumvented the issue of whether Robert Lincoln would give permission for his mother's release or not. Dr. Patterson couldn't afford bad publicity—he was in financial trouble already. When the "Mary Lincoln Is a Prisoner" article came out—and it would undoubtedly contain the words *habeas corpus* somewhere in its text—all those other families who were keeping their female relatives in Bellevue would begin to pull *them* out, too. Sooner than see that, Patterson would shove Mary Lincoln out the door, and at that point Robert would dare not put her elsewhere . . . not unless he wanted to learn the *real* meaning of public embarrassment.

Oh, oops, we happened to squish a Negro in the process, but at least Mrs. Lincoln is free! Hip hip hooray!

Sorry about your job, and your career, and all. . . .

Even a white attendant guilty of that kind of betrayal couldn't hope to find another position of trust, much less a patron willing to teach him. But a white man would at least have the option of seeking a post as a guard—if he really wanted to go on working with the insane—or of going west and looking for work in California or Oregon, far away from the close-knit circles of the Association of Medical Superintendents of American Institutions for the Insane.

A white man could usually get another white man to at least listen to him when he said, "I didn't know. I'll never do it again. . . ."

His salary of sixty dollars a month, joined to what Lionel

made in the stockyards and the income from Cassy's laundry business, was barely enough to make the rent on the house, buy firewood and soap for the laundry, and feed the dozen-plus members of the household. He knew a white man would be paid far more—a railroad porter would make more—but he had looked on the work as the road to better things.

And now there was nothing.

He debarked from the local train at the Twelfth Street station and for a time simply stood on the platform, the hot reek of the city beating on him, crushing him. For two years now the knowledge that he could go back to the green quiet of Batavia had sustained him every time he walked east toward the hellhole streets between tracks and packing-yards.

Now he could not face the thought.

For the first time since he'd left the Army he thought, *I really need a drink.*

Walking into the wrong neighborhood grog-shop, of course, could get you killed, if you were Irish or black or Hungarian or whatever the local regulars were not. But he knew there were saloons all along State Street near the levee and the yards where they didn't care if you were black or white, male or female, human or a pig escaped from the stock-pens, provided you had money to pay for your liquor, and one of these was Flossie's.

Flossie's was a three-story brick building rammed in between two other three-story brick buildings in the block called Coon Hollow. Flossie herself, a blowzy harridan who'd run a parlor-house in New Orleans during the War and a string of brothels in Mobile immediately afterwards, kept a bordello on the upper floors and, according to Lionel, owned the panel-house next door where the customers were robbed systematically rather than intermittently. Flossie's bar-room was long, dark, and nearly empty at this time of the day—four in the afternoon—furnished with rough tables and chairs at which gamblers plied their trade in the evenings.

He bought a whiskey from the slatternly waiter-girl behind the bar and then another, and retreated to the dimness to think about what he was going to say to Clarice.

What he was going to say to Cassy.

At this time of the day, it was mostly the sneak-thieves and pickpockets of the levee, the strong-arm men who made their living selling "protection" to local shopkeepers, the whores from upstairs jolting down preliminary drinks to get them through their first few johns of the evening. A man came in with two girls—the man dark-skinned but with the features of an Italian or a Spaniard, the girls white and barely pubescent—and the waiter-girl behind the bar said, "You better vamoose, Dago; you know better than to bring those little chickabiddies in here."

"You jealous they'll take your customers?" sneered the pimp. "Wouldn't be hard. Give us a couple toots of shock for the girls, and a whiskey for me, and I mean *all* whiskey, not that camphor shit you dole out to the niggers."

John settled back against the wall—after a preliminary check to make sure there wasn't anything walking up it just then—and cradled the faintly camphor-smelling whiskey between his palms. He knew what they cut liquor with in places like this and didn't much care. Griffe Moissant's booze would be the same, closer to home, and there'd be the chance of walking into Lionel there or, God forbid, Phoebe.

He closed his eyes, listening to the voices. So many of them with the smoky inflection of the South: Missouri, Mississippi, Louisiana. So many men, like himself, like Lionel, who'd come north looking for something other than sharecropping the land they'd once worked on as slaves, and more coming in every day.

And finding nothing. Since the banks had collapsed two years ago a man was lucky to have a job sweeping blood off the killing-floors into drains. And those jobs, he knew, went to those who knew people in the yards already. As the voices drifted to him in the saloon's gloom he heard those of men coming in after hunting work, or laboring a few hours stacking lumber or slapping pork in cans amid clouds of steam and pounding machines that could take off a hand or a finger if you blinked....

More men, who hadn't even found that.

"I hear Mushmouth lookin' for a couple boys to help him knock off a big place out by Douglas Park." John glanced up as the voices passed his table, a couple of laborers listening to a dapper weaselly man whom Cassy had pointed out to him once as an enforcer for one of the protection bosses. "You boys lookin' for a few dollars?"

And later—how much later he wasn't sure—he overheard someone say, "Three dollars a day, they askin'! Three dollars to stay on that corner, without them runnin' me off... Some days I don't shine three dollars' worth o' shoes!" The man who was speaking looked at least seventy years old. John wondered how much he had to pay for rent on top of that three dollars, and if he had a family to support.

Get used to it, he thought, his eyes going to the men crowding around the bar as their shift ended at the yards, or slumped morosely on the benches around the room. Three card-games were in progress, run by slick-looking men in flashy suits with diamonds on their stickpins and fingers. In the back room, the click of billiard-balls could be heard, and men's voices, loud with anger and drink.

This is your world now, the only world you're going to have. Luck gave you a single open door, and you let that chance slip away.

Because you pitied a woman who treated you like a human being when no one else did—and because you trusted her friend.

Despair brought the taste of bile to his mouth, and the metallic nastiness of whatever the waiter-girl had given him.

This place, and the house, with Cassy and Mama and all the children, and the stench at the back of the yards. These would be the limits of his experience. And of Cora's, too, when she grew up.

He knew he was getting very drunk, but couldn't remember why he should care. Like Mrs. Lincoln, he had nowhere that day to go. He could smell the stockyards from here, and hear the constant, clanging roar of the trains as they rolled through not three blocks away.

Already it seemed to him that everything he'd gone through and worked for since the War's end was dissolving like a coat of cheap whitewash in the pouring rain of reality.

This was the world into which he had been freed.

The world in which he'd believed that it was possible to make a life for himself.

I was the insane one, he thought.

Dago the Pimp was back, with another girl this time. She couldn't have been as old as Selina, and her round, scared, pretty face reminded him heartrendingly of his sister Lucy— before Lucy had taken to drinking and whoring. One of Flossie's strong-arm men went over to talk to Dago, shoving him. The girl clung close to him, staring around her in desperation, and one of the yard-men went over to her in his shirt and pants all gummed with dirt and dried blood, and pinched her shallow breasts as he talked to her.

It was as if John watched someone else lurch to his feet. One of Flossie's girls intercepted him: "Ain't seen you 'round here before, Handsome." She was "bright," as the white men said. Her hair had been straightened with lye and dyed vivid red and her dress was cut away nearly to the nipples. She was fleshy, like a light-brown satin pillow.

"Excuse me," he said politely, and stepped around her. He caught the blood-caked slaughterer by the wrist and heard himself say, "You old enough to be that poor little girl's daddy. You should be ashamed."

The man turned around, baring broken teeth at him. Dago broke off his argument with the house strong-arm and said, "Now, my friend, that little girl knows more about pleasin' a man than any ten other nymphs of the pavement, and she'll be more than happy to prove it to the both of you." He seized her arm so that his fingers dug into the tender skin. "Won't you, sugar?"

"You get the fuck out of here, Dago, and take your whore with you!" screamed the red-haired girl who'd followed John from his table. "Or I'll tell Flossie!"

"You can stick Flossie up your—"

The red-haired whore snatched a bottle off the bar, smashed it on the bar's edge, and slashed at Dago. Dago's little nymph screamed, and the next second, it seemed, the barroom erupted into violence. Someone—John was never sure who—grabbed him and hurled him back against the bar, the edge gouged his back. The young girl screamed again and John lunged to drag her out of the sudden morass of struggling limbs and slashing glass and steel that had churned into life in the cavelike semidarkness.

Something struck him and he fell, rolling, his old instincts kicking in. He tucked to protect his belly and face as a boot smashed into his ribs, and another caught him glancing on the side of the head. He smelled fresh blood and spilled beer and someone tripped over him, even in the corner against the bar into which he'd rolled. There was shouting and a man bellowed, "Oh my God, oh my God . . . !" the way he'd heard men shriek when they brought them into the hospital tents with their intestines dangling. Then shock caught up with him and he felt himself sinking, colder and colder, down into the earth, to come out chilled to the bone, and aching all over into sudden quiet, near-darkness, and the stink of blood.

John started to sit up and, as it had in the tent at Camp Barker years before, nausea seized him and he rolled over fast, choking as vomit spewed from his lips. A thick Irish voice said, "What d'we got here, Sleepin' Beauty?" and men laughed.

One of the dark shapes in the now nearly empty barroom reached him in two strides—blue-clothed, like the Union soldier all those years ago, with a nightstick instead of a rifle in his hands. John raised his hands to show them empty and the policeman struck him, casually and with full force, slam-

ming him back to the floor and sending lancing agony
through his right arm.

The next moment his hands were jerked behind him, and
the pain blacked out his mind. When he came to, he was lying with his cheek in a puddle of beer-diluted vomit, hand-
cuffed and looking at the three policemen gathered around
the two bodies in the middle of the floor. A woman was talking, shrill and furious—

"—I pay my money to the stationhouse and this sure as
hell isn't the kind of service I expect—"

It wasn't until one of the cops dragged the bodies closer to
the single gaslight still burning near the bar that John recognized Dago the Pimp, with his throat cut from ear to ear and
his whole flashy green suit a single black wash of gore.

The other body was that of his little whore.

HE WAS TAKEN TO THE TWENTY-SECOND PRECINCT HOUSE on
Maxwell Street, and in the morning—night had somehow
fallen while he had mused in his camphorene-induced haze
and the fight had taken place at close to eleven—was taken to
the jail of the Cook County Courthouse on Clark Street,
and indicted for murder.

And passed a week in Hell.

He'd had a little money in his pockets when he'd risen
from his table at Flossie's, but there was none there when he
was arrested. His watch, hat, and jacket had vanished, too.
One of the men in the jail-cell with him was a thick-
shouldered angry laborer named Klauswijz who knocked
John's head against the brick wall and took the meager plate
of food he was given—the other men simply moved aside
and watched—and thereafter stole food from him whenever
it was brought. Anyone with any connection to the protection gangs or gambling bosses had, naturally, been bailed out
on the night of their arrest, so the cells were populated by the
pettiest of independent criminals, smash-and-grab thieves or

thugs for hire, too mentally deficient or too far gone in drink or drugs to be of use to anyone: angry, sullen, violent.

One of the men in the cell turned out to be a cousin of Dago the Pimp. John kept very, very quiet about why he was there.

It seemed to him that he never slept that first week. There were four bunks and eight men in the cell—two men slept on the floor in spite of the roaches and the rats. John sat in the corner near the latrine bucket with his arms folded around him and simply tried not to speak to or look at anyone; thirsty, nodding with exhaustion, legs and arms cramping from days of inactivity, his right wrist puffed up and hurting so that the pain sometimes made him faint.

"They won't even expect me at home till Wednesday," he whispered one night, half-delirious, to Bailey, one of the two other black men in the cell, a scared and rather simple-minded youth who divided his share of the water with him after Klauswijz snatched his away again. "I could be hanged by then."

"Don't break yourself into a dew of sweat about that, boy-o," remarked a wizened Irish drunkard who'd taken over one of the upper bunks. "They're not gonna get 'round to tryin' the likes of you for weeks.... You kill a nigger or a white?"

"I didn't kill anyone," whispered John.

The Irishman crowed with laughter. "Sure, and neither did I!" There was dried blood caked all over his shirt.

By the following Friday morning John would have been willing to be tried and convicted if only for the chance to get out of the cell and walk. When the guard came to the bars and said, "Wilamet? Somebody here to see you," he nearly fell, his legs and body were so cramped and his mind so hazy with exhaustion and hunger.

Cassy was waiting for him in that long room where prisoners were brought, always supposing there was anyone on earth who wanted to see them. John had been there more than once, when he and Cassy had gone to bail out their mother. There was a table and some broken-down benches. The Courthouse was barely four years old—rebuilt after the Fire like everything else in this part of town—but already the visiting-room had the soiled drabness of hard use and neglect, the smells of dirty clothing and dirty flesh, expectorated tobacco, and cigar-smoke.

Most of the visiting women matched the men who were in the cells. Nobody with any money or any connections had anything to do with the Cook County jail.

Even without his glasses—which had also disappeared at Flossie's—he could see the anger that stiffened his sister's body when he told her he'd been sacked. "God damn it, am I the only one . . . ?" she rasped, then stopped herself, breathing hard. He saw her big, knotted hands ball on the grimy table. Saw how she made herself relax. "Are you okay, brother?"

"I think I broke my wrist—broke it or sprained it. Cassy, they got me for murder, for killing a pimp and his girl. I didn't do it, I got caught in a brawl at Flossie's, when I come to they were dead already—"

Cassy whispered, "Jesus." For the first time in her life, she sounded hopeless, and scared.

Cassy, who would walk up and spit in the Devil's face.

That, as much as his own fear of what would happen when he was brought up before a court of white men, felt like the crushing weight of a tomb falling on his shoulders.

She straightened her back. He could almost see her gather up a mouthful of spit. "What're we gonna do?"

"Get in touch with Mrs. Myra Bradwell," said John, and realized, with another cold jolt of shock, that he had no idea where she lived. Panic flashed through him, then he thought a moment, and said, "She's the wife of Judge Bradwell. Somebody here will be able to tell you where to send her a letter, or somebody at the Chicago *Times,* or the *Chicago Review of Law.* They'll be in the City Directory."

Just being out of the cell, being able to move, to talk to his sister, revived something inside him, that had been numbed by days of shock and thirst and pain. One foot in front of the other...

I got away from Blue Hill Plantation, and got Mama all the way to Washington without being caught. Anybody who could do that should be able to get through damn near anything.

He drew a deep breath.

"You tell her that I got sacked—and I got into this trouble—because I helped out her and Mrs. Lincoln." He braced himself for Cassy's spitfire retort, but she said nothing. Squinting across the table at her, he saw that her fear for him had even swamped the anger of him losing his job.

She loved him, he realized. Loved him more than the thought of their home, their survival as a family. Those paled for her beside fear for his survival.

The understanding of the depth of her love—and of his love for her—was honey and sunlight, in the midst of Hell. It burned his eyes with tears.

"And you think that's gonna get this white woman to lift a hand?" Cassy's voice was bitter.

"I do, yes. Cassy, please." She'd dealt with too many wealthy white women who wanted their sheets and petticoats washed right away and not starched too much, to have any high opinion of the breed. "She'll help," he said.

Cassy sniffed.

"She's got to know lawyers. She's a lawyer herself. She owes me."

"I got lots of white ladies owe me," retorted Cassy, getting to her feet. Through the haze of myopia John saw she was wearing her Sunday-go-to-meeting dress, faded sage-green chintz, the neatest she had. Like armor against the dirt and poverty and scorn of the jail. "And if they didn't need me for somethin' else, not a one of them would pay me." She reached across the table, and took his left hand.

"You keep strong, John. We'll get you out. With or without your white lady lawyer friend."

When John got back to the cell, Klauswijz and the boy Bailey were both gone. Before evening their places were taken by a gambler—who was bailed out within hours—and a morphine addict who proceeded to vomit, purge, and howl for the remainder of the day and night, but at least John got his own share of water and food. The gambler brought a newspaper with him, and left it behind. It contained a letter to the editor from Judge James Bradwell, accusing Dr. Patterson of treatment "calculated to drive Mrs. Lincoln insane" and a threat to come knocking on the "prison-house" doors with a writ of *habeas corpus.*

That night he slept like a dead man, and dreamed of the tangled woodland battlefields of the Wilderness between Crown Point and Richmond. Dreamed of searching through the woods, and finding dying soldiers as they lay sobbing amid hackberry and weeds. Dreamed of carrying them back to the ambulance-carts, with their blood dripping down his back. He saw the dim shapes of the dead-carts above him, the piles of bodies heaped like cordwood. A tall man in shirtsleeves was working there alone, lifting the dead onto the cart, and as he came nearer John saw it was Mr. Lincoln, wearing a butcher's bloodied apron, his hands and arms crimson to the biceps. Every time he turned, John saw the gaping wound in the back of his head, where Booth's bullet had smashed through the skull.

John asked him, "Did you know this was going to happen?"

"I guessed it," said Lincoln. "Yes."

"Was it worth it?"

Lincoln bent to help John load a corpse onto the cart. It was the little whore who'd stared around her in such terror at Flossie's, the little girl who so resembled Lucy. The older man stood looking down at her for a moment, then sighed like a death-rattle. "I think so."

"Even for this?" The fog was thinning. The battlefield lay exposed, stretching as far as anyone could see, filling the world. Smoke drifted, with the stink of blood and sulfur. Flies roared in black clouds. This then was the glory of the coming of the Lord, John thought: bodies lying like the trampled skins of grapes, wrath hanging like a poison over the stricken field. Somehow he knew they'd be picking up the bodies of the slain for months, for years. His mother was out there dead somewhere, and Cassy and Lionel and Lizabet Keckley and Frederick Douglass, and men and women not yet born. "None of them asked to die. They asked only to live."

Lincoln said, "We all die, John." And with a self-conscious gesture fingered the wound in the back of his head, looked at the blood on his hand, then shrugged and wiped it on his trouser-leg. "Would you go back if you could?"

John grinned up at him. "Not a chance."

And Lincoln grinned back, suddenly young. "Neither would I."

Chapter Sixty-seven

"I DO NOT KNOW WHAT I AM GOING TO DO WITH YOU!" Robert slapped the newspaper down on the bench beside Mary, the strained violence of his movement speaking volumes for a lifetime of restricting what he felt and how he reacted. A lifetime of dealing with Mary. Of being pointed at as Abraham Lincoln's son.

He'd come on her in the rose garden, striding up the gravel drive—Mary had seen Argus let him in at the front gate, had seen by the way he walked that he was furious. She'd considered going into the house and making him ask Dr. Patterson to bring her to the parlor, where at least he couldn't shout and rail at her, but a kind of weary anger kept her in her seat.

Let him shout, she thought. Though Dr. Patterson had only told her that John Wilamet had "decided to quit us," she knew Robert must have had something to do with his dismissal a week ago. And her anger at the loss of her friend—at the loss of the only person in this place who truly had her good at heart—had fire-cured the hard knot of strength within her that had somehow gotten lost in the soft haze of her medicines. She found that even in cold blood, she no longer really cared whether Robert was angry at her or not.

She picked up the paper and glanced at the place to which Robert had folded it open.

"Why is it necessary that you do anything with me?" she asked quietly. "Because you can't endure the thought of having a mother who travels around the country without a male protector? Or a mother who is interested in politics and writes letters to newspapers? Or is it just that you don't like the sight of me spending money that you think of as yours?"

"We've been through this before, Mother." He spoke as if trying to conceal a painful carbuncle whose existence was beneath the dignity of Abraham Lincoln's son. "You think that by getting your friends to bring calumny down upon Dr. Patterson and his family—none of whom have ever done you the slightest harm..."

"Not done me *harm*? Not done me harm, to suggest to you that the best thing that you could do with an embarrassing female relation is to have her declared mad and locked up? In *his* private madhouse, at the rate of two hundred dollars a month...Or did you find Bellevue with a pin and a City Directory?"

Robert's blue eyes shifted, then returned to hers aflame with indignation. "It didn't happen like that at all. Dr. Patterson's brother examined you in Washington, when you had your carriage accident. Dr. Patterson was one of several doctors I consulted about your sanity."

"The only one who runs a private institution and was looking for patients to fill it up, I daresay. And on the subject of calumny, you have been calling me insane—in the public newspapers, no less—since the time I began fighting for Congress to give me the remainder of your father's salary so we could have something to live on while that dilatory hog Judge Davis collected the interest on your father's estate. You called me insane while I tried to get a pension to live on at a time when Congress and every wealthy businessman in the East were shoving handfuls of greenbacks and house-deeds into Sam Grant's pockets for doing less to save the Union than your father did, and at far less cost to himself. Don't think I don't know that you were calling me insane to your cronies at Harvard and in the Army as well."

"You *are* insane!" he shouted at her. "Good God, Mother, you should have seen yourself when you came off the train last March, raving that I was going to die! When you were wandering around the halls of the Grand Pacific in your nightdress, swearing that voices were speaking to you out of the walls!"

Tears filled Mary's eyes and with them, the blinding urge to turn on him her old weapons of sarcasm and hysterics, of guilt and shame. Instead she said, "Obviously, I was ill, and now am better. You can ask Dr. Patterson, or his son, if I have had any such delusions while I have been here. I reserve the right to remain eccentric—I never noticed anyone trying to lock up your Uncle Levi when he'd go on shouting rampages, or for heaven's sake Cash Clay. . . ."

"The only reason no one has tried so far to lock up Cassius Clay is because they're afraid he'll shoot them in the process."

"The only reason no one has tried to lock up Cash," said Mary firmly, "is because he is a man. And a man can make as much of a jackass of himself as he pleases, writing letters to newspapers or switching political sides or speaking to mobs of freedmen urging rebellion against Reconstruction . . . or keeping a harem of Russian dancing-girls and driving his poor wife to distraction and divorce, for that matter. And half the members of Congress, over the years, haven't been much better."

She folded the newspaper with James Bradwell's letter in it and set it again on the bench at her side, and shaded her eyes as she looked up at her son. "But a woman is considered mad if she spends her own money to excess, or loses her temper too often and too loudly, or seeks communication with the souls of those she loved in life, in order to comfort her grief."

"If she hands all her money to charlatans who claim to be the 'media' of that communication, yes, I'd say that was insane," snapped Robert.

"But it is *my money.* If I were to hand it all to the Catholic Church, or to the Freedmen's Relief Association—or to the clerk at the jewelry counter at Marshall Field's, for that matter, like some women I could name—it is *my business,* and not yours."

And she saw him stiffen up with stubborn anger at the

idea that any doings of his female belongings—whether mother, wife, or daughter—were not his business.

She went on, "My sister tells me that you wrote to her warning her that Myra Bradwell was the 'high priestess' of a 'gang of Spiritualists' who were trying to get their hands on my money. And that she is in perfectly good health, and not—as you specifically told me—that she was too ill to have me go and stay with her."

"I did not say *specifically* that she was too ill."

She promptly fished for the letter in her reticule, and with blotches of anger staining his cheekbones Robert raised his hand. After a moment he said, "I was only thinking of you, Mother. This place is good for you. You said yourself you have ceased having those delusions, and it is because you have been living quietly here, and not exciting your brain with the confusing distractions of travel and of those da—" He caught himself from swearing, and corrected, "—those wretched table-tappers who do nothing but raise the passions of women to such a degree that they result in derangement."

"You mean they raise the passions of women to such a degree that they result in disagreement with men," retorted Mary. And then, as Robert opened his mouth, she added, "As you just said yourself, we have been through this before, and we shall probably never agree. But there is a law of *habeas corpus* in this state—"

"You damned—wretched—women, quoting the law..."

"The law that you'd rather we didn't know about? As slaveholders preferred that their chattels not learn about it? I expected better of your father's son!"

Mary stood, and shook out her black skirts. The morning was growing hot. The scent of the roses swathed her like a veil, as if the sweetness were intended to mask the dim screams coming from the house. That would be Mrs. Hill, strapped in a hydrotherapy tank.

"There is a law of *habeas corpus* in Illinois, Robert. And I *am* going to get out of this place. As I'm sure that neither of us wishes me to come live with you and your *lovely* wife—"

her voice twisted with scorn "—perhaps it would be best if you stopped lying to my sister, and Mrs. Bradwell, and Dr. Patterson, and accepted that fact. It is possible for me to be sane in places other than the one you sanction, and to get help from sources other than those of which you approve."

"I will not have you running about the world creating an embarrassment for the Lincoln family!"

"Your embarrassment is your own problem, Robert, not mine," she pointed out icily. "Please feel free to disown me. And if at any time in the future I start hearing voices coming out of the floor, or begin having delusions of men following me—that is, men other than those *you* have hired yourself—you may call in your mad-doctors to examine me again. But not until that time. May I take this?" She held up the newspaper.

Robert turned from her without a word, and walked stiffly away down the gravel drive to the gate. She watched him go, her heart aching. Not with the loss of the man, she realized. For years, she understood now, he had been a stranger to her. Maybe he always had. But she was losing the sturdy boy who'd run through the leafy aisles of the vegetable garden on Jackson Street, the boy the other children had called Cock-Eye, the boy who'd darted about the steamboat deck to look at the paddles, and the young man who'd written to her wild with excitement: *The other boys said how proud I must be, to have him for my father. . . .*

Her heart went back further, to the rainy November night and the silence of Simeon Francis's house; Lincoln's weight pressing her body into the worn sofa. The hoarse gasp of his breath, the brush of his lips on her face, the fire reflected in his gray eyes.

Life is short. We don't know what the future will bring. I don't want never to have done this. . . .

She realized that she still felt the same way. That if she could go back, and erase everything that had passed between that night, and the tall angry figure striding from her down the garden path, she would not. It was all precious to her, every moment, the painful along with the sweet. The lie that she had told had made Robert what he was, and what he would go on to be: the whole of their relationship implicit in those few impulsive words that she could not take back, once they'd been spoken.

Everything that had come of that lie seemed to settle into her heart, like wings folding. It was what was. For the first time in over thirty years, she felt no shame, only a profound sadness.

Robert was gone. With him he was taking Mamie, and the other children Young Mary would bear: Abraham Lincoln's grandchildren. *Her* grandchildren.

With him he was taking the past, and whatever future that she might have had, with Abraham Lincoln's only surviving son.

And though a tear crept down her face for that vanished future, she was still glad that she had done what she had done, and had what she had had.

CASSY AND CLARICE BOTH CAME TO THE COOK COUNTY JAIL on Saturday to visit John, and again on Sunday with Selina and Phoebe and a box of apples and hard-boiled eggs. If there had been any repercussions or rage on Phoebe's part— or Cassy's, for that matter—about money and the future, they had taken place at home. Just the knowledge that his family knew where he was, that they cared about him enough to endure the streetcar ride and the walk in the brutal August sun, made the jail-cell bearable.

On Monday a young white gentleman named Leeland turned up. A lawyer, he said, and a friend of Mrs. Bradwell, he was willing to argue John's case. In the crowded visiting-room he listened to John's account of the evening at Flossie's, and took notes. This was more than was being done, John couldn't help noticing, by the sparse scattering of pro bono attorneys pulled from the court roster to help the more deserving or endangered of the other prisoners.

One of these, a stout sleepy gentleman in an appalling checked suit, kept shaking his head at his client's impassioned protests of innocence and saying, "I'll do what I can, Mr.—uh—Mr. Belker—but you understand I mostly do probates, not murders...."

He also couldn't keep from noticing what was obvious even without his spectacles: that he was the only black man in conversation with a member of the legal profession, probates or otherwise. He guessed—his guess a near certainty—that without Myra Bradwell pulling in a favor, he'd have been arguing his own not-very-convincing case in court.

"Oh, they haven't got a leg to stand on," said Leeland, when John had finished his account of what little he'd seen of the fight. "The police had a couple of bodies on their hands and wanted to make an arrest to impress their sergeant. I'd wager they don't even have any witnesses, other than the flatfoot who made the arrest."

"That'll be enough to get me hanged, if we don't have at least one witness that I was knocked out on the floor," pointed out John grimly. "And you're going to have your work cut out for you finding one. I surely don't advise you to try going into Flossie's alone and asking questions."

"Good God!" Leeland looked horrified at the thought. "I know better than to do that. But we'll be all right." The young lawyer gave John a cheerful slap on the shoulder. "Half the time, when the judge hears that there's going to be an attorney for the defense at all, he just drops the charges, especially if there's no witnesses. I'll see what I can do."

He stood—he'd talked to John for all of about five minutes, an eon in that room and those circumstances. The man at the next table seemed to be vainly trying to state his case in a language his attorney didn't understand. Leeland said, "Mrs. Bradwell told me to get you off, and she'll never speak to me again if I don't."

"You work for her?" John stood also—the bored-looking guard came forward, to take him back. When John moved, the manacles on his wrists jangled on the battered wooden table, rubbing older scars. He was surprised at how angry it made him, to wear chains again.

"In a manner of speaking." Leeland resumed his stylish new derby with a flourish. "She got me work in her husband's office when I first started out, and had no money, and let me earn extra writing articles for her newspaper. I owe her."

As he walked John back to the cell the guard muttered, "Lawyers for niggers, what'll they want next?"

Through the next nerve-wracking week he was keenly aware of how lucky he was, as he saw some of those who'd been in the holding cell before him taken away. He heard from others about the cursory trials that lasted barely twenty minutes, testimony from policemen, storekeepers, bartenders who merely shrugged off the questions put to them by the accused, or answered with wisecracks that drew grins from the jury.

The fact that he knew he wasn't going to have to get up and question a couple of white cops who wanted to impress their sergeant with their detective abilities eased his mind considerably, but did nothing to reduce the furnace of sour anger burning within him. He would—probably—walk out of here with his life, but there remained the question of where he would go when he did. And in the weeks in the cell, he saw what he had always been able to turn away from before: the sheer extent of what poverty did, to those whom no one regarded as quite human enough to employ.

To all intents and purposes, John understood that he was back at Camp Barker yet again, being told off by Washington ladies' yard-hands and beaten up by Irish teamsters.

All because he had tried to help the woman whose husband had freed him. The woman who had treated him kindly, on his first day in the Promised Land.

JOHN HAD FEARED THAT MR. LEELAND'S CASUAL REMARKS about the charges being dropped were a mere justification

for not putting himself to the danger of going out and looking for a witness, but it turned out that the lawyer had a
clearer awareness of the courts' corruption than John did.
On the eighth of September—almost a month after his
arrest—he was taken out of his cell, informed that the
charges against him had been dropped, and let loose onto the
streets of Chicago. He was bearded, filthy, and shaky with
lack of exercise. Through the two-mile-plus walk to the grid
of dirty alleyways between train-tracks and stockyard near
the levee, he had to stop repeatedly to regain his strength and
his breath.

If the breezes hadn't been cool that day off Lake Michigan
he wasn't sure he'd have made it.

At the house—where everyone had been living on oatmeal because Lionel was carrying the whole family on his
slender wages—John had a bath in Cassy's used laundry-
water, shaved, and slept for twenty-six hours. When he
woke, the first thing he saw was Phoebe, sitting beside his cot
with a fan of braided newspaper in her hands, keeping the
flies off his face.

The following day he walked back uptown to Michigan
Avenue, to pay a visit to Myra Bradwell.

The house was three stories, fronted with brown brick,
reminding him a little of those he'd seen in New York. He
had to squint to see the house number. Griffe Moissant had
lent him a pair of glasses and they weren't nearly strong
enough. A German servant answered the door, and she
looked him up and down in horror. He wondered if a white
man, clothed in the clean but shabby second-best suit that for
a miracle Phoebe hadn't pawned for medicine-money, would
have been asked over the threshold.

"Yes?"

"I'm here to see Mrs. Bradwell. Would you please tell her
that Mr. John Wilamet from Bellevue Place is here?" A little
awkwardly, because his arm was still in a sling, he put one of
his cards on her tray.

Put that in your pipe and smoke it.

The woman's expression clearly indicated that only super-human Christian charity prevented her from pointing out that she had knickknacks to dust and could not afford the time to be announcing Negroes to Mrs. Bradwell. When she closed the door in his face John kept his temper by counting the seconds. It was six and a half minutes—far longer than it would take for a woman to climb a flight of stairs and grunt a visitor's name—before the door was opened again, and the maid said grudgingly, "Please come in." She took his hat with the delicacy of one who expected it to be lousy and put a piece of newspaper on the marble-topped rosewood hall table before setting it down, then followed him up the stairs like a detective trailing a prospective shoplifter.

John was sorely tempted to turn around and yell, "Boo!"

"Mr. Wilamet, I am delighted to see you!" Myra rose from her desk, strode to the door to meet him. The room—a bright little chamber above the kitchen that in any other house would have been a sewing-room—was clearly her fortress and sanctum, lined with shelves that bore law-books stacked neatly on their sides, long inky newspaper galleys, docketed folders of papers, and a dozen big commonplace-books of clippings. Wooden file cabinets and an old but spot-less desk took up most of the room. There was one chair for a visitor and one at the desk, a bright rag rug, and pots of ivy on the sill of the windows that ran the length of the room and gave a view of a rather overgrown garden below.

On the wall, bordered in black, was a sepia ambrotype of a little girl in a white dress, with bunches of fresh asters in the vase in front of it.

Myra went on in her brisk voice, "Leeland told me Monday Judge Hertford was dropping the charges. Old Hertford's always ready to save himself trouble. I don't blame you for resting a few days before coming to see me."

Monday, he thought dourly. And yesterday—the day of his release—had been Wednesday. Two days, before they'd gotten around to actually letting him go. It figured. He was lucky they hadn't lost the papers until Christmas.

"You're so thin, my poor boy! And your arm . . . I'm afraid you've had a most dreadful time. But Leeland is truly a marvel. You're lucky to have caught me—I'm leaving this evening for Springfield, to be there tomorrow when Mary arrives at her sister's house."

"It's settled, then?" He wasn't really surprised. He'd followed the bitter interchange of letters in the papers, which Cassy and Clarice had brought him almost daily, including the quite masterful article by Franc Wilkie in the *Times*. Caught between Robert Lincoln and fear of public disgrace, Dr. Patterson had put up as much of a fight as he could, but the conclusion, John had guessed, was foregone.

"There will be universal satisfaction to know that Mrs. Lincoln has been restored to her reason and to her friends," proclaimed one journal; and another, *"When a woman spends her own money lavishly and appears a little different from others she ought not to be placed behind iron bars. She has borne all and wronged no one."*

Dr. Patterson had written in a letter to the *Tribune*, *"I am willing to record the opinion that such is the character of her malady she will not be content to do this, and that the experiment, if made, will result only in giving her the coveted opportunity to make extended rambles, to renew the indulgence of her purchasing mania, and other morbid manifestations."*

"DR. PATTERSON," James Bradwell had responded in a final blistering letter to the *Chicago Post and Mail*, *"IS A VERY PECULIAR MAN. . . ."*

"Robert is frothing at the mouth." There was rich satisfaction in Myra's voice. "I've received some of the most frigidly polite letters in the English language from him, once he saw that he could not keep his mother under lock and key where she would be forced to stop spending the money that he's counting on, and behave the way he thinks a real woman ought to. I must say, he certainly doesn't have his father's way with words—or his mother's either, for that matter. It was Wilkie's article that did the trick, though!"

She turned back to her desk, where she laid hands on it at once, already neatly cut and tucked into a folder.

"That's what set off the round of support. You know there were ministers who made her the subject of sermons, demanding her release? Probably preached by the very same ministers who execrated her a few years ago for trying to sell off her old dresses. But there's nothing like a good newspaper campaign to force an issue. . . ."

"You might have told me."

At the hardness of his tone, her hazel eyes narrowed.

"I daresay I might have," she replied evenly. "Would you have helped, if you knew?"

"If I'd known that it would cost me my job? The sole support of my wife, my mother, and my child? I don't know."

He saw her face change, all the triumphant ebullience leaving it, and that lawyer mask with which he was so familiar emerging, like the skull through the skin. "Is that why you're here?" she inquired. A lawyer's voice, like the face, that gave away nothing: every word precisely graded so as to offer not the slightest handhold to an opponent.

He wondered if Lincoln had gotten like that in court, and then realized, *Of course he had.*

"If you mean, am I here to ask you for money, no." And to his complete surprise—because he hadn't had the slightest idea of what he was, in fact, going to say to her, he went on, "I'm here to thank you for sending Mr. Leeland to get me out. I probably owe him—and you—my life. Black men get very brief trials in this town."

She inclined her head, still watchful. "If you thought I would have abandoned you after the help you gave me and Mrs. Lincoln, you can't have formed a very complete picture of my character." She was still angry.

"To tell you the truth, Mrs. Bradwell, in the twelve years that I've been a free man—and the fifteen years I was a slave—I learned the hard way never to completely trust whites, because so many of the things that go into making up

their characters are...not things that I—we—have experience with. It's sometimes hard for me to read whites. Mostly,
on Maxwell Street, we just know what's done to us."

His eyes were on hers as he spoke—and it was still strange
to him, to look into a white woman's eyes after half a lifetime's training not to—and it was her gaze that fell.

After a moment she said, "Won't you sit down, Mr.
Wilamet?" She reached for and rang the silver bell on her
desk. "Heidi... Please bring coffee for Mr. Wilamet and myself," she told the maid and took her seat at the desk, turning
her chair to face him as he sat down. "I'm sorry," she said
simply. "I was quite wrong not to trust you... not to consider the results of my action more carefully than I did. You
must admit I was justified."

"I admit you were justified," replied John quietly, and ad-
justed Griffe's glasses, which were too narrow and gave him
a headache. "But you were also wrong."

Myra's lips tightened, and John recalled her words on the
train from Springfield, about how the feminists in the abolition movement had been betrayed by those men who
thought they could win if they separated freedom for black
men from freedom for all. Enough to make a woman carry a
grudge, if she didn't know too much about how those black
men got treated after their much-talked-about Freedom finally came through.

"Yes, I was wrong," she told him. "And even giving you
back a future isn't sufficient payment, if I've damaged that future beyond repair. What can I do for you?"

"I don't know. What *can* you do for me? Besides coloniz-
ing me to Africa."

Myra laughed, just as Heidi came in with the coffee-tray.
The maid's face was like stone as she set it down, but John
guessed she'd have a few words to say to the cook about their
mistress's eccentricities in welcoming a Negro as an equal.
He wondered if the cup he drank from would be accidentally "broken" in the interests of "cleanliness," while Myra
was in Springfield.

"How well do you write?" Myra asked. "How clearly? Most lawyers want clerks with some legal training, but I can certainly bully one of my husband's staff into taking you on as an assistant clerk. The pay won't be much...."

"It's better than rolling cigars," said John.

Myra looked surprised.

"Or sweeping a saloon—which are just about the only jobs a black man can get in this town, unless he knows someone. And black men never know anyone, except other black men."

"Rather like being a woman," she replied drily. "A woman seeking employment—other than prostitution or sewing—encounters exactly the same thing. They take one look at *you* and say, 'Oh, you're black.' They take one look at *me* and say, 'Oh, you're a woman. You have a "nervous constitution" and can't be trusted not to—' "

She broke off. "Mr. Wilamet," she said, with a different emphasis on the words, "how well do you write? Because I need articles for my newspaper about laws concerning the treatment of the insane—particularly women. You worked at Bellevue—and as I recall you said you worked at the Jacksonville asylum as well. Do you think you could research in the law and medical journals to write about the abuses there, in the light of your own experience? Again, the pay won't be much."

"Again," said John, "it's better than rolling cigars."

He stepped out the door of Myra Bradwell's home into sunlight, and wind blowing across the spangled surface of the lake. Beyond the trees of Lake Park a train rolled by along the dark cindery line of track between water and land, noisy even in this fashionable neighborhood. A policeman walking his beat eyed him, but didn't cross the street. John wondered if, in between writing about madhouses, he might slip in a few articles about the Cook County jail as well.

He realized that for the next few years he'd be working with Myra Bradwell.

Not how he'd pictured the Promised Land.

But it was a start.

Feeling as if he'd found a dollar in the streets of wartime Washington to carry back to Camp Barker, he set off down Michigan Avenue for home.

Chapter Sixty-eight

"I TRUST EVERYTHING IS TO YOUR SATISFACTION, MRS. Lincoln?"

Dr. Patterson's voice was stiff, as he stood in the doorway of her little room, an indistinct shape against the gaslights of the hall. For the past month—since he had learned from Robert the identity of the Mr. Wilkie whom Myra had brought to see her—Patterson had been hard put to be polite to Mary, lecturing her several times a day on her untruthfulness, as if it were a mark of insanity to mistrust one's jailers. Every time she turned around, she'd encountered Gretchen or Zeus or Mrs. Patterson, scribbling notes of her behavior.

Searching, she knew, for evidence that she was insane, and that Dr. Patterson and Robert were right.

Lately—since Mr. Wilkie's article had appeared—this had ceased. But she still felt anxious, as if everything she did would be used against her.

Patterson went on, "Your son will be here in the morning, to escort you to your sister's house. I have made arrangements for your trunks to be shipped at the end of the week. I hope you know what you're doing, in insisting on leaving Bellevue, Mrs. Lincoln...."

It was a rhetorical opening to a lecture on the virtues of lotos-eating, but she responded sweetly, "That is the entire case at issue, Doctor, is it not?"

He pokered up exactly like young Mr. Presby used to, when Mary had pinked a hole in the tutor's Yankee self-righteousness. He said, "Good-night, Mrs. Lincoln," and stalked off down the hall.

She closed the door. She could hear Amanda moving around in the adjoining room. Packing, she supposed.

Amanda had agreed to accompany her as a nurse to Springfield, for despite—or perhaps because of—or in addition to—her reduction in her medicines, Mary still felt far from well.

Her back, neck, and shoulder still hurt; her privates itched and she still had to use the toilet a dozen times a night (and wouldn't *that* be a pleasure with Elizabeth's room next to hers!). She still quarreled unreasonably with whoever crossed her path some days, still had those strange moments of feeling detached from her body, of feeling she was on the verge of losing herself.

And that was, she supposed, what her life would become. Amanda was one of the few who had agreed with John Wilamet's judgment that no more than two watered spoonfuls of medicine were to be taken on any one day, no matter what she said or felt. Mary knew this was best, but no day went by that she didn't think, at least once: *Just one more spoonful, because my back is extra bad today....* She thought about the long years ahead and shivered.

It had been easier to put such thoughts away when she'd had John to talk to. Myra had told her that Patterson had dismissed the young black man assisting them, and that he'd later gotten into trouble—wrongfully—with the police: that she was getting one of Jamie's law cronies to help him. Once she got to Elizabeth's, she reflected, she'd ask Myra where to write to him, perhaps even see him. On the days when the cravings were so bad, it did her good to talk.

On the nights like tonight, the thought of seeing Myra, or John, or one of her other friends was the only thing she could hold on to, like lights glimpsed in a wilderness of dark.

If she went back to taking more medicine than she should, Robert would be able to lock her up again. This time forever.

The little warm stir of anger—of fight—helped. *I'll show him.*

In nine months, Myra had told her, they'd be able to go to court and have the judgment of insanity lifted from her.

In nine months she'd be truly free.

And then, I will return to Europe, where Robert will not be able to touch me. Where he'll never be "embarrassed" by me again.

She closed her eyes, recalling the warming sunlight of Italy, the tumbled bronze-purple hills of Scotland, London's rain-gray streets. The wooded hills above Frankfurt, its cobbled lanes and the bright-hued dresses of the ladies strolling along the Zeil in the chill sunshine.

Nine months of living with Elizabeth, whom she had not seen in ten years. Of living under the same roof as Ninian, as she had when she was twenty-one.

Nine months of coming downstairs every day to the double-parlor where Dr. Henry had sat by the fire: *He is a man whose heart is stronger than his body.* . . . Nine months of crossing the porch where Ninian had stood in the snow and told Lincoln to relinquish his sister-in-law's hand.

We cannot always be children under our fathers' roofs. . . .

Nine months of eating dinner in the dining-room where Lincoln had slipped on her finger the now-too-tight gold band that said, *A.L. to M.T. Nov. 4 1842 Love Is Eternal.* Of seeing his gray eyes looking out of every shadow at her.

Of knowing that Merce Conkling and Julia Trumbull and her perfidious sister Ann and all the other false friends of former days were whispering about her over their afternoon tea.

She did not know how she was going to endure it.

Nor could she even contemplate how she was going to live through the years to come.

That night she dreamed about Lincoln.

She was in the carriage with him again, under the dappled shade of the Washington dogwoods. She thought, *No! Not this again . . . !* unable to bear the thought of what was coming. To sit beside him in the theater, to hear the crack of Booth's pistol and feel her husband's arm jerk in her grip, then the weight of him slump down on her shoulder. "We must both try to be more cheerful," he was saying, and looking up, she saw again how worn his face was, how lined with four years of sleepless nights, four years of sorrow. "With our dear Willie's death, we have both been very miserable."

"I have been very miserable," said Mary firmly, and took his hand. "And not just because of Willie's death."

He looked surprised, because this had not actually happened, nor had she ever dreamed of stepping out of the actual past before. This memory of their last afternoon together had always been too precious to alter, even to evade the grief that followed. He put his arm around her then, and sighed. "I know," he said. "I am sorry, Molly."

She could feel the warmth of his fingers through the gloves they both wore.

"You did the best you could," she told him quietly, and rested her head on his shoulder, thankful that this dream didn't include the cavalry escort. "And you did a hero's work. But you abandoned me. You left me behind—left me out of your life. After all our years together. And then you left me alone."

It was the thing she had always longed to say to him, in all those darkened parlors, in all those ghostly rooms where the music of far-off violins had whispered across the Veil between the worlds. She never had, for it would not do, to let anyone know the truth about him: that like other men he was a man, capable of temper and thoughtlessness, and of ignoring or disappointing his wife.

It would never do to let anyone know the truth about her: that her wholehearted love had been mingled, all along, with anger, frustration, and the selfish, devouring need to have more of his love than he would give. More than he *could* give.

Maybe more than anyone could ever give.

She had never known how to break past this: first because he would be great, then because he was President, and finally because of the death that had raised him to martyrdom and herself to the thankless role of a martyr's wife.

And he had never appeared to her, as Tad and Willie and

Eddie had, in those hazy, glowing spells that she now recognized as opium-dreams.

He asked gently, "Do you think I really wanted to leave you, Molly? In the end?"

In life she would have wept, but in her dream she seemed to have control of both her temper and her tears. "No. And I know I'm not an easy woman to live with. I could have done better. . . . But so could you. I know you didn't mean to hurt me, but you did. I wish I could say that I never meant to hurt you. . . . I am sorry that I *did* mean it, sometimes."

He smiled at her, as he had when she'd work herself into a fret about a fancied slight or some day-to-day crisis in their Springfield days, and squeezed her shoulder gently with one long arm. "It happens. I recovered."

The sun was sinking, and looking past him, she saw that they weren't in Washington at all, but driving along the Richmond road on the outskirts of Lexington. She saw Henry Clay's house, Ashland, among its beautiful gardens, and the low brick shape of Rose Hill on the other side of the road. But the countryside that lay beyond them was the Illinois prairie, as it had been when first she and her father had taken the stage up from St. Louis, empty, baked, and golden in the fading evening light.

She took a deep breath, and said, "I'm sorry I lied to you. About Robert, I mean."

"Bob's a good boy," said Lincoln. "And a fine man. He has his own path to walk. You did for him what you could."

"I just didn't want to be alone." And hearing her own words, she smiled her rueful sidelong smile. "And now after all that, here I am, alone anyway."

"We're all alone sometimes, Molly," said Lincoln gently. "Sometimes that's the way we need to be. We all do what we have to do about it. Like the old farmer said, some days you get the bear and some days the bear gets you. I am purely sorry that I made you unhappy—and glad that I could make you happy, when I did. Promise me you'll do what you need to do, to be as happy as you can."

She sighed, and answered, "I'll do what I can."

"That's my Molly."

They were coming into Springfield, passing the Globe Tavern, where she glimpsed an empty carriage standing waiting for her, and a gaggle of loungers listening to a story-teller in the darkness of the porch. In the flare of torchlight as they went by the tavern's doors she saw that it was John Wilamet driving the carriage in which they rode—Myra, she thought, must have gotten him that job after he'd been dismissed from Bellevue. His eyes met hers and he smiled.

Then Lincoln drew her to him, and kissed her in the sunset's amber glow, the strength of his arm so familiar, the taste of his mouth what it had always been. They held each other like adolescents in the first wild springtime of love.

The carriage turned down Second Street, and Mary saw Elizabeth waiting for her in the dim glow of the porch lamps, Ninian standing tall behind her. Myra was beside her, and Robert, looking like he'd been sucking a lemon. In the soft blue twilight with its thick scent of honeysuckle, she glimpsed other forms on the porch: Lizabet Keckley, she thought, and handsome young Elmer Ellsworth in his Zouave uniform, and Stephen Douglas like a dandified little bantam rooster, and Dr. Henry and Cash Clay.

The carriage drew to a halt, and Lincoln opened the door and swung lightly down, holding out his hand to her to steady her on the high step.

"You can't come in with me?" Mary asked, though she knew that wasn't allowed. "Even for a little?" He shook his head.

"I'll meet you a ways down the road."

Mary smiled at him, gathered up her petticoats, and stepped down. She was wearing, she noted, the pink faille that she'd had on that first evening in Springfield, when her father had gone looking for Ninian and drunken old Professor Kittridge had come over to lecture her on the evils of slavery.

She looked up at Lincoln and smiled. "I'll look forward to it."

"As will I."

He took off his hat and leaned down to kiss her, then sprang up into the carriage again. "You have a good time, Molly."

Not at all sure that she would, Mary walked up the path to her sister's house through the dream's blue twilight, trying not to look back.

ON JUNE 15, 1876, THE CHICAGO COURT REVERSED ITS DECISION and declared Mary Todd Lincoln sane. She left Springfield in September, traveling to New York with her great-nephew Lewis Baker and thence to Europe, where she settled in Pau, a pleasant town at the foot of the French Pyrenees. For four years she lived there alone, alternating between profound self-pity and the comfortable solitude of an expatriate widow. Though always a recreational spender, she never again ran into serious debt and always kept meticulous track of her money through a financial manager. She traveled to Italy and through southern France, and even stayed out of politics (mostly).

When former President Grant and his wife stopped in Pau in December of 1879 on their round-the-world post-Administration trip, Julia Grant claimed that she had "not learned" of Mrs. Lincoln's presence in Pau until the night before they were leaving town, and it was "too late to make her a visit" or invite her to any of the receptions, parades, or banquets given the war hero by the city fathers.

In 1880, her health and eyesight failing, Mary returned to Springfield. There she lived as a semi-invalid in four rooms of Elizabeth's house: bedroom, sitting-room, and two rooms in which to store the sixty-four trunks whose weight nearly caved in the floor-boards. Her relatives describe her as living alone in the darkened rooms (kept dim because of corneas literally abraded from half a lifetime of tears), compulsively sorting through the contents of her trunks. But when President James Garfield was assassinated in 1881 and his widow was given a pension of $5,000, Mary assembled helpers and rushed to Washington to demand parity. She got it, plus back payments, plus interest.

She collapsed on the eleventh anniversary of Tad's death—July 15, 1882—and died of a stroke the following day, which was the thirty-third anniversary of her father's. Robert came to the funeral, and inherited close to $58,000.

Mary was buried with Willie, Eddie, Tad, and Mr. Lincoln in Springfield.

Robert Todd Lincoln lived to be eighty-three, serving as President of the Pullman Company and dying a millionaire. He was Secretary of War, to James Garfield and Chester A. Arthur, and his objections and obstructions about sending support to the Greeley Polar Expedition of 1884 have been blamed for the disaster that overtook the explorers. From 1889 to 1893 he was the U.S. Minister to Great Britain.

In 1881, Robert Lincoln was among President Garfield's party at the train-station when Garfield was shot by a disappointed office-seeker, and was present at the President's deathbed. In 1901 he happened, purely by chance, to be in the crowd at the Pan-American Exposition in Buffalo when Leon Czolgosz shot President William McKinley, and thereafter refused all invitations to the White House or to any occasion on which he would be in the same room as the President of the United States.

He selectively pruned his father's papers, burning some and putting others under seal not to be opened until twenty-one years after his own death.

He died in July of 1926, and in keeping with his desire to be perceived as a man in his own right and not as Abraham Lincoln's son, lies buried in Arlington National Cemetery, on the hillside just below Robert E. Lee's house.

His estate threatened Myra Bradwell's granddaughter with a lawsuit until she sold them not only all of Mary Todd Lincoln's correspondence with Myra, but all of Myra's correspondence with Mary, and the article that she was writing about the events of July–September 1875. All of these were destroyed.

AUTHOR'S NOTE

The Emancipator's Wife is a work of fiction. I've made sur-
mises about the way things may have happened, and the possible reasons events took place, that cannot be substantiated,
but I've tried not to portray anything contrary to docu-
mented events. As all historical novelists must, I have taken
my best guess at those occurrences or motivations for which
there are no records.

Nowhere have I found any biographer who came out and
said that Mary Todd Lincoln had a substance abuse problem.
Given the list of her known ailments—an unspecified "female
problem" resulting from Tad's birth, migraines, menstrual
problems, what sound like allergy-related sinus headaches,
and injuries from her carriage accident in July of 1863—it
would be astonishing if she didn't. Opium and alcohol figured
prominently in most over-the-counter medicines in that era,
and her biographers agree she took them in quantity: one
friend described her as pouring dollops from five or six various bottles into a glass and chugging the result. Before the
early twentieth century, no manufacturer of the various female cordials, soothing elixirs, and patented cure-alls was required to list anywhere the percentage of narcotics that these
"medicines" contained. Many, many women of stronger will
and character than Mrs. Lincoln ended up addicted.

It is also a fact that although she became seriously delusional during the period after Tad's death, when she was

solitary and had little to occupy her time, nowhere have I found even a hint that she suffered delusions either while she was incarcerated in Bellevue Place, or following her release. In fact, after she emigrated to Europe in 1876 she also kept herself clear of major debt.

Did Mary Todd entrap Abraham Lincoln into marrying her? Looking at the manipulative chicanery she later indulged in with White House funds, and with promises dealt out to get her debts paid, I can only say that I wouldn't put it past her. She loved him deeply and possessively. She waited for him for twenty months after their breakup in January of 1841 while he tentatively pursued at least two other young ladies. Several of Lincoln's friends attested to the strong streak of physical passion that underlay his iron self-control. When they started spending time together again—unchaperoned and late in the evening at Simeon Francis's house—Mary was a month shy of twenty-four, approaching old-maid territory by almost anyone's standards. They were married on a half-day's notice and their son Robert was born nine months less four days later.

Was Mary Todd Lincoln really insane?

She was undoubtedly eccentric. It's generally held now that she was bipolar—even people who loved her describe her as being subject to wild and abrupt mood-swings, starting in childhood; friends and neighbors interviewed by Billy Herndon in Springfield, and Lincoln's two secretaries Hay and Nicolay, agree that she had a horrendous and perhaps hysterical temper. Recent biographers have suggested the effects of untreated diabetes as well. After the deaths of three of her children, and two separate incidents of major trauma—having her husband's brains blown out while he was sitting beside her and later having the Chicago Fire come within three blocks of her less than ninety days after the loss of her beloved son—she was, if nothing else, a candidate for serious therapy. Though I have been able to find no specific account of what Mary did during the Chicago Fire, her delusion, reported at her trial, that "the South Side of the city was on fire" sounds a great deal like a flashback of post-traumatic stress syndrome.

Descendants of the Todd family to whom I've spoken say that the family tradition is very clear that both Mary and her brother Levi were "crazy."

The Spider Incident is completely fictitious, but there was certainly friction between the second Mrs. Todd and her husband's children by her predecessor. There may be no more to Elizabeth's departure from the Todd home in Lexington before her marriage at the age of seventeen than overcrowding, but the departure of all four of the first Mrs. Todd's daughters seems more than coincidental. The fact that Mary was sent away to boarding school a mile and a half from her father's house sounds like a compromise to deal with some underlying problem.

John Wilamet and his family are completely fictitious, but I have tried to be as faithful as I could to the experience of post-Reconstruction blacks.

BARBARA HAMBLY
Los Angeles, 2003

ABOUT THE AUTHOR

BARBARA HAMBLY attended the University of California and spent a year at the University of Bordeaux obtaining a master's degree in medieval history. She has worked as both a teacher and a technical editor, but her first love has always been history. Barbara Hambly is the author of *Patriot Ladies, A Free Man of Color, Fever Season, Graveyard Dust, Wet Grave, Sold Down the River, Die Upon a Kiss, Days of the Dead,* and *Dead Water*.

If you enjoyed Barbara Hambly's acclaimed novel *The Emancipator's Wife*, you won't want to miss any of her beloved novels. Look for them at your favorite bookseller.

And read on for an exciting early look at her next novel,

HOMELAND

coming soon from
Bantam Books.

Ok averas taps — 35" x 43"d

oman High — 20" to 22'

& tag to Bottom 35" to 40"d

4 5 6

ONE

MERCY

WHEN THE DEAD ARE BURIED—THAT'S WHEN SECRETS come out.

Sometimes it's things people haven't talked about for forty years, out of respect or fear or pity: things like whose son Cousin George *really* was, or why Aunt Charlotte never talked about her first husband. Sometimes it's only parts of tales, which have to be fitted together if they're to make sense, and not all the pieces are present. Sometimes when the tales are complete, you wish you'd never heard them.

Some of the tales are never complete.

I didn't know this when I was thirteen, and my mother and I took the train to Tennessee for my grandpa Andy's funeral. But as the green mountains surrounded us I saw her weep—Mama, who never wept, except over books, or when my piano teacher played a certain song that I later learned had been popular just before the War...and I knew that my guess was correct, that Mama had been to this place before, though she never talked about it.

The same way she never talked about the War.

When we lived in Paris, the other little girls at Mrs. Allard's American school on the Rue du Faubourg Saint-Honoré were always talking about how the Yankees burned their parents' plantations, or how their fathers or uncles had been shot by Rebels in battle. None of us was old enough to actually remember the War clearly, but Thalia Innes called me a "yellow-eyed Yankee" and told the other Southern girls that it was my "side" that had killed her mother and her grand-mother, and had driven her poor father out of Charleston and impoverished her family. (Relatively impoverished—even at the age of six, I knew Mrs. Allard's wasn't cheap.) I put a lizard in her dinner pail—they used to bask along the top of the high brick wall that surrounded the school's garden—but long after we'd left Paris for London, and then returned to the United States, the remark still hurt.

In a way, it still did hurt me on the train to Tennessee, though we'd been back in the United States then for almost five years.

That, and the dreams of my tinier childhood, from which I'd wake weeping and desolate because of other things I'd been called.

At Mrs. Allard's, the Southern girls could name each general who had defended the Lost Cause, and give blow-by-blow accounts of battles their fathers and uncles had bled in. The Northern girls in their turn whispered about the way those fathers and uncles had whipped and tortured their slaves, and could tell long stories about how this black woman or that one had been torn from her children and sold away—not that any of them had ever spoken to a single black person in their entire lives.

Neither faction had a single good word to say about my grandpa Andy.

The Northern girls would ask me sometimes, "Did you really live in the White House?"—which we had, for about a year, my mother being at the time a sort of governess to the President's grandchildren. I didn't remember Grandpa Andy very well from those days, except that he was like a big black-maned lion, fierce and lovable. He always smelled of bourbon, but I never saw him drunk. He'd left the Presidency by the time Mama, Papa, and I returned from Paris in 1871, and since that time we'd seen him only once, when he came east to testify at a hearing in Washington, and we'd taken the train down from New York City specially. He'd been ill on that occasion and his hair was graying, but he was still filled with the raw, boisterous energy I recalled from the days when he'd go charging around on his hands and knees among his grandchildren—his *real* grand-children, and those of us, their friends, who all called him Grandpa.

And now he was dead.

I knew that Mama wept for him as the train steamed through Charlottesville, Lynchburg, Bristol, deep in the folds of the Smoky Mountains on the Tennessee border—but I sensed, I don't know why, that her tears came from deeper memories, too. I asked, "Are you all right?" and her hand tightened over mine, but she didn't speak.

As we got out of the train at Greeneville I was struck by the baroque lushness of the trees, the grass knee-high in the vacant lots under drumming August heat; of how thick the shadows were. Mostly I was struck by the stillness, the quiet, as we walked up Main Street from the depot, down the hill and up the hill and down the hill again, with the black rail-road porter behind us carrying our bags. I was used to Paris and New York City. The green mountains crowded close around the little town. Beyond a block or two of brick buildings near the depot, Greeneville was barely a village, each house sitting back among its own gardens, its own trees. I looked down Church Street and Summer Street, and could see the woods only a few blocks away.

Mostly I was aware of Mama's silence. When I peeked up behind me at her face, there were tears again in her eyes, un-shed this time. Her eyes themselves—translucent green, like a mermaid's—had the quality of looking past the new brick buildings, the repaired shops and unweathered fences, the breathless density of the Tennessee summer, to a different time and place. I knew she was seeing it as she'd seen it first, whenever that had been.

Or as she'd seen it last.

FLORRIE OPENED THE DOOR FOR US AT THE BIG BRICK HOUSE AT the other end of Main Street. I hadn't thought of Florrie for years, but she was just the same as she'd been in our White

House days, a smiling young woman now instead of a smiling teenaged maid. "Miss Cora," she said to Mama—they stood for a moment facing each other on the threshold, then Mama stepped forward, took Florrie in her arms.

"Thank you, ma'am," Florrie whispered, her face pressed to Mama's shoulder. "Thank you—"

So much for the Northern girls' tales about *all* slaveholders mistreating their human chattels . . . or casually selling their bond servants' children away to the slave dealers. I know it was done, and done a lot: Grandpa Andy had purchased Florrie's mother and uncle as children at a public sale. It just wasn't the whole story.

"How is Miss Eliza?" Mama asked, and Florrie shook her head.

"Duke," Florrie called out past us to the porter, "you take Miss Cora's things round the side. Good Lord, Miss Cora, that's never Miss Mercy?"

"If it isn't," replied Mama gravely, "some evil person switched children on me on the boat back from France." Florrie looked taken aback for one second—Mama's straight-faced jokes often catch people by surprise, maybe because she's so beautiful nobody expects her to have a sense of humor. Then she chuckled, grief for a moment leaving her face.

"It's good to have you in the house again, ma'am." She stepped back from the doorway, ushered us into the modest front hall. "Mr. Broadstairs didn't come with you?"

"He doesn't do well in the heat." Mama smiled tenderly at the thought of Papa, who had been seasick all the way across the Atlantic and would get queasy even on the train from New York City out to our summer cottage on Long Island—which was where he was now, with my baby brother, Harry. As they spoke, I looked around me at the house Grannie Eliza had always spoken of as the Homestead.

I thought it small, considering that Grandpa Andy had been one of the richest men in Greeneville, not to mention President of the United States. The door to the right of us was closed: Sarah Stover—Grandpa Andy's *real* granddaughter, unlike me—later told me that was Grandpa Andy's bedroom, where he'd lain the day before until they took him to lie in state in the courthouse a few blocks away. To the left, the parlor was small and cavernously dim, cluttered up with too many chairs. Sarah's mama, my Aunt Mary—only she and Aunt Martha were no more truly my aunts than Grandpa Andy had been truly my grandfather—had, with Aunt Martha, been receiving visitors all day, and the sight of those chairs brought Grandpa Andy back to me sharply: that gruff, deep voice, the smiling dark eyes marked with lines and folds of pain he never talked about. I clenched my teeth hard, though I don't know why I was ashamed—and deep-down afraid—to have Florrie or anyone see my tears.

Florrie loved me. Mama loved me. Yet graven in me, so deep I no longer remembered why, except in those awful dreams, was the imperative: never *ever* let *anyone* see how I felt. It would only make matters worse, if they—and I didn't even know who *they* really were—saw me weep.

The White House in Washington was a big, ramshackle old mansion, filled to bursting not only with Grandpa Andy's family—which when I was four included his surviving sons, grown-up Robbie and thirteen-year-old Frank, his daughters and their children and the one son-in-law the war had left alive, and us—but Florrie and *her* family as well. Yet the heart of the household had always been Grannie Eliza's parlor. It had been a guest bedroom back when President Lincoln was there, and we always called it the Guest Room. In any other household I'd have thought it strange to see a huge bed draped with purple and gold sitting in the parlor, but the old frontier custom seemed to fit with our family: besides, it wasn't as if we had rooms to spare.

Grannie Eliza was seldom well enough to leave the house, and looking back, I don't think I ever saw her outdoors. Yet it was she we all went to, that tall, thin, dark-haired woman whose haunted dark eyes so often bore the marks of sleeplessness but who always gave you her full attention, listened to whatever you had to say. I'd heard Mama tell Papa on any number of occasions, after letters from her, that she was slowly worsening, so I wasn't really shocked when I followed Mama into her bedroom and saw her. Just very, very sad.

She got up and crossed to us, took Mama in her arms like a daughter. "Darling." She was dressed in mourning black, and wore a corset, though I guessed she hadn't been downstairs when the guests came, and though it had been altered to fit her (I could see the tucks at the shoulders), it still hung slack on her skeletal frame. Her stripped, husky voice barely had any sound left to it. "Mercy," she said, and her gaunt face warmed up into a smile. "Or should I say Miss Broadstairs?" I started to curtsey and she cocked an eye at me, as if to say *Don't you play jokes on your old grannie, child,* then gathered me into her arms. My eyes burned again as I understood that she wouldn't be long in following Grandpa Andy to the top of Signal Hill outside town, where he would be buried in two days' time.

Over my head, she asked Mama, "Are you all right?" And there was a tone in her voice that told me, without even looking up, that it wasn't Grandpa Andy's death, nor anything in the present, that she was asking about. As if she knew about the tears Mama had shed on the train.

It's my father she means, I thought—I *knew*—and a queer shiver went through me. My real father, not Henry Broadstairs, who'd been Papa to me since their wedding in Paris when I was five.

To my knowledge, I'd never even heard his name.

In her most pleasant voice, Mama lied, "Yes, I'm all right. It's just . . . It's been a long time."

Grannie Eliza sighed, and put her arm around Mama's waist. She said, "It has been that."

Two

Cora

Pennsylvania and Maryland
April 1861

CORA AND EMORY POOLE TOOK THE CARS OF THE NEW YORK and New Haven Railroad south, with the April sunlight spangling the water of the Long Island Sound and Cora barely able to keep her eyes off her husband. She felt her face crimson every time she looked at him: *Why didn't anyone tell you what it was like to lie naked in the arms of a naked man?*

Her mother would have blenched with shock, and given her a stringent lecture on the sin of such reflections—something no decent girl, married or not, even experienced, much less returned to, reveling, again and again.

And her father would have grieved that she could give way to such things for even a moment, in the light of what had happened—was happening—to the nation.

Everyone else in the passenger car around them was talking about the Rebel seizure of Fort Sumter, and the President's call for volunteers. About the unthinkable, feared and dodged and threatened and averted at the last minute, for so many years. The Southern states had finally, actually, risen in arms against the government. Had seceded from the Union, broken the world's only democratic republic in two.

Only days ago, just before the wedding in New Haven, Cora had seen her scholarly father weep at the news. Her wedding itself had passed like a dream, filtered through a state of sickened shock. Yet now she had only to move her head, had only to catch a glimpse of her new husband's profile as he bent his attention on the *Boston Transcript,* for all recollection of the crisis to be swept away in a torrent of impure thoughts and scalding shame.

"They've got to get the government out of Washington," insisted the man in the seat behind them. This was a ladies' car, in which the gentlemen accompanying their wives were supposed to be on their best behavior, but that thought—like her own womanly modesty—did not seem to be proof against recent events. "God knows what that stupid gorilla Lincoln's thinking about, that he hasn't given orders already—"

"Fucken Christ Jesus, man, what good you think gettin' out of Washington will do, if Virginia rebels as well?"

The nation is coming apart. Secessionists have taken control of the governments of seven states. The country I've grown up in, the world I've known—the culmination of human political and moral progress, shattered—

And all she could think about was the way triple candle flame had glimmered over Emory's flanks last Sunday night. All her mind held was the salt-musk savor of his flesh, his triangular smile like a little "v," and the gentle slide of soft cotton across her nipples as he'd drawn her nightgown off over her head: *Let me look at you. I want to see the most beautiful girl in the world. . . .*

I shouldn't be thinking this. Even without the admonition of God and her mother, even without the sickening tragedy that had befallen the nation, Mrs. Wollstonecraft—her literary mentor and patron saint—admonished in her *Vindication of the Rights of Woman* (which Cora's friend Elinor Westcott had sneaked from the library of the Hartford Female Seminary when they were both fourteen): *Calmly let passion subside into friendship* . . . when *two virtuous young people marry, it would be better if some circumstances checked their passion.*

It had made sense, when Cora had first read those words in that text that had opened her mind with words of joy and steel. From earliest childhood, she had been aware—even had her mother not told her so in no uncertain terms—that boys, and later men, saw her in terms of her beauty. In terms of passion. In animal terms, not those of the human soul. Because she was beautiful, her mother said, Cora must be careful. Her beauty had been given to her by God as a test, an added yoke of sin that it was her burden to carry, the way God had seen fit to test her friend Deborah Haskell with a stunted left hand, or her brother's wife, Betsy, with hives every time she ate strawberries. Eve had been the most beautiful woman in the world, her mother said.

Cora was aware she was blushing again, and tried to summon up some cooling quotation from Virgil or Aristotle to put into perspective the wave of warmth that swept her flesh. But all she could remember was Catullus, whom her mother had forbidden her to read: *Da mi basia mille, deinde centum. . . .* Her father had had a copy in his study at Yale. *Give me a thousand kisses, and then a hundred more.*

So the ancient Romans had known this, too, this languid, excruciating fire.

Let him kiss me with the kisses of his mouth, for his love is better than wine.

"December was the time for calling up troops, not now!" ranted the man behind them. "If that pantywaist Buchanan had sent men in to arrest everybody at that damned secesh convention of theirs, we wouldn't be in this fix!"

Emory was listening, and Cora saw the muscles of his jaw twitch as he struggled not to get up and demand of the would-be politician how they thought the right of a state to free itself from Britain's rule was different from the right of that same state to free itself from Washington's, if its own people voted to do so. The lapel of his well-cut gray frock coat bore a badge of red, white, and blue ribbons, which men and young ladies had been handing out on the railway platform in New York—the whole depot had fluttered with banners in the same patriotic colors—but his training in the law had given her husband an acute awareness that the argument was not all on one side.

She asked, "Is there further news from Washington?" to draw his mind away, knowing that if Emory did stand up and challenge the pair of loudmouths, his soft Tennessee drawl would shut their minds to the content of his words, badge or no badge. Had he only remarked *The sun is shining,* they'd have shouted him down.

He was a Southerner, thus automatically in their eyes a secesh.

"It says here they're calling a special session of Congress." He took a deep breath, and she observed the change in the focus of his eyes. Hazel eyes, almost golden, like autumn sunlight when it slanted through the woods behind her parents' farmhouse, and all the more tawny against the corn-yellow of his hair. "There've been rallies in Richmond, and Governor Lechter of Virginia's told Lincoln he can go whistle for his troops. What did Lincoln think was going to happen? That Lechter would *give* him men just on his say-so?"

Let him kiss me with the kisses of his mouth. . . .

"What are they going to do about Congress?" asked Cora. "About the Senate seats of the Southern states? The senators all walked out, didn't they? All but one."

"All but Andy Johnson." There was a glint of pride in Emory's eyes as he spoke of the Senator from Tennessee. "Whatever they do, it'll tell us what the Republicans' plans are. I'll be curious to see if those seats get filled with good Republicans, appointed by the men who ran Lincoln to office."

When Cora Smith had first seen Emory Poole, in his rustic Sunday best, his homespun checked shirt, work boots, and slouch felt hat, she'd been struck by the animal quality of him: a young golden panther who'd accidentally strayed in among the grave dark-suited New Englander boys at Yale. She'd been sixteen then, and in her third year at the Hartford Female Seminary.

He was the first Southerner she had met.

Now in his gray Boston tailoring, his gold hair trimmed and tamed, he looked every inch the young lawyer his studies had guided him to be. At her father's recommendation, he would begin his clerkship next month at her uncle's firm in Boston, where her brother Brock had just been taken in as a partner. In the five years Emory had spent in New England,

Cora had seen that panther-eyed mountain boy change. She had seen his levelheaded logic win out over the underlying violence that seemed to be so integral a part of the world in which he'd grown up. Had seen his inarticulate craving for wisdom find voice, honed by the sharing of ideas with educated men.

Had it not been so, she thought he'd have remained too alien for her to approach, even to speak to. Scholarly and fastidious like her father, Cora could barely imagine the world Emory spoke of, on those few occasions when he'd even mentioned his childhood in the tangled hollows of the East Tennessee hills. And had she not had in her, she reflected now as he took her gloved hand, the taint of impure curiosity that was her lasting shame, she supposed she would have drawn away from him, struggled harder, that afternoon last spring when she'd come to visit her father at Yale. Emory had walked her to her boardinghouse from the station, and halfway there had taken her in his arms.

THEY CHANGED TRAINS IN TRENTON, TO THE PENNSYLVANIA Central Railroad, and spent the night in Philadelphia. When they reached Baltimore—to change again from the Penn Central to the Washington, Baltimore, and Annapolis Railroad—it was to find the news everywhere: Virginia had seceded from the Union.

"I can't imagine they'd stop the trains running, even if there was a vote to secede," Emory pointed out reasonably. "You and I can't be the only people who need to cross Virginia soil."

"Might not secessionists try to seize the railway lines? If Lincoln has called up volunteers, surely the quickest way to move troops would be by rail?"

"You have a point." Emory's expression reminded her of her mother judging the saltiness of broth. "I'm not sure how they *could,* though, with the track all different widths on so many lines." He folded the *Harrisburg Patriot* across his knee as the train lurched into motion. VOLUNTEERS! VOLUNTEERS! trumpeted inch-high letters across the front page. Elsewhere, a fragment of text caught her eye: *"Conspirators now in arms against the Federal Government..."* *"Never did a deluded people commit a more egregious blunder..."*

The rhetoric of newspapers had always made Cora uneasy. It reminded her too sharply of her friend Elinor Westcott's father, when he was trying to justify not paying his boat crews as much as Cora's uncle Mordacai paid his.

"We may have to travel part of the way by carriage or coach. Julia's wedding isn't till the first." Emory's voice paused just a moment on the name of his childhood love. "Are you agreeable to that?"

He was probably right. Even a crisis in the constitution of the United States didn't necessarily mean there would be war. But for almost ten years, Cora had been reading in the newspapers of armed militias—each claiming the backing of law—fighting savagely in Kansas over whether slavery was to be made legal in the Territories.

There was no way of telling what might happen before she and Emory reached Tennessee.

I am a rational woman and Emory's equal partner, Cora told herself firmly. *Would Mary Wollstonecraft, or Lucretia Mott, or any of the other women who have stood forth for the rights of women to equal treatment before the law, shrink away where a rational man fears not to tread?*

And there was more to this journey, she sensed, than simply Emory's desire to see an old sweetheart wed to his best childhood friend. *How would I feel, if I had not seen Papa and Mama, Brock and Oliver, for five years? Not to mention Elinor and Deborah and all my other friends?*

If I had not seen my own homeland—not seen Deer Isle—for that long? Not heard the wind in the pine trees on the ridge above the house, or heard the gulls crying over Webb's Cove when a wind comes up in the morning?

She couldn't imagine it.

The wedding of Julia Ashford—"My first love," he'd declared, and struck his breast melodramatically—was, she suspected, the occasion Emory had chosen to make peace with the world he had fled. A doorway through which to return to speaking terms with the father of whom he would only say, "He's a strange man."

It would be easier for him, she guessed, with her at his side.